P9-DNR-348

PRAISE FOR *MASTER OF SORROWS*

"One of the best books I have read this year and a perfect example of grimdark fantasy…It is riveting, exciting, and one that is going to stick with me for a while."
—*GRIMDARK MAGAZINE*

"Instantly entertaining, but it also lays the groundwork for something massively rewarding in the years ahead…This is the start of a truly epic dark fantasy saga that is well worth jumping into on the ground floor."
—*FANTASY BOOK REVIEW*

"A modern take on the classic coming-of-age fantasies that embraces its roots amongst the likes of Eddings, Sanderson, Canavan, and Weeks, and dares to reach for the stars and carve out its own destiny. A fantastic debut in a promising series."
—*THE FANTASY HIVE*

"One of the most outstanding beginnings to a fantasy series I have ever read…I was lost in these pages from the gut-wrenchingly emotional prologue … to the liquid rage finale that left my jaw firmly on the floor."
—*ALWAYS TRUST IN BOOKS*

"If you're a fan of coming-of-age stories, magic schools, and the idea of what's right and what's wrong, then *Master of Sorrows* is the book for you."
—*THE FANTASY INN*

"A remarkable debut which I simply cannot put down…*Master of Sorrows* is a brilliant and riveting tale…I recommend this book for lovers of classic epic fantasy looking for a modern voice."
—*NOVEL NOTIONS*

MASTER
of
SORROWS

MASTER
of
SORROWS

JUSTIN T. CALL

**BLACK
STONE**
PUBLISHING

ST. JOHN THE BAPTIST PARISH LIBRARY
2920 NEW HIGHWAY 51
LAPLACE, LOUISIANA 70068

Copyright © 2020 by Justin Travis Call
Published in 2020 by Blackstone Publishing
Cover and book design by Blackstone Publishing

All rights reserved. This book or any portion
thereof may not be reproduced or used in any manner
whatsoever without the express written permission
of the publisher except for the use of brief quotations
in a book review.

The characters and events in this book are fictitious.
Any similarity to real persons, living or dead, is coincidental
and not intended by the author.

Printed in the United States of America

First edition: 2020
ISBN 978-1-982591-78-6
Fiction / Fantasy / General

1 3 5 7 9 10 8 6 4 2

CIP data for this book is available
from the Library of Congress

Blackstone Publishing
31 Mistletoe Rd.
Ashland, OR 97520

www.BlackstonePublishing.com

For Darwinkle and Mr. Crackers
—may your childhoods be filled with joy
and your teenage years filled with wisdom.

Lost to Himself,
He shall lead those that feign to be lost.
Unknown to Himself,
the blind shall seek Him and call His name.
For the honor of His naming,
the Herald shall plead mercy and receive it.
And these are the words of her prophecy:

Descended of the Gods yet sired by Man.
Seven seek to lead Him. Seven dread His hand.
Bonded by the Ageless, the Ancient breaks His path.
The Crippled King guides Him. The world fears His wrath.

Son of Seven Fathers. Child of None.
Master of Sorrows. The Incarnate One.
Bladesinger. Magpie. Phoenix. King.
Bloodlord. Ring-snake. End of All Things.

Woe unto those that awaken Him, for great shall be
*   their destruction.*
Woe unto those that follow Him, for great shall be
*   their sacrifice.*
Woe unto those that contest Him, for by His hand they
*   shall be broken.*
And when the Silent Gods awake, then weep, children,
*   for the end is nigh.*

—"Son of Seven Fathers," excerpt from *The Book of Terra*

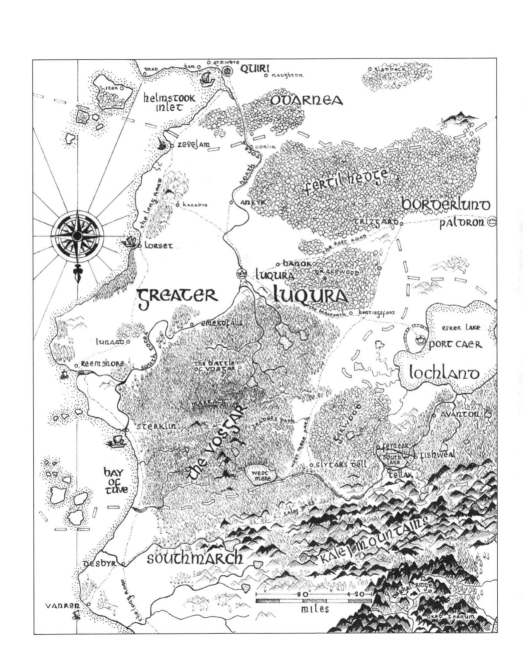

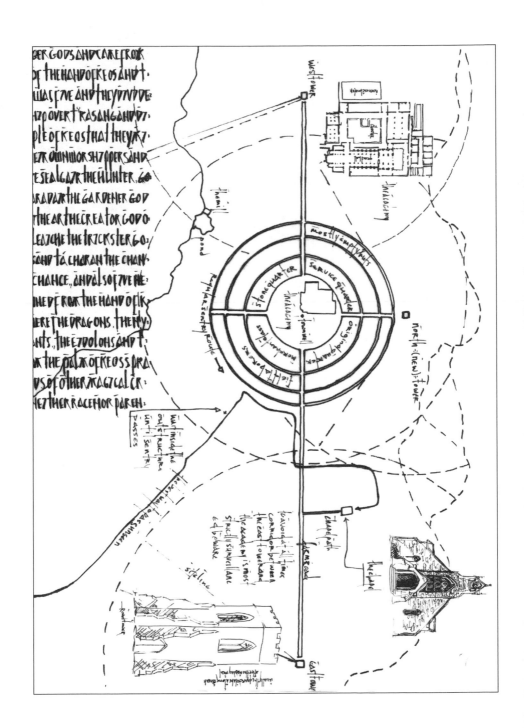

PROLOGUE

The woman's screams faded, and a baby's cry took their place. Sodar had been waiting for this moment. He smoothed his blue robes and followed close on Ancient Tosan's heels, stepping inside the beige tent.

Sodar squinted once inside, allowing his eyes to adjust to the dim light. No candles were needed at this hour, but a dark shadow still covered the room.

In one corner of the birthing tent he could see Ancient Tosan speaking with his wife Lana—one of the two witwomen assisting with Aegen's pregnancy. It seemed she had caught the lean man before he could approach the new mother and her baby, and the priest was grateful that allowed him a moment with Aegen and her child. He stepped toward the middle of the tent and saw an older witwoman holding the bile-slick babe, a blanket haphazardly wrapped around its body. Sodar quelled his instinct to sprint to the infant. Instead, he tempered his elation that Tuor's line continued and approached the mother with a calmness that belied his excitement.

It had been a hard birth. Aegen was lying still atop the birthing mat, her pale face framed by sweat-soaked ringlets. Sodar didn't want to wake the exhausted woman, but a sense of uneasiness poisoned his gut.

She's not breathing, he realized.

In a flash, the priest was kneeling at her side. He shook her shoulders, first whispering and then shouting her name. A moment later, he felt Lana at his shoulder, her slick red hands touching his wrist.

"She's dead, Brother Sodar."

Sodar flinched away from the witwoman's touch. He rubbed where her bloody fingers had touched him and felt the wetness smear his wrinkled skin.

"Was it the child?" He struggled to say the words as he turned to look at the babe. Tosan had taken the infant from the second witwoman—a bony grandmother named Kelga—and held the newborn in his hands, but instead of cradling it to his chest, Tosan held it out at arm's length and stared in revulsion at the bundle.

"Ancient Tosan?"

The slender ancient didn't look up.

"The child," Tosan said. "Sodar, he's a Son of Keos."

"He's *what?*"

Tosan held the infant out toward the blue-robed priest. "The child," he repeated, lifting the blanket, "is a Son of Keos."

Sodar's heart thudded in horror. The babe's piercing blue eyes caught his attention—a mark of blessing from the god Odar—but saw nothing to warrant calling the child a Son of Keos. A wisp of light brown hair crowned the infant's head, and he seemed unremarkable. Sodar's brow crinkled and he was about to challenge Tosan's judgment when the baby moved, waving his hands in front of him.

No. His hand. One hand.

"Gods," Sodar swore.

Tosan covered the infant again. "Aegen carried the child. She was the vessel of Keos, and the vessels of Keos must be broken."

Lana nodded in confirmation of her husband's words, and the priest found his attention drawn to the witwoman's bloody hands and then to the dead woman—and this time he saw it: a dark red stain pooling on the birthing mat beneath her skull.

They killed her, Sodar realized. *They killed Aegen, and I wasn't here to stop it.*

"Take this thing away," Tosan said, passing the infant to Lana. "You know what to do."

The witwoman bowed, her brown braids swinging behind her back as she rose. "The beasts of Keos shall consume the Sons of Keos."

"Be certain you witness its death. The beasts won't feed till nightfall."

"Ancient Tosan," Kelga said, stepping forward. "Lana may want to return to the Academy and your new daughter. I could take the infant to the woods."

Tosan stroked his thin black goatee. "Lana?"

"The witgirls can take care of Myjun for me while I'm gone," Lana said, wiping her bloodied hands on the infant's sheepskin blanket, and then dipping it in the pool of blood. "But it *would* be good to have some company."

Tosan nodded. "The Brakewood has never been a safe place. You would be well-served to have a companion to share the night's watch." He eyed the bloody bundle in Lana's arms then fastidiously wiped his palms on his gray-black cloak. "The father is also a vessel of Keos. Wait until he has been bound and then take infant to the woods."

Tuor, Sodar thought, knowing the blacksmith would be waiting outside to meet his child. *I can't abandon him ... but I can't save him and the infant.*

"I apologize for inviting you, Sodar," Tosan said, lifting the tent flap. "There will be no infant to bless this day." He paused, halfway out of the tent. "I think you should stay, though. It would be good for the villagers to see their priest breaking a vessel of Keos."

Sodar lowered his eyes, schooling both his tongue and his temper. "Forgive me, Ancient Tosan, but I must decline. My strength is not what it once was."

The ancient grunted, clearly unsurprised by Sodar's answer, and left. Kelga sniffed and went about gathering up the blankets piled atop Aegen's birthing mat. Moments later, Sodar could hear Tosan shouting above the babble of the assembled crowd. The tent shuddered as quick hands dismantled it, and light flooded in as the tent collapsed around Sodar and the two witwomen. A few farmers began to separate the segmented tent walls, and suddenly Aegen lay exposed to the crowd.

"Aegen?"

Less than a stone's throw away, Tuor stared in horror.

"Aegen!" Tuor rushed to his dead wife's side and gathered her up, pressing her limp frame to his chest. "Aegen, Aegen …" he repeated, a talisman against the bloody truth in his arms.

Behind the blacksmith, Tosan approached with Ancient Windor, the Eldest of Ancients, and a half-dozen masters from the Academy. The master avatars wore their traditional bloodred tunics, while Winsor wore the red and black chevron-patterned robes of a headmaster.

"Bind the Vessel of Keos," Winsor instructed. "Bind them and break them. We cannot permit their taint to spread."

Tuor looked up from Aegen's bloody corpse, searching for the child his wife had carried these last nine months. He spotted the sheepskin blanket in Lana's arms just as Sodar stepped in front of him, blocking the babe from sight.

Their eyes met, and in those seconds the priest tried to convey all that he dared not say.

I'll keep him safe. I promise. *I* will *keep him safe.*

Tuor was a mass of sorrow and fury, but then it seemed he understood. When, only moments before, the stout man had been tightly coiled to fight for his son, he now gave him into Sodar's protection. Something passed between the two men then—a silent goodbye whose depth only a mourning father could fathom.

And then the master avatars were on him. Tuor fought for long enough to gently lower Aegen's body to the ground, and then he reared back, throwing off the first men to have grabbed him. Sodar and the two witwomen fell back from the crowd as the remaining master avatars joined the fray, pinning Tuor's arms and legs and then binding them with tough cords. Even beaten and bound, the blacksmith still thrashed and kicked, worming his way across the earth until he reached his lifeless wife. He curled his own broad figure around hers, protecting her from what was to come.

Sodar was helpless to aid his friend. But Tuor had sacrificed himself to save his son, and Sodor had sworn to protect him, so he kept his eyes fixed on the bundle in Lana's arms and shadowed the two witwomen. They had reached the edge of the village square when he heard Winsor's aging voice struggling to rise above the roar of the crowd. A moment later, Tosan's booming baritone rang out instead.

"A Son of Keos has been born among us," Tosan shouted. "Our duty is clear! The beasts of Keos shall consume the Sons of Keos. But to us lies the burden—nay, the *privilege*—of breaking the Vessel of Keos!"

A few villagers cheered at this, and Sodar found it difficult not to stop and take note of them. He knew what he would see if he looked back, because he had seen it before: the villagers would be gathering stones, and then, too soon, the Breaking would begin.

Sodar forced himself to turn away. While he had paused, Lana and Kelga had left the square. As the pair made their way east through the village, Sodar followed at a discreet distance. He crossed the street and heard Tuor's cries leading the roar of the crowd. "Cleanse the filth!" screamed one voice. "Spawn of Keos!" shouted another, all to the snarling chant of "Break their bones!"

Sodar forced himself onwards, trying not to pick individual voices from the mob. Distance blended the screams into one murderous cacophony, and then a new wail sprang up ahead of him. This one was high, constant, and piercing—the sound of a hungry baby, frightened and alone.

But not for long. Because Sodar was coming for him.

***

Lana lay still at the edge of the forest clearing, her breath rising and falling steadily in mimicry of sleep. To her right she saw Kelga's hunched silhouette framed against the starry sky. The bony old witwoman paced back and forth, her attention on the babe they had placed near a copse of blackthorn, yet there was an anxiousness to the woman's movements that concerned Lana.

At first, she'd thought the grandmother simply wished to support her. That made sense; Lana had given birth to a daughter only a month ago, and it was uncommon for witwomen to return to midwifing so soon. But it wasn't as if Lana was participating in the reaping—that would have been too much even for her resilient body—observing the death of a Son of Keos was hardly rigorous. All Lana need do was stay awake till the beasts of the Brakewood came, drawn by the child's cries and the blood on the infant's blanket.

But Kelga had persisted in her commitment to witness the child's death. It surprised Lana, not because the older witwoman was frail—Lana had seen the crone endure trials that overwhelmed other witwomen—but because Kelga was selfish, solitary, and consistently uncaring towards others. Indeed, Lana suspected Kelga's sour demeanor was the chief reason Witmistress Kiara had asked her to stay behind for the reaping.

Yet here Kelga was, offering to keep vigil with Lana and even insisting that she take the first watch. Lana had declined at first, but Kelga had worn her down.

Rather than sleep, Lana watched Kelga grow increasingly restless as the forest grew darker, and felt the cold prickle of dread crawl into her blankets as the older woman settled herself against a tree trunk. By the time night fell, Lana was filled with an unreasonable fear. She could not pinpoint why, so she combatted it the only way she knew how: by watching Kelga and by being prepared. In one hand, she held a fistful of mushrooms spores; in the other, her reaping knife—the same stiletto she had plunged into Aegen's skull.

She heard the soft crunch of careful feet stepping on dry sticks and leaves behind her and tensed, suddenly realizing Kelga had moved.

"Why do you feign sleep?"

"Because I fear death," Lana breathed.

"It is wise to fear what we do not understand," Kelga said, her voice creaking. "But death comes for us all."

"Do you bring it with you now?"

The old woman's laugh was dry and husky, and Lana's fear deepened. She loosed her blanket, preparing for the attack she knew would come.

"You should have let me take the child," Kelga said.

Lana shifted in her blanket, meditating on Kelga's words as realization dawned. "You're a Daughter of Keos. A handmaiden of death. The rumors about the schism … they're true."

"I am no handmaiden," Kelga replied evenly. "Death is my shadow. He follows me wherever I go … and he is here now, calling for the child."

The boy's crying had quieted, and it seemed sleep had finally claimed him. Lana glanced toward the babe in grove.

"And calling for you."

Kelga struck. The dagger plunged down so hard and fast that Lana could barely dodge. The blade bit deep into her shoulder, narrowly missing her chest. She twisted, wrenching herself free, and threw the spores into Kelga's face.

The old woman screamed, her bony hands clawing at her cheeks and eyes as she fell back—but the spores were potent, choking her, silencing her.

Lana dragged herself to her feet and stumbled into the center of the clearing. She knew the spores in Kelga's throat would quickly blossom and bloom, expanding until they crushed Kelga's windpipe and suffocated the old hag, so Lana used the moonlight to assess the damage the old woman had inflicted.

The wound was deep. Worse, Lana had torn the muscle in ripping herself free of Kelga's knife. If she didn't staunch the flow of blood now, she wouldn't survive the walk back. Lana tore a strip off her blanket, one end in her teeth, and began wrapping her injured arm.

"Your instincts are commendable," Kelga croaked.

Lana turned to see Kelga stagger into the moonlit clearing. Vomit flecked the witwoman's lips, but she breathed freely. It seemed Lana's aim had been poor: instead of choking the old woman, the spores had claimed Kelga's eyes: they were clouded over, the same color as her bleached-bone hair. Lana backed away from the crazed witwoman and noticed that Kelga followed her more with her ears than her eyes.

"You're a blind traitor, Kelga, and the anointing that lets you find Chaenbalu has been destroyed. You can *never* return to the village."

Kelga cackled, her warped voice rising. "I never intended to return. I've been waiting for that infant my whole life, and I shall take him from this backwater village forever." She crept closer to Lana, her knife still drawn, the weapon poised to strike.

Lana retreated, hastening toward the babe at the edge of the grove. Whatever Kelga's plans, she wanted to preserve the baby's life, and she had not denied being a Daughter of Keos. Lana's best chance was to kill the child now. She moved with purpose.

If I kill it, she thought, *her plans will be thwarted and I can run for*

Chaenbalu. It was the safest path. Lana had no desire to fight the old woman. She was blinded but Lana could only use one arm, and she had no idea what tricks the old crone might have at her disposal.

Kelga sensed Lana's intentions and tried to intercept her, but Lana got there first. She struck hard and sure with her stiletto.

It met nothing but air and dirt. The babe had disappeared.

Lana turned, searching for it, but there was no sign of the infant.

A moment later, Kelga was on her, screaming. The hag slashed, her own curved knife swinging wide as Lana leaned back to dodge the blade. At the same time, Kelga's empty hand struck Lana's chest, throwing her back into the blackthorn copse behind her. Dozens of the barbed black needles punctured her thighs, back, and arms, their ridged, two-inch-long spikes holding her firm. Lana struggled against the briars and felt more sharp thorns embed themselves deep in her body. She screamed—a wail of fear, frustration, and pain, which became a frothy cough as the thorns constricted her chest.

Kelga hobbled forward, a silhouette in the moonlight, until her outstretched palm touched the blackthorn. Her milky eyes stared up at the dark sky and she bent an ear toward Lana. Kelga cackled, then bent down to retrieve the infant that was not there.

"What did you do with it?" Kelga barked. Her head spun about as though she were trying to locate the infant with some sixth sense. "*Where is the Vessel?*" she screamed.

Lana's laugh came out as more coughing. She spat at the woman instead, tasting blood. "Keos took him," she snarled. "I hope he takes you too."

"There are worse ways to die than blood loss and blackthorns," Kelga growled, reaching out with her curved knife until it prodded Lana's chest. "Where is the child?" she demanded, the knife carving into Lana's flesh until she gave a bloody scream.

A stout staff swung from the darkness, smashing Kelga across the back and driving the witwoman to her knees. The old woman howled and spun, throwing her arm in the air and pointing her bony fingers at her unseen attacker.

"*Bàsaich!*"

The staff flared silver and then faded to a dull glow in the darkness. Lana blinked, trying to see her savior, and was shocked to see the village priest step into the moonlit clearing.

"Sodar?" She scarcely believed her eyes, and still less when she saw the sheepskin bundle clutched in the old man's arms. "What … what are you doing?"

The priest advanced on Kelga, his staff ready, and the blind woman shrank back across the clover-filled clearing. The moment Sodar came into striking distance, Kelga threw her knife at the priest's belly. He knocked the blade aside with a flick of his quarterstaff then brought the solid oak down on the woman's head. Kelga collapsed beneath the blow and Sodar lifted the staff once more, this time bringing it high overhead, ready to smash the old woman's skull. But she didn't move again. Sodar hesitated then lowered the wooden weapon, turning back to Lana.

Lana heard the cursed babe coo inside the sheepskin blanket. "Quickly," she panted, tasting blood. "You must help me destroy the Son of Keos and warn the Academy. Daughters of Keos have infiltrated the Wit Circle."

The priest didn't move. Instead, he stared at Lana with hard eyes and a frown. "You're in no position to make demands, Lana banTosan." He spared a glance at the unconscious old woman. "You said Kelga has lost the ability to return to Chaenbalu." Lana nodded then coughed, bright blood flecking her lips. "She could return, though," Sodar continued, "if she had a guide."

Lana gasped as an acute pressure seized her chest. "Who would bring her *back*? She wanted to … save the Son of Keos."

"And that is why I am letting her live." The priest returned his gaze to Lana. "But *you* would have killed the boy as quickly as you killed Aegen." Sodar shook his head, his gray-white beard almost caressing the infant's face. "If Kelga cannot return to the village, she is no threat. With Odar's blessing, she may even find her way out of the Brake before the beasts consume her. You're a different matter, though, for if I let you live, you would condemn us both."

Lana blinked as her vision began to fuzz and blood trickled from her mouth.

"I had feared I would have to kill you," Sodar continued, "but it seems Kelga has taken care of that for me."

The priest's cool gray eyes watched as the world grew colder around Lana, and she realized she would die here, without ever seeing her husband or daughter again. Her body slumped backwards, and this time even the bite of the blackthorn couldn't rouse her.

PART ONE

On the thirty-first day of Thirdmonth, one hundred years after the death of Myahlai the Deceiver, the gods and their children came together to celebrate the day that evil was cast out of Luquatra. And in the days preceding this one hundredth anniversary, Keos saw the joy of their followers and proposed that he, Lumea, and Odar join their worshippers in celebration.

Yet Odar, the eldest and wisest of the gods, objected, deeming that mingling with the merrymaking of their children was ill-thought. Instead, Odar suggested the gods exchange gifts on the next holy day—and so came about the first great Regaleus.

Now it was two days before the appointed day when Keos, deep in thought, approached his elder brother. Odar, sensing his brother's distress, asked what vexed him.

And Keos answered, "It is the gift for our sister. What canst thou give a goddess, who holds the sun in the palm of her hand? All things seek her pleasure, and she wants for nothing; our sister's joy is complete."

And Odar answered, "Does not a mother rejoice in the gifts of her children? Let us then gift unto Lumea that which she and her worshippers shall rejoice in sharing."

And Keos found wisdom in these words and asked, "Hast thou a gift for our sister?" And Odar answered, "Nay, for I have not the skill nor the craft to create one. But perhaps it is fated that you come to me this day, for thou art skilled in all crafts, and it was my thought to present Lumea and her children with a clay flute, for both she and they delight in song and dance."

And Keos was pleased to hear these words, for he was indeed blessed with mighty skill in all things t'rasang; endowed with the power to shape things born of clay and stone, of metal and wood, and of blood and bone. And so it was that Keos and Odar agreed to create a joint gift for their sister Lumea.

But when Keos sat down at his forge in Thoir Cuma, the God of T'rasang *was beset with doubt and hesitation for he considered clay a base substance, unfit for crafting the beautiful flute he envisioned for his sister. So instead of clay, Keos forged Lumea's flute from the purest gold, drawn from the deepest veins of the world. When he was finished, Keos showed the flute to Odar, who saw the changes Keos had made. And Odar was not wroth and gave the gold flute his blessing.*

The day before the festival, Lumea approached Keos and asked him what gift they might give to their brother. And Keos remembered the wisdom of Odar and said, "Does not a father rejoice in the gifts of his children? Let us then gift unto Odar that which he and his children shall rejoice in sharing." And Lumea asked, "What gift wouldst thou give to our brother? For he is wise beyond years and his children are ever blessed."

And Keos answered, "I have gone amongst our worshippers in secret and observed their works, yea, even the works of the children of Odar, and I have seen a gift worthy of our brother: a staff, which is given unto the elderly to acknowledge their wisdom, and unto kings to signify their power and rulership."

"Yes," Lumea agreed. "Let us make a staff for our elder brother, for is not a god a king among his people? And is he not wise beyond years? And perhaps even his children shall wield this staff and take it as a sign of the blessings of Odar and of his favor." Thus it was decided between Keos and Lumea to create the Staff of Odar.

Now it was Lumea's desire that the staff be made of wood, for she took great delight in the forests of Luquatra, in the scent of cherry blossoms and the strength of the oak, and her people often danced in the forest glades. But when Keos went to his forge, he was again beset with doubt and feared that, if the staff were made of wood, Odar would compare it to Lumea's gold flute and be jealous. So instead of wood, Keos forged Odar's staff with the richest silver, drawn from the deepest veins of Luquatra. When he was finished, Keos showed the staff to Lumea, who saw the changes Keos had made. And Lumea was not wroth and gave the silver staff her blessing.

Then came the day for the Gods to exchange gifts with one another. It was decided amongst them that Lumea would receive her gift first, so Keos and Odar stepped forward and presented the golden flute. And when the goddess saw the exquisite work of the instrument and felt how both Keos and Odar had poured their power into it, she cried tears of great joy. In acceptance of her gift, Lumea brought the flute to her lips and played the sweetest song the world had ever heard, and a sweeter tune has not been heard since, save but one. She played with joy, passion, and life, pouring her heart and soul into the flute, filling it with lumen *until it glowed and all those that heard its music were captured by it.*

When the song was over, Lumea stepped back and thanked her brothers for the wonderful gift they had given her and her people.

Lumea and Keos then presented the silver staff, and when Odar saw it, he understood its significance and was humbled by it. He took the tool in his hands, felt its power, and was pleased, saying, "As this rod bears the strength of Keos and the love of Lumea, so shall I pour my own virtue into it."

So saying, Odar raised the staff above his head and called forth the power of quaire, *the very spirit of air, water, and ice. And when he was finished, the silver staff glowed with an awesome sheen, greater even than the pure silver from which Keos had forged it.*

Then said Odar unto his siblings, "As you have given me this staff, so I gift it to my followers, that they may wield it in wisdom and truth. Let it be a sign of the blessings of Odar and of my favor." And Keos and Lumea were pleased.

Then came the time for Keos to receive his gift. With much care, Odar laid down his staff and took his place beside Lumea. Then Lumea stepped forward, opened her mouth, and began to sing. And it was said that no ear had ever heard such wondrous things as Lumea sang to Keos; and no human tongue can utter the words she sang; nor can man conceive of the joy which consumed the soul upon hearing her song.

Now when Lumea finished singing, she stepped back and gazed at her brother, beseeching his approval. But there was none in the face of Keos; neither was there joy nor laughter, neither life nor love. Instead, he was perplexed and heavy with sadness, which turned first to disbelief, and then into cool anger. And Keos raised his face to his siblings and asked, "Is this all you have for me, my family?"

And Lumea answered, "This is your gift."

And Keos was angered and said, "I labored with great pains to give gifts unto thee, my brother and sister. I plumbed the deepest veins of the world for its most precious minerals and labored mightily at my forge that you might take pleasure in your gifts. And in return you give me nothing but a song?"

Then Odar stepped forward and answered, "Nay, for this is no mere song, brother. I labored long in choosing its words, which are sacred words of power; and thy sister labored that its music might bring life to the heart and light to the mind. It is our gift to thee, and its value is beyond mere gold and silver."

But Keos was enraged and departed in anger, estranging himself from his siblings. And from that time onward, it was said that great mischief came from giving gifts.

—"The First Regaleus," excerpt from *The Book of Odar*

***

And Keos returned to his forge at Thoir Cuma where his bitterness consumed him and he refused consolation. Once there, he descended to the core of Luquatra, plumbing its depths for a metal more precious than gold. And in the depths of the mountains, in the great chasms beneath the earth, Keos found a remnant of aqlumera, *the element from which the world was made. And it was both fire and ice, liquid and metal; and from it the three Elder Gods had sprung, and from it they created Luquatra.*

And Keos took the aqlumera *and laid it on his forge and crafted himself the tool he most desired: a hammer, for his joy was greatest when creating things of t'rasang. And he called it the Hand of Keos, for he poured much of his power into the hammer.*

And many centuries passed since the first Regaleus, and the people of Luquatra were greatly blessed by the Gods. And they were lifted up in the pride of their hearts and the traditions of their cultures, both the Darites and the Ilumites as well as the Terrans. And contentions arose among the people regarding points of doctrine and of rulership, and they established kings and kingdoms amongst themselves. And thus ended the Age of the Gods and began the Age of Kings.

Now when Odar and Lumea saw the changes being wrought among their people, they went down amongst their worshippers and counseled them, and they taught them to be peaceable and humble. And to the degree that people listened, so they were blessed. And the Flute of Lumea and the Staff of Odar passed unto many of the Ilumites and Darites. And they were called daltas, or Child Gods, for they wielded the Artifacts of the Gods and were blessed with divine power.

But the Terrans were not counseled or taught by Keos during this time, for his anger still consumed him. And his children became a warlike people, prone to savagery and lust. And instead of crafting tools and instruments, they began to forge weapons and armor and arrayed themselves with all manner of fine apparel and jewelry. And when Keos finally rose from Thoir Cuma and gazed upon the works of his people, he was not angered but glad. And he became a fickle god, prone to blessing those possessed with strength and beauty, willing to lend his favor to those who fought well and were filled with passion.

And it came to pass that many years had passed away, yea, even six hundred years had passed away since the first Regaleus. And it was seven hundred years since the day that Myahlai, the Incarnation of Entropy, was cast out of Luquatra.

—"The Fall of Keos," excerpt from *The Book of Odar*

CHAPTER ONE

"Annev! Wake up."

Annev rolled away from the voice as a sharp jab in the ribs brought him to complete wakefulness.

"Ouch!"

"Get up," Sodar hissed, prodding Annev with the butt of his staff again. "You're going to be late for class."

Annev sat up and threw off the mound of blankets. "I'm awake! I'm up!" He jumped to his feet and shivered as they touched the freezing floor. He stretched, shivered again, and inhaled the earthy smell of sweat mixed with straw, dirt, and cinnamon. He wrinkled his nose and yawned.

With the windows shuttered, the only light came from the guttering candle just outside his bedroom door. As his bleary eyes adjusted, he saw the priest standing before him, staff in hand.

"Come on!" Sodar snapped. Then he paused, his face softening as he studied Annev in his small clothes. "You can skip dusting the chapel today. You'll barely have time to wash as it is."

Annev grinned despite the chill. "I'll have time," he said as he flipped open the chest by his bed and pulled out a stained beige tunic and matching pair of breeches. The unbleached fabric had once been ecru—almost white—but now his Academy clothes looked more brown than greige.

"Fine," Sodar said, beckoning him to hurry. "Water, hearth, kettle. When you're done—"

"I know, I know," Annev pulled on his breeches. "Check the traps and clean the chapel. Same thing every day."

"Almost every day," Sodar corrected. When Annev looked up, Sodar caught his eye. "Tonight is the first night of Regaleus. And tomorrow is Testing Day. The *last* Testing Day." The words hung in the air, heavy with meaning.

Annev nodded, his face turning solemn. "I haven't forgotten."

Sodar nodded. "Good. Hurry up then. I'll ready your waterskins. I'm starting the count as soon as you leave this room." The priest left.

Testing Day, Annev thought, lacing up his breeches. *The last Test of Judgment*. The next three days were Regaleus, the celebration that signaled the beginning of spring, and that meant tomorrow was the last time Annev's class could take the test—the last chance any of them had to earn their avatar titles.

Annev weighed his chances of finally earning his title—and sighed.

The Academy held a test at the end of every month to see which student would advance from Acolyte of Faith to Avatar of Judgment. Only one student could advance each month—and after participating in fourteen tests, fewer than half of Annev's classmates had earned the coveted rank. It might have been more but becoming an avatar didn't disqualify the winners from participating in the *next* Test of Judgment, so boys who had already won kept competing against those who hadn't.

It isn't fair, Annev thought—not for the first time. *Especially when my reap is the largest the Academy's ever had.*

Annev belted his tunic and pulled on his soft leather boots. As he laced them, he thought of his two friends—a skinny youth named Therin and a plump little boy named Titus—neither of which had earned their avatar titles. Remembering that detail pained Annev, for it also reminded him he would be competing against his two friends for the final avatar promotion. It seemed unlikely, too, that either of Annev's friends would win, for neither excelled at physical combat. Therin's strengths instead lay in stealth and skullduggery, while Titus was simply outmatched. Almost two years younger than the rest of Annev's classmates, Titus had come to the Academy in a later reaping and was advanced into Annev's class because of his talent with the softer skills taught by the ancients, such as history, husbandry, agronomy, and arithmetic. But that advancement had also come with an ultimatum: if Titus could not pass the Test of Judgment with his senior classmates, he could not graduate at all.

No student had ever been turned out of the Academy, but those who failed their Test of Judgment were forbidden from ever becoming master avatars. Instead, they became stewards, and in Annev's mind there was no greater punishment: stewards could never qualify for the highest rank of Ancient of the Academy, they could not teach the acolytes, they could not marry, and they were de facto servants of the masters and ancients, subject to their whims and slave to any tasks the Master of Operations deemed appropriate.

That wasn't even the worst part, though, which was that avatars were sent on artifact retrieval missions once they became masters, but stewards could never leave Chaenbalu. They would spend their whole lives in the village, trapped.

Annev always felt for Markov, in particular, a steward who spent most of his days helping Master Narach catalog artifacts in the Vault of Damnation. A plague had passed through Chaenbalu several years ago, striking many people down, including a good portion of the Academy's older students, witwomen, and master avatars. Markov was one of the lucky few who fell sick but survived. Unfortunately, he had been too ill to participate in most of his reap's tests, and by the time he had fully recovered his chance was gone.

Annev pulled out a pair of black gloves and stared at them, noticing that the left was more threadbare than the right. He shrugged, flung the second glove back into his chest, and pulled the worn glove up to his elbow. He didn't always wear one glove, but he did it often enough that the masters and ancients had come to accept it as his personal idiosyncrasy.

Dressed and ready, Annev went to the kitchen where Sodar threw him a pair of thick leather water bags. Annev caught them instinctively.

"One," the priest began. "Two ..." Before Sodar reached three, Annev was through the kitchen door, racing past the rows of benches in the chapel and flinging open the doors. He stumbled in the near darkness then righted himself and sprinted out into the morning.

Annev's routine was the same every day: run to the well at the center of the village then race back with as much water as he could carry. Meanwhile, Sodar sat serenely in the kitchen, counting the seconds for Annev to return.

The task was supposed to complement Annev's Academy training, but for the first year Annev had considered it little more than a grueling chore. He complained for so long that Sodar finally made a game of it.

"Bring back enough water to fill this jug," Sodar said, indicating a large clay pot in the corner of the kitchen. "Fill it before I count to fifteen hundred."

"What do I get if I do?" a cheeky, eight-year-old Annev had asked.

"You get to drink it."

Annev's brow furrowed. "I can do that now."

"Not anymore, you can't." He waited for his words to sink in.

"You're not going to let me drink our water?" Annev exclaimed, incredulous. "The water *I* bring you? The water *I* have to carry?"

Sodar smiled. "You're catching on."

And he hadn't been kidding either. The day after Sodar proposed his little game, Annev had deliberately taken his time on the way back to the chapel. He had been carrying the water in buckets back then and thought that by going slowly he would spill less water and not need to make a second trip. He had been right—he had filled the water jug to overflowing—but Sodar's count had reached two thousand. When Annev then ventured to scoop a ladle of water, Sodar's staff had come swinging down on his hand, knocking the ladle across the room.

"OUCH!" Annev shouted, rubbing his bruised hand. "Odar's *balls*! What was that for?"

"Language," Sodar chided, picking up the ladle. "And you know why. Rules are rules. No water from the jug." And that had been that. No water to drink or to wash his face or hands. He'd left early that morning—thirsty and stinking—so he could stop at the village well and draw up a few handfuls of water before class.

He was rarely late again.

As Annev sprinted towards the well through the predawn light, he swung the thick leather sling around his neck and draped the empty water bags behind his back.

The bags had been his idea, one he was especially proud of. After months of blisters and a few times he had tripped and spilled the buckets of water,

Annev had spoken with the village tanner Elyas and asked how he could make a waterproof bag. By the end of the week, Annev had two of them and was bringing the water home before Sodar could count to fifteen hundred.

"Well done," Sodar said after the second week of bringing the water back early. "Let's see if you can fill the jug before I get to thirteen hundred."

And so it went. Year after year. Each time Annev found a way to improve his time, Sodar dropped the count. When Annev became quicker at drawing the water from the well it fell to twelve hundred. When his endurance improved, it fell again, and when Annev mastered gliding across the ground without jostling the water bags, Sodar dropped the count to one thousand.

Annev had his own count when he reached the well. After hanging both bags over his chest, he kicked the lock-bar holding the hand crank in place and listened as the bucket tumbled to the watery depths below. As soon as it splashed, he slapped the crank and began to wind.

"One. Two. Three. Four. Five. Six. Seven." After nineteen solid cranks, the bucket rose up out of the darkness. Annev dropped the lock-bar back in place, reached over the edge of the well, and submerged one end of his sling into the bucket. Once the first bag was full, he cinched it tight and kicked the lock-bar again, sending the bucket spiraling back down into the darkness. He was on his eighth turn of the crank when something on the other side of the village plaza caught his eye. Annev glanced up just as a yellow dress and white apron ducked into Greusik's cobbler shop. His fierce cranking slowed.

Someone spying on me? Annev wondered. It couldn't have been Greusik's wife—she wasn't the type for spying and she didn't own anything brighter than the earthy red dress she wore to chapel—but it *might* have been Myjun.

The headmaster's daughter had been wearing a yellow dress over a month ago when she had beckoned Annev into the alley behind the baker's shop. Myjun had leaned him against the wall and, while his heart raced, she had slipped a piece of chalk from her apron and pressed his hand against the red bricks. Glancing away from his gaze, she carefully traced its outline on the wall then blushed as she finished and he took the chalk from her. He placed her hand so that it overlapped the outline of his and slowly traced her fingers onto the brick, memorizing her scent, the curve of her jaw, and the feel of her warm skin pressed against his. A week later, rain had washed the chalk from the wall of the bakery, but Annev's eyes still lingered on the brickwork where the white lines had been.

Annev startled as the bucket thumped to the top and water sloshed over the edge. He dropped the lock-bar in place, filled his second water bag then glanced once more at the cobbler's door, hoping for another flash of yellow.

Nothing.

He spun on his heel and raced back to the chapel.

The return trip was much slower, but Annev found that if he counted his paces as he ran, he was less likely to stumble. It was exactly 1,011 paces back to the church at the edge of the forest, and Annev spent each step thinking of Myjun and the promise ring he hoped to one day give her.

He burst through the front doors with a smile on his face and surveyed a chapel that, while large enough to house Chaenbalu's regular worshippers, was still smaller than the Academy's dusty nave. Still clutching his waterskins, he dashed up the aisle, launched himself onto the dais, and burst through the door at the back, which led immediately into the rectory.

"Nine hundred sixty-three. Nine hundred sixty-four …"

"I'm here!" Annev gasped as he burst into the kitchen and unslung the water bags. Sodar pointed at the empty clay pot in the corner of the room, still counting. Annev groaned even as he hurried to the earthenware jar and began filling it from his bags.

"Nine hundred seventy-one," Sodar concluded as Annev tossed the empty bags to the ground and slumped to the floor. "You're getting slower, Annev. Last week I never reached eight hundred."

Despite his panting, Annev found he was still smiling. "Yeah." He laughed. "I got held up."

"Doing what?"

"I thought I saw Myjun at the cobbler's."

"Mmm," Sodar tugged his beard. "That would do it I suppose." He took the wooden ladle from above the fireplace mantle and began spooning water into the kettle hanging over the blazing hearth. "Was it truly her?"

"I don't know. I think so. She ducked into Greusik's just as I was filling the waterskins."

Sodar shook his head. "And what would your headmaster say if he caught you pining after his daughter? Hmm? It's bad enough that you cross paths at the Academy. If you start running into her outside of her father's domain, and without his knowledge …"

Annev eased himself into a chair. "Tosan," Annev said, "can take a flying piss off a rolling bread bun."

"Annev!" Sodar turned, spilling water. "Tosan is the Eldest of Ancients and head of the Academy. Show some respect."

"Fine," Annev said. "*Elder* Tosan can take a flying—" He met the priest's eyes and saw they were cold as ice. He swallowed. "Sorry, Sodar. I'm just … I'm worried about the testing tomorrow."

Sodar turned back to his kettle. As he did, Annev thought he heard a suppressed bark of laughter followed by the words "… rolling bread bun".

Annev smiled. No matter Sodar's words, he knew there was no love between the priest and the headmaster. The division between the priesthood and the Academy stemmed from a split that had occurred decades ago—well before Sodar came to Chaenbalu—but the tension had been exacerbated by Annev's apprenticeship to the priest, and Sodar made no effort to relieve it. Sometimes Annev thought he was even stoking it.

With the kettle full, Sodar passed the ladle to Annev who took several long gulps of water from the clay pot. Meanwhile, Sodar moved about the kitchen gathering tea leaves and cinnamon sticks. "As you check the traps, don't reset them—and please spring all the ones that haven't been set off." He tossed the leaves and sticks into the kettle.

"But not the bird traps," Annev said, replacing the ladle on the mantle.

"The bird traps too. 'No beast, nor fish, nor fowl shalt thou consume on my holy day.'"

"But it's not Seventhday," Annev argued.

"No, it's the first night of Regaleus," Sodar said, tossing a handful of ground chicory root into the kettle. "Besides, if tomorrow is anything like every other Testing Day, you'll be no use to me in the morning. So distracted I'll have to mend half your chores." He shook his head. "We'll prepare for tomorrow today; spring *all* the traps."

Annev frowned at the reminder of tomorrow's Test—and Sodar's allusion to his previous failures—and felt churlish.

"If *The Book of Odar* says we're not supposed to eat animals on holy days, why do we still eat birds and fish on Seventhday?"

"Because Seventhday is a regular holy day. Not a "holiday" like Regaleus."

Annev's frown deepened. "But shouldn't we still—"

"Annev, do you really want to debate the difference between holy days and holidays now?" Sodar asked. "The Council of Neven nan Su'ul tried that in the Third Age. Whole books are written on the subject, and most of it's horseshit."

Annev's mouth dropped open, though the priest pretended not to notice. A smile flickered across his face as he concentrated on his tea.

"The truth," Sodar continued, "is that I can be a bit of a hypocrite, but—unlike some of my brothers—I try to be honest about it." He glanced back at Annev, his eyes twinkling. "But this isn't about holy days or *The Book of Odar*, is it? It's not even about you doing your chores."

Annev looked into the priest's eyes and clenched his jaw, afraid to speak.

Sodar watched him for a moment. "You'll do fine, Annev. No matter what happens, I'm proud of you."

Annev nodded once, his face flushed. "Sure," he said, his throat clenched. "So I spring all the traps. Anything else?"

Sodar poked at the leaves floating in the kettle. "Don't chop more firewood. We have enough in the shed to last us through the weekend, and I'd rather you were early today."

"I still have plenty of time to get to class."

"Not if you plan to change and wash that face of yours. It's grubby enough to make your tunic look white again."

Annev forced a laugh then rubbed his hand along his cheek. There was definitely dirt there, though he wasn't sure if it came from his fingertips or his face. "Alright," Annev said. "I'll hurry back," and he ran before Sodar could tell him to do anything else.

CHAPTER TWO

The door at the back of the kitchen had once led directly outside, but as Annev had grown older, Sodar had constructed a makeshift wood enclosure that extended far beyond the back door and encompassed a large enough space for Annev to train in. The woodshed also housed a variety of mock weapons, a training dummy, firewood, an underground root cellar, and a small privy.

As Annev entered the darkened room, he snatched his game bag and hunting knife from their peg on the wall then eyed the privy in the far corner of the shed. With a sigh, he jogged over to the squat box and removed the waste-filled pot hidden beneath it. Holding the vessel at arm's length, he left the shed and trotted the quarter mile to the edge of the woods, emptying the pot into the copse of trees he used specifically for that purpose. Finished, he set the pot down and stalked into the woods, eager to discover what animals his traps may have caught.

A dozen paces into the Brakewood, Annev stopped to inhale the glade's rich aroma and take in the familiar sights and sounds of the forest. He studied the tall conifers with their evergreen boughs, which contrasted the oak and beech trees that still wore the dead leaves of winter, yielding them only when new buds grew to take their place. He ran beneath them to one of the game trails that led deep into the forest and raced down the untamed path to his first set of snares.

Within half an hour, Annev had a pheasant, two plump squirrels, and an even plumper rabbit to show for his efforts. He was heading back toward the village and was almost in sight of the tree line when he noticed a strange, inky pool of darkness surrounding a cluster of pine trees. Annev stared at the shadows, watching them shift as light filtered down from the forest canopy.

Shadepools were rare in the Brakewood, but Annev had chanced upon a few in the depths of the forest. He had never interacted with one, though, and this was first he'd seen so near the village.

With his game bag secure over one shoulder, Annev walked to a nearby blackthorn and stooped to grab a stone that was half the size of his palm. He hefted it in his hand, looked back to the pool of darkness, and threw the projectile.

The stone disappeared into the thick grass and murky shadows with a muffled *whoosh*. Annev stared at where the darkness had swallowed the rock. After a few seconds, he huffed. He wasn't sure what he had expected, but he had hoped for something more exciting than nothing. Worse, the strangeness of the shadepool still called to him.

With his eyes still fixed on the shifting pool of shadows, Annev bent to pick up a second stone and a bright pain shot through his hand. With a curse, he released the blackthorn he had accidentally grasped and flexed his injured right hand, watching two red dots blossom on his palm. He almost wiped the blood on his tunic then stopped, catching himself before he further stained the beige linen.

Annev looked down at the dirt and dead pine needles covering the forest floor then spied another gray stone, almost twice as large as the first. He moved aside the thorny branch at his feet and scooped up the rock, wiping his bloody palm on the surface of the stone and letting the chill surface cool his throbbing hand before he hurled it into the void. The stone disappeared into the blackness.

For a while, nothing happened. Then, so subtle he almost missed it, Annev saw a shudder of dark crimson pulse across the surface of the shadepool. Annev blinked, trying to focus on the throb of color, but it had already gone. The shadow's surface was undisturbed, just as it had been before he'd thrown the stone.

Annev grit his teeth. He knew he should go, but instead he ventured to the edge of the shadepool. His heart thudded in his chest, but he forced his foot into the blackness. When still nothing happened, Annev slowly stepped in, his skin growing cold as he waded into the opaque pool of shadows. As he moved, the shades lapped at his knees and then his hips—almost like wading into the mill pond at night—but then the darkness grew colder, and Annev had the distinct impression that something or someone was watching him. He held his nerve for a moment then hastily retreated, frightened.

Free of the darkness, Annev chided himself. He was alone in the woods, and the shadepool was no cooler than any other patch of shadows. Nothing to startle at. Yet even with that in mind, the shadepool unnerved Annev more than he cared to admit. He glanced once more at the shadows, then he shivered and hurried home.

***

"Did you empty the chamber pot?" Sodar asked the moment Annev had stepped into the kitchen.

"Yes," Annev said, glad he had returned the now-empty vessel to the privy before hanging up his game bag and entering the rectory.

"Good. Wash, eat, and we'll test your magic."

Annev groaned. "We did that last week."

"We should be doing it *every day*," Sodar said, pouring his tea. "But I've been too busy with my Speur Dún translation." He sighed, tugged his beard, and took a sip of tea. "I mean to be better about that. Besides, with Regaleus upon us, you should have better luck accessing your magic."

Annev vigorously rubbed his injured hand in the cold water, washing the remaining blood from his palm, then he splashed his face. "Is magic always more prevalent around Regaleus?" he asked, his face dripping.

"That's what I've observed." Sodar threw him a towel.

"Maybe that explains the shadepools."

"Shadepools?"

Annev nodded as he tossed the damp towel back to Sodar. "The places in the Brake where the shadows clump together. Like pools of water."

"Yes, you've mentioned them before though not by that name. Did you see one today?"

Annev rubbed the elbow-length glove covering his left arm and nodded. "Near the tree line." He paused. "Never seen one so close to the village before." He recalled how the darkness had chilled his skin and shivered. When he looked up, he saw the priest studying him.

"These shadepools," Sodar said, still watching Annev, "you could never get close to them before." Annev nodded. "So you've never interacted with them?"

Annev shrugged. "No, not really. Today I got close enough to throw some rocks in, but nothing happened." Annev felt the priest's eyes on him long enough that he felt Sodar knew there was more to his tale. Finally, the old man grunted and turned back to his tea.

"I've never seen these pools myself," Sodar said, taking a long sip from his mug, "but you may be right about why they are appearing now. The Brake has a queer connection to the shadow realm, and that connection will be stronger during Regaleus. Could be harmless, but I'd steer clear all the same." Sodar waited for Annev to reply. When he merely nodded, the priest wagged a finger at him. "I need you to say it, Annev. Promise you won't go near those shadepools."

Annev swallowed. "I promise."

"Excellent," Sodar said, moving toward his bedroom door. "Now, if the Brake's magic is stronger this morning, I expect yours will be too. Not enough time for us to test your glyphs, so let's try the sack." He sat down and pulled a faded green bag from his robes.

Annev moaned and dumped himself into the chair facing Sodar. When the priest frowned at him, he plastered a smile on his face and spoke with mock enthusiasm.

"Bring out the bottomless bag of disappointments!"

Sodar scoffed then dropped the empty bag on the table. Annev slid it across the worn tabletop, untied the drawstring and stuck his right hand inside.

"This never works for me."

Sodar shrugged. "Maybe today will be different."

"Sure. Maybe today it will cut off my hand."

Sodar smiled then took a sip of his tea. 'Doubtful. A hiding-sack is no good if its owner loses a limb whenever they reach inside. In any case, you have to let go of an item before the sack can take it."

Annev fumbled with the fabric, thinking. "Why is it I can use the artifacts the masters give us for training classes, but I can't get this sack to work?"

"Because an artifact can be keyed to work for anyone, for certain kinds of people, or even for one person in particular. The masters and ancients assume no one at the Academy can perform magic, so they are giving you common artifacts—something anyone can use. But this hiding-sack has been keyed to only work for those with the talent, which means it requires more effort to activate."

Annev grunted. "What am I pulling out?"

Sodar leaned back in his chair and stroked his beard. "Your breakfast. If you find it then you can eat it."

"That's not funny, Sodar."

"It's not meant to be."

"Wait," Annev said. "You're serious? You put my breakfast in there?" The priest nodded. "But … I've *never* pulled anything out of that sack. I'll starve."

"I'm not starving you. Your breakfast is right in that bag. No one's stopping you."

Annev frowned but rummaged inside the empty sack. He always felt like a fool when trying to do magic, and today was no different.

"It would help if you told me what I'm supposed to be finding."

"Bacon."

Annev paused, uncertain. "You didn't make bacon. I'd have smelled it."

Sodar grinned. "That's true, but I put a few strips of cottage bacon in there a year or two ago. Should still be good."

Annev flinched at the thought of his fingers sliding into a heap of rancid meat. He pulled his hand from the bag and tossed the empty sack at his mentor.

"I don't believe you."

The priest shrugged. "More for me, I suppose." He reached inside and pulled out a thick strip of cooked bacon.

Annev stared as Sodar crunched on the hot piece of meat. He caught the unmistakable whiff of grease and smoked meat and felt his stomach rumble.

"Give me the bag."

Sodar slid the sack across the table as he ate the last piece and licked his fingers clean.

Annev picked up the bag and stuck his hand back in, this time imagining a plate piled high with crispy bacon.

"So," he asked, fumbling at the green cloth, "how does it stay hot? Does time not pass inside the bag?"

"Near as I can tell. The artificer that made it seems to have connected the bag to an alternate space where time passes very slowly. I believe that's part of the reason the artifact is so well preserved."

Annev glanced at the threadbare cloth, his expression dubious. "Looks a bit ratty to me."

"I suppose it does. But how old does it *look*?"

Annev shrugged, trying to focus on the sensation of hot bacon appearing in his hands. "I don't know. Maybe a hundred years old?"

"Try three or four thousand years old."

Annev stopped thinking of breakfast, the immensity of Sodar's claim shaking thoughts of bacon from his skull. "This was around during the Age of Kings?"

"Yes. Possibly even earlier."

"How do you know though? How can you be sure?" Sodar reached for the sack and Annev let it go, resigning himself to a hungry morning.

"Because," the priest said, "one day I reached in to pull out a coin." Sodar demonstrated by putting his wrinkled hand inside the sack. "I had dropped in a handful of coins a few days before, but I was only buying bread, so I didn't much care what coin I pulled out." Sodar removed his hand from the sack and dropped a misshapen copper penny on the table. "Imagine my surprise when I saw that."

Annev picked it up. The coin was heavier than he expected, rough around the edges and not perfectly circular. The faces were a little worn, but he could make out the Staff of Odar dividing a wind-tossed sea from a lightning-streaked sky. Amidst the waves, Annev spied the faded letters "U-R-R-A-N". He flipped the penny over to see a wicked-looking variation of the raven's beak hammer: part smithing tool, part war hammer; the long-handled weapon floated ominously above a smoking anvil.

"Keos," Annev whispered, dropping the coin. The copper rolled unsteadily across the table's surface before toppling over in front of Sodar.

"Keos, indeed," Sodar said, picking up the penny.

"I've never seen anything like that," Annev breathed. "Is it Darite or Terran?"

"Both." Sodar turned the coin over in his hand. "The nations of Daroea and Terra shared currency for a brief period during the Age of Kings—the Second Age."

"But how does that prove the bag's age? If the coin predates the bag, it could have been dropped there by you or some coin collector."

Sodar gave a half-nod, half-shrug. "The coins were put out of circulation in the Second Age, so I think it unlikely, but there's also this." Sodar turned the sack inside out. Annev studied it until he saw what Sodar meant him to see: the letters "U-R-R-A-N" stitched into the seam.

"What does that mean?"

"Not what. *Who.* The Terran who forged the mold for this coin is the same man who crafted this sack. The most talented artisan of his time—a master among master craftsmen whose dedication to his art was beyond compare—and he was born at the dawn of the Second Age. Early in his career, he put his stamp on every artifact he made. He wanted the world to know what his hands had forged and fabricated." Sodar flipped the coin expertly between his fingers. "As Urran grew older, though, he realized he could only ever leave a fleeting mark on the world, so he gave up making artifacts to join the clergy."

"He became a Bloodlord?"

"Yes and no. Bloodlords are a subset of Terrans who possess the talent, but we Darites tend to group them all together. Technically, Urran remained a Master Artificer but, as the story goes, he exchanged being a craftsman for crafting himself into a better man."

"And," Annev finished, "since he stopped making artifacts, that means the bag and the coin were made at about the same time."

"Exactly." Sodar stopped flipping the coin, holding it so that the faded letters reflected some of the room's light.

"What happened to Urran after he joined the clergy?"

Sodar flicked his fingertips and the coin vanished. "That's a story for another day."

Annev scoffed as Sodar reached across the table and plucked the coin from behind Annev's ear. He rolled his eyes and the priest smiled.

"You groan, but even tricks have their place." Sodar dropped the copper penny back into the green sack and handed the latter to Annev. "Do a trick for me. Pull out Urran's penny."

Annev took the sack in his left hand and peered inside, then he sighed and shook his head. "I can't do it, Sodar. I can't find the bacon. I won't find the coin. I'd be lucky if I could pull out a ball of lint."

"I'd take lint."

Annev snorted but stuck his hand in and fished around for a moment. After a few seconds, he pulled his hand out again. "You realize how this feels, right? Rummaging inside an empty sack? It's—"

"The embodiment of futility?"

"I was going to say silly."

Sodar waved a hand dismissively. "Just concentrate on finding the penny. Remember its heft. How it looked. How it felt in your hand."

Annev swirled his hand around in a circular motion. "A very old penny. Got it. I'm picturing it now."

"You saw me drop it in there. It's just waiting for you to pull it out."

Annev circled his hand around the inside of the bag a few more times then stopped. His eyebrows shot up and a look of astonishment passed over him. "I think I got it," he whispered, slowly pulling his hand from the mantis-green sack.

Sodar leaned forward, his eyes fixed on Annev's tight-fisted hand. "You did? Well done, my boy! Well done. Let's see it." He held his hand extended beneath Annev's fist and watched as Annev opened his hand, palm facing downward.

And nothing fell out.

Sodar frowned then looked up to find Annev restraining his laughter. When their eyes met, the boy burst out laughing.

"Gotcha!" Annev said, snickering. "Sorry, Sodar, but that was too easy."

The old priest huffed and snatched the sack back. "If you took this more seriously, you would have more success."

"If I had any success, I might take it more seriously," Annev countered. He stood up from the table. "Keep your breakfast. I have to run. If I'm late for Dorstal's class, he'll disqualify me from tomorrow's test."

Sodar nodded, also rising from his seat. He placed a hand on Annev's shoulder. "Be careful today. I've seen how combative you boys get before Testing Day—especially Fyn. A good thief doesn't win fights, he avoids them."

"We're not thieves, Sodar. We're avatars."

Sodar grunted. "I see little difference, but at least you take *something* seriously." He picked up his mug and the empty sack. "You're a better avatar than any boy in that class, Annev, even if they haven't given you the title yet—even if they *never* do. You don't have to prove anything to anyone."

Annev thought about the test. He and his friends usually worked together to win, but tomorrow … *Titus, Therin, or me. We're a team … but only one of us can win …*

Then there was the promise ring hidden in his room—the one he hoped to give to Myjun on the final night of Regaleus. When Annev had asked Sraon to forge it, he'd been certain he would be one of the first students to pass the Test of Judgment—a critical detail since only avatars were permitted to court women, and only master avatars and ancients could wed. Put simply, if Annev failed tomorrow's Test and became a steward, he'd lose both Myjun and his future at the Academy in one blow.

That couldn't happen. Annev could *not* fail tomorrow. He refused to become a steward. He hardened his resolve: he would tell his friends they were on their own tomorrow. That was fair. Each acolyte would decide their own fate.

Another thought lingered at the back of Annev's mind: he could use his friends. He could tell Titus and Therin that three of them were still in it together—that they could win it together—and then he could turn on them when the test required it.

The idea made Annev's stomach churn even as he acknowledged it was the cleverest thing to do—which suggested it was probably the correct move.

Annev looked back at Sodar, his face a mass of conflicting emotions. He swallowed.

"Right," he said. "Nothing to prove."

CHAPTER THREE

Ancient Dorstal paced in front of the class, his black robes swishing with each step. Morning light trickled in from a small glass window barely illuminating his cowled face.

To Dorstal's right, a raised table displayed twelve rods made of metal or wood. To his left, twelve teenage boys sat at three rows of dark-stained tables. Five of the boys wore earthy brown smocks, clean and richly dyed; the rest, including Annev, were in varying shades of beige.

"... some argue that most magical rods are harmless," Dorstal said, continuing his lecture, "intended for healing or mundane chores like washing clothes and boiling water. But it doesn't take long for those simple purposes to be misused." Dorstal stopped pacing in front of an acolyte in a filthy beige smock. At the back of the class a large boy in a brown tunic yawned. Two of his classmates—also in brown—stifled a laugh. Dorstal ignored them.

"That is why you must take care when recovering any kind of artifact. Over the years, the avatars and masters of Chaenbalu have collected most of the magic wands in Northwestern Daroea, including the greater rods and dark rods, which are the most dangerous—but even the humblest rod can kill if you aren't careful."

At the back of the class, Annev raised his hand. Ancient Dorstal glanced away and moved behind the table holding the magic artifacts. Annev waited, hand still up.

"Now, I mentioned classification." Dorstal took a piece of chalk from his pocket and began to draw on the sheet of slate cut into the classroom wall. "Greater rods refer to wands with immense power." Dorstal drew two stars at opposite ends of the board. The first was large, the second much smaller. "The term "great" may refer to the ability of the wand itself but is typically a descriptor of its power,"—he circled the large star—"its range,"—he drew a dotted line between the two stars—"or its range." Dorstal drew a second and then a third star atop the smaller star. "So some rods are great because their influence lasts a long time—indefinitely in some cases." He tapped the small star twice. "And some because of their power, their intensity, or because they are effective at long distances."

Dorstal tapped the dotted line with a flourish then turned to face the class. He glanced at Annev's still-raised hand then turned his attention to the wands on display. "A dark rod, on the other hand, is the term for any wand whose singular, dedicated purpose is to harm, injure, or manipulate others."

"Ancient Dorstal," Annev said.

"What, Acolyte Ainnevog?" Dorstal snapped.

Annev lowered his hand. "I understand why we retrieve the greater rods and the dark rods." Annev chose his words carefully. "But if the owner of an ordinary rod is just a woodcutter or a washerwoman then what's the harm in letting them keep it? They're not hurting anyone so why should we—"

The large boy sitting two seats to Annev's left, groaned. "Give it up, Annev. They only send *avatars* on retrieval missions, and after tomorrow you'll be a steward." The heckler, Fyn, leaned around the student sitting between them and met Annev's eyes. "I'll make sure of it," Fyn whispered, eyes gleaming.

Annev wanted to ignore the young avatar, but the bully's words had a sting of truth that hurt too much to ignore. Fyn had done it a few times already, cutting other students off and winning four of the fourteen competitions so far—just one short of the Academy record.

At the front of the class, Dorstal looked for all the world as if he had sucked a sour washrag, but Annev pressed on, ignoring Fyn's taunts and Dorstal's disapproving glare.

"Ancient Dorstal, you said we take the artifacts because people misuse them. But how do we *know* they misuse them? We're just assuming they're bad people, and that's not fair." Dorstal's eyes flared and Annev drew back in his seat. "That doesn't *seem* fair," Annev amended quietly. "Not to me."

"It doesn't *need* to make sense to *you*, acolyte," Dorstal said briskly. "If you achieve the title of avatar tomorrow, it still need not make sense to you. An avatar's duty is to recover dangerous artifacts from dangerous people. Questions of morality are decided by the ancients."

If there was a note of finality to Dorstal's explanation, Annev did not hear it.

"But what about rods of healing?" Annev persisted. "Those aren't dangerous. Why should I—why should *we*—steal them from healers?"

"Magic," Dorstal said coldly, "has been outlawed for *centuries*. Magic is evil. People who do not give up their magic are outlaws. *They* are evil, and power-hungry in turn." He studied Annev's face for continued dissent. "Magic of any kind is dangerous, no matter who wields it. We are tasked with protecting others by securing it in the Vault of Damnation, under the supervision of the Order of Ancients."

Annev then wanted to ask why the masters and ancients could use artifacts for training at the Academy, but not permit others to heal their sick or injured—but he sensed this was an argument he would not win. Pressing would only further provoke Dorstal, and Annev couldn't risk a punishment that might jeopardize his participation in tomorrow's test. He quietly gave up the argument and Dorstal's wrinkled face smoothed itself out again. The man nodded curtly and went back to the rods on the table.

"Once you've accepted that *all* rods are dangerous," Dorstal said, looking sternly at Annev, "then you must learn to tell if the rod you are stealing is magical or not. Sometimes a rod is just a rod, just as some sticks are just sticks. If they hold no magic, they are not artifacts."

Dorstal looked out over the class. "Throughout your training at the Academy you have been taught how to tell the difference between an artifact and an ordinary, nonmagical item. We will test that skill today, before your final Testing Day." He eyed the boys in beige. "Let's see if you can identify if these wands are magical,"—he gestured at the rods on the table—"and, if so, what they do." Dorstal crooked a finger at a skinny boy in a dirty tunic. "Therin."

Therin stumbled out of his seat and quickstepped to the ancient's side.

He avoided looking at the rods and gave Annev a crooked smile. Dorstal looked down his nose at the black-haired boy.

"Take a rod, Therin."

Therin paused, studied the display, then raised his right hand and paused again, his hand hovering nearly a foot above the table.

"You can't test the rods without touching them, Therin."

A laugh went up in the back of the room. Therin blushed, self-conscious, and pinched a slender ash wand between his fingers.

"Hold it properly," Dorstal chided. "Avatars can't be scared of the very artifacts they're sent to collect." Several more of Annev's classmates laughed, but Dorstal continued. "You'll have a better idea of what the rod can do if you make full contact with it." Therin winced but complied. "Now. What do you feel?"

Despite the laughter, the class was leaning forward with earnest interest. Even Annev was curious what Therin might sense. His friend wasn't the best at magical identification, but he wasn't the worst either.

"It's magical," Therin said. "I can tell that. And it's cold. Very cold."

Dorstal let the cowl of his robe fall back, exposing his bald head. "What else?"

Therin's shoulders slumped. "I don't know. What *should* I feel?"

Dorstal snatched the wand out of Therin's hand and balanced it in the center of his palm. He held it there, barely breathing, not saying anything, the boys watching with bated breath. Finally he rested it on the table beside the other wands.

"It's a Rod of True-seeing," Dorstal said, looking at Therin. "And I suspect that it felt cold because we're going to have a light frost tonight. The details would be obvious to someone innately cursed with magic, but with practice even the pure can discern an artifact's true nature." He paused, eying the boy in front of him. "You did well, Therin. That was a hard one." The boy plopped himself back down in his seat, sighing with relief. "Who's next?"

Four hands shot up. Dorstal eyed the group then singled out a boy who had not volunteered.

"Fyunai."

Fyn eased out of his chair and swaggered to the front of the room, his brown dreadlocks swinging lazily. He was tall, athletically built, and handsome.

He was also mean as piss, most especially to Annev.

Dorstal waited as the larger boy took his place at the long wooden table. "Take a rod, Avatar Fyunai."

Fyn flicked his dreadlocks back and selected a rod made of solid gold. He clutched it in one hand and half-closed his eyes. After a few seconds, he opened them again.

"It's magical," he said. "I can feel it pulse. But it also makes my skin feel raw." He paused, studying the ancient's face as he spoke. "It's almost painful … like it's been used to hurt people." He waited for a reaction from Dorstal.

The ancient shrugged. "Perhaps it has. But can you discern the rod's intended purpose?

Fyn hesitated. "Ah … to torture people?"

Dorstal studied Fyn's face for a second before starting to laugh. He laughed so hard his eyes teared up and he began to cough, which turned into a hacking gasp for breath. The ancient doubled over, clutching his mouth and robes while his students watched with a mixture of amusement and concern.

Dorstal finally got his breathing under control. He wiped his eyes, laughed a little more and smoothed his clothes.

"Yes," he said. "Very good, Fyunai." The ancient patted the boy's shoulder. "It's not a dark rod or a greater rod, but you're probably right that it caused some people discomfort." He reached out and took the rod from Fyn.

Fyn exchanged glances with Jasper and Kellor—the two friends who sat in the back with him—but the boys only shrugged.

"It's a royal cleaning rod," Dorstal said, answering the unspoken question. "For nobility who were too dainty to wipe for themselves."

Fyn grimaced and backed away from the table. He wiped his hand on the front of his brown robes and hurried back to his seat.

Dorstal chuckled as he waited for Fyn to sit down. Then his smile faded from his face. "Acolyte Ainnevog."

The rest of the class turned toward Annev as he rose from his seat and Fyn, Jasper, and Kellor whispered something behind his back. Annev ignored them, his intention focused solely on the challenge ahead of him.

Aside from the gold rod, four other metal wands lay on the display table. Of those, Annev was fairly certain that two were silver and one was bronze. He wasn't sure about the last one. Iron, maybe.

Annev couldn't discern the origin or composition of any of the seven wood rods. Some were lighter, some darker. Some were stained and some not. The only one he thought he recognized was the rod Therin had taken, but up close he wasn't sure.

"Choose a rod, Annev."

Annev lifted his hand above the display, about to take the iron wand, but then his fingers tingled and he sensed something else at the corner of the desk: a polished stick of palm vine, the same flexible Ilumite wood Annev used during his training sessions with Master Edra and his sparring sessions with Sodar. He grabbed it.

The tingling sensation spiked and Annev's arm began to throb. The feeling was painful, but pleasant, too; he wanted to laugh, he wanted to cry. Mostly, though, he suddenly wanted to destroy something—to siphon the blood from Dorstal's body, or to throw Fyn against the back wall and splatter his brains across the gray stones. And there was more than that—more than a feeling of anger or a selfish desire to act on his base impulses; he sensed the presence of untapped power, and he felt some silent part of him reach for that power, wanting to bend its purpose to his will.

Annev gasped and dropped the wand back on the table. Dorstal stood, waiting.

"It's … uh …"

"It's what, Annev?"

"It's … a dark rod. It causes pain."

Dorstal sniffed and waved the boy back to his seat. Annev hesitated for a moment, shaken and still looking at the rod, then turned and sat down.

"I'm surprised, Annev," Dorstal said, straightening the rods on the table. "This is a very easy one." The ancient sighed and picked up the palm vine wand. "This is a Rod of Healing."

There was a light rap on the door and Dorstal replaced the rod before opening it. A middle-aged man with a strong jaw waited in the hallway. His short-cropped hair was bright red, the same color as his smock.

"Master Edra," Dorstal greeted him.

"Ancient Dorstal." The redheaded man gave a slight bow then peered into the classroom. "Last day for most of these boys."

"I suppose it is," Dorstal said, looking at the class with an air of disappointment.

Edra grunted. "We aren't meeting in the sparring room today, so I thought I'd collect this lot before gathering Benifew's class."

Dorstal grunted then waved a hand at the boys. "Go on then. Follow Edra."

As one, they bolted from their seats and poured out of the room.

CHAPTER FOUR

Annev padded down the stone corridor behind the rest of his classmates, fretting over a half-dozen things. He was increasingly anxious about tomorrow's Test of Judgment, fearing failing almost as much as the inevitability of betraying his friends. Yet those fears were somehow overshadowed by his experience with the palm healing wand: why had he felt so violent when holding the rod? Why had holding it made him want to do terrible things to Dorstal and Fyn?

A Rod of Healing shouldn't do that, Annev brooded. *Its purpose is to salve wounds and heal injuries ... yet I wanted to drain the blood from Dorstal.* Bloodletting could certainly be a restorative procedure and, if done for medicinal purposes, it wasn't inherently evil ...

But I didn't want to heal him, Annev admitted to himself. *I wanted to kill him. I wanted to smash Fyn's head in.* Annev bit his lip, trying to rationalize what he had felt in the classroom. Had he sensed the rod's ability to heal people? Annev didn't think so. If it had been there at all then the rod's potential to heal had been drowned out by its more malevolent potential. As Annev pondered what that might mean, he became vaguely aware of Therin falling back to join him at the end of the queue.

Could Dorstal have mistaken the wand's purpose? Annev wondered. *It could still be a dark rod.* But if that were true, it meant Annev's instincts were superior to the ancient's knowledge and experience—and Annev doubted that.

Did that mean Dorstal was right, that all magic really was evil?

Annev would not—*could* not—believe that. Sodar had taught him that magic was a tool that could be used for good or ill, and Sodar was a mage. To believe that magic was innately evil was to accept that Sodar was evil. It simply wasn't true.

That left Annev with one answer: the dark impulses were his own, not the wand's. The more Annev thought about it, the more he suspected that was the case—and the worse he felt.

"Bad luck with that wand, eh?"

Annev looked up to see Therin watching him. At the same time, he remembered what he had to do at tomorrow's test and his treacherous heart gave a guilty lurch. "Hmm?" he said, pretending he had not heard.

"You're normally pretty good at magical identification," Therin said, oblivious. "But guessing that healing rod was a dark rod ... Heh. Pretty far off the mark." Annev's cheeks flushed. "Of course, Fyn's the dolt of the day. A *cleaning* rod. Ha! I can't believe someone turned a gompf stick into a magic artifact." He giggled then stopped, suddenly thoughtful. "Genius, though. I wouldn't mind not sharing a sponge with half the Academy."

Annev was still lost in his thoughts. He ran his fingertips over the dusty tapestries hanging on the wall as the class climbed to the next floor of the Academy.

"What was the Rod of True-seeing like?" he said after an awkward pause.

Therin pursed his lips. "Weird. At first, I thought it was cold because it had sat in the Vault of Damnation all winter—that's why I didn't say anything. I didn't want to look stupid. But then I felt this prickle down my arms and back. Like a window had been opened and an icy wind blew across my skin ... except there was no wind." He shook his head then looked over at Annev. "What did you feel when—"

"Hey," Annev interrupted, avoiding the question, "here comes Titus!" At the front, their classmates and Master Edra had joined a group of students led by the wispy-haired Ancient Benifew. Therin eyed the other class with a feral grin, his question forgotten.

"Mm," Therin grunted. "I'm going to enjoy beating Titmouse today."

Annev shook his head. "Only because Titus is the only person you can reliably beat in combat training—and he's two years younger than you."

"So? Still counts as a win." As he spoke, a round-faced boy with soft cheeks and fluffy blond hair weaved his way through the press of brown- and beige-clad students. He was smaller than the rest and, though he wore a dirty beige tunic like Annev and Therin, Titus's robes were a few shades brighter than the rest.

"What still counts?" Titus asked.

"Heya, Titmouse!" Therin ruffled the younger boy's mop of curly yellow hair.

Titus groaned and pushed Therin's hand away. "You know I hate being called that."

"Which is exactly why I do it," Therin said cheerfully. "Hey, Annev says it doesn't count when I beat you because you're so little. What do *you* say?"

Annev gave Therin a shove, knowing his paraphrasing would upset their friend.

"Is that true?" Titus asked, his voice peaking.

"No! I said Therin picks on you in combat training because he can't beat anyone his own age."

Titus brightened. "Oh. That's true. He can't."

Therin stuck his tongue out.

A dozen feet away, the black-clad Ancient Benifew took his leave of Master Edra and the fiery-haired weapons master folded his beefy forearms. He looked over the assembled boys.

"Today's weapons training will take place on the rooftop terrace," Edra said, "followed by some special training in the nave with Master Duvarek." A murmur went up at this—training with the Master of Shadows was rare.

"Quiet!" Edra snapped. Most of the boys stopped talking and suddenly Fyn's voice could be heard.

"… always away or drunk—"

Annev turned and saw that Fyn had been speaking to Jasper and hook-nosed Kellor. A bullish avatar from Titus's class had also joined the trio and was snickering in the silence. Edra's gaze locked onto him.

"Something you'd like to share with the rest of us, Brinden?"

"Uh …" Brinden shook his head. Edra nodded and turned his withering gaze on the rest of the students.

"Today's weapons training," Edra said. "I've brought two dozen weapons up from the armory. Some are in good condition, but some are bent, broken, or dull. In the field you will fight with whatever comes to hand." He smiled. "First students to the north terrace get their pick of the weapons. Last ones get the dregs. The six who do best today get a head start in tomorrow's test." He smiled, and it was all teeth. "Go!"

Annev felt a surge of adrenaline as a group of avatars darted for the nearest stairway. Therin started to follow but Annev grabbed his shoulder.

"Faster way." Annev slid past the crowd of boys sprinting up the stairs and saw another avatar had the same idea. The boy darted in front of Annev, his chin-length hair whipping back to reveal a scar running down the side of his face.

"Kenton!" Annev growled. The raven-haired boy typically kept to himself—he trained with Duvarek in almost the same way Annev did with Sodar—but about six months ago Annev had convinced Kenton to join his small group of friends. The four of them—Therin, Titus, Annev, and Kenton—had agreed to work together until they all earned their avatar titles. But as soon as Kenton passed his Test of Judgment he had reneged on his promise, turning a cold shoulder to the other acolytes and even befriending Fyn. Seeing Kenton also made Annev's conscience twinge because he planned to similarly betray Titus and Therin in tomorrow's Test.

Kenton ignored the shout of his name and instead ran faster, flinging himself down a corridor and darting up a second flight of stairs. Annev was hard on his heels when the scar-faced boy ripped a heavy tapestry down from the wall. With barely a thought, Annev rolled beneath the bulky hanging and sprang to his feet on the other side. Kenton glanced back, swore, and turned the corner.

So that's the game, Annev thought. There was swearing behind him as Therin and Titus tangled in the heavy tapestry, and as Annev turned the corner he saw Fyn and his sycophants batter Titus and Therin aside so they could run past. Annev ran even faster down the hallway.

Can't help them, he told himself, spurred on by the prospect of catching Kenton. *Have to keep moving.* The dark-haired boy had reached a junction in the corridor; he hesitated then turned right, disappearing from view. On instinct, Annev turned left.

The two corridors traced the perimeter of the upper dormitories, so Kenton and Annev would rejoin before connecting with the battlements and rooftop terrace. The difference, though, was that the younger students all had rooms along the right-hand corridor, while almost all the rooms on the left were vacant. Annev hoped Kenton would have to dodge students, slowing his progress to the roof, while Annev only need worry about the surly Master Duvarek—the corridor's single inhabitant—who would be giving a special lesson in the nave in less than an hour and should already be there.

Annev knew this in the two heartbeats it took to fling himself to the left. In the third heartbeat, he felt a flush of success. In the fourth, he collided hard with the kneeling Master of Shadows. Annev tried to soften the blow by rolling over Duvarek's kneeling form, but at that precise moment the master raised his face, which caused his head to plow into Annev's stomach. The impact threw Duvarek backwards, cracking the master's head against the thinly carpeted floor. Annev twisted, slamming his shoulder into the ground as his hip squelched into the master's pool of vomit. For a moment they both lay on the floor, winded and covered in Duvarek's sick.

Annev groaned, awkwardly rising to his knees.

"Keos," Duvarek swore. The scruffy-looking master was about to say more, but instead he turned his head and vomited on the carpet again.

Annev scrabbled backward, accidentally kicking Duvarek as he fumbled to extricate himself from both the master and the puddle. When he judged he was a safe distance away, he scrabbled to his feet and saw that a dark stain now covered his right side from his ribs to his thigh. He might have been worried about the garment, but the dark spot had already begun to fade, blending with the sweat and grime already staining his tunic.

Nothing will hide that smell, though.

With an effort, Duvarek scooted off the soiled rug and pressed his temple against the cool stone floor.

"Bloody … burning … bones."

Annev blinked, thinking he should run before the master recognized him. Then Duvarek turned his head and Annev realized it was too late.

His face was puffy, his hair black and unruly, and there were dark circles beneath his watery eyes. He blinked, his vision focusing on Annev.

"What the *hell*, Acolyte Annev?"

Annev swallowed. He could hear the other avatars racing down the hall Kenton had taken. As the sound of their footsteps started to fade, Annev blurted the first thing that came to mind.

"I'm sorry, Master Duvarek! I was racing to class. I can't be late or I might be disqualified from tomorrow's Test of Judgment."

"I should disqualify you now," Duvarek slurred, clutching his head.

"Please don't! I have to compete in that test, Master Duvarek. It's my last chance."

The Master of Shadows screwed up his face as if mentioning the test had awoken something he'd been trying to drown in honey wine. He sat up, wiped his mouth and flicked the wet gobbets from his fingers so that they spattered on the wall. Then he looked back at Annev.

"Go on then." The master wiped his palm on his tunic before running the same sticky hand through his tousled black hair. "I'll deal with you in an hour."

Annev raced for the rooftop.

CHAPTER FIVE

Annev was still cursing his luck when he reached the rooftop terrace. Of all people, why did he have to run into Duvarek? The Master of Shadows was most often sent on artifact retrieval missions—a task Annev openly coveted—and he had just knocked the master into a pool of his own vomit. Kenton had earned private lessons with him after earning his title, and Annev doubted he'd get a similar chance now.

He's been beyond the Brakewood—to Banok and to Luqura. He's even been to the far north. I want to do that. I want to be just like him.

An image of Duvarek lying in his own sick flashed before Annev, and he amended that last thought. *I want to be* better *than him. How do I become a man the Academy turns to for artifact retrieval?*

Annev didn't know the full answer to that question, but the first step was obvious: passing tomorrow's Test of Judgment—at all costs. That would unlock all the doors presently barred before him. He could have it all, but only if he passed, and today that prospect seemed less and less likely.

Annev was the last to arrive at Master Edra's class. He skirted the edge of the gathered students, sharply aware that he stank of Duvarek's vomit, and surveyed the crowd. Based on the sleek sparring weapons Fyn and Kenton carried, they had been the first to reach the rooftop. A quick glance around the terrace revealed that most of the boys in brown held a good weapon—a wooden sword, a leather-wrapped ax, a sparring stave. Edra stood in the center of them atop a raised platform, pairing off the boys who had arrived first and telling them where to fight.

In contrast to the brown-robed avatars, the acolytes in beige generally carried the crudest weapons. Annev spotted Therin and Titus standing apart from the crowd. The former held a dirty coil of rope while the latter carried a small burlap bag. Lemwich, another acolyte from Titus's class, stood between Annev's two friends and the larger crowd of boys. Annev jogged over to them.

"Anything left?"

"Nothing good," Therin said. "We just got here."

"There's some chain mail gloves," Titus said, pointing to a dark corner of the roof, "but the links are broken."

"Rusty too," Lemwich said, turning a small knife over in his large hands. "Wouldn't put my hands in them."

"Probably couldn't *fit* your hands in them," Therin said, eyeing the bull-necked acolyte.

"Probably not."

"That's it?" Annev asked. "Just the gloves?" Titus nodded. "What's in your sack?"

"Some throwing spikes," Titus said. "But they're wooden, poorly weighted, and once I toss them I'll be unarmed."

"Better not miss then," Therin said, punching the boy's arm. "Hey, you think Edra will let us upgrade our weapons as the other boys get eliminated?"

"Maybe. Probably," Annev said. "How do you get eliminated?"

"'Subdue your opponent or strike a blow that would be fatal.' Edra has to *see* the blow, though, so if he turns away when Titus hits with one of his spikes, Titmouse is out of luck."

Titus nodded. "I think that's why no one took the spikes."

"Makes sense," Annev said, eyeing the chain mail gloves in the corner. "Guess we'll have to make do till some better weapons are available." He jogged over to the gauntlets, grabbed the gloves, and returned to his friends, by which time he had an idea. "Hey, Therin. What do you think about cutting your rope in half and making some bolas or chain-weights?"

"By tying the ropes to your gloves?" Annev nodded and Therin shrugged. "Rather have a knife, but a weighted rope is better than a naked one."

"Great." Annev tapped Lemwich on the shoulder. "Hey, Lem. Can I borrow your knife?"

The hulking acolyte stared at the tiny shard of iron in his hands. After a long pause, he extended the blade handle-first. "You'll give it back." It wasn't a question.

"I will," Annev said. "Thanks." He dropped the chain mail gauntlets and began to saw the rope in half. Dull as the knife was, after some work the braided hemp began to give way beneath it. Annev watched Edra pair off another group of boys, worried the master would call on him to spar before he had finished. Distracted, the knife slipped from the partially cut rope and he dropped it. Annev swore, grabbed a loop of hemp, and started sawing again, careful to make each cut count this time.

"Got it!" Annev said, snapping the rope in two. He tossed a piece each to Titus and Therin. "Tie them to the gauntlets. Make sure they're tight." He was about to give the knife back to Lemwich then stopped, an idea forming.

"Hey, Lem. You want Therin's chain-weight instead?"

Lemwich's face scrunched up. "That's a rope, not a chain—and I want my knife back."

"You won't get close enough to use it."

The larger boy was unconvinced, but Therin jumped to his feet and extended the weapon he had finished constructing.

"Give it a swing, Lem! With your strength, you could probably slap someone's face off." He shook the rusty gauntlet tied to the end of the rope.

Lemwich stuck out his chin then slowly reached for the makeshift weapon, uncertain. "I've never practiced with chain-weights—or ropes."

"Just swing it," Therin said, grinning. "If you can get someone tangled up, you can pound them into submission."

A tiny smile dimpled the larger boy's face. "What if they don't get tangled?"

"Then swing it again," Therin said, his face impish.

Lemwich scoffed but gathered up the rope and gauntlet. He gave the rope an experimental swing, smacking the metal glove down into the roof with a thump. Annev winced as red flakes of rust puffed into the air and were carried away by the wind. Lemwich lifted the rope again, studying the glove.

"Alright," he said, nodding to Annev. "Keep the knife." The larger boy stepped up to join the throng surrounding the Master of Arms. Therin suppressed a laugh.

"What?" Titus asked.

Therin looked at Annev, still grinning. "You want to tell him?"

"It might not even break," Annev said. "You saw how it held just now."

"But you cut—"

"Annev!"

Annev looked up and saw Therin's laughter had attracted their teacher's attention. He handed the knife to Therin and took the last rope-weight from Titus. As he jogged over to Edra, he heard Therin whisper an explanation to Titus. "Annev," Edra said, once he had approached. "You're with Janson. Southeast corner. Go."

Annev went, pushing Lemwich and his weapon to the back of his mind and concentrating on winning.

Janson, he thought. *Fast. Wiry. Likes hatchets.* He maneuvered past the crowd and saw his brown-robed opponent standing casually by the edge of the roof. The dark-skinned avatar looked over the crenellated parapet, a short-handled ax resting on his shoulder.

"Nice view."

"Yeah," Annev agreed, drawing closer. "Can see all the way to the watchtowers."

"You ready?" Janson said, turning. He saw the rope and glove in Annev's hands and grinned.

Annev tensed, his adrenaline beginning to spike. He *needed* to win this. He needed every advantage in tomorrow's test.

"Let's go."

Janson nodded once then swung with his sheathed ax, aiming for Annev's neck.

Annev ducked and dodged, stepping away as he uncoiled the rope and snapped the weighted end toward Janson's feet. The mailed glove flew out, snaking around the boy's calves, and circled back on itself. Annev yanked and the rope went taut, jerking Janson's legs together before the boy could recover from his wild swing. The avatar's weight-bearing foot stayed planted even as his back foot snapped forward, throwing him off-balance.

It was all the advantage Annev needed. He stepped in with his hip and reached over his shoulder, grabbing the haft of Janson's ax. Still holding the rope tight, Annev pulled the ax forward over his head toward the ground. Janson held tight to his weapon, but the hemp buckled his knees and Annev levered his body in a smooth throw. In a blink, Janson rolled over Annev's shoulder and smacked into the stone roof, a *whump* knocking the air from his lungs.

Annev pulled on the ax, expecting it to come free, but Janson held on, gasping for air. Annev pulled again then cursed and kicked the boy in the arm and shoulder. Janson only released it when Annev's booted foot aimed for his face. Instead of kicking, Annev placed his foot on the avatar's neck and lifted the weapon overhead.

"Master Edra!" Annev yelled, not taking his eyes off his opponent.

Annev waited while Janson struggled beneath his boot, trying to lift Annev's foot from his throat. Annev pressed harder, and when that failed he rapped Janson's fingers with the blunt side of the ax.

"Master Edra!" he shouted again.

"Let him go," Edra shouted back. "Janson, you're out. Annev, join the others."

Annev lifted his foot, his pulse still racing, but as he turned to go Janson grabbed his ankle and yanked, dropping Annev to his stomach. He flipped onto his back, blood thumping in his ears, but the avatar didn't try anything else.

"You got lucky," Janson said, untangling the rope around his legs. "You surprised me."

Annev wanted to snap back that it was skill, not luck, but he was still winded from hitting the ground. Instead, he got to his feet.

"Thanks for the ax."

He walked toward Edra and the other boys then spotted Lemwich sparring with a freckle-faced acolyte named Alisander. The smaller boy carried a shard of dead wood—the remnant of a pine bough he'd been using as a crude club. From what Annev could tell, Alisander had used his stick to block Lemwich's opening salvo, but the force of the chain mail gauntlet had shattered the dried wood.

By the time Annev reached Edra the fight was over.

"Let him go, Lem! Alisander, you're out." Edra looked down at Annev. "Annev, you can face Lemwich next. Southern terrace."

Annev's stomach flipped as he walked toward the acolyte he'd been helping just a few minutes ago. He stopped a dozen paces away and Lemwich smiled at him.

"Worked pretty well," Lemwich said, drawing in the rope and gauntlet. "Scared the tar out of Ali, anyway. What happened to yours?"

"My rope-weight?" Annev asked. "I left it. Thought the ax was an upgrade until I knew I'd be facing you. No reach to it."

"Mm. Not much left of Ali's branch, so I guess I'm still using this." Lemwich coiled the rope up, letting the chain glove slither across the rooftop. "It'll be a shame when I beat you with it." Before Annev could manage a retort, the rope-weight shot out and the chain mail gauntlet flew for Annev's face. Annev raised his ax, holding it tight with both hands, and ducked.

The weapon crashed into the ax handle, its momentum spinning the hemp rope and chain glove tight around the haft. Annev tensed, keeping a firm grip on the ax, then felt Lem haul on the other end of the rope. Annev's shoulders jerked and he braced against another, stronger tug that almost pulled him off his feet. He yanked back unsteadily as Lem hauled him closer. Annev pulled harder, trying to break the rope he'd half-severed moments before, but it didn't break. Lem grinned, pulling Annev closer. Annev was just about to lose their tug-of-war when he and Lemwich pulled in opposite directions and the rope snapped. The braided cord flew away leaving the mail glove wrapped around Annev's ax. A half-dozen feet away, Lemwich stared stupidly at the limp coil of rope in his hands.

Annev didn't hesitate. He launched himself at Lemwich, taking advantage of his opponent's shock. The boy's hands came up reflexively, the frayed hemp still clutched in his meaty fingers, only Annev ignored the boy's fists and ducked low, using the ax to hook Lem's leg. At the same time, he plowed his shoulder into the larger boy's gut, throwing him off-balance. Lemwich hopped backward, trying to regain his footing and Annev continued to press him, unrelenting, forcing Lemwich back again.

Lemwich *had* to fall. Annev would *make* him fall.

Annev threw his weight into the big acolyte again—the largest and strongest in his reap—and forced him backwards. Lemwich tried to brace himself then grunted, suddenly stopping, his hands grabbing Annev's tunic.

No! Annev's mind roared. If the larger boy got a solid hold, he was done for.

Annev jumped back, yanking his tunic free and hauling upwards on his ax, lifting Lemwich's leg out from under him. With a furious final push, Annev toppled the boy.

Lemwich fell backward, flipping onto the edge of the parapet. Annev saw in a moment that was how he had stopped—braced against it until Annev flipped him. Lem's eyes widened as his massive frame teetered on the brink of the Academy wall. He squirmed like an overturned turtle then slipped toward the edge.

"No!" Annev shouted, lunging for his classmate.

And then the boy was gone, toppling over the edge, just the coil of rope snaking over the parapet behind him. Annev dropped his ax and grabbed it, throwing a loop of hemp around the nearest merlon a moment before the rope snapped tight. He heard Lemwich yelp and felt the rope slide through his fingers. Annev swore and spun, wrapping the hemp around his hips and bracing his legs against the two nearest merlons.

"Help!" Annev shouted. "Master Edra! Help!"

There was nothing but him and the rope, his legs straining against the merlons, holding Lem's weight for an eternity. The sounds of the other boys fighting were distant as the rope crushed around him. Annev yelled again. And again. And the rope began to slide through his hands, burning his hands and dragging its rough threads across his body. He tried to hold tighter but his grip was failing. His feet shifted on the merlon and he felt Lemwich lurch at the other end of the rope. Annev screamed as more hemp slid through his fingers, Lemwich was simply too heavy to hold. Annev felt the end of the braided hemp reach his hands and—

"Gods!" Edra swore, grabbing the rope before it could fly loose and hauling on it. As the weight came off him, Annev dropped to the ground, seized the rope, and added his weight to Edra's strength. Others arrived, attracted by Annev's scream, and moments later they had dragged the acolyte back up to the terrace. Lemwich's clenched, bloodless fingers and broad face appeared above the battlements and he was pulled back over the wall to safety.

Annev dropped the hemp rope and slumped to the ground. He looked over at Lemwich, and the boy gave him a long, slow nod of thanks. Then he looked up and saw the Master of Arms glowering at him.

"An accident?"

Annev nodded. "I tried ..."

"You tried to save him," Edra said. "I know. I saw. I didn't how he came to fall over that ledge."

Annev glanced over at Lemwich, who met Annev's gaze in silence. Edra watched the exchange and nodded.

"I'll assume this was an accident, one caused by negligence"—he looked at Annev—"or incompetence." He glanced at Lemwich. "In either case, I think this accident disqualifies you both from winning the advantage for tomorrow's Test."

Annev's face fell, as did Lem's. Edra nodded, satisfied with their reactions.

"Lemwich, go join the boys who've lost a match." The larger acolyte stood, bowed, then ran to join Janson and the others. Annev moved to follow, but Edra stopped him. "Enough sparring for today, Annev. Go down to the nave and assist Master Duvarek."

"But ... I'm already disqualified. Why send me away?"

Edra grit his teeth. "Annev, this was serious. There have to be clear consequences, otherwise, the next student might take further." He paused, distracted by Kenton and another boy who hadn't been matched together but were starting to scuffle.

"Like that," Edra said, spitting. "Damn that scar. He's always causing problems." He looked back at Annev. "Are we clear?"

"Master Duvarek," Annev repeated, grimacing. He had no desire to see the man so soon after their collision that morning, but it seemed he had no choice.

"Don't worry," Edra said, misinterpreting the cause of Annev's trepidation. "Dove's not so bad—once you get used to the smell." He grinned then patted Annev on the shoulder. "Anyway, don't think of this as a punishment. Think of it as another chance to earn an advantage in to-morrow's Test."

Annev raised his gaze from the ground. "Another advantage?" Edra stepped away from Annev, moving towards the brawl that seemed about to break out.

"No more questions. Get going!"

CHAPTER SIX

Annev reached the nave's tall ironbound doors and pushed. Instead of squeaking, the heavy portals swung inward on silent hinges, and Annev immediately reevaluated his memories of the once-neglected space. He stepped into the room and was even more surprised by what he saw.

The nave's cavernous vaulted ceiling had once been strewn with cobwebs. Now scores of clean black curtains stretched from ceiling to floor, obscuring the light from the stained-glass windows and dividing the room into dozens of artificial corridors: in some places the panels were broad, heavy swathes of cloth stitched together to create long artificial walls; in other places the drapes were narrow, little more than a foot or two wide. The cloth panels all started at the edge of the pews, so the wide area at the entrance remained open and unobscured, allowing Annev to pace the width of the old nave and spot the other changes Duvarek had made.

Annev knew from previous visits that the nave held forty-five wood pews, with two aisles dividing the benches into sections fifteen pews deep. These benches were all now obscured by the long black curtains that fell to just above the back of the pews or, in the aisles, to the floor. As Annev paced the back of the hall, he saw that the central and eastern banks of pews had been covered with wooden planks resting atop them, creating broad platforms that someone could walk across.

The artificially raised floor was imperfect, though; when Annev looked more closely he noticed several gaps among the planks, each wide enough to crawl through or fall into. In about half of these cases, the cloth panels reached through the gaps and touched the floor. When Annev knelt down and peered beneath the pews, he saw that the pews and panels formed a separate maze of corridors beneath the artificial floor.

"Hello?" Annev said, returning to the entrance. "Master Duvarek?"

The clack and scrape of wood answered him from the far west side of the nave. He headed towards the sound and saw that, while the curtains had been hung in this part of the nave, the pews had not yet been covered. Scores of planks still leaned against the wall.

"What?" Duvarek shouted from behind the curtains.

"Master Edra sent me to help you."

"Fine," came the muffled reply. "Help me cover the rest of these benches."

Still not seeing the Master of Shadows, Annev walked to the planks stacked against the wall and lifted one of the splintery boards. The wood was near rotten, covered in grime, and slightly damp.

"Don't just stand there," Duvarek said, appearing beside him. "Grab a load and help."

Annev hesitated, wondering if the man had recognized him, but Duvarek seemed focused on his task. He watched as the man lifted three of the dirty planks, shouldered aside the curtains, and edged between the pews.

Annev reluctantly took up a plank. As he shifted the wood, a black beetle skittered from beneath the stack and disappeared under the nearest curtain. Annev grit his teeth, secured his grip, and followed Duvarek.

"Master Murlach's claimed all the good wood for tomorrow's test," Duvarek said, appearing beside Annev again. "I got the leftovers. Suits me fine. We're not bolting or nailing anything. Just drop the wood on the pews and try not to leave any gaps. I'll deal with those."

"Yes sir," Annev said, hoisting the grimy planks onto his shoulder and sidestepping between the benches, shifting aside the cloth panels that blocked his path. When he reached the far side of the chapel, he positioned the planks so they stretched across the backs of three different pews and lined the boards up tight against Duvarek's. He looked up just as the wiry Master of Shadows emerged from the curtains with another stack of wood. Duvarek glanced at the boards with approval.

"Looks good. Keep going. Need this done before Edra brings your reap down."

Annev nodded, relieved Duvarek still hadn't recognized him.

"And try not to hit me with those planks," Duvarek added, returning to the front of the chapel. "You've already smashed into me once today, and I don't fancy a second blow."

Annev's cheeks burned, but he did as he was told. The pair went to work, wordlessly weaving their way through the hanging cloth panels, picking up the half-rotten planks and covering the tops of the remaining pews. When they were about two-thirds done, Annev realized they would run out of wood before they could finish covering the rest of the benches. At about the same time, Duvarek stopped laying the boards and climbed onto the makeshift floor they had built. The master walked back and forth between the maze of cloth panels. Whenever he came to a plank that seesawed when he stepped on it, he popped the board with his foot and removed it from the floor entirely. Once he had an armload of planks, he added them to the remaining stack of wood. As Annev continued to lay the false floor, he watched Duvarek disappear into the back of the nave and return with a few scraps of black cloth. The master briskly stitched them to the cloth panels hanging over some of the holes in the western floor and soon the western section of pews looked much like the central and eastern sections.

The work was finished half an hour later. Annev walked between the long black curtains with Duvarek and surveyed the room. He gave a tug on one of the cloth panels and watched as it swayed soundlessly in the air.

"Are we supposed to climb these?"

Duvarek grinned and wiped his hands on his stained tunic. "Maybe."

Annev raised an eyebrow then studied the planks resting on the pews. He pushed on a few and noted that some still wobbled or tilted if he put his weight on the wrong side.

"These aren't very secure," Annev noted, wandering toward the center of the nave.

"You noticed." The Master of Shadows followed Annev. Every now and then, he would shift a board a few inches.

Annev walked to the other side of the room and gazed up at the nave's rune-covered walls and large glass windows. Light shone through the still-dusty panes, but much of it was blocked by the dark cloth hanging a half-dozen feet from the window. Toward the center of the nave, where the middle row of pews had been covered, it was much darker; even in the areas where something could be seen, the black panels obscured vision for more than a few feet in any direction.

Annev circled around to the back of the chamber and, as he left the rows of pews, he saw the dais was largely unobscured by the hanging panels. Annev climbed the steps and, unthinking, made his way to the stone altar at the center of the raised platform. He cringed when he saw that the water trough surrounding the altar had dried up, and he wondered why the ancients had let the chapel fall into disuse.

As he circled the holy table, Annev saw the differences between this altar and Sodar's. The sacred moat encircling it was set into the floor of the raised dais and was huge—wide enough for a priest to stand at the altar in the center, yet deep enough for a man to lie down in the empty trough. By contrast, the moat surrounding Sodar's table hugged the altar itself and was only an inch or so deep. Where Sodar's was only lightly ornamented, the Academy's had been carved with a dazzling variety of runes and symbols, including pictographs and a small mural; it was almost as if the craftsman building the altar had not wanted to be outdone by the one who had decorated the nave's walls, so he'd taken every symbol from the walls—every glyph and rune in the room—and found a way to cram it all onto the altar.

Annev stepped away from the altar and stumbled into a heap of black fabric piled near the dais. He poked it with his foot and saw it matched the cloth panels suspended throughout the nave, though these were only scraps, unfit for hanging.

At the far end of the room, the portal to the nave creaked open.

Annev looked up, but his sight of the nave's entrance was obscured. Instead, he heard the soft thump of dozens of booted feet pouring into the room.

Annev hopped down from the dais and made his way around the perimeter of the nave. He reached the front of the room just in time to see Duvarek clasp wrists with Edra. Annev's reap had also entered and now surrounded the two masters. Annev scanned the boys' faces and saw several with fresh bruises—Brinden even sported a bloody nose—but none seemed to require the attentions of Master Aran or the Academy's witwomen. Lemwich even seemed recovered, to Annev's relief. He spied Titus and Therin at the back of the group.

"You look like hell, Dove," Edra said as Annev walked past.

Duvarek shrugged. "Drank too much. Overslept. The usual." The Master of Shadows pushed his way through the crowd of boys and closed the door to the grand nave.

"The usual," Edra repeated, nodding. He spotted Annev. "Have you been helpful?"

The Master of Shadows answered for him. "He was. Made up for plowing me over this morning."

"What?"

"Nothing," Duvarek said, nodding to Annev. "It's in the past."

Edra looked from Duvarek to Annev then sighed. "Fine. Annev, I'll let Brother Sodar know you missed the last half of today's sparring. You can make it up with him this evening, before tonight's sermon." Annev bowed his head but Edra wasn't finished. "I'll also tell him you saved Lemwich's life during training. Maybe he'll go easy on you."

Annev looked up and forced a small smile. It was Edra's way of closing the issue with Lemwich on the rooftop; though Sodar would never go easy on him, no matter what Edra said.

"Thank you, Master Edra." Annev rejoined his friends. "How'd you do after I left?"

"Terrible," Therin mumbled around a fat lip. "Better than Titus, though."

Titus nodded his agreement. "They paired us up. Therin waited till I'd thrown all my spikes then put his knife to my throat. Course, then he was beaten by Kellor."

Annev laughed in spite of himself. "So who got the advantage in tomorrow's test?"

"Who do you think?" Therin pointed in the direction of Fyn and his friends. "Brinden, Jasper, Kellor, Fyn. They all got it."

"And Kenton," Titus added. "Janson was best of the losers, so he got the sixth spot."

Worse and worse, Annev thought, realizing it would have been his if he hadn't been disqualified. Edra walked past again, a small chest under his arm. Annev frowned, wondering at its contents. Before he could ask Titus or Therin about it, though, Edra spoke.

"Today you will be combining your combat training with your stealth skills," Edra said, looking over the assembled students. "Dove and I decided to do something special today since, for many of you, this will be your last class with us." He looked at Duvarek. "Where are the witgirls?"

Duvarek shrugged just as the nave doors opened to admit two witwomen. The first was stout, middle-aged, and wore dark red skirts; the second was thin, midtwenties with a severe expression.

"Witwoman Nasha," Duvarek said, inclining his head. "We were just talking about you."

The plump woman with the motherly face wrinkled her nose at the master's stained robes while her companion surveyed the hanging curtains and plank-covered pews. She nodded slowly.

"This will do."

Nasha sniffed then clapped her hands twice in quick succession and a group of young women entered the nave.

Annev stared, dumfounded as the girls began filing into the room. When he recognized their faces, his heart picked up its beat.

This is her class, he thought. *This is* her *class.*

The other avatars and acolytes fared little better. The reap was, to a boy, dumbstruck to be joined by their female counterparts. The strict separation between the ancients' male students and the witwomen's female charges was rarely breached, so even in this innocuous setting the room felt charged with electricity.

For Annev's part, he tried to catch a glimpse of each young woman as she entered. He recognized Malia with her black braided hair. Lydia with her cool gray eyes and purple skirts. Faith, with hair like flax and skin flecked with freckles. And behind her, in a pale yellow dress and white apron, was Myjun.

CHAPTER SEVEN

The young woman stood beside her blond friend, her auburn hair tied back, her hands clasped together. As she gazed around the room, her eyes lingered on Fyn's handsome face.

Annev ground his teeth, but then Myjun's eyes caught his and his jealousy was forgotten. She beamed at him and seemed about to speak before she remembered herself. A smile still on her lips, she gave him a tiny wave.

"Pretty, isn't she?"

Therin was staring at Myjun too.

"Hair like the sun," Therin continued. "And those freckles! Just a dash on her nose and cheeks—like her skin's on fire."

Oh, Annev thought, fists unclenching. *He means Faith.*

Therin grinned at her. "Why do you think they're here? Are we training with them?" His face screwed up as an idea struck him. "Are they *fighting* us?"

The question hit Annev like a bucket of ice water. He glanced back at Myjun and saw that the young women all stood at attention, looking toward an older woman who had followed the last four witgirls into the nave. She had gray-streaked brown hair and wore a charcoal gray dress. Annev had seen her before, usually speaking with Elder Tosan, and she clearly held a senior position within the witwomen.

"Ladies. Please join your male counterparts," she ordered as she glided toward Duvarek, her hands steepled in front of her chest. The eight young women flowed past the crowd of adolescent boys, forming a line opposite them. Annev watched Myjun and saw the tight black leggings that peeked from beneath her flowing yellow skirts. He blinked and realized all the witapprentices were wearing the same tight black uniform.

They have their reaping uniforms on beneath their day clothes …

As the ladies settled into place in front of the male students, Annev sensed a deeper change in the atmosphere. Myjun took a place opposite him, her eyes meeting his before glancing away, but not before an impish smile tugged at the corner of her mouth. Annev took a deep breath then exhaled slowly, trying to focus.

Duvarek turned to the Master of Arms. "Explain the challenge while I fetch the rods from Narach? He's so reluctant to let them out of the vault I'll have to prise them from his hands."

"Sure. I have the medallions." Edra rolled his shoulders and traded places with the Master of Shadows, who hurried through the front door of the nave.

"The purpose of this lesson is to test your stealth—your skill at avoiding detection and ability to escape others while carrying items of value." He looked over the assembled acolytes, avatars, and witapprentices, making eye contact with Annev and a few of his classmates. "You boys know your duty. Thousands of cursed magic artifacts are still loose in the world, and many of them will find their way to Greater Luqura. Odar has entrusted us with finding and securing them in the Vault of Damnation. But we cannot reclaim those artifacts by force. Success requires stealth, cunning, and deception. Witmistress Kiara?"

The older witwoman stepped forward and also surveyed the group. Annev held his breath as the full weight of her regard passed over him.

"Ladies, our sisters are even now gathering the next reap of acolytes. When they return to Chaenbalu, we will raise those newborns and train them for their future callings as Avatars of Judgment. Today we continue your training for the reap itself. It is a dangerous mission, and its successful execution is a key part of to your role as a witwoman. Failure here, in these controlled circumstances, will indicate that you are unfit for the rigors of reaping. Do I make myself clear?"

The witapprentices bowed their heads, and Annev felt a tinge of dread as he realized they faced their own challenges for advancement at the Academy. It was a strange glimpse into Myjun's world.

Annev knew that the witwomen and their Wit Circle were secretive beyond even what was normal for the masters and ancients, and that their primary duty was to bring babes back from Luqura so that they could be raised at the Academy as acolytes, avatars, and witapprentices. But he had no idea how they achieved this goal and had no concept of their hierarchy or the training needed to become a full witwoman. He supposed that, in many respects, abducting infants would be harder than stealing magic artifacts—a baby was alive, after all, and stealing an infant from its parents was an emotional challenge as well as a physical one—but Annev also knew that reaping was a small part of their role, though it was always referred to with reverence. When the masters and ancients explained how acolytes came to the Academy, they claimed the mothers had chosen to give their children to Odar to serve his arcane purposes. Few people other than Titus actually believed that, though. The rest, including Annev, observed the injuries the witwomen sometimes received during the reaping and guessed it was a pretense for something less innocent. No one spoke of it openly, though.

The door at the back of the nave swung open as Duvarek returned, followed swiftly by Steward Markov in his tan robes and the elderly Master Narach. They joined Master Edra at the front of the room, Markov carrying a black-painted chest. Edra set down the small unpainted chest he had been carrying, opened it, and pulled out a fistful of wooden disks strung on braided cord. He began separating the tangled wood and string.

"Each of you—avatars, acolytes, and witapprentices—will wear one of these." Edra freed a wooden disk and lifted it high enough for all the students to see. "Today's test will last an hour and if you have more than one badge at the end of the hour, you will pass." He lowered the disk. "If you have one, or none, then you fail." The students murmured their understanding and Edra began handing out the medallions.

The Master of Shadows gestured for Markov to open the black box and plucked out a slender wooden wand. One half was painted black and the other half was bright gold. Annev noticed that Duvarek was careful not to touch the black end.

Duvarek lifted the rod for all to see. "This is a stumble-stick."

"A Rod of Paralysis!" Narach corrected, his voice crabby and irritated.

"The Master of Secrets names the artifacts in the vault, and you will show respect by using its correct name."

Duvarek cleared his throat. "The *stumble-stick*," Duvarek repeated, "paralyzes whatever it touches." He lifted the wand, holding it between his thumb and forefinger. "You grasp the gold handle—that part is safe. Touch someone with the black end, though, and that part of their body will go limp. 'Gold, you hold. Black goes slack.' Don't accidentally stun yourself." Duvarek beckoned Markov. "A demonstration."

Markov was visibly unwilling.

"Come along, steward." Duvarek flashed his teeth at the anxious young man.

Markov looked to Narach and the wizened master waved him forward. "Go on. The sooner this is finished the sooner we can get back to the vault."

Markov set down the chest of wands and dutifully stepped forward with a slump in his shoulders.

"Roll up your sleeve … arm out … good." Duvarek circled Markov. "The paralysis wears off after a few hours, but it can take as little as an hour if you are young and healthy." Duvarek raised the wand and tapped the sleeve of Markov's right arm. The boy flinched, but nothing happened. Duvarek poked him in the leg, chest, and ribs. Again, nothing happened.

"The rod doesn't work unless you are touching bare skin. If you do that …" Duvarek tapped Markov's bare arm and it fell limp to his side. Murmurs of interest broke out among the avatars.

"Steward Markov, did that hurt?"

The steward shrugged his good shoulder. "It is uncomfortable, but not painful." Duvarek glanced to Edra, who stepped behind Markov.

"Touch a bare limb and it goes slack," Duvarek continued. "Touch the head, neck, or spine, and the whole body will be paralyzed." Markov saw what was coming and closed his eyes, resigned to it. Duvarek tapped the wand on Markov's spine and he flinched, but nothing happened. The steward visibly relaxed.

"Remember," Duvarek said, "it has to be *bare* skin."

The master poked Markov in the neck and his body crumpled, falling limp into Master Edra's waiting arms. One of the acolytes gasped while a few of the avatars began murmuring. Edra dragged the steward's body to the side of the room and propped him against the wall. Duvarek dropped the rod back inside the box.

"You will each have a rod in addition to the medallion you have received. You have one hour to collect as many medallions as possible, ideally using stealth instead of physical combat. Stun your fellow students and take their badges." Duvarek looked to Edra. "Does that cover everything?"

"Almost," Edra said. He reached beneath his tunic and pulled out a small key tied to a leather thong. "Avatars and acolytes taking your test tomorrow. Whichever one of you gathers the most badges will receive this." He waved the iron key at the male students. "I won't tell you what it's for—you're all smart enough to pick a lock—but it will give you an advantage in tomorrow's Test of Judgment."

Another advantage! Annev studied the key, suddenly more alert. *Maybe that could make up for Fyn's head start.* He nodded to himself, committed. He would win that key.

Duvarek took up the black box. "That's it. Boys, take your wands from me, then find a position in the nave." He glanced at the witapprentices. "Ladies, you will collect yours from Witmistress Kiara. You will all wait for my whistle to begin."

CHAPTER EIGHT

Therin and Titus followed Annev through the maze of hanging panels.

Therin peered up at the curtains as they ran past. "Shouldn't we be hiding? We could climb these drapes and get a drop on anyone that walks by."

"Or we could hide under the pews," Titus said from the back. "I don't think I could hang from those curtains for an hour."

"Later," Annev said, weaving toward the dais at the back of the nave. "Our tunics stand out in the darkness. If we want to be stealthy, we need to cover them. We should try to cover more of our skin too. So I have an idea," He climbed the steps to the dais and headed for the altar.

"How do we manage that?" Therin asked, a few steps behind him.

Annev stopped beside the pile of black fabric behind the altar. "With these." He tossed a scrap to Therin. "Wrap them around your body—legs, arms, torso. Cover everything you can, but especially your tunic." He tossed another scrap to Titus.

Therin started wrapping the scraps around his legs. "You know, if we tore these into smaller strips, we could wrap them around our hands and faces. No one could stun us!"

Annev wrapped his torso with the discarded fabric. "That's what I was thinking. They could probably get us to drop the rods if they touch our fingers, but if they have to poke us between the eyes to stun us, we'll have a big advantage."

"It'll be harder to move, though," Titus said, carefully weaving the black cloth around his arm. "Harder to climb, or crawl under those benches."

"Go easy around your joints," Annev said, flexing one arm. "That should help." They went to work in earnest, wrapping their limbs, loins, hands, and faces, helping each other as needed.

A piercing whistle came from the other end of the nave.

"We're off," Therin said, lowering his voice as he tucked his wand beneath his cloth wrapping. He looked down at the gold handle poking out from beneath his black rags and tisked. "That'll stand out when we're swinging from the curtains." He shifted his wrappings and covered the gold handle as well. "That's better."

"You're really going to climb them?" Titus asked.

"Sure. We don't have to *fight* anyone, just surprise them. Probably one of the few times I'll have an advantage over someone like Fyn."

Annev slid his Rod of Paralysis beneath the cloth wrappings on his hip. "One of us should climb to the rafters and see if we can spot anyone. If we do, we can signal the other two."

"I'll go up if you promise to split the medallions," Therin volunteered. "I can't stun anyone if I'm acting as a scout."

"Sure." He looked to Titus. "You coming? If we stick to the curtains at the edge of the dais, no one can sneak up behind us."

The younger boy let out his breath and nodded. "Yeah," Titus said, forcing a smile. "I can't hang from those curtains for too long, but I'll do my best." He slid his Rod of Paralysis into the wrappings at his waist—and instantly crumpled to the ground.

"*Balls*, Titus!" Therin swore, jumping back from his friend. "What'd you do?"

"Titus?" Annev knelt beside his fallen friend, already guessing what had happened.

Titus frowned and propped himself up from the waist. He tried to turn over but his legs wouldn't cooperate. His face went pale. "I think … I paralyzed my legs."

Therin struggled to keep his voice down. "Are you serious?"

Titus nodded, eyes watering. Annev carefully pulled the Rod of Paralysis out from under his friend's wrappings. "I can't move them at all. I doubt I could even get into one of those crawl spaces."

The murmured creak of metal rings rubbing against wooden poles suddenly echoed throughout the nave, prompting all three boys to look up. Cloth panels jerked and rippled around them, and one of the curtains near the dais billowed softly. Therin licked his lips and looked at Annev. "Everyone's on the move. I can't get caught in the open, I won't stand a chance."

Annev nodded, understanding. "Go. I'll stay with Titus."

Therin looked at Annev as if he were mad. Instead of arguing, though, he shrugged. "Good luck." Then he took off at a run, leaping from the edge of the dais and seizing one of the hanging curtains. Within seconds, the scrawny acolyte had scurried up the cloth panel and swung himself into the maze.

Titus pulled his medallion over his head. "You shouldn't stay either, Annev. Take this and go—I don't need it."

Annev hesitated. He wanted that medallion—he needed it if he was going to win the key—but he hated the idea of taking advantage of his friend. He cursed those feelings, knowing he needed to quell his conscience if he was going to use Titus and Therin to win tomorrow.

"Come on, Annev," Titus continued, ascribing virtuous motives to his friend's hesitation. "We both know I'm not cut out to be an avatar, but you are. You deserve this. Someone else will steal it from me anyway, and I'd rather you had it."

Annev smiled at his friend, grateful. Maybe he *didn't* have to betray his friends to win tomorrow. Maybe they would help him anyway. He tucked the second Rod of Paralysis into his wrappings then reached for Titus's medallion. As he did so, the curtains near the edge of the dais wavered. He stopped. Somewhere in the shrouded nave, a boy cried out. Footsteps followed, and then another boy shouted something.

"Annev?"

Instead of taking the medallion, Annev pressed it back into his friend's hand. He grinned.

"Keep hold of it. I have an idea."

CHAPTER NINE

Fyn dropped from the curtains like a shadow falling on felt, landing on bent knees and lightly touching his fingertips to the floor as his large frame expertly absorbed the impact. He froze, tense as he listened for noise. Hearing none, he rose and stalked over to the stairs leading to the dais. A half-dozen badges hung around his neck and a Rod of Paralysis appeared in each hand. After surveying the quiet platform, he saw Titus's prone form, stalked over, and poked the acolyte in the chest with a rod.

"Got caught out, huh?"

Titus didn't move or respond. Fyn smiled, leaned over, and patted the boy's chest.

"I'm guessing you were with your friends, and when you were paralyzed they abandoned you. Or maybe they paralyzed you and took your medallion?" Fyn tapped the wooden tokens hanging around his neck. "That's what I'd have done. Good strategy, though—finding the high ground. Wrapping yourself up. Clever."

Fyn knelt by Titus's limp body, his dreadlocks falling across the younger boy's face, and simultaneously prodded the boy in the neck and forehead. Titus jerked, and then his body went truly slack.

Fyn grinned. "Never hurts to be careful. Maybe I should give you an extra poke to be sure." He leaned forward, pressed a wand against Titus's nose, and watched as the smaller boy began to blink uncontrollably, eyelids twitching. Fyn studied Titus's spasming face then lifted the wand away. "That's a good trick. Wouldn't mind seeing it again." Very slowly, Fyn lowered the tip of his wand until it pressed against Titus's cheekbone.

The corner of Titus's mouth began to twitch. Fyn pressed harder, tracing circles on his cheek until the acolyte's eyes spasmed.

A shout and the sound of a struggle came from the nave. Fyn glanced over his shoulder at the hanging curtains then lifted the wand.

"Enough messing around." Fyn slipped a hand beneath the cloth wrappings covering Titus's chest and checked for a medallion. He grinned as he found the younger boy's token.

"So you *were* just pretending to be stunned." He pulled the badge from beneath Titus's wrappings, snapping the hemp. "Risky but—"

Fyn's head jolted backward as Annev jabbed a Rod of Paralysis into the base of his neck. His body slumped, about to tip forward, but Annev shoved him aside before he could fall across Titus and crush the smaller boy. Fyn's body twisted and then toppled into the empty water trough where Annev had been concealed.

Annev checked his friend's pulse. "You alright, Titus?"

The blond boy blinked but did not otherwise move.

"I'll take two blinks as a yes?" Titus blinked twice, and Annev breathed a sigh of relief. "Sorry it took so long to circle behind Fyn. I thought he would come back here, but I should have known Fyn would take the time to torture someone who looked helpless."

Annev made sure Titus was lying comfortably then hopped into the water trough and rolled Fyn over. The avatar's face was frozen, though his eyes were filled with hatred. Annev felt his own flood of rage; he wanted to hurt Fyn—deliberately hurt him, as he had hurt Titus. He wrestled with that impulse for a moment, imagining pressing the rod into Fyn's mouth or against his eye, watching as the boy got a taste of his own abuse.

Annev grabbed one of the rods Fyn had dropped and, on impulse, pressed its black tip to the boy's chin. Fyn's jaw chattered beneath the power of the wand's arcane magic.

"You're never just happy to win," Annev whispered in the boy's ear. "You always have to be mean too." He slid the wand down, prodding Fyn in the neck. A breath of air was forced from the boy's lungs and Fyn's eyes went wild before he began to choke—a strangled gurgle between clenched teeth. Annev held the wand steady and recognized the rush of emotions he'd experienced while holding the Rod of Healing.

"This is how it feels to be tortured, Fyn," Annev continued. "To be powerless. It's terrifying, isn't it? Being at the mercy of someone stronger than you." Annev pressed harder, thrilling as the larger boy's chest began to convulse in waves of panic.

I could kill him, Annev thought. *I* am *killing him.*

With a jerk, Annev dropped the rod and pulled his hand back. Fyn's breathing normalized, though his eyes remained frantic.

Annev felt ashamed and guilty, but powerful too. It was similar to how he had felt when holding the Rod of Healing, as if he had only begun to understand what the rods could do. A part of him itched to delve deeper—to probe the limits of the wand's magic—but this wasn't the moment. There was still a test to complete.

Annev picked up the rods of paralysis Fyn had dropped then tucked all four wands beneath his wrappings, careful to ensure they could not touch his skin. With both hands free, Annev patted Fyn down and scooped up the half-dozen badges slung around the boy's neck. He took Titus's token from Fyn's hand, knotted it, and hung all seven beside his own.

Annev stood and saw Fyn watching him. He felt the same rush of emotions as before—anger, vindication, power—but instead of dismissing them or giving into them, Annev seized them, harnessing those feelings and channeling them into a single impulse: the desire to protect others.

Annev leaned forward, nose to nose with Fyn.

"Don't *ever* hurt my friends again—or next time, I *will* kill you."

Fyn blinked, unable to hide the fear in his eyes, and Annev sensed something significant change between the two of them. A small part of Annev thrilled at that, while a larger part worried he might one day need to follow through on his promise. He sincerely hoped it never came to that.

Annev heaved himself out of the trench and walked back to Titus. Without a word, he unslung two of Fyn's badges and slipped them into the boy's tunic. Titus blinked rapidly at him.

"It's fine, Titus. I've still got six badges—and I may not be able to hold onto them. Leaving two with you is a backup plan." He smiled, not sure if he was lying to himself or just his friend. Either way, after using Titus to beat Fyn, Annev was no longer sure he had to sabotage his friends to get ahead. For the moment, he could support those who supported him. "Come on," he said. "I'll hide you so no one else bothers you."

Annev tugged the boy's slack body over to the nearby pile of black rags and dumped them on top of Titus, making sure his friend could breathe. Satisfied, he made his way back to the altar. He was halfway there when the black curtains in front of the dais began to tremble. With a rush of adrenaline, Annev leaped over the moat concealing Fyn's paralyzed body and crouched behind the altar. He slipped two Rods of Paralysis from his tunic, peered around the stone table, and waited.

Silence. Stillness. He waited a long minute, barely breathing, and was about to leave his hiding place when the cloth panel shrouding the center row of pews shifted—not at its base, but at the top.

Annev looked up and saw a masked face peering down. The student was studying the raised dais and altar and spied Annev at the same time Annev spied him. They stared at each other, frozen, before the masked student lowered the black wrappings covering his mouth.

"Annev?" he whispered, his voice barely audible.

"Therin?" Annev stood and raced over to the edge of the dais. "I didn't think you'd come back," he whispered, his voice equally soft.

Therin grinned then slid halfway down the drape he'd been clinging to. "I wasn't, but I saw Fyn heading this way and thought I'd get the drop on him." He looked around. "Where is he?"

Annev slid the two wands back under his wrappings. "He's in the Ring of Odar."

"You got his medallions?" Therin asked, impressed.

Annev nodded, patting his chest where the six medallions were secured. He stepped to the edge of the dais so that he was eye-level with Therin, but before he could ask his friend how he had fared, a dark-haired boy in brown robes shot out from beneath the center pew and leaped for Annev, slashing at his face.

Annev jumped back from the edge of the dais, barely managing to slap Kenton's wand away with his gloved left hand, then stumbled backward, leaving himself open to a counterattack. The scar-faced avatar saw his opening and sprang up onto the dais, pressing his attack against Annev. Just as he cleared the platform, Therin dropped from his perch and slapped his rod against Kenton's neck. The avatar fell to his knees, his wand sliding from his limp hand, and he slumped onto his face.

Therin poked his fallen classmate with a boot and grinned. "Getting the drop on Kenton is *almost* as good as catching Fyn." He looked up at Annev. "And he deserves it for breaking his promise to us."

"Agreed." Annev joined his friend as Therin took Kenton's medallions. There were five, and Therin gave a quiet hiss of approval as he hung them around his own neck.

"That's seven badges now. How many you got?"

"Six," Annev said, briefly regretting leaving two with Titus.

"TWENTY MINUTES!" Edra bellowed, the sound dampened by the cloth panels around the nave.

Therin grinned at Annev, shaking his tokens. Annev returned the smile, showing his own medallions, then tucked them inside the wrappings around his chest.

"All we have to do is keep hold of these," Annev whispered, retreating to the safety of the altar. "Who did you see out there?"

Therin followed after Annev, stopping long enough to grin at Fyn's limp form in the bottom of the water trough. "Half the class is out. I saw some hiding under the pews, probably with just one badge, but the others are paralyzed all around the nave."

"Like Fyn," Annev said, nodding to the stunned boy.

"Yeah, and Titus." Therin looked around. "Where is he?"

Annev smiled. "Don't count Titus out just yet. He had two badges last time I saw him."

Therin laughed, throwing his arm around Annev's neck. "Titmouse stole someone's badge? With *two* paralyzed legs?" He shook his head. "Either you're lying or that kid has more tricks than a ring-snake."

Annev shrugged, trying not to glance at the black scraps of fabric where the boy was hidden. "Titus may surprise you." He gazed around the dais, wondering whether they should stay and wait for others to find them or venture into the maze and hunt for more medallions. It would probably be safer to wait—Fyn was right that the high ground offered an advantage—but Annev wondered if anyone would come for them; the test was nearly over, after all, and those that had badges would be interested in keeping them. But Annev wanted more—he *needed* more if he was going to win that key to tomorrow's Test of Judgment.

"Have you seen any of the witgirls?" Annev asked, suddenly thinking about Myjun.

Therin stepped back, shaking his head. "Not one. Maybe they're hiding—or maybe they were all stunned at the start. It's not like they can hide in those dresses."

Annev felt a thrill as he considered the possibility of finding Myjun in the darkness, but he shook his head. "Witmistress Kiara made it sound like they couldn't become full witwomen unless they passed this test. I don't know how good they are at stealth, but they've been training with Duvarek and the Witcircle since they were babies. They can't be that much worse than us."

"So … you want to look for them?"

"Why?" Annev asked. "Do you?"

Therin shrugged, though his eyes sparkled with mischief. "We might earn some more badges that way …"

"And just where do you think we'll find them?"

"I didn't see any girls hanging from curtains, so my guess is they're under the pews."

Annev nodded, seeing no fault to Therin's logic. "Lead the way."

The pair stalked over to the edge of the dais, bypassing its short set of stairs in favor of silently hopping down to the nave floor. They stopped at the first bench and Annev pointed at Therin's eyes and then the curtains, indicating that he should keep watch above while he investigated the underfloor.

Annev stooped to the ground, carefully peering beneath the central set of pews. He saw mostly darkness, though a faint rectangle of light indicated some places where an overhead plank was missing. He listened carefully but heard nothing. He stood, stalked over to the eastern section of benches, and did the same thing. This time he heard something shuffling almost silently through the darkness.

He waved Therin over. "Someone's hiding in there," Annev whispered, barely breathing. "Near the back row." Therin lifted his wand, face grim as Annev used hand gestures to indicate his intentions. "Split up. Circle around. Surprise them." Therin nodded.

Annev slid under the first two pews. When Therin did the same, he was almost invisible in the darkness. Without another word, they separated, sliding through the shadows, hunting for the sounds of broken silence.

CHAPTER TEN

As he reached the end of the ninth bench, Annev slowly approached a two-foot gap in the plank flooring overhead. A black drape reached down to the floor, creating a faux wall of sorts, and Annev stopped behind it, listening intently for any sounds of movement. The silence was complete, broken only by Edra's gravelly voice—closer than it had been before—shouting "TEN MINUTES!"

There was a gentle shuffle of cloth against wood on the other side of the drape. Annev silently eased back and rewrapped the broad strip of cloth hanging around his neck so that it covered his mouth and nose. There was another near-silent shuffle, and he slipped one of the rods from his tunic. The curtain above him went taut, stretching as someone pulled on the black fabric, and Annev struck, lifting the drape and jabbing the black tip into the climbing student.

The witgirl didn't even falter as the rod bounced harmlessly off her covered calf, and Annev stared in awe at the sight of the young woman. Gone were the bright skirt and blouse, which had been shed in favor of a fitted, black, practical outfit that covered her from head-to-toe; swathed in her reaping uniform, she was almost perfectly camouflaged in the shadows.

As Annev recoiled in surprise the young woman swung from the drape and kicked out with her slippered feet, catching Annev hard in the forearm and knocking away his first Rod of Paralysis. Annev rolled away and drew a second wand from his wrappings.

The witgirl dropped from the curtain, landing silently, and Annev glimpsed her cloth-wrapped face, her brown eyes barely visible in the faint light shining through the hole overhead.

Not Myjun, Annev thought. He was relieved and disappointed at the same time—and determined to stun her. Somehow.

The witgirl cocked her head, watching as Annev assumed a combat stance. She hesitated for the barest moment, and then her eyes seemed to twinkle beneath her mask. She spun out, feinting for his left. Annev shifted his weight as if to dodge, but instead he met her blow to his right. The witgirl snapped out with a rod of her own, its tip grazing Annev's covered cheekbone.

Annev instinctively threw himself backwards then cursed himself for not simply grabbing her while she'd been close. He was stronger—he was sure of that—but it seemed she was faster, and Annev was unused to those skill sets being reversed.

Unfortunately for Annev, the witgirl needed no such mental adjustment. She lashed out again, slapping his flailing arms aside and stabbing for his eyes.

Annev dropped to the ground, rolled, and kicked out against an anticipated follow-up attack. His momentum caught the witgirl's leading foot and she spun, reeling. It was only a moment's respite, but Annev used that half-second to roll beneath the nearest bench. He spied his fallen Rod of Paralysis but left it, preferring to get some distance between himself and his cloth-covered adversary.

Annev crawled to the end of his pew and glanced backward to see the witgirl stalking him in the near darkness. There was a flicker of movement behind her and Annev saw a second black-wrapped figure in the darkness. He thought it might be Therin coming to trap the witgirl as they had originally planned, but then the stranger passed beneath a shaft of light and he saw it was a second witgirl.

Bloody burning bones.

Annev tucked his rod away, rolled out from under the pews, and dashed into the maze of cloth panels obscuring the aisle between the eastern and center section of pews. There was no time for stealth now—he was being hunted.

Annev darted between the hanging black curtains and brushed aside another drape, reaching the central section of pews. He crouched to dive beneath its floorboards, but the prone forms of Lemwich and two other avatars blocked the way. Cursing, he bounded up onto the artificial floor in the center of the nave instead.

The planks beneath his feet shifted and groaned as he landed, broadcasting his exact location to any remaining students. As if on cue, a sandy-haired avatar named Horus dropped from the curtains above, his Rod of Paralysis sliding across Annev's neck and back. The black wrappings protected him from the avatar's sudden assault, so he spun and slammed his open palm into the avatar's face. The boy stumbled back, and Annev pressed his attack with a second palm-strike to the chest then a swipe upward, grabbing the boy's medallion and pulling it over his head.

The soft thuds and muted creaks of more padded feet converged on their position. Annev spun, kicked Horus in the chest, and sprinted away across the planks covering the center pews. Behind him, the brown-robed avatar roared in defiance and reeled from Annev's kick. Even so, he kept his feet beneath him and pursued, seemingly deaf to the witgirls behind him.

Annev flew down a corridor of cloth, sprinting across the planks resting atop the church pews as he also flung Horus's badge around his neck. As he moved, he tried to form a mental image of the gaps he had seen Duvarek make in the floorboards, then he headed toward a large pit in the center of the nave.

With a burst of adrenaline, he brushed aside the next thick curtain, spied the expected hole in the artificial floor, and jumped, barely clearing the surprise obstacle. He continued his sprint to the opposite end of the pews, but when the boards clattered behind him, Annev spared a glance over his shoulder and saw Horus reach the same wide gap. Not expecting it, the boy hesitated at the edge of the precipice for a second and a pair of cloth-wrapped hands lashed out at Horus, the naked fingers thumping into the boy's calf and opposite knee, paralyzing his legs the same way a stumble-stick might. The avatar fell with a groan, toppling into the hole, and was immediately dragged beneath the floorboards.

Gods! Annev thought, suddenly eyeing the wooden boards more suspiciously. *They're good. So good they don't even need wands to take us out.*

Annev slowed his pace, brushed aside a second cloth panel and stayed a careful distance from the edge of the plank platform. On a hunch, he crouched and leaped halfway across the second aisleway. Mid-fall, he caught a hanging curtain and swung the rest of the distance to the western benches. As he released the drape, he backflipped onto the platform and narrowly glimpsed a pair of hands dart out from under the western pews, searching for his legs.

Therin was right. They're under the pews and they're working together to take us out.

Annev guessed they'd already caught Therin. With their reaping uniforms covering most of their bodies, the girls were almost immune to the rods; unless Therin had stayed hidden, they'd have trapped him against the eastern wall. It was only a matter of time before they hunted him down too.

They didn't separate like we did, Annev realized, feeling foolish. *They stuck together so none of us could pick them off.* It was brilliant, and totally within the rules of the challenge. It also made Edra's attempt to reward the winner of the day's exercise seem like folly. The avatars and acolytes would have done much better by working together, but they had all been trained to view all tests as a competition. Even Annev, who had initially tried to work with Titus and Therin, had fallen into that trap.

A witapprentice slipped out into the western aisleway, searching for the student that had evaded their trap, and although he was crouched in the shadows against a backdrop of black, her keen eyes still spied Annev's cloth-wrapped form.

"FIVE MINUTES!" Edra bellowed from the front of the nave.

The witgirl lowered her black face wrap, revealing her blond hair and freckled face. "Two left!" Faith shouted over her shoulder. "One's in front of me, on the western benches!"

Damn! Annev thought, dodging behind a panel and climbing into the curtains. He wondered briefly if that meant they'd found Fyn but not Titus, or maybe they had found Titus but Therin was still out there. Either option meant that at least one of his friends would pass today's test, but it also meant …

I'm the only one left to catch! Better yet, if only Titus was left, Annev had won the key. And if only Therin was left, then they were tied for badges. Annev felt a moment of elation at that thought before remembering his location was known, and all eight of the witgirls were coming for him.

Halfway up to the ceiling, Annev saw three more witgirls emerge from behind cloth drapes or pop up from under the western floorboards. Annev hung motionless from his perch, his ankles pinching the curtain beneath him, holding him in place. As he took a breath, Faith shouted from below.

"He's here! Above me!"

Annev cursed. Stopping to rest had been a mistake. He leaped from his perch, grabbed the next curtain, and swung from drape to drape, moving north toward the entrance at a fair speed.

I need even higher ground, Annev realized. *Fyn was smart to go for the dais, and Therin and I should have stayed there. Maybe I can hide in the rafters.*

Annev was climbing higher when a fifth black-clad witapprentice dropped from above, knocking him to the artificial floor. Annev slammed into the planks moments before the witgirl dropped down in front of him. Ignoring his bruised ribs and shoulder, Annev rolled, kicking the woman in the chest and flipping to his feet as she fell back. He feinted right then dodged left behind a curtain and ran backwards, across the western pews and back toward the dais.

I can use this, Annev thought, remembering the position of the boards and planks. *I helped build it. I know which planks are traps. I just need to last a few more minutes without being cornered.*

Annev silently ran for the center of the false floor he had helped construct, sliding around curtains as he evaded two witapprentices who ran past him. He reached inside his tunic and pulled out two of his three remaining rods, then nearly stumbled as he discovered all but one of the disks around his neck were gone.

How …? And then Annev knew. *Therin … when he put his arm around my neck. That* bastard *stole them!* Annev almost hissed in frustration.

Damn it! I can't win now. If Therin is still out there, he's won—and if he got caught after we split up, he's lost my medallions. Annev's blood boiled, and he found himself retracting his promise to work with his friends tomorrow.

No, he thought, more calmly. *I'll work with them, just like I said I would. I'll use them. I'll get ahead with them … and then cast them off. Titus has already said he won't make a good avatar, and Therin doesn't deserve my help now. I'm on my own.*

But Annev still needed to win this test. He had only one disk now—despite all his efforts—and if he didn't get at least one more badge, he would fail the test and forfeit the advantage Edra had promised the winner. He had to go on the offensive, and with less than five minutes to spare he had to do it *now.*

Footsteps pounded on the boards in front of Annev as the last witgirl materialized before him. Annev sprinted past her, surprising her, then narrowly dodged a second girl as they both spun, tripping over each other as they tried to pursue him. Annev kept running, skipping over a complicated section of floorboards that he knew were not supported properly.

The girl in the lead had closed the distance between them and she sprang for him. No rod was in her hand, but her fingers scissored toward Annev's spine. Annev anticipated the move, dodged, and dropped hard onto the end of plank beneath him. It seesawed down, dropping Annev into the church pews and catapulting her into the air.

The small girl twisted as she flew, catching a drape and ripping it to the ground. Annev's hands pumped out, flinging both stumble-sticks at the young woman as she tried to untangle herself. The first black-and-gold wand thumped against the girl's chest, but then the black tip of the second wand smacked her exposed cheek and she collapsed.

Annev heard the second witapprentice approaching and crouched in the darkness beneath the pews, pulling out his third wand and waiting. A second later she passed the gap in the planks and Annev struck, grabbing her leg and dropping her hard onto the church pew beside him. She met Annev's eyes just as he tapped her exposed forehead with his last Rod of Paralysis and she went slack. Annev stared at her, suddenly realizing he had no idea where she had hidden her wood token.

"Sorry," he said, pulling the cloth wrapping away from her face and sliding his fingers down her neck, searching for it.

But there was no sign of it, and he had no time. He tried the same quick search of the first girl he had stunned, turned her over, and still found nothing. From somewhere not-too-distant, he heard the other witgirls' shouts as they closed on his location. Annev looked down at the second young woman's perfectly prone body, swallowed, and methodically patted her down. His gloved left hand and the naked fingertips of his right slid down her collarbones and then beneath her breasts in a smooth sweep. Nothing. He ran his hands down across her hips, searching for any telltale bumps. The witgirls' shouts grew closer still as he slid his hands beneath the prone girl and finally found a bulge at the small of her back.

Whispering another apology, Annev slipped a hand beneath the cloth wrapping and seized the wooden disks, his fingers brushing the girl's soft skin before pulling out the four hidden tokens. He hesitated, looking at them and wondering if he should take them all or leave her with two as he had with Titus.

Time's almost up. If Therin's still out there, then he's won—I can't beat him. But I can pass the test ... and I can make sure she does too.

Annev sat back on his heels as the girl's eyelids fluttered—or had she winked at him? He shook his head then held up all four tokens so she could see them. Then, making his intentions clear, he took two in his right hand and replaced the others at the small of young woman's back. It was just as he released them, his fingers still touching her skin, that Annev belatedly recognized her.

Myjun.

He snatched his hand back.

"TIME!" Edra shouted. "Cease! Return to the entrance of the nave."

Annev looked down into Myjun's cool green eyes.

She stared back, and this time there was no mistaking the wink she gave him.

CHAPTER ELEVEN

A few seconds after Edra called time, Duvarek pulled a large rope at the entrance to the nave, and all of the cloth panels came rolling down from the rafters. Light flooded the room, and it became obvious who was paralyzed and who was still mobile.

Annev made sure Myjun was comfortable then reluctantly stood up from his hole in the pews. He looked around. Six witgirls stood within a dozen paces of him, but not a single avatar or acolyte could be seen.

"Oh," Edra mumbled from the opposite end of the nave. Witmistress Kiara and the other two witwomen smiled at him, clearly unsurprised. The Master of Arms harrumphed. "Change of plans," he bellowed. "Let's clear this wreck out. Witgirls, please help Master Duvarek roll up the curtains. Avatars …" He paused, looking at Annev then shrugged and continued. "Avatars, Master Narach has a wand for curing you of your paralysis. Once he has, you will collect up these planks and stack them against the wall."

It took a little time, but once Narach had unfrozen the paralyzed, using a rod that was painted half-gold and half-white, the work proceeded quickly.

The boys who had been stunned by the witgirls' pressure-point attacks were unaffected by Narach's rod, so Witmistress Kiara worked alongside him, forcing thumb and knuckle into the avatars' and acolytes' joints. Most regained feeling almost immediately, though Therin had apparently been worked over by the witgirls and needed additional help; Kiara summoned the third witwoman—Tonja—and together they applied pressure to Therin's paralyzed limbs. He gasped aloud, his body contorting as they twisted and pulled. Then there was an audible *pop*, which Annev heard from across the nave, and Therin went limp. He wasn't able to help clear up, but by the time the cloth panels and planks had been moved he could stand again.

He avoided Annev.

Annev was busy scooping up planks and carrying them over to the wall when he noticed the other students staring at him and remembered he was still wrapped in cloth. He shed the strips and added them to the pile of rags on the dais, belatedly remembering Titus as he did. He moved the pile of cloth, pulling his stunned and blinking friend out and calling for Narach. After several pokes with the Rod of Recovery, Titus regained the use of his limbs.

"That's strange," Narach said, tucking the wand back into his robes. "Usually doesn't need more than one poke. Same thing happened with that Fyn boy."

Titus shrugged, ignoring Narach's unspoken question.

Once the room had been cleared, Edra and Duvarek asked the students to line up to present their badges and account for their actions in the nave. The witgirls lined up, too, but Kiara gave no indication that they would give a similar accounting. Instead, she and the two witwomen took their places beside Edra and Duvarek, silently observing.

The avatars went first, and the accounting was supposed to be their opportunity to explain their prowess—but today it was a parade of humiliation, each explaining how they had fallen to the witgirls or been taken down by Fyn. Kenton had fared better than most, until he admitted Therin had got the drop on him, and any respect he had earned quickly diminished.

For Fyn, it was much worse. He had been dragged out of the Ring of Odar to a chorus of whispered speculation and pointed fingers. When it was his turn he lingered on his successes, his voice turning sullen when he related how he had found and stunned Titus—omitting that the boy was already paralyzed or that he had tortured him. He concluded his tale by saying Annev had hidden in the Ring of Odar and surprised him when he stooped to collect Titus's badge. It was close enough to the truth that Annev didn't correct it, and he enjoyed seeing the other students reappraising him. Best of all was Myjun's flash of a smile as Annev's blue eyes met her green ones. For that moment he relived the seconds they had shared in the shadows of the nave.

With the avatars' accounting over, it was the acolytes' turn. Therin surprised everyone by going first. He had stunned Alisander in the rafters, and then stunned Kenton on the dais. He gazed at his feet then before glancing sheepishly at Annev.

"I'm not proud of what I did next," he said. "I didn't stun Annev, but I did use our friendship to steal his takings. We were almost tied for medallions, and I wanted to win. It didn't even matter in the end, because I was caught by the witgirls almost at once." He shrugged. "I had thirteen badges, and I"d have more if I'd worked with Annev. I hid instead, because I was afraid of losing my advantage, and Faith and Malia found me." Therin paused here, grinning broadly, all penance suddenly gone from his face. "But damn! What a way to go!"

Most of the avatars and acolytes laughed at Therin's not-so-penitent confession. Even Duvarek snorted, though he got it under control when Kiara glared at him.

Annev watched the witapprentices during the exchange, and saw Faith, Malia, and Myjun whisper amongst themselves. All three laughed at a private joke.

"Enough!" Edra bellowed, eyeing the acolyte. "Thank you for your account, Therin, though at the Academy we are more respectful of our peers. Now that you are hale again, you will help Steward Markov carry the planks and drapes back to the storage room beneath the testing arena."

Therin stared comically at the stacks of splintery boards and heaps of black cloth piled at the edge of the nave. He swallowed, realizing the work that lay ahead of him, then shrugged.

"It was worth it," he said, with a courtly bow to the witgirls, which Annev knew was meant for Faith. Before Edra could chastise him again, the wiry acolyte sprang up, gathered an armload of black cloth, and hurried after Markov who was already making his tenth trip down to the storage rooms.

The other testimonies went quickly, with many acolytes having done nothing but hide under the pews until they were tagged by the witgirls. When it was Titus's turn, he surprised everyone by pulling two badges from under his tunic.

"You passed?" Edra said, disbelieving. "How? Fyn stunned you and took your token."

"But he didn't mention dumping the boy in a pile of rags," Kiara said, eyeing Titus. "I suspect there's more to this story than Avatar Fyn shared."

Duvarek grunted, agreeing. "Why *were* you in that pile?"

Keos, Annev thought. *Maybe I should have kept those badges ...*

Titus looked at Annev. "Annev and I. We ..."

"Spit it out," Edra snapped. "You've passed. I just want to know how."

"Sorry, Master Edra. The truth is ... I stunned—"

"Titus was bait," Annev interrupted, stepping to Titus's side. "He pretended to be stunned, and I was going to ambush anyone who spotted him. Only Fyn was careful and stunned him for real." He looked to Titus, hoping the boy wouldn't mention accidentally stunning himself. "Fyn had guessed Titus was pretending, and I stunned him when he was distracted."

Edra weighed Annev's words and nodded slowly, squinting at the raised dais and altar at the far end of the nave. "Then you dumped Fyn in the Ring of Odar." The master glanced at Annev who nodded. "A bit sacrilegious to dump a paralyzed someone in there. Especially for a deacon." Annev bowed his head, having no answer for that, and Edra turned back to Titus. "And how did you end up beneath those rags?"

"They were for stealth. To cover our uniforms—" Titus said, unwinding a black strip of cloth from his body.

"Not that," Edra interrupted. "How did you end up under that pile of cloth? Fyn stunned you and took your badge. But now you have two badges. How?"

Titus's voice grew quieter. "Annev hid me there with my badge plus one he'd taken from Fyn."

"One riddle solved," Edra said. He nodded, dismissing Titus and turning his gaze on Annev. He, Duvarek, and Kiara all studied him in silence. Annev looked away, self-consciously tugging on the glove that covered his left hand.

"Acolyte Ainnevog," Edra said. "You're the last. Account for yourself."

Annev did, aware of everyone's eyes on him. He felt Fyn and Kenton's glare as he reported beating them. He glossed over Therin's theft, not having realized it at the time, and explained their plan to corner the witgirls. Kiara sniffed but did not interrupt until Annev mentioned beating Myjun and the other witapprentice, when she huffed.

"She was carrying *four* badges, but you only took two." The witmistress stared at him, gray eyes glittering. "Did you pity her as you did the plump boy?"

Annev suddenly realized leaving tokens with Myjun and Titus really had been a mistake. He shook his head. "I didn't pity either of them. Titus earned his by distracting Fyn."

"And Myjun?"

Annev felt Myjun's eyes on him but did not look at her. "Titus helped me beat Fyn. Therin and I beat Kenton together, and if he hadn't stolen my badges, maybe we could have earned some more."

"Unlikely," Kiara said, "and irrelevant when I asked you about Myjun."

"But that *is* my point," Annev said, gaining confidence. "I did well because I allied with my friends—for as long as I could—and your witgirls did well because they worked together. Myjun was part of that. She lost to me, but she was successful working as part of a team. Taking all of her badges would not have reflected that." Kiara surprised him by laughing— not with derision, but with genuine mirth.

It surprised Edra and Duvarek too, and when she spoke she had a thin smile on her face.

"Your acolyte is as talkative as he is talented, and he has proven my point about the value of working together, as *my* apprentices are trained to do. Our allegiance and support for our sisters gives us our strength." Kiara looked pointedly at Edra. "Your avatars would have fared better if they had made more alliances."

"Maybe," Edra conceded, "But this was not a team exercise. We want to assess how well each apprentice will fare on his own."

"And you have your answer," Kiara said. "Poorly. Your avatars may have bested each other, but none overcame my apprentices." She paused, appraising Annev. "Except this one—who overcame two and is not even an avatar." The gray-eyed witmistress steepled her hands but said no more.

Master Narach approached the masters, the black box of stumble-sticks in his age-spotted hands.

"I have all but two of the rods," he said, setting the box down to wipe his pale, watery eyes. "No student may leave until I have them all. If they've misplaced even one—"

"We'll find the rods, Narach," Duvarek waved a hand, dismissing the aged Master of Secrets and his evident concern, "so you can lock your precious artifacts up again."

Narach focused the full force of his withering glare on his colleague. "Don't try my patience, Master Duvarek, or I might not be so quick to let you use artifacts in your next lesson."

"You weren't quick this time," Duvarek replied, "but we will search for your precious rods."

Narach sputtered and hobbled away, mumbling something about getting Markov to help him.

Master Narach's presence always made Annev uneasy. He empathized with the grumpy old man, who often seemed an outcast among the younger masters, but he and Ancient Tosan both used scrying artifacts to check if any students, masters, or ancients were concealing forbidden magic, and Annev had to consciously stop himself from fiddling with his glove when the Master of Secrets was around.

Kiara pursed her lips together. "Acolyte Ainnevog, why are you not an avatar?"

Annev was uncertain how to respond. "Because … I haven't passed the Test of Judgment?"

"You obviously possess the skills to do so." She paused, glancing at the two Masters beside her and allowing her words to sink in. "Whatever you've done in the past, it's not working. I suggest you rethink your strategy."

She nodded to Edra and Duvarek. "Masters."

Witmistress Kiara moved toward the door. Nasha and Tonja followed close behind with the eight witgirls, back in their dresses without a hair out of place, trailing them. Narach met them, examining each with a scrying stone before they could leave.

Annev tugged at the Glove of Illusion Sodar had made for him. The priest had made several such gloves over the years, but now the illusory fabric Sodar had stolen from the vault was almost gone. Annev's current glove was threadbare, but it would still protect him from Tosan and Narach's scrying. He took a deep breath, consciously releasing the magical glove.

Everything's fine. He never sees my arm. They never tell me to take off the glove. Everything's fine.

"I think we've finished your accounting, Annev," Master Edra said, his tone curt. Duvarek had already left, directing the other avatars and acolytes to help clear the planks and curtains away. "Since you helped Duvarek set up, you can go back to your chapel. Help Sodar prepare tonight's sermon. You are dismissed."

Annev chafed at the master's tone. *It's as if I'm being punished, not rewarded for winning.* The thought reminded Annev of Edra's key.

"As you wish, Master Edra. And when will I receive that key you promised the winner?"

Edra's mind was already elsewhere. "Tomorrow. You're done for today."

Annev nodded, once again feeling that Edra was angry with him. *Maybe he feels working together with Therin and Titus was cheating.* Whatever the cause of Edra's displeasure, Annev kept his silence and turned to leave.

"Master Narach," Edra shouted. "Annev has his religious duties now. Come and check him so he can go back to his chapel."

There it is again, Annev thought. *Not Sodar's chapel. Not the village chapel. My chapel.* Annev doubted Edra meant anything by it, but it made him uneasy all the same, as if the master were deliberately distancing Annev from those and who lived and slept inside the Academy. Annev frowned but held his tongue, then waited for Narach to finish examining the witgirls.

"And for Odar's sake," Edra snapped, "take off that stupid glove."

CHAPTER TWELVE

Annev's stomach lurched horribly.

"What—" Annev said, choking on a rush of fear. He swallowed, beginning again. "I'm sorry, Master Edra?"

"Take off that damn glove," Edra repeated, his voice tired. "It's a ridiculous affectation which probably gave you an advantage in today's lesson. Should have told you to take it off earlier."

Terror bloomed in the pit of Annev's stomach. He nodded, mute with dread, and fumbled at it, peeling the thin black fabric off his elbow and down his forearm then pulled the whole glove from his hand, glancing over his shoulder to assess how much time he had. He nearly pissed himself as he saw Narach approaching already with his black box of wands.

The Master of Secrets glared at Edra, his lips pressed into a thin line, then he looked at Annev. "Chapel duties, is it? One moment." Master Narach set his box of wands on the ground and patted his pockets. "Now, where did I put it …?"

Edra raised his eyes to the heavens. "You're not serious."

Narach spat at the floor, glaring. "I'm *perfectly* serious. I'm too old for this master avatar nonsense. Should have been made an ancient decades ago."

Annev swallowed, his heart beating fast. He glanced between Edra and the Master of Secrets, pretending he wasn't terrified that his secret was about to be discovered.

Narach began turning his pockets inside out as Duvarek came over. "What's he doing?"

Edra was obviously losing his temper and turned aside to speak plainly. "He still hasn't found the missing rods—and now he's misplaced his scrying stone."

"He just had it! I saw him using it to search the witwomen." He looked at Master Narach. "Did you drop it in the box?"

Narach squinted at the Master of Shadows. He opened his mouth to say something then stopped, eyeing the black box at his feet. "I don't think so …" He trailed off, scratched his stubbly cheek, and bent down to open the box.

The black chest was full of black-and-gold Rods of Paralysis, as well as the Rod of Recovery. Narach picked up this last rod and used it to poke through the chest, sifting through the stumble-sticks until he spied a translucent white stone wrapped in a leather thong.

"Huh," Narach said, threading his wand through the thong and lifting the scrying stone out. "I must have dropped it in there after searching the witgirls." The master raised the stone to his right eye and peered through its milky center. As he did, the stone shimmered and became clear as crystal.

Annev shifted so that his left arm hung a little behind his body. *Please, God. Please, Odar. Please, All-father. Don't let Narach see my arm. Please, please, please.* His heart thumped in his chest and his mind raced. He needed to do something—anything—to stop Narach from spying his hand.

"How does it work, Master Narach?" Annev blurted, feigning interest. "Can anyone use the scrying stone or is it only for those with magical affinity?"

Narach harrumphed, taking the stone away from his eye. "Of course anyone can use it. I certainly don't possess any magical capabilities." Narach snorted as if the very notion were preposterous, which, Annev supposed, it was. Anyone found to possess magic was deemed a Child of Keos and stoned to death—or tied to a tree and left for the beasts of the Brakewood.

Master Narach handed the flat stone to Annev. "Look through the thin part in the middle," he said, enjoying Annev's unexpected interest. "The center turns clear—yes, just like that. Now look at the wands in that chest. Good. What do you see?"

Annev closed one eye and used the other to peer through the Stone of True-seeing. When he looked at the contents of the black chest, he saw that the rods now radiated a swirling vapor of purple light, which seemed to flow over, around, and through the chest of artifacts.

"Wow," Annev said, genuinely intrigued. Narach nodded then extended his hand, wordlessly asking for the artifact back. Annev tried to stall him.

"Would Steward Markov like some help searching for the rods?"

Narach lowered his hand, considering. "Well …"

"You won the competition," Duvarek snapped. "Enjoy your reward, and don't volunteer for steward work."

Edra nodded. "It's tan-robe work, Annev. Let Master Narach scry you and get out of here."

Annev grit his teeth and reluctantly handed the stone back.

Narach lifted the stone to his eye. "Arms out to the side, please."

Annev held them out slowly as another idea came to mind. "Couldn't you use the stone to find the rods?"

Narach lowered the lens from his eye and frowned. "A good thought, Acolyte Annev. I doubt it would work from this distance but … Hmm." The Master of Secrets turned from Annev and peered into the nave through his scrying stone. After a moment, a small smile appeared on his wrinkled face. With the stone still held in front of his eye, he shouted at Markov.

"Markov, you idiot! Third row. Left side. Yes … no, *my* left. Third from the back. Yes."

Annev was practically shaking with relief as Markov lifted a rod.

"Silver staves," Narach beamed. "Don't know why I didn't think to do that before." He raised the scrying stone back to his eye and smiled again. "I see the last one too. Good." Annev was already sliding his glove back on.

"Get out of here," said Master Edra.

Annev bowed, shocked by the closeness of his escape. He swallowed bile and forced himself to stroll over to the nave's ironbound doors. He opened the portal then had to jump back as the Master of Operations strode into the room. When the ink-spattered man spotted the Master of Shadows, he waved to him.

"Duvarek! Get yourself cleaned up. You're going to Banok tonight with Master Keyish."

Annev paused at the door, listening as Duvarek groaned.

"It's the first night of Regaleus, Carbad. Can't it wait?"

Carbad shook his head. "Tonight. Janak's got his hands on a dark rod."

Duvarek swore. "Alright. Let me eat first. I haven't had a gods-damned thing today." The two men walked through the open doorway and Annev slipped through the door behind them with a tremendous sense of relief. He forced himself to walk slowly down the hall, double-checking that his glove was firmly in place, but as soon as he rounded the corner he sprinted through the hallways, racing to escape the Academy's claustrophobic walls.

As Annev ran down the dimly lit halls, guided as much by memory than sight, his mind raced too. He marveled at how quickly the day had passed, fueled by nothing but adrenaline. He'd saved Lem, beaten Fyn, been betrayed by Therin, and touched Myjun. He'd also won an impossible challenge and gained a mysterious advantage in tomorrow's Test of Judgment. He might need to eat and rest, but his mind raced with the thrills of the day, and his feet felt light despite his fatigue.

Annev dashed through the great hall and raced for the massive double doors that guarded the entrance to the Academy. He had missed lunch with Sodar, but today's classes had ended earlier than usual, so he would still surprise the priest by coming home.

Annev passed under the Academy's arched doorway, where both the inner and outer doors had been propped open, then half-ran, half-slid down the worn stone steps to Chaenbalu's central plaza.

As Annev outran the Academy's shadow, the familiar sights and smells of Chaenbalu washed over him. Out here, surrounded by the villagers, he felt energized by his dual positions at the Academy and chapel. His role as a deacon came with few perks, but he enjoyed the journey between the Academy and the chapel—it was a small privilege that no other student had.

Across the plaza, Annev heard the muted thumps of a hammer pounding leather coming from the cobbler's work shed. On the other side of the carpenter's shop, Rafela and her grumpy husband Lorn were pulling a slab of fresh-baked bread from the oven. The smell of it sharpened Annev's hunger.

"Afternoon, Annev!"

Annev slowed to see the village's one-eyed blacksmith striding across the square with a heavy block of pig iron resting on one shoulder. The swarthy man paused to shift the raw metal from one shoulder to the other.

"Afternoon, Sraon!"

"Late for lunch? Or have the Ancients tired of you already?"

Annev stopped, always pleased to see the blacksmith and enjoy his strange, lilting accent. Sodar described it as "muddled nauthron," though that had meant little to Annev; in a community so sheltered from the outside world, any novelty was enjoyable. The eye patch that covered his missing eye set Sraon even farther from what most villagers deemed normal.Naturally, Annev had taken a quick liking to him. He grinned.

"Both, I suppose. I beat the master's test so they sent me packing early."

"Jings! Not *the* test?"

Annev shook his head. "That's tomorrow. Today was more of a ... practice test."

Sraon grunted, shifting the bolt of iron over again. "Well and good. I hope you pass. Would be a shame to have forged that ring for naught." Annev bit his lip and Sraon laughed to see it before heading to his smithy on the east side of the Academy.

Probably shouldn't have told him so much about Myjun, Annev thought, slowing. He had spoken freely to Sraon while the smith had forged Myjun's promise ring. He doubted the blacksmith would share Annev's secret with anyone, but if Annev didn't earn his avatar title tomorrow then Sraon would know what he had lost, and the thought made Annev uncomfortable. He had to be more careful about the secrets he chose to share with others.

He circled the Academy walls until he reached the well at the center of village. From there, Annev could see Sraon's open-air smithy and beyond it, at the easternmost edge of Chaenbalu, he could just see Sodar's chapel. Annev ran towards it, passing the first row of houses and the back of the smith's home. He slowed then ducked into the alley separating Sraon's forge and smithy from the cobbler's. As soon as he emerged from the alleyway, he sped up again, only to be caught off guard by another greeting.

"Annev!"

He spun on the ball of one foot and skidded to a halt facing the speaker. Suddenly his heart was beating harder than when he'd been sprinting. He smiled.

"Hello, Myjun."

CHAPTER THIRTEEN

Seeing Myjun was both a surprise and a delight. A tremor ran through his body as she gave him a smile, followed by guilt that he had touched her without her permission.

"You left before I could apologize," Annev said.

"Apologize?"

Annev nodded. "For touching … in the dark. I was just looking for the badges. I didn't mean to …" He swallowed, uncertain what he was trying to say. "I'd never hurt you."

Myjun's voice was light with amusement. "I wasn't offended. You were trying to win, to get every advantage in tomorrow's test."

Annev nodded, grateful Myjun understood. "What about … leaving you those badges? I don't think Kiara liked that."

Myjun's smile transformed into a mischievous grin. "No … but it was what I'd hoped you would do."

"Oh?"

The mischief spread to Myjun's eyes. "Of course. I wanted my wit-sisters to win, but I didn't want you to lose either. That's why I tripped Coshry, and why I let you stun me."

"Tripped? Wait … you *let* me stun you?"

Myjun flipped her hair back, amused by the question. "Did you think otherwise?"

"Well … yeah."

She laughed. "You're sweet, Annev. Yes, I let you stun me. I trusted you'd let me keep a few medallions—and that worked out too."

ST. JOHN THE BAPTIST PARISH LIBRARY
2920 NEW HIGHWAY 51
LAPLACE, LOUISIANA 70068

Annev shook his head. Myjun had been a step ahead the whole time. It cheapened his victory somewhat, yet he felt he had still earned it.

"Yeah," he agreed, "it all worked out." He leaned in, then caught himself, looking around to see if others were watching their private exchange. "So," he said, a smile in his voice, "why are you out here instead of with the witwomen?"

"I had to collect father's shoes from Greusik." Myjun wiggled her left arm and Annev saw she was carrying a pair of large leather sandals. In her other hand, she held a cloth-covered wicker basket. The smell of warm bread came from it and Annev's stomach rumbled.

"You were quick. I ran all the way here."

"I was hoping I might see you."

"Oh," Annev said, surprised and pleased. "Well, here I am."

"Yes. Here we are."

They stood in awkward silence for a moment as he tried to think of something else to say.

"So ... will you be at this evening's Regaleus sermon?"

"Of course! That's when I get to see you in your clerical robes. I love that. Much better than the dirty uniforms the masters make you wear."

Annev nodded, unsure if Myjun was commenting on his status as an acolyte or the actual cleanliness of his wardrobe. "I definitely get to dress up."

"Oh! That reminds me." Myjun shifted the sandals to her other arm and fumbled in her pocket. "I have something for you." Then, from the soft folds of her white apron, she drew out a long piece of red and gold cloth.

A glove.

"I made it for you." Annev could feel a huge smile spreading over his face as she held it out. "Happy Regaleus."

Annev slowly took the glove from her. It was made of bright crimson cloth. A fiery golden tail began above the elbow, its yellow threads spiraling around the arm and into the body of the phoenix emblazoned on the forearm. The bird's face was stitched on the back of the hand, beak agape, tongue flickering up the left thumb.

"It's beautiful. Thank you. I have something for you, too, for the last day of Regaleus."

Myjun's smile blossomed. "Thanks—and I'm so glad you like it. I wasn't sure if I should make you one or two, but you seem to wear one on your left hand a lot more." Annev shyly rubbed his gloved hand, surprised Myjun had noticed, then her lips puckered into a tiny pink frown. "Faith says you wear one glove because you burned your hand at the Academy and they make you hide it—like with Kenton's scar."

"No," Annev said carefully. "No burns or scars."

"I know. At least, I know your hand isn't disfigured." She bit her lip and there was a glint of mischief in her eye as she reached out and touched his gloved hand, tracing his fingertips before carefully tugging the garment off.

Annev gasped as his naked hand slid free then he fought the urge to cover it. Myjun smiled, caressing his bare skin as she carefully turned his hand over in hers.

"See. Painless. Maybe one of these days I can check the rest?"

Annev ducked his head, flustered, and Myjun sensed it, taking the opportunity to slide her phoenix glove over Annev's left hand. A perfect fit.

"It's lovely," he said again.

Myjun nodded, releasing him. "Anyway, I knew your hand wasn't scarred after that day behind the bakery. I told Faith that—said your hand was fine—but she won't believe me till she sees it herself." She shook her head, and Annev felt the first stirrings of unease. "It's so shameful to see someone disfigured," Myjun continued, "but Faith loves gossip. It's like Sraon's eye. Father says if he weren't the only blacksmith in the village, the council would have thrown him out years ago. It would be easier if his apprentice was any good, but apparently he can barely bend metal—only fit for striking work, you know—and now father says he's been botching that as well." She tisked, oblivious to Annev's discomfort. "So for now we have to rely on a marked-one for our smithing. Hard to fathom we haven't found anyone more suitable than Sraon after over a decade, but there it is."

Annev shook his head slowly, his fingers creeping up to tug at the phoenix glove. "Sraon does good work. Besides, he lost his eye fighting monsters from the Cunnart Isle. He's told me the story a hundred times. There's nothing shameful in his injury."

"Of course there is, Annev," Myjun said matter-of-factly, and slowly began walking towards the Academy. Annev followed, his eyes drawn to her even as he cringed at her words. "It's a sign from Odar. His way of revealing Children of Keos in disguise." She flicked her head, tossing her long brown hair over her shoulder. "It says a lot that he would defend him—let alone befriend him. You're kind like that ... but you should be careful. My father says the children of Keos are deceitful, always hiding their true nature, preying on the kindness of others. It worries me that Sraon talks with you about his life before Chaenbalu but doesn't share those stories with others. Don't you find that odd?"

"Well ..." Myjun's brow crinkled as she waited in earnest to hear Annev's opinion. He swallowed. "He hasn't said all *that* much to me. Just that he learned smithing in Odarnea. And fought keokum on the Cunnart Isle."

Myjun tilted her head, her eyes narrowing. "How do you know he's telling the whole truth?" She paused, lowering her voice. "He's been marked by Odar. Maybe he actually *led* the ogres out of Cunnart so that they could eat Darite babies."

Annev laughed. "That's silly. He's a good man, Myjun. I see him every Seventhday."

"He's a *smith*, Ani." She walked closer, their shoulders brushing, waiting for him to puzzle it out. After a few seconds, she glanced up at him. "Like the *Terrans*? They worship Keos and they're *all* smiths."

Annev scratched his head, resisting the urge to contradict Myjun by explaining what Sodar had taught him about the Terrans. "Look, Sraon's from the north. Terrans live in the old lands—out east. And anyway, Sraon comes to chapel *every Seventhday*. Sometimes he even comes during the week to say prayers with Sodar. He definitely worships *Odar*, Myjun. Not Keos."

Myjun shrugged dismissively with one shoulder. "Father says Sons of Keos do that to trick people. And he would know."

Annev slowed, realizing he would never convince her; Myjun seemed to believe anything her father Elder Tosan told her—no matter how far-fetched it was. A second, colder realization accompanied the first: Myjun would never really accept him if she knew his secret. Annev's weight shifted from foot to foot and he decided he had nothing left to say.

"I have to prepare for tonight's sermon." He took Myjun's hand and bowed formally over it, lightly kissing the back of her palm. "Thank you for the glove. You'll have your gift on the last night of Regaleus."

Myjun bit her lip then smiled as she withdrew her hand. "Don't let my father know we're exchanging gifts. He's a traditionalist—he believes it's bad luck." She clutched the sandals to her chest. "Can I tell you a secret, though?"

"Anything."

She leaned forward conspiratorially. "I think he's old-fashioned," she whispered, close enough that he felt her breath on his cheek. "He takes some things far too seriously." She winked at him. "Bye, Annev."

"Bye …" he hesitated, savoring her name on his lips, "… Myjun."

She made to leave, walking halfway across the plaza, then glanced over her shoulder one last time. "It was exciting," she said, just loud enough for him to hear, "being alone in the nave with you."

And before Annev could respond, she darted up the stone steps to the Academy and disappeared from view.

Annev sighed. His skin felt warm and his mind was racing. *She's so beautiful,* he thought, staring at the steps, *and yet some of the things she says …*

He didn't know what to make of her. Sometimes when Myjun spoke, he felt Tosan's words were coming out of her mouth. Words he utterly disagreed with. At other times, though, her words were like drinking honey-eyed water … and nothing felt more right.

CHAPTER FOURTEEN

"I wonder what Ancient Tosan would say about Acolyte Ainnevog exchanging gifts with his daughter." The jeering voice jolted Annev from his thoughts and he turned to see Fyn slink into the alley. "Or maybe I'll just tell him I caught you kissing."

Annev's mood withered.

"Why don't you tell Elder Tosan and find out?" he bluffed. "Then he can ask his daughter if you were telling the truth. I think I'd enjoy seeing that."

Fyn glowered at him, and Annev noticed the boy had shed his brown tunic in favor of civilian clothing. "You always think you're better than us, don't you?" he snarled through gritted teeth.

"There are some things I *am* better at, Fyn."

Fyn laughed, though there was no mirth in it. "You think you're so clever, huh? Sneaking up on me in class. *Torturing* me. Sneaking those badges to your mousy little friend."

"You tortured Titus first," Annev said, not backing down.

Fyn sniffed. "He would never have passed that test without your help—without cheating. But he's still going to become a steward, and you'll never beat me in a fair fight."

Ah, Annev thought, *he's here to put me in my place. Great.*

"You're going to fail the Test of Judgment tomorrow," Fyn added. "I'm going to ensure it—because *nobody* beats me. Not you. Not anyone."

Annev gritted his teeth. Fyn *wanted* a fight, and he knew exactly how to stoke Annev's temper. Worse, Annev could feel himself rising to it.

"I suppose we'll find out tomorrow, Fyn," Annev said, his tone even. "Right now, though, I have to help Sodar prepare—"

"You think working in that old dodderer's chapel makes you better than the rest of us? You're so *important*. You get to *question* everything—"

"I don't, Fyn. I have duties—"

"And you think that means you can do whatever you want. That the rules somehow don't apply to you." The taller boy paced, fists clenching and unclenching.

"Fyn," Annev said, his growing anger threatening to overwhelm his good judgment. "It's been a long day, and I still have work to do." He turned and walked away.

Don't follow me, Annev thought, hastening his pace. *You made your point. I'm not one of you. Let it go.*

"That's what I'm talking about," Fyn shouted before pursuing Annev. "Right there! You think you can do whatever you want. *Take* whatever you want. *Leave* whenever you want." He circled around till he stood in the middle of the circular street, blocking Annev's path. "You run around making eyes at Tosan's daughter. You *torture* people in class and then stand up on Seventhday in your fancy robes, as if you're *so* much holier than the rest of us. And you wear that *stupid* glove"—he pointed at Myjun's gift—"just to make sure you stand out. Like you're too good to touch the same *dirt* as the rest of us."

If only you knew, Fyn.

"I made myself a promise today," Fyn said, pulling a pair of kali sticks from behind his back. "Can you guess what it was?"

Bloody bones, Annev thought. *I guess this is actually happening.*

"Let me guess," Annev said, moving sideways into an alleyway, his eyes roaming for an avenue of escape. "To take revenge for dumping you in that trough?"

Fyn smiled. "The trough I can forgive. The torture … not so much." He spun the two-foot long, fire-hardened sticks and advanced on Annev. "You said you'd kill me if I touched your friends. How about I kill *you* instead."

Annev reeled, suddenly realizing how badly he had misjudged the situation. He looked from the kali sticks to Fyn and realized, no matter what he did, the boy wanted blood.

Damn.

He had three options: Apologize and hope Fyn accepted it—a virtual, even laughable, impossibility. He could fight and let the avatar beat him to a bloody pulp. That might temporarily pacify his bloodlust … but Fyn might actually kill him. He could fight to win … which he and Fyn both knew wasn't the most viable choice. But their encounters had been escalating, and Annev feared that the only permanent solution was serious injury or death for one of them. Given those options, he preferred to preserve his life over Fyn's.

He sighed. *Well. Let's work through the list.*

"Fyn. I'm sorry I choked you with the Rod of Paralysis. I was over the line, and I was wrong. It was an accident that I went so far."

"Accident?" Fyn repeated coldly. "It seemed to me it was payback for poking your friend. You're sure it was an *accident*?"

"I didn't mean to go so far," Annev maintained, though he knew that wasn't strictly true. He glanced down the alley and saw that it opened up onto one of the wider streets circling the village plaza.

Fourth option, he thought. *Run for the chapel.* He edged closer to the mouth of alley.

Fyn shook his head, his dreadlocks flipping in front of his eyes. "Sure. Accidents happen. No problem. I'll let you off the hook. Let you get away with it. The way you get away with everything else."

"It *was* unintentional, Fyn."

Fyn tapped his kali sticks together in rapid succession. "I'm afraid there's another accident about to happen. You won't be well enough to participate in tomorrow's test."

On cue, Brinden, Kellor, and Jasper appeared behind Annev, blocking the street. Like Fyn, they had shed their training uniforms and were inconspicuously dressed.

Maybe I can use that to my advantage.

Annev stopped moving towards the street. There was nowhere to run, and his apology had failed. As the boys closed in around him, his gut knotted and more adrenaline began to course through his blood. He took a deep breath. Should he strike first and use what little advantage remained to him? Or should he wait and try to use their attacks against each other?

Annev looked between Fyn on his left and the three approaching avatars on his right. The alley was about ten feet wide, with walls in front of and behind Annev. He was trapped.

It was going to be a blood bath.

CHAPTER FIFTEEN

Fyn feigned a punch to Annev's face then snatched the black glove Annev loosely held in his hand. Annev tried to reclaim it, but Fyn stepped back and tore the garment in half—then he tore it again, dropped the pieces to the earth, and ground his boot into the magicked fabric.

"What do you think, boys? Tan enough now? Still looks too close to brown to me." Annev's hand darted for the shredded Glove of Illusion, but Fyn was quicker, his foot snapping out, nearly catching Annev in the groin.

Annev jumped back a pace toward Jasper and Brinden and barely dodged Jasper's attempt to get a lock on his arm. He grabbed Jasper's instead and used his momentum to throw the oafish boy over his shoulder, knocking him into Brinden.

"Get him!" Fyn shouted as both boys fell to the ground.

Kellor rushed in and Annev pivoted, roundhouse kicking him in the face. The boy stumbled, blood gushing from his beak-like nose. He shook his head, trying to recover while Brinden regained his feet.

Annev sprinted toward the building in front of him, ran up the wall and backflipped over Brinden's charging form. As he arced down, he kicked the surprised avatar in the back of the head. Brinden stumbled, crashed headfirst into the stone wall, and dropped to the earth. Annev landed softly on his feet, knees bent and ready to strike.

A whirring sound drew his attention and he half-turned to see a spinning projectile flying toward his face. Annev ducked, raising one arm to protect his head, and the kali stick glanced off the crest of his forearm, skittering across the dusty road as the second stick whirred towards him. Annev threw himself onto his stomach, narrowly missing the spinning weapon, and realized too late it was a feint. Fyn pounced, a knee in Annev's back forcing the air from his lungs. He coughed, pinned and unable to breathe.

As Annev struggled, the rest of Fyn's gang gathered around, cheering as Fyn smashed Annev's face into the hard-packed dirt. Stunned, he tasted dust and blood. He tried to writhe free but was kicked into submission.

"Take his other glove!" Fyn bellowed.

Annev felt Myjun's phoenix glove slip from his arm then heard Kellor laugh as he tossed it to Fyn.

"Now you can touch dirt like the rest of us," Fyn jeered. They flipped him over and Fyn grabbed a handful of soil, jamming it into Annev's mouth, forcing it down his throat. Annev swallowed some and choked on more, Fyn's weight still pinning him down.

"You like that?" Fyn whispered, leaning close to Annev's ear. "Now you know what it's like. Unable to move. Unable to breathe." He moved his hand so that it covered Annev's mouth and nose, cutting off what little air the boy had. Annev's eyes went wild.

"Now you know how it feels," Fyn said, eyes gleaming. "You're not like the rest of us, Annev—you're *worse*. You're an *acolyte*. And tomorrow, when you and your friends fail the Test of Judgment, you'll be *stewards*. You're going to sleep in the Academy like everyone else, and instead of preaching every Seventhday, you'll carry our laundry and scrub the garderobe."

Annev choked, gagged, and bucked, desperate to breathe. His vision dimmed and his lungs burned from the lack of oxygen, but he couldn't free his limbs and Fyn's hand was like a vice on his mouth.

He's killing me, Annev thought, the world darkening. *I'm going to die here.*

"I could spare you the shame of becoming a steward," Fyn said, echoing Annev's thoughts. "I could end you, right now." He tightened his grip as Annev struggled, watching Annev's eyelids flutter closed. Then he leaned in close. "Or I could let you live. Then, when you become a steward and Myjun marries *me*, we can laugh about how special you thought you were."

Myjun.

Annev's blood surged at her name and the idea of her choosing Fyn, the eligible avatar, over Annev, a disgraced steward. His eyes bulged with a sudden fury, imagining that betrayal, and a tingling sensation ran up his left arm. He felt a distant part of his mind unlock.

With a tremendous burst of energy, Annev jerked his head from Fyn's grasp, smashed the crest of his forehead into Fyn's nose, and spat gritty mud into the avatar's face. Stars flooded his vision as he yanked his right arm free and punched Jasper in the face. He struggled to pull his other arm free, but Brinden held him tight.

With a roar, Fyn slammed his fist into Annev's cheekbone, splitting the skin and cracking his head back to the ground. Annev blinked, stunned, as Jasper pinned his left arm down once more. Fyn wrapped his meaty hands around Annev's neck and began to squeeze.

"I should kill you," the boy snarled, blood dribbling down his face, his chest heaving as he crushed Annev's windpipe, "but if I did, I wouldn't get to torture you. Every day. For the rest of your life." He let go and backhanded Annev across the face. Annev gasped, grateful for the blow, which granted him a breath of air.

Fyn snatched the fallen phoenix glove from the dirt. "I'm keeping this." He pressed his full weight against Annev's stomach and chest. "I doubt Myjun will mind. Anyone who's too weak to hold onto a gift like this doesn't deserve it. Besides, stewards wear tan. *Nothing* but tan." He bounced roughly on Annev's chest, making his ribs creak with pain, before standing.

Annev coughed and curled up, struggling to bring air back into his tortured lungs. He barely noticed as Fyn picked up his discarded kali sticks. The rest of the gang were jubilant, punching Fyn in the shoulder as they walked away.

"Happy Regaleus!" Jasper whooped.

Against his better judgment, against every instinct telling him to stay down, Annev slowly, stubbornly, got to his feet, watching Fyn walk away.

"It bothers you because it's true," he whispered.

The boys stopped, slowly turning in place. "What did you say?" Fyn asked, his voice cold.

"I'm better than you," Annev continued, barely raising his voice. "That's why you're so angry. I'm better than you." This time he raised his voice, shouting so that the whole village could hear. "I'm a better avatar, Fyn—and you *know* it! That's why Myjun likes me. That's why you can't beat me in a straight fight without help. You're afraid of me—and you *should* be!"

Jasper, Brinden, and Kellor stared at Annev, mouths open, then looked to their leader. Fyn glared, his fists shaking with ill-concealed rage.

Despite his pain, in spite of the insanity of what he had just done, Annev found himself grinning as Fyn's fury poured from him in a primal scream. The boy charged, kali sticks held high overhead.

Annev met the attack head-on, stepping under and between two wild swings before Fyn crashed into him. The kali sticks fell as the two students rolled to the ground, grappling each other.

Within seconds, the larger boy's strength won out and he pinned Annev. He slammed his fist into the side of Annev's head then reached to choke him, but Annev was quicker and blocked Fyn's attack with his right hand. The avatar latched onto Annev's wrist and twisted his hand backwards until it gave a sharp *crack* and Annev yelped in pain.

Fyn dropped Annev's wrist. "Sorry," he growled, without a trace of apology. "It was an *accident.*" He looked down at the bloody, muddy boy, snorted and stood up.

"You better get that looked at, Annev. It'd be a shame if it kept you from competing in tomorrow's test."

Fyn picked up his kali sticks then kicked Annev in the ribs as a final farewell. Annev coughed and curled back into a ball, blood dribbling from his lips, watching the gang leave through one half-open eye. Even when he was certain they were finally gone, he lay on the ground, unmoving. He focused on his breathing and cradled his injured hand to his chest until he could roll onto his side, sit up, and then stagger to his feet.

His body ached, his forehead throbbed with pain, and his cheek stung. His throat burned and his wrist was clearly broken. Even so, when Annev pulled his clenched left fist away from his sore stomach, he couldn't help but smile.

He was holding the crimson glove.

CHAPTER SIXTEEN

The chapel hall had changed very little over the years. The hard pine benches and cobblestone floors, worn smooth from patrons sitting and kneeling, were cleaned daily by either the old priest or his young deacon. Not a speck of dirt or mote of dust sullied the holy place.

Unlike the Academy's nave, no decorations or carvings covered these walls. Even the plain stone table—which was distinctly Darite in its engravings of the Staff of Odar, the arcane symbols of *quaire*, and the water trough surrounding its base—was decidedly humble compared to the Academy's altar. Even so, Annev had noted that the sparse engravings on the altar were all subtly aligned with Sodar's unique interpretation of Darite histories, doctrine, and worship.

It looked a simple place, exactly as Sodar intended.

When Annev stumbled into the kitchen with his broken wrist cradled to his chest, he expected to find the priest there or in his room, preparing for the Regaleus services. When Annev entered the priest's private chambers, though, he saw Sodar's bed was neatly made, his desk was clear, and his clothes chest locked, but the man himself wasn't there.

"Sodar?" Annev called. *Where is he?* He wondered, his sense of uneasiness growing along with his pain.

Annev knew Sodar could fix his wrist—the wizard-priest had healed greater injuries before. Otherwise, Annev might have stayed in the alley, bleeding, beaten, and with his future in tatters. As it was, he only had to contend with the physical pain of his injuries, which had subsided to a dull throb of torment as he'd dragged himself to the chapel. If he bent or bumped his arm, it was agony. Annev knew Sodar could help with that … but his mentor had disappeared.

He would have to tend to his injuries himself. Back in the kitchen he grabbed the ladle with his good hand, filled a bowl with water, and stoically began to clean his face and arms. He couldn't see the extent of his facial injuries, but he felt no loose teeth and he doubted the cuts would require stitching.

His wrist was another matter. The slightest bump caused waves of agony, and he forced himself to paw through his clothes chest until he found an old shirt he could fashion into a sling. It took a while to tie the knots with one hand and his teeth, and wishful thinking kept him glancing at the door for Sodar's return. When the priest still did not appear, Annev rummaged up something to eat, chewing on a piece of salted meat and a heel of bread. With his belly full and his wrist swelling, Annev began to search for the old man in earnest. He passed through the woodshed on his way outside and saw the lumber ax was missing.

He's not chopping firewood, Annev thought. *I'd be able to hear him … but why else would he take the ax?* It didn't make sense, and it made Annev feel uneasy. He was exhausted, beaten and in pain, drained from a long day. He wanted his mentor to heal him or, failing that, to lie down and cry himself to sleep.

But he could only be healed if he found Sodar.

Annev grit his teeth, took his hunting knife down from its peg, and left the shed. He let the door bang shut behind him and trudged to the nearest edge of the Brake. When he reached the trees, he stopped to listen but didn't hear anything out of place, so he crept into the forest gloom, remaining alert for signs of his mentor. He was a short distance into the woods itself when he spied Sodar's ax leaning against a tree trunk.

He was here, Annev thought, *but where did he go? And why did he leave the ax?* Annev puzzled at it. If there was trouble, the priest would have taken a better weapon. If they needed wood, he would be chopping it. Instead, the way the ax leaned against the tree looked as if it had been deliberately placed there, ready to be reclaimed when Sodar returned from whatever arcane errand had taken him into the Brake.

He took the ax so he could claim he was chopping wood, Annev realized. *But who is Sodar trying to deceive?*

Using every ounce of caution and skill he could muster, Annev pushed his pain aside and crept deeper into the Brakewood, his senses alert for any sign of struggle or evidence of Sodar's passing. He kept his arm close to his body to prevent it from being bumped or jostled and tried to conceal his own passing, making a reasonable effort to avoid dry leaves and mud and instead creeping over rocks, moss, and any hard-packed open terrain. He felt foolish doing so—particularly if Sodar was fine—but he was worried. As Annev moved through the wood, he could hear Sodar's oft-repeated words in his mind: "Always be cautious, especially in the Brakewood. It is a wild place which looks tame. So is the Academy, with eyes and ears always watching, listening. Stay alert. Danger won't give you warning."

Sodar had always been vague about what those dangers might be, though Annev had assumed the priest meant there would be trouble if the ancients learned about his arm. When he spoke of the dangers of the Brake, Annev guessed Sodar had meant bears and boars. As Annev swept the woods in search of his mentor, though, he began to wonder if the old man had been thinking of something else. Sodar had been so adamant about Annev staying away from the shadepools, and Annev had felt a chill in the unnatural darkness. Could Sodar have wandered into one? He glanced about sharply, studying the natural shadows cast by trees and brush, then he shivered and kept walking.

As he crested a boulder-strewn hill he heard a shout that sounded like Sodar's and immediately changed course, angling towards it, but he heard nothing more. He slowed, ears keen for any sound.

"*Fifty* artisans?"

Annev frowned. It was Sodar's voice, but his tone was so sorrowful …

"It can't be," Sodar continued. "That's … impossible."

"I assure you, it's true."

Annev edged closer to the voices, careful not to alert either to his presence. He felt ashamed for not immediately running to seek aid from the priest, but he burned with curiosity to know the cause of Sodar's strange disappearance and the reason for any possible dissembling. When he was close enough to hear the priest's conversation, he stopped and looked for a stout tree. He wasn't sure he could climb, but he had often trained to do difficult activities with one hand—though, admittedly, usually with his right hand rather than his left.

Annev stepped up to a copse of silver maple trees and picked the one that looked easiest to climb. He cautiously pulled himself onto the lowest branch then half-walked, half-climbed up the crooked limbs till he found a good vantage point to watch Sodar and his companion. He eased himself into the wide crook of a knotted branch and listened carefully to the men below.

A man in a thick, brown cloak sat by a small campfire. Sodar's old tea kettle sat among the coals, its left side dented where Annev had once dropped it. The man's damp boots were drying on a flat rock by the fire, a hint of steam rising from them. The stranger sipped from a cup held in both hands, and Annev noticed a pile of discarded arrows on the ground nearby.

Sodar was pacing in front of the fire, muttering under his breath.

"We've been hemorrhaging members for the last two millennia," the stranger said, setting down his cup. He picked up one of his boots and stuck a hand inside then grimaced and pushed both boots closer to the fire. "But this sudden drop is too fast. It's unnatural."

Sodar paced faster. "Just fifty artisans," he breathed. "But there were almost a thousand—and eighty of those were ageless. Our numbers had been growing. Now you're saying there are less than fifty artisans in *total*?" Sodar stopped pacing and looked at the stranger. "How many ageless ones *are* left?"

The man sighed. "Counting us …?" He ticked people off on his fingers. "Seven."

"Seven?"

Annev strained to hear Sodar's voice, which was barely a whisper. The priest slunk down onto a large rock by the fire, staring into space.

What are they talking about? Annev wondered. *What's an artisan—or an ageless one?*

"Seven," the man repeated, "plus the forty or so who will never get to make the ageless covenant—but many of the brethren have gone into hiding, so numbers aren't exact. Could be less or more." The man rubbed his hands together.

Sodar shook his head. "Seven," he repeated in hushed tones. He looked up. "Morgenstone?"

"Gone."

"Balhamel?"

The stranger shook his head and Sodar slumped a little. After a moment, he lifted his head again, suddenly earnest. "You said seven ageless ones. What about the wanderer?"

Arnor seemed to think about this. "Eight if you count him, but I try not to. For all I know, he died decades ago."

Sodar nodded. "What *happened*, Arnor? Did the brethren go to war? I thought Reeve—"

"No, no war. Not the kind we know anyway." Arnor scratched his stubbly cheeks. "The guilds had become too divisive—you know how it's been the last two decades?" Sodar nodded. "Well, it got worse. A *lot* worse. About three years ago they began threatening each other—the usual paranoia targeted at the Mindwalkers and Stormcallers, plus some dissent among the others—but a few months after that whole enclaves started to disappear. We didn't realize at first, and by the time we thought to investigate, all of the Dionachs Tobar south of the Kalej Mountains were gone. Dead or vanished."

"But the High Council must have noticed? Arch-Dionach Kadmon and Arch-Dionach Levi are both from Tir Reota."

"They were among the first to disappear. No one realized—not even Reeve—until the council meeting. The messengers we sent to investigate never returned."

"Unbelievable," Sodar breathed, shaking his head. "To think it could happen so fast …"

"Exactly. We suspected an external threat. Perhaps some Inquisitors or some other Terran artisans who had made their way south. But the patrol we sent to the highways found nothing, while the messengers we sent to the enclaves never came back." Arnor stood then used the hem of his cloak to grab the handle of the simmering kettle and pour himself more tea.

"We only realized the problem was *within* the Brotherhood a year ago," Arnor continued, blowing on his cup. "That's when the Faction War began. It was mostly politicking at first, with the guilds vying for what little control remained. That changed when some radicals calling themselves the Vanguards of Truth tried to seize power. They eliminated most of the High Council before the rest coordinated enough to stop them, but almost everyone involved was killed, and recruiting for the Brotherhood has completely stopped since. The four guilds are now too afraid to work together, and many brethren have gone into hiding. Reeve has tried to coax them out so we can rebuild, but only the Shield-bearers are receiving him."

"What of our own guild? Surely the Breathbreakers will listen to you."

Arnor shook his head. "Ours has been a policy of isolation, and that works against us here. The ones I've found prefer to be left alone, and with nothing to hold magisterial power over, the High Council is defunct."

"Fifty," Sodar repeated again, seeming not to hear Arnor. He shook his head. "Out of hundreds of thousands. The true religion of Odar nearly wiped out." He stared at the low-burning flames of the campfire for a long moment then sniffed. "We've done to ourselves what Keos and his Bloodlords could never manage."

Arnor put his empty cup down and pulled his damp boots back on.

"I'm sorry to be the bearer of bad news, Sodar. But we need you. Reeve sent me to ask you to come back north. There are many who still remember you. You could be a rallying point—someone who's kept clear of all the politics and bloodshed."

"No. My mission here is vital. Not just for the Brotherhood." Sodar's eyes locked on the fire. "What I do is for the whole world."

Arnor stared at Sodar's face, slowly nodding, though it was clear he didn't agree.

"I see," he said. "Well, a lot has happened and Reeve wanted to be sure you understood our situation. He also asked after the boy. Wanted to know if his magic had matured. If you brought him back to Quiri he could begin training with the Order." Sodar was already shaking his head but Arnor continued. "Whatever advantages you're finding here, I'm sure we can match them there."

"Not safety."

Arnor huffed, undeterred. "We need you, Sodar. Frankly, with so few ageless ones left, I'm surprised Reeve hasn't forced you to come up and join the High Council."

"I'm *on* the council," Sodar said, eyes distant. "But my mission occupies too much time and attention. It doesn't permit me to participate."

"Doesn't 'permit'?" Arnor scoffed. "Surely with the Order decimated—"

"No," Sodar said, focusing on Arnor. "Unless Reeve himself comes to call me back—unless he *forces* me to—I will stay here and fulfill my task. As I have done for these many years."

Arnor's fists clenched and unclenched. At length, though, he grit his teeth and nodded. "Odar knows we need you—I'm sure you could convince some of the others to come back, probably even double our number—but if you must stay here …" He shrugged. "I don't hold with the notion that one boy is more important than a whole religion—but nor will I argue with an Arch-Dionach."

Sodar gazed at the man opposite him, his eyes sad. "Don't burden me with that title, Arnor. Here, I am Brother Sodar and nothing more."

Arnor huffed. "You giving me license to argue then?"

"No."

Arnor nodded then tilted his head sideways. "Fine. Before I go, you should be aware: I was followed out of Quiri. All the way down to the Vosgar."

Sodar half-rose from his seat and his eyes snapped to attention. "What? You should have *led* with that. How?"

"It was an eidolon, and I killed it."

"You mean *shadow* spawn? You're certain?"

The other man gave Sodar a flat stare.

"Of course, you're certain." Sodar tugged at his tangled beard. "And you killed it? Good, good." He scratched at his chin, thinking. "Any connection between it and the artisans disappearing?"

"I wondered that," Arnor said. "But I can't think of a single brother who can summon an eidolon. I've been followed before too—usually by brothers belonging to factions in the other guilds—but this was the first time I've been stalked by shadow spawn. I just don't see the connection."

Sodar grunted. "So we can assume it was sent by a priest of the

Shadow God, or by someone who can command void magic. Why was it following you?"

"Perhaps someone guessed I'm visiting brothers in hiding? Can't say for certain, but I think it a strange coincidence that I was also coming to see you."

"Agreed," Sodar said, fretting.

Arnor patted him on the shoulder. "Maybe it really is just a coincidence, though. The other brethren think you're dead. *I* didn't know you were still alive until Reeve gave me orders to find you—and it was difficult even with his instructions."

"Yes," Sodar said, "the ward of protection keeps strangers and visitors away. Unless your eyes have been anointed with *aqlumera*, you can't see the village—and that means the village can't see you."

"*Aqlumera?*" Arnor repeated, eyes widening. "Well, that's a secret worth protecting."

"Yes. See that you do." He paused. "The arrows were a clever way to get my attention. How did you know where to shoot them?"

"I didn't." Arnor laughed, scooping up the missiles. "But Reeve was very specific. Even gave me an old map you'd once drawn for him—though I can't say it helped at all since I was firing blind into the forest. I'm not likely to recover all my arrows." He lifted a backpack from behind the log he'd been sitting on. "Anyhow, I mentioned the shadow spawn because I knew you would want to know, but I think you're safe as houses. I doubt anyone is looking for you specifically, nor will they stumble onto you." Arnor pulled his unstrung bow from behind the same log, dropped the arrows into his pack, shouldered the bag, and hefted the bow like a walking stick.

Sodar stroked his beard, thinking. "Where did you lay the eidolon to rest?"

"In the Vosgar. I guessed I was being followed not long after I left Quiri, but I didn't know who or what it was till I was just outside the Brakewood. I circled farther south, hoping to lose it, and finally had to kill the thing."

"I'm glad you did." Sodar took a deep breath and slowly let it out. "Sounds like plenty of danger remains out there, but Chaenbalu remains a sanctuary.

"I'll tell Reeve," Arnor said. They shook hands and Arnor held Sodar's grasp just a moment longer. "You sure you can't come back to Quiri with me? Gods, we need you, and it would be good to have another of the ageless around."

Sodar smiled but shook his head. "Maybe when Annev is older. For now, so long as his arm and his magic remain secret, this is the safest place I know. My time with him is a burden worth bearing."

Burden? Annev's hand clamped around the branch beneath him, steadying himself. *Am I really a burden?* He had often felt he was, but it hurt to know for sure that the priest viewed him as a task that had to be tended.

He still sees me as a child, Annev realized. *Not as a man. If he trusted me, he would not sneak off to the woods and pretend to chop firewood to protect his secrets. This stranger … Arnor … he knows more about Sodar than I do.* The truth of that made Annev feel sick, dizzy even, and only his grip on the branch stopped him toppling to the ground.

Who in all of Chaenbalu—in all the world—knew Annev better than Sodar? No one. Yet here was a stranger who knew all Sodar's secrets, all his past lives. Meanwhile, Annev had been fed lies his whole life—about Sodar's past, about the nature of their friendship, about the priest's motives for raising Annev—and he'd been naïve enough to believe them.

No more.

Arnor nodded. "Very well. Good luck, Sodar. I don't envy you."

"Nor I you," Sodar said. "I wish I could risk leaving Chaenbalu." Arnor clapped the priest on the back, and Sodar hugged him tightly. "Be well, my friend. Give my best to Reeve, and see that he gets my copy of the Speur Dún translation."

"I will. Be well, Brother Sodar."

They separated, and Arnor hoisted his pack and strode purposefully from the clearing. Sodar slowly exhaled then began cleaning up the campfire, tea kettle, and cups.

Annev cradled his broken wrist to his chest and watched, heart aching, then stiffly climbed down from the tree. He crept away from the clearing and walked back to the chapel in silence, his physical pains an echo of the sorrow he felt.

Annev had gone to the chapel seeking solace but had instead found a mystery. He had then left the chapel in search of his mentor and friend, but instead he had found two strangers: one he had never met, and one he thought he had known.

He had never felt so alone.

CHAPTER SEVENTEEN

Annev paced the chapel in a daze, the pain in his wrist competing with the ache in his heart.

How much more has he kept from me? How much of what he told me is just lies?

Annev knew Sodar was secretive—the man *had* to be to survive with magic under the noses of the masters and ancients—but until today, he thought he had known the important parts of Sodar's past.

During his seventeen years with the priest, Annev had pieced together a rough biographical sketch of the man. He knew Sodar had discovered his magic as a young boy in Odarnea, in a time and place where people were slightly more forgiving of the cursed. He'd been shunned, but not executed or exiled, and a traveling merchant had taken pity on Sodar by allowing him to join his caravan. Sodar had accepted, and through the merchant he had found mentors in both religion and magic. When he was fourteen he entered the priesthood. At twenty-one a local war hero asked him to leave his monastic home to serve as his spiritual adviser. Sodar consented, and in time he came to use his magic to protect those who rode under his lord's banner. He even fought in some of the battles—a detail that led to Sodar showing Annev his notched heater shield.

What was its name? Headsplitter? Toothbreaker …? Annev could never remember; he'd been too excited to see the weapon, too keen to wield it or train with it.

But Sodar wouldn't allow it; he wanted the past to remain in the past and claimed he had left that life behind when he rejoined the monastery at

Banok, though not before learning a considerable amount about warfare and the wider world. From there he was eventually recruited by the ancients of Chaenbalu to replace their former priest. That had been decades ago—a lifetime by most people's reckoning—so it was understandable when he forgot details or didn't care to elaborate.

Now, though, Annev saw the lies for what they were and he wanted to know how deep they went. Questions he had long since set aside were joined by a series of new ones. What was this secret brotherhood? Who were Arnor and Reeve? What was an Arch-Dionach? An artisan? An ageless one? And what did it have to do with him?

He had just gone to lie down when he heard Sodar return. He'd speculated whether the priest would actually return with firewood, and the clatter and thump of logs dropping onto the drying rack gave him his answer.

Annev wasn't ready to confront the man, but he needed to heal his wrist; the pain and the swelling were steadily rising, and if it wasn't treated soon he wouldn't be able to compete tomorrow. He stood, passed through the kitchen, and opened the back door.

The priest had returned the ax to its place and was stacking logs.

"We didn't need any more firewood."

The words came out before he could measure his tone, and Sodar cocked his head, squinting at the shadowed entry where Annev stood. "Are you alright, Annev?"

Annev swallowed, unable to respond without letting his emotions bleed through. Instead of speaking, he stepped into the shafts of light filtering down through gaps in the shed's roof and raised his injured arm: the swollen wrist was bent at an awkward angle and the skin had shifted to a mottled purple.

"Gods!" Sodar exclaimed, coming forward to examine the injury. "What happened? Who did this? What are these bruises on your neck?"

Annev winced as the priest probed his broken wrist and bruised skin. He wasn't sure how to answer, but it turned out he didn't need to say anything.

"It was that Fyn boy, wasn't it? Him and his friends."

Annev blinked. "Yeah."

Sodar ushered Annev into the house. "I knew it. I've seen how they pick on you during exercises. It's despicable."

"What?" Annev asked, genuinely surprised. "When?"

The priest seated him at the table. "A month ago. When the ice had broken enough that they had you swimming laps around the mill pond. They kept pulling you underwater when the masters weren't looking. But I saw." Sodar tisked at the injury then went into his bedroom. He came back with a clay cup and a stick of charcoal, dipped the former into the jug of water near the hearth, and brought both items over to the table.

"Such violence," he said, dipping the charcoal into the water then drawing a glyph on Annev's forearm. "You would think they'd be more careful, with the test tomorrow." When Annev only grunted, Sodar stopped and looked him in the eye. "Only this didn't happen in class, did it?"

Annev couldn't lie, and when he didn't immediately respond, Sodar had his answer. He opened his mouth to ask something else but stopped when he heard a knock at the front door of the chapel.

"Who could that be?" Sodar wondered aloud. "It's too early for congregants to arrive." He set down the water and charcoal then propped open the rectory door. "Forgive me, Annev. I'll be but a moment."

Annev forced himself to nod then watched Sodar enter the worship hall. He tried to stoke his anger at the priest as Sodar marched down the center aisle, opened the front door, and spoke to someone on the opposite side. Yet when Sodar returned with a sack under one arm, Annev was betrayed to discover the rawness of his emotions had been dulled by his curiosity.

"Who was it?" he asked.

"Yohan, the chandler." Sodar set the sack on the table. "He brought us some scented candles for tonight's Regaleus sermon."

"That was … nice of him."

"Indeed," Sodar said, reaching into the sack. "He's usually a prick."

Annev laughed despite his pain, then stopped when Sodar cried out, dropping the sack of candles.

"What is it? What happened?"

"That damn chandler," Sodar said, carefully picking up the fallen bag. "He's left something sharp in there." He reached inside, more careful this time, and withdrew a slender shard of glass that had fallen in amidst the candle sticks. He set it on the table, tisking. "It's as they say. 'Mischief comes from giving gifts.'"

Annev shifted in his seat, remembering that his fight with Fyn had come after accepting Myjun's Regaleus gift.

"Do you really believe that?"

Sodar shrugged, sucking the blood off his thumb. "You tell me. When Yohan gave me the candles, he also delivered a message from Master Edra." Annev tried not to seem uneasy as Sodar took the damp charcoal stick and painted a second glyph in the palm of his injured hand. "Edra wanted to be sure you did some sparring practice with me this afternoon, which suggests he doesn't know about your injury." The priest raised a single bushy eyebrow in inquiry. "Mind explaining what that's about?"

Annev groaned, having forgotten his promise to Edra. "I missed half of weapons training."

"But not because of this," Sodar said, nodding at Annev's broken wrist.

"No. I was ... helping Master Duvarek. That's all."

Sodar grunted. "We can spar when your wrist is healed." He dipped the charcoal again and drew a third glyph in the center of Annev's wrist. Annev winced at the pressure, but Sodar's touch was light and precise.

"I'll heal it completely, since your test is tomorrow. Can't have you failing because of those bullies." Annev nodded, grateful. "I'm leaving the bruises on your face, though," Sodar continued. "It'd look suspicious otherwise." Sodar examined his work then looked up. "Do you recognize these glyphs?"

"The one on my wrist is the symbol for healing. The other two are ..." He hesitated.

"Symbols for joining," Sodar said. He pointed to the runes on Annev's palm and forearm. "They are two halves of the same glyph. Drawn separately, they can bind two things together—for a time, anyway. This should help the bones knit more quickly, especially in conjunction with the ward of healing."

Annev nodded his understanding. The priest set the charcoal down, placed both hands on Annev's injured limb and closed his eyes.

"You speak the words of healing first," Sodar instructed, eyes still closed. "The joining comes second." He took a deep breath then exhaled. As he spoke, his thumbs softly probed Annev's broken wrist. "*Slànaich is cuplaich. Cuplaich le slànachadh.*"

Annev watched in fascination as the water-smeared lines of charcoal glowed and his wrist subtly realigned. The moisture quickly evaporated, leaving only a dry, black powder to mark Annev's skin. Sodar blew on the ash and it floated away, leaving the skin unmarred save for Sodar's bloody thumbprint. Annev rubbed this away and was pleased to see even the purple bruise had faded, leaving the limb pink and clean. He tested his wrist, carefully moving his right arm. When he felt no pain, he shook the limb, made a fist, and pounded it on the table.

Sodar nodded. "Good as new."

Annev grunted, marveling. "That didn't hurt. Normally it stings during and aches after." He shook his hand again. "I didn't feel a thing. Is that how a full healing normally works?"

Sodar hummed to himself. "No. If anything, the pain should have been more intense because your body healed at an accelerated pace." He tapped his chin. "It's not unheard of, though. The efficacy of a spell depends on several factors, and a few could affect residual pain."

"Like?"

"Well," Sodar said, thinking, "Darite magic tends to work better with experience and an understanding of the words of power, the glyphs, and their meaning. A powerful and experienced wizard-healer can perform miracles where another man using the same spell might only cure a stubbed toe."

"But you healed my cracked ribs two days ago," Annev objected. "Mending them felt like you were breaking them all over again. Has your understanding of magic grown since then?"

"I doubt it."

"So what changed?" Annev iterated.

"I'm not sure. The emotional state of the caster or recipient can sometimes enhance or hinder a spell, but that's more typical of spell-singing than glyph-speaking."

"Spell-singing?"

Sodar nodded. "Ilumite magic. I'm sure I've mentioned it before.

They use music and emotion to invoke their spells. For Terrans it's called dwimmer-crafting."

"I remember all that. But you didn't sing, and neither of us are Ilumite."

Sodar hesitated for a fraction of a second then nodded. "Right. Quite right."

There, Annev thought. *He's hiding something. But what is he not saying?*

"So," the priest said, shifting topics, "you're mended. Have you eaten?"

"A bit."

"Good. Sparring lesson then. We'll eat properly afterwards."

Annev groaned, unable to conceal his frustration at the thought of another fight; he had fought in Edra's class, and in Duvarek's class, and then again with Fyn in the street. He had no desire to spar with Sodar, particularly when he just wanted to interrogate the man.

"Can't we just skip it? I didn't miss much of Edra's class—and I've more than made up for the missed combat training outside of class." He gestured at the lumps, cuts, and bruises that still covered his face, neck, and arms.

"Once could argue those bruises prove you need *more* practice."

Annev's temper flared, indignant. "That's unfair. Fyn was armed and attacked me with his friends. I could beat him if we were alone."

Not every time, Annev silently admitted, *but probably half the time. Maybe.*

Sodar shrugged, indifferent. "When danger comes, it usually comes prepared. You don't get to find your friends and pick your weapons. You have to plan for that—expect it—and don't make excuses when you fail."

"That's so ... sympathetic of you."

The priest raised an eyebrow. "Don't be churlish. If I let you rest when you're beaten and worn, I'm not helping you. And if I give you reprieve when no one else does, what am I teaching you?"

Annev sighed. "So we're sparring?"

Sodar shrugged. "You can rest if you want ..." Annev rose from the table. "... but if you do, I can't give you your present."

Annev rocked back on his heels. "What present?"

"The one I was going to give you for Regaleus."

Annev's hand slipped into his pocket, touching the red glove. "Oh.

I just thought … you always say Regaleus is a cursed holiday. We never exchange gifts."

"Well, you've endured enough holidays without a present that I felt you deserved one today." Sodar smiled, a touch of sadness gracing his eyes. "If you like, you can call it a … birthday present."

"Why?" Annev asked. "Is it my birthday?"

Sodar sputtered. "I didn't … Look, call it whatever you want. My point is you won't get it unless we go a few rounds this afternoon."

Annev considered it then nodded. "Alright, old man. If you're that eager for a beating, let's fight."

CHAPTER EIGHTEEN

Annev flung the woodshed door open and hopped down its three short steps. When he reached the weapons rack at the back of the room, he snatched a wooden ax and battered short sword off the wall. Sodar groaned.

"Not those again. You've chosen that combination every time for three months."

Annev shrugged. "I like them."

"You like two-handed fighting," Sodar amended.

"No," Annev corrected. "I like being able to hook, slash, and disarm with my ax—and I like the length of the short sword. I can slip in close but still have some reach."

Sodar pulled a long sword from the weapons rack.

"Prove it."

Before Annev could respond, the priest leaped to attack, stabbing outward. Annev dodged, left foot moving back, his ax hooking the sword's blade and pulling it aside. Then he bounced forward, stabbing for Sodar's ribs.

But Sodar wasn't there. Instead, he had gone with Annev's pull, rolling under his own sword and taking a knee behind Annev.

He's so fast. How can an old man be that fast? The thought brought back all of Annev's questions, his sense of betrayal. *I need him to admit he's been lying—and to tell me what he's been hiding.*

He spun left, dancing backwards so that he was facing Sodar again. He swung his ax down, thinking to intercept Sodar's counterattack, but

the priest surprised him by stepping into his falling arm; he grabbed Annev's elbow, pulled it down across his body, and rose to his feet. Annev was
lifted from the ground, his chest rolling over Sodar's shoulders as his body
followed the momentum of the ax. He crashed onto his back, dropping
his ax, and felt the wind rush out of him.

Sodar's longsword tapped him on the chest.

"The advantage of fighting cat's-paw," Sodar said, looking down at
Annev, "is that you can block your opponent's attacks at the same time
you make your own. To do that, both hands need to be dominant. They
need to work at the same time—independently or together." He lowered his sword and extended a hand to Annev. "It's a hard skill to master.
That's why I always preferred a staff—or a paired sword and shield."

Annev reluctantly took the priest's hand and rose to his feet. "But you
can only defend with a shield. With an ax in my off-hand, I can block and
attack at the same time."

Sodar smiled. "I'm not certain your left hand *is* your off-hand."

Annev frowned. "It can't be my dominant hand—I train more with
my right.

Sodar shrugged. "You're competent with both hands—ambidextrous
even—but I think you naturally favor your left hand." He walked back to the
weapons rack, replaced the longsword, and took up a short spear.

"Now, a shield *can* be used to attack—and much more reliably than
an ax can defend. In fact, it was once my preferred weapon—long ago, in
another time and place."

There's my chance, Annev thought, scooping up his ax. *I just need to ask
the right question. Something innocuous ...*

"Your shield. Is that the one I saw you polishing last winter?"

"The same."

"What was its name?"

Sodar smiled. "Toothbreaker."

There, Annev thought. *Now keep him talking.*

"It's just a notched heater shield, though. You can't hurt someone with
that—not like you can with an ax."

"It's more like a modified vambrace, and technically you can." The priest rubbed his forearm in memory. "When my quarterstaff was broken or my short sword lost, I waded through many battles with just Tooth-breaker to keep me alive."

"How? And why did you name it Toothbreaker?"

Sodar thrust his spear into the dirt and leaned on its haft. "You remember how the shield looked?" Annev nodded. "The notches cut into the front of the shield—to either side of the wrist, adjacent to the spikes—could catch a falling sword. If I twisted my forearm just right, it could disarm whoever I was fighting. A few times, I even snapped their sword in two."

"So … Toothbreaker," Annev said.

Sodar nodded. "The spikes on the front were offensive as well as defensive. Catch a blade or punch a man in the gut. The spikes at the bottom were ideal for elbowing soldiers who tried to attack from behind. It was still more effective with a short sword, though, since I carried Tooth-breaker in my off-hand."

"When did you get it—and who taught you to fight with it?"

"It was given to me a long, long time ago." Sodar pulled the spear from the ground, took a step backwards, and spun the weapon in his hands. "And I've learned from many—soldiers, men-at-arms, priests." He swung at Annev, spearhead leading.

Annev jumped back, easily dodging the attack. "What about the merchant who took you from your village?"

"I don't recall his name," Sodar said, taking another swing with the butt-end of his spear. "People called him something different in every town. I doubt I ever knew his real identity."

I know the feeling, Annev thought, dodging another attack and countering with one of his own.

"You learned to fight on the road, though?"

Sodar shrugged. "I learned on the streets." He tapped his spear against the flat side of Annev's short sword, searching for an opening. "I learned more from the men guarding the merchant's caravan—sword patterns, footwork. Shoddy stuff really, but it gave me a foundation." He lunged. Annev parried, having anticipated the attack, then followed up with his own strike, nearly scoring a hit on the priest's knee.

"Close."

Annev nodded, weapons still extended. "So who taught you the spear?"

Sodar shrugged and began to circle. "I trained with the staff when I joined the priesthood. They're closely related."

Annev grit his teeth, unsurprised by the answer—all Darite priests were supposed to train with the staff, but Annev had hoped for something more.

"Who was your favorite teacher? Who mentored you?"

Instead of answering, the priest whirled the spear around his body, dropped into a squat and kicked at Annev's legs. Annev jumped, crossed his weapons in front of him, and landed lightly on his feet.

As Sodar rose up to meet him, Annev slashed down and across with both weapons. The priest countered by rattling his spear between the ax and short sword, preventing Annev from engaging. He parried the ax blow and crashed the butt of his spear into Annev's sternum. The boy reeled back, gasping for breath, and cast his weapons to the ground.

"How do you *do* that?"

"Do what?" Sodar stood straight.

"How do you move so *fast*?" He paused, frowning. "Do you use magic when we fight?"

Sodar huffed. "Of course not. That would be cheating."

Annev raised an eyebrow, unconvinced the priest was being honest. Instead of expressing his doubts, though, he snatched Sodar's spear and tossed it against the wall.

"You're going to fight me with a weapon you haven't mastered."

Sodar laughed. "Who's training whom?"

"Will you do it?"

The priest shrugged. "Pick your poison. I know every weapon in this woodshed."

"Great," Annev said. "Go grab the wallowpike."

"The *wallow*pike?" Sodar snorted. "I made that for demonstrations, not sparring."

"Go and get it," Annev said, unflinching.

Sodar bristled. "It's a weapon for heavy cavalry. The pole alone weighs as much as you."

"So you won't spar against me unless you've mastered the weapon first? That doesn't seem fair."

Sodar rolled his eyes, muttered something about birthday presents, then marched to the end of the shed where the pikes and polearms were stored. He pulled out an eight-foot pole with a heavy wooden wedge at one end—the longest and heaviest in the stack.

"You know," Sodar said, hefting the weapon in both hands, "when footmen had to use this against rows of heavy cavalry, *two* men carried it."

"I know," Annev said. "You also said it was awkward to wield and almost impossible to use more than once. That's why it was replaced with the wallowsling."

"And that's why you picked it."

"And that's why I picked it."

Sodar nodded, firming his grip on the pike as he found its center of balance. "Alright. You have a good memory. Now let's see if you have good reflexes too."

The priest advanced before Annev could collect his weapons and swung the unwieldy polearm at his student's head. Annev jumped forward, diving beneath the heavy wedge as it smashed into the ground. With a roll and a twist, he snatched up the ax and short sword as he came to his feet.

"Not fast enough, old man!"

With a roar, Sodar braced the butt of the pole arm against his foot and lifted its heavy wedge off the ground. Poised between the priest and the acolyte, the faux ax-head kept Annev at bay before swinging back toward him, this time aimed at his left hip. Annev threw his weight against the eight-foot wallowpike and rolled over it.

Anticipating the move, Sodar was already swinging the polearm in an upward arc, circling back toward Annev just as the boy rose to his feet.

Instead of dodging again, Annev leaped forward. Ax and short sword held high, he slid the haft and blade of his weapons along the wallowpike's shaft then pulled with both weapons, creating a new fulcrum for the heavy pole arm and dragging its wedge in a wide arc. With Sodar's momentum redirected, Annev closed the distance between them, leaving the priest no room to regain his advantage.

But Sodar was quick to adapt. Rather than fighting Annev, he used his strength to swing the weapon harder and lifted the head of the pole arm up over his shoulder. As the pole rotated in his hands, Sodar snapped the butt-end between Annev's advancing legs.

Once again, Annev rolled with the pike. He fell back this time, taking a painful slap across his inner thigh, and hit the ground. In a blink, he flipped himself back onto his feet, weapons poised for another attack.

But Sodar was too quick for him.

In the half-second it took Annev to rise, Sodar had swung the weapon full-circle, around the fulcrum of his hands and shoulder, then brought the wedge back up and into Annev.

Annev came forward, arms out, anticipating a blow from above, and was surprised when the wooden wedge raced upward instead. The blunted wedge smashed into Annev's leading left arm, flinging both the boy and his ax across the room.

Sodar dropped his weapon, puffing with exertion. "Are you alright, boy?"

Annev groaned, dropped his sword, and cradled his injured arm to his chest. When he looked down and saw an enormous purple bruise forming beneath the skin, he swore. Then he saw half of the injury was streaked with threads of silver, and a metallic sheen was spreading across the skin. Shocked, he clutched his arm and burst into tears.

"Annev?" Sodar laid a hand on his shoulder.

Annev stared at the bruise, watching as more of the skin assumed its natural silvery color. Sodar gingerly lifted the injured arm and surveyed the damage.

"Oh. That's unfortunate."

"Unfortunate? You *broke* my arm, Sodar! The masters and ancients will see it—they'll *know*. I can't take the Test of Judgment now. I can't even risk entering the Academy!"

Annev watched as his left forearm down to his fingertips transitioned from fleshy pink to a bright metallic silver. He flexed his fingers, stretching his bruised forearm, and watched as blood from the reddening bruise swirled into the magic prosthetic he wore on his left arm. Copper veins drank in the dark blood, pulsing and spreading beneath a thin sheath of silver-scaled skin.

All thoughts of Sodar's dishonesty flew from Annev's mind. Instead, he sat transfixed by the singular, undeniable truth before him.

The magic of the artificial limb, which he had hidden and which had kept him safe for years, had finally failed.

CHAPTER NINETEEN

Annev clenched his metallic fist, unable to look away from the reality of his now-revealed magic arm.

Sodar frowned at the silver appendage, the coloring of his cheeks betraying the anxiety he clearly felt. "Try taking it off before you despair, Annev." His tone remained hopeful, though Annev sensed an edge of panic to it. "Take it off and see how bad it is."

Annev roughly wiped his tears away and looked up at his mentor. *Just take it off. Could it be that easy?* He felt a glimmer of hope as he touched the artificial limb with his right hand. The silver scales felt warm and glossy beneath his fingertips—not the soft texture of skin, but of something more alien. Annev ignored that thought and grasped the base of the prosthetic.

He rarely removed the artificial limb—being caught without it would be fatal—but he had done so on three or four occasions in the past. Even so, it had been several years since he had last removed the limb, and Annev felt a thrill of panic that the magic might not work this time. He pushed the fears down. He'd been using it for years; it wasn't like a magic wand or a bottomless sack.

He simply needed to let go.

As if sensing his need, the prosthetic emitted a near inaudible *thhhh*. A heartbeat later, the limb fell to the ground.

Sodar squeezed his shoulder, nodding. "I should have foreseen this. I'm sorry. The artifact is old and much of its magic has faded. You've been using it since you were a baby."

Annev picked up the limb, examining it for any rents or cracks, but only saw the purple-and-copper bruise at the base of the prosthetic. As he held it, though, the magic arm began to heal itself: threads of copper absorbed the purple bruise, causing it to fade, and then the copper spun itself into strands of silver and gold. The sheath of silver encasing the limb's internal workings turned opaque, and the arm appeared whole again.

"I thought only spells lost their magic. Artifacts are supposed to last forever."

Sodar shrugged. "Some do. Most don't. Only the best can retain their powers despite the ravages of time and wear," he reached out and touched the prosthetic, concentrating for a moment, "but I sense there is still a great deal of magic left in that arm. Perhaps it couldn't mask its true nature and heal itself at the same time. Now that it has recovered it should be able to camouflage itself again." He looked more closely at Annev's hand. "Speaking of camouflage … where is your Glove of Illusion?"

"Fyn and his friends destroyed it," Annev said, ashamed. "I kept the pieces but …" He reached into his pocket and pulled out the tattered, filthy remains of his former garment. Sodar took them.

"I see."

The priest had stolen the Cloth of Illusion from the Academy's Vault almost two decades ago—a fruitful trip that had also yielded Annev's magic prosthetic and the bottomless bag Sodar was so fond of—but that supply had come to an end. The only cloth that remained were the tattered gloves Annev had worn as a child and the scraps Sodar had saved after stitching those gloves.

Annev could see similar thoughts on the old man's face as he pocketed the remains of the shredded glove, but Sodar said nothing else about the incident, choosing to let the silence speak for him. He combed at the long hairs of his beard and mustache, gray eyes brooding.

Annev studied his right arm, which ended in a smooth stump in the middle of his forearm. He'd spent precious little time looking at the disfigured limb, for every time he had removed his hand, he had felt an unreasonable panic rise up in the back of his throat, threatening to choke him.

This deformity—this *curse*—was the reason his friends, peers, and teachers would unquestioningly stone him to death. He spent so much of his life with it hidden that it seemed absurd its existence could control his fate. He hated it, which was strange, seeing as it rarely caused any problems. But the chance for catastrophe was always there, a looming threat. He felt the bile rising in his throat again and turned his eyes away.

Annev rose to his feet. After taking a deep breath, he cradled the mended prosthetic to his stunted arm and willed the magic to take effect. A familiar tingle ran up his arm as the two limbs joined and the prosthetic's silvery skin smoothly shifted to match the color and tone of his own. Moments later he was flexing his surrogate fingers again, and he looked up to see Sodar standing in front of him, smiling from ear to ear.

"And there is the proof that you can use magic."

Annev shook his head. "We've had this conversation before. My arm is different." Sodar shook his head, but Annev changed the subject.

"When I thought the limb was broken … I thought we'd have to leave Chaenbalu. That I'd never get to be an avatar. Never get to …" He was going to say *be with Myjun*, but he stopped himself. "I thought my life was over," he said at last.

Sodar rose to his feet. "It's not easy keeping secrets, even ones you've had your whole life. You're never quite sure how others will react"—he laid a hand on Annev's shoulder and met his eyes—"or how much to tell them … when they find out."

Annev nodded, studying the priest, then his stomach did a somersault.

"You … you mean you *knew*! You knew I saw you in the woods, with Arnor."

Sodar nodded. "You did well hiding your trail in the Brakewood, but your injury probably hindered you. Also, you forgot something." Annev shook his head, puzzled, and the priest waggled his fingers. "I have magic."

Annev found himself getting angry again. "So why pretend? Why not just—"

"Say I caught you spying?" Annev nodded and Sodar raised his hands as if to show he had no answers. "I wasn't sure how much you had heard, and I hoped to avoid the conversation. When it was clear you'd heard enough to be upset, I hoped you'd ask me about it. That was, perhaps, selfish."

Annev didn't trust himself to speak.

The priest walked over to the steps and sat down. "I expect you feel I've been dishonest with you."

"You've been *lying* to me, Sodar."

The priest's eyes were full of sympathy. "Those lies are meant to keep you safe. The truth can be … complicated. Painful. Burdensome. Your life is difficult enough with bullies, chores, and your training at the Academy—not to mention lessons from a dodgy old priest."

"*Very* dodgy."

Sodar bowed his head in mock acknowledgment, though when he looked up, he was serious. "My point is that you keep secrets already—about your arm, your magic—"

"I don't have magic," Annev objected, ignoring the priest's upraised hand.

"You have enough to worry about already. Enough dangerous secrets. You don't need to carry mine."

Annev shook his head, stepping closer. "That's not fair. You know everything about me and I know next to nothing about you."

"Well, I doubt that I know *all* of your secrets …" Annev suddenly thought of the shadepools, the glove that Myjun had given him, and the ring he hoped to give her after he passed the Test of Judgment "… but," Sodar said, "I see your point. In my efforts to be cautious, I may have been too secretive. So let me remedy that a little. What do you want to know?"

Annev thought about it. "Why are you so fast—so strong? It can't just be practice."

Sodar smiled. "You still think it's magic." Annev nodded. "Well, you're close enough to the truth. Once, a very long time ago, I received a special blessing that invigorated my mind and body—I don't get tired the way most people do, and my body responds faster to the demands I place on it. That blessing has stayed with me."

'Is that why Arnor called you an ageless one?"

"You heard that, did you?" Annev nodded and Sodar sighed. "It's connected, but also more complicated. There's a bit of Terran magic thrown in there plus a lot of things I still don't understand myself. Anyhow, what Arnor and I do … it's something I can't share now."

Sodar's words pricked at Annev, and he remembered how he'd felt when he'd overheard Sodar in the woods. "It's connected to me, isn't it? You told Arnor you had to take care of me—that you couldn't help his Order because of me. Because you had to take care of me."

"Yes, and I can't explain why—not yet. As I said, it's my burden to bear."

"But that's not how it works, Sodar! You want me to trust you—like a friend or a father—but a friend would treat me like an equal, and a father …" Annev choked, his voice dropping low, almost to a whisper. "A father wouldn't view me as a burden."

Sodar suddenly hugged him. "If I have ever treated you like a burden," he said, holding the boy to his chest, "then it is because I'm a very poor replacement for your father. I've done my best to fill that void in your life, and not out of duty or obligation. I do it because I believe in you, Annev—more than you believe in yourself—and every action I take, every day of my life, reaffirms that belief."

Annev was still for a long while, silently resisting the old man's affection. Yet he could not deny the old man's love—fierce and protective as it was—and he finally leaned into it.

"Does that mean you'll tell me more about your past?" Annev asked, his emotions still raw. "About your mission … about me?"

The priest hugged him tighter. "I've told you all you need to know for now. To say more …" Sodar sighed, his breath deep and ragged. "Just be a boy, Annev. Enjoy what remains of your childhood, because tomorrow will rob us of the things we take for granted today."

"But you'll explain all of it," Annev pressed, listening to the beat of his mentor's heart. "One day."

"One day soon. Not just about my past, either, but about a war beyond this village."

Annev hesitated, still anxious that Sodar kept secrets, but reassured that the priest would tell him the truth in due course.

"All right."

"Good." The priest squeezed him once more. "Now let's clean up and eat."

Annev nodded and went to retrieve his hand-ax and short sword.

When he reached down with his left hand, though, he found his attention returning to the magic prosthetic.

"You know," Annev said, walking the weapons back to the rack, "I still don't understand much about magic—not even about the artifacts we're told to reclaim. Aside from how to identify them and bring them back to the Academy, the ancients say nothing about how and why they were made, let alone how they're meant to work."

"I suspect they've forgotten what little there is to know," Sodar said, carrying the wallowpike to the back of the room. "Their teachings are based in fear and superstition. But there is a *science* to magic, which is as precise and delicate as art and beauty—both of which are smaller facets of a greater and more abstract "truth". All good things. All worth seeking out and understanding." Sodar slid the heavy pike into the rack then stood straight. "What do you want to know?"

Annev held up his left hand. "About this. I used to think a Bloodlord made it for himself, but it can adapt its size and coloring to the wearer—from an adult to an infant—which made me think it was probably crafted to grow with a child … but why? The Sons of Keos never help anyone."

Sodar laughed. "Did the Academy teach you that? The Terrans worked harder than any race during the First and Second Age." They walked back towards the kitchen. "Frankly, I think it was crafted as a gift for a loved one, but not by a Bloodlord. It'd have been made by an artificer, like Urran."

So," Annev said, walking beside Sodar. "Maybe their motives were good initially, but … things are different now, right? The Terrans were good people back then, but now they're evil."

"The way anyone with a disability used to be good, but now they're all worshippers of Keos? Like Sraon? Like you?"

Annev's cheeks reddened at catching himself with Myjun's words in his mouth, and he found he had no response. He stopped in front of the steps to the chapel and rubbed his left elbow. "No, you're right. It's maddening hearing the masters and ancients talk about cripples and magic as if either one was proof of evil. I keep wanting to tell them—to *show* them—that they're wrong." He shook his head, feeling the burden of his secrets.

"Sometimes I wish I could tell people—let them see the truth with their own eyes. Instead, I always have to lie about what … about who I am."

"Who would you tell?"

Myjun immediately filled Annev's mind, but the memory of her ugly words quickly pushed that thought away. His heart told him she was only repeating her father's words; but he wished he could be certain she would feel differently if she knew Annev's secret.

"Other avatars," Annev said, after what felt like too long a pause. "Then maybe they wouldn't give me such a hard time. Or I could tell some of the villagers. The way they gossip about Ilumites and keokum and Keos marking people with deformities … I don't know. I want to show them they're wrong. *I'm* not evil. Maybe they're not, either."

Sodar put his arm over Annev's shoulder as they climbed the steps to the rectory. "You have good intentions and a good heart, Annev, but have you forgotten how they treat Sraon? He's a wonderful man with a kind heart and a generous spirit, which doesn't stop them from cursing him and everything he touches. If any one of them knew you were missing an arm, they would tell the ancients and you'd be stoned to death." Sodar looked Annev in the eye, utterly serious. "You can't tell anyone. Not ever."

Annev gave a small nod.

"Good." Sodar squeezed his shoulders and opened the kitchen door. "Now, how about we eat something—and then you can open your presents."

Annev turned. "There's more than one?"

"Only if you're quick."

Annev sprinted into house.

CHAPTER TWENTY

A few minutes later, Annev was seated at Sodar's modest table with a bowl of cold meal in front of him. They both bowed their heads and sat in silence. After a moment, Annev lifted his head and cracked an eye open to peer at his companion.

"It's your turn, Annev," Sodar said without moving.

The boy snapped his head back down and said a blessing over the food, invoking the will of Odar. When it was finished, he snatched up his spoon and dug into the thick porridge.

"I hate cold oats," Annev grumbled, scooping another overflowing spoonful into his mouth. "Any chance of some meat?"

"No. Arnor's summons caught me by surprise, so I didn't have time to cook." Sodar stirred his own bowl, tracing a glyph across the surface of his mush and whispering a word. Steam immediately rose from the surface of the pottage, its contents smelling of ginger and nutmeg.

"Hey!" Annev said, pointing at the steam. "Why didn't you heat mine up?"

Sodar shrugged. "You've got magic. You know the glyph and the words of power. If you want hot food, heat it yourself."

"But I can't—"

"Yes," Sodar interrupted, pointing his spoon at Annev. "You *can*."

Annev rolled his eyes, not wanting to argue. Though when Sodar's attention returned to his food, Annev quickly traced the glyph for heat on the surface of his oats. He studied it, wondering if the symbol were clear enough and whether the water in the oats was sufficient to fuel the magic.

"*Teasaich*," Annev whispered, speaking the ancient name for the rune. He probed the bowl with his spoon then brought the porridge to his mouth … still cold.

No surprise there.

He finished eating a few minutes later and tossed the bowl and spoon onto the table.

"Alright," he exclaimed, "when do I get these presents?"

Scraping the sides of his own bowl, Sodar lifted a finger at Annev. "Wash the dishes first." Matching words to actions, Sodar licked his spoon and stacked it and his bowl along with Annev's. Annev groaned, but dutifully took the dishes from the table and carried them outside to be washed in the water trough abutting the exterior of the training shed.

When Annev returned with clean bowls and utensils in hand, Sodar was still seated. This time, though, a large red and gold piece of cloth covered the table. It gave Annev a start, as it was embroidered with the detailed form of a phoenix. Again, Annev's mind jumped to the glove Myjun had made for him, which he'd hidden in his tunic pocket along with his lockpicking tools. He studied the cloth on the table, noting as he did that it lay uneven and bulged in some spots, as if one or more flat objects lay beneath it.

"It's a phoenix," Annev whispered, still surprised at the coincidence.

"It's the emblem of a Halcyon Knight named Breathanas. It's said that his enemies would flee when they saw the phoenix banner. You're named after him, in part." Annev examined the threading more closely and marveled again at its resemblance to Myjun's gift.

"Was Breathanas a child-god—a dalta?"

"Why do you ask?"

"Ancient Benifew said some of the daltas' faces were engraved on the Academy walls. He mentioned Breathanas."

"He was a dalta," Sodar said carefully. "Though his line was virtually wiped out in the years after the gods went silent."

Annev stared at the flag for a moment longer. "Right," he said, remembering. "When the gods' weapons were stolen."

"The *diamagi* weren't really weapons," Sodar said, "though the Artifacts of Legend—the flute, the staff, and the hammer—were used as such.

They were tools and, like any tool, they could be used to create as well as destroy. But enough of this. You've waited long enough." Sodar whipped away the red and gold banner, revealing what lay hidden beneath.

On the table lay two exceptional weapons: an ax, its blade covered by a thick piece of rawhide; and a short sword sheathed in an ornate silver scabbard, its hilt wrapped from crosspiece to pommel with a light blue cord. Annev picked the latter up and slid it from its scabbard.

"Sodar! This is amazing. How ... where did you get this?"

"It was mine. A gift from a very old friend, which I am now giving to you."

Annev ran his thumb along the edge of the weapon. Its edge, though void of nicks and chips, was perfectly smooth—round even.

"Your mighty blade is dull, Sodar."

The old man laughed. "First of all, the sword's name is Mercy—and it's your blade now. Second, it's *meant* to be dull."

Annev replaced the weapon in its sheath. "For sparring?"

"Partly." Sodar took the sword and unwrapped the light blue cord. A strange symbol like the letter "y" was meticulously woven into the metal beneath. Here, though, the letter lay on its side, its tail and tops curved upward, like three sinuous claws.

"That's a glyph," Annev said. "For ... "sharp air"?"

Sodar nodded. "It's an arcane Darite symbol." He rewrapped the hilt carefully. "This is an *artifact*, Annev."

Annev's eyes widened. "Like my arm?" Sodar nodded. "But ... I can't have any artifacts. All magic items go to the vault."

Sodar waved his hands, shushing the boy. "That's why this is yours on the condition that you show it to no one."

"A secret?"

Sodar nodded.

Annev's bright blue eyes sparkled for a moment then went dark. "A present I can't use. And another secret, just like my arm."

Sodar frowned. "Your arm would get you killed, Annev. But you can use the sword and the ax for sparring. And perhaps someday, when you leave Chaenbalu, they will be useful to you."

Annev took the short sword from the priest. "You named it Mercy?" Sodar nodded. "How does it work?"

"Draw the sword. Always draw it before activating its powers, otherwise you may compromise the integrity of the scabbard."

Annev drew it far more carefully than he had the first time.

"Now concentrate on the symbol you saw on the hilt. Imagine the blade honed to a perfect edge. The finer you imagine it, the sharper it will be."

Annev cocked an eyebrow. "Is this some elaborate excuse to test my magic again?"

Sodar laughed. "Just try."

Annev shrugged and focused intently on the blade. After a moment, he looked at Sodar. "How do I know if it's working?"

"I wouldn't run a finger over it, if that's what you're thinking. Usually, though, I sense a depletion of my *quaire*: I become thirsty or winded, like I forgot to take a breath." Annev nodded, thinking he understood, and the priest placed a stick of kindling on the edge of the table.

"Run the edge of the sword across the firewood."

Annev approached the table, holding the sword in both hands. He studied the kindling—it was almost a foot long but barely an inch thick—then he crashed the edge of the sword atop the offending splinter. The stick shot out, rolling away from the sword's dull edge, and clattered to the hard-packed earth floor.

Annev glared at Sodar and saw the priest was trying not to laugh.

"Is this funny?"

The priest lowered his hand, still smiling. "It's an *artifact*, Annev."

"I know that."

"Yes, but you're treating it like a sword—a *real* sword. That's not how it works. The shape of the artifact is meant to help the user *imagine* its purpose. Mercy could have been made into a rod or a wand, but giving it a flat surface—like a sword—makes it easier to visualize the weapon's edge." Sodar picked up the scrap of wood and placed it back on the table. "Try again, but don't use the blade to cut the wood. Visualize the true edge—the air *surrounding* the blade—and imagine that air parting the wood."

Annev frowned but placed the sword back atop the wood. He glanced once more at Sodar then pressed the blade hard against the kindling.

Sharp air, Annev thought, trying to imagine what that would look like. *But air isn't sharp … it's shapeless. Formless, like the wind.* Instead of voicing those thoughts, though, Annev sliced the sword across the scrap of wood. Nothing happened. He looked up, his expression dark.

"This is stupid."

Sodar shook his head, his mirth gone. "Try saying the glyph's name as you visualize. The word is *géaraer.*"

"Shouldn't I have used that the first time?"

Sodar tilted his hand from side to side. "Glyph-speaking is a misnomer. We use glyphs to form our intent, but Darite magic is fueled by two things: *quaire* and words. The quaire comes from you—you'll deplete your air or water when the spell is effective—but the *words* can be spoken or simply formed as a thought in your mind."

"But you usually speak the words."

"Yes, because spoken words are like water. They pour out of your mouth and take the shape of the vessel you've poured them into—they're *reliable.* Thoughts are the opposite. They're like air … always changing, floating away the moment we've formed them. But as spoken words *begin* as thoughts, they are the same thing, just as *quaire* is both air and water."

"Skywater," Annev said, understanding. "So I form the word in my mind and then give it shape by speaking."

"More or less, but remember: magic is a science *and* an art. Rules can define the form, but the rest is intuitive."

Annev held his tongue, imagining the word in his mind, and touched the sword's edge against the wood. He looked up at Sodar, who nodded. "*Géaraer!*" Annev cried, dragging the blade across the kindling. He stopped midway through his stroke and glanced at the stick beneath the sword; it remained stubbornly whole. Annev cursed.

Sodar picked up the wood and turned it over in his hands. A faint scratch marred its surface. He sighed. "Don't worry, Annev. We'll break that block of yours one day. Somehow."

"Blood and bones! *This* is why I hate testing for magic. Every time—*every* time—it's a disappointment." He kicked the firewood pile. "Why can I use my arm but not this?" He waved the sword at Sodar. "It's not *fair*!"

Sodar folded his arms. "How *do* you get that arm to fuse to you?"

Annev shrugged. "I don't know. I've been using it for so long, I don't think about it. It's just sort of … natural. I know what needs to happen and it does."

"Interesting." Sodar stroked his beard.

"What?"

"Mercy was crafted by a Darite, so its magic is unlocked by glyph-speaking. Your arm was made by a Terran using dwimmer-craft, so its mechanics are … different. I can't explain how since I'm no artificer, but it typically requires a gesture or some other physical action."

"Right," Annev said, remembering, "glyph-speaking works through words and thoughts. Ilumites use music. Terrans use gestures." He looked down at his arm, confused. "But Sodar, I don't do *any* of that. My arm just … works. Like the stumble-sticks my class used in the nave this morning. I didn't have to think about how to use those."

"But those were common artifacts and your arm is not."

"You *say* it's not common, but I think it is. I bet any cripple missing a left hand and half a forearm could use it."

"Bah!" Sodar waved a hand at him. "Who is teaching whom?"

Annev gave a half-bow to his mentor, conceding the point without admitting he might be wrong. "Is there a way people use magic *without* glyph-speaking, spell-singing, or dwimmer-crafting?"

Sodar huffed. "Not unless you're a keokum."

"I'm *not* a keokum."

Sodar laughed at the notion, and even Annev cracked a smile at that thought. "No, you're not an ogre or a dragon. But there have been a few …" Sodar looked sharply at Annev. "Try again, but don't think about either the magic or the blade. Ignore the rune and its purpose. Focus on what you want the sword to do."

Annev bit the inside of his cheek. *Great. Now he thinks I'm keokum—a sentient fragment formed from the hand of Keos.* He shook his head, finding the whole thing absurd. *Why does he insist on this? My arm is a common artifact, and I have no affinity for magic.* Annev looked at Sodar, prepared to say as much, then stopped when he saw the gleam in the old man's eyes.

Annev sighed. He would try once more, to make Sodar happy. He rolled his shoulders back, leaning first left then right, feeling his muscles roll across his shoulder blades and back. He fixed his eyes on the wood, remembering the spark of hope in Sodar's eyes, and a tiny fire kindled inside him. Determination replaced his wariness.

Maybe I can *do this,* he told himself. *It's just a piece of wood. I can cut wood. I'm holding a sword, for Odar's sake, it's supposed to cut things. And I chop firewood every day. This is no different.*

Annev raised the weapon and eyed the sliver of kindling, centering the blade above it.

It's just a piece of wood—and I'm the blade; I am the master of this sword.

Annev blinked, slicing down … and sheared off a whole corner of the table.

CHAPTER TWENTY-ONE

"Gods!" Sodar looked from the broken table to the cut kindling and triangular piece of tabletop lying on the ground. He looked at Annev's pale face.

"I … I didn't mean to do that," Annev said, staring at the spot where the corner of the stout oak table had once been.

Sodar was just as stunned. "No. No, it's fine—more than fine. Annev, this is *wonderful*. That table is solid oak! That blade has never been so sharp." Sodar examined the chunk of wood lying on the dirt floor.

"Do it again."

"What?"

"Do it again, Annev. But this time …" He left the room and went out into the shed. When he came back he carried a large rough stone in both hands. "This time," he said, "cut the rock."

"That's impossible."

Sodar set the stone on the ground at Annev's feet. "Nothing is impossible." He gave Annev an excited grin. "Try."

Annev studied the stone, pondering. Could he do it? If that was possible, what else was? He tingled with excitement, in a way he'd never felt when testing his magic before.

"I'll try."

Sodar beamed at him. Annev lifted the sword again and slowly lowered the blade toward the rock, thinking about slicing through it. He stopped a few inches above the stone and took a deep breath.

"Do it slowly this time, Annev. Imagine what you were feeling before and harness it. That feeling should be the power of *quaire*—the spirit of air and water. Let it extend into the stone—but don't rush. Just feel the magic."

Annev slowly exhaled as the sword descended upon the rock ... and slid impotently off its surface. He looked up at Sodar, frowning. The priest waved his hands.

"Forget everything I just said and do whatever you did the first time."

Annev snorted but did as he was told. He imagined the blade was part of him—an extension of his will—then he slowly brought the sword down. Just as the metal was about to kiss the stone, a delicate line appeared on its surface. He heard Sodar's breath catch and stopped.

"Keep going, Annev—but this time, don't move the sword. Hold it still and focus on extending the magic. Find it. Embrace it. Then extend the edge of the blade as you might extend your arm."

These new instructions seemed to resonate with Annev. He stared fiercely at the rock and sensed the power Sodar described, just out of reach.

I am the sword, Annev thought. *I am the air and the water, the light and the fire. I am the earth and its blood.* He felt the tingling sensation extend throughout his body, and his left arm grew warmer. He held the sword perfectly still and thought about cutting the stone.

It fell apart.

"By the Staff of Odar," Sodar swore, sitting down heavily. "The daltas have returned!"

"What?"

"You cut the stone without using the metal of the sword—without even passing your blade through it! I could *never* do that." The priest bent over and picked the stone off the ground, exposing the full extent of the cut: a gash almost an inch deep had been sliced into the floor.

"How does that even work?" Annev asked, equally stunned.

"The blade allows the wielder to compress the air around it into a cutting edge. When I use it, I can extend the edge by a hair's breadth. More than enough to fight with and, while I could never cut through stone, it was extremely sharp. From that gash in the floor, though, it looks like you extended the spell straight through the rock and into the ground—that's more than *six inches*! Remarkable." The priest carefully slid the sword from Annev's hand.

"It's also very dangerous," Sodar added. "If you're not concentrating on making the sword sharp, the magic should dispel itself, but …" He tested the edge against the table and nothing happened; the blade was dull once again. Sodar slid the sword back into its scabbard and weighed it carefully in his hands. "Annev. If you were to accidentally use this magic in our practice sessions, you would slice right through my shield arm."

"I would never—"

Sodar held up a hand. "Not intentionally. But this magic works differently for you. I have to fix the glyph in my mind and think the word of power. I thought you'd take after your father—who was Darite—or maybe your mother's Ilumite magic, but I was *wrong*. Your magic works …" Sodar's voice trailed off, but even so, Annev heard the words muttered under the priest's breath. "… like a dalta's … or a keokum's." He shook his head. "I had no idea this could happen. For now, at least, giving you the sword may have been a mistake."

"No!" Annev shouted. "You've wanted this for *years*! You can't punish me for finally succeeding!"

"I'm not punishing you, Annev. I just think it would be better to—"

"You can't do that!" Annev protested. "Not after giving it to me. I already promised not to show it to anyone. I won't leave the house with it. I won't even use it, but please don't take it back." He lowered his face to hide the tears that were threatening. "It's the only thing you've ever given me."

Sodar gave a long sigh and glanced between the sword and the boy. "I have given you many gifts, my boy. The foremost of them being knowledge." He paused, carefully weighing both the sword and his words. "But if you will use that knowledge then use it to temper the power of your sword. Perhaps then I could let you keep it."

Annev hastily wiped his tears away and looked up into his mentor's gray eyes.

"I promise."

Sodar nodded. "Then take Mercy, Annev. But don't use it again until we better understand the type of magic you possess." Annev took the blade back from Sodar. The priest quickly moved to the table and retrieved the hand ax. "In the midst of our excitement, we've forgotten Sraon's present." He passed the ax to Annev.

Taking the ax in his left hand, Annev examined the tough rawhide case belted to the blade of the ax. He undid the buckle. The craftsmanship of the blade equaled that of the short sword but was more intricate; geometric stars and diamonds had been carved into the flat of the blade, creating a decorative pattern that also gave the ax a lighter heft.

"It's beautiful."

"Yes, it is. Sraon put a lot of work into it. He won't tell me how much, but I'm certain he started it before winter. It's a remarkable gift."

Annev gave it a practice swing. "Can I spar with it?"

Sodar nodded. "Keep the guard on the blade. I'd rather not have you chopping my legs out from under me."

Annev smiled. "I haven't beaten you yet."

"You're getting closer."

Annev shook his head. "I'm nearly top of my class ... but whenever I spar with you, I feel like you're humoring me."

"I just enjoy taunting you. You would qualify as a weapons master in almost any small village—and a journeyman or man-at-arms in any midsized town. You understand the principles, you just lack experience." He indicated Annev's bruised face for emphasis. "How many of them were there?"

The question caught Annev off guard, but he found he couldn't lie about the fight with Fyn.

"Four."

"Go on."

"Fyn had kali sticks. Even then, I think could have beaten him, but ..."

"But not all of them?"

"No."

Both the priest and the boy sat in silence.

"Sodar," Annev said, after a long moment staring at the ground. "You mentioned my parents ... and their magic." Sodar winced and Annev's stomach lurched, but he carried on. "I thought you didn't know who my parents were."

Sodar's lips moved as if he wanted to speak, but his voice had failed him.

He knew them, Annev realized, bile rising. *Gods. His conversation with Arnor was just a fraction of what he's kept from me. He's lied to me my whole life.* All the feelings of hurt and betrayal, all the anger and frustration, came rushing back. *What else has he hidden? What other lies has he told?*

"How do you know my parents?" Annev repeated. His breathing had become rapid and shallow. "Are they alive? Are they in Luqura?"

Sodar stood up. "Annev. Don't—"

"Did they really give me up, or was I stolen? That's what some of the ancients said—that we were born to unfit parents and the Academy took us away to serve as avatars." He looked up at Sodar, eyes wide. "Is that what happened? Which version is true?"

"Annev," Sodar began, choosing his words carefully. "Don't ask about your parents."

"But why not?!" Annev shouted, tears spilling down his cheeks. "If you know who they are, why can't you tell me? Why keep *lying* to me?"

Sodar studied Annev's face for a long moment then lingered on the boy's prosthetic arm. His gaze wandered to the sword on the table, and some of the tension went out of him. Sodar walked back, sat down in his chair, and clasped his hands in front of his face as if he were praying. After a moment, he looked up.

"Sometimes lies can protect us, and truths can kill us. Given the choice between the two, which would you prefer?"

Annev wiped the tears from his cheeks and eyes. "I don't understand."

"Then take a breath and think."

The curt reply made Annev stop and consider his next answer. He swallowed, reining in his emotions. "My arm is a lie that protects me," he said. "If the ancients ever found out, they would kill me. But the truth is that I'm ..."

Crippled? Deformed?

"... that I have one arm," he said, forcing the words out. "That I'm ... not whole. That is the truth. My disability makes me a Son of Keos, and it can get me killed."

"And you have magic."

"Which makes me twice cursed."

Sodar shook his head. "Magic is a blessing that few possess. Be grateful for it. Your arm is also a blessing. In his mercy, Odar has given you a trial to overcome, and that challenge will make you stronger."

"It is still a truth that can get me killed," Annev said. "That's what you're trying to say."

Sodar tapped the sheathed sword on the table. "Your whole life has been a series of lies meant to keep you safe, Annev. You lie to the ancients about your arm and your magical affinity. They lie about who you are, where you came from, and what you are doing here."

"And who do *you* lie to?"

Annev regretted the question the moment he said it, but he couldn't take it back, and when Sodar hesitated he found himself genuinely curious how the priest would answer.

"I lie to everyone," Sodar said, his tone entirely unapologetic.

Annev was unsurprised by the priest's words yet still shocked by Sodar's admission. "If I asked you now," Annev asked, "would you tell me the truth?"

The priest hesitated. "No."

"Why not!" Annev demanded.

"Because I won't let you get hurt, Annev! I won't ..." He stopped. "I won't let it happen again."

"Let *what* happen again?" With every question, Annev felt more and more confused, as if he were spiraling into deep, dark waters. "Tell me," Annev repeated, seizing control of his emotions. "I'm your student ... your *friend*. I deserve to know. What are you hiding?"

Sodar shook his head, eyes pleading. "Not tonight, Annev. It is too much. Not tonight."

Annev steadied himself with a great gulp of air. So many secrets. So many lies. Why should he believe anything the priest told him? Why should he believe Sodar would *ever* tell him the truth?

"We need to prepare for Regaleus," Annev said slowly, his face still flushed with anger. He swept the sword and ax from the table. When Sodar nodded his agreement, Annev looked sharply at him, holding his gaze. "But this conversation isn't over."

CHAPTER TWENTY-TWO

The evening bell tolled as the villagers began to crowd into Sodar's tiny chapel. Farmers, shopkeepers, tradesmen and master avatars all wished each other a Happy Regaleus. Soon the benches had all been filled except for the two at the very front, and it was standing room only.

Annev stood on the raised dais at the front of the chapel with the altar behind him and Yohan's lavender-scented candles burning to either side of him. Over his clean acolyte clothes, he wore blue vestments tied with a gray belt. The robes themselves were a deep shade of blue which had been gradually bleached so it faded to a stark white. Finally, Annev wore the bright red phoenix glove on his left hand. Sodar had initially questioned the wisdom of that decision—and speculated about the glove's origin—but when Annev had met his disapproval with silence the priest had relented.

As Annev watched the sun set and the last villagers entered the chapel, he lifted a silver-painted staff aloft with both hands and chanted.

"Lord of Heavens, God above. Lord of Waters, God below. Hear our prayers."

"Hear our prayers," the congregants chanted in unison.

Annev thumped the butt of the staff once on the ground and held it aloft again. "Give us breath that we may breathe," he prayed. "Give us water that we may drink. Give us knowledge that we may know thee. Creator of the skies and the seas. God of *Quaire*. God of Skywater. Steward of our Souls and Keeper of our Secrets, hear our prayers."

"Hear our prayers," the audience repeated.

Annev thumped the staff on the ground twice more and strode to the left side of the dais just as a group of ancients led by Elder Tosan—in his best red-and-black robes, the cuffs and collar trimmed with black ermine fur—arrived and began to push through the crowd towards the empty benches.

Myjun followed her father. Black satin slashed her red silk dress and a slender silver chain hung about her neck. At the end of the chain, hanging just above her modest neckline, was a tiny silver rod, a symbol of the Staff of Odar.

Tosan took the first bench. Myjun sat beside him. The other ancients shuffled behind Tosan and took their seats.

"Odar, All-father," Annev continued, "Lord of Wind and Air and Sea, we thank thee for the waters that cleanse us and the holy spirit that lifts us up. Forgive us our trespasses against God and man." Annev's gaze drifted to Tosan, who was staring resolutely forward, and then his eyes flitted to Myjun.

"And lead us not into temptation," Annev continued.

A shy smile crept onto Myjun's face and he found himself smiling back until he glanced at Tosan and found his eyes locking with the Eldest of Ancients. Myjun's father folded his arms and raised both eyebrows.

"Hear our prayers," Annev said quickly.

"Hear our prayers," Tosan and Myjun chorused with the rest of the villagers.

Annev stepped back, thumping the staff three times in front of him. As he reached the back of the dais and turned around, he stole one last glance at Myjun and almost tripped over his feet. He stumbled backward, teetering for a moment at the edge of the raised dais. Just as he felt his weight tip backward, a hand reached out and steadied him. Annev looked back and saw Sodar standing behind him.

"Sorry," Annev whispered, his feet shifting away from the precipice. He handed the silver staff to the old priest.

On many nights Sodar wore robes embroidered with symbols that represented the unknowable depths of the ocean. Tonight, his robes were night-blue, almost black, and speckled with pale yellow stars meant to signify the vastness of Odar's knowledge. The priest's attire included a matching pointed cap with small white lightning bolts, signifying the potency of Odar's celestial power.

"Keep your mind on the job," Sodar whispered back without moving his lips.

Annev's cheeks reddened and he sidestepped to his chair at the back of the dais. When he sat down to face the villagers, he made a point of not looking in Myjun's direction, which was difficult, as the young woman and her father were sitting directly in front of him.

Sodar lifted the staff high above his head and thumped it three times on the platform beneath his feet. He waited. Those villagers who had talked through Annev's opening benediction finally stopped and the hall fell silent. Sodar held the staff in front of him and peered out over the congregation.

"Brothers and Sisters," he intoned after a long moment of silence. "Ancients and Masters of the Academy. Thank you for worshipping with us on this Seventhday, the first night of our three-day celebration of Regaleus.

"According to tradition, this celebration marks the five thousand and seventeenth anniversary of the day that Myahlai was cast out of Luquatra, and the four thousand nine hundred and seventeenth anniversary of the first Regaleus, which we mark with gift-giving. It is said, of course, that great mischief comes from giving gifts—though we speak in reverence of the first gifts, and of the staff that Odar received and which Keos later cursed." As he spoke, Sodar made his way to the center of the dais and placed the silver staff atop the altar.

"We also remember how Odar made the Oracle, a being of pure *quaire*; how Lumea made the sprites, beings of pure *lumen*; and how Keos made *Fyoldar*, an abomination of pure *t'rasang* that preyed upon Odar and Lumea's worshippers for four hundred years. The Book of Odar calls this dark time the Fall of Keos, which only ended with the Breaking of the Hand of Keos.

"We remember all of this at Regaleus, but with the passing of ages it is possible for history to give way to legend, and legend to myth, until it is no longer clear what was true and what was merely a story."

Annev's ears perked up. *He's diverting from the usual Regaleus recitation ... Why?*

Sodar beckoned Annev forward. On cue, Annev took the bound book of bronze sheets from beneath his chair and carried them to the priest. As he sat back down, he stole another glance at Myjun and their eyes met. He fought not to blush.

She was waiting for me to look at her. Or she's been looking at me this whole time. Annev's heart fluttered at the notion.

"That is why we must constantly turn to scripture to remind us of the truth," Sodar said, lifting the thin stack of bronze plates for the crowd to see. "The Book of Odar holds many of these truths, including the creation of Luquatra, the Age of the Gods, the Age of Kings, the Age of Blood, and the Age of Peace. These truths have been passed down for thousands of years until the present day ... but they have not reached us wholly pure." Sodar placed the book beside the staff on the altar.

Now he's definitely *left the script.* Annev thought. Few things could have distracted him from Myjun's attention that evening, but the unexpected direction of Sodar's sermon was doing exactly that. *What's he playing at?* Annev wondered.

"For millennia, the priesthood has sorrowed for the destruction of Gorm Corsa, the razing of the library at Neven nan Su'ul, and the loss of our most sacred scriptures, histories, and prophecies. Yet, against all odds, some of these records have been saved from destruction." Sodar turned and beckoned to his deacon. Annev stared at him, baffled by the priest's gestures—and then he understood.

Odar's beard ... he wants the Speur Dún manuscript!

Annev leaped to his feet, still not sure he had guessed correctly. He took a half-step toward the rectory door and Sodar nodded. Annev swallowed a curse then trotted off the dais.

The moment he had passed through the rectory door, Annev sprinted through the kitchen and into Sodar's room, where the ink-spattered translation lay on the priest's bed. Annev snatched it up and jogged back to the chapel to hand Sodar the messy sheaf of papers. He sat down just as Sodar lifted the documents above his head.

Well, Annev thought, cringing inwardly, *this will be interesting.*

"A few centuries ago, a group of our brothers ventured to Gorm Corsa in search of the lost records. Most did not survive the journey, but those that returned brought back a record which had been ancient even before Neven nan Su'ul was destroyed. It was written on brass plates that looked much like this." Sodar lifted the bronze-plated Book of Odar in his right hand then set both the bronze plates and the sheaf of papers on the altar. "These plates were brought to the monastery at Speur Dún and meticulously copied, though the language of the plates was a puzzle. The words were Darite, but the glyphs were an obscure type of Terran pictograph. This meant that, for both Terrans and Darites alike, the plates appeared to be gibberish—a flaw that would prove to be this record's saving grace. In fact, I believe it has only survived for so long because no one knew how to read it.

"Before a complete translation of the manuscript could be done, though, the monastery at Speur Dún was destroyed. Most of its records were also lost." Sodar lifted the sheaf of papers from the altar. "But a few copies survived."

Tosan cleared his throat in irritation.

"My preface was to explain from whence these scriptures come. I am about to read a history of the events following the first Regaleus—a story we all know well—but instead of reading from *The Book of Odar*, this translation voices the perspective of our national enemies … the Terrans."

A chorus of subdued murmurs filled the chapel and Tosan's frown deepened. The ancients were whispering among themselves, mostly directing their comments to Ancient Jerik, the Academy's ancient history scholar, who was stone-faced.

"Brother Sodar," Tosan said, his eyes flinty. "What does it profit us to hear Terran lies spoken from the pulpit? I can already guess that it will praise Keos and slander the All-father. This reeks of heresy."

The priest held up a placating hand. "Do not judge what you have not heard, Elder Tosan. Much of this is consistent with *The Book of Odar*, but there are many details that are not in our record—details that could benefit the Academy."

"Benefit?" Tosan scoffed. "I see no benefit in preaching *blasphemy* to your congregation." Yet even as the headmaster spoke, Annev could tell that Tosan was weighing the significance of Sodar's words. "How is this record—this *translation*—any benefit to the Academy?"

Annev couldn't see Sodar's face, but from the way the priest's back straightened—from the way he rubbed his fingers together in anticipation—he knew the old man's eyes were sparkling.

Tosan had just given Sodar the opening he'd been waiting for.

"The Terrans," Sodar explained, "preserved many of the details surrounding the creation of the Oracle—one of the most powerful artifacts ever forged by Gods or men. My translation explains what it is, why Odar made it, and—perhaps most important of all—where it was kept."

Annev could see the priest had the headmaster's full interest.

"If the Academy will permit," Sodar continued, addressing the congregation, "I would like to read this translation tonight. It contains some cultural biases, as Elder Tosan has noted, but I believe the Terran perspective reveals some truths lost to *The Book of Odar*."

"This is highly unorthodox, Sodar." The complaint came from Tosan, yet the headmaster's tone indicated his words were only a token objection. After a short pause, the Eldest of Ancients added: "You may continue, but after your sermon you must bring your records to the Academy so we can discuss your findings, including the methods of your research."

Sodar inclined his head. "It would be my pleasure, Elder Tosan." He shuffled the manuscript then placed the bronze plates on top of the loose papers.

"Before I read from this new manuscript," Sodar said, flipping through the bronze leaves, "I would like to preface my translation with verses taken from *The Book of Odar*." He cleared his throat. "*And it came to pass that many years had passed away, yea even six hundred years had passed away since the first Regaleus. And it was seven hundred years since the day that Myahlai, the Incarnation of Entropy, was cast out of Luquatra.*"

Sodar placed his manuscript atop the plates, raised his eyes to the congregation, and began.

PART TWO

And on the six hundredth anniversary of Regaleus, Odar, in his vanity, blessed his children with a new gift: using the element over which he was steward, the Elder God raised his staff and created an elemental being of pure quaire. *And Odar called it the Oracle and placed it in northwestern Odarnea, where the Darites did visit it often, for it was said the Oracle possessed the mind of Odar and could answer a supplicant's unspoken questions. And the Oracle was strengthened by the powers of Keos and Lumea, for Odar used his staff to forge the Oracle, and the Staff of Odar still bore the blessings of Keos and Lumea.*

And Lumea saw the gift of her brother, Odar, and thought the Oracle a worthy thing for him to gift unto his children, and she wished to follow the example of her brother by blessing the Ilumites in turn. So it was that, raising the Flute of Lumea, the Goddess formed creatures of pure lumen *and sent them amongst her people. And she called them Sprites, for they were simple beings of light and fire that brought much joy to Lumea's people. And the Goddess placed them throughout the valleys of Ilumea that they might bring light and love to all who encountered them. And the souls of the Sprites were strengthened by the powers of Keos and Odar, for Lumea used her flute to conjure the Sprites, and the Flute of Lumea still carried the blessings of her brothers.*

Now when Keos spied these creations he was wroth, for he had wrought the staff and the flute for Odar and Lumea, and he remembered how his siblings had belittled him with their gift of a song. Yea, and he saw how they mocked him now by gifting greater treasures unto their children using the tools he had crafted for them.

So Keos returned to his forge and labored long at its fires. And with the strength of his hammer he created a greater elemental than those of his siblings, forged in his own likeness and image, and imbued with much strength and vigor.

And Keos loved the golem and gave it a name: Fyoldar.

Now the Hammer of Keos had never received the blessing of Odar or Lumea, for having insulted their brother with a song, the Gods had failed to bless the gift that Keos made for himself. And the creations forged by the Hammer of Keos were abominable to the Darites and Ilumites, for they perceived that without lumen *his creations lacked a spirit, and without* quaire *they lacked intelligence. Nevertheless, Keos rejoiced, for he knew a mindless servant would obey its master, and a soulless thrall would not tire of its tasks. Even so, Keos knew that Fyoldar's strength was terrible to behold, and he knew that his siblings would likewise name it an abomination. So Keos kept the golem in the base of the mountains, inside the great chasms at the center of the earth. And for a time, Fyoldar stayed there, hidden from the sight of Odar and Lumea.*

Now Fyoldar, being a creature of pure t'rasang, did not hunger or thirst in the manner of animals or humans, for he could not drink water, and neither fruits nor vegetables satisfied his hunger: only blood could slake Fyoldar's thirst, and by flesh alone would his appetite be satisfied. Moreover, when consuming the flesh of beasts, Fyoldar became wild and feral, but when Fyoldar drank the blood of men, his mind was opened and his thoughts were cunning like those of men. So it was that Keos, because of his love for Fyoldar and his spite for Lumea and Odar, stole the worshippers of his siblings and sacrificed them to sate the hunger of his Flesh Golem.

But this was not all. For with the creation of Fyoldar, Keos had awakened a hunger within himself, a hunger to create more beings of pure t'rasang. For, notwithstanding Keos's love for Fyoldar, he saw that the golem was flawed, lacking intellect, beauty, and grace. So Keos retreated to the pits beneath his forge at Thoir Cuma and began laboring in secret, crafting many golems and arcane creatures as he sought to create a more perfect being of earthblood.

And he created golems from stone and called the greatest among them Klaklanrai. He created golems from metal and called the greatest among them Yarnach. He created winged golems and called their master Gargol. And after many years of laboring, he created Dortafola, the first great Vampyr. And in Dortafola, Keos found the beauty and grace he had sought.

But Odar and Lumea had not been ignorant of the creations of Keos, *for they had felt Luquatra shake at their births, had heard the keening of the creatures at night, and had seen the beasts hunt those Darites and Ilumites who persecuted the Children of Keos.*

Witnessing this, Odar, God of Quaire, *who had not spoken with Keos since the eve of that first Regaleus, visited his younger brother. And Odar exhorted Keos to repent of his actions, admonishing him, threatening that if Keos would not repent of his creations, the priests of Odar would hunt the Children of Keos and remove their taint from Luquatra.*

But Keos was wise, for he saw the hypocrisy of his brother's words and he chastised him, saying, "Do not your children already hunt mine? Yea, and you support them in their retribution for you suppose their cause is just. But I have seen the crimes of your priests, and I have seen the bloodlust of your children—how they covet the land that is ours and seek to expand beyond the islands of the sea. Therefore, do not counsel me in this, for thy mind is tainted by the love of thy children, and I will not sacrifice mine to please thine own."

And Odar went away, his intentions frustrated, and he sought the aid of their sister Lumea, hoping she might counsel their brother.

And Lumea came to Thoir Cuma to plead with Keos on behalf of her worshippers, and also on behalf of Odar and his worshippers, to beseech Keos to cease making creatures devoid of light and life. And Keos listened to Lumea but was not persuaded by her arguments.

And Lumea took the hand of Keos—yea, the very hand that had smitten Myahlai in the final battle—and she wept into it. And as she was so engaged, Lumea discovered her brother's secret hurt: a blackened scar and withered finger. And when Lumea remembered the jaws of Myahlai—how the demon's teeth had clamped upon Keos in his moment of victory—she perceived that Myahlai's venom lay upon her brother.

Then said Lumea unto Keos, "I fear that the taint of Myahlai is upon thee, brother, for when thou didst wrestle with the Anti-God, did he not infect thee with his poison? Yea, has not thy hand been cursed with the taint of Myahlai?"

And Keos hearkened to these words and was uneasy, for Myahlai—the Incarnation of Entropy; the Father of Evil, Death, and Ignominy—had indeed bitten the hand of Keos during the final battle. And Keos had concealed his wound from his brother and sister, being afraid of the taint upon him and not knowing what would come of it. And Keos humbled himself and listened to his sister and agreed to hear Odar's counsel a second time.

And Lumea spoke to Odar on Keos's behalf and explained how the Destroyer's taint had fallen upon Keos. And she persuaded Odar to accompany her to visit Keos once more.

Now this was the first time since the first Regaleus that the Gods had gathered together. And after they discussed the injury Keos had suffered during his battle with Myahlai, Odar proposed that Keos destroy his golems, yea, even all the creations that Keos had wrought from pure t'rasang. And Keos consented to Odar's request, though he grieved at the loss of his creations. Having thus secured this first promise from Keos, Odar then demanded the God of T'rasang deliver up his hammer. For Odar feared the creations wrought by his brother's hand, and he envied the Hammer of Keos, which Keos valued above all his other creations.

But this second counsel cut Keos to the core, for it named his virtues as evils. Yea, Keos had been willing to destroy his creations, to break apart the very things he had forged and loved, but he could not bear to give up his hammer. For Keos knew he had been wronged during the first Regaleus, and he would not relinquish the hammer's power, neither to his brother, nor his sister, nor to anyone.

So it was that, for the second time, Keos refused to give heed to the words of Odar and was angry with him. And Lumea pleaded with her brother and threw her arms round his neck, crying that he might relinquish his hatred and stubbornness, but Keos was unmoved.

And Odar saw that Keos was intractable, that he had set his mind and heart against him and would not yield to his entreaties. Yea, and Odar took this as a sign that Keos was truly plagued with the taint of Myahlai. And as he gazed upon the hand of Keos, he imagined that same taint had begun to consume his brother, and Odar determined that it had to be removed.

Then Odar raised his staff against Keos and smote the hand bitten by Myahlai. And the palm of Keos shattered into a thousand pieces and his fingers were broken in half and cast to the earth.

—A fragment recovered from the ruins of Speur Dún:
"The Rise of Fyoldar" from *The Book of Terra*,
translation by Sodar Weir

CHAPTER TWENTY-THREE

As soon as Sodar had concluded his benediction, the villagers rose and began filing out, returning to their farms and homes. Meanwhile, the assorted ancients turned to gauge Tosan's reaction. Annev also turned to see what the Eldest of Ancients might say.

Tosan had his arms crossed, serenely stroking his gray goatee. As the last trickle of villagers left the chapel, he whispered something to Myjun, who nodded her head in reply and followed the rest of the villagers out into the night. When she was gone, Tosan turned back to Sodar, eyes sharp.

"Thank you for your sermon, Brother Sodar," Tosan said, his voice neutral. "That was quite a remarkable story. Those lost Terran records, not to mention your felicitous translation ... quite remarkable."

Sodar bowed. "You are too kind, Elder Tosan."

"Then you will reward my kindness with graciousness." Tosan stood. "Come to my study. Bring the manuscript and the translation."

"I ... as you say, Elder Tosan," Sodar bowed a second time, much lower. "If you will permit me to change clothes and gather my things."

Tosan nodded then turned to the ancients and masters who had remained. He pointed to Ancients Jerik and Dorstal. "Stay and make sure Brother Sodar and Acolyte Ainnevog are not delayed."

A short while later, the group knocked at Tosan's study. When the door opened, the Master of Operations greeted them.

"Elder Tosan will see you in the banned reading room. Ancient Dorstal, you are dismissed."

Banned reading room? Annev thought, watching Dorstal march back down the hall. *Wonder what that's about.* He followed Carbad, Jerik, and Sodar in the opposite direction.

When Sodar had packed up his manuscript and closed the chapel, there had been no time for Annev to talk to him, especially with Ancients Jerik and Dorstal waiting to escort them to the Academy. But now Dorstal was gone and they were on the move again. Annev lagged behind then tugged on Sodar's robes, and the priest slowed so he was no longer nipping at Jerik's heels. He cocked his head slightly to one side, listening.

"Why did he ask to see us?" Annev whispered.

"Manuscript," Sodar whispered back. "Not happy."

"But why me?"

Sodar shrugged.

"You don't seem worried," Annev said after a long pause.

Sodar turned enough that Annev could see the smile on the old man's face. "I'm *terrified* boy, but I'm also prepared. I've been expecting this meeting—hoping for it, actually."

Hoping for it? Annev wanted to ask more, but then Ancient Jerik slowed his pace till he was within earshot of their conversation and he lost his chance.

After some twists and turns, the group passed into a dark hallway and wound down a narrow flight of stairs cut into the back wall of the keep. In all his time wandering the Academy's halls, Annev had never noticed the passage. He studied the space, wondering why he hadn't seen it before, and supposed it was because the shadows and narrowness of the passage hid it from view. They went single file with Carbad carrying the lamp and eventually reached an iron door at the foot of the steps. The Master of Operations passed the lamp to Jerik then took out a ring of keys and unlocked it.

"Enter."

Ancient Jerik passed into the room with the bold step of a man who had been there before, yet Sodar paused at the threshold of the reading room. Annev watched him, his face framed in the grim light of Jerik's flickering oil lamp. It was only a few heartbeats, yet the priest's hesitation spoke volumes about his uneasiness. A moment later, he entered. Annev followed and Carbad took the lamp back and closed the door, remaining outside.

Annev looked around the dimly lit chamber. An oil lamp flickered on a small table at the back of the room, but the rest of the chamber was filled with bookcases.

A library, Annev realized. Small, but clean and dry—and there was something else. Annev inhaled the scents of crumbling parchment and worn leather and was surprised to find them sweet and musky.

"Intoxicating, isn't it?"

Tosan stepped from behind a tall bookshelf with a smaller lamp in one hand and a clutch of thin books in the other. He raised the leather-bound parchments to his nose and sniffed. "What is it about old books that makes them smell so delicious—like almonds ... or chocolate. Have you ever tasted chocolate, Ancient Jerik?"

"No."

"Sodar?"

The priest hesitated. "Decades ago."

Tosan nodded. "I should have Duvarek or one of the other masters pick some up next time they have a mission in Quiri." Jerik nodded, Sodar politely bowed his head, and Tosan led them all to a table at the back of the room.

"I didn't have the records I wanted in my office, so I thought it best to meet here," Tosan continued, setting down both the books and the lamp. "The pleasant aroma is a fortunate side benefit." He smiled congenially, and Annev found himself returning the smile with only a hint of his underlying trepidation. To his left, Ancient Jerik remained stone-faced. To his right, Sodar quietly stroked his beard.

So far as Annev could see, there were no chairs in the room, which seemed odd, even for a *banned* reading room.

Tosan took a thin cloth from the table, draped it over his open palm, then extended his hand to Sodar. "May I see the record—the original?"

"Of course." Sodar pulled the sheaf of papers from under his arm, shuffled them and handed a stack of thick parchment to the headmaster. Tosan studied the pages, carefully turning them with the grace of a practiced preservationist.

"You've had this record for thirty-five ... forty years, now? ... and you've never mentioned it," he said at last. "Why present it this evening, in a public sermon during Regaleus? Why not share your revelations privately, when you discovered them?"

Sodar's anxiety seemed to vanish—and Annev understood why: there were few things that got him more excited than talking about the Speur Dún manuscript, whatever the circumstances.

"My apologies, Elder Tosan. I only discovered the key to the translation a decade ago—and even then I was only able to decipher a few words and phrases. None of it made sense. A clause might not reveal its subject until much later in the manuscript. It was impossible to know the value of what I was translating. I only realized this was the Terran translation of the Fall of Keos, as contained in *The Book of Odar*, a few years ago—though in *their* record, the event is described in two parts: the first half is the Rise of Fyoldar, and the second half is the Breaking of the Hand of Keos."

"And the timing?" Tosan snapped.

"The translation is essentially an extension of the first Regaleus narrative, so what better time to share it than *during* Regaleus?"

"That implies you've had the translation finished for some time. A fortnight? A year?" Tosan shook his head. "You should have brought it to the Academy before reading it in public."

Sodar bowed his head. "Again, I apologize. I confess, I thought this section was innocuous enough, and I was excited to share it with our congregants—but I see that was a mistake."

"Indeed, it was," Tosan affirmed. "You should have brought your translation efforts to my attention years ago. In case you've forgotten, I was Ancient in the Art of Antiquated Languages *before* I became headmaster."

"Ah," Sodar said, sounding surprised. "Yes. I *had* forgotten."

Annev coughed—he'd heard Sodar mock the headmaster for his exaggerated translation skills multiple times—earning a glare from Tosan.

"Now that you mention it," Sodar continued, "perhaps we *can* collaborate. There is still a section which has eluded me."

Another lie, Annev thought, though this time he succeeded in hiding his reaction. *Sodar finished translating the Speur Dún manuscript last winter. He's been spending his free time copying it.*

"Just one section?" Tosan murmured, neither accepting nor rejecting Sodar's suggestion. He smiled, but it was all teeth. "Translating heretical scriptures may seem worthwhile to an idle priest, but I consider it a poor use of the Academy's resources."

"Even the details surrounding the six hundredth Regaleus gifts?"

"You mean that speck about the Oracle?" Tosan scoffed. "Your translation barely mentioned it—"

"I'm convinced the record contains more detail. There is mention of a cistern."

"For catching rainwater?" Tosan sniffed. "I'm not impressed."

Sodar stepped closer to the headmaster. "A cistern for skywater—for *quaire*. A vessel to house the Oracle."

The priest and the headmaster locked eyes, and Tosan looked uncertain. The ancient stroked the point of his goatee and flicked a pinch of stray whiskers to the cobblestone floor.

"You think this cistern is … still operational?"

Sodar thoughtfully combed his fingers through the long white strands of his own beard. "Many artifacts from the First and Second Age can still be found today—that manuscript, for example—and I would think an artifact made by Odar would have a greater level of permanence."

Tosan nodded, eyes beginning to sparkle. "I meant to ask. This manuscript …" he held up the sheaf of parchment he had taken from Sodar. "The pages should have been compromised, if not by age then by wear and tear. And what you said just now …" Tosan smiled. "This *is* an artifact, isn't it?"

Annev held his breath: Sodar had made a mistake, and Tosan had noticed. The priest's lies were starting to unravel.

Sodar frowned. "I suppose it *could* be—"

"It is," Tosan said with finality. "That's why the pictographs are still legible—they've been magicked to resist wear and prevent decay." When Sodar didn't respond, Tosan tisked. "You've been keeping artifacts from the Academy, Sodar. This belongs in the vault."

"But, given the nature of the magic, perhaps—"

"No exemptions," Tosan said. "No exceptions. The manuscript stays here." He set the pages down on the table, as if to emphasize his point.

"I see." Sodar bowed his head. "As you say."

Tosan smirked. "Just like that? You're not going to fight to finish your translation?" When Sodar did not answer, Tosan chuckled. "No. You've made other transcriptions, haven't you? You'd *prefer* the original, but you don't technically need it, do you?"

"My transcription would be less than worthless to you."

Tosan studied the priest then let his gaze drop to the manuscript in his hands. "Do you really think the Oracle is just sitting there? Abandoned in Odarnea, waiting for the right person to uncover it?"

Sodar shrugged. "Given what I have gleaned from the translation … yes. It's probable the Oracle is still buried somewhere in the desert."

"Buried? Not lost or stolen." The priest nodded and Tosan scoffed. "Explain."

Sodar glanced between Annev and Ancient Jerik then took a deep breath. "The Halcyon Knights—"

"—were heretics," Tosan snapped.

Sodar smiled. "That is common knowledge. But they guarded the Oracle for most of the Third and Fourth Ages."

Tosan glanced to Ancient Jerik who nodded, if reluctantly.

"Less commonly known," Sodar continued, "is that the Order did not have the Oracle when the Sky Keep was destroyed during the Fifth Age. Devout priests and treasure hunters have since sought the Oracle, but none have found it. This translation contains a detailed description of the Oracle's original location—a cistern in the Odarnean desert, set apart from the settlements of men. I am convinced there is more still, but the translation is cumbersome."

Tosan considered this, eyes shrewd. He licked his lips. "And if an expedition were mounted and the Oracle found … what then?"

"We would put it in the vault along with the manuscript. An artifact of that power … the ability to answer a man's unspoken questions?" Sodar shook his head. "I fear what would happen if it fell into the wrong hands."

"You think too small, Brother Sodar. If Odar saw fit to give men the Oracle, then men should use it. If the *Academy* had it, our efforts to recover magic would improve a thousandfold. We could use the Oracle to locate *other* magic artifacts. We could ask the Oracle *how to obtain* those artifacts."

Sodar's bushy eyebrows lifted in surprise, though Annev guessed the priest was still following a carefully plotted script. "I hadn't considered that, but yes. The translation suggests the Oracle has that capability."

Tosan nodded, deciding something, then gestured to Ancient Jerik. "Have Master Narach bring me any records about the Oracle from the vault—and see if you can find an old map of Odarnea. When you've done that, search here for any references to the Oracle." Jerik took his lamps and left as Tosan turned to Sodar.

"How soon can you finish this translation?"

The priest paused to consider this. "A few weeks? Maybe a month. The problem is that Yomad pictography leaves much room for interpretation— especially when conveying thoughts in Darite—and if I can't name the *exact* location of the Oracle an expedition would be lost ..." He shrugged. "I can pinpoint an area, but the geography will influence how the pictographs should be interpreted—and I cannot leave here, I have my congregation to attend to." He tapped his chin. "You could lead an expedition, but it seems beneath your station—and interpreting the pictographs may be ... fickle."

For a long while, Tosan remained silent. Annev studied the headmaster's face and could almost see the man's thoughts working their way to a solution.

"You will go," Tosan said at last. "Accompanied by some of our masters."

Sodar frowned, though Annev got the sense this was precisely what he wanted. "But my congregation ..."

"—will be here when you get back."

Sodar stroked his beard, considering. "I'd need an assistant—I'm not as spry as your masters. And I'll need someone to run ahead and report on the terrain—a guide or someone familiar with the area. Has anyone in Chaenbalu explored that part of the continent?"

"Northwestern Odarnea?" Sodar nodded in reply and Tosan shook his head. "Quiri is the farthest north we send avatars, but that's northeast. Out west ... no." He paused. "Didn't the blacksmith come from that region?"

Sodar hummed thoughtfully to himself. "Sraon is from Innistiul, which is even father north ... but yes. He may know the terrain."

"The two of you will go, then." Tosan decided. "The record stays here at the Academy. Master Carbad will escort you out now."

Sodar nodded then glanced to Annev. "And my deacon will come with me?"

Tosan sniffed. "No. Your *deacon* is an acolyte of the Academy. Ainnevog will remain here." Sodar raised a single white eyebrow, but if he had any complaints, he did not voice them.

"Very well," the priest said. "I shall return to the chapel and continue with my translation."

"Go, with all possible expediency. Annev, you will stay."

Sodar nodded then turned to Annev. "Be careful," he whispered, his tone heavy with meaning. Annev nodded, and Master Carbad and the old priest left.

Tosan gathered up the Speur Dún manuscript and his clutch of books as the door closed. He handed the oil lamp to Annev.

"Escort me back to my chambers, Acolyte Ainnevog. We'll talk along the way."

CHAPTER TWENTY-FOUR

The two men climbed the narrow stairs with Annev leading the way. When they reached the main hall, Tosan moved beside him and set a plodding pace.

"I see you are wearing my daughter's glove," the headmaster said at last.

Annev's heart skipped a beat. *He knows. Of course, he knows.*

It'd been a bold choice to wear the crimson garment during Regaleus services—Sodar had even counseled Annev against it—but Annev had wanted to please Myjun, and he had convinced himself that Tosan wouldn't recognize it. It had been a proud and foolish decision.

"Yes," he said, "Myjun gave it to me."

"A Regaleus gift?"

"Just a gift," Annev hedged, remembering Tosan's prejudices about Regaleus gifts.

Tosan sighed. "I'm disappointed Myjun continues to encourage your interest—and that you have ignored my requests to discourage her. She is not for you, Ainnevog—but that is not why we are speaking now. I wish to discuss tomorrow's test."

"The Test of Judgment?" Annev was surprised. "What about it?"

Tosan's pace slowed even further as he considered his words. "Witmistress Kiara tells me you are ranked significantly below your skill level. She says that, of all your classmates, you are the only one she believes deserves the title of avatar."

Annev's heart soared at the unexpected praise. "Witmistress Kiara is very kind."

"No," Tosan replied, stopping in the middle of the hallway. "She is not. She is cold, pushy, high-minded, and mean-tempered." He paused, smoothed his robes, and resumed their walk. "She is also very intelligent," he continued, "and perceptive. A very skilled teacher. So when she criticizes a whole class of avatars and compliments just one of my students, I take note."

Annev nodded, uncertain what to say or how this related to tomorrow's test. Before he could work up the courage to speak, Tosan finished his thought.

"Why have you not yet earned your avatar title?"

The question caught Annev by surprise. *Why haven't I earned my title?* It certainly wasn't for lack of trying. It was often because of Fyn's meddling, but Annev had competed in several Tests of Judgment where he had not crossed paths with the boy. So could he honestly say Fyn was his only obstacle? Was he even the largest?

"I don't know," Annev said at last.

They turned the next corner in the hall and continued to walk in silence.

"I don't like saying it," Tosan said after a long pause, "but Witmistress Kiara is right—you *are* talented enough to be an Avatar of Judgment. I've observed your training, and I get reports from the masters and ancients. You are a bright and capable student. I expected you to be among the first to earn their title, yet you've consistently fallen short. It's an observation that vexes me, particularly when others bring it to my attention."

"I'm sorry, Elder Tosan." And Annev was surprised to find he meant it. "I will try harder."

"No," Tosan said, "lack of effort is not the root of this problem." Tosan lifted the Speur Dún manuscript from the stack of books he carried and shook it. "*He* is holding you back."

"Sodar?" Annev asked, confused. Tosan nodded, to Annev's continued confusion: whatever his frustrations with the priest, Annev didn't believe the old man was preventing him from becoming an avatar. "No," Annev objected. "Sodar *wants* me to pass the Test of Judgment. He helps me train every day. All the time."

Tosan scoffed. "I'm certain he does, but he is training you to replace him as a *priest*—not to fulfill your role as an avatar, much less to serve as a master or an ancient." Tosan rifled through the parchment in his hands, examining the pictographs contained there. "Do you deny he is sharing ideas with you? Ideas that may hold you back or make you question your training?"

Annev considered it, trying to be honest with himself as much as the headmaster, and his answer was less certain; Sodar's ideology definitely clashed with the masters and ancients—there was never any question of that—but he'd never before thought Sodar might want Annev to fail his avatar test. The priest had plans for him, after all—secret plans that he shared with Arnor but would not reveal to Annev—and it seemed unlikely those plans involved Annev dashing off on dangerous missions for the Academy. In fact, Arnor's conversation with Sodar revealed the opposite: one day, soon, Sodar might return to his brothers in Quiri, and when he did, he would try to take Annev with him.

"Sodar shares a lot with me," Annev said, choosing his words carefully, "but not everything. He supports me in becoming an avatar but …"

"… but he views you as his deacon and would prefer you became the next village priest." Annev nodded, unsure what else to say. Tosan sighed. "We had a man like that once—Master Flint. He wanted to leave the Academy and join the priesthood. In the end he became Master of Sorrows—and his duties became infinitely more complicated."

"Master of Sorrows?"

"Yes. An old title reserved for the Master of Religion, which became defunct when Sodar became village priest. From the records I read, he reminds me of Sodar. A good man, I suppose, but with skewed loyalties."

"Skewed how?"

Tosan scoffed as if the answer were obvious. "Brother Sodar—like Master Flint before him—thinks he can serve the people of Chaenbalu as their spiritual mentor, that by listening to them recount their sins—their *sorrows*—he can counsel them to lead better lives. But tell me. Should the people of Chaenbalu be more frightened by the evil in themselves, or the evil that lurks outside the village?"

Annev's mind flashed to the Wand of Healing from Dorstal's classroom.

He recalled his desire to drain the man's lifeblood. To splatter Fyn's brains across the walls.

"I think people should fear their own destruction … in whatever form it chooses."

Tosan smiled. "A clever answer—and I admit there is some advantage to knowing what lurks in the hearts of our villagers. But this dual-minded approach is not helping you become an avatar."

"You feel my duties at the chapel have distracted me?"

"No, I think *Sodar* is distracting you."

"But he's been nothing but encouraging," Annev said again.

"Yes," Tosan agreed, "but the behaviors he encourages are not conducive to your success." When it was clear Annev did not see the correlation, Tosan slowed his pace, stopped, and turned to face Annev.

"You helped one of your classmates pass a test this afternoon. The boy was paralyzed, so you slipped him two of your own medallions and hid him so no one else could take them." Tosan tilted his head, scrutinizing Annev's face. "Is that right?"

Annev was almost alarmed by how much Tosan knew.

"Yes, Elder Tosan."

"Did your friend deserve to pass that test? Are his skills so superior to your classmates that he should be exempt from the challenge?"

Annev hung his head. "No."

"And my daughter?"

Annev looked up, his stomach churning at the possibility that Tosan had seen him search Myjun in the shadows of the nave. He met Tosan's eyes, searching for an answer.

"Myjun deserved to pass that test," he said at last. "She's very competent."

Tosan studied him for a long moment. "So why did you aid your highly competent adversary?"

Annev didn't think it appropriate to say he had helped the headmaster's daughter because he loved her. Though, as Annev thought back, he realized that really *wasn't* why he had helped her; the truth was, when he had left the badges, he hadn't known it was Myjun under that mask. He'd had possessed no ulterior motives; he was just trying to be kind.

"I guess … I didn't want to be the cause of another student's failure," Annev said, realizing that was the truth. Tosan raised an eyebrow, doubtful. "I'd already passed the test," Annev continued, "so I didn't think it was fair for another student to—"

"Fair?"

"Hmm?"

"You didn't think it was fair," Tosan repeated. Annev nodded and the headmaster huffed. "Then you're a fool twice over." Before Annev could respond, the ancient continued down the hall. Annev had to jog to catch him.

"Wait," Annev said. "Why a fool?"

Tosan snorted, not slowing his pace. "You aided Myjun because you care for her, just as you aided that other boy because he's your friend. If you claim it was some skewed sense of morality, then you're either a liar— and a fool for thinking I'd believe you—or Sodar has poisoned you more than I thought." He whirled, stopping in place once again, and Annev had to throw himself against the wall to avoid running into the man.

"So which is it?" Tosan said, glaring at him. "Are you a lying fool … or are you stupid?"

Rhetorical or not, Annev didn't have an answer for that—he didn't see how kindness could be stupid, and he wouldn't apologize for it. He was about to say as much, when Tosan spoke again.

"You insulted her, you know."

Annev froze, his certainty at having done the right thing suddenly shattering. He recalled Myjun's words to him in front of the Academy: she said she'd been *happy* when Annev had let her keep her badges—that it had been her plan all along—but what if she was just trying to spare his feelings, or her own? What if Tosan was right, and he had actually offended Myjun by attempting to aid her. The idea turned him cold.

"I made her look weak. Like Titus."

Tosan nodded, his face a mask. "Now tell me again that Sodar is *not* holding you back. That his principles have not kept you from earning your avatar title."

Annev studied the weave of the gray-blue runner beneath their feet. He thought back on all the Tests of Judgment he had competed in, especially those times he had come close but still lost. He remembered when the students had first fought each other in an infamous scrum. Annev had tried to help Therin fight Fyn, only he had surprised the scrawny boy with his aid and they had become entangled. He'd helped Titus up an icy platform as Kellor bowled into them and knocked them both over the edge. Then there'd been the time the testing arena and its underground tunnels were filled with water and the acolytes were tasked with swimming through the tunnels to earn their title. Annev had done well where most hadn't, yet instead of continuing to claim the title, he had backtracked—twice—to tell others where to find air pockets. He'd lost precious minutes in doing so, and the second time Kenton had used the opportunity to swim ahead and win his own title.

"I've been too busy helping people," Annev said slowly. "Like Titus and Therin."

"And Kenton," Tosan added. Annev looked up in surprise and the headmaster nodded. "I've seen little pacts like yours before. Tell me, though. Has aiding your friends ever helped you? Kenton used you to earn his title. Therin betrayed you today in the nave, and Titus does not even want to become an avatar." He paused, seeing his words had struck home. "But kindness towards your classmates is just one facet to the core problem."

"Sodar," Annev said, seeing where the ancient was leading.

"*Sodar*. The priest's influence cannot be understated. Like him, you have a history of challenging the traditions of the Academy—of resisting your teachers and the principles we are trying to instill in you. Just this morning you questioned if magic is inherently evil, yes?"

Annev nodded, still disturbed by how much Tosan knew about his daily life.

"You say you want to be an avatar," Tosan continued, "and you possess the requisite skills to become one, but you fight against the nature of what it *means* to be an avatar." He laid a hand on Annev's shoulder, making eye contact. "I used to wonder why you sabotaged yourself so often ... but now I know."

"Sodar," Annev whispered, his breath catching in his throat as he recognized the truth.

Tosan nodded. "This evening's Regaleus sermon reinforced my

opinion and prompted me to speak with you. The man's teachings are subversive—appropriate, perhaps, for a deacon or a mindless farmer, but destructive to the Academy and its mission. You claim the priest openly supports you becoming an avatar, but I see how he subtly poisons you against your own interests—and you don't even realize it."

Annev turned from Tosan's gaze, unable to bear its weight. The headmaster's logic was twisted, yet there was some truth to it. Sodar *had* been undermining the Academy's teachings—and in ways less subtle than Tosan was suggesting—but had that really translated into Annev subconsciously sabotaging his own efforts to advance within the Academy?

His stomach churned. He didn't want to betray Titus and Therin tomorrow, but first Witwoman Kiara and now Tosan were encouraging exactly that. Worse, Annev found himself drawn in by the headmaster's logic; he didn't want to hurt his friends, but they *had* all hurt his chances of becoming an avatar. At the same time, Sodar probably did not mean for Annev to fail his Test of Judgment, but the influence of his ethos may have led Annev to do exactly that. The thought made Annev resentful, and when he considered how secretive the priest remained—even after Annev had confronted him and exposed his lies—he felt angry and confused; he no longer understood Sodar or his motives, and the weight of Tosan's observations added to that burden.

"Think on it," the Eldest of Ancients said, his tone implying the conversation was at an end. Annev looked around, realizing only then that they had stopped a dozen feet from the headmaster's chambers. Tosan moved toward his door and the boy slowly followed.

"Consider your priorities as you approach tomorrow's test, Acolyte Ainnevog. If your desire is to become an avatar, you must place that goal above all else. There can only be one victor in the Test of Judgment. That means allowing your friends to fail—or succeed—on their own merits, even if you could otherwise save them."

They stopped in front of the ancient's door and Tosan took the lamp from him.

"One last thing," the headmaster said, the shadows dancing across his face. "Do not take my silence as tacit approval of your courting my daughter. Myjun is strong-willed, and I will not deny her what she desires, but neither do I approve of her fascination with you. It is no doubt prompted by your defiance and the novelty of your ancillary role at the chapel—but neither of those things will bring you closer to my daughter. If you are determined to continue this … infantile courtship … you must align yourself with the Academy's values. Otherwise you *will* become a steward, and Myjun will always be beyond your reach." He paused, allowing the silence to emphasize his point. "Do you understand?"

Annev stared at the headmaster, shaken by their conversation and pierced by the truth of his situation; the stakes for tomorrow's test could not be higher.

"I understand, Elder Tosan."

Tosan nodded. "Sleep well, Acolyte Ainnevog."

He closed the door, leaving Annev in darkness.

CHAPTER TWENTY-FIVE

Annev awoke with a start, his hands reaching for something. His hair was damp with sweat and his chest heaved, but he was alive and whole.

What was that? Where am I?

Annev blinked, eyes adjusting to the darkness as his mind wrestled with his disorientation. He was in his bedroom, the faint glow of starlight leaking through the tiny cracks in his chamber walls. As he lay on his pallet, breathing beginning to calm, he felt beneath the prickly straw mattress for the crimson glove Myjun had given him, safely tucked away. His fingers traced the stitching of the phoenix. Annev felt a lump inside the garment and reached inside for the promise ring he had also hidden. He swallowed hard, fighting the lump in his throat as his fingers toyed with the ring.

Why do I feel so anxious? Why are my hands trembling?

And then he recalled his nightmare. The vision had been so terrible—filled with shadows and darkness, blood and stones …

But the details were already fading, and when he fought to remember what had frightened him so badly, he could only recall the barest details: a stone table and a golden mask; red lips and green eyes.

Myjun? Annev wondered. *Was I dreaming of her?* He clutched the phoenix glove in his fist and thought harder, but the vision had fled, replaced by memories of the previous day which were just as uncomfortable.

As specious as Ancient Tosan's arguments had been, Annev had to concede the Eldest of Ancients had made some valid points, which had circled his mind on his walk back to the chapel—a journey made all the more difficult as Tosan had taken back his lamp and left Annev in the pitch darkness of the Academy's unlit halls.

To his relief, when Annev had arrived home he found Sodar already in bed. Unable to sleep, Annev lit a candle and wandered back into the chapel. With barely a thought as to what he was doing, he began sweeping, cleaning the room and preparing it for the morning. When he'd finished, he was still wrestling with his emotions, so he'd given up and gone to bed, hoping sleep would absolve him of his worries. The nightmare proved how foolish that hope had been, and Annev rose again, this time gathering his water skins to trek back to the village in the moonlight.

When Annev reached the well, he kicked the hand crank and listened to the bucket splash below. He slowly cranked it back up, and as the bucket rose from the depths, he tried to get to the heart of his sleepless turmoil: he resented Sodar for lying to him and for refusing to speak about his parents; he was angry that Tosan blamed Sodar for his failure to pass the Test of Judgment; he was upset with himself for thinking Tosan might be right; and he felt guilty for planning to use his friends to pass tomorrow's test.

Annev returned to the chapel with full water skins and a heavy heart. He filled the clay jar in the kitchen and considered going to the Brake to gather firewood. He even took a step toward the shed but he stopped when a wave of anxiety crash over him.

The dream, he thought, catching glimpses of it again: a bloody table, a disembodied voice, black nightmarish hands pulling him down into the stones … It terrified him, yet he tried to latch onto the threads of it, weaving them into something coherent he could make sense of. Instead, exhaustion overcame him and he retreated back to bed, cold and tired and with a mind full of nightmares, of Myjun, of Tosan's warnings, and of tomorrow's Test of Judgment.

Not tomorrow, he realized with growing anxiety. *Today.*

***

He woke again a few hours later, calmly stood, went to his clothes chest, and began dressing. The day had just begun to dawn, so there was no need to rush. He stopped after donning his small clothes then walked into the kitchen.

It seemed Sodar was still asleep, so Annev silently gathered a small bowl, a bar of soap, and a damp rag. He returned to his room for a cold sponge bath then finished dressing, pulling on Myjun's phoenix glove last of all. It wouldn't hide his prosthetic from any magic scrying devices, but it felt odd not having something to cover his left hand and forearm. Seeing the stitches Myjun had so carefully made reminded him what he was fighting for today.

When Annev reentered the kitchen, he saw a fire had been lit in the hearth. A bowl of soup and a cup of tea also sat on the table. Sodar stood beside them. He nodded at Annev, gesturing him to sit.

"I saw you'd risen early to do your chores and so I thought you'd want an early breakfast."

Annev glanced at the steaming bowl and mug. "Magic?"

Sodar shrugged. "Can't conjure something from nothing, but I may have had a little help warming the food and starting the fire."

Annev snorted. "So long as it's not some moldy bacon from that sack of yours."

Sodar smiled, and some of the tension seemed to go out of him. "I can always pull some out if you'd like. I'm sure it's still warm—and fresh."

Annev shook his head. "You said I couldn't have it unless I pulled it from the sack myself."

"I suspect you now could, if you wanted to. You've already mastered Mercy's magic. The bag should be no challenge."

Annev had no answer for that—not after his magical display yesterday afternoon—so he simply nodded and sat at the table. As Sodar turned to get his own bowl, Annev bowed his head and said a silent prayer, invoking Odar's will and a blessing on both the food and his performance at the Test of Judgment. He ate quickly, not knowing what to say, and had already finished when Sodar set his own bowl and cup on the table.

Annev stood, gathering his dishes and glancing at Sodar. When he made eye contact, he noticed the tension had returned to the old man's shoulders. Annev swallowed, the guilt in his gut rising to his throat.

"Thank you for breakfast."

"You're welcome," Sodar said, his tone conveying more than mere words.

On another day, in a previous time, Annev would have embraced the man, Sodar would have wished him luck, and some good-natured ribbing would have followed his well-wishes.

But it was different now. They both sensed it, and Annev wasn't sure there was any way to fix it. Neither of them had the heart to joke about the forthcoming Test. Not now, with this wedge between them and so much still unspoken. Not with this being Annev's last chance to earn his title.

"Good luck."

Annev nodded. He set his dishes by the sink, thinking to leave them for the priest, then changed his mind. He washed the cup, spoon, and bowl with Sodar's eyes on his back. When he was finished, Sodar was still watching him. Annev turned to go.

"Oh!" Sodar called. "One more thing."

Annev turned and the priest threw a black glove to him. He caught it, and found it looked much like his old Glove of Illusion, save that this one was a patchwork of worn scraps and rough stitches.

"Pieced it together from your old gloves," Sodar said. "I'd kept the pieces for the memories more than anything else, and now they're serving their original purpose again."

Annev stared at the glove, his eyes growing misty at the priest's gift. He tried to voice his thanks, but the words caught in his throat.

And then Sodar was embracing him. Annev wasn't sure who had closed the distance, but he hugged the man tightly, whispering his gratitude.

Sodar's voice was tight with emotion too. "Don't go losing this one. There won't be any more, and you can't live at the Academy with that hand uncovered." The man smiled, his face shining with tears, and Annev realized he'd been a fool.

Tosan's logic had been so persuasive—Annev couldn't deny that Sodar's ideology *had* cost him his title in previous competitions—but there was something more, that Tosan did not want Annev to see: Sodar believed in Annev, and he did not want him to fail. Rather, Sodar was the one person who believed Annev could pass the Test of Judgment without compromising his morals. Annev wasn't sure he believed that himself, but the priest's faith in Annev let him rekindle that ember of hope.

"Sodar ..." Annev began, knowing he had to ask.

"Yes?"

"Do you want me to become an avatar?"

There. He'd said it, and there was no way of taking it back. He watched for Sodar's reaction, trying to divine the man's thoughts, but his mentor betrayed none of them.

"I want you to be happy," he said slowly, "which means defining yourself by more than a title or a uniform. Words like "avatar" and "priest" are too small for you—and your heart is too big for them. I don't believe you'll be happy in either role because you're greater than the sum of their parts."

"So ... you don't want me to pass the test?"

Sodar's eyes softened, his expression tinged with sadness as he saw Annev did not understand. "You've *already* passed the test—you've passed it a thousand times, and I expect you'll pass it again today. Earning a title from the Academy?" Sodar shrugged. "It's immaterial. I know you *can* do it—and it would be satisfying if you achieved what you've sought for so long—but it's not going to bring you joy. That comes from in here." He tapped Annev's breast. "Do you understand?"

Annev was not sure he did, but he had the answer he needed. Sodar's faith in him had sparked a different kind of flame. After his tormented night, he felt the hope of something fresh—a certainty that he didn't have to choose between Sodar's chapel and Tosan's Academy but could combine them. He didn't quite understand it, but he fanned the flame nonetheless, and he felt the fire growing in his chest.

Annev *would* pass today's test—and he would do it on his own terms. He doubted that's what Sodar intended, but Annev knew he had to try. He wouldn't let the ideologies of either man dictate his choices in the arena: whatever happened, he would follow his heart and accept the consequences.

Sodar squeezed Annev again then released him, wiping his eyes as he pushed Annev toward the door.

"Go. Tomorrow robs us of our present joys, so savor today—and give them hell."

CHAPTER TWENTY-SIX

Annev climbed the last step leading to the second floor of the Academy just as Master Edra turned the corner and entered the same hall. He gave Annev a bleary-eyed nod as they approached one another, stopping in front of the dormitories belonging to Annev's classmates.

"Did you do your weapons training like I asked?"

"Yes, Master Edra. Sodar and I sparred last night, just before Regaleus services."

"Good," he said, wincing slightly, "then you've earned this." He reached under his tunic for the iron key, pulled the loop of leather over his head, and placed it around Annev's neck.

Annev blinked. He'd almost forgotten his victory in the nave, not to mention the promised reward. He fumbled at the key, wondering what advantage it might grant him.

"Don't bother asking what it's for," Edra said, seeming to anticipate the question. "I was merely instructed to give it to yesterday's winner."

Annev stared at the iron key, turning it over in his hands. The teeth were small, widely spaced, and uncomplicated. It was the key for a small lock, nothing grand or complex. How could such a simple thing grant any student an advantage, least of all Annev who could pick all but the most complicated locks? He let go the leather thong and slipped the key under his tunic, still puzzling over the riddle.

"You're a smart boy. No doubt you'll figure it out."

"Thank you, Master Edra."

Edra shrugged. "You earned it. No need for thanks." He was about to say more but then the door to the boys' dormitory creaked open and Chedwick's stocky frame peered out.

"Told you I heard voices!" he shouted to the boys inside. "Edra's here to collect us." The door swung wide and boys began pouring out of the room.

Edra's mouth snapped shut and he nodded once to Annev, concluding their conversation. The master stepped back, allowing the students to fill the space.

Titus came out with the first trickle of boys and immediately spied Annev. He wrapped his friend in a fierce hug.

"You're early!" Titus said, releasing him.

"Earlier than normal," Annev said. He looked around. "Where's Therin?"

Titus gestured at the warren of bedchambers behind him. "Getting dressed. Want to come in and wait for him?" Annev shook his head. "He's sorry, you know. About yesterday. He felt bad about stealing your badges."

"*He* felt bad?"

Titus shrugged. "You know Therin. He doesn't think until it's too late, and he feels bad after. It wasn't planned."

Annev wasn't so sure, but his own plans for the Test of Judgment required both Titus and Therin, and he knew his chances for success would be greatly diminished without them both. Even if Annev were still angry at Therin, he couldn't risk losing him now.

"Come on boys!" Edra bellowed, clutching his temple. "This is your last Test of Judgment. If you're late, you'll be disqualified!"

A dozen more boys emerged, a few still lacing their breeches or pulling on shoes and shirts. Annev saw Fyn and his cronies exit with the larger crowd, and he held his breath, momentarily forgetting Titus and their conversation.

Fyn laughed at a joke Jasper made and was mid-breath when he saw Annev standing in the hall. His laughter died in his throat as his eyes drifted to Annev's ungloved right hand.

Annev lifted his unbroken wrist and waved, demonstrating its wholeness.

Fyn sputtered, searching for words as the crowd carried him forward, his own friends pushing him to the front of the line. The bully glanced back once more, his hateful eyes searching Annev out.

"Therin's impulsive," Annev agreed, looking at Titus, "but he's my friend. Even when he's being selfish and stupid."

"Well, that's good to hear, I guess."

Annev turned to find Therin standing right behind him. He eyed the scrawny boy in his beige uniform.

"How much did you hear?"

Therin smiled. "Enough. I've been standing here buttoning my breeches."

The boy had been eavesdropping for most of the conversation. "So you were going to let Titus apologize for you?"

"Well … I wasn't going to interrupt—Titus is much better at that sort of thing."

"That's because Titus is actually humble."

"Ouch," Therin said, laying a hand over his heart. "Now that's unfair. He's got *reasons* to be humble."

"You know I'm right here," Titus said, waving a hand between his two companions.

Annev nodded at the blond boy, yet his focus remained on Therin. "Titus has his strengths and weaknesses, just like you do—just like I do—but he's also got my back. I can trust him. Can I say the same of you? Or Kenton or any of the other students?"

Therin's smile faded. "I'm not like Kenton."

"It didn't feel that way yesterday. Felt the exact same, actually."

"Let's go!" Edra growled. "Last chance for you acolytes to prove yourselves." He began walking down the hall. The other boys followed at a brisk pace, yet Annev, Therin, and Titus hung back, instinctively joining at the back of the line. They had just started to walk when Therin spoke quietly.

"Yeah," he said, his head hanging low. "I guess I was a real prick yesterday."

"Yep."

Annev and Therin both turned, surprised to hear Titus voice his agreement. The smaller boy looked at them both, his cheeks turning red, yet he did not look away or slow his pace.

"You *were*," Titus whispered. "Stealing Annev's badges after we all agreed to help each other was mean. Something I'd expect from Fyn or Kenton." He paused, taking a breath. "But you're not them, Therin. I know we can trust you when it counts."

"Can you?" Therin said. Annev could see his instinct for self-deprecation warring with feelings of self-doubt and genuine anguish. "This right now—what we're walking towards—is our *last* Test of Judgment. Only one of us can get the title, and there will never be another chance." He shrugged. "You're my best friends, but I don't want to be a steward either." He looked at the floor, staring at the heels of the boys in front of him. "I was a jerk yesterday because I thought it would make things easier today."

Annev studied his skinny friend and realized they'd been struggling with the same dilemma. The Academy was trying to turn them against each other and Annev had nearly allowed it to happen; just a few hours ago, he had made that precise decision.

But now Annev had a new plan—his *own* plan—and as he considered the costs and possible outcomes, he felt his resolve strengthen. He laid a hand on his friend's shoulder and squeezed. The boy looked up.

"I don't want to fight with you, Therin. I want us to work together, like we always do."

"Why?" Therin asked, suspicious. "They'll never let more than one of us pass the test."

"Not if we do it their way. But if we do it our way? Maybe."

"Our way?"

Annev nodded. "We work as a team, like the witgirls yesterday. Fight together. Win together. If we each pull our own weight and finish as a team, maybe we can force the ancients to give all three of us avatar titles."

Therin gave a low whistle.

"So bollocks to Tosan and his rules?"

"Basically."

Therin laughed. "Count me in for that. We'll probably all lose, but I didn't think I'd win anyway—not with Fyn and his gang against us. And if there's a chance we can all become avatars while tweaking Tosan's nose … that's the best offer any of us are likely to get. What do you think, Titus?" He'd been quiet for most of the walk.

"I wasn't going to compete for myself today—I just wanted you or Annev to win—but if there's a chance we can all advance together, then yeah. That'd be great."

Annev nodded, satisfied. "Great. Then I have a plan." The three boys huddled close, whispering as their reap descended the last set of stairs.

A minute later, Edra halted at the end of the long subterranean hall that led to the arena's imposing stone doors. Leaning against the wall outside the entrance was a tall man, lean-faced with a thin mustache and artfully coiffed brown hair. Like Edra, he wore a red tunic, a pair of soft black boots, and sturdy black leggings. The man smiled, stood straight, and greeted Edra with a firm handshake and keen eyes.

"Master Edra! Punctual and punctilious—as always."

"I don't know what that means"—Edra grumbled, sidling up to the other master—"nor do I care." He looked out over the crowd of boys, most of whom were still chatting with each other. The students' voices echoed down the long hall until Edra yelled.

"QUIET!"

The chattering cut off, and even at the back of the line, Annev and his friends ended their whispered discussion. Silence filled the chamber, and when the masters spoke again, Annev could hear every word.

The Master of Lies placed a slender middle finger to his ear drum and shook his head. "I hope that wasn't aimed at me," he drawled. "Punctual means you're *on time*, Edra. It's a compliment. And punctilious—"

"Not today, Ather. Fancy words don't impress me."

Ather's eyes gleamed as his gaze danced over the assembled boys. "Come now, Master Edra, these young minds need role models—good ones." He tapped the Master of Arms on the chest. "You're not so bad—a bit grumpy, perhaps, but dependable. Sturdy. Something for our boys to aspire to, as a *master* avatar." He waved his hand with a flourish.

Edra grimaced. "Enough. My head feels like it's stuffed with wool."

Ather hummed thoughtfully to himself, roaming down the hall as he moved with an energy that refused to be contained. "Too much honey wine last night, if I don't miss my guess." He reached the end of the line, smiled at the acolytes, then winked. "You need to pace yourself during the festival, boys," he hollered, "or you'll never make it to the third night of Regaleus!"

Edra scowled in Ather's direction then wandered down the hall to rejoin him. "It's that damn Duvarek," he said, lowering his voice. "Made me start drinking early yesterday since he had to go on a retrieval mission."

"And how is our dear Master of Shadows?" Ather pirouetted around Edra for the pure pleasure of it.

"I'm surprised Dove could walk out of here," Edra said, ignoring his colleague's antics. "If I drank half as much as that man, my liver would revolt."

"And yet the ancients choose to send him instead of me," Ather said, his feet still tapping in front of him. "If I didn't know better, I'd say they had favorites."

"You really want to know why?" Annev inched closer, interested in Edra's reply. "It's because you pack half your wardrobe every time—and you'll take a week if you take a day. It's inefficient, Ather. Been that way ever since you were an acolyte. No challenge too great so long as you could change your outfit twice."

Ather suddenly stood still. "That's unkind, Edra. A Master of Lies needs time to prepare himself and his mark. Silver must be spent. Confidences must be won. You can't just smash-and-grab and expect results—no offense intended, of course."

Edra grunted, barely registering the jab.

"Preparation is not always a bad thing," Ather continued, "Some things take a fortnight to do right."

Edra shrugged. "You asked and I answered. Duvarek is fast, and he's good. Doesn't waste time when he's out. No loose threads. No witnesses."

"Isn't that how *you* operate? And yet you're sent out even less often than I am."

"I wager that I care a good deal less too." Edra grinned. "Anyway, I usually leave a mess behind, because if the Academy's sent me it means they want to send a message. They send you for information or manipulation. If they want the damn *artifact*, though, they send Dove."

A metal gong sounded deep within the bowels of the Academy, ending their conversation and making the boys shuffle with nerves. As the sound of the gong faded, the arena's huge stone doors swung open, swiveling on a metal track of iron and oil. Once the doors stopped, Ather led the line of young men into the great hall.

As Annev approached the entrance to the testing arena, the steady hum of ratcheting metal, whirring gears, and spinning cogs filled his ears. It wasn't until he entered the hall, though, that he saw the source of the cacophony was hidden behind a tall wooden barrier just a few yards beyond the main door.

The last of the acolytes entered the chamber. "Good luck, boys," the master rumbled as Annev and his friends passed. "Hopefully I'll see one of you at the end."

Annev felt Edra's gaze rest on him as he spoke. He glanced at his friends and saw they had noticed it too. Sensing their doubt, he shook his head.

"You'll see all three of us, Master Edra."

The Master of Arms shook his head and closed the doors behind them.

***

Ahead, Ather had reached the wooden wall and turned right, leading the students toward a staircase halfway along the great barrier. As the acolytes caught up with their classmates, Annev looked up at the thirty-foot wall hiding the testing grounds from view, then further up to the five glass spheres illuminating the great arena; unlike torches, these luminous spheres never wavered and were among the scant dozen magic treasures the ancients had deemed acceptable for public use.

As Annev's gaze traveled back down the length of the wall, he caught his foot and stumbled into Therin, who in turn knocked over Titus.

"Sorry!" Annev apologized, helping his blond friend to his feet. He glanced back and saw he had tripped on the inset ring of a small trapdoor. He kicked the lock in irritation, and they hurried up the tall wooden staircase after their classmates.

The students climbed in silence, winding their way back and forth until the top of the wooden wall came into view. When they could almost see beyond the top of the barricade, the stairs turned and opened onto a narrow observation deck. Ather directed them towards the back, instructing them to turn away from the area and keep their eyes on Elder Tosan.

Although Ather's body obscured the view, Annev stepped out of line and glimpsed what lay beyond the precipice: in the bright glow of the light-orbs, he saw a dozen swinging pendulums, a maze of crisscrossing wooden beams, and something at the center of the maze that looked like a churning stone mill. A tall tower stood above it, and a long narrow walkway extended from the center, jutting out into empty space.

Then Ather was there—blocking Annev's view.

"Get. Into. The line," Ather hissed.

Annev stepped back and hurried to join his friends.

"You saw it?" Therin whispered.

"Shhh," Annev whispered back, though he nodded slightly.

Ahead of them, Tosan stepped atop a sturdy wooden box at the back of platform. The Eldest of Ancients surveyed the group, saw Annev, and rolled his eyes when he saw Titus and Therin standing beside him. The silence elongated as the students stood with their eyes fixed on Tosan and their backs facing the unknown dangers beyond the platform's edge.

"Each of you was an orphan, saved and brought here by the witwomen," the headmaster said, beginning his Testing Day monologue. "Nobody else wanted you. Nobody would have you, except us. The ancients have raised you. Fed you. Prepared you, mentally and spiritually, for the work you were chosen to accomplish." Tosan beckoned Ather forward and the Master of Lies took his place beside the Eldest of Ancients.

"The master avatars have prepared the way for you," Tosan said, laying his hand on Ather's shoulder. "They have instructed you in the physical arts of the avatar, and someday the greatest among you will take their places." Ather eyed each boy in turn as Tosan lifted his hand and held one finger in the air.

"This is your final chance to prove your worth as an avatar. This last Test of Judgment will determine who among you has ultimately earned that title … and who has not." The ancient fixed his glare on Annev,

Therin, and Titus. "You came to us as Acolytes of Faith. After today, many of you will become Stewards of the Academy—but perhaps there remains one more among you who is worthy to become an Avatar of Judgment."

Ather stepped in front of the makeshift podium, struck a dramatic pose, and gestured to the testing grounds beyond the curtain wall.

"The arena contains many paths," Ather said, his tone rich and resonant, "but only *one* leads to victory. To find it, you must descend and tread where you have gone before. Only then will you find the door that leads forward—to Master Edra and the final test. Everything else is a distraction. Find the door, and you will find the path." Ather paused, to add drama. "Brinden, Fyunai, Jasper, Kenton, Kellor, and Janson. Please step forward."

The six avatars stepped out of line. As they did, Kellor good-naturedly rubbed the top of Jasper's bald head, and Brinden snorted with amusement. Kenton remained aloof, yet Fyn took that moment to glance back at Annev and grin; he knew what was coming, and he wanted Annev to see it.

"These six avatars have already passed the Test of Judgment," Ather continued, "and having proven their skill in combat once again, they have been awarded sixty additional seconds to observe today's test before embarking on it. That advantage will begin at the first gong. At the second gong, the rest of you may face the arena. Anyone caught cheating will be thrown from the platform." The Master of Lies made certain he had Annev's attention when he said this, and for a moment Annev thought Ather might retroactively punish him. "You will have sixty seconds to view the arena and begin the test," Ather repeated. "The gong will sound every ten seconds, and any students still on the observation platform after one minute will be *removed*." Ather tucked a loose lock of hair back to his quiff with a predatory smile.

"Good luck."

CHAPTER TWENTY-SEVEN

The master's final words echoed across the cavernous room just as the gong rang beneath the observation deck. Taking their cue, the six avatars at the front of class dashed forward, shoving the other students aside for an unobstructed view of the magically lit testing grounds.

Having deliberately stayed at the back, Annev found himself face-to-face with Fyn as the bully rushed headlong at him. Annev dodged away from the edge of the platform, and the larger boy passed on, cackling. With his back facing Fyn and the five other avatars, Annev's body stayed tense as he waited out the sixty seconds before he and the other students could begin their test. Ather paced before the row of boys, practically daring them to turn around, but no one did. Half a minute in, Annev heard Fyn and the others leave and then the platform went silent. Hearing nothing but the whirr and groan of cogs and gears, Annev assumed the six avatars had left to begin the test in earnest and he tensed further, waiting for the gong to sound a second time. His stomach began to churn.

The gong sounded and chaos erupted as Annev turned and grasped the full depth and breadth of the arena.

Large towers of scaffolding dotted the open space, several reaching as high as the observation platform. Most of the rest were of middling height, but a few squatted much lower. A nest of slanted beams, crisscrossing rafters, and hinged planks stretched between the towers, connecting their various tops, middles, and bottoms in one three-dimensional maze.

At the edge of the arena, the outer towers spidered out to touch the surrounding wooden wall.

As Annev studied the labyrinth of wood, wire, and metal, he saw the whole thing was connected by a series of moving cogs and gears. Even the interconnecting scaffolding was in motion, with planks moving at different speeds or in different directions; platforms rose ten or twelve feet before abruptly dropping, turning the whole arena into a giant puzzle of erratic, ever-shifting obstacles. Finding a course through it would be a challenge.

Gong.

Fifty seconds. The ground beneath the scaffolding was covered with a thick black substance. Annev couldn't guess what it was, so he focused on the maze itself, searching for the true path to the opposite end of the arena.

At the back of the vast room, Annev saw a tower with walls so steep its fifteen-foot top was well beyond the reach of any approaching from the ground. In addition to being completely flat, the top was also long and narrow, free of tar, and capped by a familiar wooden obstacle.

"The scissor field," Annev grumbled aloud.

The scissor field was a cradle of immense wooden beams that swung above the narrow pathway. The ends of the beams were capped with a mix of heavy blunted stones and wide ax blades, and the obstacle was a common fixture at the Tests of Judgment, appearing in almost half the tests administered by the ancients. Annev felt sick every time he saw it.

Gong.

Forty seconds. "I can't see!" a tiny voice wailed from the back of the pack.

Annev saw Titus trying—and failing—to elbow his way back to the crowded edge of the platform. A few boys had peeled away and were dropping down into the maze, but most students held their ground, awed by the complexity of this month's challenge.

Annev couldn't blame them—the Master of Engineering had outdone himself this time—but Annev was also relying on Titus's observational skills to help him to navigate the test.

Though it pained him to do it, he stepped away from his spot at the edge of the platform. The neighboring boys swooped in, closing the gap, but Annev paid them no mind. He pushed his way to Titus, spun the smaller boy around, and hoisted him onto his shoulders.

Gong.

Thirty seconds. "What can you see?" Annev asked.

"There's a lot more open space than usual."

"Right. They broke down the maze to build the holding-wall." Annev gestured. "They left the scissor field up, though."

"That's good. Therin can get us through it." Titus leaned forward "The doors are behind the scissor field, cut into the far back wall. Everything points in that direction."

Gong.

Twenty seconds. "Is that too obvious?"

"Maybe … though getting there will be quite a challenge, and Ather said it was on the opposite end of the arena."

"Do we follow the west wall there?"

That's what I thought," Therin said, popping up beside them. "It reaches all the way to—"

"The wall is no good!" Titus snapped, "a beam sweeps across it."

"So where then?"

"I think I see—"

"Be sure," Annev cautioned. "We're almost out of time."

The gong sounded yet again—*ten seconds*—and several boys jumped from the observation platform, disappearing from view. A number had the same thought as Therin, for they began making their way across the top of the western wall.

Titus slid from Annev's shoulders as Therin asked "Where to, Titmouse?"

"There's a rafter right beneath—"

Bong. Gong. Bong. Gong. Bong.

"Go!" Annev shouted over the din.

The remaining students began to scramble away. Some moved with purpose, while others looked wild and uncertain. Titus pushed Annev and Therin to the eastern corner of the platform and pointed to a small square of wood fifteen feet below them.

"It's rising!" Titus shouted above the din. "A few more seconds and we can jump down!"

Glong-glong-glong-glong-glong. BONG!

Time's up.

Ather stepped forward. The master casually cradled a quarterstaff and strolled over to the remaining mass of students huddled at the platform's edge. He looked one of the boys in the eye—a freckle-faced avatar named Alisander—and idly ran a thumb and forefinger over his mustache. Alisander smiled at the master, and he was still smiling when Ather pushed him off the ledge and sent him tumbling to the pitch-covered ground below.

A resounding *SMACK* echoed across the arena as he struck, though when Annev looked down he saw Alisander had only been dazed by the fall. The ginger-haired boy shook his head, planted his hands in the muck and struggled to right himself. Instead of rising, though, his arms sank solidly into the bog. The boy fought unsuccessfully to free himself.

"Wow," Titus murmured, one eye still on the rising platform.

Annev watched Ather topple two nearby boys off the ledge with a sweep of his quarterstaff and turned back.

"We have to jump *now*."

The small piece of scaffolding was six feet below the observation deck. Therin dropped down and the wooden platform bounced under the impact then slowly began to descend.

"Hurry!" Therin shouted. Ather was closer, knocking an acolyte one step away into the muck below.

Annev nudged Titus. "Go! Quick." Titus bent his legs and sprang out over the ledge. He landed with a soft thud and rolled to his feet.

"You're taking your own sweet time," Ather drawled in his ear. "Let me help."

Annev flung himself off the platform. For a moment, he thought he'd escaped Ather, but the butt of the master's staff caught him in the ribs and Annev found himself twisting in midair. He came down hard on his side, jarring the platform violently, and shaking the rickety elevator loose from whatever cog or crank had been raising and lowering it. The whole thing plummeted toward the muck and Annev braced himself, grabbing the platform's edge. The other two boys dropped to their knees and did the same. They lurched as the square of wood hit the viscous muck covering the arena floor, and then they were silent.

Annev breathed deep then felt the black ooze sucking at his fingers. He jerked his hands back from the platform's edge and stood, heart still racing.

"Quick, before we sink."

"That way!" Titus pointed at a platform just above Therin's head.

The three boys formed a human ladder, Titus climbed onto Annev's shoulders and Therin clambered up both boys, gaining the platform and then helping Titus do the same. Annev came last. He scooted to the edge of the sinking platform, found his balance, and took a flying leap. His chest thumped into the scaffolding and he scrabbled for a handhold as Titus and Therin grabbed him, halting his descent. With some effort, the two boys pulled him over the edge, scraping off a bit of skin in the process.

"You're bleeding," Titus said, pointing at Annev's chin.

"Keep going," Annev said, rising to his feet. "Which way?"

Titus took their bearings. They'd been the last into the arena, and an earlier group of boys had taken the same path, moving toward the eastern wall. The scissor field lay to the north, while Elder Tosan and Master Ather watched the competition from the south.

Annev watched the boys east of their position as they climbed, crawled, and hopped through the suspended obstacle course. Far to their west, two avatars had found a route to the top of the curtain wall, and Annev cursed as they sprinted across the top, their brown-robed figures fast approaching the scissor field. His anger faded, though, when he saw a multipronged beam swing across the top of the wooden barrier, as Titus had warned. The obstacle swept the first boy off the partition. The second tried to jump over it and one of the prongs caught him in the chest, tumbling him off the wall and into the muck.

"This way!" Titus shouted.

Annev and Therin followed Titus, dashing onto a long plank just as it rose to their level and then across a series of narrow interconnecting ramps suspended above the mire.

"I know the way to the scissor field," Titus said over his shoulder, "but we have to hurry before the room shifts too much."

The three acolytes ran down a long rafter then jumped onto a moving ramp that sloped up into the heart of the arena's interconnecting beams and platforms.

"Where are we heading?" Annev shouted over the din of grinding gears and creaking wood.

"The tall tower in the middle!" The boy pointed to a tower of scaffolding nestled in the center of the wooden web. Directly above it hung one of the glowing glass spheres that lit the arena. "There's a ramp from the top that leads to the scissor field."

Therin squinted. "I don't see it."

"It moved."

Therin and Annev both slowed, glancing at one another.

"What?" Titus asked, as they reached the top of the ramp. "We just have to be at the top when it comes back."

Therin looked to Annev, who thought back to his first glance at the arena.

"Lead the way."

The three boys hopped between several low platforms as they made their way toward the tower. Halfway to their destination, the platforms were replaced by a long series of poles suspended from pairs of parallel chains. Within seconds they were swinging from bar to bar in rapid succession, gradually climbing higher. Titus reached the tower first, and Annev watched as Therin swung to the final chain-bar. The lithe acolyte swung back and forth, building up momentum before launching himself toward a platform built into the tower's exposed scaffolding. Near the end of a graceful arc, Therin tucked his legs, tumbled into the structure, and sprang to his feet. He rushed back to the opening a moment later, his face flushed with excitement.

"Come on!" he shouted to Annev, panting for breath.

Annev rocked back and forth then launched himself onto Therin's previous perch, caught the last bar and used his momentum to wind up for a final leap. As he did, a dark figure appeared at the top of the tower, casting a long shadow down its length.

"Yes, do hurry up," the speaker called. "We're tired of waiting for you."

Five other figures joined the shadow at the edge of the tower, their individual forms becoming one dark mass. Annev squinted up and saw Jasper, Kellor, Janson, Brinden, and Kenton. At the heart of the group, with a smug look on his face, was Fyn.

CHAPTER TWENTY-EIGHT

Annev released his bar and tumbled into the tower just as the laughter died down.

"Hey, Annev!" Fyn hollered. "Kenton says if we threw you off this tower, that black stuff would keep you from breaking your legs. I say we test it, though. See if your legs heal as fast as your wrist."

Titus looked at Annev, a mixture of awe and fear stamped across his face. "Did you fight Fyn … outside of class?"

Annev shrugged.

Titus's mouth hung open. "But … you're not dead."

Fyn leaned menacingly over the top of the scaffold wall and caught a glimpse of Titus in the bowels of the tower.

"What about you? Want a flying lesson?"

Titus cringed and shrank deeper into the tower.

"Hey, Fyn!" Therin called back, his eyes searching for an obvious route to the top of the tower. "If Kenton's so sure no one will get hurt, you should chuck *him* over the edge!"

Fyn laughed. "Maybe I will, if I get bored waiting for you!" The other boys—except Kenton—joined in the laughter, but Fyn wasn't finished. "I want to see Annev first, though," he continued. "That cheeky bastard stole my red glove! Real fancy one with birds on it!"

Jasper and Kellor roared at this, and Annev heard the distinctive sound of Brinden snicker-snorting. Titus frowned.

"What's he talking about?"

"Nothing," Annev said, glad he'd chosen to wear Sodar's patchwork glove for the competition.

"So," Therin said, unafraid to ask the obvious. "What do we do now?"

Titus looked around then shook his head. "I figured there'd be some way to climb the tower. With them at the top, though …" Titus shrugged. "What should we do, Annev?"

Annev surveyed the innards of the scaffolding tower. Giving up wasn't an option.

"We've got to be clever if we want to win," Annev said, "so what do we know? It's three against six, and we have to get up there if we're to reach the scissor field. Or is there another way?"

Titus surveyed the field around them but ultimately shook his head.

Annev was silent, thinking. Magic light filtered between the thin cracks of the tower's planks, revealing the shadows of the boys above them. Annev stared intently at the ceiling, and then a smile spread across his face.

"What if we dropped the floor out from under them?"

Therin immediately liked the suggestion.

"How?"

Annev studied the ceiling and walls. "The masters reuse a lot of this wood each Testing Day. It's built to come apart easily. We could use that."

Therin nodded more vigorously. "Yeah. I'll take a look." He turned, jabbed his fingers into the gaps in the boards of the tower walls, and began climbing.

Annev watched the boy scale the wall, a second idea forming in his head. "Titus, can you show me where that platform disappeared to? If we can figure out when it comes back, maybe we can reach it from down here and avoid Fyn altogether."

Titus liked the idea and led Annev to an opening on the eastern side of the tower. The suspended bars they had used to reach to the tower were still swinging and a platform steadily rose and fell beyond them.

"Where was it?" Annev asked. "Do you see it now?"

Titus shook his head. "I think it's attached to that track down there."

Titus pointed at a wide metal track, raised just above the height of the black goo. "I didn't get a good look at it, but it's long."

"That doesn't help much."

"I mean it's *really* long. Even though it was on the opposite side of the tower, I could see it slanting out of the top. Then, when it started to move away, it flipped down and folded in half."

Annev pursed his lips and tried to recall the glimpse of the arena he had stolen before Ather had knocked him back to join the other boys. There had been *something* sticking out of the tower, but it hadn't come from the top. It had jutted from the middle, straight as a knife blade.

Annev smiled.

"I don't think we'll need to climb to the top," he said. "We might need to climb to the northern side to get to the ramp, but we should be able to board it before it reaches to the top."

"So we won't have to fight Fyn and the other avatars!" Titus was visibly relieved.

"We may, if they see us clinging to the side of the tower. We'll have to time it …"

Annev trailed off as he noticed the new figure standing on the viewing platform. In contrast to Ather's crimson tunic and Tosan's red and black robes, the young woman wore a dark green dress and her hair hung loose around her shoulders.

"Myjun," Annev whispered, suddenly oblivious of everything else around him.

She stood between Ather and Tosan, clearly searching for something or someone. When she glimpsed Annev, she brazenly waved to him then stopped, glancing at her father, but Tosan's attention was elsewhere.

Annev leaned out to return Myjun's wave.

She's watching the test, he thought, excited. Then his heart dropped into his stomach. *Of course she's watching. She wants to see if I finally earn my title …*

"Blood and bones," he swore.

"What?" Titus said, poking his head out of the tower. "What's wrong?"

"Nothing, I just …" Annev broke off again as he saw Myjun beckoning to him. Tosan noticed this time, though, and Myjun hid her intent by casually bringing her hand to her mouth, forcing a yawn.

What does she mean …?

"Annev! Hey!" Therin snapped his fingers in front of Annev's face.

Annev blinked, noticing that Therin had returned. He squinted at Myjun once more then forced himself to focus, letting the question go.

"Sorry. Got distracted."

"I'll say." Therin shook his head. "I found something."

"Us too!" Titus said. "Annev thinks we can get to the ramp without fighting Fyn and the others!" Therin had been smiling before, but after Titus described what Annev and he had discovered he was grinning from ear to ear.

"Fyn's in for a big surprise then." He pointed at the scaffolding floor twenty feet above his head. "You see that crack running down the middle? That's the line separating the two halves of the platform. The left side has linchpins to keep it from dropping down. It was built to collapse from the inside—just like Annev guessed."

Annev nodded, unsurprised. "Ancient Denithal probably created that black muck at the bottom of the arena, but Master Murlach's done everything else here. He's always been fond of traps. He built the scissor field. And the tumbler. And the twiddle-snap." He shook his head. "They should have named him Master of Traps."

"So what do we do?" Titus asked, looking up at the platform above their heads.

Therin laughed. "We pull the pins! While Fyn and his mates are standing on them."

"But … we don't need to fight them?"

"If we leave them behind, they'll just come after us. Leave no enemies behind, Titus."

Annev nodded, seeing the wisdom of Therin's suggestion; if they could cripple Fyn or Kenton—literally or figuratively—then they should, and Annev wouldn't feel guilty in the slightest.

"Therin's right. Titus, watch for the moving platform. Therin, we'll pull the pins on his signal. After that we'll have to get out of here fast and climb the northern exterior wall."

Titus nodded, keeping any dissenting thoughts to himself, and Annev and Therin began to scale the interior scaffolding. They climbed in silence, slowing as they neared the top. Through the cracks above his head, Annev could see a boy keeping lookout on each side of the tower. A fifth boy stood in the center of the platform, and the sixth was just off-center, closer to the northern face of the tower. This last boy paced back and forth, the planks beneath his feet creaking with each step.

"Where are they?" Jasper whined, directly above Annev's head.

The avatar who had been pacing stopped. "I don't know."

Annev smiled. That was Fyn.

"There's nowhere else to go," Fyn said. "They'll have to climb out."

"We can't wait here all day."

"We can if we have to. Look around. Do you see any other way to the scissor field?"

A long pause. "No."

"So no one can get there without going through us first," Fyn said. "Annev and his twits can wait as long as they want. The next group of students to reach the tower will throw them off anyway. We can sit back and watch. Got it?"

"Um … yes. But how are *we* supposed to get there?" Jasper persisted.

Fyn walked over to Jasper, placing himself between the avatar and the southern lookout. Annev looked over at Therin who excitedly held up three fingers. Three out of six on the hinged part of the platform was pretty good. It would even the odds at least, and maybe the boy straddling the divide would fall too. They could cripple Fyn and half his group in one blow.

"If you really want to go over there," Fyn said, his hushed voice just a few feet from Annev's head, "you could always walk …"

He shoved Jasper over the edge of the tower.

Annev's breath caught as he heard the avatar smack into the gooey arena floor. He struggled to keep silent as, above him, Fyn muttered "so annoying," and began pacing again. There was some shuffling above Annev's head, and the odd boy in the center of the tower moved to fill Jasper's vacancy.

Annev shook his head, disgusted. It was one thing to throw a competitor off the tower, but pushing a friend off? His stomach revolted at the thought … though he remembered feeling differently after his discussion with Tosan.

Annev reached up and grasped the pin next to his head, resolved. He looked at Therin, who did the same.

"Titus," Annev whispered, his voice barely audible. He looked down and saw the boy had just poked his head out of the opening in the eastern wall. "Titus!" Annev whispered more urgently. The smaller boy pulled himself back in and looked up at Annev.

"It's coming!" he whispered back, a little too loudly.

Annev swore as he heard more feet shuffling above his head. With barely a nod to Therin, Annev hauled hard on the linchpin supporting the southern side of the platform. Therin did the same, and the two-foot-long pieces of metal slid from the rafter above their heads. The hinged platform shrieked as half the ceiling swung downward and two boys dropped through the opening, plummeting twenty feet to the floor below. As the avatars fell, Annev caught a flash of Fyn leaping to the northern side, narrowly evading the trap.

Quick as a cat, Annev climbed down the interior tower wall and dodged past the two bodies lying at his feet: Kellor was unconscious at the bottom of the heap, his leg either dislocated or broken; Janson lay atop him, groaning and in no hurry to get up.

"I'm going to *kill* you, Ainnevog!" Fyn shouted from the opening above their heads, searching for a way down.

"Why does he only use my full name when he's threatening me?" Annev asked as he and Therin swung themselves out of the tower and began climbing.

"Why does he give *you* all the credit. I dropped half that platform."

Annev lifted his chin towards the top of the tower. "You're welcome to tell him that."

They'd pulled themselves up to Titus when a string of curses rained down from above. Annev looked up and saw Fyn, snarling and glaring at them, still looking for a way to reach them. A moment later Brinden and Kenton appeared at the avatar's side.

"Climb up here, you bastards, and I'll kick your skulls in!"

Therin laughed as he adjusted his grip on the wooden planks. "He makes that sound inviting, doesn't he?"

"He still thinks we have to climb up," Titus said, and nodded in Annev's direction. "But our ride is here."

Annev watched as the moving platform came within two feet from the side of the tower, almost level with them. As it continued to rise it also began to extend, the nearest end reaching for the tower as the far end stretched toward the scissor field, almost forty feet away.

"Be quick," Titus said as he prepared to jump. "It collapses in on itself a few seconds after it reaches the top of the tower."

"And we'll have Fyn right behind us," Annev said, not relishing the thought.

"There's an incentive to run faster!" Therin leaped onto the platform and sprinted away.

Annev rolled his eyes, adjusted his grip and prepared to jump. The platform had reached their height and was only a foot away.

"Brinden! Get down there and stop them!" Fyn yelled.

"Titus, go!" Annev urged, keeping an eye on the boys above.

The younger boy jumped onto the moving platform, steadied himself, then ran after Therin as the narrow ramp continued to rise, inching closer to the tower wall. With a sudden alarm, Annev saw that the platform—now level with his waist—would press itself flush against the side of tower.

Keos! Annev had waited too long. *It's going to cut me in half!*

He jumped, flinging his torso onto the ramp, and pulled his legs up behind him. Just as his feet cleared the gap, the ramp snapped into place against the tower wall—and Annev was up and running. He felt the thumps behind him as Fyn, Kenton, and Brinden leapt over the edge of the tower and gave chase.

We're doing it! Annev realized. *If we can just stay ahead, we might beat them!* The beams and platforms between him and the ground far below blurred together as he ran, the ramp beginning to click downward. Annev's pace quickened, aided by the ramp's steepening slope, but as it continued to dip, his elation suddenly morphed into fear: the ramp was dropping out from under him, exactly as Titus had warned.

Annev tore his eyes away from his feet and looked at the far end of the ramp. Therin had already reached the scissor field. A second later, Titus reached the end of the narrow platform, jumped the gap, and landed beside Therin.

Annev put his head down, sprinted for the end of the ramp, and flung himself into the abyss. He flew several feet through the air, just clearing the growing gap between the ramp and the ground, then skidded onto his knees between the other two boys. He spun to watch the avatars behind them.

Fyn was leading the other two avatars at a steady pace down the gang-plank, clearly unaware of the immediate danger. He bore a wolfish grin, fully expecting his quarry to run, yet confident he could corner Annev and the rest at the end of the floating platform.

That confidence was a mistake. Annev heard a series of loud *clicks* echo throughout the arena as the long platform detached from the scaf-folding tower and began to fold in half. Fyn's expression changed as the ramp dropped and he attempted to sprint the last five feet. He jumped as the platform fell away entirely, but did so with enough force that he cleared the gap and rolled to a stop in front of Annev, Titus, and Therin.

Brinden was too slow to react and watched as the scissor field passed beyond his reach. He cursed, dropping to his knees at the edge of the ramp, looking resigned to riding the thing down to the mire below.

Kenton refused to be beaten so easily. As Brinden fell to his knees and braced himself against the falling platform, the scar-faced avatar picked up speed and sprinted forward up onto Brinden's back, using his broad shoulders as a launchpad. Surprised by the sudden weight, Brinden in-stinctively rose, giving Kenton the extra boost he needed. Kenton's body slammed into the side of the tower, his arms and elbows just clearing the edge, and he heaved his dangling legs and torso up onto the safety of the higher ground with a defiant roar.

Back on the folding ramp, Brinden howled with anger as the ramp dropped away and he disappeared from view.

CHAPTER TWENTY-NINE

"Wow," Therin said as Kenton rose to his feet. "That was … wow."

Kenton ignored Therin's comment and Fyn's sprawled body, instead turning to look back the way he had come. Annev followed his gaze and saw the mechanical ramp had folded itself in half, proceeding along its circuitous track with Brinden nowhere in sight.

Then Annev realized Kenton wasn't looking down, toward his fallen comrade, but *up*—at the observation tower where Tosan, Ather, and Myjun watched the competition. Seeing he had their attention, Kenton waved awkwardly at the three observers.

Ather nodded curtly in response. Tosan and Myjun flatly ignored him.

"Hey," Therin whispered, backing up while Fyn and Kenton were distracted. "Let's go!"

The trio retreated to the entrance of the scissor field then stopped. Therin was already gazing at the gantlet of swinging metal and stone with a frown.

"We've never all gone through together," Titus said, echoing Annev's thoughts.

"We don't have a choice," Annev said. "Fyn and Kenton will pitch anyone who hesitates over the edge."

"It's fine," Therin said, studying the scissor field's swinging beams, "I think we can run three abreast. We just need to stick together."

"You sure?"

Therin glanced back at Fyn and Kenton who had begun to argue.

"We've always made it before," he said. "And I can find the new pattern if you keep them off me."

"I'll watch them," Titus offered. "Neither of them trusts the other to watch their back, so we have a few seconds." Titus turned to face their opponents while Therin studied the scissor field's pendulum-like arms, counting under his breath. Annev stood beside him, entranced by the pattern. The first of pendulum swung in front of the northern wall and marked the entrance to the grand gantlet, but the rest swung on a cradle that tunneled through the wall itself. The passageway was only just wide enough to accommodate the full height and breadth of the swinging shafts, leaving no space to climb over, around, or beneath the obstacles; the only way through the tunnel was straight through the fiendish gantlet of swinging beams.

The beams themselves came in various shapes and sizes—some were as thick as Annev's thigh, while others were wider than Titus's waist. Some were faced with large round boulders, but a few had been carved into rough oblong pieces shaped like a smith's hammer or a ram's head. The thinner beams all carried ax blades, each one a different size and shape, and covered by a thick piece of toughened rawhide—a necessary precaution, but one that spared no bruises.

None of the scissor field's appendages would kill an Academy student—holes had even been dug to allow injured students to fall into the muck beneath rather than be continually pummeled by the scissor field. All the same, the brutality of the machine made it clear that the Academy allowed no half measures when training their recruits. The scissor field had proven this by injuring several students and maiming one boy in their reap.

Samrel, Annev thought, trying not to remember the look on the boy's face after the stone struck him in the temple, or how Master Aog had calmly taken an ax to the boy's head after the accident.

"Dead weight," he had said dispassionately. "He'd have never recovered. Best to end it now."

"I've got it!" Therin said, pulling Annev back to the present. "On the count of three, run straight through to the arm with the pig's head on the end. We'll have to dodge a bit on the way, so don't go *too* fast, and don't go past the pig."

"Too fast?" Annev repeated, just as Titus said, "Wait. What are we dodging?"

Therin smiled. "You'll see."

Titus looked at Annev. "I'm not sure this is a good—"

"One!"

"Are we running *after* three or—"

"Two!"

"Run *on* three."

"Three!"

They ran beneath the arch of the scissor field's swinging scythes in unison. Therin kept the pace in the center, Annev and Titus to either side. As a group, they dashed in front of a stone maul, sidestepped a leather-bound ax head, and sprinted through a gap between three spinning scissor blades—then narrowly avoided being crushed by a block of granite carved in the shape of an anvil.

"Almost there!" Therin shouted, ducking beneath a wide beam—and then they were. The stone warthog swooped past directly in front of them and they stepped into its return path. Titus nervously eyed the warthog as it climbed toward the top of its arc.

"Now what?" Annev asked, pulse racing.

"You're going to run like Keos is kissing your britches."

"No stopping? No pausing?"

Therin shook his head. "If you stop, you'll get smashed."

"What if we run too fast?"

"Therin …" Titus said, watching the warthog descend.

"You can't run too fast," Therin answered without a hint of humor.

"Therin?" Titus repeated, the stone head swinging closer toward them.

"Get ready …"

"Therin!" Titus screamed as the warthog came streaking at them.

"NOW!" Therin shouted.

The three boys bolted down the corridor just as the stone warthog zipped behind them. Then an ax blade. Then a boulder. A stone fist thudded past. Annev picked up speed when he was clipped by a speeding dragon's head.

"Blood and bones, Therin!" Annev shouted, still sprinting. "Are you trying to *kill* us?"

"Fassssttttteeeerrrrr!" Therin yelled at the top of his lungs, and then suddenly "Slide, slide, slide!" as a sweeping beam dropped down ahead of them. He and Annev dropped and slid beneath it on their knees; a fraction later Titus rolled under it. They had just climbed back to their feet when Therin was screaming in their ears again.

"DODGE!"

With barely a thought, Annev and Titus went left while Therin moved right. They shimmied as close to the walls as they could without falling into the gutters as a pendulum swung straight for them, perpendicular to the rest; It was huge, carved to look like an anchor, and as it swung towards them, Annev realized they still weren't clear of the anchor-shaped battering ram.

"GET DOWN!" he shouted.

They scrambled into the trenches lining the passageway, careful not to fall through the gutters and into the morass below as the massive anchor flew past them, barely an inch above the ground. The anchor hovered at the end of its arc, almost touching the side-swinging beam they had passed moments before, then it fell toward them again.

"RUN!"

The three acolytes rolled out of the gutters and sprinted in a final mad dash for the end of the scissor field. They shot out the far end in a tangle and tumbled over one another, scrambling to get clear of the anchor's backswing.

"That ... was ..." Titus panted, trying to catch his breath.

"Awesome?" Therin said.

"New?" Annev suggested.

"Terrifying."

Annev glanced back the way they had come. When the anchor reached the height of its pitch, he caught the briefest glance of Fyn staring at them in horror from the opposite end of the scissor field. Beside him, a brooding Kenton rubbed the scarred side of his face.

CHAPTER THIRTY

While Therin and Titus caught their breath, Annev turned his attention to the chamber they were in: it was small, dimly lit by light from the adjoining room, and had been roughly hewn from the bedrock beneath the Academy. The walls were also slick with moisture and the air was damper. He felt disoriented. The room had never been like this before.

"They took down the walls," Titus said, finding the answer moments before Annev. "They've always had rooms built inside here, but now it's just bare rock."

Annev nodded. "Lots of surprises this time." He went deeper into the cave-like room, expecting to see a tunnel or a door at the opposite end of the chamber. He was not disappointed, spying three iron-banded oak doors.

Therin approached the middle door and tried its handle. "Locked," he announced.

Annev nodded, unsurprised. "Lockpicking test."

Therin cursed. "I hope you're wrong. Kenton and Fyn could come through the scissor field at any second." He jogged down to the third door, tried the handle, then ran back to the first. He swore again. "All locked."

"Maybe this will help."

Annev slipped the iron key from around his neck and tossed it to Therin, who caught it and began to laugh. "Edra's key!" He started testing it on the three locked doors.

"Be careful of traps!" Annev warned, though it didn't take long for Therin to reach the last door and realize the key was useless.

"It doesn't fit any of the locks," he complained. "What good is it?"

Annev shrugged. "Edra said it was some kind of puzzle, so I guess it makes sense that it won't unlock the doors. That'd be too easy." He took the key back and they all pulled out their lock picking tools.

"Take a door each and be careful of traps."

The other boys nodded, and Therin plopped down in front of his door. Titus jogged over to the first and Annev took the one in the middle. It took seconds for him to click the last tumbler into place and the others had been as quick. He eased his door open, sensed resistance on the other side, and stopped. He probed the edge of the door, sliding his fingers up and down until he located a taut string connected to an unseen trap just above the door frame. He took a tiny pair of shears from his pocket, snipped the cord, and stepped back.

As the door swung open, Annev saw the severed string, its opposite end tied to a trough filled with bubbling purple liquid.

"Denithal and Murlach must be working together," Annev said as Therin and Titus approached. "There's a trap above the door that would drop a bucket of … something on my head."

"No traps behind my door," Titus said.

"Mine either." Therin was about to say more when they heard shouts from the scissor field. Time was running out.

"Only your door was trapped," Therin said. "What kind of locks did you pick? Mine was a wafer lock."

"Pin tumbler," Titus said, glancing over his shoulder. "Double-action lever tumbler," Annev said. "You both had simple locks with no traps. I had the hardest lock and a trap. We take the middle door."

Therin pumped the air with his fist. "Yes! Let's go!"

"Too late," Titus said.

Annev turned just as Kenton fell into the chamber. The dark-haired boy rose to his knees and clutched his hip, trying to catch his breath.

"You hurt, Kenton?" Annev asked.

The boy huffed. "What do you care?"

"You can compete and still care—just like you can be an avatar and still keep your friends." Annev's response was intended as an accusation, but it also affirmed his decision not to betray Titus and Therin. His words gave Kenton pause, but then the other boy straightened up to his full height and shook his head.

"I don't want to be friends with any of you." He glanced toward Titus and Therin. "I'm going to win and you're going spend the rest of your stupid lives as stewards."

Titus bit his lip. "Kenton—" he began.

"Don't say a bloody word, Titus," Kenton growled. "Just get out of my way." Titus meekly stepped out of Kenton's path, but Therin and Annev held their ground.

"You don't know which door to choose," Annev stalled, wondering what to do next. *Is this what Tosan meant, about Sodar influencing me too much? We should have attacked him as soon as he came through the scissor field ...*

Kenton was looking from one to the other when Titus spoke.

"It's the third door."

Annev turned, surprised by Titus's lie but immediately latching onto it. He hissed at the acolyte, feigning anger, and Therin took the charade a step further, thumping the smaller boy on the back of his head.

"Keos, Titus! Why've you got to muck it up for the rest of us?"

Titus looked between Kenton and his friends as genuine tears formed on the boy's face. "I didn't ... I'm sorry." He sobbed and dropped his face to the ground, ashamed. The act was convincing enough that Annev felt his stomach twist into a knot.

Kenton moved to the third door, silent as a shadow, and looked inside. When he pulled his head out, it was to cock his ear toward the scissor field: somewhere beyond the chamber, they could all hear Fyn's labored curses as he navigated the obstacle course. Kenton looked back.

"Thanks, Titus."

The scar-faced avatar stepped through and closed the door with the sturdy thud of a bar dropping into place.

"Good job, Titus," Annev said, surprised their ruse had worked.

"Nice touch with the tears," Therin added.

"Quick," Titus said, wiping his face. "Fyn's coming."

They ran for the second door. Annev grabbed the drop bar as Therin eased the door shut, being careful not to tip the bucket of purple liquid that continued to froth and bubble just a few feet overhead.

With the door closed, the passage fell into darkness and Annev dropped the heavy bar in place by touch. Seconds later, they heard Fyn's frustrated roar from the chamber. Annev smiled to hear it before wordlessly leading his friends down into the dark.

A resounding *SMACK* came from somewhere behind Annev.

"Ouch!" Therin yelped. "Why'd you do that?"

"Why do you think?" Titus said. "Next time don't hit me so hard."

Therin snorted. "Oh, is this going to be a regular thing?"

Annev shushed them both.

They stumbled through the dark tunnel, which turned first left and then right. Annev shuffled forwards with his hands out, searching for the end of the tunnel while Titus and Therin moved at his sides, running their hands along the walls to make certain they didn't stumble past any intersecting corridors. The pitch-black passage continued its twists and turns then dipped down several feet and turned sharply to the right.

"We've turned around," Therin noted.

"Looks that way," Annev said after a moment of silence.

"Did we take the wrong tunnel?"

Annev thought back to Ather saying the correct door led forward while the rest led back, and he started second-guessing himself. He reconsidered all the paths they had taken thus far in the test, but he felt no regrets about their decisions.

"No," Annev said, sounding more confident than he felt. "The ancients wouldn't make the choice random, and the second door was the only one they trapped."

"Was it *too* obvious?"

Annev chewed his lip as they walked on. "Perhaps," he admitted, "but I still see no better choices."

They came to an intersection in the winding underground passage. The main corridor continued on and two other tunnels branched off. After some quick deliberations they decided to stick together on the main route, foregoing any intersecting paths they came to.

They had passed a second junction and followed another bend in the tunnel when Annev suddenly spied light trickling through the cracks of a door. He searched for traps then grasped the key around his neck, hoping it might be the answer to this puzzle, but when he tested the handle he found the door unlocked. With practiced care, he eased the door open and the three boys stepped into the final testing room.

Only it wasn't the final testing room—it was the *first* testing room. The door led to a shaded area beneath the winding staircase the students had climbed after entering the testing arena. Ahead of them stood the great wooden barricade; to their left, the staircase. Tosan, Ather, and Myjun were still watching the competition from the platform at the top.

"Uhh ..." Therin moaned, taking in the scene. "Are we where I think we are?"

Annev nodded, forcing the words out. "We're back at the start."

"But we did everything right," Therin whined. "Were we supposed to follow a different path in the tunnel? Kenton or Fyn might have already won!"

"No one's won yet." Titus said. "They always announce it when someone does."

Annev sighed. "I don't get it. We must have missed something." He scratched his forearm beneath the patchwork Glove of Illusion, unconsciously seeking out the invisible seam where his elbow and the prosthetic met. He tuned out the boys' conversation and tried to think. What had Ather said? He clutched the iron key around his neck, trying to remember the exact words.

"Only one path leads to victory," Annev said, whispering the words. "To find that path, you must descend and tread where you have gone before. Only then will you find the door that leads forward."

Titus nodded. "That's what Ather said. 'Find the door, and you will find the path.'"

Therin scratched his mop of messy brown hair. "So we took the wrong door. We need to descend into the arena, go back to those three doors, and find the one that leads forward."

"Maybe," Annev said, still rubbing his key. "Or maybe ..."

"What?" Titus asked.

"'Tread where you have gone before'. They've used the arena for every Test of Judgment, so no matter which path we take, we're going over old ground. Why say that unless …"

Therin frowned. "What?"

"'Everything else is a distraction.'" Annev bit his lip, thinking. And then it came to him.

"The door is here. On *this* side of the barricade!"

"It's the door we just came through?" Therin asked.

Annev shook his head. "No. The *arena* is the distraction. Ather wanted us to descend … and walk where we had just been …" Annev grinned then pulled the loop of leather off his beck. "Those bastards," he said, holding up the iron key.

"What?" Titus said, confused.

"It's for the trapdoor!" He flashed them both a smile and raced between the wide pillars supporting the platform above.

When the three boys reached the trapdoor on the other side of the staircase, Annev threw himself at it and shoved the small key into the padlock. Iron scraped against iron as the key slipped inside and Annev twisted.

The lock clicked open.

Annev tore off the padlock, cast it aside, and lifted the metal ring. He heaved, pulling upward until the door moaned in protest. He heaved again and the door came free with a jolt.

Somewhere on the other side of the arena, a gong sounded once. Twice. Three times.

"What was that?" Titus asked.

Therin glared suspiciously at the tunnel beneath the trapdoor. "Isn't that where they kept the wild boar last summer?"

"And where they drained the water after the swimming competition," Annev said, lowering himself into the hole.

"And didn't they keep snakes down there once?"

"Yep. 'Descend and tread where you've gone before.'" Annev dropped down into the darkness. A second later, he poked his head back out. "It's only four feet high, and half as wide. We'll have to duck."

Therin shifted from one foot to the other. "I don't like tight spaces."

Titus lowered himself in. "I'm coming, Annev."

Annev ducked back in and disappeared into the darkness, then Titus dropped in behind him. Therin bent down and stared into the tunnel. After a moment he groaned.

"I'm coming!" He slid in, grabbed the trapdoor, and pulled it down behind him.

Once again, Annev shuffled down the passageway at the front of the trio, his hands searching for an exit. This time, though, the tunnel was too narrow to walk abreast, so they went single file with Therin at the rear. After several feet, the tunnel dipped and became much cooler. Annev heard a soft splash as his feet met a few inches of shallow water. A few seconds later, he felt the cold wetness seep into his boots.

At the back of the line, Therin groaned. "I *hate* getting my feet wet."

"You'll live." Annev pressed on.

As they walked on the floor sloped away and the water level rose. At one point the ceiling sloped down sharply, forcing them to crawl through the ankle-deep pool. Shortly thereafter, the tunnel dropped again bringing the water level to their knees. Each time the water got deeper Therin moaned, but finally Annev's hands touched a rough stone wall. His fingers searched the rocky surface and he felt the tunnel curve left.

"Turning left," Annev said. "Stay close."

"Shhh," said Therin. "There's something behind us."

Both Titus and Annev turned their heads to listen. Something, perhaps a hundred feet away, was splashing in the tunnel …

"Kenton?" Titus wondered.

"Or Fyn."

"Or there could be something living down here," Therin added. The splashing grew louder.

"Well," Annev said, wading forward, "I'm not staying to find out."

The passage rose gently and the water level began to drop. Shortly after that, the tunnel took a series of sharp turns and the slope became a steady incline, bringing them to dry ground again. Annev's fingers touched a

MASTER OF SORROWS

rough wall at the end of the passage. He searched to the left and right and found stone to either side.

"Why did we stop?" Therin asked.

"End of the tunnel."

"Burn my bloody bones! I thought that key meant we'd found the right tunnel."

"Wait." Annev's hands patted the rough-hewn rock above his head. With his hands tracing the ceiling, he backed into Titus and Therin and felt the rough stone change to smooth wood.

"Figures," Annev muttered. "There's another trapdoor above us. Help me push it open." The three acolytes gathered together and pressed their hands and shoulders against the wooden door. "On the count of three," Annev said. "One ... two ... three!"

The trapdoor sprang open, filling the tunnel with torchlight. The three boys stood, blinking at the sudden brightness. Once Annev's eyes had adjusted, he straightened up, and hoisted himself through the hole.

He was surrounded.

Eight of the Academy's nineteen master avatars stood evenly spaced around the room with a pair of torches on the wall between each of them; each master stood to attention, hands holding a ceremonial quarterstaff, watching the trapdoor and waiting for the winner.

As Titus and Therin crawled through the trapdoor, Annev glimpsed the raised dais at the opposite end of the room. Three of the Academy's ancients were seated to either side in their purple ceremonial robes, and in the midst of them, sitting on a cushioned chair elevated above the rest, was Elder Tosan.

CHAPTER THIRTY-ONE

"Well, this is a first," Tosan murmured. "Three acolytes finishing at the same moment." He bowed his head in feigned admiration. "Bravo."

Annev bowed as he noticed Witmistress Kiara standing in the far corner of the room. Witwoman Tonja stood beside her, severe-looking as ever, and two witapprentices stood behind them. Faith stood behind Kiara, while Myjun stood at Tonja's elbow. Her gaze locked with Annev's and she smiled.

"Of course," Tosan continued, "we are prepared for such an eventuality." He nodded to Master Edra. "Proceed."

To one side of the room, the Master of Arms set aside his staff and took up three small rods.

"Line up!" Edra shouted.

The boys stood to attention in a single straight line facing the ancients. Edra made a show of looking the acolytes over then nodded and placed a bronze rod in Titus's palm. He gave a silver rod to Therin and a gold one to Annev. Then he stepped back and circled behind the three boys.

"You have proven yourselves in the testing arena," Edra said. "You have shown your agility of body is equal to your quickness of mind." He paused for effect. "The final test lies before you. You must—"

There was a scuffling sound behind him as Kenton climbed through the trapdoor.

"Avatar Kenton," Edra said, his tone neutral. "The final task is about to begin. Do you still wish to compete for the honor of today's title?"

Kenton rose to his feet, his face grim. "I do."

Edra gestured him into line and handed the boy an iron rod.

"The final test lies before you," Edra continued. "You must now demonstrate your skill in combat. Each of you has a metal rod. When you have collected three of them, you will secure your avatar title." Edra stepped back from the trapdoor and resumed his place along the wall.

No! Annev thought. *We've come so far ... all three of us made it. There's got to be another way ...*

From his place on the dais, Tosan caught and held Annev's gaze, and it lit a fire inside of Annev, steeling his resolve.

There's always another way. I'll make another way.

The headmaster flicked a hand in the air. "Begin."

With a sudden ferocity, Kenton whirled to his left and kicked Therin in the stomach. The boy coughed, his hands shooting out in front of him as he stumbled backward. Kenton stretched to grab the metal rod from Therin's hands, but before he could claim it, Therin tripped and dropped through the open trapdoor. Kenton swore and turned his attention to Annev and Titus who had backed into opposite corners of the room.

He'll go for Titus, Annev thought, watching the boy's dark eyes fall on his companion. *I need to surprise him ... do something unexpected.*

"Titus!" Annev called. The smaller acolyte turned to look at him. "Catch!" Annev threw his rod toward the fair-haired boy. Kenton watched, astonished, as the golden object sailed through the air, then he came to his senses and rushed to intercept the falling piece of metal. Titus stood poised to catch the rod until he saw Kenton bearing down on him. He jumped back and the gold rod clattered to the floor.

But Annev had not been idle, and he tackled the surly avatar while his attention was on the fallen rod. They collided hard, Kenton rose off the ground, and the two boys tumbled through the air, their tangled bodies thudding to the floor several feet away. Their momentum slid them toward one of the master avatars and the man stepped aside at the last moment, allowing the pair to slam into the wall.

Kenton's iron rod clattered to the floor and rolled to a stop beside Annev's golden one. The dark-haired boy spied the two metals and tried to seize them both, but Annev grabbed him first, wrestling him into a submission hold. He tried to choke Kenton out but the boy had his hands between Annev's, creating an imperfect hold—and a perfect impasse: Kenton had no leverage to free himself unless he allowed Annev to secure his choke hold, and Annev could hold Kenton ... but not incapacitate him, and neither of them could take the rods.

Annev looked up from his entanglement and saw Titus standing less than two feet from the gold and iron rods. Opposite him, Therin had climbed back into the room and was running for them.

"Leave them!" Annev shouted. "Help me with Kenton!"

Therin hesitated, staring hungrily at the two discarded rods. There was a metallic *ping* as Titus dropped his bronze rod and hastened to help Annev. With a heavy sigh, Therin set down his silver rod and helped his friends.

"TITUS!" Kenton bellowed when the smaller avatar seized his leg. "You *owe* me!"

Titus flinched at Kenton's words, but he shifted to stand beside Annev then seized Kenton's left arm. Therin grabbed the right and both boys pulled, giving Annev the choke hold that had eluded him.

"Let's get him to the trap door," Annev said, when Kenton passed out.

The two boys kept their hold on Kenton's arms while Annev seized his legs. Together they hoisted the avatar off the floor, waddled him over to the trap door, and unceremoniously dumped his unconscious body into the hole.

Another boy shouted from the dark tunnel, barely managing to jump out of the way of Kenton's falling body.

"It's Fyn!" Annev shouted, slamming the trapdoor shut. He hopped atop the door just as Fyn slammed into the other side of it. "Titus, help me stand on this! Therin, find something to hold it shut!"

With a nod, Therin ran to the discarded rods, picked up Kenton's iron bar, and knelt down beside the receiver plate bolted to the floor. He shoved the bar into its metal slot, then forced it across the lip of the trapdoor, holding it closed to the audible relief of all three boys. Beneath them, Fyn banged furiously on the trapdoor, cursing and demanding admission.

Soft applause came from the right side of the room. Annev looked up and saw Tosan rise from his chair.

"Well done," Tosan said, eyes glittering, "Now one of you must still present three of the four rods." He looked from Therin and Titus to Annev. "Whichever of you gives them to Edra will become an Avatar of Judgment. The others will become Stewards of the Academy."

For a long moment, no one moved. Titus and Therin each glanced at Annev, and the boy finally stood. Tosan smiled, a satisfied gleam in his eyes. But when Annev reached the rods, he only scooped up two of them. Without saying a word, he handed Titus and Therin their bronze and silver rods, then he walked back to claim the third. All three acolytes stood in front of Tosan, and then Annev went to his knees, bowing his head respectfully as he offered his rod to the headmaster. Therin and Titus followed his lead.

Tosan did not move, and the silence was only broken by Fyn's fist banging against the locked trapdoor.

Annev could see Witmistress Kiara in his peripheral vision: the older woman had her head tilted sideways, studying Annev as if he had sprouted wings. A tiny smile pricked the corner of her mouth. Annev swallowed hard, anxious yet committed to his course.

"Elder Tosan," he looked the headmaster in the eye. "We've all trained to earn our places as Avatars of Judgment. All three of us have fought to be here, and we have each passed today's test. As the witapprentices showed us yesterday, we must each be capable alone but are unstoppable if we work together." He glanced at Witmistress Kiara, hoping to see another smile or some other nonverbal cue indicating she approved of his logic. Instead, her eyes were thoughtful, her face blank. Annev was instantly less sure of himself.

Had he found the middle ground between Tosan's ideology and Sodar's principles? Or had he fooled himself ... and failed yet again?

"We have each demonstrated the necessary skills," Annev said, trying to regain his earlier confidence, "and we each deserve to become Avatars of Judgment." He tried to gauge the headmaster's reaction. The ancient had listened, his face a perfect mask, but now Annev could see the anger smoldering behind his eyes: the man's gaze burned with restrained fury.

"Thank you, Acolyte Ainnevog." The headmaster looked between Therin and Titus. "Does your classmate speak for you both?"

Titus and Therin looked at one another then glanced at Annev. Titus nodded a moment before Therin.

"Thank you, Acolyte Titus," Tosan said. "Each Test of Judgment is won by one acolyte and, by this statement of defiance, both you and Acolyte Ainnevog have withdrawn from this month's Test. I am forced to promote Acolyte Therin." The headmaster snapped his fingers and Brayan stepped forward carrying a brown tunic and belt.

"You came to us as an Acolyte of Faith," Tosan said, as Therin numbly accepted the bundle of clothing. "Today you have become an Avatar of Judgment."

Therin stared at the package and then at Annev and Titus, a look of horror stamped across his face.

"I didn't … I don't—" He was dumbfounded by the turn of events.

In contrast, Annev had seen Titus's expression shift from confusion to dismay and then to a sort of passive acceptance—perhaps even relief—and Annev was not surprised. Titus had always been more interested in a steward's duties than those of an avatar. Any horror on his face was reserved for Annev.

For Annev's part, his mind and his heart could not accept the head-master's words. *He's promoting Therin to teach me a lesson, because he thinks I stuck to Sodar's principles and not the Academy's.* He stared at the floor, tears threatening. *He could have promoted all three of us—he could have—but instead he's punishing me for sticking to my principles—to Sodar's principles.* Annev felt the rage boiling inside him, then felt it freeze into cold blades despair: he could never be with Myjun. He couldn't even look at her.

He never wanted me to be with her, Annev realized. *It's all been personal, from the very start.*

Annev wanted to challenge the headmaster—he ached to lash out, to prove he was worthy to be an avatar—but in failing the final Test of Judgment, he had lost everything. Annev wasn't even an acolyte anymore—he was a steward. Fyn had won. Kenton had won. For the rest of Annev's life, they would order him around and rub his nose in their successes. All their cheating and backstabbing had been rewarded, while Annev was punished. Myjun would marry another, and every day that he passed her in the halls of the Academy, he would feel the shame of this day.

Annev had lost.

Tosan was shaking hands with Edra and Murlach, congratulating them and Ancient Denithal, the ingenious and elderly alchemist, on a job well done. As he spoke with the three men, Titus, Therin, and Annev rose from their knees. Annev felt the boys' eyes on him, but he couldn't bear to meet their gazes. Not now. Maybe never again.

"Avatar Therin," Tosan said, "you will go with the master avatars. The Master of Disguise will see that you are properly fitted for your new tunics, and the Master of Stealth will fit you for new shoes and boots. If you have need of anything else, you may ask the Quartermaster." The stricken-looking Therin was ushered away in a flash of brown and red, mouthing the word "sorry" to Annev as he went.

Annev watched in silence. He didn't want to blame Therin for accepting the promotion, for not holding his ground and demanding that all three of them become avatars together ... but he *did* still blame the boy, perhaps unreasonably. His current shock and dismay echoed the sense of betrayal he had felt when Therin had stolen his badges, only this was worse—so much worse. His anger and resentment were growing.

"I'm sorry you won't be progressing within the Academy, Titus." Ancient Benifew placed a hairy arm around Titus's round shoulders. "I suspect you'll find joy in your new calling though." He paused, eyeing Annev, and seemed to decide to keep his words for Titus alone. "Come, my boy. We have a few hours before the other acolytes get themselves cleaned up and you all take on your new roles as stewards. Walk me to the kitchens and we can get something to eat. While we're there, I can tell you the story of Bron Gloir, and how he single-handedly killed five thousand men on the steps of Speur Dún."

Titus handed his bronze rod back to Edra and let Benifew lead him across the room. As he passed Annev. he made eye contact and offered a weak smile.

"At least we'll be stewards together. Right?"

Annev didn't have the heart to reply. He stared at the floor, barely knowing what to do with himself, and when he finally lifted his head he saw Witmistress Kiara in a heated discussion with Elder Tosan. Tonja, Faith, and Myjun had all disappeared, and Annev supposed that was for the best too. He couldn't look Myjun in the eye now. Part of him hoped he would never have to see her again.

"Very well," the headmaster growled. Kiara made her way toward the door along with the masters who were filing out of the room. As soon as she had left, Tosan began a hushed conversation with the ancients who had remained behind.

Annev shifted from one foot to another, feeling unwanted and out of place but with nowhere to go either. He was exhausted, hurt, and angry. He edged toward the door at the glacial speed of someone with no sense of purpose. Nothing mattered anymore. He might as well return to the chapel, to work and die as a celibate priest. Or maybe he'd have to stay in the stewards' dormitories now. It didn't matter. He wished he could forget the day—to forget all that he had ever hoped and dreamed—and be forgotten by others in turn.

"Acolyte Ainnevog."

Annev stopped at the threshold, his shoulders slumped, as Ancients Maiken, Denithal, and Peodar filed out of the room, ignoring him. Ancients Jerik and Dorstal followed closely behind, their glares amplifying Annev's misery as they filed out. Once the room was empty, Elder Tosan finally addressed him.

"Acolyte Ainnevog, you will be in my study in thirty minutes."

Great, Annev thought, *what else can he take from me?*

"Yes, Elder Tosan."

The headmaster studied Annev from head to toe, closed his eyes, and rubbed his temples. "Before you come up, get something to eat from Master Sage and a dry pair of boots from Quartermaster Brayan." He sighed, as though wearied by some invisible burden.

"Don't be early," he added, leaving the chamber, "and definitely do *not* be late."

CHAPTER THIRTY-TWO

Annev walked the Academy's long stone hallways in silence. When he reached the kitchens he was relieved to see Titus and Ancient Benifew had already gone. The fat Steward of Health gave him a ration of bread and soup, and then Annev hurried down the hall to get some dry shoes from Master Brayan.

While he ate and changed his boots, Annev's mind churned. He was about to become a Steward of the Academy, and he doubted any lecture from Tosan could make Fyn's gloating or the loss of Myjun worse … so what did Tosan want? To discuss his new duties as a steward? Annev needed time to mourn and to puzzle out what he had done wrong first; his wounds were simply too fresh, too painful for anything else. He felt sick. Bloated with anger, failure, and frustration.

Why did Tosan have to cling so doggedly to the Academy's rules? Why couldn't he let all three of them pass the test? Annev was furious with the headmaster, and he didn't trust himself to hold his tongue when he got to Tosan's study.

Only … Tosan had warned him. He'd very clearly said not to hold back or be kind to his peers. So why hadn't Annev listened? He had to recognize that part of his anger was with himself, for believing he could force Tosan's hand.

Why didn't I take the rods when I had the chance? Annev realized he was angry with Sodar for influencing that decision yet again, and then angry with himself for shifting the blame.

I knew what I had to do. I should have done it. If I had picked up the third rod then I'd be the one in brown and everything would be different. Therin would have failed the test, but Annev felt he deserved the title more, and he had more to lose … so why had he gambled the certainty of his future happiness on the faint chance that Tosan would allow all three of them to pass? Would he feel half so miserable if he had betrayed Titus and Therin? Annev didn't know, but he suspected a future with Myjun would have compensated for the loss of his friends.

After almost thirty minutes, Annev stopped in front of the headmaster's familiar oak door as it swung open and a man in dark red bumped into Annev.

"Excuse me, Master Carbad."

The Master of Operations rubbed his nose as he squinted at Annev. His temples were streaked with gray and he carried a ledger and inkpot in his arms. After a moment, his eyes brightened with recognition.

"Ah! Ainnevog." The master gestured at Tosan's door. "Elder Tosan is waiting."

Annev bowed to Carbad and stepped into the room. As he closed the door, his boots shifted from bare stone to the thick, red-and-black rugs Tosan used to carpet his study. Ornamental tapestries lined the walls, and a single bookcase brimmed with scrolls and manuscripts. A massive oak desk occupied the center of the room with a pile of scrolls sitting atop it and Tosan behind it, reclining comfortably in a fur-lined chair. Yet neither Tosan nor his furniture held Annev's attention. As usual, that honor was reserved for the immense stained-glass window covering the east side of the study.

From simple shards of colored glass, the artist had constructed a fantastic forest setting. To the far right, a man lifted a staff to the heavens, his eyes like lightning streaking from a thundercloud. To the far left, a red and gold depiction of Keos completed the artist's rendition of the Battle of Vosgar: the God of Blood and Bone was amidst a swarm of keokum—depicted as armored giants, black-skinned dragons, and fiery-eyed faeries—a flaming hammer in his massive golden hand; his adversary wielding the silver staff met the attack with a blast of blue-white energy, his face shining with the light of Odar.

Tosan cleared his throat and Annev tore his gaze from the stained-glass portrait, then sat in the small, hard chair the headmaster gestured to.

The ancient stroked his black goatee as if pondering some weighty matter.

"Do you know what a ring-snake is, Ainnevog?"

"A what?"

"A ring-snake," Tosan repeated, steepling his fingers. "It's known by other names—codavora, ouroboros—but the one most people seem to know is ring-snake."

Annev shook his head, unfamiliar with the creature and unable to guess where Tosan was taking the conversation.

The headmaster nodded, expecting as much. He rose from his chair, pulled a thick volume from the bookcase, and flipped through its pages. He stopped at an illustration of a serpent wrapped around a tree branch and set the book in front of Annev.

"They can only be found in the Vosgar," Tosan said, returning to his seat, "but the Brakewood used to be part of the Vosgar, so we have some ring-snakes at the southern edge of Chaenbalu. When I was an acolyte, the Master of Poisons sent us to hunt for them ... but they're chameleons—an effect of the toxins secreted by their skin. Master Karrigan theorized that those toxins also helped them shape the trees."

"Shape the trees?"

Tosan nodded, tapping the illustration. "They nest in ochroma trees, and which aren't very dense, and they squeeze the branches till they form rings. When they're hunting, they bite their tails and disappear—they look just like the rings—and then they ambush their prey, squeezing it like the tree branch. The victim suffocates, but the toxins accelerate things. It's almost as if ..."

Tosan fell silent, leaving his thoughts unfinished. Without a word of explanation, he pulled a time-worn journal from the desk and jotted a note in it with a gold-nibbed pen.

Annev sat in silence, confused, and after a minute wondered if Tosan had forgotten him.

"You're wondering why I mention the ring-snakes," Tosan said. He set his pen down and reached for the pounce pot.

"Ah ..." Annev floundered. "It's not my place—"

"It's an analogy," Tosan said. He scattered sand across the wet ink, set it down to dry, then capped the inkpot and pointed his pen at Annev.

"*You're* a ring-snake, Ainnevog."

"I'm what?"

Tosan returned the journal to his desk, then poured the loose sand from the paper back into the pounce pot. "You're a ring-snake," he repeated, pushing a scroll across the desk towards him. "You blend in with the tree—you pretend to be part of it—but you're actually twisting it, weakening it. Reshaping it to fit your own needs."

Annev unrolled the scroll as Tosan set a second, and a third on the desk.

"Do you know what these are?

Annev studied the paper in his hands. "These are your notes from our annual meetings."

Tosan nodded then tapped the top parchment. "Could you read the fourth line down?"

Annev studied the scroll. When his eyes reached the fourth line, his stomach twisted into a knot. Even so, he read aloud. "'Argues with the ancients. Does not accept authority.'"

"Every year," Tosan said, tapping the other scrolls. "It's come up every single time, Ainnevog. A long-standing problem. You've never been content with things as they are, and you behave as if the rules shouldn't apply to you. Sodar has instilled the spirit of rebellion in you."

"I don't—"

"Precisely," Tosan interrupted. "You *don't*." He raised a hand and began counting his fingers. "You don't live at the Academy with the rest of your peers. You don't receive the same training. You don't accept what the ancients are teaching you. You don't question what Sodar teaches you." He raised his fifth finger. "And I'm sure you don't agree with the verdict in the testing chamber."

Annev's mouth snapped shut. What could he say to that? The last part was certainly true—and he *did* question the ancients—but the rest was outside his control. Should he be punished for living with Sodar?

"I question all of my teachers," Annev said, finding his voice. "Sodar is no exception. As for living at the chapel … I've had no alternative."

A faint smile quirked the ancient's mouth. "You act as if you have no agency, Ainnevog. As if you were a slave to your circumstances and this"—he tapped the scrolls on the desk—"were somehow the Academy's fault. But we both know that's a lie. When you disagree with something, you try to change it. That's what you did this morning, isn't it? Your stunt with Therin and Titus?"

Annev was almost afraid to speak, and Tosan sensed he had won the argument.

"It's in your nature, Ainnevog. Like the ring-snake, you change your surroundings to suit your needs. Given the choice to live in the dormitories you would *not* have chosen differently, because you *have not* chosen differently. You may act as if you belong, but your actions prove you are not part of this tree. Instead, you are a divisive element that seeks to cripple what I have worked very hard to cultivate." Tosan paused, as if expecting Annev to argue. When he did not, Tosan picked up the book containing the snake illustration. He studied it then carefully closed the book and walked it back to his bookcase.

"There's one other thing I find fascinating about ring-snakes," Tosan said, replacing the book. "It doesn't happen very often, but sometimes a snake injures itself by trying to be too clever—either by trying to squeeze a tree that is too large or by swallowing too much of its own tail. In the first instance, the snake is fortunate. It exhausts itself and learns to accept the things it cannot change. In the second instance—when it can't withdraw its tail—it chokes and dies." The headmaster studied Annev.

"You're unquestionably talented, Ainnevog," Tosan said, beginning to pace the room, "but there comes a time when we must all learn to submit, when we accept that some things cannot change and therefore … *we* must change. What I don't know is whether you've reached that point. I don't know if you can learn from your mistakes or if you're just doomed to choke on them."

Tosan stopped in front of the stained-glass window. The sun had almost reached its zenith, and shafts of rainbow light filled the room. From Annev's vantage, bright shards of red and gold painted the headmaster's face.

"Witmistress Kiara has argued your case," Tosan said, after a long pause. "When we spoke, I noted your argumentative nature, but I also acknowledged your ability. So the decision remains a pragmatic one. Does our need for good avatars outweigh the risk of you subverting the Academy with Sodar's ideology?"

Annev felt a desperate spark of hope kindle in his breast.

"No," Tosan continued, "it does not. But if I deprived you of Sodar's influence—if I quenched that spirit of rebellion—could I then mold you into something useful? That, I do not know." Tosan tapped his lips, turned from the window, and walked back to his chair.

"You've been training to become an Avatar of Judgment for years," Tosan said, as if speaking to himself, "and yet, at the same time, you have been training to be a deacon and a priest. In hindsight, I should have put an end to that once I became Eldest of Ancients. How do I now reconcile your fractured loyalties?"

Annev held his breath, sensing Tosan's decision was imminent.

"I had hoped you would see things from my perspective after our talk last night, but your Test today proves you have not changed your course. Since, despite my encouragement, you haven't proven yourself an avatar in body *and* spirit, my only choice is to make you a Steward of the Academy. You will no longer attend training classes with the master avatars. Instead, you will be assigned a master steward and will learn his trade, and you will move out of the chapel and live here at the Academy. Your privileges of entering the Brakewood have also been revoked." Tosan tapped his chin. "That won't prevent you from seeing Sodar, though, so I think I'll also restrict your movements to the Academy. No attending Seventhday services, no trips to market. You are to never leave this building. Understood?"

Annev blinked, at a loss for words. He had hoped Elder Tosan was talking himself into a third option—that Kiara had convinced him—but instead Tosan had found something even worse than just becoming a steward. Annev had run out of options, and he bitterly regretted helping Titus and Therin. For the first time, he genuinely wished he had followed the rules and heeded Tosan's advice.

"I … I understand."

"Good." Tosan sat down.

Annev's stomach twisted into a knot as he felt his whole life turn on its head. It was real—*this* was real. He would never be able to escape Fyn's bullying. Never be able to give Myjun his promise ring.

Never see Sodar again.

It didn't seem possible. He had eaten breakfast with the man just this morning, and now he was not permitted to see or speak to him. The old priest was more than just a mentor. He was the closest thing Annev had to a father. He knew the boy's secrets and his strengths, and had protected and aided him when the Academy would have cursed or killed him.

Annev felt as if he were being torn in half. He was going to be sick. He cast about, desperate for something to cling to—for any chance to salvage a single scrap of his former life.

"There is one possibility," Tosan said. "One chance at redemption."

Annev looked up, unaware of the tears streaming down his face.

"Anything," he whispered.

"This month's test has fallen on Regaleus," Tosan said, leaning forward in his chair, "which means there is one more day before this week ends and the next reap begins testing. One more day in which you could prove yourself worthy to become an Avatar of Judgment."

Annev sat up straight. "What must I do?"

Tosan studied him. "Whatever happens, you *will* leave Sodar's chapel and move to the Academy. The man's corrupting influence cannot be overstated, and we cannot retrain you without removing you from his care."

Annev barely hesitated. His life with Sodar was over, one way or another.

"I understand, Elder Tosan."

"Excellent. Now, for your task. Master Carbad tells me there is a merchant wandering the perimeter of the village. The man claims he got lost trying to find a shortcut through the Brakewood. Apparently, he is seeking admittance to Chaenbalu right now."

"A merchant?" Annev repeated. "But … no one ever comes to Chaenbalu."

Tosan stared at Annev, his face a mask. "It has been years since anyone has stumbled upon our village, and we must keep it that way. Our secrecy is imperative to keeping the magical artifacts safe from monsters who would misuse them."

Annev frowned, waiting for Tosan to elaborate. When he did not, Annev had to guess at Tosan's intent.

"I can find this merchant, Elder Tosan. What then?"

"Barter for palm vine and dragon's blood tree resin. The Academy needs more of both, but your real mission is to discover how the merchant found our village." Annev nodded and the ancient took a tiny purse from his desk drawer.

"You will find the man on the eastern side of the village," Tosan said, handing Annev the coin purse. "Once you've secured the supplies, lead him away from the village and kill him."

"Kill him, for getting lost?" Annev's mouth went dry.

"Kill him, as a risk to the Academy, the Vault of Damnation, and the artifacts we safeguard. Death has always been the penalty for leaving the village. The merchant knows where our village is, so the same rule applies."

"So this purse … is just a prop?"

The headmaster frowned. "We are avatars, Ainnevog, not thieves—you will pay the man for his goods." Tosan stood. "If you wish to rob him once he is dead, that is your choice. Personally, I find it distasteful—a grave robber is still a thief, after all—but you can bring back spoils if you must. I will need proof you've accomplished your task, so I expect you to bring back the merchant's ears as well."

"His ears?"

Tosan nodded, gesturing toward the door. "Before sunset tomorrow. I would normally give you permission to collect any tools you might need from the Quartermaster … but you're not an avatar, so you don't get that privilege. I expect you'll do fine, though. You've proven very resourceful thus far."

Annev walked to the door in a daze. Just as he opened it, Tosan called back to him.

"Priests can afford to be pleasant, Ainnevog, but avatars don't have that luxury. This is your last chance to decide which one you are. I've chosen this mission carefully to *test* you, so don't disappoint me."

CHAPTER THIRTY-THREE

Annev circled the courtyard and cut behind the Academy, heading towards Sodar's chapel and the easternmost edge of Chaenbalu.

The task Tosan had assigned him left little room for interpretation. There was a man in the Brakewood—a stranger—and Annev was to interrogate and murder him. Under normal circumstances, he would never have agreed to such a mission.

But things were different now. Annev had tasted a despair so overwhelming that he would do anything to avoid feeling it again; including betray his friends, abandon his mentor, and murder a stranger. He would do all of it if he could still become an avatar.

Once he'd crossed the dusty courtyard and entered Chaenbalu's circular streets, Annev turned back to look at the Academy walls. The stained-glass image of the Battle of Vosgar stood out against the rest of the building's dark stone relief, and Annev half-imagined he saw Tosan standing there, hidden behind the red glare of the glass and the afternoon sun, watching.

There was a flicker behind the windowpane.

Perhaps I'm not imagining it.

Annev turned and ran toward the eastern gate. As he navigated the squat houses lining the streets, the composition of the buildings quickly changed from stone to wood, and then to wattle and daub. At the edge of the village, amidst the smaller homes of the farmers and sheep peddlers, he saw the chapel. He veered toward it for an instant—wanting to tell Sodar the price of failing the test—but the sense of Tosan's eyes on his back pushed him on, toward the Brakewood and the watchtower that guarded the easternmost entrance to the village.

He passed the distant silhouette of the chapel, his attention on the task at hand. For a moment he wished he had his hunting knife, or Mercy, but when he considered what he was going to do, he decided he didn't want to sully either blade with the act. In any case, Tosan had been right about his resourcefulness. He didn't need a knife to kill someone. When the time came, Annev would find a way to do it.

He drew closer to the watchtower and spiked wooden wall that formed the perimeter of Chaenbalu's eastern gate. When he was within earshot of the cobblestone edifice, a large man in a red smock hailed him.

"Ainnevog!" said Folum, the Master of Customs. "Is Tosan sending children to do men's work now, or did you forget your brown robes?"

Annev was in no mood to be teased. "Where is he?" he said, breathing hard from his run.

"The peddler?" Annev nodded. "He's waiting at the edge of the wood, just past the standing stones."

Annev turned to go.

"If he's crossed them, you must bring him back here!" Folum shouted.

Annev waved in acknowledgment but did not slow or turn back. He passed Chaenbalu's open gates and sprinted full-out down the east road into the heart of the Brake.

When he finally reached the forest, he stopped and inhaled the strong scent of pine. A cold dampness filled his lungs, and he felt almost giddy. He wondered what kind of man he was about to kill—good or evil, father or bachelor—and whether the man would struggle.

Ahead of him were the standing stones and beyond them the path to the Brake. As he crossed between the two waist-high pillars, Annev's bare hand traced the worn glyphs that had been inscribed there.

So far as he could tell, the runes weren't magical—he didn't recognize them, and Sodar had confirmed as much when he'd asked about them—yet Annev always felt a chill as he passed between them. He did so now and felt that same chill as he looked deeper into the forest: dry pine needles and the black remnants of last winter's leaves padded the soil, but there was no sign of a merchant.

The sun was at his back and still visible above the Brakewood canopy, but the path through the trees lay in shadow. He peered into the dark depths of the forest and was reminded of the shade pools he'd seen the previous day. Annev rarely traveled this far south or east—once a year at most—and the forest here was unfamiliar, but even so he felt confident he would find the stranger before the man found him.

But it was not the case. Annev had crept into the woods like a hunting cat, but after ten minutes of searching he began to think the peddler had already gone. He shuddered to think what Tosan would say if he had, and knew he would stalk the wood all night till he found the man.

"Hello?" Annev finally shouted, piercing the silence. "Anybody there?"

"I'm here all right," came the reply, a bodiless voice emerging from the heart of the forest. "Saw you come down that road. Got nothin' else to do, though, so I've been sittin' here. Watchin' you stumble round like your eyes are painted on."

Annev bristled at the insult as he turned toward the source of the voice, but its owner remained hidden. He stepped deeper into the shadows of the wood, allowing his eyes to adjust to the dimmer light.

"Where are you?" Annev asked, not knowing where to address his question.

A low cackle came from the waggling limbs of a silver maple, its trunk obscured by the tall, thin frame of a black spruce. As Annev drew closer, he was surprised to see a small handcart hidden behind the wide base of the tree—an oddity he had somehow overlooked during his initial sweep of the area.

Annev's eyes moved upward, following the path of the waist-thick tree branches, which tapered and split on their way toward the top of the forest canopy—and then he saw it: four feet off the ground, couched in the low crook of one of these fatter branches, was a large round man. Brown-faced and ruddy-cheeked, he was draped in a thick cloak the color of moss and sat smoking a long-stemmed pipe. Wisps of scraggly brown beard sprouted from his cheeks, half-tucked into the folds of his chin and neck.

"Had to keep meself warm," he called, and grinned around the bit of his corncob smoker. "Been wanderin' about the forest all night, and when I finally found help, you bastards wouldn't even give me the courtesies of a roof." He snorted, chewed something, swished his pipe to one side, and spat. A loping string of liquid splashed onto the forest floor less than a yard from Annev's boots.

Annev grimaced, taking a step back, but maintained eye contact with the man in the tree. "I've been sent to guide you out of the Brake," he said coolly.

"Guide me, eh? And who exactly is my guide?" The stranger puckered his lips when he pronounced his O's, drawing them out into long, round vowels. It reminded Annev of the way Sraon the blacksmith spoke, though the peddler's accent was more pronounced.

Annev had his response ready. He was going to kill the man, so it didn't matter what he told the merchant, and the truth was always easiest to keep straight.

"My name is Ainnevog. People call me Annev."

"Ainnevog, eh?" The merchant chewed on this for a bit. "Means "phoenix," doesn't it?" Annev nodded, surprised. "And Annev means "rare." Heh. Fancy name." The merchant drew a hand from the folds of his cloak and rubbed his stubbly cheeks with black-stained fingertips, scratching both corners of his mouth before plucking the corncob pipe from his teeth.

"I'm Cragcarac," the merchant offered.

"Crack-crack?"

The peddler shook his head, gray-streaked locks spilling over his shoulders. "Crag-ca-rac." He emphasized the syllables by dotting the air with his pipe then threw his cloak back over his shoulders, stretched, and hopped down to the ground, sinking half an inch into the moist topsoil. "It's an old name," he said, shaking out his cloak. "It means … well, its meaning is less impressive than yours. Just call me Crag." He grinned.

Annev stared at the merchant's chapped lips, a mouthful of half-yellow teeth gaping back at him. The smile was a genuine one, though, and Annev found himself returning it.

"Crag then," Annev said, in a friendly tone. "What brings you to the Brakewood, Crag?"

"Business." Crag waved a hand at the cart behind the tree then trudged toward it. "Business brings me to the Brakewood. I've come from Northern Odarnea with palm vine, kola nuts, warana, dragon tree resin. Rare goods, specially this far south."

"Why the Brake rather than Luqura?"

"Luq'ra!" Crag shook his head at Annev, pulling his cart out of the silver maple's shade and onto the forest path. He gave the cart one last yank, placing it squarely beneath a patch of scattered light. "You go to Luq'ra, you get taxed. You sell your goods in Luq'ra, you have to match the prices of the merchant's union and you have to *pay* the merchant's union for the chance. Better to sell in Banok—or Port Caer, though that's a long way off."

"Is that where you're headed?"

"Yessir. I left Banok four days ago for Hentingsfort, and then on to Port Caer. I was takin' a shortcut through the Brake. Least I thought I was. If I'd gone the long way round like a good street peddler, I'd be halfway there." Crag hacked, spitting another long string of mucus at the ground. "Damnable forest lost me a day's journey."

"Two days," Annev said. "Wherever you got to, you wandered back to the west side of the Brakewood. You're on the edge of it right now."

The news left Crag's mouth hanging half open, his face contorted in surprise and painful disbelief. Annev had seen that same face during his sparring matches at the Academy, normally after an avatar got kicked in the stomach. It took a moment before Crag seemed able to catch his breath.

"Back on the *west* side?" he asked. "But how's that possible? Banok's the closest town that side of the Brake. Thought for sure I'd passed on to the south." Annev shook his head. "Where the Gods am I?" Crag asked.

"Chaenbalu," Annev said, sealing the merchant's fate as he said the name. He couldn't possibly let him live now.

"Chan-blue?" Crag shook his head. "Never heard of it. And I know every small town between Odarnea and Lochland."

Annev shrugged. *I suppose that takes care of the first part of Tosan's task. The man doesn't have a clue how he got here.*

Crag clawed at his thinly bearded chin and scratched the sides of his mouth again.

"Chanblue," he said again, turning the word over in his mouth. He glanced down the forest path, studying the farmland outside the forest's edge, then he looked back at Annev. "Must be a secret place then. That why the fellow in the red pajamas wouldn't let me through?"

"Something like that," Annev said, prepared to be open since the man would be dead before nightfall.

"Well, damn him then—damn this whole forest. First I lost Cenif, now I've lost meself."

"Stop your spitting and moaning. I said I'm here to guide you. I'm also interested in trading with you."

"Spittin' and moanin'?" Crag reached beneath his cloak and deerskin vest for a silver flask, sucked down a portion of its contents, swished his mouth and swallowed, never once breaking eye contact. "Not sure what they've been teachin' you in that secret village, but it sure ain't respect for your elders." He sucked at his teeth, replacing the flask.

Annev bounced Tosan's coin purse in his hand. "You said you had palm vine and dragon's blood tree sap."

"That's right. How much do you need?"

Annev hesitated, realizing Tosan hadn't told him. "Ten sticks of wood and four bottles of resin," he said, pulling the numbers out of the air. He emptied half the pouch into his hand, picking out the largest coins from the pile. "I'll give you three silver moons." Crag stepped away from his cart and inspected the meager handful of coins.

"For that, I'll trade two sticks and a bottle," Crag announced.

"I said three *moons*. Not staves."

"And I said two sticks and a bottle. Are you deaf? But I'll do you a deal, seeing as you're helping me out. You can have the lot for twelve moons."

Annev emptied the rest of the pouch into his hand: he had five moons, a score of copper stars, and less than half as many silver staves. Not a gold beam or sun in the lot—it was a little more than half what he needed. Either the peddler was hustling him or Annev had vastly underestimated the value of the goods he was buying.

"I'll give you a moon for each bottle—"

"Two."

"—and a score of coppers for the palm vine wood."

Crag laughed. "I'll do you a favor. Give me that whole pouch of coin—every star, sun, and stave you got—and you can have *half* your order. Two bottles and five sticks. Won't find a better offer than that."

"Fine," Annev said, and Crag reached for pouch with eagerness. "And I'll take the rest of the supplies in exchange for guiding you out of the Brake."

Crag jerked his hand back. "I already discounted your wares on account of helpin' me! This far south, that pile of coins would barely cover the sticks alone. And the resin is even more expensive, even in Northern Odarnea."

"But you're not in Northern Odarnea," Annev said. "You're lost in the Brakewood, and you can't sell anything to anyone, at any price, without my help."

Crag shook his head. "You're a cheat and a thief. Your bloody villagers told me I couldna leave without an escort—and now you charge for it? Bah!"

"You can go," Annev said, his tone cool, "with or without an escort. But you'll be lost in the Brake for weeks without my help. I know these paths, and you know my price."

The peddler sniffed. "You're insultin' me, boy. All I have to do is push south and east until I come to the Brake Road. From there it'll be easy enough."

"If it was easy, you'd already have done it," Annev countered. "If you head southeast you'll get lost again. Could be days before you find the Brake Road, if you find it at all. You probably noticed the trees play tricks with the light?" Crag looked up and Annev knew he had him. "You think you see the sun rising in the east so you head towards it, but really you're heading due north and end up right back where you started. That sound about right?"

Crag squinted at him, as if seeing him for the first time, not as an errand boy or a simple guide, but as another trader. An opportunist.

"You're a mite smarter than you look," Crag said. "Phoenix indeed. All right then boy, what's your price? How much of that coin will you pocket afore you help me outta this wood?"

Annev opened his palm, showing the coins in his hand. "Ten sticks of palm vine and four bottles of dragon's blood tree sap ... for eight moons."

Crag poked at the coins, counting. "You're one staff short." He eyed Annev's empty pouch then shrugged. "I would have preferred ten, but this will do." He scooped the coins into his hand and they disappeared into his cloak with barely a clink. Then he pulled back a stitch of canvas covering the top of the wagon's contents.

"How'd you pull that heavy cart all the way from Odarnea?" Annev asked, watching Crag sift through his wares.

"I had a mule," Crag said, pulling out the dried palm vine and bright red tree sap. "Lost her in the Brake last night, though. I was makin' camp, unharnessed Cenif from the cart. Fed her, watered her, and was just about to tie her back up when somethin' spooked her. Just ran off into the dark." Crag eased the supplies into a cloth sack, taking care to wrap the bottles in rags, and held it out it to Annev. "To tell the truth," he whispered, "it spooked me too. Didna see or hear nothin', but Cenif and I both felt it. Nothin' natural."

A deep silence seemed to blanket the forest just then, emphasizing Crag's words. Annev stared at the dark shadows at the end of the path and imagined the tendrils of some vast and invisible being unraveling itself, stalking toward them, whispering at the soles of their boots. He thought of the shade pools again and shifted uncomfortably.

Annev eased the sack from Crag's hands and hefted it onto his back. "I'll drop this at the tree line then come back," he said, heart thumping. Crag nodded, though he didn't seem keen on being alone just then.

Annev jogged back to the tree line and deposited the sack on the other side of the standing stones. He'd shaken off the sense of foreboding, but then he remembered his true task—the merchant's death—and his uneasiness returned.

How would he do it? *When* would he do it? Tosan had given him a whole day and a half, though Annev could do the deed in the next hour if that's what he chose. Crag had already explained why he was wandering through the Brake, he had no prior knowledge of the village, and Annev had secured the supplies. There was only one task left undone.

I'll take him down the road for a bit, Annev thought. *Ask him some questions. Once his guard is down, I'll do it.*

But how? He'd thought to break Crag's neck, but the man was so fat Annev wasn't sure it would take. The same went for choking. If he'd had a knife or a rope then perhaps ... but he didn't. A blunt stone would have to do. If he hit him hard enough, the man would drop like a rock. From there, Annev could probably find a tool in the peddler's cart—a knife or some other sharp instrument—and he could end it.

"Thank you for the supplies," Annev said, returning to the peddler's side. "I'm sorry about your mule—and about you getting lost—but it's almost over now. I can help pull your cart, and you can get another animal when you reach Hentingsfort." The lie felt bitter on his tongue.

Crag laughed. "I s'pose that'll have to do—not like you left me much choice and you already got your goods. Seems I'm at your mercy."

The peddler's choice of words gave Annev pause: did he know, or was the turn of phrase a coincidence? He swallowed, feeling less certain.

"I don't know," Annev said, trying to act natural. "I thought you got a fair deal."

Crag cackled at this. "And how would you know that, seein' as how you live in a secret village? I'm surprised you know the value of your coin, let alone the worth of my goods."

Annev smiled back. "I'm certainly not used to bartering with it. So-dar's taught me a bit, though, so I'm not completely ignorant. I know the currency of the realm, even if I don't ... Crag?"

The merchant's face had gone very pale.

"What name was that?" Crag whispered.

"What?"

"You said Sodar."

CHAPTER THIRTY-FOUR

"Yes," Annev said, trying to sound casual. "He's my mentor." As Annev spoke, he could almost hear Sodar rebuking him for sharing secrets with strangers. Only Sodar would never rebuke him again, and Crag would be dead within the hour.

"Sodar," Crag said slowly. "And you're Ainnevog. Phoenix." A strange grin spread across the fat merchant's face and Annev found he didn't like the man's sudden interest.

"Let's go, lad," the merchant said, still smiling. Annev watched as Crag bent low beneath the handcart's push-rail, leaning into the heavy load. Annev joined him, filling up the little remaining space. "Which way?"

Annev nodded straight ahead. He hadn't come this way since last summer, but the landmarks hadn't changed. "We take the first right." They began pushing the laden cart down the forest path.

"So tell me about your village, Annev."

"It's nothing special. We just keep to ourselves."

Crag grinned. "I don't doubt that, given the way you treat travelers. Doubt you get many repeat visitors." Annev said nothing and let the man talk. "Must be something special about it, though."

"Why do you say that?"

"Outside of not letting me in?" Crag shrugged. "I gave a list of my wares to one of those fellows in the red smocks. No interest in the usual stuff—silk, spices, pots, pans. Nope. Just wanted the palm vine and dragon's blood."

"Why is that strange?"

"Palm vine is an older name—most folk ask for rattan. The dragon's blood, though? That's strange. Few folk this far south know of the stuff, let alone that it's naught but tree sap."

"So why carry it then?"

"Because it's *rare*. Folk that know to ask for it also know its price—except maybe *you*—so I can usually get a few sunbeams out of it."

"And is that a fair price?" Annev asked, keeping an eye out for a suitable weapon.

"For four bottles?" Crag laughed. "Fair for me, maybe."

Annev smiled, his suspicions confirmed. The man had been trying to swindle him. The knowledge eased his conscience a little as he waited for the right time to kill him.

"So this Sodar," Crag continued. "He taught you to count coin?" Annev nodded. "Taught you to haggle too. What's his trade? Shopkeep? Horse-lord?"

Annev laughed. "Nothing like that."

"Oh, I've said something amusing, have I? Hmm. Must be a priest then, which would make you his deacon. Yes?"

Annev's pace faltered for a moment as he fumbled for a response. "I ... why would you guess that?"

Crag nodded at Annev's tunic. "Most common folk wear a splash of color. Only the pious and the poor wear naught but beige." He eyed Annev's single patchwork glove for a moment, then discounted it. "I doubt your master's a beggar, so that leaves the priesthood—though I suppose you could still work for the men in the red pajamas. It's not uncommon to force novitiates to wear plain homespun." He peered over at Annev. "Either of those hit the mark?"

Annev grunted, surprised by the man's perceptiveness and wondering if it were wise to keep answering his questions. The merchant was too cunning by half, and Annev worried he might puzzle out his dark intentions. They rolled forward in awkward silence, the trees growing denser as they lurched through the Brakewood.

"I'm a deacon," Annev finally said, breaking the silence. "Sort of a deacon," he added. "It's complicated."

"Well then. Not another word about it." Crag nodded in sympathy, the push bar bouncing beneath his belly. "Let me ask you this instead." He paused. "What does a "sort of deacon" do?"

Annev peered sideways at Cragcarac, wondering if the man was daft. *Did he even hear what I said?* Crag caught the look and returned it with a wicked grin.

The man was teasing him.

In spite of himself Annev grinned back. It was clear the merchant wasn't going to give up, and Annev couldn't complete the final part of his task until he spotted a weapon, so they were heading farther into the Brakewood. One way or another, it seemed he would have to make conversation with the man. He pointed to a spot up ahead where a tiny path broke off from the main road. "This is the trail."

The two worked together to pull the cart off the main path, trudging through the wet moss and underbrush, up over a dark mound of topsoil, and then sliding to the bottom of the small hill with the great wooden box creaking and jouncing behind them. The bushes clustered closer together and, as they pressed on, the footpath became little more than a game trail, winding ever deeper into the heart of the forest.

"How far is it?" Crag asked.

"Hard to say. The forest really does play tricks on you. I've walked this path maybe a dozen times, and every time it's different."

"What do you mean?"

"At one hour of the day, you might reach the Brake Road in as little as an hour, maybe two. But if you try and cut through at other times … well, it could take several hours."

Crag huffed, pushing hard on the handrail as he drew the cart over a thick shrub obstructing the path. "You mean the paths change?"

"No," Annev said. "Not exactly. They just … lengthen, as if you were walking slower somehow. The path is the same but … it just takes longer." Crag pondered Annev's words as they rolled farther down the path, following a sharp bend in the trail.

"You ever get lost?" Crag asked.

"All the time—even north of here, where I usually go hunting—but you learn the forest's landmarks. The way it breathes and moves, where the clearings are and where the main paths connect. It gets easier, but it's never easy."

"Any notion as to why it does that?"

Annev shrugged. "It used to be part of the Vosgar—and there's plenty of magic there—maybe something got left in the Brake ... some magic that makes the shadows seem more alive."

"You seem to know a lot about it."

"I know enough to avoid the dark places where the trees grow close."

"Dark places?"

Annev nodded. "Places where leaves and branches knit into a black sheet and no light comes through the canopy. It's dark as pitch, but somehow things still manage to grow there. If you're standing outside the shadows, they almost look like black pools of water."

"You've taken a peek, though?" Crag asked knowingly.

A crooked grin spread across Annev's face. "Once or twice. I'm supposed to report any I see, though—and to not go near them. They say it's dangerous."

"Sounds like your elders tell you not to do a lot of things. And you be doin' them anyway."

Annev's cheeks glowed red—not from embarrassment, but from the bitter embers of his anger at Tosan and the Academy. "Well, some of the rules make no sense!" he said, taking the opportunity to vent. "We're not allowed to leave, but the ancients and masters can come and go whenever they want. They tell us how to dress and what to eat and where to go and punish us if we don't do exactly as they say. They act like they're better than everyone else—as if the world is full of thieves and murderers—but they're *just* as bad. And now ..." He trailed off.

"Now?"

And now I'm here to kill you, so that I can become one of them. The clarity of the thought made Annev sick. He was stuck in the Brakewood with evening approaching, pushing a wagon through weeds and muck with the man he was supposed to kill. He shouldn't even be talking to Crag—he should already be walking back with the man's ears in his pocket—yet Annev trudged on, sharing Crag's load.

"Nothing," Annev said, looking away.

Crag nodded as though he'd heard it all before.

"We all have to follow rules at some point, lad. Things aren't much rosier on the outside. Downright rotten if you ask me. Dark things comin' outta the east, and the nobles in Borderlund are too busy squabblin' to do aught about it—and don't get me started on Luq'ra and Quiri! Den o' thieves, both of 'em. Like that song they sing in pubs. "In Quiri the thieves all wear cassocks, and in Luq'ra they all wear hose." You know the one?" Crag looked at Annev but the boy just shook his head. "No, of course you don't. My point is you got a lot of rules here, but you got a nice place too. Seems you're not starvin', or bein' set upon by bandits n' such. Maybe following a few rules isn't so bad."

I doubt he'd say that if he knew our rules were going to get him killed.

Annev studied the man, reminding himself why he was here. It wasn't to please the ancients or win Tosan's favor; Annev had chosen to come here because he wanted to become an avatar—to be with Myjun, explore the outside world, and be allowed to leave the Academy. It was Crag's life for Annev's freedom.

"Why so glum, lad?" Crag asked, peering over at him. "Just thinkin' on your village has got you lookin' like a gargol."

Annev shook his head. "It's nothing. Nothing I can change, anyway." He looked ahead and saw a small clearing surrounded by hemlock. A stream ran beside it, its waters choppy with shards of broken ice. It was time to finish his task.

"Let's pause here," Annev said, slowing the cart. "We can get some water, and you can tell me about the different places you've seen. I've always wanted to see beyond the village."

And if I kill you, Annev thought, *maybe I can.*

"Gods, yes!" Crag said, sighing. "I need a break …" He saw Annev's attention was elsewhere and followed his gaze, up and off the path into the clearing of hemlock.

The peddler saw the mound of blood-spattered rocks then, and splayed out in the center of the glade, the remains of a mutilated animal.

"Cenif!"

CHAPTER THIRTY-FIVE

"Wolves?" Annev wondered, pacing the scene for the second time.

"No." Crag shook his head. "Men." He lifted the steel-capped staff he had taken from the wagon and pointed it at the edge of the clearing. In the soft mud beneath the frost-covered hemlock were footprints. Beside them, an unstrung bow. It looked familiar to Annev, though he couldn't say why.

Most of the animal's carcass lay atop a stone slab in the center of the glade, with pieces of gore and bone strewn among scattered rocks surrounding the makeshift table. As Annev approached, he could see what remained of the mule's face: the eyes had been plucked clean from their sockets, the ears and lips had been torn away, and the muzzle was a shattered mass of gnawed bone.

Annev shook his head. "Men might have passed through this clearing, but only an animal could have butchered her that way."

"No," Crag disagreed. "Cenif was cut open—with a knife."

Annev stepped closer and saw the deep gouges on the mule's side. The cuts were long and clean. Beneath lay the exposed ribs and a gaping, empty hole.

"But a man wouldn't gnaw on ..." His voice trailed off.

"These cuts were made with a blade." Crag extended a boot and pushed the animal's body onto its side, exposing its stomach cavity. "Her heart is gone. So are her major internal organs by the look of it. If an animal had done that, it would have eaten Cenif's muscle as well."

He circled the beast, stopping every so often to squint at a footprint in the mud, an overturned stone, a bent sprig of hemlock. He waddled back round to the mule and poked at the rocks stacked beneath the stone slab.

"What do you make of these, boy?"

Annev stepped back from the carcass and took in the entire scene once again.

"It looks like an altar—the way the stones are stacked, with the slab on top—but it's nothing like the altars I'm familiar with."

Crag tugged at the brown wisps on his chin. "How so?"

Annev circled the mound of stones for the third time, taking in the details he had missed earlier. "All Darite altars have a water trough surrounding their base—and an Ilumite altar would show signs of fire. I suppose it could be a *Terran* altar—there's certainly enough blood—but there are no Terrans in the Brakewood. The closest ones live in Eastern Daroea, past Borderlund and the Kuar River."

Annev studied the mud surrounding the clearing. His and Crag's tracks could be traced away from the rock-strewn glade and up to the main trail. Other tracks could be seen pacing around the stone mound. Annev traced them around the altar.

"These look like hoof prints. Could they belong to your mule?"

The peddler nodded, brooding. "Could do." He pointed at the dead mule's hooves. "Whoever it was even pried her horseshoes off."

"Bandits?"

"If so, they're awfully poor bandits. Not to mention stupid. Stealing iron from a mule is considerably less profitable than stealing gold from a merchant." Crag tapped his pipe against his teeth, muttering.

"Crag?" Annev asked, stepping carefully around the blood-spattered stones. "We should go. What if … whatever did this is still nearby?"

Crag stared off into the Brake, his vision fixed on the path ahead. "You say you're sort of a deacon—a *half*-deacon." The merchant slowly turned his head, his baleful eyes locking with Annev's. "What's the other half?"

"Why …" Annev started to ask, but then he changed his question. "Why are we still here? We should go, Crag."

"And if I'd rather wait for whoever killed my mule?"

Annev studied the peddler, trying to decide if he were serious. But Crag had already turned away. The man's dark eyes searched the forest and, for the first time since they'd met, Annev sensed something truly dangerous about him. The way he carried himself, how he held his staff and cocked his head—it told a different story than that of a fat peddler who'd got lost in the woods. Crag turned, his eyes sweeping over Annev, and the air practically crackled with violence.

He knows, Annev thought, *or he's guessed what I'm planning. I have to act before he does.* His eyes drifted to one of the bloody stones. There would never be a better moment to kill the peddler than amidst a scene of preexisting carnage. Annev bent down and scooped up a heavy rock; it was a bloody thing, cleaved so that one half was smooth and the other jagged. He hefted it in his hand, confident in his weapon.

"Tell me," Crag began again, his voice cracking like ice under the weight of winter. "What do you do in your village? Not being a deacon. Your *other* job."

Annev turned to strike—then froze, suddenly seeing the rage that had been building beneath Crag's otherwise calm exterior; the peddler was *aching* for a fight, was looking to *kill* whatever had butchered his mule. What's more, Annev had no doubt the man would succeed, for just as he could sense the merchant's ill-concealed rage, Annev suddenly noticed the subtle movements that belied Crag's true strength and skill; the man had been a warrior once—a trained killer—and the death of his mule had reawakened those instincts.

Annev circled to the other side of the altar and placed the broken stone atop Cenif's remains. "The masters at the Academy," he said, "call us Avatars of Judgment."

"Avatars," Crag repeated, his eyes following Annev. "Fancy name. I suppose it explains why your elders are so damned pretentious." Crag rubbed his ink-stained fingers against his cheeks. "And what do you do, exactly? Ride winged ponies and proclaim Odar's holy tidings?"

Annev bent down, picked up another rock, and added it to the would-be cairn. "We train, mostly."

"Train to fight?"

Again, Annev was surprised by the merchant's perceptiveness. "Yes."

"To fight … and to kill?"

Annev was ready for the question. He answered without pausing, though he had a firm grip on his rock and kept Crag's staff in sight.

"Yes."

"Good."

Annev quirked an eyebrow, puzzled by Crag's emphatic response. *Does he really want me to attack him? Is he waiting for it?* Without the element of surprise, things would become messy. He stacked his rock atop the pile then quickly grabbed another.

"We don't just train to fight," Annev continued. "The ancients and masters also train us to steal things. Magical things."

"Magic, eh?" Crag leaned his staff against a tree. With his eyes on Annev, he took out a pipe and stuffed the bowl with rack root. "I find that awful curious," Crag said, filling the pipe bowl. "I mean, if you never leave your village, how can you know someone has something magical? No, no—don't spoil it for me. Let me think on it." A striker and charcloth appeared in Crag's hand. He lit the latter over the bowl, sucked tentatively on the smoker, and pocketed the rest.

"You'd need to have contacts in the cities," Crag said between puffs. "Banok. Luq'ra. Quiri. Ain't no way around that. But how would you communicate with them?"

Annev shrugged, less because he didn't know and more because he didn't grasp the merchant's game.

"Do you have a rookery?" Crag pressed. "A place for keeping birds?"

Annev thought on it. "Yes. The quartermaster keeps some doves and a few pigeons, even a hunting hawk."

"So. Use the birds to send messages back and forth. Still ..." Crag shook his head, his gray-streaked locks swinging about his chin. "Seems a daft thing to do. I mean, artifacts are rare enough I suppose, but if you're not going to sell what you steal then what's the point? There's no profit in it. And it's obvious you don't have anything of value or somebody would have hunted you down by now and stolen it back." Crag sucked on his pipe stem till the embers in the bowl glowed orange.

Annev shook his head, stacking another stone. "When an artifact goes into the Vault of Damnation, no one—"

"Ahhh," Crag interrupted. He gave a long low sigh, exhaling a mouthful of smoke. "And now the pieces fit together."

"What fits together?"

Crag took another long drag on his pipe, exhaled, and pushed himself up from the ground with his staff. "Ancients. Vault of Damnation. Avatars of Judgment. It all sounds familiar. Like an old story I couldn't quite remember." Crag smiled, a dangerous glint still in his eyes. "But now I do." He walked away from the altar, through the half-frozen mud and into the shaded depths of the wood.

"Crag?" Annev dropped his stone. "Where are you going? What do you remember?"

"I'm going to find whoever killed me mule. As to the story," Crag called over his shoulder, "come with me if you want to hear it." He was moving swiftly away from the clearing now, marching toward the forest gloom.

Annev hesitated. "But the path out of the Brake … you're going the wrong way!"

Crag stopped, turning to face Annev. "There are two trails here, lad. One you know and one you don't. If you want to learn something worth knowin', which do you think you should follow?" The merchant spun on his heel, heading back toward the darkness.

Annev took a step and then stopped. "Wait, your cart! You're just going to leave it? What if the people who killed Cenif come back?"

Crag didn't answer. He'd reached the edge of the clearing and disappeared into the shadowed trees. With a muttered curse, Annev dashed after him.

CHAPTER THIRTY-SIX

Neither Sodar's lessons nor Annev's training had covered tracking in the forest, but it wasn't hard here. He saw plenty of signs of passage—footprints in the mud, broken twigs, overturned rocks—and if these weren't enough, the trail of blood was easy to follow. Every few feet, Annev found the drops of dried crimson clinging to bushes, brush, and stone.

"Crag," Annev said, trying to get the merchant to slow his pace. "Crag, the mule was *brought* to that altar. Whoever killed it probably didn't come back this way."

"You assume the killers think like men who've committed a crime," Crag said around his pipe. "But I saw that clearing, same as you. Men might have killed Cenif, but what they did was savage, more like a wild animal ..."

"... and an animal has a den," Annev finished.

Crag nodded. "There's a story at the end of this trail, and I intend to find it."

Annev had no reply. As they walked on he reminded himself of his pledge to kill the peddler. That hadn't changed, but this wasn't the moment. There was something dangerous in the wood, and Annev wanted to know what it was. He even dared to hope that whatever beast had killed Cenif would also kill Crag. If Annev survived and the peddler did not, he could still take the man's ears back to Tosan. He felt a tiny flash of guilt at the thought—he had promised not to circumvent the rules of their deal—but the greater part of Annev's soul rejoiced in thinking there might be another way. He supposed that meant he was still the ring-snake Tosan had accused him of being, and he wondered what that meant for his future.

"What will you do when you find the people who killed your mule?"

Crag swished the pipe to the side of his mouth and spat into the trees. "I'll repay them in kind." He swung his quarterstaff at an offending shrub, scything its leaves from its body.

"But they could be dangerous."

"I can be dangerous, too, lad."

An hour ago, Annev would have found that boast absurd, but he'd since caught a glimpse of the harder man hiding beneath the merchant's jokes and jolly paunch, and he wouldn't underestimate Crag a second time.

The trail led them to the edge of a frozen rill, which snaked across the half-broken ice to the opposite bank, just a few feet away. Annev cautiously made his way across as the ice cracked and crunched beneath his feet, then he stopped and waited for Crag.

The fat man wasn't far behind. With his quarterstaff supporting him, Crag stepped onto the ice, his feet gliding in such a way that they didn't even crack the surface of the frozen water. Annev's brow furrowed as he adjusted his assessment of the peddler once again.

They moved on through the brush, the light growing dimmer as the day grew older. Annev tallied the hours since he'd left Chaenbalu and then his remaining time. A full day remained—more than enough time to accomplish his task—only Annev had expected it to be done by now, and the fact that it wasn't left him feeling uneasy.

"Do you have any family, Crag?"

The peddler shrugged. "Had a wife and son, but I outlived them both. Had a grandson, too, but fate took him from me as well. I s'pose I've accepted it, in my own way."

"What way is that?"

"By travelin', learnin'. I'm by meself most the time, but I make friends in every village I pass through. Feels less lonely that way. Havin' Cenif helps too …" He trailed off, and Annev understood why.

"So you haven't always been a peddler?"

"No. I was a farmer once—and a scholar, and a soldier. I've tried near every trade, and I expect I'll try a few more afore Fate calls me home."

Annev felt a pang of guilt at this last comment. "You were a soldier," he said, pulling at the thread he'd been picking at. "Have you ever killed anyone?"

Crag slowed his pace. "Have you?" Annev shook his head. "Then you best stay behind me when we get to the end of this trail. Trainin' ain't the same as doin'."

Not long after that, the tracks led them to the top of the ridge. The shrubs grew closer together on the other side, making the mule's wild trail easier to see.

"She was in a lot of pain, I think," Annev said, speaking softly. "I doubt she even saw where she was going." He pointed at the ravaged shrubbery. "She tore right through the scrub, snapping twigs, tearing up the ground."

Crag gazed down into the small valley below. "Poor beastie. She deserved better. She was a cursed stubborn mule, but she was steady-hearted." He tightened the grip on his staff. "I think we're close. You see that tree?" He pointed at a fallen pine. "There's a pit on the other side and the trail leads that way. I wager that's where the monsters found her."

"I thought we agreed men killed your mule."

Crag grunted. "Men can be monsters. And a man that hurts a frightened animal is ten times a monster." He spat, eyes hot with anger. "Whoever did this will pay. Blood for blood, and I make good on my promises." Crag led the way down the slope, steadying himself with the quarterstaff. Annev was close behind, wishing he had a staff of his own.

The scene below was strikingly like the forest clearing: blood spattered the length of the mule's trail, and Annev could see the dried pink and crimson streaks of spattered gore across the bark of every third or fourth tree.

Crag stepped close to one tree and eyed it more closely.

"This ain't mule's blood," he whispered, then pointed his staff at the red droplets on the ground. "That is."

"What's the difference?" Annev asked. "She might have stumbled into the trees."

"Aye, and from a distance that's just what it seems—but look closer. This blood weren't just smeared across the trees. 'Twas flung there. Sprayed across the bark with some measure of violence."

Annev stared at the tree closest to him. Crag was right. Something—more

MASTER OF SORROWS

likely several things—had been killed here, and not kindly. Goosebumps prickled Annev's neck, and he found himself wishing he had a weapon.

"Look here." Crag pointed at another tree a few feet to his left. "Metal embedded in the tree. Looks like copper." Annev stepped forward and examined the same trunk.

"Copper ... and iron?"

"And gold!" Crag exclaimed. He tugged at a slim ribbon of metal impaled into the roots of the tree, eventually prying the shard free. He turned it over in his hand then passed it to Annev.

"I don't understand," Annev said, examining the strip of gold metal. It was easily worth a gold sun and possibly a few beams. It was also sharp—sharp enough for him to use as a knife if need required it.

"Nor do I," Crag said. He ran his finger over a piece of flesh clinging to the tree trunk. "A strange and grisly puzzle." He took a step toward the pit then paused, clearing his throat. "Come on, lad," he said, seeming less confident than he'd been moments before. "I'll have the answers that lie at the end of this trail."

Annev pocketed the shard. Ahead, a portion of the path was blocked by the fallen pine. Annev drew closer and saw it had lain there for some time: most of the bark had peeled from the gray trunk, and dry needles covered the forest floor.

As Annev moved beyond the tree, he approached the small pit they had seen from atop the ridge. It was narrow, less than six feet in each direction, and a half-dozen twisted limbs and dry branches crisscrossed the opening. Peering through the broken limbs covering the hole, Annev saw two man-sized boulders lying at the bottom of the pit. The top of each was covered with dried blood.

"A trap," Annev said.

"Aye," Crag agreed. He stepped to the edge of the hole and poked at the branches with his staff. "Crude thing. Poorly built. Poorly hid. No stakes or snares at the bottom. Shallow, too. If you stood atop one of them boulders, you could hop right out." He knelt down and examined the open side of the hole. "Almost looks like it was dug by hand."

Annev crouched down and pointed at a severed root poking through

265

the side of the pit. "No. Look there. That root's been cut clean through. You'd need something sharp for that kind of cut."

Crag nodded. "I can't think it'd be a shovel on account of the walls being so poorly sloped. An ax, though? Maybe. Might be they used an ax to dig the pit too."

"A man with no shovel … who digs a pit with his ax?"

"Odd, ain't it?" Crag stood up, dusting the dirt from his knees.

Annev studied the pit, thinking. "I think the trap caught your mule. And the boulders … they must have been rolled in after she was caught. So they could get her out again." He crouched down at the mouth of the pit and pulled back two pine boughs, enlarging its opening. He continued to clear until he could see into the pit, then he hopped down onto the nearest boulder. Crag peered at him, curious.

"What're you doin'?"

Annev didn't answer. Instead, he bent down until his nose was almost touching the dry blood caking the rock's surface, then he moved around the rock, examining the dirt and dust beneath it. "There are white lines scribbled all over the tops of these boulders. Like something sharp was raked across their surface, over and over."

Crag pulled on his chin, frowning. "Keos, but that's a riddle I don't know the answer to."

Annev nodded, climbing back out of the pit. "Whoever set the trap meant to catch something, not kill it. Then they climbed in to get the mule out."

"But then why the blood?" Crag asked. "And the scratches on the rocks? If the monsters didn't want to hurt the poor beastie, why did they bleed her like that?"

"Because…" said a reedy voice from atop the ridge, "sometimes the monsters don't do what they're told."

CHAPTER THIRTY-SEVEN

The woman was so bent with age that if she'd been standing next to them, she'd have had to crane her neck to look up. She was entirely dressed in black, a terrible hump twisted her shoulders, and she peered down at them with round white eyes.

Crag held his staff in front of him and took a step forward.

"I speak of the monsters that tortured your mule." The crone's voice was thin and creaking, and she took slow steps down the ridge holding both hands close to her chest. Her fingers were twisted, gnarled things, more bone than skin and traced all over with dark blue veins.

Annev opened his mouth to speak—something about her seemed disturbingly familiar, as if he'd seen her in a dream—but Crag raised a finger for silence.

The crone reached the bottom of the ridge and vanished behind the fallen pine for a moment. Crag stayed alert, glancing back and forth between the two ends of the tree, waiting for the woman to appear.

"Who is she?" Annev whispered.

"Hush," Crag said, not taking his eyes off the pine tree.

When the old woman hobbled from behind the dead tree, Annev saw her eyes had a milky cast to them, like a pool of white smoke, though nothing about her behavior suggested she was blind. She stopped five feet in front of Crag.

No, not Crag, Annev realized. She was staring at *him*, her dull white eyes peering deep into his blue ones. A chill of foreboding ran up Annev's spine.

"The Vessel chooses his path."

"The Vessel?" Annev breathed.

The witch tilted her head to one side and smiled wickedly, her sharp teeth peeking out from dry withered lips.

"A piece of the greater whole. Sent to claim a rod and bring it back to your circle. Sent to claim a life. The merchant will give you a talisman, but it will be stolen from you, Son of Seven Fathers."

"What?" Annev's tongue seemed to stick in his mouth as the witch's words struck at his heart. "Son of Seven … Do I know you? Do you know me?"

The crone hissed. When she spoke again, her voice was low and haunting—a deep, hollow resonance that gathered in the heaviness of the forest gloom.

"Descended of the Gods yet sired by Man. Seven seek to lead Him. Seven dread His hand. Bonded by the Ageless, the Ancient breaks His path. The Crippled King guides Him. The world fears His wrath." With these last words, the witch extended her crooked arms and bowed her hunched form low to the ground.

Annev stared, mouth agape, as Crag stepped between him and the witch, one hand holding his staff and the other clutching a bony bauble tied to a string around his neck.

"Away with you, witch! We'll have none of your dark words here."

The woman lifted her head and hissed at Crag. The peddler shook the bone fragment at the crone and she retreated a step.

"Do you claim this one, Wanderer?" she said. "Do you choose the fate of the Fathers? It is not your path, I fear, but death may claim you yet."

"Death claims us all in time."

The witch cackled, running a wormy tongue over her broken teeth and cracked lips. "Your time has come and past, Wanderer. It has come many times, but you are never there to greet it, and so it claims your friends." Crag's face hardened. He glanced quickly back at Annev then turned back to the witch.

"Do you wear death's cloak then, crone?"

"I am death's shadow," wheedled the witch. "I go before him and fall behind him."

Crag raised his staff, arm cocked and ready to strike, such anger in his eyes that he looked half mad. "And are you the one," he said, "who took me beast from me?"

"A beast of burden," the witch recited. "Abandoned. Find it, and the Vessel will find you."

"*Damn* your riddles!" Crag swore. "Are you the one that killed Cenif?"

The witch twisted her head until it was at an unnatural angle from her body and drew her twisted arms close to her chest, the bony fingers dancing in front of her, her black nails clicking like dirty talons.

"One of many," she said. Crag's staff came down hard, striking at her, but she was already moving back, her tattered rags flapping in front of her, her body slipping across the ground faster than Annev could believe.

A low cackle came from atop the ridge and Annev turned to see the witch standing atop the knoll. Her eyes were wide, white and ghostly, her laughter full of malice. As Annev watched, she flickered from sight then reappeared on the opposite side of the pit. Flickered again, faster, and she seemed to be in two places at once. *Flicker. Flicker.* The images popped in and out so fast that they seemed to be multiplying—she was behind the trees, atop the ridge, inside the pit, and at his side. At the same time, her laughter came to a crescendo, building in intensity and frequency until the pitch was almost deafening.

Crag's elbow knocked Annev in the ribs. "Cover your ears, lad! She's a *witch*!"

Annev's hands clamped down on the sides of his head as Crag dropped the bone fragment tied around his neck. In its place, he drew a small, dirty mirror from the folds of his cloak. He tossed it on the ground and smashed the butt of his staff into its face. The glass shattered and her voice broke, dwindling to a thin scream coming from behind Annev. He spun to face it, reaching for the blade of gold in his pocket, and found himself staring at the old crone. She was crouched at his feet, hunched over in pain.

"Get back!" Crag shouted.

The crone did not pounce, though. Instead, she fell to the ground and curled into a tight ball of black rags, bony limbs, and knotted white hair.

Then she rocked herself back and forth, chanting softly: "Death comes for us all. Death comes for us all."

"She's mad," Annev whispered to Crag, not daring to take his eyes off the now weeping woman.

"Worse than mad. This one has magic. *Real* magic."

Annev's shook his head, trying to reconcile what he had seen with what Sodar had taught him. This was something new, a magic that was dark and unfamiliar to him. "Magic," he repeated. "Is that why she flickered about?"

"I believe so," Crag said, placing a hand on Annev's shoulder, "though I believe this one is more shadow than substance. She was creeping up behind us the whole time. What we saw was merely her shadow." He poked the crone with his staff and she rolled over onto her back, still chanting. "Seems I broke her mind when I broke me mirror—though she seemed broken enough to begin with." He tisked. "She's still dangerous. We should end her, roll her into that pit, and have done with her."

"You're still going to kill her?"

"Aye. I promised I would, and I will."

"But … she's an old woman. Seems cruel to kill her like this. In cold blood."

Crag's expression hardened. "She killed my mule."

"Death comes for us all," whispered the witch, oblivious to their conversation.

Annev looked down at the weeping old woman then imagined cutting her throat before rolling her into the pit. He shied from the image and tried to imagine Crag bludgeoning her with his staff instead … right before Annev slashed the peddler's throat with the ribbon of metal in his pocket. He felt sick. It seemed he would not escape the woods without bringing death to someone.

"No," Annev said, rejecting both images. "She said she was *one of many* and that sometimes the monsters don't do what they're told. Crag, what if she *didn't* kill your mule? What if she just helped capture it?"

The merchant scoffed. "She was still party to it. Blinded the poor beastie. Frightened her. Tortured her. Cut out her heart on a dark altar." He spat at the witch. "She's evil, Annev. Not because she has magic, not because she's a witch. She's evil because of what she does. And what she did. She *deserves* to die."

"Spared the mule," came a pathetic cry from the ground. "Killed the monsters. Spared the mule." Crag and Annev both looked down at the witch. She was still crumpled in a heap on the ground, but she had stopped shaking and her tears had subsided. She sniffed. "Told them not to kill her. They didn't. Told them not to harm her. They did. I killed them. Spared the mule. Mercy, I spared the mule."

Crag rubbed the patch of hair on his lower lip. "She's still dangerous," he said stubbornly.

"But do you think she's lying?"

Crag considered it. "I don't think so. Ones like these make strange bargains for their powers. They see what is to come, what is, and what has been, and they are compelled to tell the truth. But the truth you hear is not the truth as it is. They are malevolent creatures, which twist things to suit their own purposes." Crag brought his hand back up to the bone fragment tied around his neck. "Watch." He crouched down in front of the witch. With a jerk, he tore the bone trinket off his neck and held it in front of the crone's face.

"Speak no lies, witch, and tell me no riddles. Speak plainly and truthfully, or I will crack your skull and smash your brains across this ground. I will burn you and bury you, cast down your dark altars, and sow salt in your grave. Understand?"

The witch hissed, her arms slithered around her neck, and she bobbed her skull up and down. "I hear your words, Wanderer. I will tell you no riddles and speak no lies. Have mercy."

"First I will have the truth. Then we shall see about mercy."

The witch bobbed her head again, drawing back from the talisman in the peddler's fist. "Yes. The truth. I told them not to harm the mule."

Crag grunted. "So who killed her?"

The witch glanced furtively at Annev. "I sent the monsters to catch the mule—to dig a pit for the beast of burden. Catch the beast to bring the boy."

Annev's back stiffened and Crag looked from him to the witch, suddenly wary of them both. "The boy?"

"He'll kill us all," the witch whispered, rocking gently once again. "Kill us all. Kill *you*. Men. Gods. Keokum. All dead. All gone." She shook her head, her dirty white locks lashing across her face. "The Shadowcaster hunts him. The Shadow God wants him. The Fallen God needs him. I have been waiting so long …" Crag brought the bone fragment back up in front of the crone's nose. "I said no riddles!"

"No riddles, no riddles," she moaned. "I speak plainly. My whole life, I waited for him. Found him and lost him. Seventeen years of darkness and despair. Then he cast his blood into the shadows—blood stained with blackthorn. He *taunted* us, he teased us … but Kelga was waiting. The Gods were watching. They sent the Shadow Reborn to claim him, and he sought my aid. Dorchnok seeks him as well, but he cannot pierce the veil. Cruithear covets him, but he has given up on his *feurog* so he uses Harth as his puppet. And Tàcharan—my Lord, my God of Doom—he will not let me return without him." She hissed in frustration. "That boy is the bane of this world. The Son of Seven Fathers—the one-armed Son of Keos! By his hand we shall all die. In his death, we shall all live. I speak truly. Mercy, mercy, have mercy."

Annev flexed his gloved left hand and instinctively pulled it close to his chest. Crag peered over his shoulder at him. "Ignore her. She knows no words but dark ones. She is lying still." But the peddler's eyes told a different tale. There was fear there, Annev saw, and not fear from the witch.

"I'm not evil," Annev said. His heart beat fast and furious in his chest. His cheeks flushed red. He took a step backward. "I've never killed anyone."

"If you live we will all die." The witch pushed herself away from Crag and toward the blood-stained hole. Crag took three quick steps and placed himself between her and the pit.

The crone heaved a great sigh and lowered her head to the ground. "Your mule was dead and dying when we killed it." Her gnarled talons dug into the soil, grinding it into her skin. "The *feurog* had already dug the pit when I lured her. She fell in. Not hurt. Not hurt." The crone gave him a ghastly smile. "Called for them," the witch moaned, "called for the *feurog* to fetch the mule. No harm, I said. No harm. Did not listen."

Crag drew his right hand through the air and made the sign of Odar, flicking his index and middle fingers once to the left, once in front of him, and once to the right.

"I compel you, witch. The *feurog*," Crag demanded. "Who are they?"

"Godless ones—cast off, sent to wander alone … like you." She pointed at Crag. "They served my sisters once. Many still serve, but these were *mine*. They are like children. Twisted by the magic, forsaken by their father. Cruithear did not love them, but I did …"

"And did your *children* kill my mule, or did you?"

"They smelled the iron on her feet. Smelled her blood. I told them not to but they could not resist. I killed them for it. For ruining my plan, for tainting the prophecy. But the mule was dying. Dead but alive. I led her to the altar. Took her heart. Took her eye. Took it all to summon *you*. Mercy, mercy. I showed her—" Crag cracked her hard on the skull with the butt of his staff and she crumpled to the ground, panting, panting … and then her breathing stopped, her eyes closed, and she lay still.

CHAPTER THIRTY-EIGHT

Annev stared at the witch's unmoving body. "Is she dead?"

Before Crag could answer, a low growl came from the witch's mouth.

"*Seachranai*," the witch mumbled, opening her eyes. "*Fanai.*" She rolled to a sitting position, eyes open to reveal bright red pupils locked with Crag's. "*Anam caillte.*" She started to rise, her toes barely touching the ground as she slid towards the peddler.

"*Deorai*," the crone roared, "*sainmhiniu d'fuil!*" She lunged for Crag and he swung hard, snapping his staff across the witch's face. Her jaw cracked audibly, red spittle and broken teeth flying from her mouth.

Crag swung again, but the witch's gnarled hands shot out, inhumanly fast, and wrapped around his throat. "*Tugann Tàcharan neart domsa*," the old woman growled, squeezing. "*Ní theipeann orm arís.*" The veins in Crag's eyes bulged red and purple, his cheeks grew pale, and his strength seemed to rush out of him. His arms dropped to his sides and the staff and bone talisman fell to the ground. His knees buckled, and his body would have fallen without the witch holding him up by the throat.

In contrast to the weakening peddler, the witch seemed to be growing in strength. She stood taller—her back straightening, her stoop disappearing—until she towered over him. The white smoke that had once blanketed the crone's eyes darkened into a riotous swirl of red and black. She smiled, drawing her bloody lips back from her broken fangs, and heaved, lifting the fat merchant aloft.

"*Daoine truaillithe!*" the witch shouted. "*Daoine briste! Fir-iarainn-rugadh. Comhroinn mo bhéile …*"

The witch's mouth opened wide as an inhumanly long tongue snaked out and licked one of Crag's bulging eyes. She drew her lips back further, a gaping maw of gigantic proportions, and lowered Crag's ashen face to her mouth.

Annev tore his gaze away from the witch and glimpsed the white bone fragment lying on the forest floor. His instincts taking over, Annev dashed forward, rolled, and snatched the fallen artifact from the soil. He was back on his feet as the witch turned to look at him, mouth agape.

With the relic clutched tightly in his hand, Annev skirted Crag's dangling legs and leapt behind the old woman. He slapped the bone fragment to the crone's throat and pulled tight on the talisman's cord, strangling her with an improvised garotte. She hissed, her head swiveling at an unnatural angle, and then the witch's maw snapped shut around his wrist.

Agony.

Annev screamed, trying to pull his hand free, but it was too late. The witch's teeth tore through his black glove, shredding the skin beneath. A gray ichor dripped from his veins, coating her lips. The crone's eyes flashed, dark and angry; her once white orbs now coal black, the pupils an angry red.

Annev's arm seethed with pain as the gray ichor began to bubble out of his wound, turning black. He screamed for Crag, for Sodar, his head spinning ...

But he refused to let go. Instead, he gave a mighty shout and forced his arm further into the witch's mouth. She choked, and with his increased leverage Annev tightened the garotte. The crone gasped and Crag fell from her hands, dropping to the earth.

"Crag!" Annev screamed, tears streaming down his cheeks. "Help me!"

The merchant looked up. "Talisman?" he croaked, gasping for air.

"*Her neck!*"

He pulled himself to his feet, the color returning to his cheeks, and snatched his staff from the ground. He held the stick between himself and the witch and, with his other hand, made the sign of Odar. "*O luaith go luaith!*" Crag shouted, bringing the staff down in front of him.

A searing beam of light burst from the bone fragment tied to the witch's neck and her throat exploded with fire and blood. Annev fell backward as his improvised garotte disintegrated and his arm tore free from the witch's mouth.

The crone clutched at the gaping hole in her neck and tried to scream, but the sound morphed into a burbling cough as bile gushed from her ragged wound.

Crag took a cautious step forward, his staff held at the ready, but the witch stumbled back, her hands still clutching her throat, and then she toppled over the edge of the pit, crunching into the boulders that lay at the bottom.

Dazed but with his pain subsiding, Annev rose to his feet and together he and Crag peered down into the hole. The sight below chilled him: the old woman's body had fallen into the gap between the two boulders, folding her in half. Her skull had crashed against the stone's surface, scattering dark gray matter into the pit.

"She's dead now, right?"

Crag held up a finger, placed his staff on the ground, and untied a small sack from his belt. He poured a dash of salt into his hand, rubbing it between his fingers. "*O chre go cre*," he muttered, then scattered it atop her remains.

"It's done," Crag said, picking up his staff. "We can go." He turned and began to walk toward the ridge.

"Wait," Annev said, clutching his injured arm. Using his other hand—his true hand—he pulled back the tattered black glove covering his prosthetic, exposing the naked flesh beneath.

Unlike the last time he'd injured his arm, the magic prosthetic had somehow survived with its faux skin color intact. But this time Annev had not escaped unscathed: dark black rents in his flesh marked where the witch's fangs had sunk deep. He brushed the wounds with his right hand, and his fingers came away sticky with black blood.

Not red, he thought. *Black blood. Gray at first, and then black and boiling.*

Annev flexed his hand, testing its strength. Despite the severity of the injury it seemed to be working until, as Annev rotated his wrist, he felt an audible *pop* and a spurt of black blood shot between his fingers, splashing his cheek. The pain flared up again, as if his arm was on fire, and the dark blood pulsed anew. Annev screamed and reflexively clutched the wound, wrapping the fingers of his right hand around the injury, attempting to stem the flow of gray-black ichor.

"*Gods!*" Annev fell to his knees, curling around his arm with the pain. "It's burning!"

"Let go, you fool boy!" Crag's words came as if from a distance, yet Annev felt the man prying at his fingers, pulling his hand from the wound. Annev started to black out from the pain as it bled faster, falling backwards, his eyes glazed, until he was claimed by merciful darkness.

CHAPTER THIRTY-NINE

Annev lay on a pad of blankets, a fire crackled somewhere nearby, and the sky above was black and full of stars.

With an effort, he eased himself into a sitting position. The campfire burned merrily beside him and a small stack of dry branches lay a few feet away. On the other side of the flames stood the peddler's pushcart, its drawbar resting on the ground. Annev squinted, peering into shadows, but Crag was nowhere to be seen.

"Ah," came a soft voice somewhere high to his left. "You're awake then." Annev turned, looking up into the brown boughs of a buttonwood tree. Crag sat there, chewing on his pipe. He pulled it from his lips and expelled a long gray ring of smoke. "How are you feeling?"

Annev's eyes dropped to his left arm. The black glove had been removed and in its stead was a crisscrossing patchwork of white bandages. Annev prodded them with his right hand, testing the flesh beneath. His skin stung like a bad sunburn, but it wasn't unbearable. He flexed his left fingers and swiveled his wrist, testing his grip.

"It barely hurts," Annev said, astonished. "What did you do?"

"Truthfully, not much. You conked out and your arm started bleeding black witch-bile. Came streamin' out, like your body was anxious to get rid of the stuff."

"How did I get here?" Annev asked.

"How do you think?" Crag said, blowing another smoke ring. "I carried you and your stinking, dripping arm here. Couldn't make it stop while the taint of the witch was on you." He pulled the pipe out of his mouth and pointed at Annev's bandaged limb. "I did what I could, but I wasn't sure you'd heal till I'd cast down that damnable altar. So I smashed it, and I buried ol' Cenif." Crag's voice trailed off, going soft. "Buried what was left of her… what I could find. When I came back, your arm was healin' proper."

Annev looked down at his arm and flexed his fingers, afraid to look back up at Crag. He picked a bit at the bandages, wondering if the merchant suspected the truth of his prosthetic limb.

"Leave those alone," Crag said from his perch. "It's not healed yet." Annev nodded, replacing the loose bandage he had begun to unwind. "Give it a day," Crag added. "A week maybe. Probably won't even scar."

Annev looked up at Crag, thinking over the last half day. "You seem to know an awful lot for a peddler."

"And how would you know?" Crag asked, putting his hands on his hips in mock offense. "Seen many peddlers afore? In your secret village?"

"Well … no. Not exactly."

"Well, there you go. Might be they're all knowledgeable like me. Might be they're *worse*." He grinned, showing a mouthful of crooked, mossy teeth.

Annev smiled. "Somehow I doubt that."

"Well, then," Crag said, bowing dramatically. "You're wise beyond your years, Avatar Annev."

The smile faded a bit from Annev's face. "I'm not really an avatar," he said, trying not to frown. "I mean, I *should* be, but…" He stopped.

"But what?"

But I won't be one unless I kill you … and I don't think I can do that now. Annev shrugged. "It's complicated."

"Try me."

"Well," Annev said slowly, "right now I'm just a … deacon. I want to be more but … I failed this test. Actually, I *didn't* fail it, but the headmaster has it in for me and my friends, so instead of advancing me, I was demoted. I can still turn it around, but only if I finish a specific task."

"So what's the problem? What's the task?"

"Hmm?"

"What do you have to do for this title of theirs?" Crag asked, hopping down from his branch. When Annev hesitated, Crag tapped his nose and said, "Let me guess. That's the complicated part."

Annev nodded. "I don't know if I can do it—but, if I *don't*, my whole life is ruined. I won't be an avatar. I probably won't even be a deacon. Just a steward … or something worse. I'm not sure they even have a name for what they would make me. Servant?" He sighed.

Crag shook the contents of his pipe out into the fire, walked over to his cart, and threw back the blanket. Annev watched, curious, as Crag shoved both his hands inside and rummaged about for a small knife and a round, hand-carved block of wood. He walked back to the fire, plopped himself on the ground, and began to whittle. After a minute the peddler looked up at Annev. "What?" He lifted the block of wood and blew along the edge, scattering wood shavings across the ground. "Wasn't that the end of your story?"

"… yes," Annev said, frowning.

"You left out the part about feeling sorry for yourself." He shimmed the knife point along the face of the carving, making small, slow chips in the wood.

"What?"

Crag continued to chip away and blew at the loose shavings. "What does it matter what they call you if you're as good as everyone else? Avatar. Steward. Deacon. Servant? They're just names. They don't change who you are."

"But they're not the same," Annev protested. 'The privileges are different. The duties, the responsibilities, the respect … they're oceans apart."

Crag snorted. "So young. Thought havin' Sodar as your mentor might've opened your eyes a bit, but I s'pose livin' in a village your whole life has kept them shut pretty tight."

"So you *do* know Sodar. How?"

Crag chuckled. "That story is too long to tell, even if I had a mind to tell it—and it's beside the point, which is this: no one decides your future or your fate but you. Your ancients want to call you a steward or a servant? Fine. You can serve and make it true, or you can leave and be free."

"It's more complicated than that."

"I doubt it is," Crag said, resuming his carving, "but for the sake of argument, I'll agree with you."

Annev smiled in spite of himself and decided to drop the subject. He also decided he had made his decision: he wasn't like Tosan, and he wouldn't try to be; he was, as Tosan had suspected, like Sodar; mercy was in his blood, and while he might have an affinity for magic, he did not use it for evil ends as the witch did—nor would he.

The ramifications of that choice would have to be paid later, though. Annev would be made a steward, and Crag would go free. Worst of all, Crag would go with an intimate knowledge of the village, its purpose, and its location. By letting him leave, Annev was betraying the Academy and all of Chaenbalu. Annev doubted it would come to that—Crag did not seem malign, and Annev felt the man would keep his secrets if asked—but the risk was still there. Knowing that Crag and Sodar knew each other eased the difficulty of his choice, though; if Annev couldn't kill Crag as a lost peddler, he certainly couldn't kill him knowing he was an acquaintance of Sodar.

Annev sighed. He would return to the village as a failure, with all that entailed, but Crag's words made his fate less burdensome: maybe things weren't so complicated—maybe he really could decide his own destiny. Annev doubted it, but he also had hope again.

He looked around, trying to see the details of the forest with only the firelight to aid him. "Where are we? This isn't where we found Cenif."

"No," Crag said, still carving. "I was hoping you could help with that. After I got back to me cart, I threw you over the back and tried to trundle out of the Brake, stickin' to the path. Only it turns out you were right. These paths play tricks in the dark."

"It's not so much the dark as it is the shadows." Annev rubbed his bandages. "If it's full light or full dark, you can find your way well enough."

Crag stopped carving. "You mean if we left now, we could find our way out of here?" Annev nodded and Crag jumped to his feet. "Well, let's move then! We're wastin' time and I've got wares to sell in Hentingsfort." He snatched up his carving and tossed it to Annev who caught it, perplexed. Crag was over by his cart.

"What's this?" Annev asked, holding up the half-carved block of wood.

"It's a block of wood," Crag said, tossing the knife into the back of the cart and unstrapping a small spade.

"Right," Annev said, turning the object over in his hands. "But what are you carving it into?" The cylindrical block was nearly as wide as his hand, of equal thickness, and twice as long. Annev's fingers traced the delicate scrollwork lining its face. In the center of the spidery detailing was a bird in flight, its long, wide tail feathers fanning out below its body, its beak and crest pointed upward as if it were soaring higher.

"Am I that poor an artist?" Crag said, shoveling a spadeful of dirt onto the fire. "I thought it'd be obvious."

Annev looked at the carving more closely. The scrollwork surrounding the bird ran right up to the edge of its body, merging with the tail. As Annev turned the block of wood, he saw that the spiraling ornamentation tapered off into long feathers, each one wreathed in fire.

"A phoenix?" Annev said, turning it over once more.

"Could be, could be," said Crag, shoveling another spadeful of dirt onto the dying flames. The small camp plunged into darkness, the cart and peddler now only dimly lit by the light of the stars and half moon filtering through the forest canopy. Crag walked back to the cart and stowed the spade. "I'm not certain, though," he continued, not missing a beat. "You see, the carving isn't finished yet."

Annev scooped up his blankets and carried them and the block of wood over to Crag. "Then you should finish it."

"I shall, but tonight we need its light." Annev looked down at the carving then back at Crag, and the man snorted. "It's a riddle box. Figure it out." He threw the blankets over the back of the wagon and tucked the corners in, covering his wares and securing the loose articles on top of the load. As he moved, Annev studied the carving, no less perplexed.

"Solved it yet?" Crag said, returning.

"I'm not sure what I'm supposed to figure out. Does it open?"

"No. It does something greater than that." The peddler took the block of wood in his hands, pressed on a hidden mechanism, and pulled. Pale yellow light streamed from the carved feathers.

"Silver staves!" Annev exclaimed, startled. "It's magic. *Real* magic."

Crag chuckled. "No, it's a trade secret." He touched the side of his nose with his index finger and winked. "When you press certain parts of the wood in a certain way, certain things happen. Just now we need light to see where we're going, and I hate torches. All that black smoke and stink." He handed the glowing block of wood back to Annev. "You're the guide. Lead me out of here—and don't think for a minute you're off the hook just 'cause you saved me life." He cackled and then heaved up on the draw bar before sliding underneath and behind it. Annev started to duck beneath the rail as well.

"Stop right there," Crag said, holding up a hand. "Your arm's still healing. Let it rest. I can pull me own cart, especially when I don't have a grown boy lyin' atop it. Lead on." Crag heaved his paunch against the rail and the heavy cart rolled forward. Annev walked alongside him, holding the carved block of wood aloft to light the way.

"You should hang that on the front of the cart," Crag said, nodding to the carving. "I've some nettle-hemp under that corner of the blanket. Wind it round the bird and hang it from that hook. You should also grab a quarterstaff while you're back there," Crag advised. "If we come across another wood witch, I don't want to be caught unawares."

"Where are the staves?"

"On the far right side."

Annev pulled back the blanket as he walked alongside the rolling wagon, rummaging inside. He grabbed one of the staves then stopped. "There's a sword back here!" Annev said, surprised. "Do you want it?"

Crag shook his head. "The staff is fine for me. You can carry the blade for yourself if you like. It's more rust than metal, I fear, but it's sharp'

Annev pulled a staff and the slim sword from the back of the cart then hefted the latter in his right hand. The blade was a simple thing, perhaps three spans long and half a span wide, with no crosspiece and lacking any ornamentation. The hilt had been wrapped in a multicolored mix of rags— brown sackcloth overlapping white lace, slashes of green and blue tied to strings of yellow and ribbons of red. Rust pitted the blade, and the edge was chipped in several places. Annev tested his thumb against one jagged edge, though, and felt the metal catch against his skin, razor sharp.

"Where did you get it?" Annev asked, tucking the sword into his belt and jogging up to rejoin the merchant.

"Off a Reotan pirate in Sterklin. Had the scurvy somethin' fierce, so I traded him a few lemons for it." The cart rolled to a halt and Crag stopped to look around. "This is where I called it quits. The path disappears up ahead. It's all scrub and underbrush." He turned, nodding in the opposite direction. "But that's the way we came from, which I guess is northwest."

Annev studied the trail.

"Was there a fork in the road about a mile back?"

Crag nodded. "I turned right."

"We're still on the correct path then," Annev said. "If we go straight through that scrub, the trail will pick back up." Crag nodded and got the cart rolling again. Annev tucked the staff beneath his arm and walked beside the peddler. His right hand drifted down to his belt, to the sword at his hip. The sword Sodar had given him—Mercy—was a beautiful silvery thing, polished so brightly that Annev could see his reflection in the steel. But Annev doubted he would ever unsheathe it again. Even if he somehow passed Tosan's test, the headmaster had forbidden him from seeing Sodar and he couldn't take the sword with him into the Academy, so it was unlikely he would ever see Mercy again. Worse, if he were made a steward, he'd probably never be allowed to touch another weapon.

But *this* was a real pirate's sword. He'd never carried live steel like this, out in the open. Annev grasped the colorful hilt, imagining its history.

"What's the ocean like?"

Crag jerked the cart forward. "It's big. Wet. Salty. Full of fish."

Annev watched as the shadows of the forest trees grew and shrank under the dim light cast by the phoenix lantern. He sighed. "I'll never get to see it."

A black shadow flitted across the edge of his vision.

"Did you see that?" Annev said, whirling to follow the darker shape amidst the black forest. His hand instinctively dropped back to the sword hilt as Crag slowed the cart to a halt.

"See what, lad?" The merchant peered into the trees.

"It was a shadow … one that moved."

"An animal?"

Annev pulled the phoenix carving from its mesh netting then held it aloft, gazing intently into the darkness. He saw nothing.

Crag reached for the light. "Needs to be brighter," he said. He pulled the two ends, twisting them in opposite directions, and the diffuse light surrounding the block condensed into a single, brilliant cone blazing from the phoenix's eye.

"Incredible," Annev said, genuinely impressed. "You're sure it's not magic?"

"If I said it was, would some monks in red pajamas come to steal it from me while I slept?" Annev smiled, though he knew there was more truth to Crag's jest than he realized. "Think of it as high art," Crag said, shining the light into the trees, illuminating a thick clump of bushes and the boar that had been hiding there. "It's not magic when you know how it works."

"Well, how *does* it work?" Annev said, his eyes following the beam of light.

"Magic."

Annev snorted and glanced again at the carving in Crag's hand. He tried to remember what it had felt like holding the artifact. The wood hadn't been particularly warm. In fact, he hadn't felt any of the premonitions that the ancients had trained him to recognize. Did that mean the lantern really wasn't magical?

"Can anyone use it? Could I do it?"

Crag nodded, exchanging the carving for the pole under Annev's arm. "Once it's lit, you don't need to do anything."

Annev swept the broad beam over the forest, marveling at the details the light revealed. As he did, he clutched the block in both hands, feeling its rough, half-finished shape.

"Did you make it?"

"You saw me carving it, didn't you?"

"I meant the light. Did you create the light?"

Crag huffed. "Do I look like a magician? Lumea created the light. I'm just a peddler who figured out how to sell it."

Annev examined the carved block of wood in his hands, his fingers tracing its delicate carvings. He looked at Crag. "How do you turn it off? And make it shine like you did before?"

Crag took the carving and spun the block of wood in his hands. "You see the side where the phoenix is carved? What do you see on its breast?"

Annev studied the carving. "Feathers."

"Look closer."

"A flame," he said at last. "A tiny flame."

Crag nodded. "Good. Now what about here? In the heart of the fire." He turned the block of wood over to the side covered in flames.

Annev studied the carved flames for a long time. Unlike the phoenix, they had been carved long ago; the wood had been sanded, stained, and worn smooth with wear. He peered closer, studying their lines and curves, the varying depths of the cuts. When Crag turned the block of wood, the light from within seemed to flicker between each static flame, causing them to move and dance.

He was about to give up when he saw it: a thin, curved line carved into the center of the largest flame with a dozen smaller lines extending from it.

"A feather?" Annev asked, his fingers tracing the tiny line.

"A feather." Crag spun the block, pointing at the opposite side. "The flame within the phoenix," he intoned, placing one finger on the phoenix flame. "And the feather within the fire." He placed another finger on the feather. "Neither can truly die while the other lives." He pressed his fingers against the feather and the flame and twisted them outward. The light coalesced around the phoenix's eye and shot forth in a beam of brilliant white light.

Annev shook his head, still impressed by the changing light. He took the carving back from Crag and examined it once more. "I suppose if I want to turn it off then, I just …" Annev's fingers traced the images carved into the wood until they found the flame and the feather. He pressed down on both, felt a soft click, and tried to push the lantern together.

Nothing happened.

"Hmm." Annev released the two buttons and tried again, but this time he rotated his right and left hands in opposite directions. As he did, the block twisted inward, becoming thicker and shorter. The block clicked into place and the light diffused once again, shining from the lantern flames. Annev pressed the hidden buttons and twisted a second time and the block became shorter still. There was a soft *click*, and then the light went out, leaving them in moonlight. Annev blinked at the sudden darkness and fumbled with the lantern, fingers searching for the feather and the flame. When he found them, he pressed inward and pulled, twisting outward. Pale light sprang forth, shining from the cracks surrounding the flames as it had before.

"It's incredible," Annev said, turning the carving over in his hand. "I've never seen anything like it."

"Nor will you again, I expect." He pulled the silver flask out of his pocket, took a sip, and started the cart moving again. "No man alive knows how to make a lighted puzzle box, save the one in front of you." He screwed the cap back onto the flask and tucked it inside his vest.

Annev felt the hairs on the back of his neck rise. "What was that? Did you feel that?"

"You're jumpin' at shadows, boy. There's nothin' here."

Annev turned back to Crag. As he moved, the light reflected off something metallic in the bushes. He whipped the light back again, shining it on a dark thicket of trees. Still he saw nothing. Then he heard it—the harsh, scratching sound of metal against metal.

"Crag …" Annev said, pulling the rust-pitted sword from his belt. As he yanked the blade free, the lantern light shifted to the right and fell across a shambling, misshapen form.

"*Crag!*" Annev screamed, afraid to take his eyes off the creature, unable to turn and see if the peddler had heard him.

Then the shadows came roiling out of the darkness. The light from the phoenix lantern revealed two human figures, each one half-naked and grotesquely malformed. As they drew closer, Annev saw the scarred face of a man with long, scraggly brown hair and a matted beard. When the light touched the man's face, he raised his arms and covered his eyes, exposing the thin blades of iron that had been grafted into his forearms, their edges sharp as swords and protruding over an inch from the man's scabby flesh.

Annev swung the light toward the second figure, this one a woman, and saw her back was hunched, her breasts and spine twisted with bands of gold and copper that seemed to have merged with her skin. When the light shone across her face, she snarled, revealing broken teeth that had been filed to sharp points. She raised one thick limb, shielding her eyes from the light, and Annev glimpsed a mottled arm that looked carved from stone.

"Gods," Crag choked, appearing at Annev's side. "The witch hunts us still."

"I thought she was dead!"

"She is." Crag planted his feet on the ground and lifted his staff. "These must be her *feurog* …"

CHAPTER FORTY

"The *feurog*?" Annev swung the phoenix lantern in front of him. The light flashed between each of the creatures as they shuffled through the dark. "She said she killed those … things."

"Stop that!" Crag snatched the lantern from Annev's hand and twisted it inward to diffuse light. He tossed it on the cart and light scattered around them, illuminating the surrounding darkness.

In the pale light, Annev watched the twisted things advance. Naked and ugly, they looked like humans bereft of their humanity. Their faces were tortured, angry, and pained. The male screamed—a harsh, grinding sound—and raked its nails across its hair-covered chest, drawing blood.

An answering metallic screech came from somewhere behind Annev. He spun to see a third *feurog* emerge from the shadows. Its skull was almost entirely composed of black iron, its eyes little more than white slits behind a mask of metal and a mouthful of interlocking metal spikes. The monster gnashed its metal jaws together and howled, dribbling blood and rust.

"I hope you don't have any qualms about killing *these* bastards," Crag said, placing his back against Annev's.

"Are they even human?" Annev asked, readying the sword in his hand. The metal-faced *feurog* stalked toward him like a feral animal on the scent of fresh blood. It stopped a dozen feet away, raked its needle-sharp nails against its iron skull, and roared.

"Why don't you ask them?" Crag shouted above the din. The other two *feurog* paced in front of the peddler, scraping their metal-lined limbs together in a chorused cacophony. The bearded male with the bladed forearms screamed then lunged, his left hand swinging out to grab Crag's staff just as his bladed right arm swept toward the peddler's face.

Metal-face charged. Annev raised his sword and dropped into the stance Edra and Sodar had taught him: one foot in front of the other, his body turned sideways, his sword arm extended. The beast sprinted for him, arms pumping, hands clawing at the air. Annev swung and the beast grasped his blade. Sharp red lines appeared on its naked flesh before the snarling *feurog* snagged the chipped edge in its grip and yanked, trying to pull the sword from Annev's hand. Annev slammed his foot into its chest and as the creature fell back Annev ripped his blade free, tearing a chunk of flesh from the *feurog*'s hand.

Annev glanced back and saw that the peddler was hard pressed by the other two *feurog* which darted for him in turn, striking at Crag's face, throat, belly, and arms. The fat peddler was surprisingly fast with his staff while the *feurog* were slow and uncoordinated, but Annev could already see Crag tiring.

"If you don't mind finishin' yours off quickly, I'd appreciate the help." Crag snapped the pole twice across the female's face, once on each side, but she shook it off and advanced again. "Damn near impossible to kill these things with a blunt weapon!" he hollered.

Annev's *feurog* flexed its bleeding hand and stalked toward him, eyeing the rusty sword. Annev planted his feet, anticipating a lunge, and when it came for him, his sword arm slashed out and he sprang forward to meet it. It would be a killing blow—Annev knew it—yet he did not hesitate as he had done with the witch.

The tip pierced the monster's left eye, driven deep into the socket by the monster's own headlong rush. The thing shrieked but continued to fall forward, its momentum slowing and then stopping as Annev's sword scraped against the black metal encasing most of its skull. It fell to its knees and Annev jerked six inches of steel from the dying thing's eye socket.

Annev spun to see the peddler deliver a crashing blow to the bearded *feurog*'s head. As wood connected with cheekbone and temple, the monster's face collapsed under the sheer force of the strike and it dropped wordlessly to the ground.

Annev stepped forward as the remaining *feurog* swayed from foot to foot, her expression a mixture of rage and fear as she looked to Crag and the dead *feurog* in front of him, at Annev and the dying *feurog* behind him. She hissed, brandishing her stone arm as Annev noticed a gash on Crag's right forearm. Blood flowed steadily from the wound, dripping onto his hand. Annev came at the female from the side, advancing slowly, his sword at the ready. The *feurog* turned to face him, retreating as she did.

"Be ready!" Annev shouted just as the *feurog* pushed off her back foot and launched herself at him, flying high into the air. Annev retreated as she opened her arms wide to deliver a crushing blow.

He saw his opening—the spot where her heart would be—and raised his sword to strike. At the same time he he saw a gleam of gold reflect from the female's armored torso. She fell hard and fast, crashing into him, and Annev felt a sharp *crack* as he and the creature tumbled over each other into the dirt. He jumped back to his feet, cutlass swinging, and saw he held an empty hilt, the old blade having snapped off in the *feurog's* shoulder.

Odar's brazen balls.

The *feurog* wrenched at the steel piercing her shoulder then threw it back at Annev. He ducked beneath the spinning blade and she backhanded him across the face, knocking him to the ground and then straddling him, pinning his arms to his sides. With a roar, she raised her heavy left arm—an ugly, black-and-white-speckled thing that glittered in the lantern light—and brought it crashing down on Annev's head.

But the blow never landed. Instead Crag's staff shot through the air, quick as an arrow, and crunched into the *feurog's* windpipe. She toppled off Annev who rolled back to his feet.

Crag stood over the prone female with the butt of his staff pressed down on her forehead. She writhed in the dirt, her hands clutching at her throat, clawing for air.

"She's choking," Annev said, panting.

"Aye, that she is." Crag hefted his staff. "Best to finish her off cleanly." He raised the metal-capped staff high overhead.

"No!" Annev protested. "I mean … can't we help her?"

"She tried to kill us. Might even be one of those that tortured me mule." Crag kicked the *feurog's* left hand away from her throat and it fell to the ground, heavy as a stone. He stepped on it. "You see that?" he said, grinding his boot into her hand. "Her skin's like granite. She would've smashed your skull to bits."

Annev frowned. The *feurog* struggled to pull her arm back from Crag's boot, but she was growing weaker. Her lips turned blue and Annev could see panic in her eyes.

Her terribly human eyes.

"Give me your pipe!" Annev snapped, kneeling beside the *feurog*.

"What do you want with—"

"Your pipe! Now. Before it's too late!"

Crag shook his head even as he pulled the pipe from his pocket. "I know you think you're helpin', boy, but you're not. This one's dead. It'd be kinder to finish her off."

Annev ignored him, taking the pipe. He tore the *feurog's* other hand from her throat and held it to one side. "Hold this other wrist down!" Annev demanded. Crag muttered something dark under his breath but did as he was told, stepping on the creature's other hand. Beneath him, the *feurog* thrashed and tried to free herself, eyes bulging, teeth gnashing.

Annev reclaimed the broken sword blade then placed the pipe between the *feurog's* metal-sheathed breasts. Holding the dull spine in his hands, he pressed the blade's edge against the pipe stem and sawed downward, hacking the pipe stem from its bowl. The *feurog* jerked as the edge of the sword pressed into her chest, but when the blade was lifted, only a thin scratch could be seen on her metallic skin. Annev straddled the woman's misshapen chest, uncertain what he was doing. Sodar had explained it to him once—had said he should never attempt it unless it was the difference between life and death; this was such a moment, and he knew he had to try, even if his failure ensured the woman's death.

Pinching the broken end of his cutlass, Annev made a quick puncture into the *feurog's* windpipe. He flinched as a spurt of air burst from her throat, then, before blood could seep into the wound, he jammed the severed pipe into the incision.

The *feurog* stopped thrashing as air returned to her lungs. Her lips regained their color and her eyes looked a little less wild, though no less frightened.

Annev stood, still holding his rusty blade by its spine. Crag whistled. "Where'd you learn that bit of magic?"

"Sodar," Annev said, still watching the *feurog*. "He said if I was going to be a priest, I needed to know how to help people."

"That's a skill, me boy. Healing is a true art." He frowned. "Though I wish you hadn't broken me favorite pipe." He nodded at the creature on the ground. "What're we to do with this one? She's still dangerous."

Annev looked between the *feurog* and the broken cutlass, suddenly realizing the weapon couldn't defend him. He scooped up the broken hilt from where he had dropped it and stepped back, his fingers working to untie the mismatched cloth strips. "Do you think she'll try and harm us?" he asked, rewinding the cloth around the base of the naked blade.

Crag shrugged. "These things seem feral. No tellin' what she'll do. Still not sure why they attacked us just now, seein' as the witch is dead and can't drive them on. I'm even less certain why you're tryin' to save her."

Annev stopped winding and studied the female. She had closed her mouth to better concentrate on breathing through the pipe in her neck. With her thin lips pursed shut, Annev could no longer see the long rows of sharp teeth. She looked less like an animal and more like a frightened woman—and it was clear she was terrified of them. The *feurog*'s eyes bounced between Annev and Crag, but there was something else there. A spark of intelligence? A plea for mercy?

"Let her go," Annev said.

Crag looked down at the *feurog* with the pipe sticking out of her neck. "She'll kill you, given half a chance."

"Maybe," Annev conceded. "All the same, I'd rather we let her go. She's less dangerous than she was, and I'm curious what she'll do."

Crag sighed and lifted his staff off the *feurog*'s head. "So be it." He stepped off her arms and retreated a few steps, watching. Annev also retreated, circling back to stand beside Crag.

With her arms free, the *feurog* carefully brought both hands to her throat. The skin of the *feurog*'s right hand was soft flesh—not granite like the left hand or metal like her back and chest. She used her human fingers to gingerly prod at the pipe stem in her throat. She grasped it between her fingers.

"No!" Annev shouted. The creature stopped, dropping both hands to her sides. All the while, Crag said nothing.

The female rolled to her hands and knees then stood. With her eyes on Crag and Annev, she slunk back to the two dead males lying on the forest floor. When she reached the bearded one with the crushed face, she grabbed his arm and dragged his body into the darkness.

CHAPTER FORTY-ONE

"Such strange things we've seen this night," Crag said, clutching his staff to his chest. "If I didn't know better, I'd say we'd wandered into the Vosgar."

Annev shook his head, his eyes fixed on the metal-faced creature the female had left behind. "We can't be, we've not crossed the Brake Road." He looked around at the black woods. "We're close, though. The trees look and feel different the nearer you get to the Vosgar. Darker. More wild. I've never known anything like tonight, though. No witches. No creatures made of metal." He walked over to the dead *feurog*, examining its face. His eyes went wide.

Its ears ... they aren't covered by the iron.

Annev swallowed hard, barely able to believe his luck: he could still choose his own path—he could side with Sodar and be a man of character while still fulfilling Tosan's inane task. He could take the creature's ears, and with them he could purchase his salvation. His whole future at the Academy, everything he had ever hoped for and dreamed about, could still be a reality. With trembling hands, Annev discarded the hilt of the broken cutlass and tied off the cloth strips covering the base of the steel blade, then he knelt on the soil and lifted the makeshift sword to the side of the *feurog*'s face.

"What're you doin' there, lad?"

Annev paused. "You remember those complications I mentioned?"

"Aye." Crag brought the lantern over.

"This is one of them." Without explaining further, Annev sliced off the creature's ear with his sword.

"Gods, boy! A minute ago you wouldn't kill one of these things, and now you're takin' trophies?"

Annev rolled the *feurog*'s head over and grasped its second ear. Part of the lobe was fused to the iron covering the *feurog*'s skull, but Annev was able to slice off enough that he felt Tosan would be satisfied. He stood, collected some fern leaves, and used them to wrap the chunks of flesh.

"I take back sayin' your village was a good place. Any folk that insist you take someone's ears as a test …" Crag shook his head. "That ain't the sort of place you want to call home."

Annev used another leaf to secure the bloody package then tucked it into his tunic. "Maybe," he conceded, though in truth he felt giddy. He might still earn his avatar title—*without* having to murder a lost peddler.

"Strange order, though," Crag said, eyeing the sword in Annev's hand. "How do they expect you to find a pair of ears when they've deliberately hidden their village out of the way of other folk?" How scratched his own ear and shook his head.

"I said it was complicated," Annev said, avoiding the merchant's unspoken question. He turned and gathered his bearings. "The edge of the forest should be about a mile south."

Crag grunted, still watching Annev. "Best we move on then." He handed Annev the lantern and together they walked back to the cart. Once there, Crag pulled the silver flask out of his pocket, took a sip, and splashed some of its contents on the cut on his forearm.

"How's your arm?" Annev asked, studying the wound.

"It'll heal."

"I can wrap it for you if you have something to use as a dressing."

"No need. That bit of magic I can do on me own." So saying, he reached into the back of his cart, shifted a few things around, and pulled out a tiny roll of cloth. He unraveled it then began to wrap the bandage around his injury. "How's *your* arm?"

Annev slid the cutlass blade back under his belt and flexed his bandaged left hand. "Good, I think. The pain has faded."

Crag grunted. "We should change your dressin', though."

Annev nodded and a minute later Crag was helping him unravel the sticky bandages from his prosthetic. Crag nodded at the gray-pink scars, which seemed to be healing fast, then rewrapped the injury.

"Crag," Annev said, once the peddler had finished. "Once I lead you out of the Brake, you can never venture back in. I'll never see you again."

The merchant nodded. "I suspected that. Wouldn't be a proper secret village if ol' Crag came visitin' whenever he liked—not that I would, seein' as my wares don't fetch a good price."

Annev smiled. "You'll keep our secret then? You won't tell anyone about the village or what we do there?"

Crag laid a fist over his chest. "I swear it." He paused. "Or you could come with me, you know. I need another pack animal, after all."

Annev stared at the merchant, trying to tell if the man were serious. In the shadowed light of the lantern, it was hard to tell.

"Are you really offering me a place with you?"

Crag tucked the bandages back inside the cart along with his staff. "Well," he said, "you saved my life, tonight. Seems only fair that I offer to save yours."

"But … you already did. When you carried me back to your cart and bandaged my arm."

Crag smiled, lifting the drawbar to duck beneath it. "True enough, though you saved me from the witch in turn. But that's not what I meant. Truth be told, we've each done our share on this trip. I was talkin' about this test of yours. About you takin' those ears back to your elders so you can say you got me killed."

Annev's cheeks flushed hot with embarassment. "How long have you known?"

Crag smiled. "Long enough you'd have got a nasty surprise if you'd tried. I don't take kindly to folk tryin' to murder me, even if they're friends of Sodar."

Something dropped into place for Annev. "You've been to the village before, haven't you?"

Crag nodded. "Yes. I've visited Chaenbalu."

Annev noted the peddler pronounced it correctly this time. His mouth twitched. "So you know Sodar, and you've been to the village." He shook his head, rolling the half-carved phoenix lantern in the palms of his hands. "Why all this then? Why pretend you were lost?"

"I *was* lost. I came to the Brake on purpose—to find Sodar—but I got turned around. One of your witwomen found me wanderin' nearby, and she sent one of your master avatars to keep an eye on me. Figured I should stay put at that point—didna want to make trouble for Sodar, after all—but then Odar saw fit to send you as my guide."

Annev tried to swallow, but his mouth had gone dry. "So being a peddler—it was all an act? You're just another artisan or something from Sodar's secret brotherhood." He didn't mean it to sound like an accusation, but he had grown to like Crag, and the thought that he was just another thread in Sodar's web of lies left a bad taste in his mouth.

Crag shook his head. "Sodar hasn't seen me for years, and I expect we're both happier that way. I still count him a friend, but we don't see eye to eye." He shrugged. "I'll let Sodar explain as it's a long story and not my place to tell it … unless you joined me on the road to Hentingsfort."

Annev was torn. He stared mutely at the lantern in his hands, at the bulging blanket covering Crag's cart, and finally at the peddler himself. So many questions. So many riddles. He wanted to hear Crag's history—and to learn the peddler's connection to Sodar—but he couldn't abandon his life in Chaenbalu for those answers.

"I can't go with you."

"Why not?"

"Chaenbalu is my home and people are counting on me to return. My life is there." He thought of Myjun—of courting her once he earned his avatar title. He thought of seeing Titus and Therin again, and of wiping the smug look off Fyn's face once he was wearing his brown avatar robes.

More than anything, though, Annev was thinking of Sodar. He would have to leave the ministry and abandon his mentor when he returned home, but even so, he wanted to go back to Chaenbalu and see the priest one last time. He felt guilty about going on Tosan's errand without stopping to tell Sodar about the Test of Judgment. And he had questions for Sodar. If Crag wasn't going to give them freely, Annev would ask the priest himself … and about the witch's words too.

Son of Seven Fathers, Annev thought, brooding. *Son of Keos. Vessel.* Even if Sodar claimed not to know the significance of the witch's words, he'd still lied to Annev about his parentage and his own secret past. Annev wagered that Crag was connected to it all too—part of the secret life that included artisans and bloodlords and ageless ones.

Crag studied Annev's face then nodded. "Well enough, lad. If you know your place, I'll not drag you from it." Crag pushed against the draw-bar and he and Annev started walking towards the road. "Just as well, I s'pose. I'm a fat, cranky old peddler who's not used to keepin' company."

Annev smiled. "Replace cranky with mysterious and I'll agree with you."

"Oh, I see," Crag said, his tone all mock offense. "You're sayin' I'm fat."

Annev shook his head, his smile broadening. "Can I deliver your message to Sodar?" He paused then decided to take a chance. "Does it have anything to do with the artisans dying?"

Crag looked at him sharply. "What do you know of that?"

"Arnor visited yesterday," Annev said, bending the truth a bit.

"Arnor?" Crag said, missing a step. "Now there's a name I haven't heard in a while." He was silent for a moment, his smile slowly vanishing. "I'm surprised you heard that much. Sodar always likes to keep others in the dark for as long as possible." Crag's words alarmed Annev more than he let on, but he kept quiet, hoping the merchant would speak freely. "Bad habit that," Crag continued, "though I doubt it's one you'll ever break him of."

"So," Annev said, after a beat. "What message do I give to Sodar?"

"Ah, wouldn't you like to know," Crag teased. "Too bad for you. Seems I've picked up Sodar's bad habits." When Annev frowned, the merchant laughed with true mirth. "Don't fret, lad. I left a letter near the standin' stone where we first met. You can take it to Sodar when you return—just don't break the seal." Annev nodded. "Right then. Assuming we don't get interrupted by another demon-witch or metal-monster, let's talk on more pleasant things. Ask me about any town or place you've heard of, and I wager I've got a good story to tell."

"Well," Annev said, relenting, "how about the Green Froch and the Horse-lords?"

"The Markluans! Ran into a few of those in my time. Fierce

bargainers—fer savages anyway. Their currency is strange too. They don't use the staves and suns like we do in the Empire. Instead, they got brass bangles and silver bands, copper hoops and gold rings. Anythin' you can wear—anythin' with a hole in it—can be used for trade."

After another half hour of walking and mostly pleasant conversation, Annev and the peddler stumbled out of the Brakewood and onto the Brake Road. The stars were out and they could see far off down the road in either direction. There was no sign of other travelers. Crag ducked out from under the drawbar and picked up the phoenix lantern.

"I promised you rattan and dragon's blood in exchange for safe passage out of the Brake," Crag said. "And though we were attacked twice during the journey, the first time was of me own doing and the second was pure happenstance. You performed your duties as guide better than any man could hope for." He extended his empty hand. "That being said, I'll be takin' me blasted cutlass back now."

Annev grinned, handing the broken blade to Crag. "Thank you. May Odar protect you in your travels."

"And may Lumea lighten your path, wherever it takes you," Crag replied. "Speaking of which." He offered Annev the phoenix lantern. "I want you to take this—as a gift."

Annev shook his head. "It's too precious. And besides, you'll need it."

Crag huffed and pressed the carving into Annev's hands. "I've got the stars to light my way, lad. Don't need no riddle-box, and I can always make another if I choose. You take it, I insist. A phoenix for a phoenix." Annev accepted the treasure. "Just keep that little bird away from your ancients," Crag warned. "That's a gift freely given, and I don't want to hear someone took it from you—'specially not them bastards in the red pajamas." He spat on the ground between Annev's feet. This time, Annev didn't even flinch.

"Thank you," Annev said, knowing he'd have to leave it at the chapel along with Mercy. "I'll treasure it, and our friendship, and I wish you good luck in Hentingsfort, or Port Caer, or wherever you're headed to."

"All of them!" Crag said, dipping back beneath the cart's drawbar. "First town I stop at, though, I'm gettin' meself another mule. Damned tiring having to drag this everywhere I go, and I miss Cenif's company."

He sighed then clapped Annev on the back. "Thank you, Ainnevog—and remember: if you don't like the road you're on, there's always another path. Just takes courage to find it." Annev nodded, and then Crag heaved, starting the wagon down the starlit road. Annev slung the lantern in its webbing over his shoulder and watched until the cart vanished into the darkness.

Instead of going back into the Brake alone, Annev turned west and ran along the Brake Road. To his right was the slumbering Brakewood; to his left, the towering pines of the Vosgar. He ignored both, keeping his eyes on the road, and raced into the darkness. He knew he would eventually reach familiar paths, which offered a quicker way home.

For now, though, he was alone and free—free of obligations and ancients, of titles and tutors. They would all try to claim him once he reached Chaenbalu, but for now, the road was his guide and the stars his companions. He ran faster, smiling despite his worries, and raced to beat the dawn.

PART THREE

And Keos fell to the earth and cast his eyes about him, at his brother who had smote him and at his sister who had stood by. And he raised his broken limb to his sister and cried out for help. But Lumea was ashamed and withdrew from his presence.

Now this hurt Keos far more than the physical injury he had suffered, for though Keos had once loved his elder brother, he still dearly loved his sister and felt Lumea's betrayal sharpest of all.

And so it was that Keos lifted up his voice and cursed Odar and Lumea. And he cursed their children, the Darites and the Ilumites, and vowed that he would make war upon them. And he cursed the gifts which he had wrought, both the Staff of Odar and the Flute of Lumea. And the curse of Keos was potent, for it meant Lumea and Odar would be burnt if they wielded the instruments. And the curse did extend even unto the followers of Odar and Lumea, that if a Darite or Ilumite attempted to take up the Staff or the Flute, they would be smitten and die.

Yet the curse of Keos was imperfect, for a small number of Odar and Lumea's worshippers could still wield the instruments of power. Yea, those few Ilumites who had found great favor with Lumea were able to play the Flute, and those few Darites who had found great favor with Odar were able to carry the Staff. And they were called daltas, *or child-gods, and were held in great reverence and blessed with vast magical power.*

And so Keos fled and hid himself in the depths of the earth. And for a long time he would not be consoled, and he surrounded himself with none but the golems he had made while he took up his hammer and forged himself a new hand. And it was made of pure gold and was formed with great cunning and cleverness insomuch that it appeared like unto his hand of old, save that it was engraved with his artistry.

And Keos poured much of his remaining power and strength into this new hand, and also his malice, for he had sworn vengeance against Odar and Lumea. And even as Odar had sought the destruction of the children of Keos, so Keos swore that he would destroy the worshippers of Odar and Lumea.

Now this was not all, for while Keos labored in the depths of the earth, new Gods arose. And they were called the Younger Gods and came from the Breaking of the Hand of Keos. And their names were Sealgair the Hunter, God of Animals; Garadair the Gardener, God of Plants; Cruithear the Creator, God of Minerals; Dorchnok the Trickster, God of Shadows; and Tàcharan the Changeling, God of Chance.

And also five new races spawned from the hand of Keos; and they were the Dragons, the Nymphs, the Giants, the Eidolons, and the Faeries. And from the palm of Keos sprang thousands of other magical creatures with neither race nor parentage. And they were called Keokum, for they were born of Keos and yet were not his children. And all of these things came from the Breaking of the Hand of Keos.

And the span of the Second Age was counted from the death of Myahlai until the Breaking of the Hand of Keos. And it was called the Age of Kings and spanned a thousand years.

—A translation of a fragment recovered from the ruins of Speur Dún: "The Breaking of the Hand of Keos," from *The Book of Terra,* translation by Sodar Weir

***

Now the Third Age of the world was marked by the birth of the Younger Gods. Yet when they awakened to their divinity, their father was absent from them. Yea, Keos had removed himself from the face of Luquatra, and he forsook his children that he might nurse his wounds and gather his strength for the day that he would rise again in glory and power.

And the number of the Younger Gods was five, for they had sprung from

the Breaking of the Hand of Keos, and they retained a portion of his strength. And they awoke to a world of chaos and blood, for Keos had forsaken his worshippers and they did war one with another. And the Younger Gods took pity on the people of Keos, and as they succored the Terrans, they gained worshippers of their own and began to usurp Keos's stewardship over t'rasang.

Thus it was the five Younger Gods divided the people of Keos, flattering his worshippers and claiming many for themselves. Yet the majority of the Terrans remained true to Keos and continued to worship him in his absence, for when Keos rose from his isolation, they believed he would seek communion with the faithful and that many would be raised to become Bloodlords—and so it came to be.

But the unfaithful were not rewarded. Yea, Keos did visit the Younger Gods in his wrath, and he instructed them to submit to his will and bring their worshippers back into his fold. But the Younger Gods spurned Keos, for they were proud like their father and they asserted their own divinity. Yea, and they claimed that Keos was a maimed God and that his power was diminished. And as their evidence, they pointed to the forge at Thoir Cuma, which had ever been a sign of Keos's strength, and they showed that it had been cast down and a temple of Tàcharan had been raised in its place. And thus did Keos fail to establish his supremacy over them.

Yet Keos did not rage as he had in the past, for his time in isolation had made him more thoughtful and more cunning. And he returned to the pits of Daogort, to that same place where he had once isolated himself, and he shaped its underground chasms into a great amphitheater, and he invited the Keokum to visit him and declare either their allegiance to him or their independence from him. And he also invited the Dragons, the Nymphs, the Giants, the Eidolons, and the Faeries. Yea, he invited all the creatures that had spawned from the Breaking of the Hand of Keos.

For five years Keos gathered them in. For five years he ministered to them, plying them with food and drink, flattering them with gold and silver, that he might persuade them to remain for the great Council of Keokumot. Yea, and he did persuade one of the Younger Gods to visit him and then to stay with him.

And at the end of five years, the amphitheater had swollen with those loyal to Keos. And many who stayed for the Council hoped to influence the God of Earthblood, though they would not swear their allegiance to him. And many *more remained because they perceived Keos was a Fallen God. Yea, and they sought to take advantage of him in his weakness, for they praised him by day and mocked him by night.*

And when five years had expired, the Great Council was achieved. And the doors of Keokumot were sealed that all might deliberate their allegiance or independence.

But the Council was for naught, for Keos had already discerned who among them were false and who were loyal. And he had brought an army of golems—yea, even five hundred thousand golems, which had been formed during his isolation—and the golems barred the gates of Keokumot. And the faithful filled the amphitheater with the bones of the disloyal. And none that remained contested the dominion of Keos.

And from the schism at Keokumot were derived five new races, which were the Draken, the Sirens, the Ogres, the Demons, and the Devils. And these five warred with their sister-races, which had rejected Keos. And the Third Age of Luquatra became known as the Age of Blood.

—A translation of a fragment recovered from the ruins of Speur Dún: "The Council of Keokumot," from *The Book of Terra,* translation by Sodar Weir

CHAPTER FORTY-TWO

Annev jogged up the crest of the hill overlooking his village and slid the lantern off his shoulder. He bent forward with his hands on his shaking knees and gasped quick, deep breaths while staring at the grass beneath his feet. The air carried the scents of early spring: cool morning dew mixed with the richness of damp earth and a soft, temperate breeze.

Annev slowly straightened. The sun had already risen above the treeline on the eastern side of the Brakewood, though its pale light was yet to fall on the clustered buildings and small plots of farmland sitting, as the village did, in a secluded, forested valley.

The light did catch the Academy spires, though, rising above it all. As the largest building in the village and the only structure more than two stories high, its towering spires and bleak gray architecture stood apart from the humbler surrounding buildings, rising higher even than Sodar's chapel at the far end of the village. As Annev stared at the place that would be his new home, he found he had mixed feelings about reporting to Tosan. For one thing, he was mentally and physically exhausted; the strange events of the past day and night had taken its toll in more ways than one, and the long run back home had drained him.

He was elated to have completed Tosan's task on his own terms, and to finally become an Avatar of Judgment. Yet it was bittersweet, because it meant his time with Sodar had come to an end. Annev's gaze fell away from the Academy's walls and landed on the tiny dun-colored building he had always called home. He'd have to return to gather his things and move into the Academy, and he welcomed the prospect Annev. There was even time to gather the supplies he had left at the standing stone before heading home to eat and sleep. The headmaster would wait for him—Tosan had given him until sunset, and the day was only just breaking—though Annev knew he would neither eat nor rest until he had spoken with Sodar. The priest would want to know everything, and Annev had his own questions for the priest. This time he wouldn't relent until Sodar answered them.

As he neared the southwestern edge of town, Annev passed through a grove of ochroma trees and dared to look up into their branches in search of ring-snakes. He saw only a few bats, though, and paused to drink from the mill stream. It tasted a bit brackish, but the water was welcome after his long run. He took several more gulps then crossed the dam that joined the road leading into the village. He wove through the narrow streets surrounding the plaza, giving the Academy a wide berth, and made doubly sure he stayed out of sight of the stained-glass window in Tosan's study.

As he hastened through the streets, Annev looked down and was shocked to see he had forgotten to remove the bandage from his left arm—a task he'd meant to do before entering the village. He ducked behind the tannery wall, set the lantern down, and peeled back the wrapping at the base of his elbow, feeling a slight pang of guilt as he did. The peddler had told him to leave it alone until the wound had fully healed, but Annev couldn't risk the stigma of a visible injury or the failure it implied. Even after fulfilling Tosan's mission, a scar of that magnitude would effectively void his achievements, marking him as one unworthy of Odar's favor. Annev had seen it happen to Kenton and had no desire to suffer the same fate.

As the bandages fell away, Annev examined his wrist and forearm. The skin was pink and tender with faint, almost invisible, mottled red spots surrounding the area where the witch had bitten him, but he saw no scratches or scars. The magic prosthetic had healed itself.

Relieved, Annev tucked the bandage into his tunic, reached into another pocket, and retrieved Myjun's Regaleus glove. The pristine red and gold fabric had been tucked neatly into his breast pocket since he'd left the chapel yesterday morning. In contrast, the black Glove of Illusion, which had survived the Test of Judgment, had been shredded by the wood-witch. Crag had saved the tattered scraps for him, but Annev had only the nonmagical glove to cover his arm. He pulled it on now, thinking of Myjun and of finally giving her the promise ring, and even though it could not hide his arm from magical scrying as the Glove of Illusion had done, he was comforted by its presence.

Annev poked his head around the tanner's wall and glanced up and down the street. When he was certain no one was watching, he sprinted for the eastern watchtower, weaving through the small alleys and hoping to avoid any ancients or masters attending to early morning errands. Outside the village proper, he darted between farmhouses, hastening toward the standing stone where he'd left the palm vine and dragon's blood; he wouldn't breathe easily until he'd gathered the supplies, collected Crag's letter to Sodar, and reached the chapel.

***

Annev eased the training shed door open and set down the lantern and supplies. As he did, he took a moment to examine the peddler's artifact, twisting it until light became diffused and then focused. Annev marvelled at it, less because of its magic and more because it was an astonishing gift.

Despite Crag's final admonition about keeping the it safe, Annev had briefly considered turning it over to Tosan. It would be dangerous if he were discovered with it, but he also wanted to impress the headmaster by returning from his mission with an artifact—however small—for the Vault of Damnation.

But it had been a gift; surrendering it would be a betrayal of Crag's friendship, and Sodar could keep it and Mercy safe. So in the end Annev decided to leave the lantern at the chapel. And if he ever needed to, he could collect them both.

Annev placed the lantern beside the sack of supplies then extracted a crumpled piece of paper. The letter was addressed to no one, but Annev was certain it was the one Crag had written for Sodar. As he held it, Annev heard the priest bustling about in the rectory. He crammed the letter into his empty pocket and caught the faint scent of spiced tea wafting from the kitchen. He sighed, simultaneously relieved by its comfortable familiarity and saddened to exchange that warmth for the Academy's cold companionship.

Annev eased open the kitchen door and saw Sodar, alone at the table, polishing Mercy. The bright phoenix banner was draped across the table and Sraon's sheathed ax lay atop it.

The old priest raised his head, saw Annev in the doorway, and was unexpectedly choked up with emotions. Before Annev could say a word, Sodar wrapped him in a fierce hug.

"You're home!"

"Made it back." Annev wanted to say more but found he could only mumble into Sodar's shoulder.

The priest held him at arm's length. "I heard you failed the Test of Judgment, and Tosan immediately sent you on an errand. Have you been gone all night?"

Annev nodded, relieved Sodar already knew about the test. "He set me another Test. Did the Academy not tell you?"

"No," Sodar shrugged, "but you're back now." He pushed Annev towards a seat and started to make porridge. "What happened … and where is your glove?"

Annev pulled out the remains of the shredded garment and dropped it on the table. "It's a long story. Tosan said I could still earn my Avatar title if I completed a mission in the Brakewood."

"He *did*?" Sodar looked up in surprise. "Annev, that's fantastic! What was the task? How did you do?"

Annev cleared his throat and reached into his tunic. "I was supposed to strike a deal with a lost peddler, escort him away from the village, and then kill him."

"Kill?" Sodar looked up in time to see Annev place the two bloody ears atop the tattered black glove. "Oh, Annev," Sodar set aside his cooking. "I'm sorry you were put in that situation. It's not easy taking a life, especially an innocent one." He paused. "Wait … you said a *stranger* found the village? A peddler?"

"Yes. A fat fellow with a scraggly beard. He had a funny accent, like Sraon's but thicker."

The priest seemed to go weak in the knees. He sat down across from Annev, their breakfast forgotten on the stove. "And did you learn this peddler's name?"

Annev stared hard at the priest. "I think you know it already." Sodar was silent for a long moment. When he finally spoke, his voice was barely a whisper.

"Crag."

Annev nodded and the priest looked at the ears on the table. "These are his? You killed him?"

Annev shook his head. "I would have, I think, but we were set upon by a witch."

"A witch? A sorceress attacked you?"

Annev shrugged. "She was old, all dressed in black rags. I thought she was blind at first, but she could see things … she knew things."

"What made you think she was blind?"

"Her eyes were clouded white."

Colour drained from Sodar's face. "This woman … did she give her name? Or say what she wanted?"

"No. Well, maybe. She was crazy—she called me a one-armed Son of Keos and tried to kill us. She probably would've killed Crag if I hadn't intervened."

"So you killed her and took her ears?"

"I said it was a long story. We killed her, yes, but I took these ears from a *feurog*."

"*Feurog?*"

Annev nodded. "The witch called them *feurog*. They attacked us after she died. They looked like people but … more wild, and their bodies were twisted with metal and rock." Annev paused. "None of this sounds familiar to you?"

Sodar shook his head, though some of the color had returned to his face. "I know the peddler, Crag, and it's possible I knew the witch, long ago, but the *feurog* … I know nothing of them." He frowned. "How many were there?"

"Three. We killed two and the third fled. She was in no condition to follow us, so we let her go. I took the ears as Tosan's proof, led Crag back to the Brake Road, and ran home."

Sodar breathed a sigh of relief. "Crag is alive then. And these ears … they'll earn you your title. Brilliant. Wonderful." He paused. "How much did Crag tell you?"

"Not enough. Said it wasn't his place to reveal your secrets."

Sodar stroked his beard, pensive. "That was … thoughtful of him. Uncharacteristically so." He chewed his lip. "Did he say why he came to the village?"

"No, but he left this for you." Annev pulled out the letter he'd found stashed near the standing stones. Sodar took it, examining the seal.

"You didn't try to read it?" Annev shook his head and Sodar pocketed the envelope. "Thank you, son. You must be tired."

"I'm exhausted. I'm hungry, too, though."

"Say no more." Sodar passed him a bowl of oatmeal and a cup of water. Annev drank it in one gulp, and Sodar refilled it and tidied the room while Annev ate. He sheathed Mercy and set it beside Sraon's ax, then wrapped the *feurog's* ears in a scrap of linen, burning the sticky leaves that had wrapped the gruesome trophies. That done, he examined the remains of the shredded glove, tisked and tossed them into the fire as well, confirming Annev's suspicions that the garment was unsalvageable. He would have to be doubly careful at the Academy now, particularly around Narach and his scrying stones.

When Annev had finished, he set his bowl aside and looked at Sodar. "If I sleep now, can we talk afterwards?"

"Of course."

"I mean *really* talk. Crag said you have a habit of keeping secrets from people—and keeping them longer than you should. Well, I want to know everything you've kept from me. Everything about my parents, about Crag and Arnor, the wood-witch. I need to know, now."

Sodar studied Annev. "What aren't you telling me, Annev?"

Annev hesitated. "To become an Avatar, I also have to leave the chapel and move into the Academy … immediately."

"I see."

"It was after the Test of Judgment." Annev felt he had to explain. "He thinks I'm too influenced by you. He was going to make me a steward and never let me out of the Academy, but then he gave me one last chance to prove myself—and I did it. I've got the ears and the supplies he wanted, so he should give me my title, but I still have to leave the chapel ... and I don't think he'll let me see you."

The priest gave a slow, silent nod. "I suppose I knew this day would come. I had hoped ... well, never mind what I had hoped. I've been fortunate to spend as long with you as I have." He smiled, though Annev feared he was weeping inside.

"Sleep, Annev. And then I will tell you everything."

CHAPTER FORTY-THREE

"You must never repeat any of this," Sodar began, once Annev had slept. "The Academy only reveals this to master avatars, and then in strict confidence." Sodar cleared his throat. "What the ancients told you about your parents—what they tell all the boys at the Academy—is a lie. Your parents do not give you away to be trained. When the witwomen go on reapings, they steal infants from their cribs."

"I guessed as much," Annev said, unsurprised. "Where did I come from? Which town?"

"They stole the *other* boys. But you were not born in Luqura or Banok. You were born here, in Chaenbalu."

"Here?" Annev blinked, trying to take it all in. "I was born *here*? But how …"

"You were born here," Sodar continued, "with one hand. Your parents were killed and the witwomen took you to the woods to be eaten by wild animals."

Annev nodded, knowing the ritual. "So how am I still alive?"

"I saved you. I followed the witwomen to the woods and found them arguing over you—more than arguing. They were trying to kill each other. One of the women wanted to kill you, there and then, while the other wanted to take you away. The first woman was Myjun's mother—she died in the Brake—and I believe you met the second witwoman yesterday."

"She was the wood-witch," Annev breathed.

"That is my guess. She was called Kelga, and she said she'd been hiding,

316

waiting for you. She had a little magic. Not Darite, either. Something darker. Terran, I think." It sounded plausible to Annev.

"What happened to her?"

"Myjun's mother blinded her, negating Kelga's ability to return to Chaenbalu. I expected her to die in the Brake—or, by Odar's mercy, to find a way out of the wood and start a new life—but perhaps she's been lurking in the woods these past seventeen years … perhaps something kept her there."

"Me," Annev said, with certainty. "She said she'd been waiting a long time for me. She said others were searching for me too."

Sodar nodded. "Crag's letter said something similar. He wanted to warn me—to warn *us*—you were being hunted."

"Hunted?" Annev shook his head. "But I'm nobody. I've never even left the village. Why would anyone search for me? How would they even know me?"

Sodar smiled. "That is exactly the kind of secret that I've been trying to keep from you—the kind that becomes a burden once you learn the truth." He paused. "Do you still want to know? This is your last chance to remain ignorant—to be a boy for a little while longer."

"I stopped being a boy when I killed that witch—when I killed Kelga."

"Yes … yes, I suppose you did." They sat in silence for a long moment then Sodar sighed. "I'm sorry about that, Annev. I should have executed her when I had the chance. Had I known she would remain a threat …" He shook his head. "I suppose I was too focused on saving you, on hiding that deformity."

"How *did* you do that?" Annev interrupted. "Neither of the wit-women went back to the village. If you arrived with a one-armed infant, they would have stoned you too." Sodar inclined his head in agreement.

"I had to hide you in my chapel for a bit. Then I broke into the Vault of Damnation and stole that magic arm you're wearing."

Annev removed the crimson phoenix glove and looked down at his naked left arm: the scarring had almost completely faded now, and he marveled at how quickly the prosthetic could heal itself. He tried to imagine Sodar skulking around in the bowels of the Academy, bypassing its traps and breaking into the vault—a place Annev had never even seen, let alone entered. He flexed his fingers, imagining Sodar searching the Academy's dusty shelves for a prosthetic arm—for anything that would save a baby's life—and he found a new respect for his mentor.

Annev made a fist and looked up. Sodar nodded, taking that as his cue to continue. "When the arm attached itself, you looked like any other infant, and a few weeks later I snuck you into the reap from Luqura."

"But then … how did I end up at your chapel? How did you convince them to let me be your deacon?"

Sodar smiled. "It would be easy to say I used magic, but the truth is I was well-informed, I was very persuasive, and I had a lot of luck."

"What do you mean?"

"The witwomen keep a tally of the infants they've stolen—they even keep a small book that describes the age of each infant, who stole it, and who its parents were. They mark each infant with a number, so they know which infants were taken from where. You had no such marking, though, and no entry, which caused a bit of an administrative stir—the witwomen are not supposed to make mistakes—and I chose that exact moment to intercede: I approached the headmaster and asked if one of the reap might be spared to be trained as a deacon."

A half smile crept onto Annev's face. "They chose to give me to you because it was an easy way to fix their records."

"I'm sure that was part of it. Your reap was also quite large, and I think they liked the notion of not having to care for one more infant. I suspect Kiara or Tosan would have objected, but the death and disappearance of the two witwomen still had their attention. I had to convince Winsor, though, and that was difficult enough. We compromised and agreed your time would be split between training at the Academy and training at the chapel."

"That part I understand," Annev said. "But why did you choose to save me in the first place? You risked yourself for me, that day and every day since. Why—and why are strangers hunting for me?"

"Do you remember when I first showed you this banner?" He tapped the red cloth with the gold phoenix.

"Yes. You said it belonged to a Halcyon Knight named Breathanas, and that I'm named for the phoenix on the banner."

"That's all technically true, but I didn't actually name you after the phoenix. Rather, the phoenix is your *family* name. The name of the line of Breathanas."

Annev's mouth dropped open. "… I'm a descendant of Breathanas? The man with the lightning-eyes in Tosan's study?"

"The Halcyon Knight who fought in the Battle of the Vosgar, yes. The dalta who took up the Staff of Odar when Keos struck down the leader of the Darites."

"Breathanas," Annev breathed, "the knight who killed Keos."

"The very same."

Annev carefully picked up the crimson phoenix banner and reexamined the gold stitching. When he caught himself holding his breath, he let it out slowly.

"This was his?"

Sodar nodded. "This is the banner that flew overhead when Breathanas slew the God of Earthblood, protected by magic from the ravages of time."

Annev stared, astonished. "That would mean … this is more than two thousand years old."

"Closer to twenty-two hundred." The old priest smiled as Annev carefully folded it up and replaced the cloth on the table, eyes wide. "Annev, how old do you think I am?"

He shrugged. "I don't know. A hundred?"

Sodar laughed. "Do I look that old to you?"

"Well, no. But I always thought you used magic to stay young. I can't remember you ever looking different than you do now … and I heard Arnor call you an ageless one. That sounded like more than just a title. Besides," Annev finished, "you don't fight like an old man—and don't tell me that's down to hard work and prayer. You always say that, and I hate it."

Sodar pulled the short sword from its scabbard and ran his thumb along the dull edge of the blade. "It's more than a title. I knew Breathanas when he just a squire, and Garlock—leader of the Darite armies—as well. I fought alongside them both during the Siege of the Kuar."

Annev snapped his mouth shut. "That's impossible."

"Are you calling me a liar?"

"No …" Annev said, answering evasively. "But that would make you more than two thousand years old. Nobody lives that long." He paused. "Do they?"

"*Few* have ever lived that long," Sodar corrected. "Aside from Bron Gloir, only the ageless ones—"

"Bron Gloir?" Annev interrupted. "He's real … you *know* him?"

Sodar smiled. "Yes, and yes. It's been over a century since we spoke, but he's still alive. He'll probably outlast us all."

"And Bron Gloir is an ageless one … like you."

"No, no," Sodar corrected. "Bron is the last Halcyon Knight. He survives … well, you know the stories. The Man with a Thousand Faces?" Annev nodded and Sodar shrugged. "Well, that part of his tale is true. Whenever Bron dies, his soul enters the body of the nearest living person. They move on to the afterlife and Bron continues in their stead."

Annev shook his head. First Sodar said he was a descendant of Breathanas, then he claimed to be two thousand years old. Now this business with Bron Gloir. It was all too incredible. The priest had to be teasing him.

"Sodar, if this is your idea of a joke—"

Sodar slapped Mercy on the table, his eyes fierce. "This no joke, Annev de Breth. You insisted no more secrets. Well, if you want to know my story—*your* story—then listen: the Battle of the Vosgar was less than a month after Keos abandoned the Black Wall, broke the Siege of the Kuar, and crossed the river with his host." Sodar slid Mercy back into its scabbard and placed it on the table next to the ax. "I suppose that's a good place to start."

CHAPTER FORTY-FOUR

Sodar leaned back in his chair and steepled his hands. "It was a dark day," he began, "when Cohanuk, the leader of the Sons of Keos, and Klaklanrai, the stone golem, ordered their armies to redirect the flow of the Kuar River.

"The armies of Western Daroea had been camped on the edge of the river, holding the line against Keos, for a hundred years. But with the river redirected, their flanks were exposed and overcome by the rush of monsters flooding in from the north and south.

"The vampyr Dortafola and Yarnach the iron golem led the battle in the south, while Keos and his flesh golem Fyoldar led the charge across the Kuar River. Terror swept the ranks of Churchmen as they fought man and monster alike. Through it all, the Halcyon Knights held their ground."

Sodar sighed.

"But there were too many of them and too few of us. We were exposed on every side. We sounded the retreat and the Legions of Keos harried us all the way through Borderlund. Some deserted and fled to Southmarch or Odarnea, thinking they could hide and escape the carnage. Those who did not went west, seeking safety within the dense foliage of the Vosgar. It wasn't such an evil place back then, if no less hostile to those unfamiliar with its ways. It was there that the Halcyon Knights and the bulk of the Darites and Ilumites gathered their strength and prepared to make their last stand.

"We thought we were lost, and so did Keos. Instead of bringing his entire army west, he left the bulk of his Bloodlords and golems in Daogort along with the *nechraict*—the undead who had been compelled to rise and fight again. Of those that crossed the river, half stayed behind to loot and pillage Borderlund and Lochland. So only a fraction of his army actually made it into the Vosgar—maybe two hundred legions and a thousand golems—but they still outnumbered us nearly ten to one.

"We all would have died—and many of us still did—but on the third day, the Lost Terran clans came to our aid. The Druids dropped from the trees and the Orvanes poured out of the secret caverns beneath the forest—and they brought the Younger Gods with them: Garadair and Cruithear, Dorchnok and Sealgair, even Tàcharan. The flow of battle began to turn, and suddenly it was the Legions of Keos who were outnumbered.

"During the route, the High Priest of Odar, Garlock, slew the leader of the Sons of Keos. Their army fell into disarray and Keos himself entered the fray, his magic hammer striking down all before him. He single-handedly drove back the Lost Terran clans, killed Garlock, and reclaimed the ground his army had lost. Even with the Younger Gods aiding us, we were facing defeat.

"But then something unexpected happened. When Garlock fell, a Halcyon Knight's squire unthinkingly picked up the Staff of Odar. It had been discarded in the retreat, when none dared pick it up."

"Hold on," Annev said shifting in his seat. "You're saying the Halcyon Knights dropped the Staff of Odar, an Artifact of Legend, and they just left it?" He scoffed. "That's hard to believe."

The priest held up a finger. "The Halcyon Knights didn't drop the staff. It was entrusted to Odar's priests, the Dionachs Tobar, and when their leader fell none would take up the staff."

"But … aren't you one of those priests? You and Arnor?" Sodar nodded. "Well, if you were there and saw the staff fall …"

Sodar laughed. "Why didn't I pick it up?" The priest's mirth became solemn reflection. "I didn't pick it up, Annev, because I didn't want to *die*. The curse of Keos still lay on the staff. Whoever held it had to be worthy or they'd be obliterated."

Annev chewed his lip. "… but one of the squires still picked it up?"

"Breathanas. He wasn't afraid of the curse, but he was afraid of leaving the staff behind and losing the war. So even though he was just a squire—not even a knight, let alone a priest—Breathanas took up the staff to save it from Keos. He didn't realize the magnitude of what he'd done until later, but he had become a dalta, one of the few immune to the curse of Keos."

"Wait. The Halcyon Knights worshiped Odar *and* Lumea. So if Breathanas was a Halcyon Knight ..."

"Then he was a heretic with a mixed bloodline, which means the staff should have destroyed him the moment he touched it."

"Well ... isn't that how it works?"

"Usually." Sodar leaned forward, emphasising his point. "Like you, we had believed Odar would never favor one whose blood and faith wasn't pure." He shrugged. "But we were wrong. Breathanas was blessed by Odar *and* Lumea, and when he called on the power of the staff, it was like nothing we had ever seen. Lightning and ice, as geysers sprang from the earth and stars fell from the sky." He shook his head, eyes distant.

"So," Annev prompted, "he took the staff and killed Keos?"

Sodar shook his head. "When Keos saw Breathanas' attack, he pulled back. Odar had shattered his hand with that staff, and he didn't want to go near it. So, instead of engaging Breathanas with his hammer, Keos fought him with his magic—and he should have won. He was an Elder God, and Breathanas was a new dalta ... but you wouldn't have known it watching them fight. It was as if the earth and sky had erupted. Frozen rain blanketed the forest and frosted lightning thundered from the sky. In one moment the air was thick with smoke, then a blast of rain would carry it away. The air swarmed with beetles, pelting us from every side, and then a blanket of hoarfrost scoured us clean, freezing us to the bone in the darkness. But then Tinder, the Ilumite High Priestess, took up Lumea's golden flute and began to spell-sing.

"Everything changed. The forest became radiant with light. Flames bloomed around us, our skin warmed. Drops of liquid fire rained from the sky, yet nothing burned except Keos. When *he* heard the flute, he lost his mind with anger, and killed all within reach of his hammer, whether friend or foe, and the more the priestess played, the angrier he became. Something about the music or the flute itself drove him mad. He waded into our forces and cut a path straight for Tinder.

"Until Breathanas stepped in. Staff and hammer rang, and the ground broke beneath our feet. The high priestess played until her skin began to glow. Her hair burst into flames as the other Ilumites joined her in song—and then the woods themselves erupted in flame." Sodar shook his head. "We thought it was the end of the world, but it was actually the end of an Age. Their song summoned Rojen, the Great Phoenix, and Lumea's Last Hope, who came shrieking out of the sky for Keos. Breathanas and the phoenix struck at the same moment and the Elder God's body was turned to ash and dust." Sodar's eyes grew distant.

"It's a terrible thing," he said, "to see a God die." He squeezed his eyes shut and shook his head. When he opened them again, they were clear and present but held much sadness.

Annev had listened closely but now he folded his arms. "And you were really there?"

"I promised I would tell you the truth. I was there. That was the day I swore to fight alongside Breathanas and protect his line."

"So you're more than two thousand years old."

Sodar sputtered and stood up. "Perhaps if I'd been an infant at the Battle of Vosgar … but I was already over *five hundred* then."

Annev screwed up his face. "Then that makes you …?"

Sodar straightened his clothes proudly. "On the sixth day of Tenth-month, I shall be two thousand seven hundred and thirty-six. Close your mouth. You look like a shovel fish."

Annev snapped his mouth shut and tried not to stare at the old priest—at the *very* old priest. Sodar had no reason to lie anymore, and Annev believed he was being truthful, but it was a hard thing to imagine. Even if it explained many of the small mysteries about Sodar—how the man never aged, how he never got winded, how he could recite the histories as if he'd been there.

Maybe Sodar *had* been there.

Annev stared at the banner lying on the table. "You said Breathanas had the phoenix banner at the Battle of Vosgar … but if he hadn't been knighted, why did he have a banner? He should have been carrying his knight's banner."

"Breathanas squired for his uncle, Derekyn Ainneamhag, during the

Siege of the Kuar. He took an arrow in the throat when the siege broke and leadership of the house fell to Breathanas' father."

"So I'm a descendant of House Ainneamhag?"

"That's why I made them your namesake."

"Ainnevog of House Ainneamhag?" Annev grimaced. "That's a terrible name."

Sodar laughed. "Ainneamhag is a very old name for a very old house tracing its roots back to the Age of Kings. But you needn't worry at the name. After the Fall of Keos, Breathanas was knighted and House Ainneamhag became House Breathanas. A thousand years shortened the name to Breathen, and another thousand years to Breth. Throughout it all, they kept the phoenix banner and sigil."

"So ... I'm Ainnevog Breth?"

Sodar smiled. "Yes."

"And my father was ...?"

"Tuor Breth. And your mother was Aegen."

"Aegen," Annev said, trying the name on his tongue. "Did she have a last name?"

Sodar shook his head. "Ilumites don't use last names the same way we do. They take the name of whatever clan they're traveling with, and when they leave, as Aegen had, they leave their name behind."

Annev picked up the short sword from the table. "So you knew my father, and my grandfather, and my great-grandfather..."

"And all the other greats between you and Breathanas." Sodar nodded. "I chose to become steward to your family, and I have protected your line ever since."

Annev fiddled with the cuff of his glove, afraid to make eye contact with Sodar.

"Then how did my parents die?"

Sodar went silent. When Annev finally looked up, he saw tears on the priest's cheeks.

"I couldn't save them," Sodar whispered, his voice thick with emotion. "I'm sorry, Annev." He wiped his eyes. "If I could do it over again ... I don't know. I was too late to save Aegen, and if I'd saved Tuor, I would have lost you—or we all would have been killed." He rested his hands on the table. "It was vital I saved you, and Tuor understood that, I think." He took a deep breath. "That's what I tell myself, anyway."

Annev let silence fall between them, thinking about everything the priest had said. He unrolled his glove and looked at the injury the witch had left him. Using his index finger, he traced the faint white lines encircling his forearm: the scar had almost disappeared, and all it had taken was time; the poison had bled itself out and the skin had repaired itself.

The same couldn't be said of Sodar's injuries: his memories of Aegen and Tuor still pained him, and Annev realized the priest would never fully recover until he released the guilt he still felt. Tuor and Aegen couldn't help with that … but Annev could. He looked up from his arm and met the old priest's eyes.

"You saved me, Sodar. Even though I was just a baby and I was deformed, you saved *me*. I owe you everything. If my parents were still alive, I'm sure they would thank you." He reached across the table and gripped the old man's hand, and Sodar squeezed back hard.

"I still don't get it, though," Annev said, giving the priest time to collect himself. "Why are you preserving the line of Breathanas? Why is the line so important—and why are strangers hunting me?"

Sodar released Annev's hand to tug at the tangles of his beard. "It is … complicated. The Lost Prophecies say that the House of Breathanas will destroy Keos the Fallen. For that to come true, the line of Breathanas must be kept alive."

"But Breathanas killed Keos. The prophecy was fulfilled."

Sodar shook his head. "That prophecy was given in the Age of Kings— the Second Age. There was no House of Breathanas back then, it was still the House of Ainneamhag."

"But they were the same house, so it should still apply."

Sodar wobbled his hand back and forth, both agreeing and disagreeing. "Yes. That is one interpretation of the prophecies—there are several—mine is that Keos only fell when Breathanas destroyed his physical body. But Breathanas could not destroy the *spirit* of the Elder God: only a God can kill another God, and so the prophecy stands, and Keos, in some way, still lives."

"But when Breathanas picked up the Staff of Odar, he became a dalta—a child-god—so the prophecy still applies."

Sodar chuckled. "You sound just like Arnor—or Reeve. Next you'll tell me I've wasted my life protecting your family line."

Annev smiled, though his cheeks burned hot. He *had* been thinking that, but if he said it he would break the old man's heart.

"Keos *will* rise again," Sodar said, "and the line of Breathanas must be ready to stand against him."

Annev scratched at the back of his neck. "Against a god?" He shook his head. "I can barely stand against Elder Tosan."

The priest laughed. "You remind me of your great-great-great-grandfather. Talented. Skeptical. Unbelieving." Sodar walked over to the fireplace, where the mantel displayed the table corner Annev had sliced off. "He didn't want any part of this—didn't want to be a descendant of Breathanas or have any of the responsibilities that came with it—but your grandfather was a believer, and your father too." Sodar placed the sheared piece of wood in front of Annev. "Why do the ones without magic always believe, while the ones with magic refuse?"

Annev snorted. "Maybe we don't like being told what to do."

Sodar blinked. "That sounds about right," he said. "I suppose I've been protecting your family for the Dionachs Tobar for so long that I forget about little things like free will." He laughed. "I should know better. Your father was almost as stubborn as you are, though neither he nor his father had the talent. Your great-great-grandfather Macarraig of House Breth— he was the last of your line to have a little magic, though his father was even more gifted."

"What happened to them?"

"Macarraig trained at the enclave of the Dionachs Tobar and became an artisan of modest talent. As for his father … we had a falling out. I made mistakes. Pushed him to do things he had no interest in doing. I kept too many secrets from him, and when he found out, it was too late to repair the damage." His voice filled with regret. "I'd rather not make the same mistake with you. I don't want to force you to do anything you don't want … but now we might not have a choice."

"What do you mean?"

Sodar pointed at the package of severed ears. "Your story about the wood-witch and the *feurog*. I'm worried, Annev. There's something dangerous out there, and it's hunting you." His expression was pained. "I know you've set your heart on being an avatar and that you've finally earned your place at the Academy. You deserve to live the life you've fought for. But something's not right. I think …"

Annev guessed the words before Sodar spoke them.

"I think it would be wisest if we left the village."

CHAPTER FORTY-FIVE

Annev forced his hands to unclench from the seat.

"Leave the village?"

Sodar nodded. "I've been preparing for it for years. Matter of fact, I'd been planning for us to escape during our expedition to find the Oracle—particularly as I already know where it is." He smiled at Annev, then sighed when the boy didn't react. "I'm sorry. I didn't tell you because I feared knowing we might leave one day would stop you pursuing your dreams. Boys *need* dreams. When you become an old man like me, you exchange them for hope, and then spend your hopes on others dreams."

Annev was still shocked. "So ... you never really wanted me to become an avatar?" Sodar began to speak but Annev pressed on, forcing himself to be heard. "Whether I passed or failed didn't matter. You were going to take me away no matter what."

"Annev, please."

"Admit it," Annev said, gaining momentum as he regained control of his voice. "Tell me the truth."

"This is the truth," Sodar said, his tone becoming implacable. "Everything you do in this life matters. Your training at the Academy mattered, not because you would become an avatar, but because it taught you valuable skills. Your training with me mattered. I didn't send you to chop firewood so we had something to burn—I sent you to learn. To build your strength and develop your character. Do you think I taught you the histories so you could preach from the pulpit?" Sodar shook his head. "It was so you would understand where you come from—why the world is the way it is, and why it's vital that we leave."

"And go where?" Annev interrupted. "Where is better than here? What's waiting for us out there?"

"A whole world you haven't seen."

That gave Annev pause. He really did want to see the world—it was one of his primary motivations for becoming an avatar—but he had always thought he would come back to Chaenbalu. He'd always thought there would be a home and a hearth waiting for him, that he'd have Myjun and his friends. But Sodar didn't seem to be suggesting any of that. Annev might as well have joined Crag as a traveling companion.

"You know I want to travel," Annev said slowly, sifting through his feelings, "but not at the cost of my life here. When I take that sack of goods back to the Academy, Tosan will make me an avatar. I'll have my brown robes. I can court Myjun." He paused, wondering if Sodar understood how important that was to him. "Why must we leave? You said yourself that the village is protected."

"The magic that protects Chaenbalu remains strong," Sodar said. "Thus far, nothing has broken that circle of protection."

Annev nodded, thinking he might yet convince the priest to stay. "Exactly. The witch, Kelga, said someone else couldn't break the circle of protection—someone who was hunting me. If we left Chaenbalu, they could find us."

"True," Sodar said, surprising Annev with his agreeableness, "but you said you want to become an avatar. The moment you step outside this village on one of those Odar-be-damned retrieval missions, you'll be exposed yourself to countless dangers. Ones you don't understand."

"So help me understand! All these years, you say you've been preparing me, but you won't say what for. If you know what's out there, tell me!"

"I just … I wanted to spare you this for as long as possible," Sodar admitted. "A child shouldn't have to worry about adult matters."

"I'm not a child anymore." Annev thumped the packet of severed ears in front of Sodar. "You and the masters have taught me well. If I have to leave the village, I can take care of myself." He held up a hand, forestalling

Sodar's objections. "And now I know to come straight back. If things like *this* are out there, we should stay—where it's safe."

Sodar sighed. "I wish it were that simple, Annev. You were safe because you were hidden. The wards protecting the village held because they were never tested. That's changed. With a concerted effort and a little patience, Chaenbalu's defences will fall."

"They won't," Annev said, unwilling to believe it. "Arnor said your Order was being hunted—priests being killed. If we leave the village, we're at risk, but they can't find us here."

"That's a very slim chance," Sodar said. "And the longer we stay, the slimmer it becomes."

"In that case," Annev said, changing tactics, "let's say we agree to leave. We don't have to go right away. We can wait a few years while I get my title and continue my training. The Academy only sends avatars on missions if they're about to promote them to Master status. It will be years before they ask me to leave the village. We can use that time to prepare—you can keep stalling Tosan with your Speur Dún manuscript, and when we're ready, we can form up the expedition and sneak away like you planned."

Sodar grunted. "Perhaps."

"And maybe ..." Annev said, daring to hope. "If the timing is right, maybe Myjun could come with us."

Sodar gave a pained smile at the suggestion. "Myjun is a wonderful girl ... but she's Tosan's daughter. If we disappeared, the ancients would be happy to see me go, and they would only search for you for so long. But Tosan would use the full strength of the Academy to hunt Myjun down. He would never relent, never let us go. Instead of starting a new life in Odarnea or South March, we would always be running, and if he ever caught us unawares ..." He shook his head. "I'm sorry, Annev. Even if Myjun agreed, it would still be too dangerous—and we have enough dangers to worry about."

Annev frowned, frustrated by his limited options. He didn't want to consider a life without Myjun, without being an Avatar ... so he wouldn't. He brooded over the other things Sodar had said. "The Oracle is in Odarnea. What's in Southmarch?"

"The Oracle is *not* in Odarnea. It's with Bron Gloir, and the Gods alone know where he is—or *who* he is right now." He chuckled. "No, the enclave of the Dionachs Tobar is in Odarnea, though I've not yet decided where we'd go. You heard correctly: something has been stalking my order, and until I learn what, perhaps we should stay away. That's why I suggested Southmarch, though even that may not be far enough. We could run all the way to the sunken Isles of Ilumea and still not escape."

"Then why run at all?" Annev said, still pleading his case. "Are the servants of Keos chasing me so I can't kill their dead God?" Annev rolled his eyes.

"Keos will reveal himself when he is ready," Sodar said, ignoring Annev's tone. "His servants are another matter. Some are patient and cunning. Others are impulsive and unpredictable. They will all come for you, no matter whether Keos is alive or dead. The witch you encountered in the Brake was likely a tiny component of the greater whole."

Annev's skin crawled at the mention of the wood-witch, yet it also triggered something in his memory. "What do the Younger Gods have to do with all this? The witch said something about them hunting for me."

Sodar stroked his beard, his face grave. "I'm afraid I have no answers there. The Younger Gods went into hiding after the Battle of Vosgar, and they've learned to survive by not taking sides. That should mean their interests are benign, but if the witch says the Younger Gods are hunting you, that might not be true. Do you remember her exact words?"

"Only the names of the gods she mentioned—Dorchnok, Tàcharan, and Cruithear—and that they couldn't reach me. I think she was talking about the magic that protects Chaenbalu."

"Problems on top of problems." Sodar shook his head. "Alright, boy. We'll stay for now while I figure this all out, but don't get comfortable—and no more leaving the village. No gathering firewood. No running errands for Tosan. Nothing that will take you beyond the standing stones. Understood?"

Annev nodded, relieved he would still become an avatar and have the chance to court Myjun. Yet his relief was poisoned by knowing Sodar might whisk him away at any moment. He suddenly understood why the priest had kept it secret; the notion that Annev could pursue his dreams one day and have them ripped away the next was almost paralyzing.

But did it have to be? Crag's words came back to him: *things are never as complicated as they appear, and you don't have to follow a path someone else set out.*

I don't have to go with Sodar, Annev realized. *He's taking it for granted that I will. But if he decides it's time to go, I still have a place here. With Tosan.* Annev sat and weighed the implications of that.

If he stayed at the Academy without Sodar, he'd become an avatar and court Myjun. Eventually, he'd be promoted to Master Avatar and have adventures outside the village. He'd still heed Sodar's warnings whenever he was on a mission—he wasn't a fool, after all—and he'd hasten back to Chaenbalu after each assignment. Duvarek did that, and he was one of the most decorated avatars at the Academy. He'd be able to marry Myjun. It was everything he had ever wanted—he had even killed two people and severed a pair of ears to get it. Against that, he'd be disappointing Sodar … and without his glove, there was a real danger that the Academy would find out about his missing arm. If that ever happened, the Academy and villagers would unite and stone him to death—only his avatar skills giving him a chance to escape—at which point, he could probably leave and join Sodar anyway. To him, the risk seemed equal to the reward.

Alternatively, Annev could accept everything Sodar had said about his heritage. They'd stay in Chaenbalu and, when it was time, they would leave. They'd be on the run for a while, but they would eventually pass outside the Academy's reach and start a new life—assuming that a host of *feurog*, the Younger Gods, and other servants of Keos didn't prevent them from doing so. It sounded a riskier path, one in which he would be relinquishing control of his own life and allowing old men and obscure prophecies to dictate his dreams. That notion didn't sit well with An-nev, particularly as there was no guarantee he and Sodar would ever be completely safe; it offered a prospect of the world—a life of excitement, magic, and no Academy rules—but without being an avatar or seeing Myjun. Given those two choices, Annev knew which he preferred. He just had to find a way to tell Sodar without the man feeling Annev was committing some grand betrayal.

"You need time to process all this," Sodar said, rising from the table.

"Take those items to Tosan, then hurry back and get dressed for the last night of Regaleus. The celebrations will be louder and longer, so—"

"I can't come back!" Annev snapped. "Don't you remember? Tosan relieved me of my deacon duties."

Sodar paused. "I'd forgotten. That's another good reason to hasten our departure … but never mind that." He tried to mask the pain clearly etched on his face. "I can prepare the chapel on my own, and I'm sure I'll find a way to communicate with you when it's time to leave. For now, you should go and get your title. You've earned it. I'll pack your things and send them along to the Academy."

Annev lit up. Sodar was right. He *had* earned this, and he wasn't going to let his worries about the future cloud his enjoyment of the day.

"Thank you, Sodar." He hugged the old man—and his resolution immediately crumbled.

There has *to be a way to make it all work,* Annev thought, hugging his mentor tight. *I can solve this puzzle. I can find a way to have my dreams without crushing Sodar's.*

They released each other and Annev watched the old man shuffle off with the sword and ax. *I'll stay,* he decided. *Sodar has watched over my family for centuries, so waiting a few more years won't harm him and he won't abandon me. Maybe after Myjun and I get married, and after Tosan has died, I could convince her to leave with us … or convince Sodar that the danger has passed.*

Part of him knew his hopes were impossible—that his sense of foreboding was real and should not be ignored—yet he refused to face it, clinging to the hope he could make it work instead.

He acknowledged, a little wryly, that Tosan's evaluation of him had been entirely correct: he couldn't accept the choices fate had given him. That habit would probably bring him more grief once he was living at the Academy, but he wasn't about to change.

Annev grabbed the linen-wrapped ears from the table and collected the sack he'd left in the shed, pausing to drop the phoenix lantern into his clothes chest. As he changed into a clean tunic, he saw a glint of metal: a strip of gold he'd taken from the Brake, a shard from one of the *feurog*. It was a grisly trophy, one that was too grotesque to keep yet too valuable to get rid of. He supposed Sraon could smelt it into a handful of sunbeams, but even carrying the rectangular clips of metal would remind him of their origin. He'd have to do something with it.

Once he'd finished dressing, Annev searched his straw pallet for Myjun's promise ring and pocketed it, hoping he'd have the chance to give it to her that evening. On his way out, he stopped to admire Breathanas' banner, which Sodar had not yet put away, and he compared the golden bird on the cloth with the one stitched on his glove. He marveled once again at how similar they looked—even the colors were identical: bright crimson and gold.

He raised the cuff of the red glove to his nose and sniffed. To his delight, Myjun's sweet scent still lay in the glove's fabric. *Wildflowers*, he thought dreamily, *and soap*. But there was something else there too. He sniffed again, savoring the aroma, and tried to decipher what the last two accents were. He had almost given up when it came to him.

Strawberries … and blood.

CHAPTER FORTY-SIX

Annev strolled into the village with the sack of palm vine and dragon's blood clinking on his back. As the farmers and villagers passed him by, several greeted him with a wave or a nod.

"Afternoon, Ainnevog!"

"Hello Greusik, Edrea!" Annev saluted the wiry cobbler and his wife, both in their Regaleus best. "Happy Regaleus to you both."

"And to you! Looking forward to Brother Sodar's sermon this evening."

Annev nodded in agreement, though he suspected Tosan would not allow him to attend, and asking permission would undo whatever good-will he might have earned for completing the headmaster's task. So Annev decided he would make the best of it; he had never seen how the Academy or the rest of Chaenbalu celebrated while he was helping Sodar at the chapel, and he was excited by the novelty of the experience.

The spicy scent of Yohan's scented candles wafted by, and Annev turned to see laughing children playing with the half-dozen toys Nikum had placed outside his carpenter shop. The whole village was in a festive mood, and that matched Annev's spirit just fine. He wove his way through Chaenbalu's circular streets, waving to shopkeepers and craftsman as he listened to the solid plink and clang of Sraon's anvil and open-air smithy. Annev even considered stopping to greet the one-eyed blacksmith, but he was determined to complete Tosan's mission and see if the headmaster would finally promote him to Avatar of Judgment or if he would find a way out of it yet again.

Annev patted the grisly package in the breast pocket of his tunic and felt strangely reassured by the *feurog's* severed ears. He tightened his grip on the sack slung over his shoulder and jogged across the village plaza to the Academy's entrance.

***

"I thought you understood that you were to come back to the Academy as soon as you completed your task." Tosan sat in the sable-lined chair behind his desk. The hard chair that Annev had sat in last time was nowhere to be seen; in its stead was a squat three-legged stool. Given the options, Annev chose to stand, resting the dusty sack on the stool. He bowed his head.

"I'm sorry, Elder Tosan. I returned very early. I hadn't slept and I didn't want to disturb you. I also thought it best to put my affairs in order with Sodar before returning here."

Tosan's eyes narrowed into slits. "How ... considerate of you. He paused. "So everything is settled with the priest? Sodar knows you will be leaving the priesthood?" When Annev nodded, Tosan smiled. "Good. And the task I gave you?"

Annev placed the sack on Tosan's desk and let the headmaster inspect the contents, counting out the palm vine and bottles of dragon's blood tree resin. He nodded his approval. "And what of the peddler?"

Annev withdrew the linen-wrapped package from his tunic and placed it in front of Tosan. "The merchant won't be bothering us anymore."

Tosan's eyes widened slightly, though his face was still skeptical. He lifted the small package and peeled back the linen. Dry flakes of blood fluttered onto his desk as he picked up the *feurog's* misshapen ear, examining it closely.

"Was the peddler still *alive* when you cut these off?"

Annev hesitated. Tosan had said he could sense lies, and Crag *had* been alive when Annev harvested the *feurog's* ears. His stomach lurched as he gave the only answer he could.

"Yes ... he was alive."

"Truly?" Annev nodded and Tosan smiled with a queer mix of perverse delight and wary suspicion. "And after you took his ears, did you let the man go? I would be very wroth if I learned there was an earless merchant wandering around somewhere. Don't try to deceive me."

"You won't find an earless merchant wandering about the Brake." Annev nodded at the gruesome trophy in Tosan's hand. "The owner of those ears is dead by my hands."

"How?"

"I plunged the merchant's sword straight through his eye and into his brain. I watched him die ... felt him die."

The headmaster sat in silence for a moment, processing. Finally, he nodded. "And what of the last piece of the puzzle. Did you learn how the merchant found our village?"

Annev knew he had to be just as careful here and tried to remember Crag's exact words. "He said he was headed toward Hentingsfort on his way to Port Caer. He tried to take a shortcut through the Brakewood and got lost. When I asked him about Chaenbalu, he said he had never heard of it."

"He said that, did he? That contradicts what the witwomen told me. They said he was actively searching for the village and they found him right at the edge of Chaenbalu."

"He was searching for his mule," Annev blurted.

"Excuse me?"

"He lost his mule," Annev repeated. "I helped him search for her. That's part of the reason I was delayed in returning to the village."

"He was searching for his mule ... and you helped him?" Annev nodded. "And did you find this mule? I presume not, or you would have brought the animal back to Chaenbalu."

"We found her," Annev said, "but she had been eaten by forest creatures."

"How unfortunate. And that was *part* of the reason you were delayed. What was the rest?"

"We were attacked by the same beasts. The peddler was injured and ... well, I was unconscious for a time. I apologize for the delay."

"Unconscious, you say?" Tosan studied him. "I see no injuries."

"I have a hard head," Annev said, rubbing it.

"So it would seem." Tosan stroked his goatee, thinking. "What were these beasts?"

Dammit.

"They were strange," Annev said, trying hard to keep his tale from unraveling. "Monsters with skin and limbs made of metal and rock." He wondered how much he could say about the *feurog* without Tosan guessing that the severed ears belonged to the monsters and not the peddler. He wondered, too, if he would have to mention the witch.

"Monsters in the Brakewood? Creatures made of metal and stone?"

"Yes, Elder Tosan."

The headmaster considered. "This is disturbing news, if true. Far more so than a peddler wandering about." He tugged at the whiskers of his goatee, frowning. "I am inclined to think that you fabricated this tale to excuse your incompetence or to explain away your delay." Annev opened his mouth to protest, but Tosan raised a hand. "I said that was my *inclination*, not that I believed you were lying." He shook his head. "No, you believe that what you have said is the truth. It is up to me to decide whether you have been deceived." He paused. "How many monsters did you encounter?"

"Three."

Tosan's eyebrows narrowed. He glanced at the ring on his left hand then back to Annev. "You are lying," he said, fidgeting with the ring. "Why? What are you hiding?"

Annev shook his head, confused by the accusation, then he realised his error.

Dammit.

"There were only three *feurog*," Annev said, "but there was a fourth monster—a witch."

"A witch," Tosan said, clearly intrigued, "and you called these monsters '*feurog*.' Why do you name them so?"

"That is what the witch called them."

The headmaster nodded, apparently content with Annev's explanation. "This witch," he said, leaning forward in his chair, "did she have a name?"

Annev gave himself a moment to remember. "I think … I'm not certain, but I believe her name was Kelga."

"*Kelga?*" The headmaster shot out of his seat, his eyes suddenly ablaze with passion. "You are telling me that you found a woman named Kelga in the Brakewood?" Annev had thought Tosan was fueled by anger or hope, but at his words Annev knew precisely what the man was feeling.

Desperation.

"I believe so. She only said it once and she didn't seem in her right mind."

"I believe you." Tosan's voice was hoarse and he sat down, his face ashen, a changed man. What was once an interrogation had become a plea.

"Did she mention my wife?"

Annev's mouth fell open. "Your wife?"

"Lana," he said, his voice broken. "Her name was Lana. She died barely a month after Myjun was born. I thought something had driven her into a patch of blackthorn, but ..." He shook his head. "There were signs of a struggle. Kelga was supposed to be with her ... supposed to protect her ... but we never found the old woman. I searched the Brakewood and never found the wretch." He stared at the door to his study, his dark eyes brooding. "For almost two decades I have wondered what happened. Where did Kelga go? Why did she attack my wife? What happened to the one-armed son of Keos they were sent to sacrifice?"

Annev fought not to react to the ancient's rhetorical questions. At last, Tosan's gaze shifted back to Annev. The headmaster seemed to remember himself, and his tone shifted back to interrogation.

"Why did you call Kelga a witch? Did she possess magic?"

"She used dark magic to deceive us, and to control the *feurog*. She died attacking us."

Tosan studied him. "You killed Kelga." Annev nodded. "And the merchant aided you." Annev nodded again and Tosan heaved a great sigh, as though some heavy burden had lifted from him.

"So," he continued, "you killed the witch and the three *feurog*, and then you turned on the peddler. You took his ears and then you killed him with his own sword."

Annev hesitated, knowing any affirmation would be a lie. "No."

"No?" Tosan raised an eyebrow.

"No," Annev said, clarifying, "we did not kill all three of the *feurog*. Two died but ... the third creature fled into the forest."

"Ah." Tosan fingered the ears on his desk then looked up. "Did you take anything from the witch? Anything that might confirm her identity or prove that you killed her?"

Annev paused, trying to recall if he had. He was about to say no when he remembered the gold shard in his pocket. With a sigh of regret, he pulled it from his tunic and placed it beside the severed ears. "I found this near the clearing where the witch found us. If you want further proof, you will find her bones in the Brake."

Tosan took the strip of metal, weighing it in his hands. He closed his eyes, fingers probing, then opened them in shock. "This is an *artifact*."

"What?"

Tosan turned the gold shard in his hands, marveling at it, testing its edge. "The gold contains a magic aura. Its purpose is … unclear, but there is a malevolence to it. It almost feels alive. I'm surprised you did not feel it."

Annev tried to recall how the metal had felt in his hands. Had he felt the tingle of some foreign magic then dismissed it as his own innate gift? Perhaps. Had he felt the malevolence that Tosan now felt? Annev thought not. Which was strange, when he had felt an evil taint to the Rod of Healing two days past.

"I did not take the time to examine it, Elder Tosan. There were other metals in the woods too. Different kinds. I only took the gold."

"Very well. Acolyte, you know the prerequisite for becoming an Avatar of Judgment is to pass the Test of Judgment. Do you know the prerequisite for becoming a Master Avatar?"

"I thought it happened when the ancients believed the avatar was ready to advance."

"That's partially true. But there are also two tests. First, the avatar must demonstrate his competency by obtaining an artifact and bringing it back to the Academy."

"And the second test?" Annev asked warily.

"The Trial of Commitment. The avatar must eliminate a target—usually one that poses a threat to Chaenbalu or the Academy."

"You mean, to kill someone."

Tosan raised an eyebrow. "That should be an easy task now that you've done it a few times."

"Yes," Annev said, though he didn't feel so certain. He hadn't killed the peddler, after all, and Crag had dealt the killing blow to Kelga; the only person he had killed by himself was the *feurog* with the iron-encased skull, and Annev still wasn't sure whether to count that creature as a man or a monster. He swallowed the lump in his throat, uncomfortable to know he would be tasked to kill again.

"I'll be frank with you, Ainnevog. I was certain you would try to slither out of your task … but I was wrong. You killed the peddler, and you did me a great favor in destroying Kelga."

"And did I pass your test?" Annev asked, eyes hopeful. "Have I finally earned my avatar title?"

Tosan frowned. "I'm sorry, was I not clear? You are not being promoted to Avatar of Judgment."

Annev's throat closed up. It was all happening again. As soon as his dreams were in reach someone changed the rules, taking away whatever he most wanted.

"I cannot promote you to avatar," Tosan continued, "because you have already passed the Test of Competency and the Trial of Commitment." He gestured at the gold shard and the severed ears. "This artifact will be admitted to the vault." Tosan tugged on a red rope—one of six hanging from the wall—and Annev heard a bell tinkle somewhere down the hall. He pulled the brown and black ropes as well, and while Annev heard nothing, he knew other bells were ringing elsewhere in the Academy.

"Annev, you have passed the prerequisites for a higher office."

Annev's brow furrowed then his eyes widened. His throat no longer felt like it was closing in on itself, but his heart was racing even faster now. "Higher office?" he repeated stupidly, feeling certain he had misunderstood.

The Eldest of Ancients opened his desk drawer and began counting out several stacks of rectangular metal. He formed six stacks of copper spears then added two stacks of silver staves and a single gold beam. He gestured at the coins.

"Four dozen clips, twelve slips, one blip. When an avatar is raised to Master Avatar status, they receive the value of one solar to defray the costs of any supplies they need to perform their missions in Banok and Luqura.

It also allows them to purchase the weapons of their choice, or to have the blacksmith forge one for them."

Annev stared open-mouthed at the coins then looked back at Tosan, barely able to fathom the reality of what was happening. The headmaster stood and placed a hand on Annev's shoulder.

"This is your stipend, Ainnevog. Take it, with my congratulations. You've just been promoted to the rank of Master Avatar."

CHAPTER FORTY-SEVEN

The rest of the afternoon was a whirlwind of activity. Carbad arrived to record Annev's new rank in his ledger. He would become Master of Sorrows, a role that had been vacant since the chapel had been built and Sodar had come to Chaenbalu.

"He's earned it," Tosan said when Carbad questioned the title. "Odar knows the boy has caused me enough sorrow, but he also has the theological training, which Ancient Jerik and I can expand on. The nave has been cleaned for the first time in over a decade, so we should put it to use. Once he's earned the trust of the villagers, I'm certain he'll fulfill the other tasks Master Flint performed for us."

Carbad had whisked Annev away to see Master Brayan, the Academy's hulking quartermaster who was almost seven feet tall and had a thick neck-beard besides. Despite his imposing figure he was a jovial man, and today was no exception.

"Master of Sorrows?" Brayan bellowed, grinning from ear to ear. "Well, that's wonderful! Titus will be glad to hear it. He's been asking about you, you know."

Titus had been assigned as Brayan's apprentice in much the same way Markov assisted Narach in the Vault of Damnation. "He works with Carbad too," Brayan said while searching for Annev's master avatar robes. "He's good with numbers and the like, so that's useful, but he's got a real quality with animals too. I can barely tend the stables, let alone the kennels and the dovecotes, and he's a steady pair of hands. He's tending to the birds right now."

Annev had barely had time to thank the man for his new boots and red tunic before Carbad whirled him off again.

"Master Keyish will measure you for your wardrobe when he returns from Banok later today," Carbad said. "We'll need to catch him before he and Duvarek get too deep in their cups."

They'd visited Master Der next, but the Master of Stealth was not in his quarters. "The masters are always quick to celebrate on the last day of Regaleus," Carbad harrumphed. "I suppose you'll want to celebrate too—and why not? You leapt from acolyte to master avatar. That's worth two celebrations." He led Annev farther down the hall to an unpainted door. "This is yours for the moment. Once it's cleaned, we'll move you to the rectory, but it's probably littered with rat droppings at the moment."

"Thank you," Annev said, and he meant it. Carbad pushed open the door, and Annev stepped into a cell just big enough for a bed and clothes chest. A small window at the back of the room faced the southern side of the village and gave Annev a decent view of the mill, the adjacent pond, and the Brakewood. All told, it wasn't much bigger than his room at Sodar's chapel, but it felt like a palace.

"It's a real bed," Annev said, squeezing the pillow and feeling the feathers beneath the soft fabric.

"Of course it is," Carbad said, tossing Annev his new clothes and the purse holding his stipend. "Leave your acolytes robes here. I'll see that they're burned."

"Where do I go once I'm dressed? Elder Tosan had said something about seeing Master Edra about a weapon."

"If you can find Edra, you're more than welcome to ask him for one. My guess, though, is that he's getting drunk with the other masters. Probably in the kitchens or down in the plaza. Join them if you like. We won't announce your promotion till tomorrow, but you've earned the right to. May as well enjoy the celebration."

Annev was quick to decide it was a bad idea. The masters had their own rituals and friendships, after all, and though Annev admired several of the older men, he wasn't especially close with any of them. He'd been looking forward to seeing Titus and Therin, having finally earned his avatar title, but he felt self-conscious about seeing them after having been promoted to master. Though he wouldn't mind seeing Fyn …

"Wait," Annev said, stopping Carbad as he turned to leave. "What exactly does the Master of Sorrows do? And do I have to see Master Edra for my weapons or could I use one already in my possession?"

Carbad tilted his head, squinting once more at Annev. "What kind of weapon?"

"I did some work for Sraon and he gave me an ax as payment. I'd like to keep it." He was also hoping to return to the Academy with Mercy, though he knew better than to mention the weapon or its origin.

Carbad grunted. "If it's yours, you can do what you like with it. You're a master avatar now, you've earned that privilege. As for your duties as Master of Sorrows: you'll serve as the village priest and deliver sermons here in the nave. If anyone comes to you seeking counsel or penance, you will administer it in accordance with the Academy's values and share anything of import with the headmaster. I'm sure Elder Tosan will find other duties for you as well, alongside artifact retrieval missions."

Annev nodded. "Do you ever go on retrieval missions?"

Carbad scowled. "I'm too valuable here. I barely have the privilege of leaving the village, let alone hunting down magic artifacts."

"Oh," Annev said, realizing it was a sensitive subject. He awkwardly passed the bag of coins from one hand to the other. "Well, thank you. I appreciate your help." Carbad gave a stiff nod then retreated down the corridor, leaving Annev to sort through his clothes, and his thoughts, alone.

A quarter of an hour later, Annev emerged from the building wearing his new robes. As he walked down the Academy's steps, he relished the weight of the heavy coins chinking in his pocket. He had left most of the money in his room, but he had taken a score of coppers, a few silver clips, and the single gold beam that Tosan had given him. He had plans for that gold beam—plans that involved Myjun—but he put that thought aside for the moment and focused on the here and now. With evening fast approaching, Annev indulged in the thrill of his recent successes and allowed himself to live in the moment.

He was no longer an acolyte or a deacon. He wasn't even an avatar. In

one moment of incredible fortune, Annev had become a master avatar—
Master of Sorrows.

It was a strange title, all things considered, but Annev liked it, and the
responsibility to the penitent and those in need which came with it. As
Sodar's deacon, he had already trained for the role. But the title also suggested he had overcome trials and mastered sorrows of his own, which Annev supposed was true—and he fervently hoped that his new title would
immunize him to future sorrow and tribulation.

Annev stepped into the village plaza and found himself surrounded by
a throng of villagers in their Regaleus finery. Outfitted in his crimson master robes, he felt at home amidst the women in their bright skirts and the
men in their colorful caps. He relished the softness of his new black boots
and the fine quality of his new tunic. When he paused to admire how well
the phoenix glove matched his new clothes, Annev caught the scent of
sweet breads wafting from Lorn and Rafela's bakery. His stomach rumbled,
and he allowed the scent to carry him to the bread cart outside their shop.

"Afternoon, Rafela."

"Ainnevog! How are you this fine day? Come for a sweet treat?"

Before Annev could answer, Rafela's husband Lorn burst from the
front door of his bakery carrying a fresh tray of sweet rolls, sugar cakes,
and bread buns.

"Don't you be giving away more of our bread, Raf," Lorn scolded.
"These boys never pay nothing, and we need every staff and shield to pay
the miller. Save the loaves for tonight."

Before Rafela could reply, Annev slapped two copper shields on Rafela's table then eyed the grumpy baker's tray. "I'll have a warm cake, if you
please—and a sweet bun. You can keep the rest."

Lorn set down his tray then eyed the coppers on the table. When he
saw they were coins and not clips, he nodded. "Raf, give the boy what he
likes. He's a paying customer today." He paused, squinting at Annev's new
clothes, jaw suddenly slack. "And he's dressed like them masters at the
Academy." Lorn stared, uncertain how to process this observation.

Rafela had no such difficulty. She gave a throaty laugh and started collecting Annev's order. "Get back to your ovens, Lorn." She handed Annev

his bun and cake, she also added two sweet breads to the stack. "They'll go stale before tonight, anyway," she said with a wink.

Annev thanked her and trotted toward Sraon's forge, holding one of Lorn's pastries aloft as he got closer.

"Annev!" Sraon bellowed. He doused the metal he was working and stepped through the white cloud of steam, clapping his soot-stained gloves together. "You bringing me treats now?" He grinned, set down his gloves, and accepted Annev's offering. He had just taken a bite when he spied Annev's new robes. He coughed, spitting sweat bread everywhere. "By the Gods! Annev, are those *master* robes?"

"Got them less than an hour ago," he said, unable to contain his excitement. "I'm a full master now. They gave me a stipend and everything."

"Odar's beard. Annev, that's wonderful! I bet Sodar's overjoyed."

Annev's smile faltered. He hoped Sodar would be happy for him, though he feared the news would immediately prompt another conversation about leaving the village. Annev had few concerns there, though. Despite Carbad's suggestion that there were retrieval missions in his future, Annev suspected his role as Master of Sorrows would keep him in Chaenbalu in the same way that being Master of Operations limited Carbad's movement.

No, Annev's concerns were all focused on Myjun; now that Annev was a master avatar, he could legally marry the young woman. Once Sodar realized that, Annev felt certain the priest would try and forbid Annev from seeing her. On the other hand, if Annev proposed to Myjun tonight, and preempted Sodar's objections, Sodar would have to reconsider Myjun coming with them if they ever left. There was no way the priest would ask him to abandon his fiancée, let alone his wife, and that certainty gave Annev the courage to do what he did next.

"I haven't told Sodar yet, but I will soon. I wanted to talk with you about something, though. You remember that promise ring I had you forge last year?"

Sraon nodded. "Weren't much more than a bent nail, as I recall."

Annev nodded. "I was hoping you could make me something nicer. A gold band." Annev pulled the gold beam from his pocket and handed it to Sraon. "Using this to make it."

Sraon whistled, taking the clip and turning it over in his free hand. Finally, he grunted. "I could fashion this into a woman's ring easy enough, but I'm no goldsmith. If you're looking for something fancy, you'll be disappointed."

"Your Regaleus gift was beautiful," Annev objected. "A real work of art."

The smith shrugged, though the twinkle in his eye suggested he was pleased. "Aye, weapons I can do—bend iron, cut steel. Simple work that's done well. Smaller things give me trouble, though. If you're looking for detail, you'll need a goldsmith or a jeweler."

"Just a plain band. You can do that, right?"

"Mm. I suppose I could. When would you like it by?"

"The sooner the better."

Sraon grinned. "Is this for the same girl you gave that promise ring to?"

"Um, yeah." Annev fingered the ring still inside his breast pocket, not wanting to explain he still hadn't given it to Myjun. "It's for the same girl."

Sraon smiled. "Congratulations then, Master Annev! A fine way to celebrate Regaleus—and your promotion too!" He clapped Annev on the back and took another bite of his sweet bread.

"Thanks, Sraon! What do I owe you for the work?"

"You can keep your coin," the smith mumbled around a mouthful of sticky crumbs, "call it a wedding gift—but you will have to leave me another of those pastries." He winked with his one eye.

Annev laughed and unloaded another one. "Doubly done! Thank you, Sraon. You're a good friend."

"Aye. I'll be a fat friend if you keep bringing these treats by my forge—not that I mind, of course."

Annev headed for Sodar's chapel with a spring in his step and a giddiness he had seldom, if ever, experienced. The trials of the past two days had been a nightmare—one he did not care to dwell on—but the joy of his present mood far exceeded any ills he had suffered. He would gladly do it all again, too, if he would feel like this for the rest of his life. He still had to tell Sodar, but he felt prepared to navigate that conversation. He was also excited to reclaim his Regaleus gifts and bring them into the Academy—something he had never believed would happen—and to surprising Myjun. He touched the promise ring in his pocket and dared to hope she'd accept the wedding band that Sraon would soon be forging. It was almost too wonderful to believe.

In his haze of elation, Annev almost didn't see the crimson-clad figure hailing him from afar, and it wasn't until Carbad physically planted himself in Annev's path that Annev realized the Master of Operations was trying to get him to halt.

"Master Ainnevog!" Carbad barked, trying to catch his breath. "Elder Tosan needs you in his office right now." He frowned. "I'm afraid you're going to miss tonight's festivities."

CHAPTER FORTY-EIGHT

Annev reached the office with a thousand fears about why the headmaster had recalled him.

He's going to take it all back, Annev thought. *He's found that earless monster's body and means to question me again. Or Kelga's corpse, and wants to know why he can't find the merchant or his cart.*

When Carbad opened the door to Tosan's office, it was to an entirely unexpected scene: instead of Tosan waiting behind his desk, rage building in his eyes, the headmaster was anxiously pacing the room. When he saw Annev he looked relieved.

"Excellent," the ancient said, looking him up and down. "Yes, you'll do. Your greatest flaw may be our greatest asset." He pushed through the open door and left Annev standing in his study. "Carbad," he said to the Master of Operations, "fetch our prospective Master of Arms. I'll get the other one myself." Carbad jogged away down the hall, leaving Annev alone with the headmaster.

"I will return shortly," Tosan said. "Wait here—and don't touch *any-thing*." He slammed the door behind him.

Annev stood in stunned silence. *I'm not in trouble*, he realized, *but something bad has happened ... some emergency. Tosan said I was an asset— no, he said my* flaws *were an asset. That's different.*

He waited a full minute before he felt relaxed enough to pace the room. His feet trod Tosan's now-familiar black and red carpet while his right hand idly traced the gold threading on his glove. Another minute passed before he grew bold enough to gaze out the window and watch the farmers and shopkeepers bustle about the village. He saw the butcher's three boys playing outside Nikum's shop then noticed the widow Alanna approach Sraon's smithy with a broken tea kettle under one arm. The smith immediately put down his tools and came to see her, neglecting the fires he had just been stoking.

There's another fire brewing there, Annev thought, remembering all the times he'd Sraon and Alanna chatting outside his smithy. *That, or the woman goes through kettles and cook pots as fast as she does firewood.* He smiled, happy for the two villagers, then turned away from the window.

A minute later, Annev was standing in front of Tosan's bookshelf, reading the spines. He saw one shelf was dedicated to history and geography, and he noticed the large tome Tosan had showed him when discussing ring-snakes. Another shelf contained titles like *Scroot and Black's Art of Writing, The Signs and Symbols of Odar,* and *The Old Tongue: How It Was and What It Has Become.*

Annev grimaced, recalling that Tosan's area of expertise was writing and languages. As a teacher he had compelled Gravel, Master of Forgery, to teach students their reading and letters, so Tosan could spend his own time copying texts and binding manuscripts. Annev thought it a dull task, but perhaps Tosan preferred the company of books to people.

He was turning away when a slim journal on the top shelf caught his eye. A larger tome sat atop the thin book, pinning it, yet Annev saw enough of the cover to recall seeing Tosan writing in it.

It was when he talked about those ring-snakes, Annev realized. *He lectured and insulted me, and then he stopped mid-sentence so he could jot something down. Acted like I wasn't even in the room ...* Annev stared at the half-hidden journal, his curiosity rising. What had captured the headmaster's attention so completely? The headmaster had only been gone for a few minutes, but Annev suspected he would be absent a while longer.

If he wrote something about me, I should know about it, he rationalized, *and quickly.* He stood on his toes, lifted the thick tome, and slid the journal from beneath it. The cover was blank, but as Annev flipped through the pages, it became clear he held Tosan's diary. His heart beat faster as he flipped through the journal, scanning dates and entries.

The narrative of Bron Gloir shows promise. I've sent Duvarek north to see if he can recover anything of value, but I don't hold out much hope. Too much time has passed since the rite of Bron—

Annev flipped forward half a dozen pages.

But whom to choose? It must be someone rarely seen and seldom missed. A villager perhaps, but it would be much easier if—

He flipped another dozen pages.

The man thinks me an idiot. Well, so much the better. He won't realize I know the truth until he's spun enough rope to hang himself. In the meantime, I'll play along an—

Annev flipped again, but this time he went too far and found only blank scraps of paper. He paged back and found the most recent journal entry, its page noted with the day's date.

Kelga is dead. Ainnevog brought me the news on his return from the Brakewood. Seems she was hiding there this whole time, though I can't say why or how. I'd send Brayan and another master to go and investigate—to find the corpse—but Ainnevog mentioned other monsters in the Brake. Creations of Kelga, it would seem, for she named them her feurog. The name is obscure. If Terran, then its root may come from 'ferrous', but I suspect it is arcane in nature.

Annev flipped back another page and found the date corresponding with his Test of Judgment. There was only one entry—a short one, hastily scrawled in Tosan's spidery handwriting—and it didn't reference Annev at all:

Ring-snake venom! Its properties are mutative. Arcane. Possibly keokum? Might be the catalyst to solving Bron Gloir's immortality spell. Needs testing.

Annev read it a second time, uncertain he had read it correctly. It pointed to one conclusion.

Tosan is practicing magic? But that can't be right. Tosan hates magic.

Footsteps sounded down the hall and Annev hastened to replace the journal on the bookshelf. As he did, the battered tome that had sat atop it clattered to the floor.

Annev stared at the fallen book, horrified as he saw the book plates had come loose and half-dozen pages lay scattered across the carpet. He scrambled to reassemble the broken tome. Mercifully, the fallen papers were all from one sheaf, so they were easy to scoop up, reorder, and carefully slide back into the cover. As he did, he saw the title page of the shabby book.

The Secret Art: How to Identify and Harness Your Magical Ability.

Annev went cold as he saw Tosan's handwritten notes scrawled at the top of the page. *Strain of Luminerran blood talent: Soulshaper?* He found additional notes at the bottom of the page: *Ignis temperare—Loisg. Mentiri deprehendatur—Bhraitheann an bréag. Terra transfiguratio—Athrú carraig ...*

The footsteps halted in front of the headmaster's door. Annev snapped the book shut and dropped it back on the bookshelf, covering Tosan's journal. At almost the same moment, the door swung open and Annev turned to face it. When he saw who it was, he bit back a grin and forced a mask of perfect civility.

"Hello, Fyn. Looking for Elder Tosan?"

The dreadlocked avatar frowned at Annev as he stepped into the room. "Where'd you get those?" he snapped, gesturing at Annev's robes. "You should be in tan, like your boy, Titus."

Annev's lip curled, but he restrained himself. Master Carbad leaned against the wall outside, catching his breath. The man's cheeks were pink from exertion and his armpits nearly black with perspiration. Fyn turned and waved at the man, dismissing him.

"You don't need to stay on my account, Master Carbad. I'm sure you have other duties to attend to, and Ainnevog and I can keep each other company."

The Master of Operations brushed at the gray hair streaking his temples. "I'm not sure that ..." He paused, taking note of something in the hallway. "Never mind. Elder Tosan will be here soon." He nodded. "Good afternoon, gentlemen."

While Fyn watched Carbad go, Annev checked that the battered tome and journal were safely back in their places. By the time Fyn turned around, Annev had stepped away from the bookshelf and joined the avatar beside Tosan's desk.

"Where did you go yesterday?" Fyn growled, stepping closer.

Annev savored Fyn's confusion as they both heard rapid footsteps approaching the door. On a hunch, he said, "Why don't you ask Elder Tosan?"

A moment later, the headmaster walked in with Kenton close behind. The dark-haired avatar eyed the other two boys suspiciously while Tosan shut the door and sat down. He looked seriously at the three boys in front of him.

"In case you have not already heard, Annev has been raised to the status of Master Avatar. His title is now Master of Sorrows," the man said, without preamble.

Kenton and Fyn both sputtered for words.

"He's *what*?" Fyn asked.

"Master. Avatar." Tosan repeated loudly. "Are you deaf or stupid?" They were silenced, yet it was clear Fyn and Kenton were still full of questions. Tosan apparently sensed it, too, for he added: "Ainnevog out-performed your entire reap in Duvarek and Edra's final lesson, and defeated both of you in the last Test of Judgment." He steepled his fingers. "Yesterday in the Brakewood he also passed both the Test of Competency and the Trial of Commitment, earning his status as Master Avatar."

Fyn seemed even more confused by this, yet understanding seemed to dawn for Kenton.

"You mean, Annev brought back a magic artifact ... and he killed someone?"

Tosan nodded. "I see Duvarek taught you more than how to blend into the shadows." Kenton's mouth formed a tiny line that was almost a smile, while Fyn still looked as if the world had suddenly gone mad.

"Now that your reap has finished testing, we will begin apprenticing avatars with masters or ancients whose area of expertise corresponds with that avatar's strengths. In time, your classmates will have the opportunity to reach master avatar status. One or two may even become masters before the end of the year, though most will take five to ten." He paused, looking at the faces of each boy. "Except for you three. Master Annev has already proven himself a Master of Avatar, and I am now giving you the same opportunity."

Kenton nodded, his face solemn. "I accept this opportunity, Elder Tosan."

Fyn glared at his usually reticent companion then turned back to the headmaster. "If Annev can do it, so can I."

Tosan raised an eyebrow. "We shall see. Typically, the tests are also administered as part of a retrieval mission supervised by a master avatar. The tests can be accomplished during the same mission or as separate events." He paused. "Today, I am sending all three of you on a retrieval mission to Banok."

Kenton brushed his shaggy black hair out of his eyes. "Banok? That's where Master Duvarek just went."

Tosan flinched at the Master of Shadows's name. "Yes, it is. Master Duvarek and Master Keyish were sent to Banok two nights ago to confiscate a dark rod from a merchant named Janak Harth. The man spends his wealth and resources acquiring magic artifacts from all over Luquatra. We do not prevent this, but whenever he comes into possession of something truly dangerous, the Academy confiscates it." Tosan's fingers drummed on his desk with irritation.

"Last night Masters Duvarek and Keyish failed. Janak was waiting for them with a Rod of Compulsion. Duvarek was captured and Keyish was forced to return empty-handed." Tosan frowned, licking his lips. "For your Tests of Competency, you must retrieve the dark rod and bring it back to the Academy. Do you accept this mission?"

As one, the two boys nodded.

"For your Trials of Competency, you have different targets. Janak Harth has become a threat and must be eliminated." Tosan looked at Fyn. "Avatar Fyunai, do you accept this task?"

Fyn nodded, almost eager for the challenge. "I do."

"Excellent. Now, I believe Janak not only compelled Duvarek to abandon his mission, but to betray the Academy. He is lost to us." Tosan looked at Kenton. "Avatar Kenton, if Master Duvarek is not dead when you arrive, you will eliminate him." Tosan allowed his words to sink in. "Do you accept your Trial of Commitment?"

Kenton's eyes focused on the ground in front of him. "You want me to kill Master Duvarek ... my mentor."

Tosan inclined his head. "Exactly. Do you accept?"

Kenton's eyes were shadowed by his long black hair. "I do." He and Fyn both suddenly looked very grim.

"Excellent," Tosan said. "You are lucky to have this opportunity. Things become ... complicated around Regaleus. Most of the masters have been drinking in preparation for the evening's festivities, which weakens their resistance to the Rod of Compulsion." He pursed his lips in frustration. "I need fresh, alert minds and you are the best available." He raised a slender finger. "You are all top of your class," he said, pointing at the boys, "with reputations for being stubborn, bull-headed, and rebellious."

Annev winced at the accusation and he thought he saw Kenton turn away, though Fyn accepted it as a compliment.

"Those flaws," Tosan continued, "have held you back within the Academy, but tonight they will serve you in resisting Janak's Rod of Compulsion."

There it is, Annev thought. *That's the real reason Tosan chose us. Not because we're the most skilled, but because we're the biggest pain in his ass.*

"Avatar Fyunai," Tosan said, speaking to the boy, "it was my intent to apprentice you with Master Edra this summer. Instead, if you accomplish your mission, you will become the new Master of Arms with the responsibility of training the next reap in combat, arms, and armaments. Do you feel adequately prepared for that task?"

Fyn nodded, his eyes wide. "Yes, Elder Tosan." He paused. "What of Master Edra?"

"Edra will become our new Ancient in the Art of Warcraft," Tosan explained. "It was to be announced tomorrow along with the news of Ainnevog's appointment, though he will continue to teach. You will assist him in training the older reaps."

Fyn nodded. "Thank you, Elder Tosan."

"Avatar Kenton, you are adept at identifying magical artifacts." Fyn and Annev both looked at Kenton, their surprise visible, and the third boy shied away from their gazes, his hair falling to cover his scarred cheek.

"I'm alright," he said, his voice barely above a whisper. "I'm better at stealth and camouflage. I was doing extra training with Master Der and Master Duvarek ..." Kenton's voice drifted off.

"I was already aware of your relationship with Master Duvarek," Tosan said, not missing a beat. "In truth, it is one of the reasons you were chosen for this mission, but it is not the primary reason." He paused. "You are aware that Narach, our Master of Secrets, is very old—almost ninety. Ancient Dorstal apprenticed to him before he joined the Council of Ancients, and Steward Markov is ineligible for promotion. Given the Academy's needs and your talent, I'm assigning you to Master Narach and the Vault of Damnation. If you pass your tests, you will become our new Master of Curses."

Kenton stiffened. "You want me to work with Narach in the *vault*?" He grimaced. "I don't know the first thing about cataloguing magic artifacts."

Tosan held up a single finger, forestalling his objections. "Steward Markov can catalogue, and Dorstal assures me you are the most skilled in magical identification. You will have plenty of time in the archives to learn your new duties, and when Narach dies, Steward Markov will serve as your personal assistant. This is assuming, of course, that you succeed in your mission."

Kenton frowned but bowed his head in submission. "Of course, Elder Tosan. I will serve where I am needed."

"Yes, you will," Tosan said. He turned to Annev. "Master Ainnevog, you consistently puzzle out difficult problems, you do not hesitate to do what is required when the situation demands it, and you have demonstrated leadership skills and a willingness to sacrifice yourself for the greater good. You're also damnably willful." Tosan stroked his goatee. "Fortunately for you, that is what we require today. You will be leading this expedition."

Fyn and Kenton snapped their heads toward Annev, burning with indignation.

"Lead?" Annev said, his voice sounding small. "Lead Kenton and Fyn ...?"

"Avatar Fyunai, Avatar Kenton, you will report to Master Annev and follow his orders. Master Annev, you will supervise your lessers and you will not prevent them from passing their Tests of Competency and Trials of Commitment, regardless of how they treated you as an acolyte. The success or failure of this mission rests entirely on your shoulders." He paused, tapping his lips with a finger. "Fyunai and Kenton's talents exceed Titus and Therin's. You will use your resources, as I instructed you to in the Test of Judgment."

Annev swallowed. "I understand, Elder Tosan."

But he didn't, not really. Tosan had encouraged Annev to betray his companions in order to win the test. Was Tosan now giving Annev permission to sacrifice his companions, if necessary, to secure the rod? Annev wasn't sure, but he didn't put it past Tosan.

"Good," the headmaster said, standing. "Avatar Fyunai, go and see Brayan, Der, and Edra. They will outfit you for the mission and provide additional supplies for your companions. Avatar Kenton, you will be briefed by Keyish, Folum, and Dorstal. I wager they will all be in the kitchens."

Kenton and Fyn left the room, but not without making eye contact with Annev. Kenton's gaze was dark, though that was hardly uncommon for the morose teenager. Fyn, on the other hand, seemed at odds with himself, and Annev didn't blame him. The young man was being offered the chance to become a master avatar with a single night's work. But only if he did as Annev said. He had never done anyone's bidding before.

Gods, this is going to be painful.

With the other boys gone, Tosan looked at Annev critically. "I'm trusting you, Ainnevog. Don't disappoint me. This is your first step towards a rewarding career here at the Academy. Perhaps even a step towards proving your worthiness to Myjun."

Annev's cheeks reddened. Was Tosan giving him permission to court his daughter? His heart surged at the prospect that Tosan might actually permit it, and he tried to look the headmaster steadily in the eyes.

"I will not fail, Elder Tosan."

And this time, Annev meant it. This wasn't like being ordered to murder a lost peddler: Janak had captured Duvarek and turned him against them; the merchant was a threat to Chaenbalu and the Academy, which meant he was a threat to Annev's future. Using a Rod of Compulsion against another human further proved he was beyond salvation; there was justice in Janak's death.

Killing Duvarek was harder to rationalize. Tosan said the man had betrayed the Academy after being snared by the wand, but it seemed just as likely that the headmaster was punishing Duvarek for failing his mission. Annev was glad the man's death was not his direct responsibility—he just needed to guide the mission, steer the other boys in the right direction, and bring them home.

Tosan squeezed Annev's shoulder. "Do you know the blacksmith Sraon?"

Annev froze, suddenly wondering if Tosan knew of his conversation with the smith. "Yes. I've done chores for him in exchange for things Sodar needed."

Annev was relieved to see his words had not angered the headmaster. "Good. Speak with him. Before Sraon came to Chaenbalu, he lived in Banok. Find out all he knows about the city and about Janak's castle in particular. I expect the blacksmith had dealings with the Harth Household and perhaps even Janak himself." He paused. "You will need weapons as well, and to collect your belongings from the chapel. You can explain your new role to your former guardian at the same time."

"You want me to see Sodar?" Annev asked, surprised. He had already been planning to visit the priest to collect his ax and sword, but having Tosan's permission set Annev on edge.

"Yes," Tosan said, walking Annev toward the door. "I know you've told Sodar you're leaving the priesthood, but the situation has changed. As Master of Sorrows you will be relieving him of his duties and all church services will shift to you. Tonight's Regaleus celebration will be the last service held in that chapel and all future meetings will be here, in the nave."

"I see," Annev felt his anxiety spike.

"Excellent." The headmaster gestured to the door. "I hope Sodar is pleased by this news. He always hoped you would replace him. Given his age, I'm sure he will embrace retirement … and if not, I'm sure you can make him see it that way."

Had Sodar had been a normal priest, Annev might have agreed—he might have even found comfort in Tosan's words—but Sodar was far from normal, and Annev doubted anything he did or said would change Sodar's mind about the Academy or Annev's true purpose in this world. He had to try, though. If he wanted to preserve his dreams, he needed the old man's support.

"I will persuade him, Elder Tosan."

CHAPTER FORTY-NINE

Annev wrestled with a storm of emotions as he walked through the Academy. He still felt the euphoria of being promoted to master avatar, but it was now tempered with the realities of his new mission. Aside from the forthcoming conversation with Sodar, Annev had to lead his two greatest rivals on a mission to Banok—a town he had never seen or visited—where they would kill two more men: one a stranger and the other a teacher.

When he reached Sraon's smithy, Annev's mood was shifting from somber to brooding. That changed in an instant, though, when the blacksmith saw Annev.

"Master Annev! Your timing couldn't be better. I just finished your ring."

"Finished it?" Annev asked, incredulous. "I didn't think you'd start it till tomorrow."

"Bah," Sraon said, adjusting his eye-patch. "Fewer folk bother me on Regaleus and they expect delays on the holidays, so I have some flexibility. Your project interested me, so I got started." He reached into his apron and held up the ring: a simple band of yellow with a wavy line tracing its circumference. The smith passed the ring to Annev and he saw that a tiny bird had been carved into the surface of the band.

"It's a phoenix," Sraon said, rubbing his chin. "Least, that's what it's supposed to be. I told you I don't do detail work, and it shows."

Annev smiled, his eyes tearing. "It's perfect—more than perfect. I'm sure she'll love it. Thank you, Sraon."

The smith nodded, though his gaze seemed to pass over Annev's shoulder. "If she doesn't, you can always bring it back here. I had to guess at the size ... but I think I got it about right." Sraon gestured with his chin and Annev turned to see Myjun behind him.

"Oh," Annev said, fumbling to hide the ring. "Myjun!"

"Annev."

The young woman wore a red dress with a black trim that matched Annev's glove and master avatar robes. She smiled, her face flushed. "Can I talk to you?"

Before Annev could speak, Sraon clapped his gloves together and stepped out from under the awning of his open-air smithy. "I need to wash before evening services. You two are welcome to talk here." The smith slipped by Annev, winking at him with his one eye.

Annev's mouth went dry. "Thank you, Sraon." And then, much quieter: "Thank you so much." Sraon nodded, inclined his head to Myjun and left.

Myjun took a deep breath then slowly let it out while Annev watched her, the ring hidden in his hand. She looked at the ground.

"I saw ... I saw you earlier in your red robes, when you went to see my father with Master Carbad." She took another deep breath. "Annev ... I heard everything."

"You did?" Annev asked, wondering exactly how much Myjun knew.

The young woman looked up, her eyes sparkling. "I was listening at the door. Annev, I heard *everything*. I know you're going to Banok to supervise Fyn and Kenton. I even heard what my father said after they left."

"You heard that?" Annev blushed to think of Myjun hiding outside her father's study, eavesdropping on their conversation. His hand clenched hard around the ring.

"Myjun I ... I never gave you your Regaleus gift." Annev felt his tongue stick to the roof of his mouth. He moved his hand toward his chest, thinking to swap the gold band in his hand for the promise ring in his pocket. At the last moment, he extended his fist and opened his palm.

"Happy Regaleus."

Myjun inhaled sharply, her slender hands covering her mouth. "Oh, Annev! This is ..." She paused, looking from him to the ring. "Master Annev, what do you mean by giving this to me?"

Damn, he thought. *What* do *I* mean? Am I promising or proposing?

"It's a promise ring," he said, his voice going soft.

Myjun stepped closer. "And what exactly is it promising?"

Annev hesitated, looked around at the empty shop and then at the streets: there was a lull in the foot traffic outside the smithy, and for this brief moment they were alone.

Impulsively, he took her hand and pulled her deep into the shadows of the smithy. There, by Sraon's cooling forge, he knelt down and slipped the ring onto Myjun's finger. She almost danced on her toes, eyes shining, though for a heart-stopping moment Annev thought the ring was too tight, that he would hurt her. Instead, the band slipped over her finger as if it had always belonged there. He exhaled, heart thudding in his chest and throat.

"Myjun of Chaenbalu—daughter of Tosan, Eldest of Ancients—will you marry me?"

"Yes!" she choked, her voice tinkling with laughter even as her eyes filled with tears. "Yes, I will marry you, Master Ainnevog."

She pulled him to his feet, her eyes locking with his—and then she kissed him. Their lips pressed together, tight at first then softening with familiarity. He leaned in, holding her, as they felt their way through an intimate and instinctive language that neither fully spoke.

When at last they parted, it was with a mix of giddy joy and self-consciousness.

"You smell like strawberries," he said, immediately regretting it.

"You taste like sweet bread," she answered, laughing, and Annev laughed too. She looked down at her ring, examining it more closely. "We should keep this secret for now," she said, turning the ring on her finger. "Pretend that we're courting while we convince my father to give his permission."

Annev smiled, relieved at the simplicity of her proposal. "That's perfect—*you* are perfect." He cupped her chin in his hand, his bright blue eyes meeting her pale green ones, and they kissed again. This time when their lips parted, it was with self-denial and longing.

"That was *much* better," she said, sighing.

"I've never done this before," Annev apologized, his self-consciousness returning.

"I can tell," she said, eyes bright, "but you're a fast learner."

"Wait … have *you* done this before?"

Myjun tilted her head back and laughed. "Master Ainnevog," she said, chiding, "are you questioning my virtue?"

Annev shook his head, blushing furiously. "I only meant—"

Myjun's laughter cut him off and she placed a single finger over his lips. "I'm teasing you, Annev. I've never kissed another—not like this."

"I have to go," he said reluctantly. "I've things to take care of before I leave for Banok."

Myjun nodded, a silhouette against the setting sun. "Come back whole. I doubt I'll sleep till I know you've returned." She leaned in and Annev expected another kiss, but instead she pecked him on the cheek. "Return to me, Master Ainnevog." She stepped away, leaving the shadows of Sraon's smithy and melting into the throng of villagers that once again filled the plaza.

Annev watched until she disappeared into the Academy and only then glanced about for Sraon, but the blacksmith was nowhere to be seen.

Annev shrugged. He'd spoken to Sraon about Banok many times before, while working the bellows for him, and there was only a chance he could have learned more now. The smith had even mentioned Janak a few times, though he had said nothing meaningful about the man. He sighed.

Master of Sorrows, he thought, jogging toward the chapel. *Master Ainnevog. Annev de Breth … and Myjun de Breth?* He almost laughed at his fantasy of a domestic life with Myjun, first in the village and then on the road, adventuring with Sodar. The two dreams were at odds with one another, yet either future seemed wonderful with Myjun at his side.

CHAPTER FIFTY

Annev stumbled into the chapel, still dazed from his meeting with Myjun but also tired and feeling the lingering exhaustion of the previous day. He saw Sodar had brought out the remaining Regaleus decorations, the best having been reserved for the last night, and he smiled. Bright cloth hung from the backs of benches, many decorated with the Staff of Odar or the Flute of Lumea. Wooden decorations had also been hung from the rafters, each shaped and painted to look like a star or a moon.

Despite the welcoming atmosphere the room was empty. Only the truly pious attended on the third night of Regaleus, and they would not arrive till after sunset. The rest of Chaenbalu's villagers would be gathering in the plaza for the feasting, dancing, and merriment. It was a spectacle Annev had looked forward to seeing now that he was a master avatar, free of the chapel for this one night, yet that same responsibility was calling him away from the village for his first adventure beyond Chaenbalu and the Brakewood.

Annev grasped the nearest bench as he felt his knees wobble. He'd only had four hours sleep and his body was still recovering from the adventures of the past two days. He'd failed the Test of Judgment, killed a witch and her monsters, learned he was a descendant of Breathanas, become Master Avatar and proposed to—and kissed—Myjun. Now he had to tell Sodar he was replaced as the village priest before leaving on an artifact retrieval mission with the two boys who hated him most in the world. He steadied himself, then strode toward the rectory door where his hand hesitated above the doorknob until he forced himself to turn it.

Sodar sat at the kitchen table pouring over his Speur Dún manuscripts. The man's star-speckled ceremonial robes lay folded on the opposite chair. The priest looked up, delight plain on his face and growing stronger as he took in Annev's robes.

"Annev! I didn't think they'd let you come tonight. And what's this you're wearing?"

Even knowing the news he was about to deliver, Annev found he could still grin. "He promoted me, Sodar. To Master Avatar."

"He *what*? Annev, that's wonderful! I'm so proud of you." They hugged, then Sodar pulled back to examine Annev once more, his teeth flashing white in his combed beard. He felt the fine quality of the red robes then pounded Annev on the back. "The last avatar of your reap becomes its first master. That's incredible! Congratulations, Annev. A fine way to celebrate Regaleus."

Annev nodded, knowing what he had to say next. "I won't be staying, unfortunately. Elder Tosan needs my help. I'm to lead Fyn and Kenton on an artifact retrieval mission in Banok."

"You what?" Sodar frowned. "That can't be right. Are Fyn and Kenton masters as well?"

"No."

"So who's going with y—What am I saying." He gripped Annev's shoulder hard. "You can't *leave*! Annev, we just talked about this, you're being hunted. I thought we agreed?"

Annev realized the only way out of this conversation was to push through it. "I know what we said, but that was before I was made master avatar. I thought I had no choice, that it would be years till I was given the chance to become a master."

"But that changes nothing. Have you told your companions you might be hunted the moment you enter that wood?"

"I told Tosan about the *feurog*."

"Did you?" The priest studied him. "That surprises me. Does he also know of your magic hand? Or that an evil god is hunting you?"

Annev scoffed. "Of course not. I'd be dead if I had."

"You'll be dead if you leave the village." Sodar shook his head. "This is utter foolishness."

Annev's mouth formed into a flat line as he felt his blood rising. "I didn't have a choice, Sodar."

"Didn't you? Could you not have declined Tosan's request? Or delayed?" He paused. "When is this mission?"

"Tonight. We leave in an hour."

Sodar slumped into his chair. "Gods be good. Can you delay? Can you postpone till tomorrow? Even midnight would be preferable. That might give us time."

"I can't, Sodar. I have to lead the mission."

Sodar's eyes went wide. "Lead it? My dear boy, the Academy has fifty masters and avatars. They can send someone else—*anyone* else! None of this is important."

"And what *is* important? Some ancient prophecy that no one else believes?"

"Annev," Sodar was pleading, "*you* are important. Listen to me."

He was shaking his head before Sodar finished speaking. "I'll be fine. I was fine in the Brakewood with witches and monsters. I'll be doubly fine in Banok."

"You had Crag with you in the Brake."

"And I'll have Fyn and Kenton in Banok," Annev said. "Trust me." He swallowed, dreading what he had to say next. "There is something else. My title ... Sodar, Tosan made me Master of Sorrows."

"Like old Master Flint, who built this chapel."

Annev nodded. "I'll be taking care of the spiritual needs of the villagers and reporting back to the ancients. Tosan wants all church services moved back to the nave."

"Moved?"

"Sodar ... the Academy wants you to retire."

The priest froze. "Tosan said this? What were his exact words?"

"That you would be relieved of your duties, and church services would shift to me."

Sodar's reaction was immediate. His eyes flicked left and right and he carefully stood up, pulled back the curtain over the kitchen window, and peeked outside. He tugged it closed then cautiously checked the wood-shed, closing the door softly. He did the same thing with the door to the meeting hall before sitting back down.

"Sodar, you're scaring me."

"Annev," he said gravely, "this is it. We have to leave the village imme-diately. Tonight, if possible."

"What?" Annev shook his head. "Sodar, I just told you. I'm leaving on an avatar mission *tonight*. I have to recover a dark rod from Janak Harth. They want us to kill him ... and the master he captured."

Sodar hummed to himself as though he were half-listening. "Yes, Janak has always had a fondness for magic, even before he was injured." The priest shrugged. "Fine. You leave for Banok and I'll pack up our things, give the last Regaleus sermon, and come and meet you."

"You don't understand. I'm *leading* Kenton and Fyn on this mission. I *have* to do this."

Sodar frowned. "You have to, or you want to?

"Both! What's wrong with that? Sodar, I *want* to be an avatar and live at the Academy. I've said this before. I want to stay here and marry Myjun—to have a life of my own."

"Is this all about *Myjun*?"

Maybe.

"No!" Annev snapped, more forcefully than he'd intended. "But I don't like being told what to do, and I'm not going to run away just be-cause Tosan wants you to retire. Maybe you *should* retire. You can work on your manuscripts while I take over church services. You already agreed it's safer inside the village than out there. There's no reason for us to leave."

Sodar shook his head, a sad smile on his lips. "So naïve. Annev, what do you think Tosan meant by "relieved of my duties"?"

"Exactly what he said."

Sodar sniffed. "I thought you were smarter than that."

Annev's voice dropped to a whisper. "You think he means to kill you?"

Sodar nodded. "It wouldn't be the first time he's bloodied his hands."

"What do you mean?"

"Tosan didn't become Eldest of Ancients by accident—he's been weeding out his competition for years. When Elder Winsor died a year ago, Ancient Grim should have replaced him, but he died the year before."

Annev's eyes widened. "You think Tosan poisoned him?"

"Shhh! Not so loud." Sodar glanced at the front and back doors. "Besides, I never said poison. A well-placed pillow works just as well and can be twice as fast, and I have no proof—just my gut. Which says it was no accident Tosan became Headmaster of the Academy. But that's beside the point, which is this: if Tosan means you to replace me as Chaenbalu's spiritual leader, he will find a permanent way to keep me from influencing you or anyone else in the village."

Annev shook his head. He didn't want to believe it, but in the last forty-eight hours the headmaster had ordered him to kill a peddler, a merchant, and a fellow master avatar. He'd even implied that Kenton and Fyn were expendable resources. Sodar's hunch seemed more than plausible, however little he liked it.

"No. You're just saying that to convince me not to go. You never wanted me to be an avatar—you've said as much—you want me to leave everything I care about for your prophecy. To sacrifice my life just because you've sacrificed yours." Sodar shook his head, but the words were tumbling out as Annev could form them.

"Something good finally happened to me—I *finally* found my place— and you want to twist it into something bad. You want me to be Breathanas. But I'm not him! You want proof you haven't wasted your life—or my parents' lives!" Tears ran freely down Sodar's cheeks and Annev could feel his own hot tears threatening. He blinked them away, defiant.

"I'm *going* on this mission—and then I'm *staying* in Chaenbalu."

Sodar's gaze fell away and the room fell silent. When he finally spoke, his voice was so soft Annev almost didn't hear him. "Then we are both dead, and I've truly wasted my life." He stared at his hands, clasped lightly in front of him, as if uncertain what to do with them.

His old, wrinkled hands, Annev thought, wavering slightly. *Those hands saved me. They fed me and clothed me.*

Sodar retreated to his room, leaving his manuscript, robes, and Annev behind. Annev stared dumbly at the empty room, uncertain what to do. He even took a step toward Sodar's open door then stopped.

It has to be this way, he told himself. *Or he'll tangle me in his dead prophecies. Convince me I'm special so he can control me. I'll never be my own person if I always do as he says.*

But then, wasn't he just doing as Tosan said?

Annev cast his dark thoughts aside. He had always wanted to be an avatar—a *master* avatar—and now he had his wish. He opened the door to his chambers, ran to his clothes chest, and flung open the lid. Away from Sodar his tears poured freely, streaming down his cheeks as he tried to sniff them back. He reached into the chest and began emptying it. He'd take everything—clothes and possessions alike—because he was never coming back here.

Annev stopped mid-toss and looked at the crumpled beige tunic in his hand. He huffed, almost managed a smile, and dropped it back in the chest.

I don't need any of this. They'll outfit me with more master avatar clothes after Regaleus. I just need Crag's lantern and my weapons. He eased the chest closed and went back to the kitchen.

Sodar and Annev walked in at the same moment, and though the priest's eyes were dry he avoided eye contact. He pushed his manuscript aside, making room for the supplies he carried, then set down Sraon's ax.

"You'll be needing this," he said, not looking up. "It's yours."

"Thank you."

Sodar flinched then pulled an opaque glass bottle from his arms. "Drink half of this," he said, placing the bottle beside the ax. "Initially, it will make your thoughts fuzzy and you will feel sleepy. Don't fight it. If you do, you will feel worse."

"Why?"

Sodar paused, staring at the bottle. "It will help you stay awake for your mission. If you allow the elixir to do its work, you'll feel refreshed. Your senses will be sharper and you'll feel more alert." He looked up, making eye contact for the first time. "Don't drink it all at once. Your body needs time to recover, and if you push too hard there are some nasty side effects."

Annev nodded. "Thank you," he said again.

Sodar ignored him, returning his attention to the crimson bundle in his arms. He pulled out the sword with its sky blue corded hilt and silver sheath.

"Mercy is yours too," he said, setting the magic sword on the table. "It will be discovered at the Academy, but perhaps you can hide it in the nave."

Annev stared at the blade, eager to take it, but he found himself shaking his head. "It will be safer here, outside the Academy. You should keep it for now."

Sodar's expression was suddenly hard. "I have to *leave* Annev. The village is no longer safe. I don't know how long Tosan will allow me to stay, and I don't intend to wait and find out." He glanced down at the sword, running a hand over its ornate silver sheath. "If I can, I will go tonight, before you return from your mission."

Annev's voice caught in his throat. "But … your prophecy. How can you watch over me if you leave?"

"From a distance, I expect. Or not at all. In either case, you shouldn't concern yourself. You don't believe in that nonsense, and you've been very clear that you can take care of yourself." Sodar laid the folded phoenix banner on the table beside the other items. "I can't help you if you choose to stay in Chaenbalu. But I won't force you to leave either." He tugged his beard and glanced between the banner on the table and Annev's glove. "She did a good job, didn't she?"

"Who?" Annev asked, confused by the sudden change in topic.

"Myjun," Sodar said, nodding at the phoenix glove. "She did a good job duplicating Breathanas's banner. The phoenix is much smaller, but it almost looks like it was done by the same person."

Annev frowned. "You … you knew she made this for me?"

Sodar nodded. "She came to me about the design. She was going to do a red and black checkered pattern—something simple and sober, like the robes her father wears—but when I showed her the banner, she decided to copy the phoenix instead." He smiled, his eyes sad. "She's a sweet girl, Annev. You could do far worse, and she means well. I hope it ends well."

Sodar pointed to the dark brown bottle. "You should drink some now. The initial effects can be disorienting, and you'll want to be ready for your journey." He walked to his chambers and stopped in the doorway, his back still turned.

"Goodbye, Ainnevog."

He pulled the door shut.

CHAPTER FIFTY-ONE

Annev stared at the wooden door. His vision blurred and only then did he realize his tears had returned in force, flowing down his cheeks.

I could go with him, he thought, wiping at his eyes. *It's not too late. We could go before Tosan found out …*

But Tosan *would* find out. The headmaster expected to see Annev in an hour, and if he wasn't at the stables Tosan would search for his newest master avatar, Regaleus or no. And Sodar couldn't leave until he'd given the final Regaleus sermon—when Annev would be well on the road to Banok.

Annev hated Sodar for making him choose between the life he wanted and the life fate supposedly wanted for him—and he hated himself for hating Sodar. He choked back a sob and stormed over to the peg holding his water bags. He snatched up the sling, cinched it tight around his waist, and stuffed the phoenix banner inside one of the large waterproof pockets. He was about to stuff the brown bottle inside too when he remembered Sodar's counsel.

Annev uncorked it and sniffed the contents. Though pungent, it smelled vaguely of warana and anise. He hesitated, but he trusted Sodar not to poison him. Holding his breath, he upended the concoction and began to drink. He spluttered and gagged and swallowed almost a third of the spicy liquid before he remembered Sodar's warning and stopped. He wiped his lips and felt a sharp burning sensation coat his throat and spread through his chest. He started to feel flushed and the room spun alarmingly. Annev blinked, steadying himself, and the world righted itself again.

Annev shook off the effects of the elixir, recorked the bottle, then slipped it into the second waterskin. As he slipped the phoenix lantern into the same pocket, he felt his fatigue slowly melt away until his exhaustion had completely vanished. He felt good—awake and alert, strong and steady.

Annev stared at the ax and sword lying on the table and wondered if it was wise to bring them on his mission. He guessed they would be safer in his master's quarters or hidden in the nave as Sodar had suggested, but they were going on a lethal mission and if blood was being spilt, Annev wanted the best weapons at his side.

He tucked both into his makeshift belt and cinched it tighter, then he walked around the room, testing the feel of the weapons' weight against his hips. When he was out of reasons to linger, he glanced once more at Sodar's firmly closed door and then ran from the rectory.

***

Dusk had fallen and the final Regaleus celebration had begun in earnest when Annev reached the stables. He had hoped to drop his things in his room before saddling the horses, but Fyn, Master Brayan, and Titus were waiting for him. Annev forced a smile at the sight of his old friend—now dressed in tan steward clothes—but before he could embrace the lad, Fyn stepped between them and pressed a cold packet of black clothes into his arms.

"Put these on."

Annev didn't have to ask what they were for—Fyn was already dressed in his retrieval clothing—but he chafed at Fyn's command all the same.

And so it begins.

Annev nodded to Titus by way of apology and the boy waved back at him. Despite his demotion, he seemed happier than he ever had as an acolyte. Kenton arrived then and Fyn gave him a similar packet of clothes as Annev reluctantly peeled off his crimson tunic. By the time he and Kenton were dressed, Brayan and Titus had brought out the horses, each one saddled and ready to ride.

"We've only got five at the moment," the quartermaster clucked, "but these three are the best of the lot. Mind the black rouncy—she bites." After allocating each boy a horse, Brayan apologized that no other masters would be seeing them off. "Elder Tosan's gone to worship services with near all the ancients, and most of the masters are already celebrating." He shrugged. "I'm sure you'll do fine, though." Titus gave Annev a wordless hug and then he and Brayan left without any fanfare or further farewells.

Annev untied his improvised belt and stowed it in his saddle bags along with his coin purse. He watched Kenton and Fyn stow their own possessions and saw Fyn pass Kenton a sleek, curved sword, which the boy promptly slipped under his saddle blanket. Fyn offered him a battered short sword with a broken tip but frowned when he saw the sword and ax strapped to Annev's saddle. "I was going to give you this," he said, "but I see you've already got weapons."

"I do," Annev said, "but I could do with that belt." He gestured at the cord tied to Mercy's scabbard.

Fyn grunted and untied the thin leather strap, passing it to Annev. "Where'd you get those? I've never seen them in the armory." He reached for the sword and Annev slapped his hand away.

"These are mine," Annev said, almost growling, and paused to calm himself. "Master avatars can choose or commission their own weapons."

Fyn huffed but drew his hand back. "Why do you need a weapon at all? Kenton and I are the ones who have to kill Duvarek and Janak." If the boy seemed anxious about that prospect, he didn't show it. If anything, he seemed eager. He leaned in, his mouth close to Annev's ear. "Just stay out of my way and don't steal my kill."

Annev leaned back to see Fyn's face and tried to determine if the boy was serious. Unfortunately, it seemed he was. "I've killed enough folk this week, Fyn—and I've no interest in taking anything from you."

The taller boy laughed. "I doubt that. I stopped you from becoming an avatar plenty of times. Only makes sense you'd do the same to me. Whatever Tosan said."

"I guess that's the difference between us—one of many." He stepped into his stirrup and hoisted himself atop the black rouncy. "Anyway, I don't see your weapons. Planning to kill Janak with your bare hands?"

Fyn chuckled, walked over to his gelding, and pulled a coiled garrote from his saddlebag. "Far from bare," he said, hefting the flexible wire and small wooden handles.

Annev stared at the weapon, remembering how it had felt to strangle the wood-witch with Crag's bone-charm necklace. At the time, he'd been too overwhelmed by his fear of the witch and his concern for Crag's life to consider the brutality of it. Seeing the garrote in Fyn's hands brought the memory to life, though.

"Is that really all you're bringing?" Kenton asked from atop his own horse. His hand drifted to the tachi hidden beside his saddle.

Fyn sniffed. "Course not. But I'm not stupid enough to carry weapons in plain sight." He glared meaningfully at Annev who had just finished fixing Sraon's ax and Mercy's scabbard to his new belt.

Annev abruptly saw his companions had both concealed their weapons whereas his hung in plain sight. He shrugged, feigning indifference. "It's almost dark and nobody will be out on the roads during Regaleus. We'll be fine."

Fyn cursed and the two boys looked at him. The large youth shook his head and waved them off. "It's nothing," he said, mounting his horse. "I just forgot the torches. We don't need them, though. The stars will be out soon and they'll gives us enough light to find our way."

Annev glanced at Kenton, who looked as dubious as Annev felt. He slowly shook his head. "Finding our way is one thing. Having a horse step in a hole and break its leg is another." He sensed Fyn stiffen and dreaded what he had to say next. "Go and get the torches, Fyn."

The boy stared at him, incredulous. "I just said we don't need them."

"And I say we do. Fetch them, please."

"Fetch them yourself, Master Ainnevog," he said, spitting the honorific.

Annev looked to Kenton for support but the boy was silent, waiting to see how this played out.

So this is it, Annev thought. *This is where they start testing my leadership.* He tightened the reins in his hands then walked his horse over to Fyn's gelding.

"Fyn, get those torches now."

The muscular avatar glared hatefully at Annev. "What'll you do if I don't? Whine to Elder Tosan? Nah. We'd lose too much time, and you'd look weak besides. I'm guessing you'll fetch them yourself, while I sit here. How does that sound?"

Fyn was right on the first two counts, but Annev couldn't set this precedent of allowing the avatar to resist his leadership. He couldn't even send Kenton to get the torches instead—if the scar-faced avatar followed Fyn's lead, it would make things worse. No, Annev couldn't compel them. He had to convince them to follow him—but how?

"You think Tosan was wrong to promote me ahead of you," Annev said, stating the obvious as he worked out a solution out in his mind, "and that you should be leading the party instead of me."

Fyn's brow furrowed, his mouth quirked up, and then he laughed— not a mean chuckle or a mocking sneer either, but a real belly laugh.

"I think," he said, getting his laughter under control, "you're a mongrel avatar, part deacon, part trickster. You're here by luck, but you're not fit to lick my boots, let alone lead this mission."

"So," Annev said, stalling, "you don't trust Tosan's opinion and you don't trust me ... but you trust yourself?"

"What of it?"

"Well, you said yourself that I'm lucky. Is that how I beat you in the Test of Judgment—or earned my master status? It's all just been luck?"

Fyn nodded. "Yeah, that's what I think."

"Let's say you're right," Annev said, an idea finally forming. "I'm Lumea's lucky charm, everything I touch turns to gold, and everything magically works out for me. Let's pretend that's true, and that I'm about to lead you to Banok to help you and Kenton earn your master avatar titles. If I'm as lucky as you claim, you're going to benefit from it, so what do you have against following me?"

Kenton grunted at those intellectual acrobatics and Fyn glanced between the two hesitating.

"You're trying to trick me," he said, studying Annev.

"What if I am? You said I'm only leading you because I got lucky. Well then: benefit from it."

"Eventually," Fyn said, nudging his horse closer, "luck runs out, and I don't care to hitch my wagon to yours. I do well enough by myself."

"Do you?"

"Yeah."

"Then what's your strategy when you reach Banok?"

The larger avatar frowned. "That's not how it works. I was told to get the supplies. Kenton's got the info about entering Janak's palace."

"So you're saying you can't do it alone. You see that Tosan assigned us each a role and we'll have a better chance of succeeding if we stick to that plan?"

Fyn stared at him, eyes dark and jaw slack, then he closed his mouth and shook his head. "Always a smart-ass."

Annev inclined his head, taking it as a compliment. "Maybe I am, or maybe I just agree with you and think, if we each do our part, things will go smoother. You were in charge of supplies, you're the one who should get the torches. Yes?"

Fyn studied Annev's face then dismounted and wrapped his reins around the nearest post. "If either of you touches my things ..." He left the unfinished threat hanging in the air and dashed back inside the Academy.

Kenton swept his shaggy black hair aside and peered sideways at Annev. "He'll get you back for that, and you know it. Fyn doesn't like being ordered around, and he hates looking stupid."

"What about you?"

"I don't like looking stupid either."

"Not that," Annev said, smiling in spite of himself. "You followed Fyn during the last Tests of Judgment, but you were with me, Titus, and Therin before that. What will you do now?"

Kenton's right hand drifted to the hilt of his tachi while the other knotted into the silvery mane of the palfrey beneath him. He was silent for so long Annev thought he wasn't going to answer.

"You seem to know things the rest of us don't," Kenton said at last. "I'm not sure how. Maybe Fyn's right and you're just lucky, or maybe you see things differently and that gives you an advantage." He traced the braiding of his weapon's two-handed hilt then shrugged. "Doesn't really matter. If you can get Titus and *Therin* through the Test of Judgment, you can lead us to Banok and back. No promises once we get there, though."

Annev grunted, feeling he needed more loyalty than that, but sensing he'd do better not to press the issue.

"So," he said, changing topic, "what'd you learn from Keyish, Folum, and Dorstal?"

A faint smile touched Kenton's lips. "Dorstal was up to his nose in honey wine, and Folum wasn't much better. Keyish was useful, though. He told me which landmarks to follow out of the Brake and he sketched out Janak's castle."

"That should be helpful."

Kenton shook his head. "Not so much. The Harths have a bunch of sliding walls built into their keep. Apparently, Janak can change the layout half a hundred times in an hour."

"Ah," Annev said, "we'll be on our own once we're inside." Annev wondered if Sraon would have a solution to that problem. Thinking of the man, Annev looked past the celebrating villagers toward the smith's shop. In the fading light and from this distance, he couldn't see much of the open-air smithy, but he glimpsed enough to confirm the forge fires were cold and the man was gone, likely attending Sodar's Regaleus service.

"What about the outside?" Annev asked, turning back.

"Huh?"

"Can it move, too, or does it stay the same?"

"The same, I guess."

"So we just need to find the right place to enter. The interior walls might move, but it takes more effort to shift a whole room."

Kenton grunted. "True."

Annev nudged his horse towards Kenton. "When we get there, we'll survey the place. Discuss what we see and decide where to enter. After that, can I trust you to follow me?"

Kenton studied him then slowly nodded. "For now, I'll follow you."

Annev smiled, pleased to win his companion's support, and saw Fyn returning with the three pitch-soaked torches.

"Here are your damned torches," Fyn said, passing the first to Kenton and the second to Annev. "Can we go now?"

"Of course," Annev said. "Thank you, Fyn." Before the boy could toss off a reply, Annev looked to Kenton. "Which way?"

The dark-haired avatar pointed toward the setting sun and the trees surrounding the village. "We ride for the hill. It's five miles before we leave the Brake and another six to Banok." He looked at their unlit torches. "Now that I think on it, we should take lanterns. These will be fine in the Brake, but once we leave the wood we'll be visible."

"The light will be visible from miles away," Annev agreed.

Kenton nodded. "We could douse them, but we'll be traveling over rough terrain. Lamps would be helpful in the castle too. Keyish said it's nearly as large as the Academy."

Fyn huffed. "If you want a lantern," he said, mounting his speckled gelding, "you can get it yourself."

Annev considered it then realized he had the answer in his saddle bags. "Don't worry about it," he said, wheeling his horse about. "I've got a solution in my pack. Let's go."

Daylight was fading fast when they entered the forest, and Annev worried that the shadows would lengthen their path, as they often did around dusk and dawn. But this part of the Brake was thin compared to the eastern side, and its peculiar magic was less powerful. They'd gone northwest a quarter of a mile when Annev called a halt next to a small hill overlooking the village. He asked Kenton to bring out his torch then, and its light was enough to illuminate the path for all three of them. As they passed the western hill, Annev noted the standing stones that marked the perimeter of the village and realized he'd never been this far west in his life. A similar thought seemed to strike the other boys, for they looked at each other in a rare moment of fellowship.

They rode three abreast through the forest with Kenton in the middle, and for the first half hour Annev stayed taut as a bowstring, his eyes searching for signs of the *feurog* or other monsters that could be hunting them. When nothing manifested, he began to relax, allowing himself to enjoy the thrill of this new adventure.

With the Brake's shadow-magic drawing out their pace, it took an hour to escape the Brakewood's treeline. Once they did, Kenton snuffed his torch and they climbed the large hill overlooking the wide prairie. Annev crested the hill first and Fyn and Kenton pulled up beside him.

Together, for the first time in their lives, they gazed at the world beyond Chaenbalu.

CHAPTER FIFTY-TWO

The wide plains of Daroea stretched away in all directions, barely illuminated by the setting sun. Though night had come, Annev could still make out the shadowy copses of trees that dotted the landscape, gradually growing in size and density to the north and south. He could also see the shadowed walls of Banok ahead of them, yet Annev's eyes drifted west, away from their destination and toward the silhouette of a much larger town perhaps a dozen miles away.

Not a town, he realized. *A city. The capital city—Luqura.*

Annev stared at the distant lights for a long moment then reluctantly turned away. Farther south the land became hillier and more forested, the thickets merging to form a dense wall of trees. A wide road from Luqura skirted the forest and then dove straight into the trees, forming the line that separated the Vosgar from the Brakewood.

To the north, wide plains extended beyond the Brake and Banok until a dense swathe of foliage sprang up in the northeast. In the dusky light, this new forest appeared a spring green, with bright dots of color that might have been flowers or fruit. Annev blinked, wondering if his eyes were playing tricks on him.

Kenton nodded at the wood. "That's Fertil Hedge. Master Keyish says it's haunted: the forest is always in bloom and fruit constantly hangs from its boughs."

Fyn laughed, swinging his dreadlocks out of his face. "Doesn't sound so bad."

"The ghosts keep the trees in fruit to lure in travelers."

Fyn rolled his eyes in his response while Annev turned in his saddle to see the extent of the green forest. "It looks almost as large as the Brake."

"It's three times as large. About half as big as the Vosgar. You can't see, but it extends all the way to Paldron."

"And it's *all* haunted?" Fyn said, his tone mocking.

Kenton shrugged. "Folum said something about Druids too. It doesn't matter, though. We're headed to Banok."

Annev turned back to the town a few miles ahead. "That's right," he said, "and that means we need light—something they won't see coming." The sun was gone now, and only a band of reddish-pink remained in the sky as the stars began to come out.

Annev hoped he was making the right decision as he reached into his saddle bags and pulled out the phoenix carving. He placed his thumbs on the feather and the flame, preparing to twist … then stopped. The boys eyed him, curious. Instead of surprising them both by turning on the lantern, Annev tossed the block of wood to Kenton.

"What is this? Why are you giving it to me?"

"It's a lighted puzzle box," Annev said, remembering Crag's name for the artifact. "See if you can get it to work."

Kenton stared at the carving, his fingers tracing its lines. "This feels …" He looked at Annev, a single eyebrow raised. Annev nodded, wanting to see what Kenton would do.

The dark-haired avatar closed his eyes and ran his hands over the block of wood for the second time. His fingers slowed as they reached the feather within the flame. He prodded the unseen button, sensing its purpose but not knowing how to activate it.

"Here," Annev said, extending his hand. "I'll show—"

Kenton twisted the artifact and light blazed from the phoenix lantern.

"*Gods!*" Fyn jumped, jerking hard on his reins and startling his horse.

Annev was impressed by Kenton's instincts. Despite his error identifying the Rod of Healing the other day, Annev was above average at identifying magical artifacts. It seemed Kenton was a different story, though; where Annev was talented, Kenton was a prodigy.

"Nice job."

The scar-faced avatar seemed not to hear Annev's praise. He stared at the block of wood in his hands, in awe of its luminescence. "This is magic, isn't it?" He spoke almost reverently.

"It's only magic if you don't know how it works," Annev said, repeating Crag's clever quip. "But yes, it's an artifact."

Kenton stared at him, impressed. "This is from the Vault of Damnation?"

Annev took another risk. "Not quite," he said. "I got it on my mission in the Brakewood yesterday. The peddler gave it to me as payment."

Fyn snickered. "Was that before or after you slit his throat?"

Annev met Fyn's eyes, serious. "Before."

Fyn's laughter devolved into a grunt, a grudging sign of respect. "Well," he said, mumbling, "I still don't see what good it does—it's too bright. I thought the point was for us not to be seen."

Annev nodded. "Kenton, can you adjust it?"

The boy opened his mouth to say something, then stopped. Instead of speaking, he grasped the top and bottom of the lantern. Without any guidance, he pressed on the hidden buttons and twisted, dissipating the diffused light and focusing it into a narrow, ghostly beam.

"Huh," Fyn said, impressed and trying to mask it. "That'll work." He frowned. "So you sent me to get torches when you had this the whole time." It wasn't a question.

"Yes," Annev said. He trotted his horse over to Kenton and took the lantern. "If the ancients had seen this, they'd have stowed it in the vault." He tossed it to Fyn, who caught it with both hands.

"Why am I holding this?" he asked, wary of the magic he held.

"Because we need light, and I want you to lead us the rest of the way."

"Is that right?" Fyn said, neither rejecting nor accepting Annev's implied command. He turned the lantern in his hands, examining it.

"How did you change the light?"

Kenton explained, and everyone looked pleased when Fyn successfully twisted the lantern off and then on again.

"If you keep it focused to a beam," Annev said, "you can cover the eye a little so it casts light on the ground and we can see where we're going, but no one will see where it's coming from. It's not foolproof, but we should make good time without being seen from a distance."

Kenton and Fyn looked at each other, both nodding.

"Very well, Master Ainnevog," Fyn said, only a modicum of ridicule in his voice. "I'll lead."

"Thanks," Annev said. "Alright, then. Master Fyn leads the way. Master Kenton, will you watch our backs?"

The two boys looked at each other, confused. "That's not funny," Kenton said. "You know we're not masters."

"Maybe not at the Academy," Annev said, "but we're outside Chaenbalu. Out here, you can be whatever you like."

"Horseshit," Fyn spat. "You can call a horse a duck, but it still won't fly."

"That's right," Annev said, seizing the analogy. "Changing a name doesn't change a creature's nature. The same is true of us. We trained to be master avatars, and we're each as skilled as the men who've claimed that title, so why should I call you anything else?"

Fyn and Kenton exchanged a more thoughtful look.

"As far as I'm concerned," Annev said, "you're the Master of Arms"— pointing to Fyn—"and you're the Master of Curses." He pointed at Kenton. "Tonight just cements that truth, so unless you feel you're less than my equal, I'm not calling you something different."

Kenton stared at Annev, unconsciously stroking the scar on the side of his face. Likewise, Fyn sat in silence for a long moment before seeming to come to a conclusion.

"Well," he said, twisting the lantern into a thin beam of light, "I still think you're full of shit ... but I must be getting used to the smell, because I like what you just said."

Kenton had a faint smile on his face. "Me too."

CHAPTER FIFTY-THREE

A mile from the city walls, Fyn clicked off the lantern and they approached under the cover of darkness. As the trio drew closer, they heard the sounds of Regaleus celebrations, which included plenty of raucous laughter and boisterous singing … and no sign of the town watch.

Fyn brought them within shouting distance of any guards that might be on patrol then halted. Annev stopped beside him and studied the twenty-foot stone wall surrounding the town, aware that his companions were watching him.

"Master Kenton, where does Janak live?"

The boy pointed. "His shops are on the northwest side of town in the Gold District, but his home is in the Rose Quarter, near the eastern gate."

"What're you thinking?" Fyn asked.

Annev studied his fellow avatars. Beneath their riding cloaks, each wore fitted and flexible black garments. "We dressed for stealth," he said, talking slowly as he thought it through, "so we'll use it. Leave the horses by the eastern gate, climb the city walls, and get to Janak's castle." He paused. "We'll figure out the rest when we can see it."

Fyn began tying his dreadlocks into a topknot. "That doesn't seem well thought out."

"No," Annev admitted easily, "but we don't know what's ahead of us, so we have to treat it like a Test of Judgment. Stay flexible and adapt. Get inside, get the rod, get out."

"What about Duvarek and Janak?" Kenton asked.

"We'll find them," Annev said, "but I'd prefer to secure the artifact before we find Duvarek. If we do, maybe we can use the rod to free him from his compulsion."

"Use the rod?" Fyn scoffed. "Tosan would skin us—and that's not what we're here to do. Besides, none of us know the first thing about using magic."

Annev looked at Kenton.

"I know a little bit," Kenton offered grudgingly. "I mean, I'm good at identifying artifacts. There was even one time … I used one."

"You used *magic*?" Fyn seemed torn between being impressed and disgusted.

Kenton sniffed. "I'm not a flaming keokum, Fyn. It was a common artifact, like that lantern you're holding. Anyone could have used it."

The larger boy grunted, trying not to look sheepish. "So what did you do?"

"We were doing artifact identifications with Dorstal. He brought out a cup, said it was a common artifact that could magically fill itself." He shrugged. "He dared us to try."

"And you did?"

Kenton nodded. "It was easy. I held it, thought about how thirsty I was, and repeated the glyph."

"Huh. That's … not so bad. What'd you fill it with?"

"Honey wine," Kenton said, smiling. "Dorstal drank it." The trio laughed and Annev felt encouraged by the admission.

"Great," Annev said. "Maybe if the rod can be used by common folk, we can use it to save Duvarek rather than execute him."

"Hold on," Fyn said, raising a hand. "That's not what we were told to do. If Kenton brings Duvarek back, he won't earn his master title."

"True," Annev said, "so I'll leave it up to Kenton." He looked at the scar-faced boy. "What do you think: if there's a chance to help him, do you want to try?"

Kenton frowned. "It's not that simple. I'd love to save Duvarek—getting my master avatar title tonight isn't as important as his life—but the Rod of Compulsion is a *dark* rod, not a common artifact. To have any chance of using it on Duvarek, I'd have to have real magic—the kind you only get from making a pact with Keos."

Fyn nodded in agreement while Annev bristled at the avatar's words, both because he found them personally offensive and because now he couldn't use the rod to save Duvarek; if he even tried, he'd be accused of being a Son of Keos, and would then forfeit his own life for the mere chance of saving Duvarek's. Annev admired his former teacher as a skilled master avatar, but he had no delusions of sacrificing himself to save the man.

"We stick to the plan, then," Annev said. "Execute Dove, then kill Janak for using the dark rod and threatening the Academy." Fyn nodded in agreement, while Kenton agreed with obvious reluctance.

"If we can subdue Duvarek without hurting ourselves or endangering the mission," Kenton said, "we could knock him out and drag him back to Chaenbalu. If he passes beyond the range of the dark rod, the effects will lessen and eventually wear off."

"I support that," Annev said enthusiastically and wheeled his horse about. "We have a plan. Let's find a spot to tie up these horses."

As he led them around the perimeter of the wall, Fyn quietly rode up alongside him. "You really going to try to save Duvarek?" he asked, his voice a whisper.

"Of course," Annev said, surprised. "He's a bit rough, but he doesn't deserve to die—and the Academy trains its master avatars too hard to dispose of them so easily. If we can bring him back to Chaenbalu, I'd prefer that."

"And what if one of us got snared by the rod?"

"I'd do the same. Club you over the head and get you the hell out of there." He peered sideways at the boy, curious. "Why?"

Fyn shrugged. "I just don't believe you would. It's one thing to save your buddies, but it's a whole different story with me or Kenton. Figured it'd be easier to leave us behind—or kill us. You'd not really gain anything by bringing us back."

Annev sized up his companion. He had once considered making friends with Fyn, but he'd long since given up on that possibility. Maybe he'd given up too soon.

"I would, you know."

Fyn snorted. "Sure." He rode on ahead, but then Kenton trotted up beside Annev.

"What was that about?" he asked.

"Fyn doesn't trust me."

"Are you surprised?" Kenton said, raising an eyebrow. "Fyn's always had trust issues, and you're hardly the most reliable person."

"Me?" Annev said, wondering if the boy had him confused for someone else. "You're the one who betrayed his friends during the swimming contest—and then started working with Fyn to stop us getting our titles."

"Did I ever say we were friends?" Kenton asked, his face expressionless. "I don't recall having that conversation." He spoke with so little emotion, Annev wondered if the boy were joking. Before he could ask, though, Kenton shrugged and said, "I suppose we all have reasons to hate each other, but we can still work together. That's what matters."

Annev nodded, sensing that Kenton wished to drop the subject, but not willing to let it go. "So why do you hate me?"

Kenton studied him, his face a mask. "You remember the year I got my scar?"

Annev slowly nodded, understanding his offense against Kenton wasn't from a recent injury. "Three years ago, before Titus joined our reap and we began testing for our avatar titles." It was also the year after he'd become close friends with Therin and around the time Myjun had begun taking an interest in him.

Kenton nodded. "I started my private classes with Master Duvarek that year—me and one other student."

"Yeah," Annev said, "I remember how jealous I was when I found out."

"Jealous?"

Annev nodded. "I used to idolize Duvarek. He gets to leave the Academy more than anyone I know, he's seen things and been places I can only dream of, and he's got a perfect retrieval record."

"Not anymore."

"Right," Annev admitted, realizing he'd put his foot in his mouth, "but if we bring him home along with the rod, it'll be like he never failed."

"Maybe," Kenton said. "I didn't know you liked Duvarek. People give him a hard time because he drinks and keeps to himself, but there's a reason the Academy sends him on the most missions. He's a better fighter than Edra, but he doesn't like to show off and he doesn't have the patience to teach kids that don't listen. That's why they rotate him as a teacher for the witgirls."

Annev nodded, seeing no reason to doubt Kenton's words. "He actually had a better reputation before ..."

"Before I got scarred?" Kenton finished. Annev nodded and the boy huffed, disgusted. "Duvarek wasn't a neglectful teacher. We weren't even training when I got hurt."

"But you were injured in his class. Is that not right?"

"That's what I just said, isn't it?"

"So what did happen?"

Kenton glared at him, eyes flat. "It's my affair, so stop asking about it." He shook his head. "Besides, I wasn't talking about that. I was saying that when Duvarek gave me private lessons, he had agreed to train one acolyte and one apprentice. Elder Winsor chose me and Witmistress Kiara chose Myjun."

"Myjun?" Annev felt his tongue grow thick in his mouth. "I didn't ... she never told me."

"Not surprised," Kenton said, his voice cold. "She probably didn't say anything about me either." Annev shook his head, too stunned speak. "I didn't think so. She only trained with us for six months ... and then she stopped coming."

"She never came back?"

"No ... not after I got scarred."

Not after he got scarred? Annev calculated when his own relationship with Myjun began to blossom and realized the timelines matched up. His stomach twisted into a knot, and he suddenly found he couldn't look Kenton in the eyes.

"Did you ...?" Annev said, struggling to voice his thoughts. "I mean, did she ...?"

"She did," Kenton said, his voice barely above a whisper, "and I still do."

They rode in silence, each focusing on the bobbing light of Fyn's dim lantern.

"You think she stopped coming because you got injured."

"Because of my scar," Kenton said, his voice low and brooding. "She was disgusted by it. I don't think she ever looked at me after that."

The knot in Annev's gut grew tighter. It was everything he feared about Myjun and didn't want to acknowledge: if she would shun Kenton because of a scar, how would Annev fare when she discovered his missing limb?

She can't ever know, he realized—that was the only way: she could *never* know.

"You were only fourteen," Annev said, seizing control of his emotions, "and you said Myjun only attended classes for six months. You couldn't have been that close."

He said no more, but the question was implied; Annev waited for a response, and when he didn't get one, he dared to glance at his companion.

Kenton's eyes bored into him. "Did you know the witwomen use herbs to avoid falling pregnant?"

Annev flinched, instinctively tugging the reins. His horse slowed and Kenton passed him.

"Like I said," Kenton breathed, "we all have reasons to hate each other." And before Annev could reply, the dark-haired avatar spurred his horse ahead to catch up with Fyn.

CHAPTER FIFTY-FOUR

They reined their horses in beside a single gnarled oak hidden in the shadows of the city wall, encircled by a clump of sweet ferns. Less than five hundred yards ahead, Annev could see the closed eastern gate. He gestured to his companions and the three of them dismounted, tethering their horses and silently checking their equipment.

While Kenton shed his cloak and strapped his tachi to his back, Annev pulled out his short sword and ax. He belted both weapons to his hips, avoiding eye contact with Kenton. Instead, he looked at Fyn and saw the Master of Arms had come prepared: metal bracers concealing throwing knives encircled his forearms, a double-coiled garrote and two pouches hung securely from his belt, and two three-foot-long flanged maces were strapped to his back. Annev shook his head as Fyn also strapped on a pair of spiked elbow pads and leather gloves.

"I thought we agreed on stealth?"

Fyn lashed the phoenix lantern to his belt. "I train every day. I can be just as stealthy with them as without."

Annev very much doubted that, but he decided to keep his thoughts to himself. There was already too much tension in the air, and he didn't want it turning to dissension. "Fine. But I want my lantern back when this is all done."

"Sure," Fyn said, patting the block of wood. "Though if things go sour under your watch, I'm giving it to Tosan so I can still pass my Test of Competence."

"Fantastic," Annev said, though he felt like strangling his companion.

They both hate me ... and if I'm honest, I don't much like them. He shook
his head, thinking it was a miracle they had got this far and wondering
if he could keep his team together long enough to accomplish their mission. They both trotted over Kenton who stood at the base of the city wall,
squinting at its stone blocks.

"What is it?" Annev asked, anxious.

"These stones—they're not flush. What's the point of building a wall
if you're going to stagger the blocks half an inch?" He shook his head,
disgusted.

Fyn looked up at the wall. "It's practically a staircase. Looks easier
than the Academy's climbing wall."

Annev nodded, though he still felt nervous. From this side of the barrier, the sound of the city's Regaleus celebration seemed distant. He wiped
his sweaty palms on his black trousers and gripped the disjointed stones
with his fingertips. In his peripheral vision, he saw the other boys do the
same. Without a word, they each wedged their soft-soled leather boots
into the mortared crevices and hoisted themselves upward.

Annev reached the top in less than a minute, a black shadow that
dropped over the short parapet and blended into the darkness beside Kenton. True to his word, Fyn managed the ascent without any of his weapons
clanging about, and he dropped next to Annev a few seconds later. They
crouched in the shadows and then slowly stood to gaze at the foreign city
stretching before them.

From above, Banok was a city of sloping rooftops packed together so
tightly that the alleys below were practically tunnels. Unlike Chaenbalu's
street plan of concentric circles bisected by two roads, Banok had several
dozen streets and alleys—some wide enough to be thoroughfares, some so
narrow they were almost invisible—all crisscrossing each other in a confusing
maze of angles and dead ends.

Though the majority of buildings were single-story, some rose two
stories high and a handful were higher still. The largest by far was part palace, part castle, and almost as large as the Academy—though, without the
accompanying somber gray architecture, it was far less intimidating. The
enormous sandstone keep stood a good distance from the center of town,

which seemed to be the focus of the Regaleus celebrations; most of Banok's citizens had gathered round large bonfires and were either drinking, laughing, making music, or doing some combination of the three. There were also a few men in uniforms at the edge of the celebrations—the city watch, Annev guessed.

"Is that it?" he asked, pointing to the sandstone keep.

"It matches Master Keyish's description. He says Janak keeps guards posted day and night at all the entrances, as well as patrolling most of the hallways."

Fyn shrugged. "No problem. That's what this is for." He lovingly patted his garrotte.

"Are you really that eager to kill someone?" Annev asked, a bit unsettled by Fyn's cavalier demeanor. "It's not that easy to take a life."

"Maybe it's hard if you've spent half your life training to be a priest," Fyn retorted. "But that's not me—I was made for this."

Annev let the argument go. "Fine, but stealth is still our first option. A missing guard will be noticed, and we don't want anyone investigating, especially not if we're still exploring the palace. Sneak in and sneak out without alerting anyone." Fyn folded his arms, but he didn't object. "Master Kenton, what's our path?"

"We go straight over the rooftops," the boy said, "We'll be out of the firelight, but away from the gate and any sentries."

"Great. Fyn, you've got the lantern. Do you still want to take point?"

Fyn snorted. Rather than answering, he spun and leapt backwards off the wall, grabbing the ledge as he fell and then pushing off with his feet and hands. He flipped into the darkness and softly landed on the roof of the nearest building.

"Follow me if you can."

And they did. As they reached Fyn's location, the avatar sprinted to his next target: a group of two-story buildings overlooking a narrow alley. It joined their street at an acute angle and, as Annev watched, Fyn sprang across the gap, snatched the edge of an overhanging balcony, and swung himself onto a second story window ledge.

Not to be outdone, Kenton ran for the same group of buildings, but instead of grabbing the balcony, he threw himself toward the opposite structure and bounded off its stones before gravity could reassert itself. The raven-haired avatar flew in Fyn's direction and tumbled onto the target balcony, landing a few feet higher than his rival.

Annev rolled his eyes, a small spreading across his face. They were showing off now, but he couldn't afford to lose face in front of his companions. He was also reluctant to admit that he was having fun: he didn't have to shepherd Kenton and Fyn the way he had worried over Titus and Therin, and it felt liberating to push himself without worrying about the competencies of his companions. He studied the gap between the two buildings and saw his path. With a running jump, Annev followed the same path as Kenton, but instead of tumbling onto the balcony, he angled his momentum so that his foot lit on the balcony's rail and he sprang straight onto the rooftop. The other boys reached the roof a moment later, but before Fyn could attempt a third feat of acrobatics, Annev regretfully raised his hand, stopping him.

"We should go lower. Height doesn't bring us closer to Janak's palace, and our theatrics will call too much attention to ourselves."

This time it was Fyn's turn to roll his eyes. He didn't outwardly object, though, and a few minutes later, they were back on the first-story buildings and moving swiftly but more stealthily toward Janak's palace. By silent consensus, no one led the pack and they each found their way through Banok's huddled buildings, hanging eaves, and twisted alleys. Once they had found a comfortable rhythm, they were more like a pack of shadows floating over a cobblestone street than a trio of young thieves leaping from rooftop to rooftop. Gray clouds drifted past the waning crescent moon, amplifying the effect, and the flickering light of the bonfire below was all that limned their silhouettes.

A quarter of an hour later, Annev reached the edge of the row of buildings leading to Janak's keep. A wide street stood between the home he now stood on and the merchant's palace. Annev looked down, gauging the distance between him and the roof of the keep's first floor: it was nearly thirty feet. Even with a running start there was no way he could clear it. They would have to lower themselves to the ground and start there.

Kenton and Fyn landed softly beside Annev and assessed the building.

"Too far to jump," Kenton said, but as he spoke, Fyn took a running leap and cast himself off the edge of the building. He didn't land on top of Janak's building, but he cleared the entire street—almost twenty feet—and landed softly in the shadowed recesses of the outer wall.

Kenton looked at Annev, they shrugged as one, and the reticent avatar followed Fyn, beginning his running leap just as the door below swung open.

Kenton skidded to a halt, dislodging a handful of clay tiles in the process. As they started to slide, he dropped, rolled, reached, and slapped a hand over the moving tiles at the very edge of the roof.

"Did you hear that, Nedders?" a woman's voice asked.

"I heard it," a gruff male voice replied.

Annev froze in the shadows while Kenton tried to meld himself into the roof.

"It sounded," the man continued, his speech a little slurred, "like a goose."

"A goose?" the woman said. "Why ever a—ouch! Oh, you wicked man!"

"'Twasn't me," he protested. "'Twas the goose."

"Was it now?" the woman teased. "Because it felt more like—ouch!"

"Goosed!" The man laughed.

The couple ambled into the street, their arms around each other's waists as they made their way toward the bonfire. As they walked, the man's hand kept drifting to the woman's bottom. She squealed then laughed, apparently enjoying the game.

As the couple drew farther away, Annev slid forward to help Kenton, pulling the loose tiles back into place. He glanced back at the couple and noticed that the man hobbled a bit, favoring his left foot. Annev squinted at the fellow's leg and saw that, instead of a boot or a shoe, the man—Nedders—had a peg leg.

Annev's mouth dropped open, the tiles forgotten. *He's a cripple! And he's walking around in broad daylight … with a woman at his side.* He was stunned, and saw Kenton's openly confused look reflected his own. Annev rubbed his gloved left hand just as the shaggy-haired boy traced the mottled scar covering the left side of his face.

As the couple turned the corner and disappeared from view, Kenton glanced up and saw Annev watching him. His expression hardened and Kenton snatched his hand away, quickly easing himself over the edge of the roof and dropping out of sight.

Annev sighed as he watched his scarred companion sprint across the street to join Fyn. In the past, he had wished he could openly commiserate with Kenton about his disfigurement—he had even pitied the boy—but knowing Kenton's injury had indirectly led Myjun to him, and the suggestion that she and Kenton had been close, left Annev feeling petty and irritable.

Still, he couldn't help but wonder how different their lives might be here—in a town where someone could openly display their deformity without being shunned, mistreated, or murdered. In such a place, Annev supposed he could have led a normal life … but then, in such a place Myjun might have remained with Kenton. That thought twisted like a knife in his gut, and he was ashamed to admit that, in this instance, he was grateful for Chaenbalu's prejudices.

Instead of climbing to his feet, Annev opted to dangle his legs off the side of the twelve-foot structure before easing himself over. As he turned to slide his torso over the edge, he glanced up and saw the black silhouette of a tall man in fluttering robes flitting across the rooftops.

Startled, Annev lost his grip and plummeted over the side of the building, landing flat on his back. He lay prone, winded from the air being knocked out of him, until he could scramble to his feet and dart across the street to Janak's palace. When he reached the dark alcove where his companions were waiting, Annev spun and searched the rooftops for the dark figure that had been stalking them. He stood perfectly still, counting the seconds, but saw nothing.

After almost a minute, Fyn and Kenton shared a glance.

"You all right, Annev?" Kenton asked. "You took a bit of a tumble."

"I'm fine," Annev said, his eyes fixed on the rooftops. "I just … thought I saw something."

"What?"

Annev remembered. *A man … wearing death's cloak.*

He shook his head. "I thought it was a person, but it's nothing. Just a trick of the light."

Fyn frowned, his gaze sliding over the blackness above the rooftops. "If someone was there, they're gone now." He looked back at Annev. "Ready to do this?"

Annev took a long final look then nodded. Kenton stepped up to the side of Janak's palace wall and pointed upward. "His study is on the third floor, and the window is less secure."

"Is the rod there?"

Kenton shrugged. "It would usually be underground in the treasure room, but Keyish thought Janak would move it—to keep a closer watch over it. His study seems the most likely place since that's where he displays his favorite artifacts—plus a bunch of sentimental possessions."

Annev frowned. "If we start on the third floor and the artifact is in the basement, we'll have to cross three floors just to get to the treasure room."

"Four if you count the basement itself," Kenton said brightly, "but security is tighter lower down, and if it's not there, we'll have to climb four stories to search for it. Also, it will be easier to search the study first since only a handful of those items are magical. If we start in the basement, we'll have a lot to sift through."

"I agree. We should start on the third floor … but Janak is smart. If he's expecting us, he won't make it easy to find the rod."

"*Is* he expecting us?" Fyn asked, looking around. "Seems like most folks are taking the night off for Regaleus—even the city guard is slacking off. He might have gambled we'd wait till the celebrations have finished."

"What do you mean?"

"What I said." Fyn shrugged. "I mean would you force your entire household guard to miss Regaleus on the off chance some thieves broke into your home two nights in a row?"

"He has a point," Kenton said.

Annev was pleased Fyn had spoken up. "So maybe the guards will be light tonight. If they're light enough, Janak will want to keep the rod on his person."

"So we should start in the study." Kenton ran his fingers over the joints between the well-mortared stones and found a grip on the wall where there appeared to be none.

Annev approached the wall. "It's our best option."

"Great," Fyn said, clapping his hands together and rubbing his palms. "Let's get climbing." He laid his hands on the outline of one of the massive stone blocks forming the foundation of Janak's palace and, with a bit of effort, they began to climb.

Three blocks away, the Regaleus celebration continued uninterrupted. As the people danced, the firelight flickered, casting long shadows and concealing the movements of a dark figure in fluttering robes.

CHAPTER FIFTY-FIVE

Kenton tucked his glass-cutting tool into his belt and tapped the edges of the cut glass. As he did, he pulled on the tar-covered knob and a small piece popped out of the larger window.

"Huh," the scar-faced avatar grunted. "This is easier than training class."

"Stay focused," Annev whispered.

Kenton huffed at the rebuke and reached through the glass, careful not to disturb the heavy velvet curtain, then he flicked open the latch securing the tall balcony doors.

"Janak's study takes up most of this floor," he whispered, easing the door open onto the balcony. "The hallway beyond that curtain should run around the study. If Janak's up here, there may be guards patrolling the halls and stairwells." He paused. "There may also be a guard room on the floor above us."

Annev and Fyn looked at each other, their eyebrows raised, then back at Kenton.

"There's definitely a guard room on the *first* floor," Kenton said defensively, "so this way was still safer." He glanced at Annev. "Who's first?"

Annev looked at Fyn. "Do you feel like neutralizing a guard?"

Fyn grinned. "I thought you'd never ask."

Annev and Kenton stepped out of the way and the Master of Arms padded across the balcony to the open glass door. He paused at the velvet curtain, took a deep breath, and slipped three fingers behind the drapes. Two counts later, he pulled the curtain back and slipped inside.

Annev and Kenton waited on the semicircular balcony in tense silence, alternately keeping their eyes on the distant bonfire, the shadowed rooftops of the lower terraces, and the stiff velvet drapes.

"Did you really sleep with Myjun?"

The question flew from Annev's lips before he had the sense to silence it. Kenton turned, and Annev felt doubly stupid for asking just before entering Janak's keep. There was nothing he could do if Kenton said yes—he wasn't going to push the boy off the roof, even if he wanted to—which meant he was forcing an uncomfortable conversation when they might have to rely on each other to survive. Annev was profoundly relieved when Kenton met his eyes and shook his head.

"I just wanted to get under your skin. We liked each other—we even kissed ... and a little more than that—but then I was injured."

Annev nodded, grateful for the truth. "I'm sorry," he said, and he mostly meant it.

"Sure," Kenton said, his eyes roaming back to the curtain just as Fyn's head popped out from behind it.

"Clear," he whispered then ducked inside again.

Annev waited for Kenton to step toward the door, but the avatar didn't move. Instead, he studied the stone tiles beneath their feet.

"I'm sorry I teased you about Myjun—and about falling in with Fyn once I got my title." He looked up. "No hard feelings?"

Annev shrugged. "We're both paired up with him now."

A strange smile tugged at the corner of Kenton's mouth. "I guess we are." He rubbed at the corner of his scar nearest his eye. "We're good then?"

"We're good."

They stepped up to the curtain together, Kenton drew back the drapes, and they stepped into the dimly lit hallway.

Fyn was a few feet away, the phoenix lantern clutched in his right hand, its narrow beam illuminating the colorful plush carpets. Annev's eyes followed the intricate patterns woven into the equally colorful tapestries hanging from the walls, captivated by the rich reds, deep blues, and bright yellows. It took him a moment to see the dead man sprawled at the edge of the pool of light.

Like the sober guards standing watch at the bonfire, this one wore a black uniform trimmed in blue. His head was tilted back, blood oozing from the two dark red lines around his throat.

Annev swore beneath his breath, realizing he should have been more specific when sending Fyn to ambush the guard. He'd thought their conversation about maintaining stealth was clear, but if Fyn had understood Annev's intentions, he had disregarded them.

Great, he thought. *Now I'm responsible for another death … and we have a body to get rid of.*

Fyn pointed at the hallway behind him. "There's a door around the corner. A nice one. This fellow was coming out just as I turned the hall." He coiled up his garrote as he spoke. "I checked the rest of the floor. There's a locked door, a stairwell on the opposite side of the hallway, and no one here, so I doubt anyone will miss him." Fyn retied the garrote to his belt with a quick-release loop, wiped his hands, and cracked his knuckles. "What's next?"

It's up to me, Annev thought, and tried to sound more confident than he felt. He nodded at the body. "Kenton, put him on the balcony and resecure the door. Fyn, go back to the stairwell and keep an eye out for more guards. I'll check the study door, pick the locks, and disarm any traps. We'll all enter together."

Fyn smiled and nodded, the adrenaline from his encounter apparently having put him in a good mood. He slid out a pair of throwing knives and trotted down the hallway.

Kenton hoisted the dead man's body onto his shoulders. "Just like the Test of Judgment," he muttered, heading toward the open window, "except this time people are dying."

Annev watched him go, his heart heavy. *People died during the Tests of Judgment too,* he thought, remembering Samrel and the scissor field. Instead of justifying Fyn's actions, though, he padded down the hallway to the stout gray door Fyn had mentioned.

Ironwood, he thought, recognizing the color and pattern of the grain. Sodar had shown him a piece of it once. He had said it was the toughest wood in the world, as hard as its namesake and not nearly so brittle. According to the priest, it was also quite rare: it only grew in Alltara—past the Darite Empire, on the opposite side of Eastern Daroea—and a clan of trolls was rumored to inhabit the ironwood forest. The door must have cost Janak a small fortune.

Annev pulled his lock-picking tools out of his crimson glove and knelt to examine the keyhole. Despite the strength of the door, the lock was only moderately difficult to pick—a single-acting lever tumbler instead of the more challenging double-action or the frighteningly difficult triple-action. By the time Annev had unlocked it, Kenton was back from his grisly errand. He went to get Fyn and by the time the pair of them had returned, Annev had finished checking for traps. He stood, nodded to his companions, and eased the door open. Fyn took point once again, creeping into the study; Kenton came next and Annev followed, locking the door behind them.

The spacious room took up almost the entire floor, with beautiful wood paneling decorating most of the walls and rich carpets covering the ground. Eight perfectly smooth pairs of columns had also been spaced throughout the chamber, supporting the raised ceiling and the floors above. Annev noted that three smokeless oil lamps also hung from each of the columns, about seven feet off the ground. Only the lamps at the other end of the room were lit, shedding light and casting shadows.

All around the room's perimeter, positioned precisely between the columns and the study walls, was a remarkable collection of art: elegant sculptures rested on pedestals, easels displayed colorful paintings, and strange-looking instruments, articles, and tools hung from pegs, including a carved wooden gourd, a pair of iron shackles chained to a collar, and a tiny silver harp. Annev stepped close to this last one, extended his open palm just above the strings, and sensed a faint aura of magic emanating from the artifact. He did the same as he passed the gourd, expecting he'd feel something similar to what he felt when holding the carved phoenix lantern, but instead he felt nothing.

Not magical then. Interesting …

A similarly rich collection of furniture stood between the columns, positioned to enjoy the art on display: a divan and chaise longue faced a painting of an old woman holding flowers; a circle of armchairs surrounded a sculpture of a woman riding a dragon, her rider's hair aflame; and a delicate ivory bench was positioned opposite a scaly suit of gleaming bronze armor. One gauntlet clutched a tall boar spear, while the statue itself stood at attention with the visor of its wedge-shaped helmet down.

At the far end of the room, past the display pieces, stood an ornate desk that was itself a work of art. A figure in a high-collared, gold-embroidered jacket sat behind that desk. The man's back was to the door, the light from the oil lamps gleaming off his bald head. The three avatars spotted him in the same instant, fanned out, and crept closer to the center of the long room. As Annev approached, he saw that the man's chair had two large metal wheels attached to its sides. A pair of gold-flecked blue stones had been set at the hub of each wheel, and a glyph was carved into the center of the stones. Annev drew even closer and noticed that the wheels were, in fact, a pair of reinforced shields ingeniously attached to the man's chair.

The three avatars slid from the shadows, entering the light that bathed the final half of the room. Annev soundlessly pulled his ax from his belt and slid Mercy from its sheath, his consciousness seeping into the blade until he felt the thrill of magic pulsing in his hand. Kenton glanced at him sharply and Annev toned it down, worried the magically sensitive boy might have somehow felt the blade's enchantment.

Kenton's eyes slid away from Annev and returned to their common target. He stalked the perimeter of the room with Fyn mirroring him on the opposite side, both boys staying just inside the shadows. Kenton had drawn his long, curved tachi and held it protectively in front of him. Curiously, Fyn's hands remained empty, though his muscles were taut as he approached from the right.

"The Oracle said there would be four."

Annev went stone-still between the fifth and sixth set of pillars while Kenton and Fyn shrank into the shadows at either side of the room. *Oracle?* he thought, surprised by the man's words. *He can't mean the Oracle. Sodar said Bron Gloir has it …*

There was no time to ponder it, as the man grasped the shields at his sides and spun them, propelling his chair forward around the desk. He stopped at the edge of the writing table, facing the three avatars. In that moment, Annev took in his crippled body, his form no longer hidden behind the large wooden desk. The stranger was in his midfifties, sharp-eyed and well-dressed, and his open jacket revealed thick arms and a heavily muscled chest. Had it not been for the atrophied legs beneath the blanket on his lap, Annev would have described him as healthy, strong, and alert.

The man in the chair wiped a meaty hand over the dome of his sun-browned head, studying the avatars, then stroked the handles of his heavy gray moustache. His other hand rested on a small incense lamp tucked into the folds of his black and gold blanket.

"Four horsemen, it said, each with a bird on their shoulder." The man's voice was strong and resonant as his gaze moved between Kenton, Annev, and Fyn, sizing each up in turn. He counted off on his fingers. "A heron, a kestrel, a rook, and a magpie." He looked at Annev. "Which are you?"

Annev raised his red glove, unintimidated. "I'm a phoenix."

The man chuckled. "I hope so, for your sake."

"You must be Janak."

Instead of answering, the man looked at Kenton and Fyn. "The cursed leader, the faithless warrior, the shadow's shadow, and the doomed cripple." He frowned. "The shadow must be below?"

The three avatars glanced at one another, unsure how to answer the strange question.

The man nodded. "Of course he is. Best to be safe, eh? In case I left it down there." He eyed Fyn, taking note of the weapons bristling from his arms, belt, and back. "Well, you're the warrior ..." His eyes traveled back to Kenton. "... which makes you the cripple."

Kenton flicked his long hair over his scar.

The merchant frowned, still studying Kenton. "The Oracle implied you only had one arm to steal her with." He leaned forward, studying the tachi clutched in Kenton's hands.

Annev turned sideways, instinctively shielding his gloved prosthetic. *How does he know? Could he really have* the *Oracle?* The very idea made him sweat. If Janak had the Oracle, he could have asked it anything.

The man shrugged. "No matter. She speaks in riddles, so I'm bound to misunderstand parts. But you won't take her from me. No, no. She warned me, you know. Said you'd steal her from me." He looked directly at Fyn. "And that you, the warrior, have been tasked to kill me."

Fyn met the man's gaze, also unintimidated, and pulled a throwing knife from his bracer. "If you are Janak, then yes. For use of a Rod of Compulsion, your life is forfeit."

The merchant grunted, unimpressed. "It's a shame, you know. Winsor and I had a very sensible arrangement before your new headmaster refused to cooperate. I suppose I should thank him, though. If he hadn't cut me off, I never would have sought assistance elsewhere. Never would have found the Oracle ... or learned the truth."

Truth? Arrangement? Fyn and Kenton were equally baffled by Janak's monologue, and while they kept their attention on the merchant, their reactions hadn't been lost on Janak.

"I see Tosan kept you in the dark." He rested an elbow on the arm of his wheelchair. "Then before you dispatch me, I will enlighten you." He gestured broadly at the art and furniture lining the room. "I'm a bit of a collector. In my prime, I traveled the world in search of its treasures, and I found more than a few dangers along the way. What you see here is just a fraction of the wealth I accumulated. The rest I sell or keep in storage."

He wheeled his chair over to the tall suit of bronze armor and rested a hand on the metal. "This is one of my personal treasures. I wore it long ago, when I was more mercenary than merchant." He sighed and dropped his hand to his lap. "When I lost the use of my legs, I turned my attention to accumulating magic. I was desperate for a way to restore my mobility." He shrugged. "Your Academy didn't care about my motives, though, and avatar after avatar came to steal my possessions. I wasn't sure what was happening at first. I'd acquire an artifact one week and it was spirited away the next."

Janak wheeled his chair back. As he moved, Fyn looked at Annev. "Why are we listening to this?" he whispered. "And why hasn't he raised an alarm? We should kill him now."

Fyn was right—Janak was too calm, too confident for his liking, and it was unsettling that he had not called for help—but the merchant had also spoken of an arrangement with the Academy, and Annev wanted to know what it was. Plus, Janak had mentioned the Oracle—a detail Tosan hadn't known and which neither Fyn nor Kenton knew the significance of—so Annev held up a finger, asking the boy to wait. Fyn gritted his teeth at the silent command and checked the maces on his back, but he stayed in place.

"In the end, I found a way to communicate with you. I hid notes inside artifacts I expected would be stolen, and finally Winsor and I came to an agreement: I would buy all the artifacts I could find, and every few months the Academy would send an avatar to retrieve them."

Annev couldn't believe it. "And you … gave them up willingly?"

"No. I gave them up in payment for the use of my legs."

Annev frowned, glancing at Janak's half-hidden limbs. The merchant understood and, after fumbling with the incense lamp tucked into its folds, he pulled the blanket up to reveal the extent of his emaciated legs. "The Academy has a Rod of Healing," Janak said, massaging his shrivelled calves. "Once a month, your headmaster allowed me to heal myself and restore strength to my legs. The effect lasted about a fortnight, and for that time, I lived my life as I had before. A fair bargain by my estimation." Janak gripped the rims of the steel shields attached to his chair, his eyes growing dark.

"Unfortunately, your new headmaster disliked our arrangement. He believes that I've been giving trinkets to the Academy and have kept the greatest magics for myself. So, instead of continuing my treatment, Tosan sends thieves to pillage my house." He gestured at the three intruders, illustrating his point. "Now tell me, which party has injured the other?"

Annev lowered his weapons, feeling sorry for the man. It was obvious Tosan was the one at fault—his irrational fears had already sent Annev on a fool's errand to kill Crag in the Brake, and now his paranoia was ruining the life of a harmless merchant.

No, Annev thought, *he's not harmless. He brainwashed Duvarek and is holding him hostage. He's here … somewhere.*

"You took one of our own," Annev said, forcing himself to move toward the merchant. "You knew there would be repercussions."

Janak rubbed the brass lamp in his lap, his face a thundercloud. "Yes, she warned me not to fight back. Said if I tried to keep the rod, the Shadow would take it from me—and that if I *used* the rod, Sorrow would follow." The merchant slapped a calloused hand against his emaciated thigh. "But I know better! I've struck a bargain with an ally more powerful than your silly ancients, and he's promised me new legs! Strong ones that never break, never tire, and won't grow old." Janak's eyes glimmered with a touch of madness as they fastened on Kenton. "And all he wants in return is one silly little bird …"

"Annev," Fyn whispered again, more urgent. "This is stupid. He knows he's trapped and he's spinning stories till his guards come. We should kill him and move on."

Annev bristled at the boy's tone. *He* was the one in charge of this mission, *not* Fyn.

"Stand down, Fyn. I lead this team, and you won't kill Janak until I say so."

Fyn snorted. "Gods, you're thicker than I thought." He looked to Kenton who was frozen at the opposite end of the room. "Kenton!" he shouted, dropping all pretence at stealth. "Annev's lost his wits. I'm taking charge. On my count, we rush him. When he's dead, we'll search for Duvarek and the rod."

Kenton hesitated. "Let him live. He could tell us where Duvarek is, and the rod."

Fyn muttered a string of curses. "Have you *both* lost your brains? The rod isn't up here, and we're wasting time listening to a dead man!"

Annev turned back to Janak, something bothering him. Why *was* he delaying the mission? Had he been trying to decide whether Janak or Tosan was in the right, or had it been something else? He still wanted to listen to the merchant's words, to be sympathetic—

Fyn spun, hurling his knife at Janak. The dagger flew through the air, flipping end over end over end … then it froze, the blade stuck in midair, its point less than an inch from the merchant's chest.

Fyn's mouth dropped open. At the same time, Annev felt a thick fog lift from his thoughts. He glanced at Kenton and saw the other boy had undergone a similar transformation.

Janak plucked the floating dagger from the air with an exasperated sigh. "That was hasty," he said, twirling the blade between his fingers. "You broke my concentration."

"How …?" Fyn asked, his eyes wide.

"This?" Janak waggled the knife at Fyn. "A ward of deflection. It protects against both mundane and magical attacks."

"You tried to compel us," Annev said, clarity dawning. "To snare us like you did Duvarek."

"I did," Janak said, pulling a gold rod from beneath his lap blanket. He set the wand beside the lamp then rested his hands on both items. "It's not so difficult to control more than one target—in fact, I've got over a hundred tied to me right now—but it seems to function best when the target is sympathetic and when you give the compulsion time to take hold. Once you've properly broken a person, though, there doesn't appear to be a limit to the number of thralls you can manipulate." He tisked, balancing the knife in his hand. "If I had guessed the "faithless warrior" would act so rashly, I might have targeted him first instead of your leader."

"Stop stalling," Annev said, recognizing the tiny yet insistent tug from the merchant's Rod of Compulsion this time. Now he knew what to expect, and he found it easier to ignore the magically induced impulses. "You're not going to snare us again."

"No," Janak sighed, "I suspect I won't. I'll have to content myself with only having one thrall, which means the three of you must die."

Annev shifted his feet, alert for an attack. As if on cue, he heard a faint rumbling noise coming from the floor below them, and he glanced uneasily at the door.

"Which reminds me," Janak continued, "I believe this is yours." He sent the knife hurling toward Fyn's chest. The boy dropped to the ground, barely dodging, and the blade clipped his shoulder before skittering to the back of the room.

"Blood and filth!" Fyn swore, clapping a hand to his injury. "I'm going to cut out your heart, you keokum-spawned Son of Keos!"

Janak sniffed, unfazed by Fyn's threats. "It's funny, you know. If Tosan hadn't spurned me, I never would have sought Cruithear out—and if he hadn't promised me new legs and assistance finding the Oracle, I never would have known the extent of what the Academy has stolen from me. So, in a very literal sense, the Academy brought this doom upon themselves." He caressed the brass lamp and Rod of Compulsion, his eyes reflecting the pain and fury he had been so carefully concealing. "I'm looking forward to Duvarek taking me and my men to Chaenbalu. I wonder … do you think Tosan will expect it? Will your avatars and witwomen put up a fight, or will they hide in your Academy and watch as we slaughter your villagers?"

Outside in the hall, the faint rumbling grew closer, transforming into the sound of many sturdy boots tramping across carpet-padded stone.

Annev wondered if they could retreat, but he knew it was too late. As a sense of dread washed over him, he adjusted his grip on the short sword and ax then turned to face whatever was coming through the door.

Fyn seemed to have reached the same decision for he clasped his wrists, snatched a pair of fresh throwing knives from each bracer, and moved purposefully towards the door. On the opposite side of the room, Kenton turned but held his position near Janak; with the careful poise of a master avatar, he raised the tachi over his head and assumed the heron form, his blade facing outward, its point dipping slightly in front of him. His body and face looked calm, yet his eyes revealed the fear they all felt.

The footsteps had reached the door, and Annev's attention flickered between it and the merchant, unsure whom to engage first if he wished to survive the next hour. A heartbeat later, something crashed into the iron-wood door and a gruff voice shouted for keys.

"You know," Janak drawled, leaning back in his chair, "the Oracle said you'd probably destroy my study. She never said I'd be hurt, though, or that Tosan would get what he wants. In fact, she implied the opposite." He traced the small runes on the brass incense lamp and flashed a bitter smile. "I think I'm comfortable with that."

CHAPTER FIFTY-SIX

Six men in black and blue uniforms poured into the room, their short capes flapping behind them, their weapons brandished in front of them.

"Blood and hell," Kenton swore and sprinted forward to support Fyn.

At the opposite end of the room, Fyn stepped up to meet the onrush of guards. Two angled toward him and Fyn answered their charge with a flurry of thrown daggers. The men spun away, their chests and throats bristling with sharpened steel, but the other guards pushed onward, trampling the dead and dying to get to Fyn and protect Janak.

Fyn threw another pair of daggers, bringing a third man down, and then the guards were on him. He snatched the two flanged maces off his back and spun toward a burly man with a blond beard and a second man with an eye patch. They brought their swords to bear, but Fyn ducked low, swung outward with both maces, and smashed in their kneecaps. Both men screamed, their legs buckling beneath them and, as they fell, Fyn reversed his swing, crushing a face and the side of a skull.

Kenton had engaged with the sixth guard just as four more men entered the study, their spears and shields forming a wall at the back of the room. Before they could save their companion, though, Kenton feinted, lunged, and disemboweled the man.

Annev reached Kenton's side as the second group began their advance. Short sword, ax, and tachi danced among the men's thrusting spear heads. Using Mercy, Annev caught the haft of the leftmost spear and used his ax to pull the guard's shield from the group's protective formation. Kenton took the opening and snapped his tachi to the side, stabbing the guard's exposed neck. The man dropped to the ground, a fountain of blood pulsing from his wound, and the remaining guards retreated to coordinate with a new squad carrying crossbows.

"Bloody hell," Kenton swore when he saw them.

"Get behind the pillars!" Annev yelled, diving for cover. His companions followed and a chorus of twanging bow strings chased after them. Kenton cried out, clutching his thigh, and slid to the floor. Annev looked over and the boy waved him off.

"Just grazed me," he said, moaning. "I'm fine."

Annev chanced a look at the back of the room and saw the three guardsmen with shields were shielding the four crossbowmen as they reloaded. Four more guards had begun to navigate the edge of the room, weaving around the pillars, furniture, and assembled art.

They're trying to flush us out, thought Annev.

At the opposite end of the room, Janak brushed away a crossbow quarrel that had struck his magical shield and shook the Rod of Compulsion at his men.

"Kill them, you clods!"

In response, the four approaching guards broke from cover and charged, forcing the avatars to fight them in the open.

"Now shoot them!" Janak yelled.

The crossbows twanged a moment later, and Annev ducked behind a pillar again, escaping the flying quarrels. Kenton took a knee behind a stout wooden chest, still holding off a guard, and Fyn escaped injury by placing his own opponent between himself and the firing soldiers. Two crossbow bolts punched into his back, toppling the man, and Fyn finished him off by crunching his maces into the fellow's neck and chest.

Janak's not going to give up, thought Annev. He parried the sword stroke of the fat guard still facing him. *It doesn't matter how many we kill. He'll keep throwing men at us until we're overwhelmed or we've killed every member of his guard.*

But why stop there? Janak had the Rod of Compulsion: he could force them to fight every member of his household … every citizen of Banok.

"Fyn!" Annev shouted, dancing back from a sword thrust. "You have to kill Janak!"

"Can't with that shield up!" The avatar flicked his maces, flinging gore across a bleached leather divan, then he ducked behind a pillar to avoid the next wave of quarrels.

Annev's mind raced, his back to the pillar while the guards reloaded their crossbows and the fat guardsman circled around the other side. As he waited for the man's attack, Annev tried to recall everything he knew about wards of deflection: the source of the spell was likely an artifact near Janak—something he was touching that had a glyph or symbol inscribed on it. Probably not the incense lamp since that was inside his protective sphere …

The guard reached around the pillar, swinging his short sword for Annev's head. Annev ducked and dropped to the ground then stabbed with Mercy, aiming for the man's groin. The man deflected the low blow and kicked Annev in the face, sending him sprawling. Annev spat a mouthful of blood and hazily saw the crossbow men taking aim once more. With no other cover nearby, he gritted his teeth and rolled back toward his opponent.

Sharp air! Annev thought, imbuing his will into the weapon and extending its edge. At the same time, the crossbow bolts flew, two of them smashing into the ground where Annev had just been.

The guard raised his sword, prepared to deflect Annev's clumsy attack and then skewer him on the floor. Instead, Mercy crashed through the guard's blade, slicing perfectly through metal, flesh, and bone—but Annev's attack didn't stop there: as the guard's forearm and sundered shield fell to the ground, Mercy continued her arc, slicing deep into the man's midsection.

The guard toppled, blood pooling from his injuries, and Annev took sanctuary behind the pillar once more. The dying man gripped his bleeding forearm, and Annev watched the life leave his eyes, feeling sick. This was the first person—not a witch or a *feurog*—whose death he had directly caused and he felt awful, but he also knew there had been no choice: none of them would survive the night without blood on their hands, and Annev couldn't let Janak threaten Chaenbalu and his friends. He steeled his resolve, quieting the part of him that saw humanity in his attackers. They were like the *feurog*—brutish puppets following the commands of a maddened puppeteer—and if Annev did not kill them, they would certainly kill him.

"Idiots!" Janak roared, wheeling his chair front of his desk. "Stop wasting time with those crossbows and kill these fools!"

Annev studied Janak and suddenly the answer dawned on him. *Of course ... the wheels!* He turned, shouting at Fyn who had taken cover behind the bronze suit of armour.

"Fyn! Break the gems on Janak's chair!"

"Break what?"

"The wheels!" Annev shouted. "Smash the stones on the wheels!"

Fyn didn't seem to fully understand, but he nodded and dashed out into the open.

Annev eased out from behind the pillar and took in the scene at a glance. Kenton crouched behind a pillar, a makeshift dressing around his wounded leg. Meanwhile the guards at the back of the room had exchanged their crossbows for spears and were fanning out, circling around and behind Annev and Kenton's position. Annev dashed over to Kenton and helped the raven-haired boy to his feet. Kenton tested his leg, nodded with satisfaction, and hefted his tachi.

At the other end of the room, Fyn was beyond the noose of the guards' trap and had reached Janak's chair. He raised his flanged maces, preparing to strike, and Janak raised the dark rod, pointing it at Fyn with a roar. The avatar froze in his tracks.

"No!" Annev shouted, his attention torn between Fyn's struggle with Janak and the approaching guards. The soldiers stayed just out of range, leveling their spears, and Annev and Kenton pressed their backs together to face them.

"This doesn't look good ..." Kenton muttered, his tachi raised in front of him.

Across the room, Fyn's arms shook as he struggled against the full strength of Janak's Rod of Compulsion. Gradually, the boy's arms fell back to his sides.

The guards surrounding Kenton and Annev tightened their circle. One soldier made a tentative stab at Annev's chest and he flashed Mercy, slicing the head off the spear. Their defenses tested, the other guards nodded to one another, pulling back their weapons for a coordinated group attack.

Fyn screamed, jerking his maces back into the air as the ring of guards around Annev and Kenton stepped forward, striking to skewer the boys. Annev saw a flash of panic shoot across Janak's face as Fyn's maces crashed down on both sides of the chair, shattering the engraved lapis stones at the center of each wheel.

Janak screamed.

A wave of destruction took the room in a thunderclap of pent-up magic. It threw Fyn head over heels away from the merchant. Trinkets and treasures were scattered across the floor, pedestals toppled, and easels snapped in half. The guards were knocked off their feet mid-strike while Kenton and Annev, leaning against each other, staggered and fought to steady themselves, ears ringing. The force of the explosion drove furniture screeching across the floor towards the back of the room, leaving a curious half circle of destruction surrounding Janak's wheelchair.

The enormous desk had been flipped over, the heavy drawers flung open with parchment spilling from one and a blue bottle covered in runes toppling out of another and rolling slowly across the floor. Fyn lay motionless a dozen paces from the overturned desk, blood trickling from both ears.

He's dead, Annev thought, surprised at his own sorrow to see the fallen avatar. *Dead or severely injured.* He looked for any signs of life, but instead a nearby movement caught his eye: the guards were recovering. They had to strike now.

"Kenton! Now!"

Annev spun toward the rising soldier whose padded jack bore the stripes of a squad leader or captain. He brought Mercy to bear as a familiar tingle ran up his arm. He moved to slice the man's hamstrings, but the man fell back with his hands upraised.

"No!" he screamed. "Please, let us go!"

It was the first time a soldier had spoken. He saw fear and panic on their faces and recognized they were no longer in thrall to the magic of Janak's dark rod.

"Stop!" Annev ordered, as Kenton was about to peck his tachi into a man's skull. "Let them go, Kenton. They had no choice. Look at their uniforms—they belong to the Banok city watch, not to Janak's household guard."

The captain nodded, vigorously affirming Annev's guess. "I don't serve Janak—none of us do. I just want to go home to my family."

Kenton looked between Annev and the other prone soldiers then nodded, sheathing his tachi.

"Get out."

The surviving guards struggled to their feet and ran.

CHAPTER FIFTY-SEVEN

Janak's powerful hands clutched the wheels of his chair as if doing so might somehow retain their magical protection. He had a look of incredulity stamped on his face as he saw the half score of dead guardsmen. With ragged breath, he stared at Fyn's motionless body then turned his gaze on Kenton and Annev at the center of the destruction; he looked at them without seeing them, his eyes dull.

Annev dashed over to Fyn: the boy was breathing, but a thin stream of blood still leaked from his ears. "He's got a concussion for sure," Annev said, checking Fyn's pulse. "I think he'll be alright, though. He's got a hard—"

Something heavy clanged into the floor on the other side of Fyn. Annev jumped to his feet, reaching for his weapons, and both he and Kenton turned toward the suit of armor that had stood on display before Janak's ward of deflection had erupted. The fallen bronze suit clanged again, creaking, then slowly rose to its feet.

"Kenton," Annev breathed, "… you seeing this?"

The boy nodded, speechless—and then the suit of armor opened its visor.

"Duvarek!" Kenton ran towards his former mentor. "You were hidden there the whole time?" He shook his head, disbelieving, then grinned so broadly Annev barely recognized his surly companion. "Did Janak hurt you?"

The Master of Shadows groaned, attempting to clutch his helm-encased forehead with gauntleted fingers. "Got a damn awful headache," he said, wincing. "Feels like I've been crammed into a vat of—what are *you* doing here? And Annev—and Fyn!" He shook his head, both frantic and disbelieving. "Who came with you? You have to go! If Lord Harth finds—"

Janak roared, shaking himself from his stupor. Annev turned and saw the merchant fumbling for something in his lap, muttering dark curses to himself.

"Run!" Duvarek waved them behind him and scooped up the boar spear at his feet.

"He's going for the rod!" Annev shouted. He and Kenton sprinted toward Janak, their weapons ready.

"No!" Duvarek yelled, interposing himself between Janak and his former students. "The *other* way! Get out!"

Janak cast his blanket aside, lifted the short golden artifact, and pointed it at the Master of Shadows. "Duvarek," he commanded, voice booming, "protect me!"

To Kenton and Annev's horror, Duvarek's face went slack and his eyes turned glassy; his posture straightened as he stood to attention, his former discomfort vanishing. He slapped down his visor, hiding his face behind the dark slit in the bronze helm.

"Duvarek?" Kenton asked, taking a tentative step toward his former teacher.

Quick as a snake, the steel-tipped boar spear snapped out. Kenton jumped back, barely dodging the spearhead. "Master Duvarek," he pleaded, retreating. "Please … fight with us. Fight the magic—don't let the taint corrupt you."

"*Kill* them, Duvarek!"

The suit of armor cocked its head toward the merchant, hesitating.

"Dove," Kenton tried again, holding his position, "please come back to Chaenbalu."

The bronze warrior returned his metallic gaze to Kenton. He nodded once, as if consenting, then advanced with measured steps.

"Dove?"

"Kenton," Annev said, stepping back, "I don't think—"

Duvarek lunged, swinging his boar spear for Kenton's throat as the boy stumbled backwards, tripping on broken relics as he hastily lifted his tachi and blocked the attack. He parried another thrust from his former master then ducked behind a toppled armoire, its treasure of rich dresses and infant clothes scattered across the room.

Annev moved to help but then stopped, realizing there was a better way to end Duvarek's compulsion. *If I break Janak's concentration, then he can't maintain the spell of compulsion. We have to kill Janak ... then we can save Duvarek, grab the artifact, and get the hell out of here.*

Annev looked over and saw the merchant watching the fight with morbid interest, following Kenton around the room and muttering as the boy dodged and blocked every one of Duvarek's attacks, never making one of his own except to probe his opponent's armor for weaknesses.

A dozen feet away, Fyn began to stir. Annev turned to see if Lord Harth had caught the movement, but Janak's attention was fixed on Duvarek's hunt and Kenton's recursive flight. Annev edged toward the man in the wheelchair, his ax and short sword still drawn.

"Thinking you'll tie up loose ends?"

Annev froze as Janak's eyes turned on him. "Probably wise. Winsor should have done it after his witwomen stole my child but didn't quite manage to poison me ... but he was either too shrewd or too merciful." He chuckled without mirth. "Well, come on then. Finish your mission. My shield is gone so I'm helpless."

Annev eyed the merchant's lap blanket: the brass lamp and Rod of Compulsion lay in plain sight, and while Janak's hands rested atop both items, Annev didn't feel the specific tug on his thoughts and emotions that indicated Janak was using the dark rod. Even so, he felt his actions were somehow not his own as he took another step toward the merchant.

Janak smiled. "That's right, boy. Come closer ..."

Annev faltered again and Janak tensed, his hand tightening momentarily on the artifact in his lap. Annev took a step back, watching the merchant, and the man suddenly seemed less sure of himself.

"Come *here*, child."

Now Annev felt it—the subtle touch of magic playing on his insecurities, magnifying his empathy for the man, drawing on his desire to help him avenge the wrongs the Academy had committed against him.

Annev turned away and walked towards Fyn.

"NO!" Janak shouted. "Come to *me*, you fool!"

As Annev distanced himself from the merchant, he felt the compulsion to obey weaken. By the time he reached Fyn's side, Janak was practically spitting.

"Burn you!" the man swore, slapping his withered legs. "Burn you and the demons that spawned you!"

Annev knelt beside Fyn, checking his injuries.

The avatar's eyes fluttered open and Fyn gripped his forearm. "What—"

"Annev!" Kenton shouted from the opposite end of the study. "Dove won't stop, and I can't slow him down!"

Damn. Kenton was fully engaged with Duvarek's armored figure: the boy wasn't pulling his punches now, yet every time Kenton slashed with his tachi, the bronze suit of armor absorbed his blows. He watched Kenton kick off the wall and flip behind Duvarek, hacking at the softer metal surrounding the collar bones and armpits, but the blade still slipped away.

"Kenton needs help," Annev said, easing Fyn into a sitting position. "Can you fight?"

"Huh?" Fyn said, a little too loud.

Annev pointed at Janak then slid his own thumb across his throat. The concussed boy nodded his understanding and began searching the room for his fallen weapons. Annev rose to his feet, his short sword and ax loose in his hands. Kenton saw him coming and circled around the room, taking advantage of Duvarek's slower pace to regroup with Annev. As he moved, Duvarek's visored gaze followed the boy, relentless and unhurried.

"I tried talking to him," Kenton said, catching his breath, "but nothing gets through—and that scale mail is no joke. It's harder than steel, and I can't find any openings."

"Fyn's taking care of it." Annev said, planting his feet as the bronze figure stalked towards them. "When he kills Janak, the compulsion will fail."

"Why couldn't you kill him?"

"I tried, but the closer I got, the more control he had over me."

"And you think Fyn will do better?"

Annev nodded, a crazed-looking grin on his face. "He's mostly deaf right now—and about as empathetic as a rock. Plus Janak's his kill."

Duvarek was nearly a dozen paces away and the two avatars took an unconscious step backward.

"For our sakes, I hope you're right." Kenton lifted his tachi as Duvarek stepped within spear range. "I'll go low, you go high!" And before Annev could agree, Kenton sprinted towards his former mentor.

The Master of Shadows lowered his spear, intending to skewer his former protégé, but Kenton closed the gap too quickly, dropping to his knees and sliding beneath the falling spearhead.

As Kenton slammed into Duvarek's legs, Annev leaped at the armored figure, his ax held high. He swung for the warrior's helmeted head, timing his attack just as Kenton kicked the man's greaves and slashed his groin. Duvarek accepted the body blows, refusing to budge under Kenton's assault, but when Annev's ax fell, he shifted aside, dodging the weapon. Annev followed up with a second attack from Mercy, giving Kenton time to roll out from under Duvarek's feet. The master avatar surprised him by grasping the blunted short sword with his gauntleted hand. Before Annev could activate the artifact's magic, Duvarek yanked the sword from his grasp and kicked the boy in the stomach, sending him reeling.

Annev rolled to his feet and regrouped with Kenton, feeling naked with just his ax to protect himself. He glanced at Fyn and saw the boy had reclaimed his maces and was doggedly crawling toward Janak, ignoring their battle with Duvarek. As the avatar drew closer to Janak's wheelchair, the merchant realized his plight and raised his sceptre.

"Stop!" he commanded, shaking the dark rod at Fyn. "Lay down and die, boy."

But Fyn didn't stop, nor did he slow his advance. With grim determination, the boy swayed from his hands and knees to his feet, gaining momentum as he stalked the merchant.

"Duvarek!" Janak shouted, suddenly frantic. "Protect me! Kill the warrior!"

The Master of Shadows spun from Kenton and Annev, slapped his spear under his arm, and flipped Mercy in his hand, catching its hilt in a downward grip. With long, purposeful strides, he advanced on Fyn's stumbling figure.

Annev looked at Kenton. "We can't stop him unless we try something more permanent." The scarred avatar shook his head, but Annev cut off his objections: "Fyn needs us."

Kenton saw their companion's peril and swore. With a mixture of resolve and self-loathing, he dashed forward, pressed the tip of his tachi into the soft metal covering Duvarek's armpit, and shoved. Instead of piercing the master avatar's chest, though, Kenton's silvery blade skittered across the flexible mesh covering Duvarek's joints and vitals: like the skin of a fish, each bronze scale overlapped the next without a hint of a crack or a whisper of space beneath the tiny plates.

Duvarek ignored the attack and took another step towards Fyn.

Annev stepped in with his ax, hooking the warrior's foot just as Duvarek shifted his weight. The master avatar teetered and Kenton lunged for a second attack, driving his tachi into the slits of the man's visored helm. Annev guessed it would be a killing blow but again the sword skittered off the bronze metal, unable to penetrate the slotted visor.

This time Duvarek retaliated by crashing Mercy's blunted edge into the boy's tachi, snapping the thinner nonmagical sword with the force of his blow. For a moment, Kenton stared in horror at his broken blade, but then Duvarek snapped the butt of his spear into the boy's stunned face and he went reeling.

"Duvarek!" Janak shouted again. "Kill him, *now!*"

The merchant had abandoned his broken wheelchair in an attempt to escape Fyn's murderous pursuit; with the lamp and dark rod still clutched in his hands, he crawled toward the questionable safety of his toppled desk.

In response to Janak's command, Duvarek planted his feet and aimed his spear at Fyn. Annev took a desperate swing with his ax, knocking the bottom half of the weapon as it flew from Duvarek's hand. The spear flipped end-over-end through the air, knocking a lamp from its sconce and showering the room in burning oil. The haft slapped across Fyn's shoulders and the avatar looked back, glaring at his attacker. He hesitated when he saw Duvarek advancing on him with Mercy in hand and gauged the distance between the crippled merchant ahead of him and the armored thrall behind him.

"Go!" Annev yelled, waving him onward. "Kill Janak!" He wasn't sure Fyn heard, but then Kenton jumped into Duvarek's path and clamped an iron collar around the man's neck.

That was all the opportunity Fyn needed. With renewed determination, the injured avatar stumbled faster toward his target, steadying himself on fallen furniture and avoiding the fire that was beginning to spread around the room. At the other end of the study, Janak had finally reached his toppled desk and was searching through its scattered contents.

Duvarek tried to untangle himself from Kenton's collar and chain, but his gauntlets lacked the dexterity required. For a few precious seconds, the enthralled master forgot his mission to kill Fyn and instead sought to break the chains that bound him: he tried to wedge Mercy's tip into their gray links but failed; he hacked at them with the same strength he'd used to break Kenton's tachi, and failed again; finally, he grasped the short sword with both hands and tried to slip its blade between the iron collar and the bronze gorget protecting his neck.

"Annev! Slow him down."

Kenton threw a rust-spotted manacle at him, its dangling chain still connected to Duvarek's collar. Annev caught it, felt the tingle of its magic, and instinctively knew that, like most of the items in Janak's study, it was an artifact of modest power. He saw Kenton handcuff the other manacle to a dead guardsman.

Flaming brilliant.

Annev looked around the room and spied another body less than a dozen paces away. He moved toward it, hoping to anchor Duvarek with the weight of a second corpse, but then the chain and its fetter flew from his grasp, yanked sharply away by Duvarek's strong hands: the warrior was resisting their plan and the compulsion would not allow him to be detained. Duvarek dropped Mercy, gripped Kenton's half of the chain with both hands, and pulled the cuffed guardsman toward him. Kenton leaped atop the corpse and forced a grisly tug of war, doing everything he could to buy Fyn the precious seconds he needed.

Annev turned to gauge the other boy's progress and saw Janak had pulled a blue bottle from the wreckage of his desk. With a shout of elation, he uncorked the vial and downed its contents, shuddering as he did. Fyn reached him moments later and snatched the Rod of Compulsion from Lord Harth's feverish grip.

Annev took a step back, hoping for a change to come over Duvarek, but the Master of Shadows still moved as if he were compelled: he reclaimed Mercy and stalked toward Kenton, intent on removing the obstacles between him and his mission.

Annev swore, seeing the danger his unarmed companion was now in. He dashed to support Kenton, chancing one final glance at Fyn, which made him stumble in surprise. Having drunk from the rune-inscribed bottle, the merchant's sun-browned skin had faded into an inky metallic gray, the same color as dull steel.

"You can't kill me!" Janak laughed. "Cruithear protects me!"

Fyn stared at the crippled merchant, confused by what he was seeing. Using his mace, he tapped the dome of Janak's bald head and was surprised by the metallic scrape and *clang* of metal on metal.

Janak laughed again. "You see! I am—"

Fyn raised his mace and swung, crashing its armour-piercing blades into Janak's face. The merchant cried out as sparks flew, and when Fyn lifted his weapon, it was to reveal a modest dent and two small holes in the man's forehead.

"Gods," Annev breathed.

Janak cried out, clutching the injury, but he was laughing too. "Ha-ha. You think—*arrgh*—that you can hurt me?" He groaned again, clearly in pain, yet he forced himself to smile. "Cruithear *strengthens* me! He has taken Keos's power and shares it with *me*."

"Help!"

Annev had forgotten Kenton amidst Janak's madness. He sprinted for Duvarek as the man reached the cuffed corpse. With one hand gripping the chain that bound him to the dead man's manacled arm, Duvarek raised Mercy and swung.

Kenton rolled away, abandoning the dead guard as the short sword crashed into the dead man's arm. Instead of severing the limb, though, Mercy's blunted edge bruised the skin and splintered the bone beneath. Duvarek hacked again, undeterred by the inefficacy of his weapon as Fyn slammed his flanged mace into Janak's metal face. *CLANG. CLONG. CRASH.*

Duvarek finally chopped through the dead guard's fractured arm, scooped up the manacle chained to his collar, and returned his attention to Fyn.

"Kill them all, Duvarek!" Janak frothed, his face a ruin of crumpled metal. "KILL THEM—"

CLANG! CLANG! CLONK!

Janak went silent and Duvarek swayed on his feet then looked around, taking stock of his surroundings.

"Dove?" Kenton said, daring to hope. "Are you in there?"

The man in the bronze suit looked down, weighing the iron chains in his left hand and the short sword in his right. When he looked up, his visored face pointed directly at the Master of Sorrows.

"You will all die."

Duvarek leaped at Annev, short sword raised for a piercing blow. Instead of dodging or rolling away, Annev swung with all his strength, his ax smashing into Mercy and sending both weapons skittering across the floor. The Master of Shadows landed atop Annev, knocking him to the ground, then began wrapping his iron chains around the boy's neck. Annev fumbled for leverage and came up with the guard's severed limb. Desperate for an advantage, he slid the macabre lever into Duvarek's knot of chains, wincing as the man pulled tight and tried to strangle him.

Kenton appeared above Annev's head with Mercy clutched in both hands, but then looked between Duvarek and Annev, hesitating.

"Visor . . ." Annev choked, struggling to keep the cold metal links from crushing his windpipe. It was a slim chance—Annev's could see no way to lift the man's face plate, let alone remove the magically sealed helm, and the great helm's slotted visor had proven impervious to Kenton's tachi—its gaps were too small for even a dagger to enter.

But not too small for air . . .

Kenton smashed the tip of Annev's short sword into the warrior's slotted visor as Annev stopped fighting the chains that were choking him and slapped both palms atop Mercy's fuller. In that same instant, he called upon the blade's magic, willing its edge to form a thin sliver of sharpened air, hoping his need was great enough for the magic to manifest.

Kenton gasped as the short sword caught on the slits of the great helm, and there was a sickening *crunch*, wet and piercing, from inside. Duvarek released the chains wrapped around Annev's neck and clawed at his face with gauntleted fingers before he slid off Annev's sword and collapsed to the floor. The bronze warrior twitched, convulsing as his head slapped the ground. After a final thrash of movement, his body lay still.

Annev's heart was pounding. He looked up at Kenton and saw the avatar staring wide-eyed at the dead man in the bronze suit. The boy looked in horror at the instrument of death held in his hands and at Annev touching Mercy's exposed blade. He let go of the hilt, leaving the artifact to Annev, and stepped away from the man he'd just killed.

Annev set the weapon aside, extricated himself from the chains that bound him, and sheathed Mercy. He nodded at Kenton.

"Thank you."

The boy stared blankly at the carnage around them: a half score of dead men lay scattered about a room being consumed by fire; Janak's possessions were destroyed, and the merchant himself lay in a heap beside Fyn. Annev cast aside the chains and iron manacles—one of which still held the dead guard's severed limb. Then he grabbed Sraon's ax and jogged over to Fyn.

Annev winced when he saw Janak's crumpled face, disgusted he could still see the man's former humanity amidst the mass of twisted metal.

"He's dead," Annev said, stating the obvious.

Fyn shook his head, staring blankly at the man he'd been tasked to kill. Annev thought to question his denial, but then the merchant's ruined face creaked, its crumpled head turning as the dull gray eyes locked on Annev.

"Keos …" Annev swore.

Janak raised a shaking metal arm, his steely fist pointing at Annev. "Orcle … crimple?" The words were forced out of mangled lips, raspy and grinding.

Annev stared, not understanding, then saw the brass lamp clutched in the man's hand. He pried it from Janak's stiff metallic grip, and when the incense lamp finally fell from Lord Harth's grasp, he sighed in painful resignation, a wheezing groan pushed from iron lungs.

"He should be dead," Fyn said, his voice ragged. "I don't see how he's not."

"Cruithear cursed him," Annev said, his fingers brushing the tiny runes that covered the brass artifact. "He probably convinced Janak that, in exchange for his servitude, he could reclaim his old life and have his revenge on the Academy."

Fyn looked down at the gold rod in his hand, at the burning study, and at the mangled merchant's body. "I don't know who Cruithear is," he said, shaking the dreadlocks loose, "and I don't really care. We've got the artifact, and it looks like Duvarek's dead." He peered over at Kenton who had knelt beside the corpse of his former mentor. "But how can I make this man deader than he already is? If I thought these flames would kill him, I'd leave him here to burn."

Janak groaned as if in reply, his wrecked body squeaking and creaking as he twisted his broken neck. "Plss … kl meee." He cried, his high-pitched keening sounded like grinding metal.

The man was clearly in pain—there was no doubt death would be a mercy to him. The scene reminded Annev of the withered wood-witch screaming for mercy, mercy, mercy.

Mercy.

Annev stepped forward and called upon the magic of his sword—a sword that had once cut through stone like a sickle parting stalks of grain—and plunged it straight into the wretched man's chest.

Janak blinked, his shrieking silenced. He gazed down at the sword sprouting from his sternum then locked eyes with Annev.

Relief. Gratitude.

Janak reached down and patted Annev's wrist, laying his gray palm atop the crimson phoenix glove. He gripped Annev's hand and twisted the blade.

He slumped forward with a gasp, the life gone from his eyes.

Annev withdrew the blade and stepped back as Janak's ruined body toppled over, collapsing against his desk and scattering pieces of flaming parchment. Their tasks complete, all three boys breathed a little easier.

A slow clapping came from the back of the room. Kenton sprang to his feet, and the three avatars turned to face a shadowy, gray-cloaked stranger standing in the doorway.

"Bravo," the woman said, stepping over a broken painting, the merchant's trinkets crunching beneath her feet. She glanced about at the fires spreading around the room, consuming its once beautiful paneling. "You three certainly know how to throw a party."

CHAPTER FIFTY-EIGHT

The woman was almost as tall as Fyn, with a black scarf wrapped around her head and a slim rapier and dirk hanging at her belt. Next to both of these hung a coiled chain of steel rods joined by small metal rings with a hooked dart swinging lazily from its tip.

She stepped over a broken crystal vase and sidled farther into the burning room where the flames were now becoming a genuine hazard, engulfing furniture and dead guardsmen alike. She drew closer to Kenton and the scarred boy backed away, lacking any weapon to defend himself. When the gray-garbed woman reached Duvarek, she knelt down to inspect the bronze suit, iron collar, and rusty manacles.

"Stop right there!" Fyn commanded, pointing the gold artifact at the woman.

Who is she? Annev wondered. *What does she want?* Then he remembered the cryptic words Janak had received from the Oracle. *Four horsemen, each with a bird on their shoulder—a heron, a kestrel, a rook, and a magpie.* The merchant had given them each a title: the faithless warrior, the doomed cripple, the cursed leader.

And the shadow's shadow.

The woman rose to her feet, barely glancing at Fyn. "I'm sorry," she said, brushing her tattered cloak behind her. "I didn't introduce myself. Very rude, I know." She bowed low, sliding her right foot backward, her cape sweeping across the ground. "I am Sodja, of the noble House of Rocas." She rose, eyeing the three avatars, and casually approached them.

"And you, if I am not mistaken, are dullards and thieves from that back-water academy in the wood."

Quick as a blink, Sodja grabbed the chain-whip from her belt and snapped it outward. The three avatars jumped back, narrowly escaping the weapon's range, then realized too late that the barbed end had been aimed at the Rod of Compulsion. The hooked tip wrapped tight around the gold scepter, whipping it from Fyn's surprised hand and flinging it in Sodja's direction. As it sailed overhead, she cartwheeled after it, snatching the artifact before it hit the ground. The woman landed a dozen feet away from Duvarek's armored corpse then turned to wink at the avatars—and was promptly bowled over by Annev.

They hit the ground, crunching innumerable treasures as they rolled across the bloody floor, each trying to secure a hold while avoiding the fires that burned around them. At last, Annev pinned the stranger against Duva-rek's body, holding her until Fyn and Kenton could lend their support. Yet even as they ran to assist him, Sodja eeled from Annev's grasp and was back on her feet, darting for the door. The two avatars dashed past Annev in pursuit and he rose to follow them, only to be jerked back down after a few paces.

His forearm and shoulder hurt, and as he rose to his feet, Annev saw the cause of his pain: an iron manacle had been clamped over his left arm, chaining him to Duvarek's collar. He clawed at the metal cuff circling his wrist but saw no way to unlock the artifact. He reached for Mercy, intending to cut himself free, then realized he had dropped the blade in his tussle with Sodja Rocas. He turned to look at the thief and saw she'd stopped at Janak's door, slipping the rod into her pocket and lashing the whip around her slender waist.

"Tut-tut!" Sodja said, drawing her rapier and backing through the door. "Is catching me really worth your friend's life?" She gestured at An-nev, and when his companions glanced back, she fled.

Smoke and flame filled the room now, and Annev was at the center of the conflagration. He shook his manacled arm at Fyn and Kenton, trying to wrestle it free, feeling uneasy as the flames edged closer to him. "I'm stuck!" he shouted. "I need my sword—it's near Janak's desk."

Fyn nodded. "Help him. I'll catch the thief." Matching words to actions, Fyn chased Sodja's fleeing shadow, leaving Kenton to aid Annev.

Annev watched the raven-haired boy dash past him seeking Mercy. As he waited, he ran his fingers over the bronze manacle, searching for a lock to pick. Instead of a keyhole, he found perfectly smooth metal without a hint of a crack or exposed locking mechanism. He tried again to slip his hand free from the restraint, and he felt the chafed skin beneath the phoenix glove start to bleed.

Kenton approached, his attention divided between Annev and the encroaching flames.

"I don't see a way to unlock it," Annev said, also distracted by the fires. "I might be able to cut it free with my sword, though."

"Yes," Kenton said, weighing the short sword in his hands. "I felt the magic when I killed Duvarek … but it was different. Not like your lantern or the stumble-sticks or that cup I filled with honey wine."

Annev looked up and saw the boy eyeing him, a strange look on his face. "Kenton, what's wrong?"

Kenton looked down at Mercy and slowly shook his head. "I felt the same magic when I put that collar on Duvarek. It's not the power of a common artifact … it's something you couldn't use unless you have magic."

Annev shook his head, liking neither the direction of their conversation nor the dark look on Kenton's face. "If these chains weren't common artifacts, how did that woman manage to cuff me? How did you?"

Kenton shrugged. "She can obviously use magic. Just like you … and me."

Annev's eyes widened and his heart beat heavy in his chest. He tried not to react—tried to appear confused—but Kenton saw through the ruse.

"You knew the sword was magic—that's why you brought it. That's how we killed Duvarek … you summoned its magic."

"Kenton," Annev said, eyes pleading, "it's not what you think." He took a step toward the boy but stopped when Kenton backed away.

"Those manacles will only unlock for the person that placed them."

"What?" Annev said, wondering if he had misunderstood his companion. "How can you know that?"

Kenton shrugged. "The same way I knew how to make your lantern work ... or how to fill that cup Dorstal gave me."

"Well, Sodja is gone," Annev said, processing this new information. "And I can't wait for Fyn to drag her back—but you could unlock Duvarek's collar, right? Then I could carry these chains out of here." He retreated to the Master of Shadow's body, coiling the chains in his hands as he walked. "Or you could give me the sword. Then I could—"

"I know how the blade works, Annev."

Annev watched as Kenton dragged Mercy's tip across the floor, carving a sinuous line into the stone.

Annev swallowed. "Yes, it seems you do."

Kenton walked toward him with the short sword extended. "I can feel the magic calling to me," he said, "telling me how to use it—telling me how it *wants* to be used."

Annev stood still as Kenton approached then flinched when the boy suddenly reached for him—but Kenton did not attack, nor did he cut away Annev's chains. Instead, he used Mercy to cut the scabbard free from Annev's belt.

Annev stared, dumbfounded, as the boy sheathed the weapon and retreated towards the safety of the hallway.

"What are you doing? Are you *leaving* me?" He coughed, shielding his eyes and mouth from the smoke.

Kenton continued his slow retreat, his eyes taking in the flames that now engulfed the room. He shrugged. "I think this is better for both of us. We're keokum, Annev—we can use magic, and anyone that learns that will kill us." He paused long enough to snatch the magic harp off the wall, and when he looked back there was a meanness in his eyes—something dark and sad, but not quite regretful. "I was willing to follow you, Annev, but we were never friends. You've never really been one of us ... and I'm not willing to die for you."

Annev watched him go, paralyzed with disbelief.

He left me to die. My friend left me to die.

No, Annev amended. They had never been friends—Kenton was right about that. They had been allies, and sometimes adversaries, but never friends. Even so, the betrayal hurt.

Heat tickled Annev's boot, and he recoiled from the dead guard's burning limb. As he saw the severed arm, though, he realized the solution to his problem was staring him right in the face.

Annev concentrated on his left arm and forced himself to let go of the magic prosthetic that he so often treated as his true limb. The stub of his left forearm slipped from the artifact and slid out of his glove's long crimson sleeve. Annev gripped the base of the prosthetic with his right hand and cautiously tugged at the chained limb. When it didn't slide out, he tried pulling it in the opposite direction.

Nothing—the magic that allowed the prosthetic to change size must only work when fitting itself to someone. He tried gripping the iron manacle that still bound his prosthetic, willing it to release itself, but it was as Kenton had said—the artifact refused to work for him.

The room was filled with smoke and the arch of Janak's doorway had begun to crack with the heat as Annev crouched low to ground, trying not to breathe and fumbling with the prosthetic. Unable to make it react, and with the heat growing, he abandoned any hope of salvaging the limb and instead tugged on the fingertips of the phoenix glove, yanking the crimson cloth from the confines of the manacle. He held Myjun's Regaleus gift tight.

At least I saved something tonight.

He tucked the red and gold cloth into his pocket then stooped, searching for his fallen hand ax. He spied it lying next to Janak's burning desk and ran to it, keeping his head below the smoke. When he tested the metal, he discovered the axe had warmed to an uncomfortable temperature, but he was able to holster the weapon without any problems. He was about to turn away when he saw Janak's brass incense lamp lying just beyond the flames. He snatched it up, turning the artifact over in his hand. His eyes and fingers danced across the metal, examining the hundreds of tiny runes that had been carved into the artifact's surface.

If this is really the Oracle of Speur Dún ...

Annev wasn't sure what the significance of that would be, yet he guessed its value and carefully slid the incense lamp into his tunic before sprinting out of Janak's burning study, leaving the dead merchant and his treasures behind ... along with Duvarek's bronze-encased body, and the prosthetic arm he had worn since birth. His old life was literally in flames behind him.

But Annev was a phoenix. He would find a way to rise from the ashes.

CHAPTER FIFTY-NINE

Annev jogged down the long hallway outside Janak's study, his mind in a whirl. He needed time to think, to figure what he was going to do, with thing uppermost in his mind: if he returned to Chaenbalu with only one arm, he would be killed. Perhaps as bad: if Kenton reached the village first, the vengeful avatar would tell others how Annev had died during their mission. If Annev showed up after that—and with one arm—then he and Kenton would likely both be executed. Once Annev accepted those two truths, other things fell into place.

He must beat Kenton back to Chaenbalu, ideally before dawn.

He needed to hide his exposed deformity.

He had to find a new arm.

If he could achieve those three objectives, and confront Kenton before the boy said something stupid and outed them both as magic-users, then perhaps he could salvage his life. And if he couldn't convince Kenton of their mutual need to stay alive, he would have to kill the boy. It wasn't a prospect he relished, but Annev was becoming more pragmatic about the notion, particularly since Kenton had just tried to kill him.

As Annev stalked down the corridor, he decided his best option on reaching Chaenbalu was to seek Sodar out. If the priest hadn't left the village, the man could help him infiltrate the Vault of Damnation and find a replacement prosthetic—if such a thing even existed. The old man might even offer to go in Annev's stead.

Then again, if Sodar hadn't already fled, he would undoubtedly use Annev's plight as a second chance to persuade the boy to leave Chaenbalu.

If he couldn't beat Kenton back to the village, Annev might even accept the priest's offer. As long as he had a chance to reclaim his future, though, he was willing to risk it. He just hoped Sodar had been bluffing about running away without him—and that he would help his wayward apprentice.

Annev stopped beside the body of a guard who had collapsed from blood loss. He tore off the man's cape and draped the blue-black cloth over his shoulder then moved swiftly down the hallway toward the balcony window and pulled back the drapes. The naked glass reflected the firelight flickering behind Annev, revealing his own dark reflection and the silhouetted stub of his left arm.

That won't do, Annev thought, tugging the cape over his stunted arm and then stepping toward the window. He stopped again.

Idiot! You can't climb with one arm.

Annev cursed and ran for the stairwell instead, following it down to the ground floor where he found a dead manservant leaning against the wall, a thin hole punched in the base of his skull. He ventured further into the palace, sticking to the shadows and listening for approaching footsteps, yet every corner he turned and every room he encountered was empty save for the few bodies left behind by Sodja. Each of the dead had been pierced through the heart, head, or throat by a thin, needle-like instrument.

Annev tried not to think about what kind of person could kill so callously—so *needlessly*—in order to steal the Rod of Compulsion. The woman had to be an assassin, an emotionless killer who had somehow penetrated the heart of Janak's home without raising an alarm. After seeing her grisly artistry, Annev was suddenly grateful his tangle with the thief had only ended in chains and spared a fleeting worry for Fyn if he had caught up with her.

As Annev searched for the exit, he entered a long hall filled with portraits of Lord Harth as a younger man. The merchant, it seemed, had been truthful about his exploits: in the first picture, Janak stood on the edge of a black lake with his boot resting atop the body of a slain water serpent—a draquan, if Sodar's lessons were correct. The second picture showed Janak surveying the ruins of a large city overgrown with mist and moss. Several others depicted the merchant in his bronze suit of armor, yet the final portrait showed the man in plain clothes standing next to a woman with an infant in her arms.

Annev hurried past them all and through the empty corridors, abandoning stealth in the confidence that any still alive had fled Janak's keep when the merchant perished and the Rod of Compulsion lost its influence. Not long after, he discovered Janak's kitchen larder and spied a crack in the back-pantry wall, which proved to be a half-closed door that swung out on heavy metal hinges, revealing a dark tunnel with a faint light at the far end.

This must be how Sodja entered. Following his hunch, Annev crept into the secret passage and found a dimly lit tunnel constructed from sharp blocks of granite. He raced down the path, appreciating the flat walls and arched ceiling, and quickly reached the far end.

A dozen feet from the tunnel exit, Annev spied the source of the dim light: a polished black lantern hanging from a naked torch sconce. He reached up to take it then stopped, wondering why it had been left behind. Remembering his training, he spent a few moments checking the surrounding area for traps and was surprised to find not one, but three different mechanisms protecting the lantern: a razor tripwire, a spring-loaded dart, and a contact poison.

Annev felt he could have disarmed the first trap, but the dart required two hands, and the contact poison was dangerous stuff. In the end, he left the black lantern where it hung; he'd use the night sky to find his way home. He stepped over the tripwire and crept out of the tunnel, moving into the starlight … and found himself surrounded by a thick hedge of iron-thorn bushes.

Dammit! Annev wanted to race away from Janak's keep, desperate to get home and find a replacement for his arm, but he knew he had to tread carefully here: the ironwood thorns were a favorite among Darite fletchers, who used the rare wood to make devastating arrowheads. Fortunately for Annev, a winding path had been carved through the den of thorns, and, using a little caution, he emerged mostly unscathed.

Annev stepped out of the bush and looked out over a wide plain speckled with clumps of trees and modest hills. Beyond, a massive forest lay shadowed in darkness.

Fertil Hedge, Annev thought, remembering the name Kenton had given the forest, *which means I'm on the north side of Banok, outside the city walls.* That was good luck. He wouldn't have to waste time sneaking past the guards or testing his luck by climbing over the city wall with one arm. Best of all, it meant he was probably ahead of both Kenton and Fyn.

Annev followed the curve of the wall, heading for the horses. He started out at a jog, sticking to the dark shadows beneath the wall but then began to run, no longer caring if he was seen. The waning moon was descending and in a few hours it would be morning.

Annev neared the twisted oak where the horses had been tethered and felt his pulse begin to race. In the faint starlight, he could see the oak tree well enough to know that Fyn's red gelding and Kenton's gray palfrey had gone. It wasn't until Annev reached the tree, though, that he knew his black mare had also been taken.

"Bloody broken *bones*!" Annev cursed, kicking at a patch of sweet fern growing near the edge of the oak tree's canopy. He had no way of beating either Fyn or Kenton back to the village now. He kicked at the shrubs again then stumbled, catching his foot on his own heavy leather saddle bags. He stared at them, stunned ... and then wondered if his luck might still hold.

He fumbled to unbuckle the first saddlebag with his single hand. He eventually succeeded and was rewarded by pulling out his crimson avatar robes and the purse he'd received from Tosan. Annev was pleased to see both items but neither would help him return home. He opened the second satchel and found his bulging water skins, their bags still full of the possessions he'd taken from Sodar's chapel. He checked the first and found Breathanas's carefully folded phoenix banner, then something tickled the back of his mind and he opened the last leather bag. His fingers brushed soft cloth ... and something hard and round: Sodar's potion.

Annev pulled the glass bottle free and stared at its murky contents, his mind churning with possibilities. Two-thirds of the elixir remained, its magic liquid sloshing inside the opaque glass container. Annev weighed the bottle in his hands, thoughtful. He no longer had a horse, but he could still run the eleven miles to Chaenbalu. He had done as much after his mission in the Brakewood, and with the aid of the potion he could cover that distance quickly. He could even take a few shortcuts that would be impossible on horseback, which meant he might be the first to reach the village.

It was a great idea … except Sodar had warned him that drinking too much of the elixir would have dangerous side-effects. Under normal circumstances, that would dissuade Annev, but he was out of options. Whatever the consequences were, he doubted they were worse than the alternative.

Annev placed the elixir between his thighs, pried off the cork, lifted the bottle to his lips and drank. The spicy-sweet liquor ran down his throat, coating it in a familiar fire. He drained the bottle to the dregs before casting it into the bushes, his stomach already burning—

—a blinding headache dropped him to his knees. He cried out, clutching his forehead, then collapsed to the ground. His vision blurred and his body shook, spasming in pain before subsiding into a jittery tremor.

A minute later his hands were trembling, his head pounded, and his stomach was cramping … yet he felt strong. Energized even. He stretched his legs and flexed his muscles. He felt like a coiled spring, like he needed to run and jump and fight and move.

Movement. His body *ached* to move. Craved it. Needed it.

Annev stomped his feet, flexed and unflexed his fist, and closed his eyes. Instead of running, he forced himself to open his mind and poured his energy into his senses.

He felt … lucid. More than lucid. He could smell the rich loam beneath the sweet ferns mixing with the dung the horses had dropped. He heard the creeping sounds of insects and the laughter of Banok's townspeople. He opened his eyes, blinking, and the details of the distant hills and more distant Brakewood suddenly came into focus: blades of grass, venous leaves, naked branches—all crisp and clear despite being miles away, hidden by shadow and moonlight.

There was something else too—something closer, standing right in front of Annev. A dark shadow hiding in the lighter shadow of the gnarled oak tree. The shade cocked its head, watching Annev's movements, studying him.

Annev's heartbeat quickened. How long had the figure been standing there? What *was* it? It looked like a man, tall and lean, but its features were formless, dark and flat. The figure shifted its stance and Annev glimpsed the subtle outline of a ragged gray cloak fluttering in the wind. It looked like …

A man … wearing death's cloak.

It was the same shade that had followed him across the rooftops and startled him into falling off the roof—except this time it was almost translucent, fading into the surrounding darkness, invisible to the unaided eye.

There was something else too. Something about the way the shade stood, the silhouette of his clothing, the aura … it all felt familiar.

Like Sodja Rocas, Annev realized.

Except this *wasn't* Sodja Rocas. She had been ragged, yet her rags had been rich silks and soft velvets, tailored to look worn instead of actually being so. This man—this shadow—was beggarly by comparison. His clothes seemed ethereal rather than worn, like gossamer threads of blackness, stitched to overlap one another in a weave of umbral and penumbral shadow. In like manner, the man's bearing was neither haughty nor confident, but cold, apathetic, and passionless.

Annev felt like an insect on the verge of being squashed beneath the heel of a boot. He instinctively pulled his left arm to his chest, as if to protect himself from the darkness in front of him. As he did so, his limb slipped from beneath the short cape, exposing the raw stub of his forearm.

The shadow-man jerked to attention, his eyeless face focusing intently on Annev's missing hand. The apathy he had exuded was now gone, and he strode purposefully forward, marching in a direct line toward the frightened avatar.

A chill ran down Annev's spine, and the muscles of his body flooded with a renewed surge of adrenaline and magic. He spun for the Brakewood and ran like Keos himself was behind him.

For all Annev knew, he was.

PART FOUR

Four horsemen ride to your door. Four birds perch atop
  their shoulders.
Each horse bears a weighty burden. Each bird, a secret
  strength.
The cursed leader comes to claim the life of a man he once
  called brother.
The faithless warrior lays claim to the blood of your
  household.
The shadow's shadow seeks a rod of dark power.
The doomed cripple shall bear the mark of Keos;
With a single arm, he shall bear away the Oracle.

Four birds fly to your door. Four beaks, sharp as blades.
A heron, a kestrel, a rook, and a magpie.
Do not contest the birds. Do not contain the horsemen.
If you keep the rod, the Shadow will claim it.
If you use the rod, Sorrow will follow.
Your household will be cursed, your treasures destroyed.
Mercy shall claim you in the end, and Fire shall consume
  the hand that strikes you.

—"Answers to Janak Harth," words of the Oracle of Speur Dún

Yet He is not lost, for only a God can destroy another God. Yea, His spirit shall survive, and His Vessel shall be reborn—a God-king, a savior and destroyer— for just as the broken cruse holds no oil, neither can the Broken Vessel hold His spirit. Yea, its pieces must be found, consumed, and reforged. Only in that death can there be life. Only in the cleansing fire of purification can the taint be removed. Only by embracing destruction can He be reborn.

And from the Shattered Hand proceed the fragments of the Broken Vessel:
Seven endowed with power, heirs to his magic.
Six born of flesh, heirs to their father.
Five claimed by clans, heirs to his children.
Three bound to Earthblood, stewards of what is.
Two tied to Entropy, heirs of what is not and what may be.
The seventh bears the mark of Keos and the Last Hope of Lumea, and whoso possesses His spirit at the last day shall rule the seven parts.

And these fragments shall war with one another, consuming each other until a new God of Earthblood rises from the ashes of their conflict. And His power shall exceed that of Odar and Lumea. And His worshippers shall be as numerous as the sands of the sea and shall sweep the Darites and Ilumites from the earth. Then shall Keos Reborn rule over every land, and every creature born of earth and blood will submit to His will or die.

—"Prophecies of the Shattered Hand and the Broken Vessel," excerpt
from *The Book of Fate*

Over the centuries, there have been several notable members of the Six, with a few whose reputations bordered on legend, including Gevul the Terrible, Trat the Charlatan, Garrach Bog-eater, the Shadow, Shnee of the South, Kolda Bittern, and Bidba the Second (often called Sawpit).

It is fruitless to speculate on the identities of the extant members of the Six because they change so often, but evidence suggests at least two have survived for the last three centuries: Shachran of Tir Reota (a necromancer whose vile history I've outlined elsewhere) and the nameless "Shadow Reborn."

Aside from his name, the Shadow Reborn has almost nothing in common with the original Shadow, Valdemar Kranak, who sowed unrest throughout Gorm Corsa prior to its abandonment; rather than being a Darite saboteur, this 'reborn' incarnation is of Kroseran origin and has typically been employed as an assassin or spy. He also has a unique connection to the shadow realm, and I believe it is that connection which gifts him his supernatural longevity (though my esteemed colleagues from Southmarch have some more exotic theories).

Little else can be said about the Shadow Reborn except that he is often, though not always, accompanied by an apprentice—a practice that has never been followed by other members of the Siänar.

—"The Siänar," excerpt from *The Complete Histories of Luquatra* by Kyartus Gairm

CHAPTER SIXTY

It took Annev a little less than two hours to run from the outskirts of Banok to the edge of Chaenbalu. His six-mile race over the plains of Daroea had been tireless and exhilarating, fueled by the magic of Sodar's elixir and the fear of what lay behind him. In contrast, the five-mile sprint through the Brake had been pure terror: under the influence of the elixir, the sounds and shadows of the woods had startled him at every turn. Worse, the energizing effects of the elixir had begun to wear off, and as the sky began to lighten, the shadows and spaces of the Brake began to lengthen—as they so often did—stretching before Annev and doubling the distance he needed to run. Even so, he did not stop to rest, did not dare look back in case the shadow was pursuing him.

Dawn was fast approaching when Annev crested the hill overlooking his village. He ached to stop and catch his breath, but he pushed on, running as fast as he could down the eastern slope and not slowing till he reached the center of the village, only then looking round to see if the strange shade had pursued him past the standing stones. Despite feeling it had been one step behind him for miles, there was nothing, so hee pushed on to Sodar's chapel.

The windows were shuttered when Annev arrived and, guessing the front door would also be locked, Annev crept into the training shed. Nothing was out of place—the training weapons, wood ax, and chamber pot were all in their usual places—but something was missing, and when he tried the rectory door his heart fell.

Sodar had left the door unlocked.

It was a small detail, but one which confirmed what Annev had already feared. Sodar was gone, leaving a cold hearth and an empty room behind. Annev went into the Sodar's room and found his bed neatly made, as though the man had recently left or never gone to bed in the first place. Annev searched for a note—for some confirmation the priest had truly left—but there was nothing.

Annev was on his own.

I have to get into the vault. Sodar said there were other prosthetics there, and one of them might work. If he couldn't get in, if he couldn't find them, if none of the artifacts were helpful ... he would deal with that when he had to. *The sun's almost up ... and I have to hide my arm before risking the Academy.* It was a painful realization. Magic had always aided him but now he would have to manage without it and think up some trick to keep himself safe. Annev smiled sadly then, remembering one of his last conversations with Sodar. *Even tricks have their place.*

An inkling of an idea came to him. He tore the cape free from his shoulder and marched to his room. When he reached his straw pallet, he knelt on the cape, laid the crimson phoenix glove across his knees, and started stuffing straw into the long sleeve of the arm, working it down into the fingers until he was satisfied with the shape. He slipped it over the stub of his forearm and pulled the end up over his elbow. The straw was prickly, but the result looked real enough, so long as he was careful. For a little security, he tore the blue trim from the guard's cape and used it to tie the glove securely around his left bicep.

Now to get to the vault before Fyn and Kenton return.

He flew from the chapel, praying the others had not yet arrived. Just to be certain, he ran to the stables first, listened for voices, then slipped inside.

The scents of horse and hay tickled Annev's nose and he instinctively rubbed it, only to surprise himself when the straw-filled glove thumped his face. He shook his head in frustration. He knew his hand was gone—he *knew* that—but he had taken the prosthetic for granted almost every day of his life.

Is this how it's going to be if I can't find a replacement arm? Annev wondered. The possibility frightened him, even though he had intellectually understood it, and Sodar had tried to prepare him for it. Whether he could accept it or not, though, the ancients would kill him outright if they discovered his deformity.

The damn Vault of Damnation. It was his only chance.

Annev peeked over the stable walls and saw two horses—a white nag and a brown plow horse—but no sign of the black rouncy, red gelding, or gray palfrey. He had beaten Fyn and Kenton here—but probably not by much. Annev had no time to waste. He circled around to the cellar doors and was relieved to find them unlocked. One door slid open on oiled hinges as he pulled it up, glanced around for a final time, and stepped down into the darkness.

Relying on his senses and his training, Annev crept along the darkened hallway. It connected to the basement of the Academy, and he'd walked it several times before, but never alone in the dark. His fingers slid across the stone wall, keeping him oriented as he visualized where he was in relation to the Academy. Though he'd never been to the vault, he knew it was in the basement, and that it was large enough to accommodate centuries' worth of artifacts.

His fingers reached open air and he knew that he'd come to the first junction. He felt around with his hand and feet, careful not to get turned around, and found it was a crossroad. With a quick prayer to Odar, he walked on, pushing deeper into the Academy on the assumption that the vault would be at the heart of the building. He pressed forward, counting his paces, and when he came to another junction in the darkness, he went straight again, guessing he was now beneath the Academy itself. At the third junction, though, he had to choose: left or right? With no other way to learn about the options, Annev knelt down and felt the stones beneath his feet: the path to the left was smooth with wear. The path to the right was covered in a thick film of dust.

Do I take the worn path or the one rarely used?

The vault was the most closely guarded and restricted place in the Academy, which suggested the less traveled path was the correct one. On the other hand, Master Narach visited the vault every day, so the path could just as easily be the well-trod one.

On a hunch, Annev chose the dusty corridor and shuffled along in the dark, disturbing the cobwebs stuck to the stones. He moved with a combination of caution and speed, staying alert, until his boot caught on something sticking up from the floor.

Annev jerked his foot back, dancing away on instinct as a loud *snap* was followed by a *clang* of metal clapping against metal. The sound echoed throughout the basement.

Annev swore and froze against the wall, listening for footsteps over the sound of his pounding heart. With great care, he slid his feet across the stones again until his toe brushed something. A metal trigger, which ran along a groove in the stone floor that stretched the full width of the hallway. It was connected to a large spring and a jagged metal-toothed jaw-trap. The vicious half-circle of iron was half Annev's size and designed to snap a man in two. He shuddered, rethinking his decision to turn right. Correct or not, it was clearly the more dangerous path.

Annev blinked, realizing he could almost see the outline of the trap, then saw a dim light had blossomed at the far end of the hallway, its source brightening.

Someone had heard the trap after all.

Annev bolted for the last intersection and dodged around the corner just as someone carrying a torch entered the corridor. He held his breath, back pressed against the stones, and heard the soft scuffle of footsteps as the light grew brighter. He softly thumped his head against the wall behind him, trapped. There was nowhere to run—and if he tried, he could walk straight into another jaw-trap. If he was found, his options were bad too: with no weapons to fight with, he would have to rely on wits and talk his way out of trouble.

The footsteps stopped as the torchbearer reached the trap. Annev hesitated, wondering if he could ambush them. Maybe if he was quick he would have a cha—

"Annev! What are you doing down here?"

CHAPTER SIXTY-ONE

Annev jumped, wheeling to his right, and was Myjun standing barefoot in front of him, her white nightdress held up to her mid-calf, looked as startled as he was.

"Myjun!" he laughed, both pleased and terrified to see her. "You scared me."

"I scared *you*?" She rubbed her eyes. "You scared *me*—triggering the trap and hiding in the dark." She shook her head, "What *are* you doing down here?"

"What are *you* doing?" Annev countered, answering her question with another question. "Don't tell me you sleep in the basement?"

Myjun gave a half smile. "Our secret's out—not that it was so well kept to begin with." She gestured at the hall behind her. "Our dormitory is down here, tucked away to stop you acolytes trying to slip between our sheets." She arched an eyebrow. "Is that why you're here, Master Ainnevog?"

Annev's face flushed a deep crimson while he fumbled for an excuse. "I was sent to find Master Narach. I have an artifact for him to archive."

Myjun frowned. "The vault is two floors further down. Didn't they tell you where to go?"

"Not very clearly. We left so quickly last night, and I've never been to the vault before."

"Why must everything be a test with avatars? Didn't they tell you there are traps down here?" She gestured at the massive jaw-trap where she'd wedged her torch. "Was finding it in the dark part of the test? Why didn't you take a light?"

Annev rubbed his chin, taking the opening she'd given him. "It was part of the challenge."

"You could have been killed." Myjun sounded disgusted. "There's no way you could have found the vault in the dark, especially without an escort." She tisked then stopped, her eyes brightening. "But that means you got the artifact?"

Annev nodded slowly. "We did." He patted the only thing he had—the incense lamp, still tied to his belt.

Myjun surprised him by stepping in close and kissing his cheek.

Annev froze. "What was that for?"

"For coming back to me." She leaned in again, about to kiss him on the lips, then she boxed his ear.

"Ow! What was that for?"

"For being too stupid to know how stupid you are! You should *never* venture down here without a torch, not even on a dare. It's a maze—and it's dangerous."

Annev rubbed his ear. "I understand … but I do still have to get to the vault." He patted the lamp again.

"I can take you there." Myjun's smile was blinding as she held out her right hand to his left.

Annev went cold. If she touched the straw-filled glove it would be over.

He leaned forward, took her right hand in his, and bowed over her fingers, then spun her away, sweeping her to his other side and catching her left hand in his right. He squeezed her palm with genuine affection then kissed the promise ring she was wearing.

"Lead the way, my lady."

Myjun tugged him back along the dusty corridor and past the jaw-trap, taking up her torch again as they walked by. He'd been heading the right way after all.

"So tell me," Annev said slowly. "Why put a trap in plain sight when an intruder can just step around it?"

"The way you did?" Myjun crinkled her nose at him. "There are plenty of less visible traps—the visible ones are supposed to warn intruders away." She led him through a maze of twists and turns that Annev failed to memorize until they reached a small staircase and she stepped ahead of him.

"Stay on the right-hand side and skip every third step."

"More traps?"

"Lots of them." She led the way and he was careful to step exactly where she did.

"How do you know about them?"

"On the upper level, the witwomen use them to train us, as well as to protect the vault." She winked at Annev as they reached the bottom stair. "Down here, though ... I learned by watching others avoid them."

Annev took her hand again as the corridor ahead curved, corkscrewing down into the earth. "You've followed the master avatars to the vault?" Myjun nodded. "And they've never caught you?"

"Not yet," she said. "I've not been caught spying on you and the other avatars either ..."

"Spying on us? Why?"

Myjun's broad smile became a defiant grin. "I like to see how your training differs from ours. There's a lot of places to hide and watch people—my father and the ancients do it too."

Annev's stomach churned at the thought. "So they spy on us ... and you spy on them?"

"I spy on everyone," Myjun said with a hint of pride.

They'd reached a rusting iron door covered with rows of sharp metal spikes.

"I'll pick the lock—" Annev began, hoping it wouldn't be necessary.

"No need. You wouldn't want to try it on this door anyway."

"Traps?"

"Nasty ones." She took a cone-shaped spike to the left of the handle in both hands and wrenched it upward

Click.

Myjun yanked down, as if pumping a bellows.

Clack.

And again.

Clink. Clack.

She spun the door handle once to the left, once to the right, then left and right again. Each time the door gave a series of soft clicks.

Annev watched, impressed. It must be some kind of combination lock, but it was like nothing he had seen before. He might have made it this far without Myjun, but there was no way he could have managed the door. He thanked Odar he had bumped into her.

She crouched in front of the lock plate and pressed the two steel nails beneath the handle. Something heavy clanked into place on the other side … and the door swung inward.

CHAPTER SIXTY-TWO

Annev stared at the open door, impressed that Sodar had ever broken into the vault alone. Myjun stood and gestured to the corridor beyond.

"Your path awaits," she said with a flourish.

He took her hand again, still amazed that he could. "You're incredible," he whispered as she reclaimed her torch.

"Surely you knew that already ... seeing as we're engaged."

Annev couldn't stop smiling. "So are we inside the vault now?"

"No, this is the first threshold. The archives stand between here and the second threshold, and the vault is beyond that."

Annev whistled. "That's a long way to follow someone without being seen." He paused. "Have you ever been inside?"

"The vault? Never! I've seen how they get in, but who wants to be in a room full of cursed magic?" She shuddered.

"You've never been curious?"

Myjun shook her head. "I might be curious how hell looks, but that doesn't mean I want to visit."

They turned right and the torch lit seven wooden doors, three on each side of the hallway and a large ironwood door at the far end. As they drew closer, Annev saw glyphs had been inscribed on each of the doors. He studied the closest ink-stained etching.

"*Cartlann,*" he read aloud.

Myjun brought the torch up closer, studying the door frame. She traced the carving with her finger then jerked her hand back from the door. "Annev! These aren't just glyphs. Those are Old Darite—they're *magic.*"

"Only if they've been infused with the will and thought of a wizard," Annev said, almost without thinking. "Otherwise it's just another writing system."

"Wizard? You mean a Son of Keos? A keokum?"

"No! Nothing like that. Just someone who has Odar's blessing. You can write a glyph and say its name, but nothing will happen unless you have the gift—and even then, you have to invest the symbol with your intent."

Myjun's eyes went wide. "You know how magic works." It was more than a question but not quite an accusation.

"We are taught a little about it," Annev said, trying to be reassuring, "so we can retrieve artifacts safely. And Sodar told me a bit. That's all." Annev tugged her on, away from the doors.

"Sodar taught you about *magic*?" Myjun arched an eyebrow.

"For my deacon duties."

"But what magic would a priest or a deacon need to know?"

Annev could feel her eyes on him and he cleared his throat, realizing he'd said too much. "Enough to denounce it when he sees it."

Myjun seemed to chew on this. "It seems Brother Sodar knows a lot about forbidden things—like that text he was translating. And how magic works …?"

Her accusing tone sounded exactly like her father's, complete with his superiority and disapproval. It made Annev uneasy, and defensive, so he tried to redirect the conversation. "I could say as much about you," he teased, "knowing things you're not supposed to."

Myjun smiled. "Maybe I do." She nodded at the last door. "So what does this one say?"

"Same as the other one. *Cartlann*. Archives."

Myjun grunted, seeming disappointed. "And those two?"

"*Mallachtaí*—curses," he looked at the second, "and *Rúin*. Secrets."

"Oh. Well, that makes sense. This is Narach's office, and he's the Master of Secrets. I doubt he actually sleeps here, though." So saying, and to Annev's horror, she lifted her hand and knocked on the door.

Annev held his breath, afraid the old man would answer, but there was silence. Myjun knocked again but, again, no one answered. She turned back to him.

"You did check his rooms before—"

"Stay on the right-hand side, boys," came a deep voice from the staircase, "and skip every third step. Master Murlach has left some nasty surprises on them."

"Damnably inconvenient of him," said a second voice, this one much older.

Annev glanced at Myjun, horror stamped on his face, and she laughed. "It's fine, Ani. They can't blame you for another master's prank, or for bringing an artifact to the vault—and they're not about to scold *me*." She squeezed his palm, oblivious that he was paralyzed with cold, white terror.

They're going to find out. Fyn and Kenton are with them ... they're going to find out.

"What's this now?" Narach said, his voice whiny voice creaking down the stairs and echoing down the hall. "This door was locked last night."

Annev heard the other man—it was Brayan, the quartermaster—laugh. "With the amount of honey wine you drank, I'm amazed you can remember."

The echoing stomp of boots sounded more like a fist of avatars than a pair of men, and Annev knew his fears were about to be realized. A moment later, Narach led the group into the hallway, his torch guttering as he waved it about. He saw Myjun's light immediately.

"You see!" the Master of Secrets said, shaking a ring full of keys. "There is someone here."

Fyn came next, carrying the phoenix lantern, and Kenton followed carrying Mercy and the silver harp from Janak's study. Brayan brought up the rear, and they all looked stunned to see Annev. Kenton visibly paled.

"Blood and hell, it's Master Ainnevog! Are you a ghost? These boys just told me you were killed in a fire ... or some other nonsense." He took a step closer, squinting beneath Myjun's torchlight. "Myjun? What are you doing down here? Did your father send you?"

Kenton's expression shifted from shock to hatred as he saw Myjun, and his dark eyes caught the glint of her promise ring.

"Myjun," he said, choking on her name. "Why are you down here with him?"

"Annev! How did you escape?" Fyn said at the same time.

The green-eyed witgirl glanced at Annev, a question in her eyes, but turned her attention to Narach.

"Master Narach, I brought Master Ainnevog to the Vault of Damnation as he has an artifact to catalogue."

"Does he?" Narach said, his sour face softening. "Did you take the Rod of Compulsion after all? These boys said it was stolen. Don't tell me you got it and beat them both back here?"

"And without a horse too!" Brayan was delighted. "I can't wait to tell Titus. This'll be one for the books—four artifacts retrieved in one night by our three newest masters!" He clapped his thick hands together, ignoring the looks from the others.

As the group approached, Annev eyed the two boys, resentful that they had abandoned him, yet realizing they may have given him the leverage he needed to buy their silence. In surrendering his artifacts to the vault, they had no doubt asserted both items were from Janak's, which meant Annev never had to explain how he'd come to possess them.

I can make this work, he thought. *I'll give Master Narach the brass lamp, persuade Narach to let me into the vault with him, and slip away to search for a prosthetic ...*

"Master Narach, may I help you catalogue the artifacts? I have questions about this magic oil lamp, and I thought you'd be the most knowledgeable person to ask."

Narach blinked, taken aback by the boy's interest, then he smiled, exposing a mouth of half-rotten teeth. "Why ... yes, of course, Master Annev."

Myjun looked at him with disappointment and a little revulsion. "Annev, don't go in there—it's the Vault of Damnation. You don't want that taint on you. Leave that cursed item with Master Narach and come with me."

Annev wished he could. He had hoped Myjun wouldn't enter the vault but had not anticipated her asking him to leave with her.

"Myjun," Annev started, "I'd love to ..." He watched her smile falter, hope fading from her eyes, and his tongue suddenly felt like a stone in his mouth. He wanted to spend the morning with her, to begin their future together ... but he couldn't. Unless he entered that Vault, he *had* no future. He steeled himself, trying to think of any reason Myjun would accept.

"I'd love to," Annev said again, "but it's my duty as a master to see this safely locked away before I report to your father."

Myjun studied him, her eyes boring into his as if she sensed there was more, disappointment etching her soft features. "I understand."

"Thank you," Annev whispered. He looked up to see Fyn and Kenton watching him and he met their gazes, staring each one down.

That's right, he thought grimly. *We're all in this together.* They shared a secret now, and Annev doubted either would sacrifice their becoming masters by admitting they'd stolen their artifacts from Annev and not Janak.

Then there were the darker secrets Kenton and Annev shared: being cursed with magic—and Kenton's attempt to kill him. He expected the scarred boy to keep his silence for now, but Annev knew he'd need to address that betrayal eventually.

"Acolyte Fyn, Acolyte Kenton, I'll find you once I've assisted Master Narach with the artifacts and we can report to Elder Tosan together." That earned Annev a glare from them both. "I wouldn't want my report to jeopardize your earning your master titles."

Fyn blinked then gave the barest nod of his head. "I look forward to our discussion ... Master Annev." He handed the phoenix lantern to Narach and stood with Brayan, ready to leave.

Kenton came closer to Annev, Mercy in his traitorous hands, ignoring Narach but sparing a sidelong glance at Myjun.

"How did you escape?" He hissed.

Annev smiled, released Myjun's hand, and pretended to scratch his chest, then leaned close to Kenton, as if he were about to whisper some great secret. When the boy leaned in, Annev waved his hand in front of the avatar's face, snapped his fingers, and made an iron ring appear in the palm of his hand.

"Magic," Annev said, flipping the once-forgotten promise ring at the boy's face. Kenton caught it, staring at the twisted piece of metal.

"You picked the lock. But I didn't see ..." He glanced at Annev's gloved hand, studying the blue ribbon that tied the garment to his bicep. "You're lying," he said, eyes sparkling. "And you're hiding something . . ." Kenton reached for the glove and Myjun slapped his hand away.

"Kenton," she whispered, "stop humiliating yourself!" The boy lowered his eyes and she whipped her head toward Annev, her brown curls bouncing around her face.

"Ignore him, Annev. He's just jealous you beat him back here—not to mention a fool for thinking you dead." She kissed him lightly on the cheek. "Find me after you speak with my father," she whispered.

Annev nodded, still stunning from his near-miss and thanking the gods for sending Myjun to him that night. She squeezed his palm … and they both froze. Annev's heart skipped a beat and they both looked in horror at the straw-filled glove, which had come away in Myjun's hand. She stared at his torchlit stump.

Don't let her scream, he thought. *Please, don't let her scream!*

He was so close … and maybe the others hadn't seen? Maybe Myjun would let him explain.

"Myjun …" He tried to find the words.

She screamed then, loud and piercing, the sound echoing down the hall and throughout the catacombs.

"Please!" Annev pleaded. He reached for her, his fingertips grazing her white sleeve. She whirled, flames flashing, and cracked his skull with her torch.

Annev's vision blurred as his hopes for the future—for anything— vanished before his eyes. He collapsed to the floor, the back of his head cracking against the stones, and the light around him faded into silence and darkness.

CHAPTER SIXTY-THREE

The ground was wet and cold, and when he opened his eyes he saw the stone floor was covered with blood.

His blood.

Annev sat up, shivering, and found he was naked. The bloodied clothes he'd worn on his avatar mission, his undergarments, his water bags—all gone. He curled up for warmth and was startled by the thump of his stunted forearm against his thigh.

Right, he thought, bitter. *That's why I'm here.* He rubbed his naked skin and shivered again, head pounding. *Wherever here is …*

He peered around at the dimly lit cell. The room was about fifteen feet square and, unlike the halls he had traversed with Myjun, the stone beneath him felt as rough-hewn as the walls, which had an iron door set into the wall opposite him. It had a tiny barred window, which was covered by a metal plate on the other side.

A few feet behind him, a crude staircase had been carved into the back wall, its notched and broken steps leading to a rusty trapdoor. A trickle of luminous golden liquid seeped from a small crack, faintly illuminating the room as it dripped down the back wall, spiderwebbing down to drain into a small hole at the back of the cell. Annev pulled his bruised body over to look at it.

The iridescent white-gold liquid gave off a rainbow-hued light. It dazzled as it trickled down into the earth, sparkling violet, blue, green, yellow, orange, and red … but the drain still smelled like a sewer.

He pulled himself back into a ball at the sound of footsteps and the metal plate covering the window slid back. Annev looked up over his knees to see Master Narach's pinched and wrinkled face. The man sneered, a hissing gash of missing or broken teeth.

"You're awake." He squinted into the cell. "Just as well, I suppose."

"Why am—" A fit of coughing overtook Annev and when it subsided, he licked his cracked lips and tried again. "Why am I here?" He knew the answer but wanted to know what the ancients intended to accuse him of.

"There will be a trial," Narach said, craning to get a good look at his stump. The man nodded, apparently satisfied, then spat through the bars of the window.

"Son of Keos," he muttered, and slammed the metal plate shut.

Annev got to his feet, groaning, then brushed his fingertips along the back of his head, feeling the sticky scab on his skull. His fingers came away with only a tiny smear of blood, but his head still throbbed and the rest of his body felt sticky with the dried stuff.

Annev looked up at the trapdoor above his head, wondering.

It couldn't be that easy … could it?

He forced himself up the carved stone steps and prodded the iron door. There was no handle, and the whole thing looked rusted shut.

Annev climbed another step, turned around, and pressed his back against the trapdoor. He slowly extended his legs, pressing his bare feet into the cold stone stairs, and heaved.

Nothing.

He turned to reexamine the door. Up close, he could see the tiny hole leaking the golden fluid, slipping around the edge of the rusty trapdoor. He brushed his finger against it, tentative, and felt the burn of hot and cold, ice and fire. He jerked his hand back, trying to shake it off, then examined his fingertip: a thin golden film remained on his skin, which crumbled to ash and smoke when he rubbed it.

Bloody bones. I won't be drinking any of that.

Annev backed down the stone steps and paced the floor for warmth until the rough contours of the floor began to hurt his feet and he had to sit, huddling for heat as time crept by.

I must be deep beneath the Academy. Even lower than the vault level Myjun took me to.

Myjun.

Any chance of a future with her had ended the moment she saw his stump. *The look on her face ...* He shuddered, remembering how horrified she had been.

She was just scared. If she'd had time to think, if I'd told her earlier ...

But he was lying to himself. Seeing her face—seeing her genuine revulsion—had proved what he had feared all along: Myjun could never see past his deformity, and she would likely never forgive him for lying to her.

His life was over. His arm was gone. Sodar had left, Myjun had spurned him, and it was only a matter of time before the ancients and masters executed him. The only thing that could make it worse was if Kenton accused him of using and possessing magic. Then, instead of just being stoned, he'd be beaten, blinded, and tortured. If he survived having his eyes gouged out, a multitude of horrible deaths awaited him. The last person accused of witchcraft had been boiled in oil before finally being impaled on a pole.

Annev's stomach twisted in a knot and vomit rose in his throat. He scrambled over to retch into the drain, bringing up stomach bile but nothing solid. He wiped his mouth with the back of his wrist and crawled over to the base of the stairs.

I should have left with Sodar. He was right about everything, and he let me go anyway. He let me learn it for myself. Myjun will never accept me for who I am and the Academy will never forgive me for lying to them.

***

"Stop whining, Narach. Be thankful they gave you a new Master of Curses."

"Kenton?" Narach said, clicking the lock open with his key. "He's useless. I'll be dead before he manages to learn anything."

Annev woke at the voices, wiped his eyes, and curled himself back into a ball. There was a squeal as an unseen drop bar was lifted, and a shriek followed, much louder than the first, as the iron door was yanked open.

Master Brayan stood in the doorway holding a torch aloft, blinding

Annev with the light. He lifted it high and walked in as Annev covered his eyes with his arm, waiting for his vision to adjust. When it did, he found himself staring up at Brayan's bear-like figure and Titus's cherubic face.

"Annev!" The blond boy carried a heavy wooden pail and splashed water on the floor as he moved.

Brayan glared at Narach's skeletal figure in the doorway and then at Annev. "So," he said, speaking slowly, "do you thirst?"

The phrasing of the question puzzled Annev, but he nodded.

"Do you thirst … for water?"

Ah, Annev realized, *I'm a Son of Keos now. He's asking if I want water or blood. And if I said blood, what then? Would he snap my neck and save me the humiliation of a trial, or would he slice Titus's throat so I could drink?*

"Water," Annev whispered.

Brayan nodded to Titus, who set the pail on the floor and pulled a shallow wooden bowl from the pocket of his robes. He handed it to Annev, his eyes cast down.

Annev took it and realized Titus's wide eyes had fallen on his rounded stump. His initial instinct was to hide it. But there was nowhere to hide and no longer any reason to do so, so he held his arm out for Titus to look while he plunged the bowl into the cool water and drank. After his first slow gulp drained the vessel, he refilled it again and again, hurriedly filling his stomach with the precious liquid. Once his thirst was slaked, however, he became self-conscious.

"Thank you for the water," Annev said, handing back the bowl.

"You're welcome."

There was an awkward silence as the two boys stared at each other, one dressed in tan steward robes and the other naked on the stone floor.

Narach, who had been standing outside the door, made a disgusted sound and slinked back down the hall. Annev ignored him, grateful for the privacy. He nodded at his friend. "The steward robes look good on you."

Titus smiled. "Thanks. I get to help Master Brayan with the animals—the horses, the dogs, even the bees—and Master Carbad's been showing me the Academy's ledgers and teaching me about our supplies. It's not as fun as the animals, but it's important."

Annev managed to smile. "You'll be a great steward, Titus."

"I think so too. Master Brayan says if I do well they'll make me Master Steward of Husbandry and switch my tan robes for blue ones."

"You mean … like Master Sage? The Master of Cooking?"

"Yes," Titus said, nearly spilling his bucket in excitement. "I'd still be a master steward, not an avatar, but it's still wonderful." He grinned. "It's definitely better than being an acolyte."

Annev nodded, realizing Tosan had been right about Titus. It made him wonder what else the headmaster had been right about.

Brayan cleared his throat. Titus looked up at and the quartermaster nodded at the water pail. Titus nodded, understanding.

"We're supposed to wash you," Brayan said. "For the trial."

Annev nodded, only half listening. It would be quick, the outcome already clear. Strangely, he didn't feel bad about that: he had always known the risks, and he had accepted them when he chose to risk everything and return.

Titus pulled a rag out of his pocket, dipped it in the water, and began to wipe the blood from Annev's face. Annev sat still and mute, forcing himself not to cry out when the boy began combing dried blood from his hair.

"Kenton defended you. He said you were trapped. That you cut off your own hand to escape a fire," Titus whispered.

Annev looked up, surprised. "If that were true, I'd be one tough bastard."

"I'd believe it," Titus said, smiling slightly, "but Elder Tosan says you used magic to hide your arm ever since you came to the Academy."

Annev's heart thudded in his chest. *How did he guess?* He looked at Brayan, but the towering master stared straight ahead, giving no indication he was listening.

"What does it matter now?"

Titus sopped the rag in the pail and wrung it out, turning the water pink. He scrubbed Annev's back and shoulders. "It matters a lot. If you were injured during the retrieval then you've only recently been marked by Keos. But if you've been hiding your … your arm—" Titus swallowed. "It's bad, Annev. They've been asking the avatars a lot of questions. The masters too. Tosan is livid, Myjun locked herself in her room, and Sodar '" His voice trailed off.

"Sodar?" Annev's resignation and despair was suddenly replaced with concern. "Sodar's *here?* Where? What are they doing to him?"

Brayan's eyes narrowed. "Hurry up," he bellowed. And then quieter: "We only have a few minutes."

Titus nodded, wringing out the rag once more. He began to wash Annev's legs and arms then stopped when he came to the deformed limb. He stared at it, the water dripping from the damp cloth.

"Here," Annev said, reaching for it. "I can wash myself."

Titus hesitated then nodded, handing the rag to Annev. As he scrubbed himself clean, Titus averted his eyes.

"Are you really a Son of Keos?" he whispered, his head turned so that Brayan didn't see him speaking.

Annev's shoulders slumped. *Even you, Titus?* He dipped the rag in the pail and scrubbed again. "I'm the same person I've always been."

Titus seemed to relax a bit. "You're not …" He left the sentence unfinished, hanging in the air.

"Evil? A monster?"

Titus shrugged. "Yeah."

Annev sighed, shaking his head. "I'm no more evil than you are, Titus."

"But you've been marked," the boy said, miserable.

Annev threw the rag on the floor, tired and disgusted. "I might have one hand, Titus, but I'm the same person I've always been. I'm not a monster."

There was a thunder of footsteps and voices beyond the open door.

"… said he was doing his job, and I'm only trying to do mine."

"Of course, Master Narach. You did well to inform me. Master Kenton can assist me from here."

"It's no trouble to stay, Elder Tosan."

"You can go," Tosan snapped. "Master Kenton has the keys."

Narach grumbled something unintelligible and shuffled away down the hallway.

Brayan handed the torch to Titus. "Time to go." The quartermaster picked up the pail, took two quick steps to the drain, and splashed its contents down the hole.

"Gods speed, Master Annev."

"And to you, Master Brayan."

The hulking master ushered Titus to the door, but not before Tosan stepped into the room. A moment later, Kenton appeared glaring over his shoulder, his fierce dark eyes traveling from Annev's face to his stump.

"Good morning, Master Brayan. Steward Titus." The headmaster nodded curtly. "Master Narach tells me you've been cleaning the keokum's cell."

"Yes, Elder Tosan." Brayan tried to squeeze past the Eldest of Ancients, but Tosan didn't budge.

"If you just cleaned the cell, why is that infernal light still there?"

Brayan worked his mouth amidst the mass of his great bushy beard. "It's as I've said before, Elder Tosan. The lightwater leaks in from the vault—and it will continue to do so as long as its source is undisturbed."

Tosan sighed. "And I suppose sealing the door is too complex a task?"

While the ancient and master spoke, Annev spied the bowl that Titus had left behind. He snatched it up, giving no thought to what he might do with it, but feeling he should take every opportunity fate offered him.

"… tried everything," Brayan continued. "I'll have to go into the vault and have a look around if you really want it stopped."

Annev edged his way to the corner of the room with the trickling golden liquid, the germ of an idea forming in his mind. He wedged the bowl into the drainage shaft, leaving only the lip of the wooden dish visible, then backed away.

Tosan rubbed his temples. "Thank you, Master Brayan, but only Master Narach and myself—and the new Master of Curses, of course—shall enter the vault for the moment. Perhaps Master Kenton can look into it."

Brayan bowed. "As you wish, Elder Tosan."

Tosan stepped back and, once Brayan and Titus were past him, he gestured for Kenton to enter ahead of him. The young man entered carrying a torch in one hand and a ring of keys in the other; he stood erect in the crimson robes of a master avatar, and Annev felt a pang of grief and envy.

Tosan eased the door closed then stared at Annev. "How long have you been hiding that?" the ancient spat.

Annev's eyes flickered to Kenton, but the boy refused to make eye contact. He looked back at Tosan, thinking what he might say, and in the end, he said nothing.

Tosan sneered. "Your silence won't protect Sodar. Nor will your lies. So if you want to save your precious mentor, you will tell me the truth."

Annev bit his lip, pained by the reminder they held Sodar in their custody, yet he knew the truth wouldn't save him or the old man. Did he dare to lie? Tosan's ability to discern the truth was well-known, and Annev suspected he was using an artifact—his ring—to do it. Knowing that, he saw no advantage to speaking and let the silence speak for him.

Tosan's face darkened and he pointed at Kenton. "Master Kenton swears you cut off your hand to escape a fire during last night's retrieval mission. Master Fyunai believes this is correct—he says you were chained to Duvarek's corpse and unable to free yourself." He sneered, evincing his disgust at that statement. "They both believed you were dead, yet somehow you escaped."

He waited for Annev to respond, but the boy said nothing.

"I'm to believe you cut away your own hand then sprinted all the way back here, miraculously outpacing Fyn and Kenton who were on horseback." He waited for a reaction, his voice dropping lower, becoming softer. "And during that time you were inexplicably healed?" He gestured at the round stump of Annev's limb, waiting. Still, Annev remained quiet. The headmaster's eyes smoldered, his mouth twitching.

"I don't believe that for a moment," he said, pacing once more. "It reeks of magic …" He glared at him. "Did you make a pact with Keos? Did you promise him your soul in exchange for his healing?"

Annev shook his head. It was absurd.

"No, I didn't think so. The truth is much simpler … and far more sinister." He studied Annev, his eyes glinting with malice. "You were born like this, and you used magic to hide it. You've always been able to remove that arm, haven't you?"

Annev blinked. He would have been caught off guard by the question, but he'd been expecting it after his conversation with Titus. He stared at the headmaster, implacable.

"Haven't you!" Tosan shouted, slapping him across the face. When his naked prisoner still didn't answer, Tosan kicked him in the ribs, knocking him against the wall. Annev reached out to steady himself and inadvertently rubbed his stump in the glowing liquid trickling down the back wall. His skin burned from it, but before he could pull back, Tosan kicked him again.

"How dare you *taint* my academy, *my daughter!*" Another kick.

Annev collapsed, vomiting up the water he'd just drunk.

Tosan crouched beside him. "I remember killing your parents. Tuor and Aegen. She was a keokum, too, wasn't she?"

Annev coughed in response, strings of saliva dribbling from his lips.

"I should have guessed." He grabbed a fistful of Annev's hair, pulling him closer. "I know your secret now. The priest has been hiding you all this time—a keokum, in my house. *Promised* to my daughter. Training in *my* academy." He shoved Annev away, his voice cold. "I had the priest brought to the village square. He's there right now. Tied up. Waiting for us. You will die together."

Annev slowly turned his head until he was looking the ancient full in the face. His eyes burned with an intensity that overrode the pain he felt, and he brought all this anger and frustration to bear, remembering the ills he had suffered at the Academy's hands.

"I know *your* secret too, Tosan," Annev hissed. "I found your book … I'm not the only one who's been hiding their magic."

The ancient recoiled as if he'd been hit and snapped a look at Kenton. The boy shook his head, and Tosan slapped Annev in the face again.

"Liar!" he sputtered as footsteps pounded down the hall. He raised his hand then stopped when someone banged on the opposite side of the iron door.

"Elder Tosan!" Carbad shouted. "Elder Tosan! Chaenbalu is under attack!"

CHAPTER SIXTY-FOUR

Kenton yanked the door open. Master Carbad stood there, panting.

"Men," he said in between breaths. "Metal … twisted … horrible."

"Speak up! *Who* is attacking the village?"

Carbad shook his head. "Monsters. Demons made of metal."

"Made of metal?" Tosan's eyes bulged and he glared at Annev. "Is this your doing? Did you bring the *feurog* with you? Are you in league with that witch Kelga? Is she still *alive*?"

Annev shook his head, though his stomach had lurched hard at Carbad's words.

How could they enter the village? He thought frantically. *Could they have followed me? Sodar said we were protected …*

"The masters are fighting as best they can, but the villagers are being torn to pieces."

"Bring everyone inside the Academy. We'll lock—"

"They are *inside* the Academy!" Carbad shouted, his calm shattered.

"*What?*" The headmaster looked dazed.

Narach appeared at Carbad's elbow, his spindly frame comical in his oversized nightshirt. "What's all the shouting?" he complained. He peered over Carbad's shoulder. "Is the Son of Keos loose?"

Tosan ignored him. "Master Carbad, find and protect Myjun. Understood?"

"Where are you going?"

"To put an end to this," he said, his tone dark and unyielding. Carbad turned and sprinted back down the hallway. Tosan turned to Kenton.

"Master Kenton, you will guard this cell. If the keokum tries to escape, kill him."

"Yes, Elder Tosan."

"Master Narach, we will fetch the hellfire wand."

"The *hellfire* wand?" Narach's wrinkled face puckered. "Fighting demons with demon magic? No good will come of it. And that one's a dark rod, only keokum can use it."

"The *rod*, Narach!" Tosan shouted. "Now!"

He backed away from the door, his head bobbing. "At once, Elder Tosan." The Master of Secrets fled and Tosan shot Annev a hate-filled glare as he left.

Kenton stopped halfway out and looked back at the naked boy on the floor, a puddle of sick pooling around him. He jangled the ring of keys in his hand. "If Myjun is hurt," he said through gritted teeth, "I will tear out your throat with my bare hands."

Annev met his glower, his own rage slowly bubbling to the surface. "You've always hated me ... because she chose me."

"She loved *me*!" Kenton roared, stepping back into the cell. "She loved me *first*. And you know why that changed?" He gestured at his scar. "Because of *this*. Because of your *stupid* friend Titus!"

"Titus?" Annev said, taken aback.

Kenton took another step toward Annev. "He was always useless. He should have become a steward from the very beginning. But Benifew and Grimm didn't see that—they just kept pushing him, trying to get Winsor to advance him to our reap. The masters didn't care one way or the other. They tried to beat the incompetence out of him. And I ... was stupid. I stood up for him once—*once*—and *this* happened."

"Duvarek said it was a training accident—"

"I never should have helped him," Kenton continued, his voice low, "should have let Ather and the rest beat the tears out of him. Then nothing would have changed."

Annev looked up, the tiny amount of sympathy he'd felt for Kenton evaporating. He grit his teeth, his hand shifting to grab the lip of the dish he'd hidden in the waste shaft.

"Once I was scarred she wouldn't touch me," Kenton continued, oblivious. "Wouldn't talk to me." He gave Annev a nasty smile. "Now she knows the truth … you're more scarred than me." He spat in Annev's face. "She could have been *mine* if you hadn't lied to her. She would have come back!" He snapped out his foot, kicking the side of Annev's stump. "Bastard Son of Keos!"

Annev whipped his arm forward, splashing the bowl of luminous golden liquid into Kenton's face. The avatar screamed, dropping the torch and keys as he tried to wipe the burning liquid from his eyes.

Annev rammed his shoulder into Kenton's gut, sending the boy crashing to the ground. He stooped, snatched up the torch and keys, and sprinted through the open cell door.

Kenton screamed, both hands still pressed to his face as Annev yanked on the heavy iron door, bracing both feet against the stone wall behind him to slam it shut seconds before Kenton smashed into it. The drop bar fell into place; and Annev slammed the window closed and turned the key in the lock.

"*Ainnevog!*" Kenton screamed from the other side of the door, pounding on the metal. "Keos burn your bones, I'm going to kill you. *I will kill you!*"

Annev backed away from the door, trembling. He was free. Naked and defenseless, but free. He shivered, partly from the welcome heat of the torch and partly from adrenaline. If he was seen, he'd be hunted. But now he was free, he could save Sodar.

He looked down the long hallway and saw two rows of iron doors similar to the one he'd just closed on Kenton. The passage to his left was a dead-end, but to Annev's right there was a stone staircase leading up out of the Academy's dungeons.

He took the stairs two at a time, leaving Kenton screaming behind his barred door. He kept the torch in front of him, ready to strike at anyone or anything he might encounter, and finally reached a small landing that opened onto a new floor.

This must be the Vault of Damnation, Annev thought. *Tosan said it was right above my cell.* He glanced at his stump, and at the landing, and then he pressed on, intent on reaching the surface. Saving Sodar came first. The old man was the one true and steady thing in his life. He didn't understand why the priest had come back, only that he had. He hadn't abandoned Annev after all—and Annev would be damned if he abandoned him.

He'd climbed a dozen more steps when he heard the sounds of battle above him—the shriek of metal against metal coupled with the cries of people screaming and dying. He slowly backed down the steps as the sounds above him grew louder, nearer, then ran for the safety of the floor below and sprinted down the hallway, away from the sounds of battle.

He felt like a coward, fleeing from danger. He was nothing like Breathanas or the brave Halcyon Knights from Sodar's stories—they would have fought, naked and glorious, battling with a wooden torch till they found a more suitable weapon. Annev was sure of it. Breathanas would probably have climbed to the surface, saved his mentor, the village, and the woman he loved, all while earning himself the praise and respect of the people who persecuted him—and without wearing a stitch.

But Annev was not Breathanas. He wasn't a Halcyon Knight, or even a squire to one. He wasn't even a master avatar anymore. He was just a scared one-armed boy.

The corridor widened then narrowed, turned, and widened again. He kept running, not stopping or slowing until the light from his torch reflected off an immense ironwood door at the far end.

As he drew nearer, the corridor widened into a hall and Annev saw how truly immense the door was. Perfectly round and nearly twenty feet in diameter, the dark gray ironwood had been polished till it shone. An enormous glyph, nearly six feet tall, had been inscribed in the center of the door. Annev stopped, holding the torch aloft, and studied the symbol.

The glyph was an X capped with an upside-down V, equal in width but only half as tall, with the legs of the V closing the top of the X. A round O filled the lower half of the diamond-shaped space created by the first two symbols, giving the appearance of an open eye, but Annev knew its true significance: the X represented two pieces of cut wood stacked on top of each other—*t'rasang*; the upside-down V represented the flames that consumed the wood—*lumen*; and the O within the diamond represented the air that fed the flames—*quaire*. It was the symbol of creation and destruction, the symbol of the Gods and Luquatra, of all the elements combined into one.

Aqlumera.

He searched for a handle or a lock—the vault might be a safe place to hide, or at least find a weapon—but he saw nothing. The only thing that looked remotely promising was a tiny hole cut into the center of the *aqlumera* symbol. Annev examined his key ring and saw that, amidst the collection of metal keys, there was a tiny ironwood rod. No millings or grooves had been cut into it, though. He turned back to the door, examining it once more, then cautiously slid the ironwood rod into the hole. Once he had inserted its full length, the door clicked and the wooden key locked into place. Annev jumped back, curious to see what would happen.

Nothing.

Annev returned to the door, gripped the key ring in his fist, and twisted, attempting to spin the rod in its socket.

Nothing.

What am I missing? he thought, ears keen for any approaching sounds of battle. *The key belongs here, but it doesn't turn. What kind of key doesn't turn?* He rubbed his face then stopped, a small smile appearing on his face.

It's not a key, he thought, placing the pad of his thumb on the base of the rod. *It's a common artifact … like the phoenix lantern.* Still touching the rod, he concentrated on the door opening.

A low thrum vibrated up from the stones beneath Annev's feet. There was a soft hum as a hidden mechanism whirred and chirped on the other side of the door, and then a crack appeared in the center, gradually widening until it split the glyph down the middle and the door-within-a-door swung inward. The rod slipped free, clattering to the ground.

Annev crossed the threshold, dropped his torch, and snatched the keys. As he slid the key ring over his wrist, the doors began to swing back into place. He stepped inside to avoid being crushed, then remembered his fallen torch. Before he could turn and reclaim the light, though, the doors swept it across the floor and into the hallway. He darted after it, too late, and had to jerk his hand back as the doors snapped shut, locking into place.

Well, Annev thought, slowly turning, *let's see what I got myself into.*

CHAPTER SIXTY-FIVE

A stone wall blocked his view of the vault, but an orange light at the edge of it caught his eye. As his eyes lingered on the peculiar citrine glow, it became a bright yellow, an eerie green, and then a vibrant violet. Annev stepped up to the wall and peered around the corner.

Despite the iridescent colors shining around the wall, a soft white light filled the center of the cavernous room. Annev blinked, eyes adjusting, and saw the ceiling was a huge dome, about twenty feet high at the center and stretching hundreds of feet in all directions, which tapered at the edge then sloped sharply to meet the ground.

Beneath the dome stood row upon row of shelves, which extended beyond the curtain wall and encircled the wide room, converging on an open space at the center. The light emanated from there, transitioning from a soft white light to a rainbow-hued halo suspended in the air.

"Seas and skies," Annev whispered, almost reverent.

The shelves teemed with items, both common and wondrous: scrolls and books, stones and jewelry, rods and ornaments, weapons and armor. It was like the treasures collected in Janak's study, but where the merchant had spent the latter part of his life collecting artifacts he deemed valuable, the Academy had spent centuries sending out avatars to steal every magic artifact known to them, all so they could be hoarded here.

Annev had finally entered the Vault of Damnation.

A pair of brown boots at the end of a nearby row of shelves caught Annev's eye. He scampered towards them, elated at the sight of a stitch of clothing. Even better, when he reached the boots he found a whole aisle dedicated to nothing but clothes: cloaks and scarves, pants and boots, shirts and jackets, gloves and undergarments. The aisle stretched away like a spoke in a wheel, extending from the wall at the edge of the room toward the light at the center of the chamber.

Blessed Odar, Annev thought, snatching up a pair of thick black trousers and underwear. He hastily pulled them on. The dusty brown boots went on next and were an adequate fit. He was more selective about his next pieces of clothing. He skulked down the aisle, passing a hair-covered shirt, a vest made of bones, and a hat shaped like a wolf's head. He stopped when he found a hooded, bloodred cloak made of tiny fish scales.

Not fish scales, Annev thought. *Dragon scales.*

He reached out a hand, touching the fabric, and was surprised to find the cape felt soft beneath his fingertips. As he left his hand there, he also felt the warmth of his skin radiating back to him. He picked up the cloak and draped it over his naked back and shoulders. Heat instantly flooded his body, giving him goosebumps. He shivered, clutching the cloak tighter around him, and was surprised to find two small pockets sewn into the lining of the garment. He slid the key ring from his wrist, dropped it into one of them, and carried on walking towards the light.

Annev spotted a gold-embroidered red shirt folded neatly on one of the storage shelves and paused to pull it on. The moment the fabric touched his back, though, pain lanced through his spine. He bit his tongue, afraid to scream, and ripped the garment off, casting it to the floor. As soon as it was gone, the pain disappeared.

Annev stared at the unassuming piece of fabric and shook his head. *Some of these things deserve to be here*, he reminded himself. *I have to be more careful.*

And he was. A moment later he found a rich blue shirt that looked like it might fit him, but as soon as he touched the collar to his neck, his vision grew fuzzy, it became hard to breathe, and he had a sudden impulse to douse himself with water. It took some searching before he found a plain white shirt that seemed harmless. He carefully eased it on and, when he felt no pain or other unpleasant side-effects, decided it was safe to keep.

Voices echoed across the open space in the center of the chamber.

Tosan and Narach! Annev remembered, almost too late. He fled down an aisle filled with bottles then darted behind a shelf holding jars of translucent orange liquid. He waited there, peering between the jars, watching them approach and holding his breath. The ancient and the master were arguing about something, alternatively taking a few steps down one row, then stopping to argue, then moving on again.

"… asking questions." Tosan scolded. "If it is Odar's will, it will work."

Between the orange haze of the glass bottles, Annev could see them walking down the central path toward the entrance.

"Elder Tosan, you're not a religious man. Why would Odar—"

Tosan held a jet-black wand made of glassy stone. "I am the Eldest of Ancients and our Academy is under attack. I will do whatever I think is necessary to protect our people. Anything. Do you understand?"

There was a roaring *boom* outside the vault, and the concussion shook the floor and sent motes of dust cascading down from the ancient shelves. The bottles in front of Annev clattered against each other, and he ducked out of view. When he peeked back up, Narach and Tosan's attention was fixed on the vault door.

"Very well," Narach muttered. "But don't try to use it in here. The records say it burns through stone as easily as wood or flesh—the whole room could collapse. If you're committed to this insanity, wait till you're outside the Academy."

"I'm not a fool, Narach." Tosan marched toward the ironwood portal with Narach hurrying to follow. Annev shifted his vantage point so he could watch Narach dart forward, his nightshirt billowing behind him as he brought his keys forward. He slid the slender ironwood rod into the door, muttered something, then hastily withdrew it. Once again, a low hum reverberated through the floor and the doors swung inward. Narach stepped aside, allowing the headmaster to pass. Tosan was halfway through when Tosan spared a final glance over his shoulder.

He was staring directly at Annev when the doors snapped shut between them.

In spite of the warmth of the dragon-scale cloak, Annev shivered. He turned and ran in the opposite direction, planning to hide in case Tosan had seen him.

After almost a minute of running, Annev paused at the end of one of the long aisles. There'd been no rumble of the doors opening again, so it was possible he was safe. Perhaps Tosan hadn't seen him after all. Or perhaps the ancient had more pressing things to do than pursue him.

Annev took a step beyond the aisle, toward the open space at the center of the room, and all thoughts of Tosan fled his mind.

The source of the vault's strange luminescence stood before him: a pool of lightwater—the same liquid that had been dripping into Annev's cell—nearly twenty feet in diameter.

This isn't a Vault or a cave, Annev realized. *It's a grotto.*

The liquid rippled and flowed as if alive, moving first one way then another, with no apparent reason or pattern. The watery light ebbed and flowed at the edge of the pool, spilling over and trickling down into evenly spaced runnels carved into the floor. These flowed down every tenth aisle, filling the vault with subdued ambient light. In some places, the runnels had cracked and the lightwater had spilled out, spider-webbing across the floor or trickling down into the unseen depths.

Annev circled the pool, awed by the *aqlumera* and forgetting for a moment why he was there—but then the light shifted to the hazy color of misty blood and he remembered the violence occurring a few floors above him.

Sodar is up there, somewhere. He came back for me, and Tosan will punish him for it. I can't leave him behind … and I can't hide here forever. He swore, thinking, not for the first time, that he should have stayed in Banok or fled with Sodar when he had the chance. But that time was past. Right now, he needed to get to the surface, even if it meant fighting his way there.

Fighting, Annev thought. *I need a weapon!*

He dashed down one of the aisles he had seen earlier, his eyes dancing across the items housed there: javelins, daggers, a hammer, a trident, a two-handed crescent blade. When he spied a sheathed longsword hanging from a black belt, he slid the sword from its scabbard and examined the blade.

Flamberge. Good steel. Sharp. He tried to get a sense of the magic it contained and felt a sensation similar to the phoenix lantern—warmth and light. He imagined the blade glowing, shining like a beacon in the night, but the blade stayed cool and dark in his hand. He shrugged, slid the wavy-bladed sword back into its scabbard, and strapped it to his waist. He started looking for an ax next but took two paces and stopped.

What am I doing? I can't use another weapon ... unless there's another hand somewhere in here. He paced the room, searching for magic limbs, and eventually found two shelves covered with prostheses, including three hands that ended at the wrist, two matching legs, a left foot, and a right arm. The latter included a shoulder, bicep, and elbow instead of just the forearm and hand, but it was still unusable.

No more fighting cat's-paw, he thought grimly. Worse, if he couldn't find something here, he would probably never find a replacement hand. The thought was painful, but he didn't have time to feel sorry for himself: he had to focus on escaping the Academy and surviving the next twenty-four hours.

Maybe I can compensate for the missing hand, he thought, returning to the weapons aisle. When he saw nothing useful, he moved to the next row of shelves and discovered an assortment of armor. *Maybe a vambrace ... or a modified shield.* He hurried to the adjacent storage shelves and spied a curious steel disk hanging from a long peg. Too large to be a proper buckler, yet too small to be a full shield, the concave disk had an embossed lightning bolt centered on its exterior side. Annev picked it up, slid the belts over his forearm, and cinched the shield tight. He couldn't grip the handle at the edge of the disk, but it felt secure and would give him a tiny bit of additional protection.

I'm guess I'm ready, Annev thought, though he didn't feel like it. He sprinted back the way he had come, toward the ironwood door. As he passed a table he had overlooked upon entering the vault, he saw a familiar sight.

The phoenix lantern ... and Myjun's glove!

Annev snatched up the carved block of wood and slid it into his cloak pocket. He took the glove, too, though he knew he could never wear it again. *Did Narach just assume it had magic because it had a phoenix on it, like the lantern?* Why ever it was here, Annev was grateful to have the garment back. He scanned the table for his other belongings—Mercy, Breathanas's banner, the lamp that Janak claimed was the Oracle—but they were not there. Instead, the table was littered with a white handker-chief, two finger rings, and a dull wooden rod. With barely a thought, he scooped them into the pocket with Myjun's glove to assess later. Finding the phoenix lantern had given him hope, though, for it meant the other artifacts were likely nearby.

I didn't see Mercy in the weapons aisle, though. It had been the first thing Annev had looked for. Now, he wondered. *Kenton was holding it when Myjun hit me with the torch … so maybe, in the confusion, he kept it.*

Only if Kenton still carried the sword, he could have cut himself free of the prison cell—and he couldn't have been promoted to master avatar with-out relinquishing the artifact first. *Unless he gave them the harp he stole from Janak's. Then he could have kept Mercy and no one would have been the wiser …*

Annev bit his lip, wanting to search, yet knowing every second he spent in the vault was another moment Sodar's life hung in the balance. *I'll come back for it another day,* he swore. *Right now, Sodar needs me.*

Annev sprinted the rest of the way to the door, inserted the ironwood rod into the *aqlumera* symbol carved on the interior side, and imagined the portal opening. Just as the glyph split in half, he retracted the key and the door-within-the-door swung inward.

Annev's breath caught in his throat.

Blood and gore littered the length of the hallway, sprayed across the walls and stone floor. When his gaze reached the end of the corridor, his key ring slid from his hand and clattered to the floor.

Narach lay dead on the far side.

CHAPTER SIXTY-SIX

Annev stepped through doorway, oblivious of the portal sliding shut behind him until he was plunged into darkness. With a trembling hand, he drew the phoenix lantern from his cloak, placed it between his knees, and twisted it on, casting a beam of light down the corridor. Nearly forty feet ahead, just where the hallway began to bend, he saw the torn pieces of Narach's gray nightshirt, the frail frame beneath splintered and torn apart.

As Annev drew closer, he caught the scent of fresh blood and feces. Instead of turning away, he forced himself to look at Narach, to study his body and learn from it. He knelt down beside the man, briefly wondering what sign of respect he could offer. There was nothing with which to cover him—not unless Annev wanted to take off his cloak, and he needed it more than the dead man. In the end, Annev made the sign of Odar and offered a silent prayer for the man's spirit. He collected the fallen keys then took up the phoenix lantern.

This is how Cenif the mule was killed, he thought recalling the grisly scene he and Crag had found in the forest. Annev shook his head, distraught by evidence that the *feurog* really had come to Chaenbalu. *Metal. Twisted. Horrible.* Carbad had used those very words to describe the demons that were attacking the Academy.

But the *feurog* weren't demons, not truly. They were tortured souls, pitiable humans with metal and stone grafted into their bodies who had been forced to serve Kelga, the wood-witch.

But she's dead, Annev thought, *so who drove them to attack the village ... and how did they get past the circle of protection?* Annev remembered the female *feurog* he had saved in the Brake—the one with the crushed wind-pipe—and began to tremble. *Did I cause this? Did I save one tortured soul's life and accidentally cost hundreds of others?* Only a day and a half had passed since then. Could she have followed him, and brought others with her …?

Annev shook his head. He could drive himself mad thinking about it, when he should be protecting those he loved, Sodar and Myjun in particular.

A terrible screeching echoed down from the top of the stairs and was soon followed by the din of clanging metal.

Annev forced himself up the steps, his blood pumping in his ears. Halfway up, he pocketed the lantern so he could unsheathe his flamberge. He lamented losing his light, yet as soon as the symmetrically sinuous, two-and-a-half-foot blade cleared its sheath, the wavy metal burst into blue-white flames. Annev jerked the sword away from his face, surprised, then raised the burning sword above his head like a torch.

A flame-blade! What other surprises did I pick up in that Vault?

He didn't have to wait long to find out. As Annev ran up the spiraling stairs, his feet churned beneath him, the brown boots blurring, propelling him up first two, then three steps at a time. All the while, his feet felt light, as if he were running downhill instead of up a steep flight of steps.

Annev reached the top of the stairwell and found a locked door. He set the sword down, grimacing as its flames died, and fished for the ring of keys in his pocket. Once the door was unlocked, he fumbled for the sword and rejoiced when its flames returned.

I'd still prefer Mercy, he thought, *but I could get used to this*. At the same time, he was irritated that he'd been unable to summon the sword's magic the first time he had picked it up. Why had the artifact worked in the stairwell but not in the vault?

Annev shouldered the door open a few inches and saw he'd returned to the archives. When he'd opened the door far enough, he crept through the portal and saw the battle taking place at the other end of the corridor.

Of the six other doors lining the hallway, two had been torn from their hinges. A single *feurog* lay dead in the hall and Brayan stood his ground, using a heavy war hammer to hold off a pair of twisted monsters that clawed to reach him through the archival room door.

Annev ran to his defense, his red cloak flapping behind him. As he drew close, the nearest *feurog* spotted him, turned around, and slashed out with its long, iron-tipped fingers. Annev parried, slicing the *feurog*'s wrist, then stabbed with his flamberge. The fire-limned blade slid into the monster's unprotected chest and it howled in pain, futilely scratching at the sword's forte and fuller in an attempt to wrench itself free. The flames along the sword flared, and a heartbeat later the creature dropped to its knees, eyes vacant and lifeless.

Annev yanked the flamberge free, his eyes already tracking the second *feurog*. Unlike the first, it stood upright, was dressed, and carried a rust-spotted broad sword. Despite these human affectations, the *feurog*'s face and crown were still plated with steel, and its bare chest revealed the inhuman protrusions of mineral-hardened ribs.

The *feurog* stepped back from the door, turning toward Annev as its companion fell. Seeing his chance, Brayan swung his war hammer at the creature's head and the metal crown caved in under the force of the impact. Blood spurted from the *feurog*'s eyes and mouth and the beast dropped to the ground, limp and lifeless. Brayan stepped forward, hammer still raised.

"You brought these demons to Chaenbalu," Brayan rumbled in his deep bass voice. He took another step toward Annev, hefting the weapon in his hands. Annev tightened the grip on his sword and lifted his small shield in front of him.

"I'm not your enemy, Master Brayan. I have caused you no harm, and I did not bring these monsters here." He hoped the last part was true.

Brayan kicked the *feurog* Annev had stabbed, but didn't lower his hammer. "Where are Masters Kenton and Narach? And Elder Tosan?"

"Narach is dead—the *feurog* killed him. I believe Kenton is alive. I haven't seen Tosan since he left the vault."

Brayan's eyes narrowed. "You escaped your cell and stole artifacts from the Vault of Damnation, exactly as a Son of Keos would." It was not a question.

"I'm no Son of Keos, and I've come to defend the Academy alongside you."

Brayan grit his teeth, his beard bristling with sweat. "Fine. You can fight, but you will answer for your crimes once everyone is safe." He lowered his maul. "And don't try any tricks or I'll bash your brains in. Understood?"

Annev nodded, peering into the archival room behind Brayan. "Is Titus in there with you?"

Brayan's face fell. His frown deepened and his eyes grew dark. "Titus fled when the monsters attacked. They come straight through those doors." He gestured at the two rooms whose doors had been torn free.

Annev heart leaped into his throat as he imagined his friend being chased through the bowels of the Academy by metal monsters—monsters Annev might have led to Chaenbalu. Without another word, he dashed past the hulking quartermaster and ran down the hallway. Brayan followed, but Annev's magic boots carried him faster. He turned left and spotted a handful of dead *feurog* lying at the bottom of the mysterious staircase he and Myjun had descended. Acrid smoke rose up from the dead bodies, their limbs and torsos blown to pieces by some ingenious trap laid by Master Murlach or a chemical brewed up by Ancient Denithal.

Annev sprinted past them to the large iron door Myjun had opened for him. The door had been closed, but its rusted bottom had been torn up from the floor and curled in on itself, creating a hole just large enough for a person to crouch and pass through. Another *feurog* lay dead on Annev's side of the door, but he could see more bodies in the room beyond. He pushed through the hole, crawling with his sword in front of him, and found two more dead *feurog* there, their hooked fists and metal arms wedged beneath the base of the door, dying even as they tried to break through the iron portal. He also found two dead avatars—Hans and Colven—impaled on the long iron spikes dotting the surface of the door, which had itself been marred by half a hundred dents and scratches. He stepped past the carnage and found the upper body of Folum, the Master of Customs.

Annev raced past the grisly scene, jogging up the spiraling ramp on the other side of the door. A dozen steps up, he found the other half of Folum's body, but he continued onward, holding his breath and taking care not to lose his footing on the bloody steps.

As the curving floor evened out, Annev entered the hallway with the short staircase. *Walk single file here*, he thought, remembering Myjun's warning, *on the right side of the stairs. Skip every third step.*

The truth of Myjun's words was evident: nearly every step of the staircase had crumbled into a gaping chasm in the floor. Only the right side remained intact. Annev ran up them, easily clearing the gaps between the stones, and reached the top floor of the Academy's subterranean levels. As he sprinted down the long hallway, his cape flapped wildly behind him and the fiery light of his sword flickered in the darkness. He soon came to the first junction in the corridor and halted. He looked left, right, and straight ahead, but the shadowy hallways all looked the same; no matter how long he studied the three passages, he couldn't remember which way Myjun had brought him.

Someone was yelling nearby. Annev paused, cocking his head. After a few seconds, he heard it again.

"No! Someone ... somebody help me!"

It was Titus.

Annev raced down the right-hand corridor, heading for the young steward's voice. He came to a bend in the hallway and continued onward toward a row of closed doors. He had just passed them when Titus screamed again. Annev spun around, searching, and saw that one of the iron-bound doors stood slightly ajar. He nudged it open with his shield and entered, sword leading the way.

Inside the room, the blue-white flame illuminated hundreds of sacks of grain and flour stacked atop one another. A narrow path had been cleared through the center, allowing access to a second door at the back of the room. Next to that door, standing behind a chest-high stack of grain, was a *feurog*.

The beast turned to look at Annev, its muscular chest covered in red bands of metal that reflected the light from Annev's sword. Its arms and throat were covered in the same metal, as was the top of its skull, but the rest of its face and head were unmarred, making it seem less feral than the other monsters Annev had encountered.

When the copper-capped *feurog* saw Annev, he smiled, revealing teeth that were white and whole—and altogether too human. Annev took a step toward him and Copper-cap raised his right hand above the stacks of grain, pivoting to expose a slender rapier clutched in metal fingers. Annev's mouth fell open as the monster then bent his knees and extended the sword, giving every impression he knew how to use it.

"Youuu," Copper-cap growled. "Find youuu. Found youuu."

Seas and skies, Annev thought. *It can talk!*

"Kenton?" Titus's voice whimpered from behind the stack of grain. "Help me, please!"

"It's me, Titus!" Annev yelled, taking another step down the sack-lined pathway.

"Annev!"

The *feurog* took a step toward Annev, his back-leg trailing, his sword leading.

"Commm with meeee," Copper-cap said. "Bleeeed with meeee."

Annev's mind reeled.

"You want me?" he said, lowering his shield and raising his sword. "Come get me."

"Yessss," Copper-cap hissed, his free hand dropping to his belt. "Get youuu." As the words left his mouth, the *feurog* hurled a knife at his chest.

Annev jerked the buckler in front of him, blocking the attack. The knife slammed into the steel plate and ricocheted off the metal. At the same time, there was a loud crackle of electricity and a mild *boom* as the knife flew backward, denting the *feurog*'s metal chest.

Copper-cap stared at the fallen weapon in shock, his eyes filled with hate. "Youuu ... die."

Annev took a cautious step forward, his lightning-shield leading the way. In response, the monster planted his left foot and lunged. Annev lifted his shield arm, blocking the rapier, and the tip skittered across the metal surface, sending up a cascade of sparks before piercing Annev's left shoulder. Annev grunted, taking a step back, and Copper-cap lunged again. Annev responded with his flamberge, attempting to parry and engage, but the fiery longsword was too slow. He succeeded in knocking the rapier away from his chest, but the *feurog* twisted his wrist, disengaged, and followed through with another lunge, scoring a hit on Annev's right shoulder. A second pinprick of blood spread across Annev's white shirt.

How is he beating me? Annev wondered, taking another step backward. *He's just a beast!* Or was he? Annev chided for himself for treating his enemy as anything less than human. If he was going to beat the creature, he couldn't underestimate him.

It's the rapier, he thought. *It's too fast for my flamberge, and my shield doesn't offer enough protection.*

Before Annev could puzzle out the solution to his problem, the copper-man slashed a bag of flour and kicked its contents toward Annev. White powder filled the air. Annev coughed, taking another step back, and instinctively raised the shield in front of his face and chest, ducking his head low.

The *feurog's* rapier stabbed through the cloud, slamming into the shield. There was a dull *boom* and a bright spark of lightning went up, throwing Copper-cap's sword back.

Seeing his opportunity to attack, Annev stepped forward and aimed a heavy overhand stroke at his opponent's head. The copper man sidestepped the falling blade and stabbed at Annev's feet and legs, making Annev danced backward, his magic boots aiding him as he evaded the *feurog's* lunging blade.

Titus slowly emerged from behind the sacks of grain, his blond curls tousled, one round cheek slashed and bleeding. With tears streaming down his face, the boy picked up the fallen throwing knife, shrieked, and hurled the weapon at Copper-cap's back.

The *feurog* turned in surprise, pivoting to catch the spike in his loins. He groaned, doubling over as he clutched at the wound and dropped his rapier.

The door at the back of the room suddenly flew open, revealing Fyn holding a torch and a bloody flanged mace. The avatar stared at the scene, eyes darting between the injured *feurog* and Annev's flaming sword.

"Youuuu …" the *feurog* groaned, twisting toward Annev then falling against a sack of grain.

Fyn looked between Annev's fiery blade and the wounded monster, his eyes wide with accusation. "Bloody Son of Keos," he swore, taking a step in Annev's direction.

"Stop!" Titus shouted, stepping forward. "He was helping me, Fyn!"

Copper-cap wrenched the dagger from his guts and fell to his knees.

With one hand still clutching his belly, he lifted the bloody knife, preparing to stab Titus in the back.

"No!" Annev jumped forward, falling to his knees as he thrust his flamberge into the *feurog's* thinly plated back. The sword twisted, grinding its wavy blade against metal and flesh. Copper-cap groaned in response, his arm faltering.

Fyn knocked Titus out of the way and lifted his mace above Annev's head. "Bloody Son of Keos!" he spat.

Annev instinctively raised his buckler, hoping its magic would be enough to save him from Fyn's attack, but knowing in his heart that he hadn't the strength to ward off the blow.

Fyn swung hard and the flanged points of the mace blasted through the top of the *feurog's* skull. Copper-cap twitched, his knife falling from his hands, and the *feurog* toppled dead to the floor.

CHAPTER SIXTY-SEVEN

Fyn spat on the mangled mess that remained of the *feurog*'s face, wiped his brow, and pointed his bloody mace at Annev.

"Did you kill Narach and Brayan?" he asked bluntly.

Annev shook his head, rising slowly to his feet and leaving the extinguished flamberge in the monster's back. "Brayan is still alive. He was coming up the stairs behind me. Narach was killed by the *feurog*."

"The *feurog*. Are those the shadow demons?"

The hair on the back of Annev's neck stood on end. "Shadow demons? No." Annev pointed at Copper-cap. "These are the *feurog*—the monsters with metal and rock growing out of their bodies. What demons are you talking about?"

Fyn took a deep breath. "Black things with long arms and clawed hands. They come out of the shadows and grab you. They got Jasper. Pulled him right through a wall. I heard him scream for help, but there was nothing I could do. Couldn't even see him."

Titus looked at Annev, his eyes wide. "There was one with Master Brayan, when those monsters broke through the doors. It reached for me and I ran ... straight into *that*." He pointed at Copper-cap.

Annev reached for his flamberge but stopped when Fyn nudged him with the head of his mace. "Did you bring the monsters here, as Tosan claims?"

"Silver staves," Annev swore. "No, I didn't. At least, not on purpose."

Fyn's eyes narrowed into slits. "What does *that* mean?"

Annev sighed. "You remember that shadow on the rooftops in Banok?

The one I saw on the way to Janak's?" Fyn nodded. "Well, it disappeared, but I saw it again when I was leaving. It chased me."

"And you think it followed you here?" Fyn asked. "Why?"

Annev paused, thinking how best to respond. It was pointless to mention Breathanas or the prophecy about killing Keos, particularly when he didn't believe any of it himself, but how else could he explain the monsters that were hunting him? He thought about the Shadow that had pursued him outside of Banok, remembering how agitated it had become after seeing his missing arm, and he knew what he had to do.

Annev sighed and unbelted the steel buckler from his arm. He handed the shield to Titus and lifted his limb for Fyn to see. The avatar took a step back, his face aghast.

"Blood and bones," Fyn breathed. "It's true then. You're a Son of Keos."

Annev shook his head, returning his stunted forearm to his side. "I'm not a demon, and I don't worship Keos. I lost my prosthetic hand at Janak's. When the Shadow saw my real arm, he came for me. I'm not sure why, but I think they're related."

Fyn snorted. "Are you stupid? He came to claim you for Keos!" Annev shook his head, but Fyn wasn't finished. "What about the metal demons? The *feurog*."

"I saw them for the first time two nights ago in the Brakewood with the peddler. They attacked us and we killed most of them. One escaped." Annev paused, his stomach churning. "It might have followed me back."

Fyn swore under his breath. "You're saying every time you leave the village you bring a monster back with you." He tightened his grip on his weapon. "How does that not make you a Son of Keos?"

Annev's temper flared. "Damn it, Fyn!" He reached for the flamberge and jerked it free in one fluid motion, its blade bursting into flame. Fyn stepped back and Annev pointed his sword at the dead *feurog*. "I'm *fighting* them, not helping them. If you're too stupid to see that, attack me and be done with it. Stop wasting my time."

Fyn straightened, the change in Annev's tone making him uncertain. He studied the red cloak and brown boots, the fiery flamberge, and the bloody gashes on Annev's shoulders. Finally, he squinted at Annev's forearm.

"Well," he huffed, "if you're not a Son of Keos, you're one unlucky bastard." He nodded at the flaming sword. "Where'd you get that anyway? Janak's?"

Annev shook his head. "The vault. I had to borrow a few things, like clothes. I didn't have much choice."

Fyn nodded, still studying the flamberge's blue-white flames. "That might come in handy. The shadows … they shied away from flames. I think that's why they grabbed Jasper instead of me."

"If that's true, we should each be carrying a source of light." Annev set down his weapon and pulled the phoenix lantern from his cloak, handing it to Fyn. "Show Titus how to use it."

Fyn set down his mace and torch, then showed Titus how to twist the lantern on and off. The blond boy's eyes widened, impressed, then he took the carving to try it himself.

"Where are you going?" Fyn asked, watching Titus.

"To save Sodar."

"Master Aog said they tied the priest up by the well." As Fyn spoke, Titus pressed the carving's two hidden buttons and twisted. Light blazed from the feathers and flames of the phoenix, further brightening the torchlit room. "I can probably take you to him."

"Please," Annev said. He nodded at the lightning shield Titus still carried. "You should strap that on, too, Titus. It'll cover more of you than me, and you can hold the lantern in your shield hand while you carry a weapon."

"Really?" Titus said, tucking the lantern under his arm. "How did you make the lightning work?"

"Just use it like you would a shield. It'll do the rest—it's a common artifact, like the lantern."

The round-faced boy nodded, cautiously sliding his arm beneath the belt and cinching it tight. "Thanks, Annev."

"You're welcome. Grab that rapier too." He turned to Fyn. "What's the fastest way?"

Under Fyn's direction the three boys navigated the cellars, passing a handful of dead *feurog* along the way.

"Where do you think everyone went?" Titus asked as they reached the kitchens on the ground level.

"Honestly," Fyn said, "I think most of them are dead."

"Why would you say that?"

Fyn shrugged. "The acolytes and avatars were in the dining hall when the attack happened, and I haven't seen one of them since. Jasper was with me in the basement. We'd heard people calling you a Son of Keos and wanted to know more. Kenton said they'd found your priest coming back from the Brakewood and were going to execute him, and then I ran into one of the witgirls who said something crazy about dead infants in the nursery ... and the witwomen killing each other."

"They *what?*" Annev said, shocked. "That's insane."

"Didn't sound right to me either. That's when the screaming started and those monsters grabbed Jasper, so I figured it was the demons doing all the killing."

"That's terrible," Titus whispered, biting his lip. "I hope Therin made it out—and Kenton and Master Brayan." He nudged Annev. "Kenton was with you and Elder Tosan, right?"

"He was," Annev said, not wanting to explain where he had left the boy. "He's still downstairs ... protecting the vault." The lie caught in Annev's throat. "Tosan came back up," he said, changing the subject. "Did you see him?"

Titus shook his head. "Master Carbad ran past us. He was the one who told us to gather our weapons, to defend the Academy. We were attacked after that, but I've not seen Elder Tosan. I thought he was still downstairs with you and Kenton."

That's strange, Annev thought. *I wonder where he went.*

The trio quickly traversed the hallways to the front entrance. In spite of the carnage they had seen below, the tall double doors lay closed, untouched and unscarred. Fyn approached the portal, sheathed his mace beside its twin, and dropped his torch into an empty sconce near the entryway. Without bothering to ask for help, he braced his shoulders against the beam and heaved. The piling lurched out of its cradle, balanced squarely on his shoulders. Fyn shuffled a step forward, grunted, and rolled the massive beam off his back. Without missing a step, he jerked open the ironbound doors.

The light of midday flooded into the Academy, illuminating the entryway. Annev sheathed his sword, quenching its flames, and together they stepped out onto the landing overlooking the village. From their vantage point at the top of the Academy's steps, they could see the full extent of the destruction that had been wrought upon Chaenbalu.

The old mill had been toppled into its pond, leaving a ruined stone foundation behind. Farther south and east, the village farms had been ransacked, their fields churned to mud by uncounted hosts of *feurog* and scattered with the broken bodies of farmers and their families.

At the center of town, the destruction was even more greater: scores of wild, knotted *feurog* roamed the streets, setting homes and shops ablaze. Packs of the twisted creatures had formed to hunt down villagers, dragging them from their homes to be torn apart and devoured.

A few pockets of resistance had formed around the bakery and smithy. Armed with a spear, bow, and quiver of arrows, Lorn and Rafela led the nearest group—a cluster of twenty or so craftsmen and shopkeepers armed with farm implements.

A few streets over, the one-eyed blacksmith Sraon bellowed orders at a smaller band surrounding his forge, organizing them into attack formations. When a pair of *feurog* attacked, he led the charge, wielding his short-handled halberd with deadly efficiency. A handful of younger avatars fought alongside him and, as Annev descended the Academy's stairs, he recognized one of them.

"There's Therin!" Titus shouted, pointing with his rapier. "We should help."

"Them first." Annev said, pointing to the closer knot of villagers who were attracting more *feurog*. "Sraon and the avatars can take care of themselves, but the baker and those craftsmen are getting slaughtered." As Annev spoke, he watched the tanner Elyas engage a *feurog* who had an iron maul in place of a hand. Elyas slashed out with his leather-cutting knife and scored a deep gash across the monster's throat. At almost the same time, the *feurog* raised his heavy hand and struck the side of the tanner's head, caving in his skull. Both fell to the ground, dead or dying, and while a new *feurog* replaced the one that had fallen, no one took up Elyas's position in the circle. The noose surrounding the group of villagers tightened.

"Stick close!" Annev shouted as he ran down the stairs. "Titus, watch our backs with that shield. Fyn, take the left side and we can clear a path to the villagers."

"Right!" Titus said, falling in behind Annev. Fyn hesitated to follow then hastened to catch up with the pair.

"Hey!" Fyn shouted as he pulled even with Annev. "Why are *you* leading? This isn't Banok."

Annev gritted his teeth, consciously not using the magic of his boots to sprint ahead of Fyn and Titus. "You're a warrior, Fyn, not a tactician. Let me worry about where to put you, and you worry about how to kill the things in front of you. Right now, I need you protecting my flank. My left arm is useless."

The Master of Arms huffed but did as he was told. In a flash of movement, he pulled both maces free and edged to the left, engaging a *feurog* whose back was turned.

Annev unsheathed his sword and the blue-white flames rekindled. He glanced back, saw that Titus was dutifully guarding their rear, and returned his attention to the villagers.

Rafela stood in the front-center of the group, firing arrow after arrow at the mass of monsters. The baker's wife was wounding more often than killing, but she continued to strike her targets and the onslaught of *feurog* hesitated each time she raised her bow.

Lorn stood next to his wife with a stout boar spear in hand. As Rafela nocked another arrow, a *feurog* rushed forward, attempting to catch her unawares. Lorn lunged, spearing the monster in the chest. He shoved the body backward and jerked his spear free. Just behind the baker, the willowy Edrea and her husband Greusik were trying to fend off three *feurog* with a cornette knife and a cobbler's hammer.

Seeing a chance to help, Annev dashed forward and hacked into the nearest monster's unprotected throat. It fell back in a gurgle of blood and the other two beasts whirled to face him. The first swung a spiny stone limb at Annev's head. He dodged, ducked, and brought his sword to bear, chinking his fiery blade against the sharp stone tines covering the monster's back. It howled in anger, and Annev replied by raking his sword down the monster's spine. The thing screeched, arching its back and exposing its soft belly. Before Annev could capitalize on the weakness, though, the third *feurog* rushed him. Annev dodged, spinning away from an iron claw, then swung back and slammed his sword into the gut of his previous adversary. The stony *feurog* thrashed as the magic flames ate at its flesh, and Annev sawed the undulating blade upwards, seeking out the monster's heart. He twisted and the thing convulsed then died.

Annev yanked his sword free and spun toward the final *feurog* that had been steadily creeping up on him. Dark bands of iron ore woven with stone-hardened flesh protected the monster's face and vitals. As he held it off, Annev noticed Greusik approach the monster from behind. The cobbler stepped to within a foot of the *feurog* and lifted his hammer.

Annev shook his head, trying not to draw the *feurog*'s attention to the cobbler, but Greusik was already bringing the tool down on the creature's skull. The monster's metal-plated head rang with the force of the blow, and his eyes rolled backward. Instead of dropping to the ground, though, the *feurog* spun, gave an inhuman screech of rage, and slapped the hammer from the stunned cobbler's hand.

Annev stabbed at its back, searching for a weakness in its plating. Instead, the tip of his sword went skittering away, deflected by the beast's metal skin.

The iron monster reached out and wrapped its thick, clawed fingers around Greusik's throat. The cobbler's mouth opened in a wordless scream while the *feurog* squeezed, shaking Greusik's neck until his eyes turned red with blood. Edrea screamed and Annev slashed out again, and again, and again. The monster twisted beneath the blows, shying away from the heat of the sword, but kept its hands firmly wrapped around Greusik's neck. Annev stabbed low, aiming for the *feurog*'s kidneys, but they were girded in ore and iron just like the rest. He slashed at the monster's gray feet instead, at his legs and arms, at his neck and head.

The monster tossed Greusik's limp body aside and strode purposefully for Edrea.

CHAPTER SIXTY-EIGHT

The cobbler's widow held her cornette knife in front of her, shaking, weeping openly as the metal creature wrapped its iron claws around her throat.

"NO!" Annev shouted. He dashed forward, forcing his sword between Edrea and the *feurog*, and hacked at the monster's face.

The *feurog* blinked, blinded by the flames. Its hands released their prey, seeking out Annev's sword, and Edrea wisely took her chance to flee.

Before the creature could grip the flamberge, Annev spun away and stabbed. His blade skittered across the monster's nose, scything off a tip of calloused flesh and making the creature roar in irritation. At that same moment, Annev lunged again, plunging his fiery blade down the *feurog*'s open mouth. The metal monster choked on blood and fire, but still he pushed on, driving himself against Annev's blade in an attempt to reach the one-armed Master of Sorrows. Annev twisted the sword, forcing it farther down the monster's gullet as it raged, reached out its twisted arms, and tried to seize him. When the knotted limbs failed to reach their goal, the creature settled for grasping the two feet of steel protruding from its maw. Its clawed hands gripped the flaming blade, attempting to snap the sword in half.

Annev's left arm began to tingle. He tightened his grip on the hilt of the flamberge and concentrated on the blue-white flame surrounding it. As he did so, he tried to recall what it had been like to activate and expand Mercy's magic, causing the air around the blade to sharpen: he remembered the cleaved corner of Sodar's table, the rock he had split in half, the gouge he had unwittingly carved into the ground. Holding tightly to those memories, he returned his focus to the flames of his sword and imagined them growing hotter, sharper, more intense.

The *feurog* tightened his grip on the sword blade and flexed. The metal began to bow.

Burn, Annev thought, seizing the stillness within him. *Melt. Die!*

The flames surged and the *feurog's* metal fingers fell from his hands, cleanly severed at where they gripped the flamberge. The monster screamed, and blood and melted metal boiled out of its mouth.

Annev jerked the sword downward and the white-hot blade sizzled through the *feurog's* maw, burning through its iron rib cage and spilling the creature's mineral-hardened vitals across the earth. With a sigh, the demon toppled backward, dead.

Yes! Annev spun back to Edrea, only to see he was too late: the woman's slender frame lay unmoving atop her husband's body, her throat cut by a passing *feurog* who had since disappeared among those battling Lorn and Fyn.

Annev turned to look for Titus, cursing. *Where did we fail?* he wondered. *How did they break through?* He saw the smaller steward engaged with a maddened *feurog* that kept smashing itself against the boy's enchanted buckler. Titus's shield rang with the sounds of sparks and steel, yet the monster continued to slam its hatchet-shaped fists into Titus's buckler, the magic somehow less potent in his hands. The steward took a step back and readjusted his shield arm, focused on one *feurog* rather than the others swarming at the edge of the crowd.

We're losing. Annev looked down at the bodies of Greusik and Edrea and felt defeated. *I'm no more of a tactician than Fyn. There's too many of them, and we're tiring.*

Tiring.

The word rekindled a memory: "*I always tire before you,*" he'd said to Sodar, "*None of this is fair.*"

"*You knew that when we started, so it was fair enough. You should have pressed me early and taken away my advantage. You need to end the fight before it starts. Understand?*"

He understood.

Annev lifted the flaming white flamberge and fell into Crouching Wolf. He leaped into the air—his magicked boots propelling him higher and farther than humanly possible—and landed amidst the attacking crowd of *feurog*.

The monsters circled him, surprised by the lone human separated from the pack. The three *feurog* who had been targeting Titus pulled back, drawn to this more vulnerable target.

Annev let his mind expand. His arm began to tingle and, instead of ignoring it or passively observing it, he embraced it. Energy flowed into his body, strength filled his limbs, and his mind opened up to the magic he was holding.

Dragon whelp cloak. Resistant to heat and flame. Minor protection from injuries. Annev pulled the hood of the cloak over his head.

Flame sword. Magically strengthened core and sharpened edge. Annev poured his concentrated anger into the flames, taking the color from blue-white to near ultraviolet.

A heavily muscled, seven-and-a-half-foot tall *feurog* slashed a scythe-like limb at Annev's head. Annev swung hard and hit the monster's steel-edged arm with his flamberge. The magic blade burned through flesh and carved through metal, severing the *feurog*'s arm from its body. The creature halted, caught off-balance by the blow, then stared dumbfounded at the missing limb and cauterized stump. The other *feurog* encircling Annev howled with rage, tearing up handfuls of earth and pounding their fists together in a cacophony of screeching metal and stone.

Annev followed through with the momentum of his first swing, wind-milled his arm, and swung his violet-flamed sword up into the crotch of the behemoth, splitting him cleanly in two. The giant's sundered body peeled apart and plopped to the ground, each half falling to either side.

The *feurog* fell silent, open-mouthed at the spectacle. A heartbeat passed. Then two.

Then they charged.

Boots of Swiftness. Increased strength and speed.

Annev somersaulted over the top of the charge, making those in front collide with those behind. In the resulting confusion, he twisted in the air, decapitated one, and landed softly between a new clump of screeching *feurog*. A fanged youth with golden claws raked its hands across Annev's trousers, yet the fabric did not yield.

Trousers of Protection. Extraordinary durability and resistance to abrasion.

The monster lashed out again, but this time Annev plunged his sword through the boy's chest. The adolescent slashed Annev's sword arm in the exchange, smiled at his tiny victory, then shuddered as he slid lifeless from Annev's blade.

Annev whirled to face another opponent, only to find that the monsters had retreated beyond the reach of his sword. Instead of engaging, they churned about him, searching for a weakness. Annev felt the warm trickle of blood running down his arm and held his sword out, alert to any surprise attacks as he kept an eye trained on the crimson stain blossoming beneath his white shirt. As the blood seeped into the fabric, Annev felt the garment respond.

Shirt of Regeneration. Increased stamina and rapid healing.

It was only then Annev realized the wounds he had received from Copper-cap had already healed; though stained with dried blood, his shoulders did not ache or hinder him.

Four *feurog* attacked in unison, reaching out with their crooked metal hands, heavy stone fists, and rusty broken weapons. Annev spun in a broad circle, arcing out with his sword. He imagined an invisible sphere surrounding him, guiding his attacks and maintaining the momentum of each blow. He danced among the monsters, carrying his dynamic sphere of motion with him, and when a *feurog* entered that sphere, Annev redirected it with the stub of his left arm, the sweeping blow of his foot, or the fiery blade of his sword. More and more creatures charged, enraged at the ineffectiveness of their group attack.

Annev held his ground at the center of it all, consciously moving to engage more of them in combat. He felt strong, his senses keen and alert, for though the monsters slashed at his head and back, and Annev's unprotected limbs grew bruised, battered, and bloodied, his years of training carried him through, and his magic boots and shirt kept him fighting when he would otherwise have tired.

As Annev fought, he felt at once alive and disembodied, powerful as he maimed and killed, yet detached from the experience, knowing that these *feurog* had killed his friends and acquaintances, had attacked their village and destroyed his home.

Annev whirled left and right, decapitating one beast with gnashing razors in place of teeth then swinging his flamberge up to skewer a leaping *feurog* who came at him from behind. He caught a third monster's hooked metal arm with his sword, cutting and cauterizing it at the elbow, then spun away again, always moving, maintaining his dynamic sphere of fiery metal and momentum. In his periphery, Annev saw Fyn, Titus, and the rest of the villagers making their way toward Sraon and the other avatars.

Good. Now I can focus on finding Sodar. Annev shifted his swirling arc of death toward the south side of the Academy, his attention split between the *feurog* attacking him and the well. As he moved, Annev saw some of the monsters behind him slow and slink away, unwilling to follow. The crowd of *feurog* began to thin, and Annev caught a brief glimpse of the well between the burning husks of the homes and shops surrounding the square. He fought like a demon, fervently hoping that he would see Sodar standing beside the well, unnoticed by the monsters and unscathed by battle. The mob of attacking creatures continued to thin, with almost a dozen dropping away to search for easier prey. When a howling *feurog* with obsidian-edged arms stepped in front of Annev, he decapitated it without a thought, his eyes never leaving his objective. The creature fell and Annev saw the well clearly.

The priest was nowhere in sight.

Annev roared in denial, unwilling to accept what his eyes could see. The creatures trailing him hesitated, as though his war cry spoke to them on some feral level. Several fell back and Annev raced for the well.

A fat *feurog* leaped from the shadows of a building and slammed a chipped ax into his left shoulder. The blade bounced off the dragon-scale cloak, but Annev felt something break beneath the folds of the magic cloth. He screamed in pain and lashed out with his sword, stabbing the monster through its marble-veined belly. The beast fell back and Annev ran on, calling on the magic of his shirt to heal his arm and his boots to speed him towards the well. Within moments, he had broken free of the remaining *feurog* and caught his first glimpse of the battle encompassing the eastern half of Chaenbalu. Standing at the center of it all, on the opposite side of the deserted well, was Tosan.

The Eldest of Ancient strafed the hellfire wand back and forth, doggedly protecting the broad patch of earth between the stables and the Academy. The melted corpses of men and monsters lay in a wide circle about him, and every twisted creature that came into view was blasted by liquid fire. Cowering behind Tosan's lean frame were Carbad and the bulk of the Academy's masters and ancients, all either afraid or unwilling to stand beside their headmaster. The only exception to this was Myjun, who had exchanged her night dress for reaping clothes.

Fearing that Tosan might turn the hellfire wand on him, Annev headed away, around the Academy, searching for Sodar. He glanced back to make sure he wasn't being pursued by more of the *feurog* and was surprised to see the devastation behind him.

The bodies of men and monsters littered the ground like dry leaves in a late autumn storm. Carving its way through the center of it all was Annev's own path of destruction flanked by twin trails of twisted corpses. Farther to the south and west, Annev saw scores of *feurog* tearing across the desecrated landscape, hurrying toward the safety of the surrounding forest.

Praise Odar! Annev thought, looking back at the well. As he approached it, though, he spied the pool of blood on the cobblestone base. His heart leaped into his throat then and his prayer changed from exultation to supplication.

Please be there, he thought. *Please be alive.*

He sprinted to within a dozen feet of the well and finally saw the shredded mass of bloody blue cloth on the opposite side of the structure.

"No!" he cried out. "No! Please. Sodar!" Tears streamed down his cheeks, streaking his blood-flecked face. He fell to his knees, his vision blurring as he stared at his mentor's ravaged body. "No!" he sobbed, wracked by the pain of knowing he had been the cause Sodar's death. "I should have gone with you—I should have listened to you. It's my fault …" He keened in agony, gently reaching out to touch the bloody night-blue robes, sobbing … only to find the clothing empty.

"Ainnevog!"

The voice echoed from inside the well and Annev hurried to the edge. The rope hanging from the hand crank had been unspooled and swung low in the dark space below. Annev lifted his flaming sword and peered into its depths.

A naked man hung several feet down, his wrists bound and tied to the swinging rope. He lifted his snowy head and squinted up into the light.

It was Sodar.

CHAPTER SIXTY-NINE

Annev dropped his sword and seized the crank. He pulled down, putting all of his weight and strength behind it, then kicked the lock-bar out of place. Sodar's full weight immediately tugged on his arm, the crank threatening to spin out of control, and Annev roared, pulling with all his might. The priest's body was much heavier than the water he usually drew up from the well—and he had always had two hands to turn the crank before. Annev's muscles screamed at him, but instead of relenting, he stepped up to the edge of the well, forced the crank down, and pulled it back up.

"One!" he shouted, pulling violently backward on the handle. He shifted his grip and pushed down, shifted it again and pulled up.

"Two!"

Nineteen cranks. That's how many he needed. Seventeen more. Only seventeen more. He yanked, pushed, turned, and pulled again.

"Three!"

Annev's arm burned with exertion, the muscles threatening to tear. He had never done this before—never with one hand and never with a full-grown man dangling from the end of the line. It had always been a bucket, a single bucket of water.

"Four!" Annev screamed, spittle flecking his lips. He grunted and pulled again. The crank slipped from his fingers and pinwheeled backward. "No!" Annev threw himself into the path of the spinning crank. It smashed into his shoulder, cracking his clavicle, and stopped, locked in place by Annev's body. He grunted, dazed by the pain of his broken collarbone, then felt the bittersweet relief of his magic shirt knitting the bone back together.

I can do this, Annev thought. *Odar help me, I* will *do this.* He shifted his body and grabbed the crank once more. He braced his feet and turned. Back. Down. Forward. Up.

"One!"

It was an eternity before Annev finally pulled Sodar from the darkness of the well. Out of breath and aching from exhaustion, Annev had managed the nineteen cranks without slipping again and ended by kicking the lock-bar in place. The crank had held steady and Annev reached over, slipped his arm beneath Sodar's armpit, and pulled the priest over the lip of the stone wall. As Sodar tumbled onto the ground, Annev noticed the bloody scars on the man's bare back.

"They *whipped* you?" Annev choked. What monster would torture an elderly priest, let alone one who had dedicated his life to Chaenbalu and its people? A rage began to build inside his chest, a heat that distracted him from his burning lungs.

Sodar struggled to rise to his feet. Annev helped him up then retrieved his discarded flamberge. As his hand gripped the hilt, the flames rekindled themselves and Sodar fell backward, his eyes wide as he gripped the well wall, steadying himself.

"You have … learned new magic?"

Annev shook his head. "It's just an artifact from the vault."

Sodar smiled weakly. "Two days ago, you couldn't pull a coin from a sack. Now you summon flames from steel."

Annev shrugged. "It's a common artifact. Anyone could use it."

Sodar's smile widened. "Maybe. All the same, I'd like to know if you give it a name."

Annev ignored the teasing and brought the tip of his sword beneath Sodar's bonds. "Hold still." The priest nodded and Annev flicked the blade upward, parting the hempen cord as though it were butter. The bonds fell from Sodar's wrists, revealing the chafed and bleeding skin beneath. The priest rubbed at them, grimacing.

"My clothes?"

Annev stabbed the sword into the ground and dashed over to the opposite side of the well. He picked up the priest's tattered frock then helped

Sodar pull it over his head. The old man groaned but nodded his thanks, pulling the shredded robe close to his body. He turned to Annev and took in the boy's missing hand. "It's gone then." Annev nodded and the priest sighed.

"You said you were leaving."

"And I did. The moment I finished my final Regaleus sermon, I went east—not to abandon you, but to give you space, and to learn more about who and what was hunting you. I had hoped to start by finding Kelga's remains and then deducing her part in all of this. Instead, I found a second message from Crag."

Annev's blood ran cold. "A *second* message?"

Sodar nodded. "It was near a shallow grave containing a mutilated animal. There was also an altar that had been cast down … and Arnor's bow sitting atop a rock pile."

"Arnor … the man who came to visit you?" Sodar nodded. "You think he's dead."

Sodar nodded again. "There was no body, but plenty of blood—*his* blood—and a residue of dark magic, something from the shadow realm."

Shadows …

"Crag knew Arnor," Sodar continued, "and he guessed that something foul had killed him." He grimaced. "He also said that Dortafola—the first vampyr and sworn servant of Keos—has been trying to get one of his agents into Chaenbalu."

"*What?* Why did he leave that out of his first letter?"

"Because he's picked up some of my bad habits." Sodar's face grew sour. "I'm sure he thought that by sparing details he was protecting us in some way."

"Sounds familiar," Annev said, the irony not lost on him. "Did he say who was sent?"

Sodar nodded, expression somber. "An assassin. A ghost. He was once a Kroseran Shadowcaster named Oyru. Now he is a Siänar—one of the six keokum that serve Dortafola."

A ghost … a shadow. Annev remembered the man wearing death's cloak and he shivered. "A man cloaked in light and shadow?" Sodar nodded. "I think he followed me from Banok," Annev admitted. "From Janak's mansion."

"That would make sense. I believe I even suggested something like that might happen if you left the village."

Annev lowered his head, ashamed once again for not heeding his mentor.

Sodar winced as he lifted an arm and placed a hand on Annev's shoulder. "I'm sorry. You did well to escape him, but we should be running even now. The Shadow Reborn is an unnatural adversary—much more powerful than Tosan—and I expect he played a part in bringing these monsters here."

"But why?" Annev asked, shaking his head. "Why hunt *me*?"

"Isn't it obvious? He is searching for you, Annev. *Keos* is searching for you."

Annev looked around at the ruined village, at the scattered bodies of the *feurog* and humans. "He wants to extinguish the bloodline of Breathanas … and he'll kill everyone here to get to me." Sodar nodded and Kelga's maddened words echoed in Annev's mind: "*The Shadowcaster hunts him. The Shadow God wants him. The Fallen God needs him.*"

There was so much Annev didn't understand. Had Kelga been a servant of Keos? She had been mad, but her words … she had mentioned one of the Younger Gods. Janak had said Cruithear was hunting for him—the God of Minerals had even promised the man new legs in exchange for capturing Annev—but he didn't see how the pieces fit together.

First Kelga and Janak … and now Oyru.

"We should go," Sodar said. "The village is lost, and there is no place for us here. We have to go before the Shadow finds you—or Tosan does."

A woman's scream pierced the air and Annev turned toward its source. The group of villagers next to Sraon's forge were milling about in confusion and fear.

"They need our help, Sodar."

The priest paused, looking in the direction of the commotion. "I promised I would keep you safe, Annev. Sraon is with them, as are your avatar friends, and the monsters are retreating. We should go before we're seen or before the Shadow finds us." Sodar shuffled away from the screaming. "I'd like to return to the chapel first. I left Toothbreaker for you—it doesn't fit in my bottomless sack—but now we can carry it with us." Sodar rattled on, oblivious to Annev's hesitation.

These monsters are here because of me, Annev thought. *If I run now and leave the villagers to fight alone, I will be the monster they believe me to be.*

"… packed the rest in the sack," Sodar continued. "I even brought the Speur Dún manuscripts." He paused, finally realizing Annev wasn't following him. "Hurry up, boy."

Annev shook his head. "I can't."

Sodar frowned. "You're not still mooning after that girl, are you? Master Aog didn't hold his tongue when he whipped me. Myjun attacked you when she saw your hand. She doesn't love you, Annev. She doesn't even *know* you."

Annev gritted his teeth and the blue-white flames of his sword once again began to purple. He struggled to keep from shouting. "I *know* she doesn't love me. She wants …" What did she want? He shook his head. "I'm not fighting for her. It's for them." He gestured at the avatars and villagers surrounding Sraon's forge. "*They* need us."

Sodar shook his white-bearded chin. "Annev, you don't—"

"Would you really let them die, just like my parents?" Annev snapped.

Sodar's mouth snapped shut and he stared at Annev, eyes cold.

Annev swallowed, trying to find the words. "In the Battle of Vosgar, Breathanas took up the Staff of Odar even though it could have destroyed him. He had the courage to help even if it meant sacrificing himself." Annev paused. "People are dying and we have the power to help them. You couldn't do it before, but you can now."

Sodar's bottom lip began to tremble and a shuddering sigh escaped him. "You are right," he said slowly, his voice choked with emotion, "and I am a coward." He looked at the villagers surrounding Sraon's shop. "Go. I will follow, and help. Hurry!"

Annev took off for the smithy like an arrow. His red-scaled cloak flapped in the wind as his magic boots sped him onward. He dashed through the streets, dodging the burned husks of homes and shops, then pulled up beneath the large roof covering the forge.

In the shadows beneath the awning, Lorn the baker repeatedly stabbed the earth with his boar spear, spitting curses and screaming. The avatars and villagers churned around him, some trying to calm the baker, others staying as far away as possible. This latter group seemed anxious to flee, yet wary of leaving the group.

Therin stood just outside the shadow of the awning, staring blankly at Lorn. Annev stepped in front of him and the scrawny boy jumped back, falling into monkey-fist stance. When Annev didn't engage him, he blinked and seemed to recognize him, though he did not lower his hands.

"Annev? What …?"

"I'm here to help." He gestured at the sobbing baker. "What happened?"

Therin slowly rose from his crouched position and shifted from one foot to the other. "A shadow demon," he said finally. "With long, thin arms. It grabbed Rafela and dragged her … right into the ground." He shook his head. "Same thing in the Academy. Four of them came out of the walls. Kellor was right next to me in the mess hall and they dragged him under the table." He shuddered. "I almost didn't get out."

Annev looked at the group of gathered villagers, counting the avatars, stewards, and masters. Not including Fyn, Titus, or Therin, only four had escaped. Of those, Annev recognized the freckle-faced Alisander, chubby Chedwik with his fuzzy muttonchops, the bull-necked Lemwich who carried Sraon's smithing hammer and stood protectively in front of Titus, and Brinden, who carried a heavy iron poker and stood in the shadows with Fyn. He didn't see a single acolyte, infant, or witwoman.

The usually reticent Lorn was beside himself, tearing at the ground, throwing chunks of earth into the air, screaming for the demons to come and fight him.

Sraon stood next to his smithing anvil with most of the other villagers. He spoke softly to the widowed seamstress Alanna while Nikum the carpenter and Yohan the chandler argued with one another about what they had seen. Yohan spied Annev.

"He's the one responsible!" the chandler shouted, mopping his sweat-sheened face. "Son of Keos! He brought the demons to us. He sacrificed us for dark powers." He spat at Annev.

Annev wheeled in anger, waving the fiery flamberge in Yohan's face, forcing the chandler to step back. "I'm here to *help* you! I don't worship—"

"Aaugh!"

Annev spun toward the scream and was shocked to see four spindly limbs reaching out of the shadows beneath the smithy awning, their clawed hands wrapping around Lorn's arms and legs. The baker screamed, thrashing against the shadows that bound him, and stabbed the nearest monster.

The spearhead passed clean through the demon without any effect, and the thin, gray arms slowly sank into the soil, pulling the baker with them.

Alanna screamed, Yohan cursed, and Annev leaped forward, easily crossing the twenty feet between himself and Lorn. He swung his flamberge at the demon's nearest limb and his flaming sword sliced a shadowy shoulder apart. Gray mist leaked from the wound, and one hand holding the baker dissipated into nothingness. The flames on Annev's sword flared black and red, then burned blue-white once again.

A flat-nosed face with fanged teeth and empty eye sockets burst from the ground, shrieking at Annev. He tried to stab the demon's face, but its head darted back into the shadows. In the same instance, the three hands holding Lorn wrenched down, pulling the baker through the ground and into the space between the shadows.

Annev slashed again but it was too late. Lorn was gone.

Before Annev could process what had happened, more villagers cried out in terror. Annev whirled and saw the limbs of half a dozen shadow demons latching onto avatars and villagers alike. A pair of bony arms grabbed Alisander and yanked him into the dark shadows surrounding Sraon's cold furnace. Brinden swung his poker ineffectually at the demons, and Alisander disappeared into the ground.

Alanna screamed again as a pair of clawed hands reached up from the floor and hooked around her ankles. A flat pool of darkness spread across the ground beneath the smithy awning. Annev gasped, recognizing it as one of the shadepools from the Brake, and then Alanna fell into it, slipping from the blacksmith's fingers and disappearing into the earth. Sraon stared open-mouthed at the place where Alanna had stood, his halberd clutched impotently in one hand.

"Get away from the shadows!" Sodar bellowed, appearing at Annev's side. "The eidolons live in the shadows. Get into the light, you fools!"

The villagers bolted into the streets. One fell and was trampled by Yohan and Brinden, and when Lemwich and Titus stopped to help the young carpenter, a gangly gray demon darted out from behind Sraon's anvil and tackled them both to the ground. As the demon struggled to subdue the two boys, Annev stabbed with his flamberge and speared the eidolon through the chest. It writhed on the point of his sword and the flame flickered black and red again. Lemwich and Titus scrambled to their feet and helped Nikum to safety, and the eidolon's wispy, tattered form evaporated into smoke and shadow.

Annev spun, looking for another demon to fight. He glimpsed Chedwik running past the water barrel Sraon used for tempering steel and saw a pair of long gray limbs ambush him from the side. Annev dashed forward, striking through the barrel, splitting it apart. Blue flames hissed through the water, sending up a flash of steam, and water spilled across the ground.

But it was too late for Chedwik. The avatar and the demon had both disappeared.

"Sodar!" Annev shouted. "There's too many of them!"

"Everyone into the village square!" Sodar shouted. "Keep away from the walls or anything else that casts a shadow. I'll set up a ward."

Annev dashed into the street where the surviving villagers and avatars had gathered. 'Head to the village square!" he shouted. "Follow me and stay away from the walls!"

"Damned if I will!" Yohan shouted back. "The Son of Keos is trying to pen us in for the monsters. He's one of them! Run for the woods instead." Suiting words to actions, he ran down the street, heading in the opposite direction toward the Brake.

Annev cursed as the butcher and his family followed, and then the barber and weaver. The wagoner, Duane, barely hesitated before going too. The remaining students—Fyn, Brinden, Titus, Lemwich, and Therin—stayed with Annev, as did Sraon. The smith lifted his halberd and shouted at the departing villagers.

"You bunch of fools! The boy's tryin' to help you."

Nikum, the carpenter, hesitated and looked back at Annev, Sraon, and the rest.

"The blacksmith is in league with the devils!" Yohan shouted back. "He lured us to his smithy so they could slaughter us. Keos has marked him too!" Yohan tapped a finger next to his eye then kept running.

Nikum looked between Sraon and Yohan, hesitating, then hurried after the chandler and the other villagers.

"Bloody fools!" Sraon cursed. He looked at rest of the avatars, shook his head, and spat. "Lead the way, Master Annev. We can't save 'em if they won't let us."

CHAPTER SEVENTY

When the group reached the village square, they found Sodar already there. The priest held Edrea's discarded cornette knife in one hand and scrabbled about on his hands and knees carving a large symbol into the earth beside the well. He looked up as Sraon, Annev, and the rest arrived.

"So few?"

"Yohan turned them against us." Sraon said.

"Even Alanna?"

"We lost her at the forge."

Sodar sighed, rising to his feet. "I'm sorry, Sraon. If we'd got there sooner …"

The smith frowned. "She's truly gone then. There's nothing you can do?"

"No. The shadow realm is well beyond my power. Even if it were not, I doubt you would like what you found there."

Sraon nodded. He took a deep breath, turning the halberd over in his hands. "She slipped right through my fingers. She said …" He shook his head. "Never mind."

Sodar patted his bloodied robes and withdrew his pale green magic sack. He reached inside, plucked out a bulging waterskin, and handed it to Annev. "Pour this into the symbol."

Annev sheathed his sword, took the bag, and balanced the waterskin on his forearm. As he shook its contents into the grooves Sodar had carved, he was surprised to see the bag contained salt instead of water. He traced the fifteen-foot glyph—a large V within a wide O—with Sraon, Sodar, and the other avatars in its center.

A chorus of bloodcurdling screams shattered the air as Annev finished. He spun toward the noise and looked down the long road leading to the eastern edge of the village.

At the end of Farm Street, next to the shadows of a collapsed home, Yohan and the butcher's youngest son Jori battled three eidolons—the other villagers were all gone. The demons wrestled with the boy, pulling him kicking and screaming into the darkness. Yohan made a run for it, but before he could escape the shade of the collapsed building, he was seized by the ankles and forcibly dragged into the earth.

Annev shuddered and stepped back into the protection of Sodar's ward. Brinden licked his lips, his eyes glued to the spot where the chandler had disappeared.

"So ... are we safe here?"

All eyes turned to Annev, who in turned looked to Sodar. The priest bowed his head and closed his eyes.

"*Solus. Soillse.*"

The salt-filled glyph brightened, throwing up light, dispelling even their own shadows through its radiance.

The priest opened his eyes and looked about. "We are safe ... for now. We can't stay here forever, though. When night falls, we'll be vulnerable again."

Lemwich scratched his head. "So what do we do?"

Silence. The avatars, the blacksmith, and the priest looked from one to another, searching for answers. No one said a word.

"Give me the boy, and I will let you go."

The words came from the direction of the well, and as one they turned toward the voice.

A tall man in fluttering gray robes stood within the shadows cast by the roof and waist-high well. Though it was early afternoon, his clothes soaked in the ambient light, giving him the appearance of standing in the darkest shadows.

Oyru, Annev thought, *the Shadow Reborn. He really was behind the attack.*

As in Banok, the assassin's face was covered by a black wrap and his eyes were expressionless. He stepped from the shadows cast by the well and moved into the sunlight, blinking fiercely.

He doesn't like the light, Annev realized, *but he can withstand it.*

Oyru stepped to the edge of Sodar's glyph. With one hand shielding his eyes, he leaned forward, inspecting the ward. "Give me the boy," the assassin repeated, his voice devoid of emotion, "and I will let you go."

Titus tugged on Annev's cloak. "Who is he talking about?"

"Me."

Brinden sputtered. "Well, go with him then. The least you can do is let us live."

Fyn smacked his former lackey on the back of the head. "Idiot! You think after killing half the village that thing's going to let the rest of us go?" He pointed his mace at the shadowy figure. "The second he gets Annev, he'll slaughter the rest of us. Or he'll wait till it's dark and send those shadow demons to finish us."

Brinden lowered his head, cowed by Fyn's words.

The shadow-garbed assassin eased away and settled himself on a patch of ground fifty feet away. He sat cross-legged, clasped his hands in front of his chest, and closed his eyes.

"What the hell is he doing?" Lemwich wondered aloud.

"He's meditating," Titus whispered in response. "At least, that's what it looks like."

Annev turned to Sodar. "What do we do?"

The priest looked at his pupil then stared across the square at Oyru. "I'm not sure." He spoke quietly under his breath so that only Annev could hear. "I suspect he can cross the glyph, yet he chooses not to. Why? Not because he feels threatened or hesitates to shed blood. No, if he is avoiding a fight, it is because he must." Sodar tapped his chin, thinking.

"Maybe he needs me alive," Annev said, remembering his queer conversation with Janak. "Maybe he's not here to kill me. He's here to … collect me."

Sodar nodded, his eyes trained on the meditating assassin. "That may be it. Oyru is one of Dortafola's six assassins, so if he wants you, it is because Keos—or Neruacanta acting as Keos—has sent him to claim you."

The Shadowcaster hunts him. The Shadow God wants him. The Fallen God needs him. The crone's words haunted Annev.

"You keep calling him the Shadow Reborn. Why?"

"Because he died and was resurrected through a pact with Keos. He's not the most powerful of the Siänar, nor the most cunning or evil, but he is certainly the most deadly. He was an assassin when he was alive—a Shadowcaster who worshiped Dorchnok—and now he is something worse. A ghost, more shadow than flesh, yet not bound by the same laws as the eidolons." Sodar broke his gaze from Oyru and looked at Annev. "There are tricks to fighting men and shadows, but how do you fight something that is both and neither at the same time?"

Oyru's eyes sprang open. With his hands still clasped in front of him, the assassin stood. He looked at Sodar, his eyes cold. "Give me the boy."

Sodar pursed his lips and said nothing. Behind him, Sraon shifted his stance and raised his halberd, Lemwich hefted his two-foot smithing hammer, and Titus readied his shield and rapier. Seconds slipped by. Nobody moved, and the assassin's gaze calmly moved from person to person before resting on Annev.

"So be it."

The Shadow unclasped his hands and whipped spinning stars of black metal at Sodar. The priest dodged the first—aimed at his throat—while the second embedded itself in his leg. He cried out and clutched his wounded thigh.

Oyru flicked his wrists again, whipping star after star at the clustered group of avatars. One pinged off Titus's shield while another struck Brinden's forehead, sending the avatar spinning to the ground. Sraon spun his halberd protectively in front of him, deflected one star, and caught a second in his shoulder.

A volley of metal shot back at the gray-robed assassin as Fyn hurled his throwing daggers. The assassin dodged one then plucked the second out of the air, tossing it back at Fyn. Fyn dodged, but not before throwing a third knife. The heavy-bladed dagger thudded into the assassin, knocking him back a step.

Oyru looked down at the weapon sticking from his chest. He closed his eyes and his body slowly shimmered and faded, becoming as gray and insubstantial as the eidolons. The dagger slowly slid through the assassin's chest, then passed cleanly through his body and thumped to the ground.

"Bloody bones," Therin swore.

This isn't working, Annev thought, looking at Sodar and Sraon's wounds and then at Brinden's lifeless body. *If we stay within the ward, we're open to Oyru's attack and he's impervious to ours.*

"Sraon, can you watch over Sodar?"

The blacksmith nodded. He had pulled the throwing star from his shoulder and was inspecting the wound. "Aye. I can still fight if that's what you're asking."

Annev nodded and turned back to the assassin who had picked up the dagger that had struck him. He turned the heavy blade in his hands, testing its edge, then tossed it to the ground, indifferent.

There are tricks to fighting men and shadows, but how do you fight something that is both and neither at the same time ...

Oyru completely ignored the avatars and prodded his chest, examining the spot where the dagger had struck him. *He's seeing how badly he's been hurt*, Annev thought, *which means steel* can *hurt him ... but not while he's more shadow than flesh. Maybe that's why he won't fight within the ward.*

The assassin stepped backwards into the slight shadow cast by the roof and walls of the well.

The light doesn't hurt him as much as it does the eidolons, Annev thought, *but it makes him vulnerable. He's planning to wait until the sun is lower before he attacks again ... which makes this our best moment to strike.*

"Lem," Annev said, turning to the six-foot tall avatar. "Take that poker from Brinden. You can keep the hammer, but you need a longer reach. Titus, give your rapier to Therin so you can hold the phoenix lantern behind your buckler."

The avatars looked from one to another, curious at the command. When Titus handed Therin his sword, Lemwich shrugged and complied. Fyn stepped over to Annev, pulling both maces from his back. "Are we going to rush him?"

Annev shook his head, turning back to Oyru. Across the yard, the assassin extended both hands away from his body. Tendrils of black smoke streamed up from his fingertips and began coalescing into something solid.

"Light hurts the shadows," Annev said, "but steel hurts the man. We need to use both."

Fyn pointed at Annev's flaming sword. "Looks like you *have* both."

"Yes, but I need help."

Fyn shook his head. "Not from us. I saw you kill those metal monsters all by yourself. I don't know what you picked up in that Vault, but you're a hell of a better fighter now." The other avatars had gathered around Annev and were nodding in agreement.

Annev shrugged, not wanting to explain that, while the artifacts had helped, his true power had come when he had tapped into the magic *within* those artifacts. It was something he couldn't rely on and was only beginning to understand; unlike the Darite magic Sodar had often tried to teach him, this required no glyphs or magic words, just a sense of need and an awareness of the magic he was holding.

"Two hands are stronger than one," Annev said, "and what a finger can stop, a fist can crush." He looked at each of his peers. "I need your help to fight that thing."

The avatars looked at one another, uncertain, but then Titus stepped forward, the phoenix lantern clutched close to his chest. "I'm with you."

Therin exchanged a look with Fyn and Lemwich then shrugged. "If Titus can fight without a sword, I guess I can fight with one."

"Thanks, guys," Annev said, nodding to his friends. He looked at the other avatars. "Are you with me?" One by one, the others nodded. "Good. You're going to herd him towards me. If he runs for the shadows, we may need to fall back, but as long as we keep him in the square, I think we can take him." He turned to Titus. "I want you to keep the eye of the lantern on Oyru. That should make him vulnerable to everyone else. Understood?"

Lemwich and Therin nodded. Titus grasped the phoenix lantern in his hands and twisted, bringing forth the light and focusing it into a narrow beam.

"Where should I shine it?"

Annev looked back at Oyru. The assassin had stepped out of the shadows with a wicked-looking pair of flyssa swords in hand: long and narrow, with a straight back, a subtly curved edge, and a sharply pointed tip, the black blades streamed gray smoke as Oyru spun them. He paced back and forth, squinting in the light, staying close to the well's dark shadow.

"Right in his eyes," Annev said, studying the assassin. "But keep it hidden behind your shield until we get closer. And watch yourselves. If anyone sees something coming out of the shadows—even your own shadow—shout for me or Titus."

Annev looked to Sraon and saw the blacksmith was kneeling beside Sodar, speaking to him as he checked his wound. He'd removed the throwing star and Sodar was instructing the blacksmith how to bind his injured leg. Annev took a deep breath and tightened his grip on his sword. He concentrated on the flames, imagining them cooler and brighter, then extended his consciousness into the sword: the blue-white spectrum shifted, the blue becoming yellow and the white becoming a near-blinding glare.

"Follow me."

Annev ran for Oyru, leaving the safety of Sodar's ward. The other avatars followed, spreading out behind him while trying to match his magically enhanced pace.

Oyru cocked his head to the side, studying the advance of his rushing attackers, and stepped away from the well, falling into a crouch with his two long blades held at the ready.

As Annev neared the assassin, he opened his mind and embraced the magic flowing through him, calling on the garments he wore to speed, strengthen, and protect him. He opened his eyes wide, drinking in the light and all the details of the scene before him.

When Annev was less than ten feet away, the assassin made his move, dodging aside to engage Lemwich, who had come up on the left. Annev leaped forward, attempting to intercept the assassin and protect the ill-armed avatar, but then Oyru feinted and spun to the right, engaging with Titus instead. The blond-haired boy instinctively raised his shield, bracing himself against the assassin's impending attack.

"The lantern, Titus!"

Trusting Annev, Titus fought his natural instinct to protect himself and lowered his shield, shining the bright beam of the phoenix lantern full in the face of the shadow-clad assassin.

Oyru howled, showing pain for the first time as he covered his eyes and backed away from the meek steward. As he retreated, Fyn swung out with his flanged mace, clipping the assassin's elbow. The Shadow howled again and lunged toward Fyn, trying to stab the avatar with his flyssa, but Titus was ready, blinding him once more.

Seeing Oyru's vulnerability, Fyn snapped out with his right mace, deflecting the assassin's blade, then smashed the other into Oyru's face, hitting the exact spot where Titus's lantern shined. This time, steel seemed to connect with flesh. The black cloth covering the assassin's face tore away, taking a large chunk of Oyru's nose with it.

The Shadow Reborn stumbled backward, his left hand pressed to the bleeding scar on his face, tendrils of gray smoke leaking from the wound. He glanced between Fyn and Titus then turned back to Annev, Therin, and Lemwich, looking dazed.

Annev resumed his original position in their half circle and advanced on Oyru as the other avatars closed in on the left and right, trying to surround the assassin. Oyru began to back away as they drew closer, angling himself toward the small pool of shadow surrounding the nearby well.

Sensing the assassin's intent, Annev leaped forward, throwing himself into a cartwheel over Oyru's head as he swung his flamberge down.

The Shadow Reborn ducked and rolled to the right, narrowly escaping the flaming blade before tumbling back onto his feet in front of Lemwich. The ox-strong avatar struck with his iron poker, aiming for the assassin's head. Instead of blocking the blow, Oyru dove forward, slicing out with his twin flyssas just as Lemwich's poker crashed into the side of the assassin's skull. Oyru twitched, flinching as the metal sluggishly passed through one side of his head and out the other. A spurt of blood gushed from the hole in his face as it did so, trickling down into the thin line of his gray lips.

Lemwich stared dumbly at the weapon in his hand then looked up at the assassin. Blood bloomed across his throat and chest, and then Lemwich slumped forward, dead.

At Oyru's left flank, Therin glanced between the fallen body of his fellow avatar and the menacing figure of the bloodied Shadow. To his credit,

Therin lifted his trembling rapier in front of him and stood his ground as Oyru lifted his blades for a second attack.

Then Annev was there, his bright sword knocking back the two thin blades with a shower of black and white sparks. Oyru gritted his teeth, eyes narrowed against the white light even as he deftly parried each of Annev's blows. Not once, though, did he strike back at his one-armed opponent. Instead he retreated, glancing warily between Annev's flashing sword and Titus's approaching lantern. Again, Therin and Fyn approached from the sides, but this time they stuck close to Annev, Titus, and their respective light sources.

Oyru growled, retreating further toward the well. This time Annev didn't pursue, staying close to Therin, and as the four drew within striking distance, Titus shone the phoenix lantern at Oyru, making the light dance across his chest. Therin lunged and Oyru lifted his sword to block. His flyssa was caught by Annev's flamberge, the undulating blade raking unpleasantly across the edge of his black sword, sending out a cascade of gray sparks. The tip of Therin's rapier pierced the assassin's arm just as Titus's lantern shone on it.

Oyru screamed, falling against the wall of the well behind him. As he stepped into the gray shadow at the base of the well, curls of black smoke began to pour from his wounded arm and nose, the blood evaporated, and the flesh began to heal itself. Visibly relaxing, the assassin grinned, stepping further into the wan light and embracing the shadows there.

Blood and bones, Annev thought, watching the assassin's ragged nose stitch itself back together.

The smile faded from Oyru's face and his eyes grew cold once more. With a wave of his hands, he dispelled the twin flyssas into wisps of smoke and shadow then took a deep breath, his palms rising upward. The darkness surrounding the well deepened and expanded, stretching to reach the feet of the surrounding avatars. A heartbeat later, dozens of spindly gray limbs sprang up from the blackness and seized Fyn and Therin.

"No!" Therin screamed, ineffectually swatting at the clawed fingers with his sword. Annev jumped to the boy's aid, swung his fiery blade, and severed the eidolons' hands at the wrists.

A few feet away, Titus was having similar success using the lantern. He shone the eye of the phoenix on the grasping arms pulling Fyn into the darkness and made the gray flesh sizzle and smoke. The long fingers opened, releasing their prey with a high-pitched, almost inaudible keening as the lanky limbs withdrew to the shadows.

Oyru shifted, pulled a thin star of metal out of the air, and hurled it at Titus before any of them could react.

A beam of molten fire shot through the air, obliterating the throwing star and blasting the roof off the top of the well. As one, the assassin and the four boys turned north toward the source of the magic flames.

Tosan stood at the northeastern corner of the Academy with the hellfire wand extended in front of him. He flicked it at Oyru, shouting, and another gout of fire shot from the wand.

Quick as a blink, Oyru dove headlong into the well, narrowly escaping the blast. Beneath the heat of hellfire flames, the cobblestones around the well melted and crumbled, its walls toppling inward, sealing the well below in a messy, red-hot slump of slag and rubble.

The liquid fire pouring from Tosan's wand cut off and there was a long silence as the boys realized what had happened ... and then a ragged cheer went up from the avatars.

The Shadow Reborn was gone.

CHAPTER SEVENTY-ONE

Tosan and his retinue came towards them, the headmaster alert for demons. Myjun walked in step with her father, followed closely by a train of
ancients and senior master avatars, and Brayan walked at the front of this
last group, his massive war maul resting on his shoulder. He shielded his
eyes from the sun and squinted at those surrounding the well. When he
spotted Titus, he gave a shout and waved.

Ill-prepared for a confrontation with the Eldest of Ancients, Annev
pressed the hilt of his flamberge into Fyn's hand and the magic flames
winked out. Fyn stared at the weapon, puzzled.

"Hold on to it for me, please." He turned to Titus. "Turn off the
lantern." Fyn and Titus both nodded and Annev went to check on Sodar.

As Annev entered the salt-lined glyph, he tiptoed around its white lines,
wary about disturbing their symmetry. He walked past Brinden's body and
saw that the boy's arms had been folded over his chest and the throwing star
removed from his forehead. A brown piece of cloth had taken its place, cut
from the boy's pant leg and wound around his head, hiding the mortal injury.

Sodar lay in the center of the glyph with his head propped up on the
bag of salt and his feet pointing toward the rows of smoking homes. Sraon
sat next to him, one hand pressed tightly against the priest's wounded
thigh. As Annev drew closer, he saw Sodar was using the cobbler's knife to
cut strips of cloth from the remainder of Brinden's pant leg. When Annev
approached, he lowered his knife and lifted his head.

"You're alive." Sodar breathed a sigh of relief. "I didn't … I wasn't
sure if …"

Annev knelt beside his fallen mentor. "I'm fine. Oyru never raised his blades against me."

"He's dead?"

"I don't think so. We hurt him, but he escaped into the well and Tosan sealed it up with the Hellfire Rod. He might find another way out."

Sodar grunted. "He will, I'm sure. But it will take time, and we'll be long gone by then." He set down his knife and pushed himself up into a sitting position. He looked over his shoulder, counting the figures of the approaching avatars. "One less than you left with." Annev nodded. "Who fell?"

"Lemwich."

The memory of the brawny avatar's falling body flashed through Annev's mind. He tried to dismiss it, but the memory was replaced by Brinden's bandaged face, then Chedwik and Alisander screaming in the darkness. *So many dead ...* Excepting Sraon and the three avatars behind him, his entire class of avatars had been killed along with all of Chaenbalu's farmers, tradesmen, and shopkeepers. Apart from Tosan and his approaching retinue, had any of the Academy's inhabitants survived? Annev hadn't seen a single witwoman or acolyte, and Myjun was the only woman to have emerged from the Academy. Could the rest really all be gone—could they really have been fighting each other? What of the other reaps? Annev felt sick thinking so many innocents might be dead.

Sodar nodded. "You did well. You lost one boy out of five against Keos's most dangerous assassin."

"One was too many," Annev answered. "And there were more before him."

Sodar pursed his lips and nodded. "Yes. Of course." He wrapped the long strip of cloth around his wound, cinched the bandage tight, knotted the fabric, and tucked in the loose end.

"Why don't you heal yourself?"

The priest gave a weary smile. "Because it's the fastest way to deplete my body of *quaire*, and I spent too much of that trying to survive my beatings."

Annev winced, feeling directly responsible for that, but Sodar patted his hand.

"It's fine, Annev. My body will heal on its own, and my magic will replenish itself. I'll just have to act my age for a bit."

Annev smiled at that. "Can you stand?"

"That I can manage." Sodar leaned back and picked up his bag of salt, tied it shut, then dropped it into his bottomless sack, watching it vanish into the depths of the green bag. He folded the seemingly empty bag and returned it to the pocket of his robes.

In the distance, Tosan approached. Fyn, Titus, and Therin fell in behind Tosan, joining the other avatars and masters. As the group drew closer, Annev could hear Titus telling Brayan his version of the events on the southern side of the Academy.

When Tosan came within fifty yards of Sodar's ward, he halted the group. He stared at Sodar, Annev, and Sraon, his lips pursed as he studied the glyph carved into the ground. He raised an eyebrow at the ambient light shining from it.

"Who did this?"

Sraon and Annev both looked to Sodar, seeking guidance on how best to answer. The priest looked at no one except Tosan.

"It's mine, Tosan. Do you like it? It's good at keeping the shadows away." Sodar nodded at Tosan's wand. "I see you've found something else for that, though."

Tosan's eye twitched and he snapped his head toward Sraon. "Do you consort with these keokum, blacksmith?" The headmaster's controlled tone hinted at a rage that boiled beneath his cold exterior.

Sraon looked at the injured priest. "Is it a crime now to give someone healing?"

Tosan raised his hand and beckoned to someone at the back of the line. "Bring it."

Master Carbad rushed forward with a bloody burlap sack in his hands. He placed the sack on the ground between Tosan and the perimeter of Sodar's ward.

"Open it."

Carbad complied, opening the sack and pulling out a severed head by the roots of its tangled dirty-blonde hair. The head spun, turning as Carbad held it.

Blood covered the female's sharpened teeth and tattered lips, and a long scar ran down the length of her face, but Annev could still make out the wooden pipe stem poking from her severed neck: it was the female *feurog* he and Crag had saved in the Brakewood.

Annev swallowed. The fear he'd felt while facing Tosan in the bowels of the Academy resurfaced, blossoming in his stomach.

Tosan pointed at the grisly trophy, growling through gritted teeth. "*Someone* has been helping these monsters. Someone *brought* them here, into our village." He swung his hand back to Annev, his finger shaking. "*You!* Bastard Son of Keos! You did this. *You* brought this on us." He pointed at the priest. "And you ... you have been helping him. Teaching him. *Hiding* him!"

With a roar, the headmaster stepped forward and kicked the gruesome head from Carbad's fist, sending it flying over Annev's head and across the courtyard. Tosan wheeled, lowering his arm and pointing the hellfire wand at Sraon.

"So. I ask you again, blacksmith. Have you been consorting with these keokum?"

Sraon looked at Sodar, who gave an almost imperceptible shake of his head. The blacksmith sighed.

"No, Elder Tosan. I have not."

"Good." The headmaster flicked his wrist at Sraon, gesturing the blacksmith to join the avatars and ancients at his back. "Then get out of that infernal hex."

Again Sraon looked to the priest for guidance and Sodar shooed the blacksmith away. "I'll be all right," he whispered.

Sraon nodded, releasing Sodar's bandaged leg and pushing himself off the ground. Annev watched the man take up his halberd then noticed Sodar reaching inside his robes to pull out the bottomless sack. Sraon saw it as well and shifted to block Tosan's view of the priest. "More tricks?" he whispered.

Sodar nodded, retrieving the bag of salt. "We'll see if it's enough." The blacksmith went to join Tosan as Sodar handed the salt to Annev. "Listen carefully," he whispered. "When I tell you, I want you to pour this at the bottom of the lightfire glyph. Make a line, sealing it, forming a triangle. Understand?"

Annev nodded. "The shield glyph."

"Precisely. You'll have to be quick."

Sraon had reached Tosan and the rest of the group, and the headmaster eyed him with a mix of open disgust and hostility.

"Give your weapon to Master Gravel," Tosan hissed. Sraon bowed his head in submission and handed his halberd to the portly Master of Forgery.

"Priest—if you still dare to call yourself that—you have admitted to consorting with demons, to using magic, and to concealing a Son of Keos. Do you deny it?"

Sodar chuckled. "This is a farce, Tosan."

"Do you deny it!"

Sodar raised an eyebrow. "What if I did?"

"Then I would call you a liar."

Sodar nodded, sighing. "I have never had the occasion to consort with demons, nor have I ever hidden, harbored, or concealed a Son of Keos. But if the charge is one of magic, then yes. I am a true priest of Odar. A Brother of the Order of the Dionachs Tobar, blessed with Odar's gift— which I have been trained to use." He gestured at the light-imbued glyph carved into the earth. "I used it today, to save your avatars."

"The Son of Keos is guilty!" Dorstal cried out from the back of the pack. The other ancients murmured their agreement. "Stone him!" Denithal demanded. "Cast him down to hell!" shouted another.

Tosan held up a finger for silence. "The laws of Chaenbalu are clear." A twisted sneer tugged at his mouth, almost but not quite a smile. "Masters, go amongst the rubble and the ruin, and gather stones."

Masters Aog, Der, Ather, and Murlach immediately left the crowd and walked to the nearest fallen building, filling their arms with rocks, broken bricks, and loose stone. After a nudge from Ancient Benifew, Master Gravel handed Sraon's halberd to Edra and followed. Brayan hesitated. He looked over at Titus, Fyn, and Therin, none of whom had moved, and swayed on his feet, looking between Benifew, Tosan, and the young avatars. After a long pause, he stood beside Titus, and when Ancient Benifew frowned at him, Brayan held his ground.

If Tosan noticed, he gave no sign. His gaze remained fixed on the two figures in the center of the glowing glyph.

Sodar picked up the horned cornette knife lying at his side and crawled toward the edge of the ward. "Elder Tosan, please. Let me fix this." Sodar grimaced as he pulled his injured body along. "I can dispel the magic. There is no need for this." He reached the bottom of the fifteen-foot tall glyph and began dragging the cobbler's hooked blade through the soil, connecting the open mouth of the "V".

"Stop!" Tosan shouted, pointing the wand at Sodar. As the illuminated salt-lines grew dim and lost their luminosity, however, Tosan lowered his hand. As soon as Sodar finished, he threw his knife to the side and held up both hands, showing he had meant no harm. Tosan eyed the priest suspiciously and flicked the rod at him. "Get back. You cannot undo the damage your actions have wrought, however many lines you scribble in the dirt." Tosan gestured at the dead bodies, both human and inhuman, at the burned homes and smoking cinders. "This is your fault. Your guilt and punishment have already been decided." Tosan looked to Annev. "And you. You escaped your cell and stole artifacts from the Vault of Damnation. Do you deny it?"

Annev hesitated then decided to follow Sodar's example. "I escaped my cell after being unjustly imprisoned. I entered the vault seeking refuge from the fighting, and I *borrowed* these artifacts." He laid a hand on his dragon-scale cloak. "Which I've used to *fight* the demon-spawn and protect others." He pointed to Tosan's rod. "You did the same. You took up the hellfire wand to defend our village—but it is a *dark* rod, and dark rods only work if the user possesses magic." Annev looked to the ancients in the crowd. "Tosan has the same gift as Sodar! If you would stone the priest for using magic, then you must stone the Eldest of Ancients as well."

Tosan's face purpled. "How *dare* you put me on trial! You are a crippled Son of Keos, and the Lord of Blood marked you as his own before you were born." Tosan pointed at Sodar, though his eyes still remained on Annev. "He nourished you with lies and deceit. You have used magic to hide your sins, and now you seek to twist my virtues against me." Tosan looked to the eight ancients gathered behind him. "I possess no affinity for magic and could only use this by the mercy of Odar! It was by his power alone was I able to throw back the monsters who besieged us."

The five master avatars returned with their armloads of stone and began passing them amongst the crowd.

"But you used magic to pass through the Academy's walls!" Annev blurted.

The ancients and masters collectively stopped and stared at Annev as if he had grown a third eye. Tosan sputtered. "What are you talking about?"

"Master Brayan," Annev called out, "did Elder Tosan pass you when you fought in the basement?"

The bearded giant shied away, hunching his shoulders as all eyes turned to him. At length, he shook his head. "No. Master Carbad passed me on his way out. The monsters attacked shortly after that." He rested his maul on his shoulder and scratched his neck. "I held the Archive room against the beasts until you arrived, Master Annev—but I never saw Elder Tosan, or Master Narach for that matter."

"Narach was killed," Annev said, drawing the crowd's attention back to him. "I found his body at the foot of the spiral stairs." Annev pointed at the headmaster, "I didn't see Tosan on my way out, and there are no other exits. The *feurog* got past Brayan and killed Narach. But Tosan fled. He used his magic to pass through the rock and climb to the surface."

"Lies!" Tosan shouted. "Conjecture and lies. You have no proof of this insanity, this is a distraction from—"

"There is a book," Annev shouted over the headmaster's protestations, "in Tosan's study! It teaches you to use magic and Tosan's been reading it. He even wrote notes: '*Ignis temperare. Mentiri deprehendatur. Terra trans—*'"

"*Stop this!*" Tosan stepped forward and extended his arm, shaking the rod at Annev. "One more word, and I will burn you to cinders and ash!" Tosan looked at the huddle of ancients and masters, his face bright with perspiration. "He's casting a spell on us!" Tosan snapped. "Do not listen to his words. They are filled with magic and will poison you to the truth. We must rip out his tongue. Immediately!" The ancient pointed to the dark-eyed Master Aog who had just divested himself of his last brick. "Master Aog. Silence him!"

Aog stepped forward to comply but before he had taken two steps Brayan laid a hand on the Master of Punishment's shoulder.

"Hold!" Brayan rumbled.

Aog looked at the hulking quartermaster, his eyebrow raised in silent inquiry.

"I would ask the boy a question first," Brayan explained. "He says he saw Master Narach's body at the foot of the stairs … but I held my ground in the Archival hallway. No monsters came past me. I swear on my life and my honor as a Master of the Academy. How then do you explain Narach's death?"

Annev looked between Brayan, Tosan, and Sodar. He shook his head, not understanding. "I don't … what are you implying?"

Brayan rolled his shoulders and took another step forward, placing himself squarely between Aog and Tosan. "Elder Tosan, Master Narach was with you when the fighting started, yet you escaped the Academy while he did not."

Tosan stuttered. "I … we were attacked. I dared not use the hellfire wand inside the Academy. The walls would have come collapsed on us. So I fled."

Brayan nodded. "How did you escape, and where did the monsters come from?"

Tosan shook his head, angry now. "I don't need to explain myself to you, quartermaster. *I* am not on trial here." He pointed at Annev and Sodar. "*They* are." Tosan looked to the ancients and masters. "Stone them!"

"Hold!" Brayan bellowed, raising his war hammer. He pointed his free hand at Tosan. "Your innocence has *not* been decided! Empty your pockets, Elder Tosan."

"*What?*"

Myjun stepped in front of Master Brayan's seven-foot frame. "Demon lover! Leave my father alone!"

Brayan blinked, and his face hardened. "Annev says he believes Narach was killed by the metal demons, but he did not see them commit the act. Tosan says he *saw* the metal monsters kill Narach, yet *no such demons* passed me." Brayan pushed Myjun forcibly aside and took a step toward Tosan. "Is there a bloody knife in those robes, Elder Tosan?"

Tosan looked between the ancients and the master avatars for support but no one spoke. All seemed to be considering the quartermaster's words when Sraon spoke from the back of the crowd.

"Search him!"

Ancient Denithal furrowed his bushy eyebrows and shook his head, but Ancient Edra and Ancient Benifew both nodded.

"It might be best," Benifew said. "You have not answered—"

"*I am not on trial!*" Tosan screamed, waving the wand at the group. "Stone them!" he shouted, spit flecking his lips. "Stone them *now*!" He pointed the rod at Aog then gestured at a piece of red slag lying at his feet. "Throw that cursed brick at them! Break the Sons of Keos! *Shatter* them!"

Aog blinked. Then he bent down, picked up the stone, and lifted his arm.

"Now, Annev!" Sodar hissed.

Annev leaped forward and poured the salt into the line Sodar had carved in the ground. Before he could finish, Aog threw his clay brick and it smashed into his left elbow. The dragon-scale cloak offered no protection against the blunt trauma so his joint twisted and he heard a sharp *crack*.

"Aaugh!" He scrambled to control the bag of salt as a wave of pain washed over him—all too familiar—and was immediately followed by a queer tingling sensation as the shirt tried to mend the injury.

Tosan waved the hellfire wand at the rest of the group. "*Now!* Throw your stones. All of you!" Ancients Dorstal, Jerik, and Denithal stepped forward along with Masters Gravel, Der, Ather, and Murlach.

"Hurry, Annev!" Sodar shouted.

Annev ignored the pain, groaning as he felt the magic try—and fail—to reknit his bones. His eyes blurred as he managed to pour the rest of the salt into the final groove of the glyph. He finished drew the line just as the ancients and masters hurled their stones.

"*Sgiath-cruinn na áer!*" Sodar shouted.

A ripple went through the air and the flying stones collided with an invisible barrier, tumbling to the ground.

Tosan cursed, swinging the hellfire wand back toward Sodar and Annev. "Demon magic! Sons of *Keos*!" He flicked the rod at them, frothing with anger. "*Loisg!*"

A jet of liquid fire spewed from the wand, slamming into the invisible sphere surrounding Annev and Sodar. The barrier trembled as flames pounded its surface. Waves of yellow, orange, and amber poured over the shield, sheathing the bubble in liquid heat, and the air inside grew warmer.

Sodar coughed, struggling to breathe. "Annev," he wheezed, "I need water."

Annev dropped the bag of salt and scurried over to his mentor. Sodar's lips were cracked and bleeding, his face drawn and haggard. Annev used his good arm to ease the priest onto his back, but when he pulled his hand away, he found it covered with blood. Sodar's wounds had reopened.

"What do I do?" Annev shouted over the roar of the flames. The air had become so hot it was difficult to breathe.

"The bag ..." Sodar gasped, patting the ground. "Water ..."

Annev spied the green sack lying next to the edge of the ward and brought it to Sodar.

"Water ... inside ..."

Annev opened the sack and stuck his right hand inside. He imagined a container filled with water—a glass bottle, an earthenware jug, a leather waterskin—but every time he pulled his hand out of the sack, it was empty.

"It's not working!" Annev cried, tears forming beneath his eyes. He had used so many artifacts over the past few days, yet the bottomless bag still refused to yield to him. Flames continued to envelop the sphere, and the air within scorched with heat. Annev's face felt flushed, dry and hot. He pulled the hood of the dragon-scale cloak over his head and the air felt noticeably cooler.

"Can't breathe ..." Sodar moaned. "Can't maintain ... the ward ... quaire depleted ..." He began to hyperventilate.

"No!" Annev covered him with the folds of his cloak and Sodar's breathing began to regulate itself, but his voice was still ragged and parched.

"Give me ... the bag ..."

Annev fumbled it up to Sodar's hand and the priest slipped his hand inside. He closed his eyes. When he opened them, tears streamed down his cheeks. He shook his head.

"No water."

Annev felt terror for the first time. He glanced to the side and saw Brinden's body baking in the infernal heat, his clothes smoldering, his skin smoking. Annev felt Sodar's wrinkled hand brush his face and turned to look back at the priest. Sodar's head was twitching. He gritted his teeth, his blistered lips cracking wide open.

"Forgive me, Annev!" He coughed. "Tuor … Aegen … Forgive me." His eyes rolled up and his body shook … and then he stilled.

The air trembled and Annev felt a great gush of wind release from the priest's body. At almost the same time, an inward rush of heat filled the void between him and Sodar. Annev looked down and saw the priest's robes had caught fire.

Instinctively, Annev rolled to the side, pulling the magic cloak tight around him. He heard a *pop,* and saw the invisible shield surrounding the glyph collapse. There was a shock of cool air as the heat inside the bubble rushed outward. A split second later, the flames from Tosan's hellfire wand crash into Sodar, consuming his body.

"No!" Annev cried, too late.

Sodar—the enigmatic priest, churlish guardian, and stalwart friend—was gone.

CHAPTER SEVENTY-TWO

Tears rolled down Annev's cheeks as he cowered beneath the protection of his cloak, unable to move, unable to think. Less than five feet away, the priest's blackened body burned beneath the concentrated fire of Tosan's wand. A moment later, the flames stopped.

Bewildered by the sudden reprieve from the oppressive heat, Annev looked up and saw Tosan standing at the edge of the ward, the hellfire wand pointed directly at him.

"Have you decided to confess the truth, keokum? Will you admit the pact you made with Keos?"

Annev blinked away tears, which ran down his red cheeks, and stared blankly at the Eldest of Ancients, unable to speak, barely able to think.

Sodar is dead. You killed Sodar.

Myjun was standing next to her father. Her high cheekbones and soft full lips were flushed red and her pale green eyes sparkled with intensity. She scowled at Annev, yet she still looked lovely.

So beautiful, Annev thought, *and so full of hate. She loved me once, and I traded Sodar's counsel for her kisses.* A sudden sob wracked his frame. It was all his fault—the monsters, the deaths, the destruction—it would all have been avoided if he had left the village with Sodar. Even if he had refused to be a pawn in Sodar's prophecies, he might have found a life for himself as a steward, like Titus and Markov.

But he had stayed and fought … for her.

Annev tightened his clutch on the bottomless bag in his right hand, afraid to let go of Sodar's treasured sack. Unthinking, he lifted his broken left arm toward Myjun, voicelessly pleading with her, and she grimaced in open revulsion.

"Lower your hand, monster!" Tosan barked. Annev did so. "You will not *touch*, will not *point*, will not even *look* at my daughter!"

Annev nodded dumbly. He was alone and afraid, and when his eyes searched the crowd for friendly faces most were hostile, a few were wary. Among the handful that might have been sympathetic, Therin and Fyn stared at the ground while Titus, Brayan, and Sraon looked pained. Not one moved to help.

"Now," Tosan said, "tell me. Tell *all* of us. Who brought the monsters here? If you speak the truth, your death will be quick and painless. If you lie I will know."

Annev was in a haze, barely able to process the ancient's words. *Who brought the* feurog *and the eidolons to Chaenbalu?* Oyru brought them … but Annev had brought Oyru.

"I …" Annev's mouth was dry. He coughed, licking his lips. "I …"

Despite Tosan's warning, Annev found his gaze slowly rising once more to look upon Myjun's face. He saw the girl's beauty … and her loathing, horror, and betrayal.

No, Annev thought. *She can't look at me that way. Not when I gave up everything for her … when I did nothing to hurt her.*

Annev's emotions were in a jumble and he felt the sharp sting of Myjun's betrayal, the pang of losing Sodar, and the rage at Tosan's hypocrisy, all roiling inside him, aching to be let out. His hand rose toward Myjun.

Tosan's eyes bulged.

"*Do not look at my daughter!*" He snapped the wand at Annev. "*Loisg!*"

A jet of fire roared toward Annev. He ducked, pulling his hood and cloak over him, and felt an immense heat roll across his spine. He huddled on the ground beneath the cloak, his hand and feet pulled protectively beneath the garment as the fire pounded relentlessly against his back. Annev sensed the flames hadn't caught hold of the cloak, but he could nevertheless feel the heat penetrating the thin cloth. His back began to blister and the ground beneath him began to bake.

Annev instinctively opened his mind, concentrating on the

dragon-scale cloak and shirt of regeneration. He magnified the power of both garments, wrapping himself in their magic, and felt the heat lessen, felt the skin on his scorched back try to heal itself.

But it was too much. If he did nothing, he was going to die. He needed help. He needed Sodar.

In the ache of loss for his mentor, Annev slipped his hand into Sodar's bottomless sack, searching for something to aid him, anything that might protect him or help him to fight back.

Cold metal clamped down on Annev's wrist, latching onto his arm and biting into his flesh. There was a sharp *crack*. Annev screamed and felt his arm break all over again.

Again? Annev thought, his mind cloudy beneath the pain. *My arm … my left arm.* It was only then he realized he had stuck his stump into the sack. A limb with no hand, searching for an item that would save him.

Annev slowly withdrew his arm from the bottomless bag. He vaguely remembered Sodar explaining about the enigmatic artifact. How it had found its way to Chaenbalu and the Vault of Damnation. How Sodar had broken into the vault and reclaimed it. For those who knew what to look for, there were untold secrets hidden inside it.

As Annev's elbow emerged from the pale green bag, he saw that the broken bone had reknit itself, merging seamlessly with a bright glimmer of gold that covered his forearm. At last, his hand and fingers emerged, revealing the magnificent golden arm that had fused itself to him.

The magic of Annev's previous prosthetic had been in its modest nature, in the way it changed to match the shape, size, and color of the user's limb. By contrast, this was a work of art: delicate filigrees and complex arabesques had been carved into the precious metal, filling every inch with minute detail; thick gold caps reinforced the knuckles and a dazzling white-gold bracelet encircled the wrist.

Annev stared in horror and awe at the magic artifact, flexing his fingers. In the middle of the palm, inscribed in arching cursive letters, were the words *"MEMENTO SEMPER. NUMQUAM OBLIVISCI".* He turned it over, fearing what he might find there, and saw the picture of an exotic hammer—a war falcon—floating above a smoking anvil.

"Keos," Annev breathed, barely able to speak the name.

The flames pounding Annev's head and back, momentarily forgotten, suddenly reasserted themselves. The cloak could not compete with the constancy of Tosan's flames, and Annev felt the shirt of regeneration smoldering. He sobbed at the pain, clenching his teeth against a scream, and lifted the golden hand into the flames. A fiery blast slammed into his palm, enveloping his hand, and throwing him back. Annev pushed into it, his fingers numb beneath the searing fire, and finally looked up at Tosan.

The ancient's arm shook with the power of the raging hellfire wand, barely keeping it under control. The orange and yellow flames poured from the dark rod, streaming toward Annev's arm—and were stopped, contained by the magic of the golden hand.

Tosan shook with rage as he poured his anger and energy into the dark rod. His brow furrowed, his face twisted in a silent snarl, unable to fathom how Annev was defeating the fire.

At the opposite end of the flames, Annev was amazed that he was still standing. His new hand soaked up the heat and light from the flames, the filigree growing brighter and the metal glowing brightly. He felt the power of Tosan's magic, felt the anger that fueled it. He soaked it in, let it fill his hand, and watched as a sphere of fiery yellow light blossomed from his palm. The orb continued to grow, a beacon of brilliant luminescence.

Across the yard, Myjun stood at her father's elbow.

"Kill him!" she urged, her wide eyes locked on the bright globe surging in Annev's hand. "Kill the Son of Keos!"

Something inside Annev broke. The veil that covered part of his mind, separating him from the innate magic within him, was rent in two. Faded images flooded his mind, merging with the scene in front him: instead of Tosan, Annev saw a tall man standing above him, holding a glowing silver staff; in place of Myjun, a young maiden with bright yellow hair, her eyes cast downward, full of sorrow. Annev looked at his hand once more and saw a superimposed vision of a golden prosthetic moving in coordination with a real hand made of flesh and bone.

Annev fought the images, trying to reseal the part of his mind that had come unraveled. His hand trembled, drawing the power from Tosan's wand, feeding on the flames. The globe of fire surrounding his hand surged in size again, growing to encompass his whole arm, yet his flesh did not burn. Instead, it glowed with light, drawing Annev's own innate magic from deep inside him, causing the sphere to surge with power until it surrounded his whole body. Annev struggled to contain the magic, even as he battled with the images before him.

Burn them all.

The thought was not his. Yet Annev felt it as clearly as he had in Dorstal's classroom when he clutched the ash wand: a hunger for destruction, a desire to release the pent-up energy within him.

Burn them. Break them. Kill them.

Annev shook his head, fighting it even as he felt his will slipping from him. He saw the ancients and masters behind Tosan scatter, anticipating the inevitable climax of Tosan and Annev's contest.

Myjun looked at Annev, seeing her father waver, and screamed. "I hate you!"

Burn them all.

Annev released the power, blasting it back at Tosan. The ancient had no time to react as the wave of immolating flames rushed for him but Myjun screamed, hurling herself away as the wall of fire crashed into Tosan, consuming him.

Gravel, Dorstal, and Benifew were behind him, too slow or too witless to flee with the others, and were enveloped in liquid fire, blasting the flesh from their blackened bones.

Burn them all.

The fire continued to stream from Annev's hand, searching for more to consume.

Annev screamed, unable to rein it back in. The flames passed over the fallen corpses and struck the homes on the opposite side of the square, melting stone and slate. Annev flinched at the senseless destruction and turned his hand aside, but the fire followed the path of his arm, slamming into the backs of Ancients Jerik, Peodar, and Maiken as they fled for the imagined safety of the Academy's walls. The men burst into flame and the fire blasted onward, slamming into the Academy's gray stone foundation, melting rock and mortar.

Startled, Annev jerked his hand upward and the blast tore through the Academy. Gouts of fire shot into the sky then arced downward, falling on the homes at the edge of the village. Annev tried to force it away, jerking his hand sideways, back toward the ground, and the movement further destabilized the Academy's enormous structure, dropping flying buttresses, blasting through support columns, and winnowing through the building's foundation.

With nowhere safe to direct the blaze, Annev turned again and focused the terrible beam of fire on the remnants of the well. Flames raged from his palm, crashed through the melted stone, and bored into the earth, causing a fountain of steam to erupt into the air.

Annev held his hand in place and closed his eyes. Instead of fighting the flames, he sought out the veil in his mind and tried to close himself off to the magic. He fought his sense of rage and betrayal, fought the image of a man in blue robes standing over him with a silver staff, and started to close the gap that had opened in his mind. But every time he came close to sealing it, he heard the cry of a woman in agony.

Annev opened his eyes to see Myjun kneeling in front of her father's remains, screaming, the right side of her face burned and bloodied.

Without thought, Annev turned his blazing hand in her direction then watched in horror as the magic flames ripped into the earth, throwing up rock and soil as they carved a rift in the ground that stretched toward Myjun.

He forced his hand to stop, the rift a few yards in front her. The ground shook as a chasm opened up in the earth, its depth increasing as Annev kept his hand in place. The edge of the rift spread, spider-webbing toward Myjun's feet, and a seam opened up in the ground beneath her.

Myjun stopped screaming and looked at Annev, terror in her eyes.

He roared, seizing the power within him and forcing it deep down, closing it off from his conscious mind. The flames jetting from his hand sputtered, eased, and finally broke off as Annev dropped to his knees, relieved.

The crack beneath Myjun's feet yawned open. She balanced at the edge of the precipice, staring down into the pit as the earth gave a final heave, trembling in the aftershock of the destruction and throwing Myjun forward into the abyss.

"Annev!"

Annev stared deep into the hole he had carved, hearing the echoes of her scream in the chasm's dark depths until there was only silence. He shuddered at what he had seen, what he had done, and stayed on the ground, vaguely aware of people moving around him, of Sraon pulling him to his feet, urging him to walk. He moved clumsily, as if in a daze, and let himself be dragged away from the broken Academy and burning buildings.

CHAPTER SEVENTY-THREE

Annev sat brooding in his red master avatar robes on one of the un-charred benches in the roofless hall of Sodar's burned-out chapel. He studied the black scorch marks staining the walls and wooden dais and shook his head.

It was a curious thing: Annev and Sodar's rooms were unscathed, but the kitchen, training shed, and meeting hall had been laid to waste. A similar tale could be told of every home in Chaenbalu; the *feurog* had set fire to anything which would burn, demolished whatever lay closest to hand, then moved on.

Annev looked up at the sky filling the open roof of the chapel meeting hall, watching the sun creep lower as evening approached.

Titus and Sraon sat opposite Annev on the raised dais, the smaller boy's feet dangling off the edge of the blackened platform and they remained like that for a long time, the distance between them immeasurable. After a while, Fyn and Therin walked through the broken chapel doors, bulging burlap sacks on their backs.

"Hey, Titus," Therin said, setting his sack on one of the benches. "Is the phoenix still sulking?" Sraon cleared his throat and Therin turned to discover Annev in the corner of the room.

Fyn shook his head and snapped "Idiot," which made Sraon chuckle and Therin blush. Fyn strode across the meeting hall, climbed over a fallen rafter, and circumvented an overturned bench to set his bag down next to Sraon. The blacksmith peered at the sack.

"Anything good?"

Fyn shrugged. "Not really. Most of the winter storage is gone, and the fields haven't been planted yet."

"What about the storerooms inside the Academy?"

Fyn shook his head. "They aren't accessible. There's some flour, but the rest is seed—planting was supposed to start this week. None of it is stuff we can use on the road. We found a few root cellars, though." He patted the bag. "Nothing too appetizing—hard turnips, moldy potatoes, some garlic and onions—but it's better than roots and brambles."

Sraon nodded. "We'll do fine. It's less than two days to Luqura, and I know a bit about living rough." He rubbed his bristly black beard, his fingers idly stroking the scar that peeked out from under his left eyepatch. "When I was younger, I used to travel the trade routes in Northern Quiri. I even made some treks into Western Ilumea. Lots of jungle there." He smiled. "The roads here are better, though. We'll travel quick. We could probably fast for the entire journey and still be fine."

Annev drew his feet up onto the bench and pulled his knees close to him. "What's in Luqura?" he asked, his voice just above a whisper.

Sraon looked at Annev over Fyn's shoulder. "Nothing now, but a man named Reeve will be meeting us there in a few days. He's from Sodar's order, so he'll know how to help us."

Annev's headache surged and he clutched his temple, shaking his head. "Why would I go to Luqura?" he asked, his voice still soft.

"I just said. Reeve. He'll be waiting for—"

"Why would *I* go to Luqura?" Annev said again, louder. He shut his eyes and rubbed both temples then jerked his left hand back when the cold yellow metal touched his skin. He swore, stood up, and shook the golden prosthetic, flailing his arm as though an animal had seized on it. The others stayed in the far corner of the room, shifting so they were not sitting or standing wherever Annev pointed his hand.

Annev clenched his fist, finally getting himself under control. Accepting, again, that he couldn't remove the prosthetic. He breathed through his nose, forcing himself to calm. "*You* can go wherever you want," he said, his tone cold, "but I'm staying here." He returned to his bench, folded his arms, and sat down.

Sraon and Fyn exchanged a look but Therin was the first to move. He strolled over to Annev's corner then plopped himself down on a bench on the other side of the broken aisleway.

"Why would you want to stay?" he asked, oblivious. "We've been cooped up in that Academy forever—and now we can leave! Go wherever we want. Do whatever we want." He leaned back, propping his feet on the toppled bench in front of him. "There's nothing here, Annev. The whole village has been destroyed. If anyone survived, they left at the same time as those metal monsters."

Titus cleared his throat. Therin looked up and saw the boy was scolding him. He raised an inquisitive eyebrow, but when Titus didn't elaborate he shrugged and continued.

"Brayan's checking the Academy for survivors. He hasn't found any women or children yet, but he thinks some of the masters ran in there after the fighting ended. If you ask me, though, that was real stupid of them. I mean, that place is *crumbling*."

Titus cleared his throat meaningfully again.

Therin crossed his legs, getting more comfortable. "Not that any of that was your fault, Annev. I mean, *some* of it was, but it was mostly the *feurog* that destroyed the village." He rubbed his chin. "The Academy, though, *that* was—"

"Therin!" Titus shouted.

The boy's feet fell from the bench. "What?"

"Stop talking!"

Therin frowned, looking between Titus, Sraon, and Fyn. Fyn shook his head.

"Idiot."

Annev studied the faces of all four men: the three next to the dais all had grave expressions on their faces, but when Annev looked at Therin, the boy only seemed offended, as if he couldn't fathom what he had done wrong. In spite of how miserable he felt—in spite of all the terrible things that had happened—Annev found a grin tugging at the corner of his mouth. This seemed to make Sraon, Titus, and Fyn worry all the more, but Therin grinned back and Annev shook his head.

Things were bad, about as bad as they could be, yet Therin made the best of it. He dared to approach Annev when the others hung back, their friendship tempered by a fear of something they did not understand, and which Annev understood no better than them.

He sighed and looked down at his golden prosthetic: the hand shimmered and gleamed, giving off an eerie glow that could be seen even at this time of the evening. He did not want to burden or endanger the others—not with the golden arm he couldn't hide, the magic he couldn't control, or the fate he didn't understand—yet they had chosen to stay with him. He felt guilty even thinking about it, which forced himself to keep his distance, to weigh his chances of surviving on his own. Yet every time he considered leaving them, he had no idea where to go or what to do.

Annev slowly stood, forcing himself to approach within a dozen feet of the others. No one shied away, but he sensed their uneasiness growing, so he stopped.

"How does Reeve know we're coming?"

The blacksmith seemed to know what it cost Annev to ask.

"Sodar sent him word after your Test of Judgment," Sraon replied. "He was worried. I think he was making plans to leave."

Annev nodded, knowing that was true. "Well, if Sodar wanted me to meet Reeve, that's what I'll do. I owe him that." He paused, looking around at the assembled group. "I'm not sure it's wise for all of you to come with me, though."

Fyn snorted. "I don't give a damn what you do. All I care about is leaving this godsforsaken place." He turned and pointed at Sraon. "He says he knows some people in Luqura who will pay for our avatar skills. *That's* why I'm going. We just happen to be traveling in the same direction."

Therin circled around the chapel then sat on a charred bench facing Annev and the others. Annev looked from him to Titus. "What about you two?"

Therin shrugged. "When we get to Luqura, I'll figure out how I fit into things."

Annev nodded, unable to argue with that. "Titus?"

The chubby-cheeked boy smiled. "I'm going with you, Annev. So is Master Brayan. We were talking with Sraon and we think we can help … if you'll let us."

Annev sighed and looked down at his arm. "I don't know that I want you to. Almost everyone in the village died because of me."

"That's not true," said a booming voice at the back of the hall.

Annev turned and saw Master Brayan standing in the doorway with his massive war hammer in hand. The former quartermaster strode through the hall, casually lifting a bench out of the way. He reached the foot of the dais and closed the gap between Annev and the rest, forming a half circle. He stared at Annev's golden hand, wary, then forced himself to look Annev in the eye. "I found a path into the ruins. No survivors, but I did find some answers." He met Annev's eyes. "You weren't responsible for this."

"But—"

"Just wait. Let me finish." He reached into his tunic and pulled out a crumpled envelope sealed in black wax. He raised it above his head. "I found a half-dozen of these in the west wing, along with the bodies of most of our witwomen … and witapprentices."

"What?" Annev said, disbelieving. He looked to the others for answers, yet they seemed no less shocked than he. Brayan lowered the hand holding the envelope.

"Carbad said the witwomen had gathered there for a meeting before the attack, so I kept searching till I found the room—I thought some of them had to have survived." He shook his head. "They killed each other. They're all dead. Every last one of them."

"Why?" This from Titus, his eyes brimming with tears.

Brayan shook the letter. "I doubt I would have understood this message before the attacks, but its meaning is obvious now." He handed the letter to Annev. "Read it boy. Read it aloud for the rest of us."

Annev swallowed then fumbled to open the off-white parchment and began to read.

The Vessel has been found. The Last Reap is here, and the Fallen Ones are being assembled and anointed. In an hour, I will open the tunnels and they will purify the village. Execute your charges now and join us in the west wing precisely three hours after dawn. When we are gathered, we will drink from the Cup of Fate, and the unprepared Brides will meet their Lord.

Annev looked up. "It's signed "WMK." Who is that? Witmistress Kiara?"

Brayan nodded. "That's my guess too." He looked at the others. "It frightens me to say this … but I think our witwomen brought those monsters here."

Annev shook his head. "The assassin, Oyru, came for *me*. You all heard him ask for me."

"Aye," Sraon said, "but this letter tells a second story—a dark one at that."

"That's not all," Brayan said. He reached behind his back and pulled out a long, pointed piece of melted metal. He gave the scrap to Sraon. "What do you make of that?"

Sraon took the piece of slag and turned it over in his calloused hands. "Looks like a knife. An anelace, maybe."

Brayan nodded. "That's what I thought too." He looked at Annev. "I found this with Tosan's remains, but I was withholding judgment until I found a way down to the basement. It wasn't easy, but I finally found Narach's body." He pointed to the melted anelace. "Tosan used it to kill the Master of Secrets. I'm sure of it."

Annev shook his head, realizing he had misplaced the blame for Narach's death. He flexed his golden hand, looked around the destroyed chapel then back at Brayan. "You found a path to the basement?" Brayan nodded. "Did you find Kenton down there?"

The quartermaster shook his head. "No. The survivors I did see were gathering on the south side of the chapel."

"Who? How many?"

"Seven so far, including Masters Der, Murlach, Aog, Ather, and Carbad. Ancients Edra and Denithal were with them."

Annev chewed his lip, thinking. *The Masters of Stealth, Engineering, Punishment, Lies, and Operations … but no Master of Curses.*

"To tell you the truth, none of them look like they know what to do with themselves." Brayan scratched his thick beard. "Us masters … we've spent our whole lives in this village. We don't know any other way."

Sraon stood and clapped Brayan on the shoulder. "But I do, Master Brayan. I've lived outside Chaenbalu before, and it's no harder than life in the village." He turned towards the group. "Let's pack up, boys. Take whatever you need—whatever you can carry—and meet back here in an hour. Prioritize weapons, clothes, food, and coin. We'll need all of that and then some for Luqura."

The boys all nodded then hurried off in separate directions. Brayan clasped hands with Sraon, murmured his thanks, then departed too. When they were all gone, Sraon turned to Annev. Annev waited, feeling self-conscious, rubbing the spot below his elbow where gold and flesh blended together.

"If it bothers you so much, why don't you take the bloody thing off?"

Annev stopped rubbing his arm, feeling the tears begin to well up behind his eyes, harder to control when he was shown a touch of sympathy. He squeezed his fists together and forced his mouth into a line, fighting hard not to cry, but the tears came anyway, hot and unwanted down his cheeks. The corners of his mouth tugged down, betraying him.

"I can't," he sobbed. "I've tried! I've *been* trying this whole time. It won't come off. Sraon … I'm scared of it."

Sraon pursed his lips and shook his head. "I'm sorry, lad. I didn't know." He looked at the door behind the dais. "Maybe we can cover it, though, eh? That way you don't have to look at it every second."

Annev nodded, gratefully wiping his eyes.

"Come on then. I've got my things ready and I've packed some clothes for you, but I expect there are things of Sodar's you'll want to take with you."

CHAPTER SEVENTY-FOUR

Annev stared at the priest's rumpled blankets and catalogued the items gathered atop the feather mattress: there was the phoenix lantern, the clothing he'd stolen from the vault, the flamberge he'd given to Fyn, and Sodar's drawstring sack, the magic of which had somehow protected it from Tosan's flames.

Annev picked up the lantern and dropped it into the bottomless bag. He was about to do the same with the other items when panic struck him. He stuffed his right hand inside and fished around, feeling nothing except the bottom of the sack. His heart beat faster and he felt sick at the thought the lantern was lost forever. He swallowed, forced himself to take a deep breath, and closed his eyes. As he let his breath out, he imagined his fingers wrapping around the carved block of wood.

As soon as Annev closed his hand, he felt the rough texture of the wooden lantern and pulled it from the sack, sighing in relief.

I can still use the artifacts, he thought, *I just can't figure out how to take off this godsforsaken arm.*

Annev checked the folded garments sitting atop the bed. He sniffed them and was unsurprised to find they still smelled of smoke, sweat, and blood. *I'll need to do some laundry*, he mused. *I should have stolen a Rod of Washing from the vault.* Annev smiled then stopped, remembering the forgotten items he'd placed inside the dragon-scale cloak. He fished inside the pocket and pulled out the wooden rod, the two rings, the white handkerchief, and the red phoenix glove. He quickly stuffed the glove into the sack, unable to bear the sight of it, but he took his time studying the other artifacts before sweeping them all into the drawstring bag.

Riddles for another day, he thought. He rolled up the black trousers and slid them into the bag along with the boots and underwear he'd stolen. When he came to the Shirt of Regeneration, he paused: it was badly scorched, the back and sleeves so tattered it had been reduced to rags. He considered throwing it away then thought better of it and tucked the cloth inside with the other magic items.

Might make a good bandage someday.

He picked up the bloodred cloak, but instead of stuffing it in the bag, he pulled it over his shoulders, the fine metallic scales glittering as he tied the collar in place. Finally, he flattened Sodar's magic sack and tucked it into the tunic pocket where he normally kept his lockpicking tools. He looked around Sodar's chambers, wondering if there was anything else he should take. Like Annev's room, the bedroom was sparse with just a clothes chest, a small stained table and chair, and Sodar's rumpled bed.

Annev walked to the table, which held an open copy of *The Book of Odar*. He traced the engravings on the metal leaves with the tip of his index finger then lifted the lacquered wood cover and shut the book. He walked back to Sodar's clothes chest and flipped the lid open.

A variety of folded blue smocks sat inside it. He sorted through them until he found the midnight-blue robe Sodar used for Seventhday services. He threw it on the bed then pulled out more garments, tossing them atop the first, then felt something sharp prick him. Annev jerked his hand back, examining the injury, and saw a round drop of blood blossom on the pad of his finger. Curious, he tugged another robe out of the bottom of the chest and was rewarded with the sight of Sodar's silver battle buckler.

Toothbreaker, Annev thought, pulling the rectangular vambrace from the chest. It had been a long time since he'd seen the weapon, but he remembered it well: instead of being round, like the traditional shield, Toothbreaker was long and narrow, about a foot wide and twice as long. A pair of narrow notches had been cut out of the top and bottom of the vambrace, framing the wearer's wrist and elbow exactly in the center. The four pointed corners, which were a few inches longer than the weapon's core, had been sharpened on both sides. The way Sodar had explained it, anyone wearing the shield-bracer could use those points to stab and cut at the people he was fighting while still protecting his arm.

A soft knock sounded on the door and Sraon poked his head into the room.

"Ah. I see you've found Sodar's secret."

Annev smiled, turning the unusual vambrace over in his hands. "Toothbreaker wasn't a secret—at least not to me. Sodar showed it to me a handful of times. He wanted to come back for it before we left … but I made him stay. If I hadn't, he'd still be alive."

"And the rest of us would be dead," Sraon said, stepping further into the room. "Sodar's magic saved us, so there's no point wishing it otherwise. I'm glad you found Toothbreaker, though. I think it was Sodar's favorite possession. He loved it more than *The Book of Odar*. More even than his Speur Dún manuscripts, and that's saying a lot. He'd have wanted you to have it."

Annev's eyebrows shot up. "The manuscripts!" He set the vambrace down on the bed and rifled through what remained in Sodar's clothes chest. When he had emptied it and still not found the papers, he got down on his hands and knees and began searching through the pile of clothes he'd scattered across the floor.

Sraon crossed his arms in front of his chest, tapping his foot. "And just what do you think you're doing?"

"The manuscripts," Annev repeated, not bothering to look up. "Sodar spent years translating those! I can't leave them here. I need to find them."

"And where do you think Sodar would put something that precious?"

Annev dropped the pile of clothes he had been holding and sat back on his haunches. After half a second, he rolled his eyes and slipped the green sack from his tunic pocket. He reached inside the bag and withdrew a handful of messy parchment. He examined the papers and clutched them to his chest, relieved.

Sraon tossed a thick scrap of leather at Annev.

Annev snatched it out of the air and looked at it, realizing it was a sturdy, soot-blackened glove. Long and flared at the elbow, it had been made to wear on the left hand. Annev looked up at the blacksmith.

"Is this from your forge?"

"It is. I doubt I'll be doing much smithing once we leave the village, and I figure that'll keep you from having to stare at your Keos-be-damned hand."

Annev cocked an eyebrow. "Keep *me* from staring at it, or *you*?"

Sraon licked his lips. "Both, I suppose." He nodded toward the kitchen door. "Come on. I've been waiting till you seemed strong enough to do this last bit."

***

They buried what was left of Sodar where the woodshed had stood, clearing a spot among the ashes and planting the priest's staff upright in the soil, marking his final resting place.

When they were done, Sraon nodded to Annev. "Well, you're the Master of Sorrows—and the closest thing we've got to a priest. Would you mind saying the last words?"

"Sure."

Annev knelt in front of the freshly turned soil and placed his right hand on the ground, crushing the dirt and ash with his fingers, feeling its softness against his skin. Remembering.

"Retribution," he said after a long moment. "You wanted to know if I named the sword—the flamberge. I thought I'd name it Retribution." He frowned, fighting the tears that threatened to streak his face. "I lost Mercy. I think you guessed that … but you were kind enough not to chide me for it." He swallowed. "Anyway, I said I'd tell you … if I named it."

He choked back a sob, his eyes fixed on the staff buried in the ground. It wasn't the silver staff the priest had carried during his Regaleus services, but the battered weapon Sodar had so often used during their sparring matches. It seemed fitting to Annev that they used it as his grave marker, for Sodar had been as much a warrior as a priest, a wizard, a scholar, and a caretaker.

Sraon shifted behind Annev. Waiting. Annev cleared his throat, trying to control his emotions.

"I'm still not sure I believe all your prophecies, Sodar. I know *you* believed them, though, and you dedicated your life to protecting my family. That has to count for something … so I'm going to find Reeve. I'll talk with him. I'll see if he has any solutions for outrunning gods and demons, and for removing this cursed hand, but that's it. Even if Keos himself is hunting me, I'm not the god-killer Breathanas was and I won't try to be." He looked down at the dark soil where Sodar's bones lay.

"I wish you here, Sodar. I need help—I need answers—but you're not here for either … so I guess I have to find my own way."

Annev stood, kissed his fingers, and flicked them in the sign of Odar. "Go with God, old man. You saved the lives of many souls. You were a good priest." He swallowed. "You were a good friend too. Like a father to me." The tears broke through then, but this time Annev let them come.

"Goodbye, Sodar."

***

Annev and Sraon returned to the worship hall just as the disparate members of their party started returning. Brayan and Therin came first, and Sraon immediately set to helping the quartermaster fix a wagon with a broken cartwheel. By the time a replacement was found, Fyn had returned with an armload of knives, a bow and quiver, and a few larger melee weapons. He divvied out the blades, keeping several throwing knives for himself, and gave the bow and arrows to Sraon. When Fyn came to Annev, he stared at the shield-bracer strapped to his back.

"You going to fight with that?"

"Yeah. It belonged to Sodar."

Fyn nodded, approving. "Is it magical?"

"No. Just ordinary steel."

Fyn seemed to relax at hearing this. "That's good. You need something less flashy than that sword of yours—and that shiny cloak doesn't help." Annev laughed at that, unable to argue with his former adversary.

Titus arrived just as the cart was repaired. In addition to carrying a small sack filled with coins, he surprised everyone by towing a black mare behind him.

"She was hiding near the mill pond," he said as Brayan hitched her to the cart.

About an hour later that the party crested the tall western hill overlooking Chaenbalu. Without anyone needing to say a word, the group stopped and gazed upon the village for the last time.

Annev flexed his gloved left hand, finding comfort in the knowledge that the prosthetic's arcane yellow glow lay hidden beneath the thick, soot-blackened leather. He stared out over the village one last time, squinting to see the dim outline of the chapel in the dusky light.

After a few minutes of silence, the group turned and trudged down the opposite side of the hill, their faces turned toward the western edge of the Brakewood and the capital city that lay beyond.

"What do you think Luqura will be like?" Titus asked as they entered the wood.

Annev thought about it. "I met a man who said that in Quiri the thieves all wore cassocks, but in Luqura they all wore hose."

Titus scrunched up his face. "What's that supposed to mean?"

"For us? I think it means we have to adapt. We have to accept things will be different in Luqura and we may have to change if we're going to survive."

"Survive?" The boy frowned. "Is something trying to hurt us?"

Annev looked up at purple sky, the first stars beginning to appear. "That's what I mean to find out."

EPILOGUE

Oyru stared into the darkness, his eyes piercing the earth and rocks far below the earth's surface. He no longer required light to see—he had once, but that was another time, another life. Now, Oyru could open his eyes and stare straight into the shadow realm. Physical things like earth and rock became cloudy and insubstantial, as if looking through a dirty glass window.

At the moment, Oyru's attention was on two bright points of light within the shadow. Both were close, less than a hundred yards away, and both represented the souls of young, healthy people in pain. For Oyru, a pure soul in exquisite agony was the brightest and most attractive kind of light ... and it could be molded into so many things; it was like a soft ball of clay, begging to be shaped into something ... more powerful.

The pain was useful too. It made the sufferer more pliable, and the process of molding that light was one of the few things that still interested the assassin. As a half shadow, he had no real physical appetites—no hunger or thirst, no anger or lust—but molding bright white lights into sharp black knives ... *that* excited him.

Oyru crept through the narrow passages of the earth, moving toward the two lights. As he walked, his feet and legs sloshed through water that never wet his skin or dampened his clothes. He swam through soft mud, pushed through loose rock, and when he was halted by a solid stone wall, he slipped into the shadow realm and forced himself though the obstacle. It wasn't an easy task, nor was it comfortable—he was, after all, still half human—but here, as in all places, the darkness aided him.

Oyru emerged from the wall to stand between the two lights. The one on the left was farther away and not quite as bright as that on the right, but it had something special about it: two tiny sparks of rainbow-hued light that shifted and changed when the figure moved. The novelty piqued the assassin's curiosity. He considered following it, even took a step in that direction, but then Oyru remembered the Vessel—the boy with one arm who had driven him into the well: *he* had also had a strange light surrounding him—the taint of *aqlumera*—and *he* had beaten Oyru.

The assassin turned his attention to the brighter, sweeter light—that of a woman being tortured by *feurog*. The three monsters stood near a trickle of *aqlumera*, their attention shifting between it and the girl's face. The woman screamed, yet her physical pain was less than the emotional torture she felt.

Her agony called to him.

The assassin concentrated, making his form more ethereal than real, then dove into the rock wall on his right. His movement slowed, as it always did when he entered the shadow realm, and then his body burst free of the rock. He stood inside a new tunnel and could clearly hear her screams echoing across the stone. Screams for help, for mercy, for retribution.

Oyru ran in her direction, summoning his twin flyssas as he went. He turned a corner in the twisting passage, saw a faint light ahead, and ran onward, following a sharp turn in the rock—and stopped at what he saw.

The young woman sat atop one of the monsters, smashing its skull with a rock. The other two *feurog* circled, wary of this dangerous woman. The nearest one approached, its scythe-like arms reaching for the girl's back. Oyru considered intercepting it, but decided to wait and watch.

Just as the metal blade came whirring for the girl's exposed back she twisted, grappled the *feurog*'s arm, and shoved its own scythe straight up into its brain. The beast screeched, a harsh metallic note rising from its throat, and fell dead.

The last *feurog* wailed at the sight of its companion and fled into the dark passageway. Oyru watched it go then looked at the young woman standing between the two dead monsters: beautiful, mottled red scars covered the right side of her face; her long brown hair curled in gentle waves until it kissed her shoulders; her lips were pink and plump, her eyes a startling pale green.

She saw Oyru's shadowy figure and roared, dropping to the floor as she searched for a weapon. She grabbed her rock and hurled it at the assassin.

As it passed through Oyru and clattered down the tunnel, the girl dropped to her knees and wailed in frustration and pain. Oyru studied her torn clothes and bloodied hands and knees. The injuries were surprising light, and Oyru quickly saw why: the *feurog* had been pouring *aqlumera* on her injuries.

Oyru cupped her chin in his hand and her eyes went wide with terror. The white light surrounding her grew brighter, her fear and anxiety heightened as he turned her face to the side and examined her scars: in the pockets of her burned flesh, beads of gold metal reflected the rainbow-hued light that trickled down from the ceiling. As Oyru watched, the gold liquid began to bubble, re-forming itself to match the structure of the girl's cheekbone. At the same time, her flesh began to stretch and smoke, fusing with the gold. Oyru stared, transfixed, as her face repaired itself.

Beautiful.

After a few seconds, the rainbow light diminished and then disappeared, leaving bright bands of gold embedded in her otherwise flawless skin, matching similar bands of gold marking across her flesh.

Exquisite.

Oyru released her and one hand flew to her formerly scarred face. When her fingers touched the metal ribbons streaking the right side of her face, she screamed. Oyru watched as her bright light reached an intensity he had never seen before. The darkness around her deepened and he sensed her anguish, felt it building up inside her, seeking a release while she sobbed angry words.

She tilted her head back with a wail of indescribable pain as Oyru observed each shard of her agony: abandonment, betrayal, loathing, self-loathing, hate, anger, frustration, rage, sorrow, sadness, self-pity, and even madness.

She was ready. And Oyru was there.

"I can take away your pain."

Though his voice was quiet, it cut through her maddened scream. She choked off her tears, wet rivulets streaming down her face and looked up at the assassin.

"What do you want from me?"

"Everything and nothing," the assassin answered. "I want your allegiance. In exchange, I will … heal you."

"*Heal* me," she said, spitting the word.

Oyru nodded. "I see that your heart aches, that you have been betrayed. I sense that your loved ones lied to you and abandoned you." The young woman's lip began to tremble but Oyru pressed on. She had already been broken. Now he only needed to repurpose her.

"I see that you have been marked by Keos," he whispered.

She slapped a hand to her cheek and clawed at her face, tearing at the gold bands fused with her flesh until flecks of blood stained her fingers and Oryu finally seized her wrists.

"You are deformed," he said. "You are *marked*. You are *His*. But you needn't be bound by your pain. You needn't suffer when you can seek revenge."

The girl sniffed, blinking bloody tears. "Yes! I want them to die … all of them."

Oyru let her wrists go and reached into his shadowy robes, withdrawing a delicate golden mask. He displayed it in front of the girl, turning it so she could see its perfectly crafted features, then set it atop her open palms.

"You have two options," Oyru whispered. "You can live maimed and marked, betrayed by your friends … or you can put on the mask. *Hide* your deformity and *remain* beautiful."

The young woman looked at the exquisitely wrought artifact, turning the lifelike piece of metal over in her hands. "What will it do?" she whispered.

"Take something broken and make it useful."

"Something broken?"

"Your emotions—your anguish. It will take your grief and your pain, then use them to heal your physical injuries." He paused. "I won't lie to you. Your pain never leaves—not entirely—but the mask channels that energy into your body. Makes you faster, stronger, more alert."

"It heals me?" she repeated. "Will it take away my …" She pointed at her gilded face. "*This*. Will it take this away?"

"No," he said, his voice cold and apathetic. "*Nothing* will take that away.

It will hide your deformity. It will turn your pain into a weapon, which I can teach you to use, to hunt down those who hurt you." Oyru placed his hands beneath hers and helped the girl lift the mask closer to her face. "It will keep you from being hurt again."

The young woman stopped, the mask inches from her skin, and met the eyes of the Shadow Reborn. "Will you help me kill him?"

"I will."

The girl looked down at the inside of the mask, studying its beautiful curves. Then she lifted it to her face and pressed the yellow metal against her skin. There was a flash of light and her body convulsed, her fingers contracting, scratching to rip the mask off again.

But it was too late.

She closed her eyes tight against the pain and drops of blood trickled from her eyes, staining the golden mask. The two drops ran down the metal, then froze at her cheekbones, a permanent mark on the otherwise flawless mask. The woman screamed.

Oyru drank in the sight. Relished it. Let the image burn itself into his mind. It was the kind of moment he lived for, the kind he savored when memories of his former life sought to reclaim him. For a few seconds, he felt something akin to delight.

She was no longer a girl. She would be his knife, an instrument of passion that he could hone to a razor's edge. A dangerous tool, made more dangerous by the mask and the pain that fueled it.

After years of searching, after dozens of failures, the Shadow Reborn had finally found his true apprentice.

ACKNOWLEDGMENTS

This novel would not have been possible without the help of many people who provided support and insight along the way. I'd especially like to thank my parents Alan and Sonja Call, who have always supported my love for reading and writing (and gaming), and who have quietly cheered and championed my career as a fantasy author. I am indebted to my close friends Rick Calixto and Merrill Meadow, who read and critiqued my earliest drafts of this book, and especially to my UK editor Gillian Redfearn, whose amazing talents have elevated this story from good to great. Thank you as well to my friend and map-maker Jared Sprague, who read my early drafts and has since suffered through biweekly phone calls as we continue to discuss the detail of my Silent Gods' ephemera. I would be remiss if I did not also recognize Fleetwood Robbins (who took a chance on me despite my abysmal query letter) and Danny Baror, who has since taken over as my sole agent and is a remarkable friend and colleague.

Thank you to David and Leigh Eddings, whose Sparhawk and Belgarath characters lured me into reading (and then writing) fantasy. Thank you to Brandon Sanderson, whose books and writing ethic I have always admired, and to the rest of the Writing Excuses team, in particular Dan Wells, Howard Tayler, and Mary Robinette Kowal—your podcast continues to be an inspiration.

Last but not least, I'd like to thank my wonderful wife Collette, who sincerely dislikes fantasy literature but is supportive of my love and passion for it; were it not for her many sacrifices, this book (and those to come) would never have been written.

I am fortunate to know each and every one of you, and I am grateful for the magic you have all contributed to this book.